IN THE STARS
PART II: CANCER–SAGITTARIUS

BY

DEBBIE MᶜGOWAN

Beaten Track
www.beatentrackpublishing.com

In The Stars Part II: Cancer–Sagittarius

Second Edition
Published 2018 by Beaten Track Publishing
First published 2014
Copyright © 2014, 2016, 2017, 2018 Debbie McGowan

ISBN: 978 1 78645 144 6

Cover Design by Debbie McGowan
Licensed stock images: usage is not indicative
of the models' identity, activities or preferences.
Zodiac Illustrations by Emma Pickering

Beaten Track Publishing,
Burscough, Lancashire.
www.beatentrackpublishing.com

Acknowledgements

Thank you to my wonderful proof-readers, Tracy and Andrea, for your persistence in / insistence on finding and then laughing at my dreadful mistakes, not to mention your extraordinary expertise in all matters, but in particular, those of bingo and healthcare! The Circle thank you, too!

Much gratitude to Hans M Hirschi, for checking and correcting my dodgy Norwegian / Swedish translations, even though we had only just 'met'!

Hans also writes beautiful stories – visit his website to find out more. www.hirschi.se

Thanks also to Beth, for excellent chat show related creative input. Elliot Sanchez lives because of you.

***

Excerpts from:

'The Signs', by Henry Van Dyke
The Project Gutenberg EBook of The Poems of Henry Van Dyke.

Hamlet, by William Shakespeare.
Macbeth, by William Shakespeare.
Great Expectations, by Charles Dickens.

Reproduced under the terms of the
Project Gutenberg Licence.
www.gutenberg.org

'Footprints In Your Heart', by Eleanor Roosevelt;
also attributed as
'Today is a Gift', by Laszlo Kotro-Kosztandi.
Further bibliographic information unavailable.

Dedication

For Eileen:
See you in the next one. Maybe.

And for the Dog People:
we are a transient population,
unthwarted by rain, wind, snow,
sun-baked earth and horse flies;
may the source of our insanity
remain our salvation.

Contents

"It's the time-birth-death gimmick. Can't go on much longer, too many people are wising up."

William S. Burroughs

CANCER

Learn from the crab, O runner fresh and fleet,
Sideways to move, or backward, when discreet;
Life is not all advance—sometimes retreat!

One For My Baby
Saturday 24th June

They were cruising down the middle lane when Dan saw the HGV on his inside indicate and start moving out. No time to think: in his rear-view mirror, a van coming up behind; in his wing mirror, a cabriolet fast approaching on the outside lane. He could only hope that they, too, would see him as he indicated and moved out.

If he'd stayed where he was, the lorry would have pushed him into the outside lane anyway. Instead, the shunt from the convertible caught his offside rear wing, spinning him directly into the path of the van, which swerved right, scraped along the four-by-four's nearside and set it careering sideways across the inside lane, facing the wrong direction. The front axle hit the bank of the reservation with such force that the car bounced twice before rolling onto its side.

Against the backdrop of screeching brakes and multiple collisions, the engine momentarily screamed high revs, smoking wheels spinning free in the open air, and died away to nothing.

"I'll be home by seven, babe. See ya later." The HGV driver pulled out his earpiece and glanced in his mirror to see what the commotion was. *Lucky that. Could've held me up for hours.* He unmuted the radio and continued his journey.

Low Tide
Friday 23rd June

24 Hours Earlier

Dan parked the four-by-four in the car park next to the hotel and checked the time.

"Four hours, fifty-seven minutes," he bragged. Andy didn't pass comment, his eyes glazed, staring into the distance. "I beat you by a long shot, bro."

"Yeah," Andy replied vaguely, still not really listening. Dan turned away from his brother to see what had him rapt.

"Whoa."

It had been late in the evening when they'd delivered Josh and George to their honeymoon location, and Dan hadn't got to see the bay. The view was spectacular, an expanse of exquisite golden sand stretching out to meet the white-laced edge of the glistening turquoise ocean.

"You weren't kidding, were you?"

"What's that, bro?" Andy asked dreamily.

"About it being perfect." Now they were both at it. "I wonder when the next high tide is?"

"Eighteen seventeen. The forecast's looking good, too. Offshore wind, clean three to four at eight and building. Should be some decent action out there this afternoon."

Dan raised an eyebrow. Of course his brother would know the surf forecast; he'd always lived for adventure. Sadly, these days, he mostly had to settle for imagining, or experiencing it vicariously. For instance, on the first drive down, Dan had overheard Andy telling George about the surf school on the beach, from which he could also hire a wetsuit and board if he fancied having a go.

George had responded with sufficient enthusiasm to give Andy a buzz just talking about it, although with the unwelcome side effect of making him a little subdued in the days that had passed since. Now they were here again; as long as the others were amenable, there was absolutely no reason why they couldn't hang around for a while. God knows, Andy deserved a bit of fun with all that was going on.

Dan took off his seat belt and climbed out of the car. After half a minute of waiting for his brother to do likewise, he went around and opened the passenger door. Andy gave him a vague smile.

"You all right?" Dan asked.

"Yeah."

"I'll go pay for parking. Wait here, if you like."

Andy followed him to the pay-and-display machine, drifting forward to get a better view of the ocean.

Dan dealt with the ticket and joined him. "Quiet out there."

"It won't be." They watched a group of five younger men in wetsuits, all carrying boards, saunter past and down the slipway onto the beach. Andy sighed.

Dan clapped him on the shoulder. "I s'pose we'd best go find the happy couple. Let them know we're here." As he finished speaking, his phone beeped. He read the text message aloud— "Look up and left"—following the instruction a second later. Josh and George waved at him from where they were sitting outside the bar, on a balcony overlooking the beach. He waved back and gave Andy a nudge.

By the time they got there, George was standing at the bar, waiting to buy them a drink. Andy stayed to help; Dan went outside to join Josh.

"Bloody hell! Been a bit sunny, has it, mate?"

"Yes, it has," Josh confirmed. Dan was still staring at him. "I'm guessing I've caught the sun? I can't see how. I've used about a ton of sunblock."

"It's more your hair I was talking about."

"Oh." Josh had noticed himself it had gone lighter, but he hadn't realised quite how much.

When the other men came out, they essentially performed a rerun of the conversation, which made Josh and Dan laugh. The weather was as glorious as it had been all week, and Blue was lying in the shade of the table, his long coat kinked by four days of sea water and showers.

Once they were all seated, Dan put forward his proposal. "Are you all right to hang around for a few hours? Only, surfer dude—" he glanced at his brother, who had that vacant, wistful expression again "—might fancy a quick paddle."

Josh and George looked at each other and shrugged.

"No problem here," George confirmed. "You guys are doing the driving, so whatever works for you."

Andy hadn't heard a word. Dan shoved him.

"What?"

"Go get yourself suited up."

"What?"

"I said—oh, for fuck's sake." Dan started laughing. Andy had drifted off again.

"Tell you what," George suggested, "I'll take him down there."

Josh turned and examined him. "You want to have a go yourself, don't you?"

"Yeah. I've never been surfing before."

"Why didn't you say something earlier in the week?"

"Been having too much fun eating strawberries and...stuff." He grinned. Fortunately, Josh's tan was sufficient to hide his blush.

When George had finished his drink, he got up and stopped next to Andy. "Come on, then. Let's go do this crazy thing."

"What?" Andy asked.

"Surf."

"We've gotta leave soon."

George looked to Dan for help.

"Go surf, bro. We've got a few hours before we need to head home."

"But Steph—"

"I'll give her a call now."

"And what about everyone else?" Andy sounded like he was trying to find an excuse not to go surfing, but it wasn't like that at

6

all. Impulsive he might be, but selfish he was not, and it had taken him a long time to realise his actions could inadvertently be so.

Josh could see the dilemma Andy was in, and decided to try a different approach. "George wants you to show him how to surf."

"There's a perfectly good surf school on the beach."

"And I'd like you to keep an eye on him for me."

"But there's plenty of lifeguards and—"

"Just go and bloody surf, Jeffries!"

Andy shrugged. "Oh, all right then. If you insist." He swigged back his Coke, and he and George made their way down the steps.

Dan waited until they were out of sight before he took out his phone to call Steph. "Nice move," he said to Josh.

"What? The 'George wants you to teach him' thing?"

"Yeah." He brought up Steph's number. "You've had a good time, I take it?"

"The best."

"Good to hear." Steph answered. "Hey, Steph, it's Dan."

"Hi, Dan. Are you there now?"

"We are. Just checking everything's still OK?"

"Of course. Did he take the bait?"

"Eventually."

"Good. Well, all's fine here, tell him."

"Will do. Cheers, Steph."

"Enjoy yourselves. Bye."

"Bye." Dan hung up.

Josh folded his arms. "Impressive," he said.

Dan grinned. "I learnt from the master."

"Who? Me?"

"Yeah. Sometimes you've got to play them at their own game."

"Very true." Josh sipped his drink thoughtfully. "So, if there are still rooms available, we could, theoretically, stay another night."

"Yep." Dan picked up his beer and raised it in a solitary toast.

"You'd already thought of that, hadn't you?"

"Yep." Dan swigged and emptied the bottle. "Can I get you another?"

Josh laughed. "Why not?" He watched Dan go inside and wait at the bar. He was a very different man from the rage-fuelled lunatic Josh had counselled for almost twenty years. In fact, out of the two of them, these days, it was Dan who was more balanced and in control. When he and Adele had lost the baby, Josh had assumed the anger would resurface, as Dan fought to suppress his grief rather than dealing with it. He'd even said as much to Sean. Instead, Dan had faced up to his feelings, allowed himself to mourn, and come through the other side stronger and happier.

Those things always took time and patience, and Dan had never been blessed with much of either, but there was no such thing as a quick fix. It was a fact that had always worked to Josh's advantage, because most people were like Dan—busy lives, working too hard and taking responsibility for the well-being of others, to their own detriment. It was also why Josh and Sean were sceptical of some of the more recent developments in their profession, with programmes set in stone and timely, measurable outcomes. People were unique, and most problems required a bit more than a one-size-fits-all cognitive behavioural sticking plaster that might stay put for a while, but usually came unstuck as soon as it got wet.

"What you thinking about?" Dan asked. He'd returned with the drinks, unnoticed by Josh.

"The demise of modern psychotherapy."

Dan nodded. "Glad I asked."

"Sorry." Josh picked up his drink. "I was also thinking about how much you've changed over the last couple of years."

"In what sense?"

"Only a good one. You seem to have got your head together."

Dan thought on that statement and shrugged. "Yeah. I suppose I have." He took a quick swig of his drink. "Right. I'm gonna pop back to the car, then go get us checked in. See you shortly."

Not long after Dan left, George and Andy came up the steps, carrying surfboards and wetsuits.

"Do you think they'll mind us using our room to get changed?" George asked. "We're no longer staying here, officially."

"Erm, no I'm sure that'll be fine," Josh said cautiously. Earlier, when they went to book out, the hotel had said they could leave their belongings in the room, as no-one new was coming in, which he'd thought a little strange, considering the hotel was displaying the 'no vacancies' sign. Now he knew why, but he wasn't sure whether he should reveal Dan's plans, or wait for him to come back and explain. Luckily, the decision was made for him, as Dan returned a moment later, nonchalantly swinging his car key from the index finger of one hand and carrying a large blue oblong-shaped bag in the other.

"There you go," he said, setting down the bag and holding out a plastic card for Andy to take.

"What's that?"

"That?" He nodded at the bag. "It's your board, bro." It was a statement of the obvious, but it was amusing to play along with his brother's disbelief.

"What the fuck?"

"I got it from Mum's last night."

"Was it in the car?"

"Where else?"

"How come I didn't see it?"

"Ah. That'll be down to me hiding it under a blanket. Anyway, we're in room three fifteen. Ocean Wing."

"That's next to ours," Josh said.

"What a coincidence!" Dan winked at him.

Andy frowned. "What's going on?"

"We're staying the night, bro."

"Since when?"

"Since I booked it yesterday."

Andy was about to protest, but Dan cut him off.

"It's all sorted with Steph, so don't worry. Just go and surf."

Andy was speechless.

"Cool," George said. "Bonus night."

They left their boards and went up to the rooms, George giving Andy something of a guided tour along the way, pointing out the restaurant, the gym, sauna and massage rooms, the hot tub on the balcony and the incredible pool that extended out over the cliff and terminated against a vast glass wall so that it looked like it flowed straight into the ocean. They hadn't really used the facilities to the fullest during their stay, but he didn't mention that bit.

"If you've got any plastic bags around," Andy told him as they parted company at their respective doors, "stick them on your feet before you try and get the wetsuit on. It'll be easier."

George nodded and disappeared inside. Ten minutes later, Andy knocked on the door.

"You OK in there?"

"Kind of," George muttered breathlessly. He was in the wetsuit, but there was no way he could reach the cord to zip it up. He opened the door.

"Ah, yeah." Andy smiled. "Zip's a bastard till you get used to it."

George turned around, and Andy pulled the shoulders of the suit back hard, expertly wiggling the zip up.

They returned to the balcony, this time with Andy giving George some of the tips he'd picked up over the years on how best to get in and out of a wetsuit. His old one was a nightmare to get off, and he usually did it whilst still in the water. The newer suits were a lot more flexible, which was as well—somehow he didn't think George would like the idea of stripping down to his boxers in public.

As it was, they weren't the ideal undergarment, and if Andy had been in his own wetsuit, he'd probably have gone commando. In fact, it was lucky he'd decided not to do that when he got up this morning, although his recent reminder of what had happened with Bertie in the lift was enough to ensure that most days he remembered to put on a pair of undies, even if they hadn't saved him on that particular occasion.

***

Josh was watching as they approached, his eyes slowly passing over the two men in their skintight, black neoprene suits. He blinked slowly.

"I feel naked," George said, his face burning with both embarrassment and how hot he was now he was in the sun.

"Yes, I can see why you would." Josh grinned up at him.

George leaned close and whispered, "Are you undressing me?"

"No need. I can see everything already!"

George glanced down.

Andy laughed. "Let's get out there, then no-one will be looking." He unzipped his board bag and flipped it open, revealing his longboard, with its custom shape and design—a bright red, orange and blue gradient with an Aztec-styled sun at one end.

"My word. That's vibrant," Josh remarked, holding his hand up to shield his eyes.

"Yeah, well, what can I say? It was hip back in the day. My other boards aren't quite so far out."

"It's like an explosion in a crayon factory," Dan said, watching his brother apply wax over the lurid paint job.

"What's that for?" George asked.

"Traction," Andy said. "I'll do yours, too. Helps you to stay on."

"Cool. I think I'm gonna need all the help I can get."

A few minutes later, Andy was all done, and they picked up their boards and left by the stairs, with Blue in pursuit.

Josh and Dan watched on, the other two men and dog gradually becoming smaller as they walked out towards the ocean, with Andy occasionally raising his free hand and motioning as he offered instructions to George.

Josh continued to watch them as he addressed Dan. "We haven't had much chance to speak since George's little incident in the park, with everything else that's been going on."

"I know. It's been a mad few months."

"It certainly has. Anyway, I just want to reiterate how much I appreciated your support."

"No need, mate. You've always done the same for me."

"Yes, well, it still needed saying. That was one hell of a day."

"You're not wrong there. You get migraines often?"

"Once or twice a year, at most."

"What causes them? Do you know?"

"Not for sure. When my grandma had her stroke, the consultant suggested there might be a genetic aspect to it, and it frightened the life out of me. I got the all-clear, though, so I know it's not that."

11

"That's good," Dan said.

Josh took the moment to study his friend as he stared into the distance, at Andy and George, who had reached the water's edge.

"So you've not had any since?" Dan asked.

"Hmm?" Josh's mind had wandered away from their starting point, for he had fleetingly considered just saying it. The time would have been right to do so, but the thought had quickly mutated into a hundred questions, chasing through all the potential outcomes such a statement could produce.

So, I tell Dan, and Dan tells Adele, and she tells Shaunna, who tells Kris, and so on and so forth, and they'll all know, which is what we want. But then, each time I so much as grumble about a headache, they'll be on my case—is he manic? Is he about to freak out and throw himself off a building?

Alternatively, Dan might think it selfish of me to be drawing attention to myself now, with Jess being sick, and it can wait until this trial is…over. And what if that triggers a massive episode? Is that what's been going on this week? The start of a prolonged period of hypomania? Maybe I should just get it out in the open, for George's sake.

"The migraines?" Dan prompted.

"Oh. No." Josh breathed out slowly and heavily. "That was the last one."

Dan nodded his understanding and returned to watching their surfing companions, who were too distant to be seen in any great detail, but it was apparent that Andy was demonstrating how to paddle and get up on the board whilst still on dry land, and George was copying.

Josh glanced out past them and scanned the break; the waves in the centre of the bay were smaller, and the greater number of surfers were congregated there, the majority of them using the same blue and yellow boards as the one George had acquired from the hire shop. However, the real surfing action was taking place further along to the right.

Over the course of the past few days, Josh had observed that the more experienced surfers arrived a couple of hours before high tide, indistinguishable in their wetsuits, although he could identify them by their boards. They stayed out long after the beginners had tired, so hopefully, Andy would get a good session in before the day was over.

Josh squinted and located George and Andy again; they were in the water, and Andy had waded out past George, holding his board under his arm whilst he offered further instruction.

"He showed me how to surf," Dan said. "He's actually a pretty decent teacher."

"I can imagine. He's got lots of patience."

George was following Andy, both of them lying on their boards and paddling with their arms. They stopped a little way out and turned back.

"Yeah," Dan continued. "And he doesn't take the piss, either. I'm shit at it, but he persevered until I got it as well as I was going to."

As the next wave approached, George started paddling with it but remained lying down. He repeated the action a few times, with Andy lazily drifting along beside him, pausing in between waves to explain some thing or other.

"I quite fancy the idea of having a go myself," Josh mused. "Although I'm too much of a wimp to try."

Dan nodded in agreement. "I'm more than happy to leave the adventure sports to him."

The two men paddled out again. Blue had become bored and was slowly coming back up the beach, stopping to greet other dogs and people along the way. He arrived back on the balcony and flopped down under the table once more. Josh looked up in time to see George make his first attempt to pull himself to his feet, whereby he immediately fell off his board.

"Andy'll have him riding those waves in no time," Dan asserted. He fell silent for a couple of minutes, alternating between being artificially absorbed in studying the label on his beer bottle and glancing out to sea. "I realise this is a bit out of the blue, but I want to ask you a favour."

"OK."

Dan paused and picked up his beer. "It's a biggie."

Josh nodded to encourage him, but he didn't speak for a while.

Keeping his eyes downturned, Dan frowned and swigged at the bottle. "I know you don't go in for all that marriage guidance malarkey, but I wondered if you fancied making an exception?"

"Erm…"

Josh didn't know what to say. He really, *really* hated working with couples. Granted, in the past, it had been due to not feeling qualified to do so, given that he had no personal experience of relationships. There again, he didn't have experience of most of what he treated people for, so it had always been a poor justification. He also didn't see the support he offered his friends as work—not even with Dan, although that was how they'd dealt with it in the past.

"Are things that bad between you?" he asked.

"No. They're all right, as it goes."

"So what do you need me for?"

"Well, it's like this. I want another baby. Adele wants to go back to college. God knows where that idea came from."

"Presumably, it's because Shaunna's been talking about doing it?"

Dan shook his head. "When Shaunna told her she was enrolling on a course, Adele started up on the whole 'I wish I could' routine, but she had no intention of pursuing it—said she wasn't clever enough. Then all of a sudden, she changed her mind."

"Oh, right." Josh quickly turned his attention back to the surfers. He'd evidently succeeded in persuading Adele she could go back to college if she really wanted to, so it was kind of his own fault he was in this predicament. George fell off again. "The two aren't mutually exclusive," Josh said. "Having a baby and going to college. She can do both."

"Yeah. I know that. It's an excuse." Dan made eye contact. "I'm glad we're on the same wavelength."

Josh rolled his eyes. "And *that* is precisely why I don't go in for 'that marriage guidance malarkey'. It's not nice being caught in the middle. But I'll do it, because it's you."

"Blimey. If I'd known it was going to be that easy…"

"It won't be, I assure you."

"You know what Adele's—"

14

Josh put up his hand and stopped Dan mid-flow. "That's it now. No more talking about Adele. The first rule from here on is that you both have to be present whenever you want to talk to me about each other. Otherwise, it'll head into the realm of tit-for-tat, and I'm the umpire, not the tennis ball."

"Fair enough."

Dan's bottle was empty; Josh quickly finished his own beer and went to get them another. He was starting to feel a bit giddy and really ought to slow down, but he was enjoying himself too much. He took the drinks back outside, glancing into the distance as he did so. George was up on his board again, and this time, he managed to travel a few feet before he straightened his legs and toppled sideways.

"They look like they're having a good time," Dan observed.

"Yes, they do," Josh agreed. "Cheers." He tapped his bottle against Dan's.

"So, have you been up to anything interesting that you can tell me about?"

Josh blushed. "Put it this way, I can tell you about the non-interesting stuff. As for the rest of it…"

Dan laughed. "Say no more."

"I'll probably end up saying a lot more over the next few hours. I'm feeling a tad inebriated."

"Sun and beer does that to you."

For now, they both stayed quiet and spent some time appreciating the scenery and the easiness of each other's company. With nobody else around, neither felt the need to get embroiled in their usual antics of one-upmanship.

***

Andy and George were now surfing independently of each other, with Andy having quickly got back into the swing of it. He was a very experienced and skilful surfer, and as such, a few people were watching as he paddled out, waited, and then rode back, covering vast lengths of shoreline at a time.

George was happy riding straight in on the white water of the smaller waves, along with the rest of the beginners. He'd picked it up quickly, but he was getting tired, so the next time he came close to the beach, he decided to have a rest. As he stood watching Andy, someone came up alongside him.

"Hi, George," the man said with a smile.

"Hi." George returned the smile cautiously.

"I thought you said you'd never been surfing."

"I hadn't. My friend's been giving me lessons."

"You were doing great out there."

"Thanks." They both watched the expert surfers riding along the larger waves further from the break.

"Which one's your friend?"

George pointed. "The guy with the red, blue and orange board."

"Wow. He's pretty awesome!"

"Yeah. He's been doing it for years."

A wave had just wiped out most of the surfers, but somehow Andy was still standing. He rode the wave in and stepped off his board.

"You OK?" he asked George.

"Yep. I'm thinking I might head back up to the bar, though—try and figure out how I go for a pee in this thing!"

"OK. Good luck with that. I'm gonna carry on for a while longer, if that's all right?"

"Sure," George confirmed. Andy went straight back out and was soon on his board again, ready for the next decent wave. George glanced at the guy standing next to him. "You staying down here?"

"No. I need to go do the same thing you do." They turned and walked back up the beach together. "I wouldn't normally bother."

"With?"

"The toilet. You can just do it in the sea. All ends up there anyway."

"Ew." George wrinkled his nose. They both laughed. As they got closer to the bar, George kept his focus on Josh. He was turned towards Dan but kept surreptitiously glancing their way.

"Trouble?"

George shrugged. "Come and say hi?"

"Sure."

High Tide
Friday 23rd June

Josh was trying his hardest to appear disinterested in George's return, faking enthusiasm for the conversation he and Dan were having—a quick catch-up on the past few days, during which absolutely nothing had happened.

"Hi," George called as he approached their table. He leaned down and gave Josh a kiss, dripping sea water onto his cheek.

"Hi, yourself." Josh frowned, wiping his face with his sleeve. "Had fun?"

"Yeah. It's amazing. I'd kind of like to go back in again, but I need the loo. I'm just gonna pop up to our room. Oh, and this is Will." He stepped aside.

"Hi." Will shook Josh's hand warmly.

"Hello, Will. I'm Josh."

"Good to meet you."

"And I'm Dan," Dan said.

Will shook his hand, too, and turned back to Josh. "Sorry about the misunderstanding the other day, by the way."

"Don't worry." Josh flashed him a quick smile. Will was staring at him intently, and it was making him feel uncomfortable.

George subtly cleared his throat. "OK. Any tips for getting out of this thing?"

"Pair of scissors?" Dan suggested.

Will laughed. "Yeah. That's not a bad idea. Luckily, they're easier to take off than get on, but if you're keeping it on, just pull it down as far as you need to."

"OK. Be back soon." George set off in the direction of his and Josh's room. Will waited next to the table.

"Pull up a chair," Josh invited.

"I will in a sec. I need to use the Gents' myself first." Will glanced inside hopefully.

"Past the bar and to the right," Josh instructed.

Will nodded in thanks and left.

"Misunderstanding?" Dan asked.

"Yes, although that's something of an understatement. He was chatting George up."

"Oh?"

"You sound surprised."

"I am a bit. He seemed more interested in you than George, to be honest."

"Did he?"

"Yeah."

"I didn't notice."

"The dreamy staring kind of gave him away."

"Did it?"

Dan laughed. "I'm beginning to see now why you were so shocked to find out George was in love with you."

"I know. Is it weird?"

"Yep, but you always were a bit...unique." Dan grinned broadly.

"Thanks!"

A short while later, George arrived back, having swapped the wetsuit for shorts and a t-shirt, although he had brought his wetsuit with him. There was still plenty of time to get in a little more surfing if he wanted. He could fully appreciate how people 'got the bug'. It was exhilarating being out there; he scanned the waterline until he spotted the brightly coloured surfboard. There were a couple of others with similar boards, but only one riding well.

"Has Will gone?" he asked.

Josh shook his head. "No. He went to use the loo."

"Ah, OK." As George spoke, he turned and saw Will coming over. He arrived at their table and shrugged at George's attire.

"You given up on surfing?"

"Not necessarily, but I'm knackered. After all, I'm only a beginner."

Will accepted George's justification and sat down, conspicuously the only one in a wetsuit.

18

Josh picked up on his unease, although it took him longer than usual to work out what was causing it. Once he had, there was only one thing for it. "Would you like a drink, Will?"

"I would, but I don't have my card or any money with me. I only came down to surf."

"Don't worry about that. What can I get you?"

"One of those would be great, thanks." Will indicated the bottles Dan and Josh were drinking. "I'll give you a hand."

Josh put his bottle down, and he and Will went inside to the bar.

Dan made eye contact with George. "Trust is a bloody wonderful thing."

"Sure is. It does help that Josh doesn't have the faintest clue."

"Yeah. We were just chatting about that. How the hell can't he see it?"

George shrugged. "Dunno," he said, although he had a fairly good idea. Josh didn't believe anyone was interested in him, therefore he didn't pick up on the signs he had no problem spotting if they were directed towards anyone else. Now he was aware of it, Josh was noticeably uncomfortable, as evidenced by his nervous laughter at whatever Will was saying when they came back with the drinks. To be fair to Will, he was trying his hardest to hide his attraction, but he was stuck in that strange state George understood all too well, of knowing you can't have the thing you want, yet somehow unable to leave it alone and walk away.

"Will was just telling me that the outrageous board guy is usually the kook—the idiot show-off who's loaded but can't surf," Josh explained. He gave George one of the bottles of beer he was holding.

George smiled up at him and mouthed, "Are you OK?" Josh nodded and sat down next to him.

"He *is* an idiot show-off," Dan said.

"But he *can* surf," George argued.

"Very true." The conversation paused for a few minutes whilst they watched Andy lazily traverse the length of a wave and jump clear of his board before it stopped. Meanwhile, Will's point was being well and truly proven by the two other surfers with outrageous boards, who weren't entirely useless, but certainly weren't good enough to be drawing attention to themselves.

When the conversation resumed, Will offered a running commentary on the various manoeuvres being performed by Andy and others demonstrating their sport to good effect, and it continued along those lines through to the end of their drinks. George went to the bar and returned with five bottles; he'd noticed Andy heading back up the beach.

Dan glanced in his brother's direction, observing his adrenaline-fuelled presence and slicked-back, wet hair. He rolled his eyes. "You know what's gonna happen now, don't you?" he said.

Josh laughed. "Want to lay money on it?"

They shook hands to seal the wager.

Andy came over and grinned. "Wow. That was totally fucking sick!" He put his board down and shook his head, spraying them with sea water.

"Cheers for that," George grumbled. He'd not long dried off.

"Sorry, man."

Dan smirked. "Listen to that. He's gone all surf-speak on us."

"Gnarly, dude," George said in what was supposed to be a West Coast accent but wasn't actually distinguishable from how he'd sounded when he first came back from Colorado. The other men laughed.

"So, I'm guessing you two are brothers?" Will asked Dan and Andy.

"Yep," Andy confirmed.

"Cool." Will picked up his beer, switching his focus between the surfers out on the waves and those passing by on their way off the beach, acknowledging people he knew. Dan waited optimistically, but it looked like there was no follow-up. He extracted a five-pound note from his wallet and was in the process of passing it across the table to Josh when Will had to go and ruin it—for Josh, at any rate.

"Usually, twins are both into the same kinds of stuff, but I'm guessing you're not a surfer, Dan?"

Dan snatched the five-pound note back and grinned victoriously. Josh stuck out his tongue at him.

"You wanna say it, or shall I, bro?" Andy asked.

"Be my guest."

By this point, George was laughing too much to speak, and poor Will was terribly confused. Andy sighed and turned to him.

"We're not twins," he said wearily. That made George laugh even more.

"Oh. Sorry." Will looked so embarrassed that Josh decided to come to his rescue.

"It's a standing joke," he explained.

Will mouthed another 'oh' in understanding.

"Almost everyone assumes they're twins the first time they meet them. However, they are into most of the same kinds of stuff, so you were right in that respect."

Will maintained eye contact. His attraction was still obvious to everyone other than Josh, who paused for a drink and continued gabbling—about Andy being the eldest, and how he was into extreme sports and trekking to remote locations to 'jump off mountains and stuff', whereas Dan liked his fast cars and risky business deals.

The other three men listened in for a short while but then broke away to their own conversation, which was about Dan's surprise stay-over for Andy's benefit. If he could, he'd have kept him in Cornwall for a further day, because it was his birthday on Sunday, and he knew it would be spent in places Andy didn't want to be in order to give Jess and Steph time on their own. Sadly, there was nothing to be done about it; Dan was flying to Belfast, and George was back in work.

The tide was receding and it looked pretty flat now; Andy decided to go and change back into his clothes, which once again put Will in something of a predicament. Much as he seemed keen to stay, the decision would be formalised by whatever he did next. Therefore, when Dan asked him if he'd like another drink, he shrugged, and said honestly, "I'd really like that, but I don't want to be in the way."

"You won't be," Josh assured him.

"OK. I'll get changed and stay for one more, then leave you to it. Want some help, Dan?"

"Sure."

Will followed him to the bar, leaving Josh and George sitting on their own.

"See?" George said, once Will and Dan were out of earshot.

"See what?"

"I told you he found you attractive."

"Yes. This really is uncharacteristically mercenary of you."

"What d'you mean?"

"Bringing him up here so you can make a point."

George turned away, even though it was too late to cover his intent. He should have known better. Josh nudged him with his elbow. He turned back. "It was a bit cruel of me, huh?"

Josh glanced past him, to where Andy had now joined the other two men at the bar. He and Will greeted each other with a shaka and started up a deep and meaningful conversation of the surfer variety.

"He seems happy enough."

"I guess. But do you believe me now?"

"I don't suppose I have any choice, given Dan picked up on it, too. I still can't see it."

"Man, you must've passed up some opportunities over the years."

"Maybe." Josh frowned thoughtfully. "Have I been flirting with him?"

"Nope."

"Good. I'm glad about that."

George took hold of Josh's hand and sighed in mock exasperation. "You're a very strange man," he said.

Josh smiled and kissed him. "I must be. I married you!"

George laughed. "I'm sure we've had this conversation before."

The others returned, and once Will had swapped his wetsuit for the shorts and vest he'd stashed behind a rock, the conversations continued in a typical way, with Dan asking him what he did for a living. He was a little reluctant to say at first, as he'd been working as an investment banker, until the 'credit crunch', and most people he told seemed to hold him personally accountable, even though he was but a very small cog in a vast leviathan of a wheel. Some of Dan's old university buddies had gone on to work in banking, so he understood the dilemma many found themselves in, aware that their actions were unethical and high risk but powerless to speak out or act against the might of the big finance machine.

The conversation naturally evolved into a more psychological discussion of group dynamics, risk-taking and representative heuristics, but it was Dan, not Josh, who was holding court. He had taken a course in industrial psychology as part of his degree and knew a great deal more about it than Josh did. Indeed, other than suggesting the mindset behind the financial crisis was similar to that of problem gambling, Josh had little to say, which was odd, as it was the sort of discussion that generally saw him and Dan at loggerheads, but he was very quiet.

At the next lull in the conversation, George stood up. "I'm gonna take my board and wetsuit back."

"I'll come with you," Andy said. "See if I can keep hold of mine until tomorrow, catch a few of those early morning waves before breakfast."

Will decided to leave them to it, staying just long enough for George and Andy to return so they could all swap contact details and give him some chance of returning the favour, before saying his goodbyes and jogging away in the direction of the path up the cliff.

Josh watched him leave and then flopped back in his chair, sighing so loudly that the other three men all turned and looked at him.

"I have never felt so on edge in my life!"

"Why?" Andy asked. "He seemed pretty down-to-earth to me."

"Yes, but—"

Andy interrupted before Josh got any further. "Clearly had the major hots for you, though."

"So I'm told!" Josh picked up his bottle and swigged the entire contents in one go.

"Are you trying to get drunk?" Dan asked.

"Nope." He hiccupped. "Already there." He hiccupped again and passed his empty bottle across. "Your round, I believe."

Dan passed it back. "It's yours, but I'm not convinced—"

Josh shrugged. On a second try, he made it out of his chair and staggered off towards the bar.

"Damn. I didn't think he'd make it." Dan got up and followed him, leaving Andy and George looking bemused.

"What was that about?" Andy asked.

"Beats me," George said.

They watched Josh clinging onto the bar as he ordered their drinks, whilst Dan stood next to him, talking quietly into his ear. A few minutes later, Dan returned alone.

"He's visiting the Gents'," he explained. Andy nodded and picked up one of the beers that Dan had set down. George went to check on Josh.

***

Josh was swaying in front of the urinal, singing to himself. "You OK?" George asked as he approached. Josh jumped.

"Oh, I'm fine, just fine," he slurred, the words merging into one. "But I do need to sober up a tiny bit." With much effort, he fastened the buttons of his fly and wobbled his way over to the sink.

"Dan's worried about you."

"Is he? Aw. That's nice." Josh washed his hands and wiped them dry on his trousers.

"So am I."

"No, no. It's all fine. See, all it was was…" He frowned. "Was was. What the hell does that mean?" He staggered backwards and steadied himself against the wall. "Don't let me drink anymore for a while, please?"

"I won't. All what was?"

"All what was? What was I going to tell you? Oh, yes. That's right. Dan wants me to do some of that marriage guidance malarkey. That's what he called it. A malarkey. It is, too. He said not to make a public announcement, but you know what I'm thinking? I'm thinking that it would be just the perfect time to make a public announcement."

"Joshua, you're drunk."

"Yes, George-u-a, I am." He started giggling and nearly fell over. George caught him and held on.

"I'll tell you what I'm thinking," George said. "We get you a pint of water and some food on the way out."

"Good idea," Josh agreed, nodding enthusiastically. He allowed George to guide him back to the table and into his chair.

"Stay," George commanded.

"Yessir." Josh mock-saluted and poked himself in the eye. He tried to focus on George retreating to the bar.

"You OK, mate?" Andy asked.

"Erm, yes. Too much sun in the beer. I'll be OK. George is getting me a burglar." He started giggling again, hiccupped and put his hand over his mouth. "I don't drink, you know. It goes straight to my head." He exaggerated the word 'straight' and gestured with his arm, knocking one of the bottles off the table. It rolled around the decking, spewing fizzy liquid from its neck. "Oops!" He stooped and swayed, and somehow managed to pick it up. George returned and swapped the bottle for the water. Josh smiled at him and sipped rapidly at the glass.

"I want to tell you something," he said in between sips, scanning the other men sitting around the table and doing his best to home in on Andy. "Especially you."

"Josh," George said cagily. "I think maybe now is not—"

"Shush." He attempted to put his finger against George's lips and missed. "This is for us. For you."

George took a hold of Josh's outstretched hand and looked into his eyes, beseeching him not to do something he'd regret. Josh took a deep breath in and let it go, another hiccup escaping with it. He smiled.

"I can't do it any other way. I'm sorry."

"You don't have to do it at all."

"I do." He kept hold of George's hand and turned back to Dan and Andy. They both looked very worried.

"Listen, Josh mate," Dan appealed. "Alcohol does funny things to your brain, makes you say stuff you don't really mean, so maybe you should just keep it shut, yeah?"

"No." Josh shook his head and wobbled on his chair. He stopped shaking his head and held onto the table to steady himself.

"Ten-minute rule," Andy said.

"What?"

"Ten-minute rule. You wait ten minutes, and if you still want to say whatever it is you think you want to say, then you can."

"That's a stupid rule. Who came up with that?"

"Actually," George interjected, "I think that's a really good idea. Your burger will be here soon. How about you eat first?"

"How about you stop bossing me about, seeing as it was your suggestion to start with!"

"But not like this."

Josh pulled a silly face, and George laughed in spite of what was happening.

"OK. I'll do your stupid ten-minute rule," Josh relented. He sat back and folded his arms. "Where's my food?"

"On its way."

"Good."

An uneasy silence descended, but not for long.

"Is it ten minutes yet?"

"No!"

"OK."

Silence once more. Josh took a breath in. George put his hand up.

"Don't!" he commanded. He took his phone out and set the timer running. "There. Watch that." He put it on the table in front of Josh, who was immediately entranced by the whirring digital numbers, not that he could read them particularly well.

"I can go and get my glasses on Monday," he said, still watching the display and hiccuping every so often. "They sent a text to say they were ready."

Dan and Andy briefly made eye contact. It was without a doubt the strangest evening they had ever spent with Josh. True, he'd have a few too many with the best of them, but he didn't get out-of-control drunk.

Josh's burger arrived, and he picked it up and took a bite of it, all the while continuing to watch the timer. It was now up to five and a half minutes, and he was still set on telling them. He carried on eating, pausing to count aloud through the last sixty seconds. He clicked the red 'stop' button onscreen, passed George's phone to him and took his hand, giving it a squeeze. George squeezed back and closed his eyes.

"So," Josh said, turning his attention to Dan and Andy, who were both a little less blurry now. He smiled at them, hoping to put them at ease, but it didn't work. "Firstly, I should give you some context." He paused. "Scratch that. I'll do context last. No, even better. A guessing game!" He took George's phone back and unlocked the screen. "Right. You have one minute to name as many psychiatric illnesses as you can, starting…now!" He pressed the start button and looked at them expectantly.

"Are you for real?" Andy asked.

"Yes."

"This is madness," Dan said.

Josh wagged his finger. "You need to specify the kind of madness you mean. Forty-five seconds left."

Andy frowned. "Schizophrenia?"

"Well done, Andy!" Josh said in his best schoolteacher voice.

"Erm, depression? Is that one?"

"It certainly is. Two-nil to Andy. Any offers, Dan?"

"I'm not playing," he said.

Andy scratched his head. "OCD?"

"Very good! Twenty-five seconds."

Andy couldn't think of any more. Dan sat with his arms folded, refusing to be drawn, because he was freaked out by Josh's behaviour. This was even worse than when they were waiting for George to be released.

"Ten, nine, eight…" Josh counted down to zero. "Time's up. And the winner is?"

"Please stop," George said quietly.

Josh gripped his hand more tightly. "Hey, it's OK." He leaned close and whispered in his ear. "It's all an act." George peered up, and Josh winked at him. He turned once more to Dan and Andy. "See, I wanted to show you, because just telling you wouldn't be enough for you to understand. So you know, I have had way too much to drink. However, I had to start somewhere and somewhen, so why not here and now?

"I can see by the way you're both looking at me that my actions have unnerved you. Wouldn't it be wonderful to dismiss it all as the simple and temporary effect of alcoholic over-indulgence? Of course, on this occasion, that's precisely what it is. Anyway, I don't want to drag this out any longer, so I'm just going to say it." He stopped, took a huge gulping breath of air and held it. "I have bipolar disorder." He breathed out; no hiccups this time.

"I don't know what that means," Dan said.

"Manic depression?"

"Ah. Gotcha."

Josh waited, anticipating questions. None were forthcoming. "Feel free to ask me about it."

"All that weird shit just then," Andy said. "That's like the highs, is it?"

Josh looked to George to answer, as he would know better, although he'd felt himself spiralling up towards hypomania and was still fighting to stop the tornado touching down.

"That's right," George confirmed.

"And the other pole is the depression?"

"Yes." Josh nodded.

"OK." Andy glugged the last of his beer and examined the bottle, trying to decide if he wanted another one, or if he should get an early night so he'd be up for surfing at dawn.

"What was the context you mentioned?" Dan asked.

"That I've had it since I was at university."

"Bloody hell. That's rough."

"More so for George than me, which is why I'm telling you."

"What do you need from us?"

"A promise." Josh stopped and amended. "Two promises." He looked from one to the other of the two brothers, who had always personified what his illness meant to him. It was right that they should know first.

"Yes, whatever they are," Andy said.

Josh laughed. "OK. First, I'd like your soul."

Andy raised an eyebrow. "When it thaws, it's yours."

"Awesome." Josh reached across the table and patted Andy's hand. "I'll be there, with a bucket to catch the drips," he said. Andy smiled briefly to show he understood. "Anyway. The real first promise is that you don't automatically assume everything I do is because I'm sick, because mostly I'm not, although it can get pretty bad, hence two promises. The second is that you support George when he needs it."

"How long have you wanted to tell us?" Dan asked.

"Since I was at university."

"This really is for George's benefit?"

"Yes."

Dan shrugged. "Deal."

"That easy?"

"Yep. That easy."

Wipeout
Saturday 24th June

Six a.m.

Josh had awoken an hour earlier and stumbled to the bathroom, holding his head in an attempt to stop the thumping within, like a team of tiny termites armed with pneumatic drills were trying to excavate their way through his temples. He realised he was still leaning on the sink with his eyes closed, carefully opened them and peered at his terrible reflection.

Why… If he could have done so without vomiting, he'd have shaken his head in dismay. Instead, he brushed his teeth and gargled some mouthwash, which dealt with the bitterness on his tongue, but not with his mind, as it tried to reconcile his actions of the previous evening.

Back out to their room, he glanced at George, curled up fast asleep. Maybe in a little while, he might try rejoining him; right at that moment he needed fresh air. He quietly pulled on a pair of trousers and, with Blue for company, wandered down to the beach, optimistic that a good blast of early morning ocean breeze would clear his head.

The tide was on its way in, with vast, white-tipped waves forging towards the shoreline. On the horizon, there was a single boat: a large cargo vessel with square lettering that he could almost make out from his location. He stood, arms folded against the chill, watching the three surfers weave their way through the rolling ocean. Such a wonderful peace, it was awe-inspiring.

The day was too dull to pick out any colour detail, but even so, it didn't take long for Josh to identify Andy. He was taking every opportunity the surf granted, lazily riding along one wave, before zigzagging to the next, until he was too close to the beach to come any further. Josh shivered and pulled his arms tight to his chest. It was the first morning since they'd been there that didn't carry the promise of wonderful Cornish sunshine, which was good in a way, for it would be easier to leave it behind.

Blue was snuffling between the rocks, obscured but for his tail and ears, and whatever he'd discovered had him completely transfixed. Every so often, he'd jump up in the air and go running around in circles for a few seconds, before slinking back over. Josh went to investigate. It turned out to be nothing more exciting than a washed-up jellyfish caught in one of the rock pools, a little larger than average and still alive. Once again, Blue poked it with his nose and leapt back when it stung him.

"I thought you were supposed to be intelligent," Josh said to the dog, as he did it again, and again. Josh shook his head and called him away. Together, they walked back along the beach, Josh switching his attention between Blue, who kept finding jellyfish and refused to learn his lesson, and the surfers paddling their way out, although Andy was on his way in. He spotted them and waved.

"You're up early," Andy called as soon as he was within hearing distance.

"Hangover."

"Bad, is it?"

"It's better out here. How's the surf this morning?"

"Pretty decent. I've been out since first light—the other guys were already here—decided I'd best do a dawnie, make the most of it. God knows when I'll get the chance again."

The two men remained standing, turned towards the ocean, listening to the white noise of the waves and the calls of the gulls overhead. Josh shivered.

"It's warmer when you're in the water," Andy told him.

"I'll take your word for it."

The silence resumed for a few minutes before Andy spoke again.

"Ten years. That's how long it's been since I was last here, and it's hardly changed. All right, so they've extended the hotel and renovated the bar and stuff, but the bay itself's the same as ever. Thank fuck.

"There's this place in Wales, where we used to go on holiday when we were kids. It had caves, and rock pools full of crabs. And we'd all sit on the jetty with our crabbing lines, seeing who could catch the most out of the four of us—me, Dan, Mike and Dad. That's where the competitive streak comes from. Dad should've been helping me and Dan, and instead he'd be bragging about how he'd caught more than us.

"Anyway, I was over that way last year, so I decided to go for a visit and wish I hadn't bothered. It's like someone smashing through your dreams with a sledgehammer. The cliffs fall away all the time, but they'd had such a massive collapse that the caves were no longer accessible, and they gave up maintaining the jetty years ago. The place was desolate—a ghost resort.

"When I think back to all those families down on the beach, girls collecting shells and pebbles, us lads sitting along the jetty—I was hoping the same thing hadn't happened to this place, and I'm glad it hasn't, but it worries me—looking at the hotel, and the bar and what-have-you—it all reeks a little too much of Dubai, although no surf schools there anymore. No surf, either, unless you count that bloody monstrosity in the middle of the desert."

"They've built an artificial beach in the desert?" Josh asked.

Andy tilted his head from side to side, weighing up the accuracy of the description. "It's more of a massive wave machine. Honestly, the place is nuts. They build fake islands, then cart in skiploads of marine life from elsewhere because the native marine life has been buried under tons of silt, and the ecosystem's screwed. The authorities changed the law, pretty much banning all the stuff you see here—surf schools, board hire and the like—yet nearly every single beach is privately owned by rich bastards who'll fuck the place over, move on and do the same elsewhere.

"As for the wave pool—what's the point? They might be ten foot high, but every single one is exactly the same. There's

31

no challenge. And it's a weird contradiction, when I think on, because we want to save places like this, and that Welsh cove too, but at what cost? Out there, riding real waves, you're battling nature. That's the thrill. That's the challenge.

"Shoring up the cliffs—that's battling nature, too. The difference is a surfer knows who's boss, which is why I'd rather watch this place fall into the sea than see fat cats destroy it in the name of preservation." Andy stopped talking and laughed ruefully to himself. "I tell you what, mate, there's a lot to be said for keeping the memory. No revisiting. Just move on."

The surfers had drifted away from them now. They watched for a while longer and started to stroll back towards the hotel.

"This is still a fabulous place," Josh said.

"Yeah," Andy agreed. "It is. I'm glad you like it."

"We do. And thanks for the honeymoon. It's been wonderful."

"No worries."

The silence returned, although Josh could sense that Andy was thinking, preparing to speak. After a couple of minutes, he found the words.

"I hope you've got that bucket at the ready," he remarked lightly. He smiled, but his eyes were glassy.

Josh nodded. "I thought that last night."

Andy swallowed hard, trying to dam the tears. He and Josh had reached the foot of the steps to the hotel, but Andy strode off along the base of the cliffs.

Josh followed and watched from a few feet away, as Andy balanced on the edge of a fallen rock, gripping his surfboard and taking long, deep breaths. He was trying to regain control and let out a low growl, like a strong man lifting a tremendous weight.

"I still love her," he confessed. He sighed and scuffed at the sand, burying his feet and pushing hard until his toes reappeared.

Andy was shaking—*with rage? With anguish?* Josh couldn't tell, but here he was, yet again, smack-bang in the middle of an emotional minefield. To his credit, Andy had tried not to involve him, but with their friendship group, that was just the way it happened. *Maybe it's to do with there being an odd number of people,*

32

*although…*Josh didn't want to take that thought any further and pushed it away.

"Sorry," Andy said eventually.

"Don't apologise."

"You told me, didn't you? You said it wouldn't work in the long-term."

"That's right, I did. But we can do it again if you want, or try something else?"

Andy shook his head, disappointed with himself. "What's the use? I love her, and there's nothing I can do."

Josh propped himself on the next rock along.

Andy studied his surfboard, rubbing at the wax smears. "Seeing her every day is fucking torture." He stopped rubbing and gazed out to sea, trying to make sense of his feelings. "It's like an addiction. The more I see her, the more I need her."

Josh nodded. "That's the problem with suppression. You know that saying, 'don't think of an elephant'? As soon as the thought's in there, that's all you can think about."

Andy laughed, but not in joy. "Some awful bloody elephant this is."

"You need to talk to Sean," Josh stated in a matter-of-fact tone and quickly continued, to ensure that Andy had no opportunity to interrupt or protest. "That's the other reason I told you about the bipolar, but I couldn't say as much in front of Dan. What I did with you is what Sean did with me, back in uni, when I was first diagnosed, and he was experimenting with a new technique. He shouldn't have tried it out on me, and I shouldn't have used it on you, but, well, sometimes doing the right thing involves doing the wrong thing. Anyway, he's spent years refining it since, and it works for a lot of people."

Andy frowned. He was reluctant to talk to anyone, but he couldn't carry on the way he was.

Josh got up and looked back at him. "For the record, I don't like him much, either. He's a smarmy git, and yes, he and she are well acquainted, but I have so much love and respect for him, and he knows what he's doing. He can help you. I'm sure of it."

33

Blue bounded over and shoved his nose into Andy's hand. Andy smiled and patted the dog on the head. "We never had any pets. Did you?"

"My grandma had a cat when I was little."

"Yeah?"

"He was called Claude, and he only spoke French."

Andy laughed.

"You know what I mean." Josh was laughing, too.

"Yeah. I might get a dog. When I'm settled in my own place."

"They're wonderful company."

Andy got up. "There again, would it be fair to keep putting it in kennels when I'm away on business? Probably not. Pity that."

They set off again towards the hotel. It was nearing the time when breakfast was served, so they arranged to meet in the restaurant in half an hour and both returned to their respective rooms.

Dan was in the shower, and Andy waited on the balcony, looking down on the surfers, now many more in number.

Meanwhile, George was awake but still lying in bed with his eyes shut. He opened them and glanced up at Josh as he came in.

"Morning, sleepyhead," Josh said, leaning down to give him a kiss.

"Good morning. You OK?"

"I am, actually. A bit of breakfast and I should be shot of this hangover, too. I've just been down on the beach with Andy." Josh went to the bathroom and turned on the shower. He emerged again, unbuttoning his trousers and kicking off his shoes as he talked. "He's struggling." He put his trousers on the end of the bed and pulled off his top, wandering back to the bathroom in his boxers.

George watched him in complete astonishment.

"Damn." Josh came back, unzipped his suitcase and found his shower gel. "D'you think this'll work as shampoo," he asked.

George rubbed his eyes.

"I can't be bothered to dig it out. What's wrong?"

34

"Um, nothing?" George threw back the duvet and sat up. "You're acting a bit…odd."

"Am I?"

"Yeah. Well, I say odd. It's kind of normal for everyone else, but odd for you, if you see what I mean?"

"Oh. I see." Josh smiled. "We've got about twenty minutes to both shower and get ready for breakfast."

"OK." George knew what that meant. He followed Josh into the bathroom, and they showered together—mostly an innocent experience—then dressed quickly.

Josh checked the time. "Five minutes to spare."

George kissed him on the forehead. "Well done."

He laughed. "Thanks."

Down in the restaurant, Andy and Dan were already piling plates high with a very full English breakfast. They'd chosen a table with four chairs and a fantastic view of the bay. It was a different table to the one Josh and George had kept throughout their stay.

"Oh, no!" George teased quietly. "Who you gonna stare at this morning?"

Josh looked around him, pretending to be disappointed. "I think we might be a bit too early for them anyway."

"Too early for who?" Andy asked, coming up next to them with his massive breakfast. Josh glanced down at it. Andy grinned. "Hungry work, surfing," he explained.

"I can see that."

Josh and George opted for a repeat of their breakfast choices from their first morning, with George pulling all kinds of ridiculous facial expressions at the same time as trying to convince the others that the berry compote was delicious. Whilst they ate, Josh explained to Andy and Dan about the 'sister wives', who arrived right on cue to set all four men off giggling like schoolboys. The women glanced over at them and waved. George waved back.

"Come and join us," he said.

They nodded their acceptance.

"Why did you do that?" Josh asked, watching the two women collect their breakfasts.

"Why not?" George grinned.

"They're a nice-looking pair," Andy said.

Dan got up quickly and moved away. "I'm gonna go get some, erm…" He wandered over to the breakfast buffet, trying his best to get his laughter in check. He'd forgotten what a wind-up George could be when he was on form, because he hadn't been for a long time. Now, Dan recalled all the occasions they'd got into trouble at school for giggling because of some thing or another that George had said or done, and when he and Andy were together it was even worse. Dan picked up a glass of orange juice and made his way back, walking alongside the two women.

"Hi," he said, hoping that his inane grinning would be interpreted as friendliness.

"Hi," they returned the greeting.

George had dragged a couple of chairs across from the next table. "Elise and Lorna, this is Dan and Andy," he introduced.

"Hello." Elise smiled and nodded at Dan, and then at Andy. Lorna followed suit, but the opposite way around. Andy stared, pausing only to switch from one to the other, and they both turned their gaze on him.

"Sorry—" he directed his apology at Lorna specifically, even though it applied to them both "—but you have the most stunning eyes."

Lorna giggled. So did Elise. "Thanks."

"Yes, thanks," Elise said. "It's lovely of you to say."

"Most people just stare," Lorna added, briefly glancing at Josh. He blushed and turned away. "Because we look alike, apparently."

"So everyone tells us."

"And it's so frustrating."

"Yes, it is," Elise confirmed. "'You and your sister are beautiful.' That's what they say. And of course, you don't want to appear ungracious when someone is paying you a compliment." She sighed. "But I must admit that sometimes I do get cross."

"And it makes me curse," Lorna confessed.

Andy nodded sympathetically. "I get where you're coming from. Me and Dan get it all the time, although at least we are actually brothers."

"Except," Dan picked up the tale, "since we were nine or ten, we've been about the same size, so we get asked if we're twins."

"If people ask at all, bro," Andy chipped in.

"Too true," Dan agreed.

Josh could stand it no longer. He went to get some coffee and spent a while looking over the various condiments on offer, hoping it would afford him sufficient respite to get the imminent giggling fit under control. He could still hear the conversation taking place behind him, and bizarrely, Elise and Lorna were surprised to hear that Dan and Andy got mistaken for twins. The longer Josh listened, the more he came to realise that he had been unnecessarily harsh in his initial judgement of them. They were a really lovely couple, whose 'togetherness' came from having been with each other since university. And they were expecting a baby; Elise was pregnant. It wasn't long after this news was delivered that Dan also found his way over to the coffee and tea.

"Alright?" he asked Josh.

"I'm fine, thanks. I just can't deal with those two. Not if I have to keep a straight face at the same time."

"Yeah. They're a bit…" He looked back to where Andy was recounting the many ways in which pregnant women were beautiful, which was working far more effectively on Elise than it had on Sophie. George was giving Lorna a day-by-day, highly animated account of Sophie's pregnancy and his role as birth partner. "You planning on having children?" Dan asked Josh.

"Definitely not." Even as Josh said the words, he was starting to wonder. What would he do if George *did* want children? The thought had never occurred to him before, and nor had they discussed it, not in all of the time they had known each other. "I guess we could look at fostering or adoption," he thought aloud.

"Yeah?"

"Yes." Josh frowned. "Jesus, Dan, you've gone and put a whole new train of thought in there."

"Sorry, mate. It's pretty awesome, you know, being a parent."

"But I've never wanted to be a parent. I'm not parent material. At all. I don't want to think about it." Josh continued to frown and started chewing the inside of his cheek in contemplation.

Dan tutted at him. "So stop."

"Just like that?"

"Isn't that what you've always told me when I've got hung up on something?"

"Well, yes, but I didn't think you were paying any attention."

Dan laughed, slowly shaking his head as they returned to their table, although it probably wouldn't have made much difference if they'd stayed away, as the conversation was moving along well enough without them. George had talked himself into his usual state of excitement, and Andy had become all philosophical—a dangerous mindset for him at present.

They finished breakfast and said goodbye to Elise and Lorna, who still had two more days of their honeymoon left, whereas the four men had a five-and-a-half-hour journey ahead of them, and Dan was keen to get started so he'd have time to talk to Adele about the marriage guidance idea before his business trip.

Half an hour later, they were checked out, loaded up and ready to go. The satnav reported clear roads; the forecast was for dry weather. Everything looked good for the trip home, and it was, until they were just forty-five minutes and thirty miles from their destination…until a lorry switched lanes and changed everything.

***

The silence was terrific, though not absolute: the distant hum of traffic continuing to traverse the other carriageway; the sound of several car alarms; a far-off siren… And it was warm. Too warm. No air. Hard to breathe. The seat belt cut into his left side, pressing against his chest, digging into his neck. He needed to release it in order to vocalise, to ask the others if they were all right. He could sense movement in the front, could hear rapid breathing behind, but move? Everything felt so heavy, so skewed. Maybe they'd been wrong.

So, this is what a stroke feels like.

He opened his eyes a little, enough to check they were both working; they were. *Good.* He extended the fingers on his left hand and clenched them into a fist, and repeated the action with his right hand. All working there, too. Left leg: all fine. Right leg: *ouch!* Pain, shooting up from his ankle. He opened his eyes a little more, glanced down at his legs and choked. He held his breath and tried again. *Ah. That would explain it. Trapped under the seat in front. Where am I?* He tried to think. *We were travelling... that's right. Motorway. Lorry. Crash. Dan was driving.* The full realisation hit him like a punch in the chest, and his eyes flung themselves wide open.

He tried to turn his head sideways, but the seat belt was restricting his movement. He reached out, found the hand of someone else, grabbed hold and squeezed. It squeezed back. They were both alive. He let his eyes droop shut again and focused on holding on tight to that hand.

***

Time passed by; he had no concept of how much, but it had passed. There were voices, not close, and he couldn't understand what they were saying. The shrieking was too much. It was ringing around and around his head, almost a physical sensation of pain accompanying it, but nothing compared to the pain in his shoulder. *Dislocated. Again.* If he could just get out of his seat belt...

He tried reaching with his left hand, but the pressure of the seat against his shoulder was excruciating. He braced and looked to his right: still unconscious. *Awesome. Time to be a hero again, fight the pain, break on through.* With all the willpower he could muster, he leaned his right shoulder back against the seat and reached across with his left hand to unclip the seat belt. Slumping against the door, he shuffled on his side until he could put his feet flat against the ruptured windscreen, and kicked, and kicked, and kicked.

39

The seal broke away, a gap slowly opening from left to right, or, in fact, bottom to top in their current orientation. One final boot against the middle of the pane, and the whole thing fell, crumpling and tumbling down onto the tarmac. He wormed his way forward, over the dashboard, out onto the road, squirming in agony as he crawled away from the smoking bonnet, and twisted back to see what the situation was.

"Fuck."

***

He came round so suddenly it set his heart racing. Everything was blurry, but he could still make out his brother, lying a few feet away, on the road. His first thought was that he'd been thrown from the car.

"Andy?"

No response. He shouted louder. "Andy!"

The call came back, "Yeah. I'm alright, bro."

"Thank Christ."

Dan grabbed hold of the door handle with his right hand and unfastened his seat belt with his left, slowly letting himself fall. He lifted his legs over the centre console and dropped against the passenger door. There was a hole where the windscreen had been, and he crawled through it to join his brother on the burning-hot road surface. He screwed up his eyes, trying to focus.

"I can't see."

"What?" Andy asked.

"I can't see."

"You can't see, did you say, bro?"

"Yeah."

"What?"

"Oh, for God's sake."

So, Andy couldn't hear, and Dan couldn't see. *Superb. Two wise monkeys.* And somehow they needed to check on the others. The dog was crying, and it gave him an idea. He should be able to lift the hatch, no problem at all, and get Blue out. Maybe Josh and George could climb through that way, too—if they weren't injured, if they were still—

No, don't think it.

Don't think it.

He squinted, trying to focus on the shadowy double outlines within the car, but it was no use. He couldn't tell whether he was looking at heads or headrests.

"Can you see any movement?" he asked loudly.

"Nothing."

He stood up and staggered, taking a second or two to steady himself, before meandering his way past the four-by-four, taking in the hazy outline of chaos across the three lanes, the lines of vehicles, he assumed, now queuing up behind them. That was a sign of the times. Here they were, lying on their side on the hard shoulder, and not one person had come to check if they needed help. He felt around for the boot release and pulled, relieved to find that it was in perfect working order.

Easing the hatch open, he put his hand into the space and used touch to establish that the dog was trapped under the suitcases and surfboard. Again, using touch, he lifted the suitcases out, followed by his brother's surfboard. Unclipping the dog harness proved a little trickier, but after much tracing up and down webbing, he found the clips and popped them open. Blue tried to get to his feet, but he was whining and couldn't make it, clearly injured.

"Is that you, Dan?" Josh croaked breathlessly.

"It is, mate. Are you OK?"

"Seat belt's stuck."

"I'll try and give you a hand. Let me just get the dog out first."

Dan put his arm under Blue's side and scooped him up. The dog yelped loudly in his ear and started to growl.

"Shush, Blue. It's all right," Dan tried to comfort. He carried him back to Andy and laid him down. "Keep hold of his collar, bro," he shouted.

"Will do." Andy reached over with his left arm and gripped Blue's collar, an action that made the dog yowl. Andy felt along the dog's side. "Poor little mate," he said, recognising Blue's injury as one and the same as his own. He caught sight of movement behind him. Several cars had pulled up some distance away and people were running towards him.

It was at this point Andy realised he could hardly hear a thing, for their feet made no noise as they pelted against the road surface, and their mouths were moving silently. As the woman arrived in front of him, he looked up at her, trying to see her outline against the sun shining from behind.

"I damaged my hearing in the crash," he said, in what he hoped was a normal volume.

The woman gave him a thumbs up.

"There's two more in the back," he explained.

The woman turned away; several of the other people set off across the highway towards the other vehicles. The woman hurried over to the four-by-four.

***

"Hello?" Dan called out from the back, where he had crawled through and was now trying to unclip Josh's seat belt. It was jammed tight, and he couldn't see well enough to figure out why.

"Hi. Do you need any help in there?" A female voice drew closer.

"I can't seem to get this seat belt undone." He carried on trying. He was too stubborn and competitive to give in that easily.

"The emergency services are on their way," the voice explained.

"OK. Cheers." Dan struggled on for a bit longer, but had to relent. "I'm having trouble seeing," he admitted, backing out so that the woman could access Josh.

She crouched down and stepped inside the back of the four-by-four, the glass of the nearside rear window crunching under the soles of her shoes. "Hi there." She smiled at Josh, swiftly glancing to his left, where George was pressed against the door. She reached around and put her hand in front of his face. He was breathing.

"He was conscious before," Josh whispered. The pressure of the seat belt was making it impossible to take anything more than shallow breaths, and trying to raise his voice was enough extra tension to choke him. He stayed quiet and watched as the woman attempted to pull the clip free. It had been bent in the collision and was jammed inside the socket.

"I need to get some leverage," she said. She paused, trying to decide on the best course of action.

Josh coughed and spluttered, gasping for breath.

"I'm going to try to access it from the front." She disappeared from view, reappearing in front of him a few seconds later. "OK." She climbed in and put her knee up on the side of the passenger seat. It was easier from this direction, but the clip still wouldn't budge. "I'm sorry. We'll have to wait for the emergency services." As she said it, blue lights flickered across the headlining.

"Thanks for trying," Josh whispered huskily. He'd let go of George's hand to give the woman space to work. Now he sought it out again and squeezed, but got nothing in response.

"Are you in any pain?" the woman asked.

"My foot's trapped. It's gone to sleep. Apart from that, I think I'm OK." She was preoccupied, watching George, and Josh felt his pulse quicken. That was the last thing he needed, and he tried to get it back under control. "Can you see if he's injured?" he asked.

She briefly examined George. His left leg was caked in dark, dried blood and no longer bleeding. She checked again that he was breathing, but she couldn't reach to do more than that.

"I think he's probably just broken his leg," she said. "He's breathing, so try not to worry."

A tear ran from Josh's eye, rolled down his cheek and was absorbed by his hair. He gulped and coughed. It was so hard to breathe.

The emergency vehicles were having to fight their way through the mass of cars and vans, their drivers unable to move out of the way; there was nowhere to move to. Josh distracted himself by watching their efforts.

"You just hold on in there," the woman said gently. "I'll stay until they get to you." She reached over the front seats and put her hand on top of Josh's.

He was still grasping George's hand, and he was praying, not that he believed in a god. It was more a desperate plea, that if there were some great intelligent force out there, now would be the time to demonstrate their power. The thought slowly mutated into pondering whether George's survival would require an adjustment in his belief system, and he let the strands of ideas continue to spin their web, because staying in the here and now was infinitely more awful. He was brought back to it by the sensation of cool air against the top of his hand, where the woman's palm had been resting. Now a paramedic had taken her place.

"How are you doing?" he asked.

"OK."

"All right. I'm just going to check on your friend, then we'll have you out of here. What's his name?"

"George."

"Can you hear me, George?" The paramedic tried to rouse him: nothing. However, he was still breathing and responsive to stimuli. "He's lost consciousness," the paramedic said. He called for assistance and reached into his bag in the front.

Josh started to watch, but then his attention was drawn to the firefighter above him, who had pulled the door open and was waiting on the paramedic's say-so as to whether he could cut the seat belt.

"What's your name, mate?"

"Josh."

"All right, Josh. Are you in any pain at all?"

"Foot's trapped. Chest's tight."

"Right. Let me have a look at that for you."

It took hardly any time at all to establish that Josh's foot wasn't injured. The front seat had jolted back during the impact, and it had trapped his ankle between the seat runner and the central pillar. Once the firefighter pulled the seat forward, Josh was able to move it, and the feeling quickly returned; that hurt far more. The paramedic had a listen to Josh's breathing; it was a little fast, but steady, although in the process, he discovered bruising and potential broken ribs.

Now it was a case of getting the seats out and a backboard in, and this crew was more experienced in these matters than they'd have preferred. They removed the bits of car body needed for access and had Josh out soon after. Once he was free of the vehicle, he took his phone from his pocket, where it had been digging painfully into his leg, and was surprised to find that not only was the phone still in one piece, but less than forty minutes had elapsed since the accident. It felt like hours.

Josh was wheeled towards the back of the ambulance, where Andy was already sitting inside, trying to convince the paramedic examining him that he should be given Entonox. Sadly for him, he had perforated his ear drum, and therefore couldn't have any. They gave him morphine instead, which shut him up eventually. Likewise, Josh couldn't use the Entonox, although his pain wasn't quite as severe as that caused by Andy's dislocated shoulder, so he told them he'd cope without analgesia and used a bit of mind control instead.

Meanwhile, another paramedic team was dealing with Dan, whose vision difficulties were the result of concussion, and he was now in a neck brace, sitting in the back of a second ambulance. A third ambulance pushed through the traffic to deal with the injured from the other vehicles strewn across the road, and the police had cleared the outside lane, ready to partly reopen the motorway. Josh watched it all, trying to keep his mind off the pain of breathing and what was going on in the back of the four-by-four.

The woman who had stayed with him was proving herself to be the true hero of the day. When the accident happened, she'd been on the other side of the carriageway. She'd immediately taken the next turning and driven down the hard shoulder, getting as close as she'd dared without blocking emergency access. She was a trained first aider, and once she'd done all she could to help the professionals at the scene, she asked one of her fellow helpers to give her a hand carrying Blue to her car so she could take him to the nearest vet, having left her mobile phone number with the police first.

Indeed, it was her voluntary action that had prompted others to also offer assistance, which didn't surprise Josh in the slightest. Bystander apathy was a myth; people were intrinsically good, but generally require someone to take the lead and set an example to follow. The woman had done just that, and he was overwhelmed with gratitude, amongst other things.

It was proving very difficult to free George from the car, and not because of his injuries. The position he was in made removing the seat virtually impossible. Eventually, the senior firefighter decided to cut off the roof.

Dan kept watching the vague, kind of ethereal activity of his car being hacked to pieces, and thinking how gutted he'd have been if it had happened to his convertible, surprised to find he didn't care that his four-by-four was a write-off. So long as they all came out of this alive, that was all that mattered to him now, and he suddenly remembered the convertible that was coming down the fast lane, whose driver's quick evasive action probably saved them.

He peered out of the back door of the ambulance and tried to locate the car, but he still couldn't see clearly enough, not that he recalled the colour of the car in question, although he knew the exact make and model, because it was one he'd always fancied himself. When the paramedic returned, he asked her about the driver.

"He's fine. A bit shaken, but not injured. He's giving a statement to the police."

"Can you pass on my thanks?" Dan asked.

"Will do," she said. Then she was gone again.

Breakthrough
Saturday 24th June

Traffic was slowly starting to filter past, with motorists finding it impossible not to look at the four-by-four, now devoid of its roof, and the coordinated transfer of the limp body onto a backboard and then onto a stretcher. One paramedic was holding an oxygen mask over George's mouth and nose, whilst another was splinting his broken left leg. The blood was from a long, jagged gash caused by the bent nearside central pillar, which had sprung the seat belt mechanism, embedding it a few millimetres into George's calf muscle. It was superficial, but it would need stitches.

None of that explained why George was still unconscious. He had no visible head trauma, and his breathing had remained steady throughout. Nonetheless, it was being treated as a head injury and he was blue-lighted away first, closely followed by the van driver, Josh and Andy. Dan was the last to leave the scene and had somehow persuaded the paramedics to bring Andy's surfboard along.

At the hospital, Andy was sedated so that his shoulder could be reduced. It was a procedure he'd been through twice before, so he knew what to expect, but he was still feeling anxious. Dan was placed in the cubicle next to Andy's, and the partition was only a curtain; he listened on as the doctor manipulated Andy's shoulder back into position.

"Fuck-ing-hell!" Andy shouted. He exhaled sharply. "Sorry."

"No problem. You're doing well," the doctor said. He was only young, with longish hair tied loosely into a ponytail. He moved in front of Andy again. "Ready?"

"Yep." Andy closed his eyes and held his breath.

"Keep breathing," the doctor told him. It made no difference. "I see you're a surfer," he tried instead.

Andy answered with a suffocated, "Yeah. Kinda."

"I'm a paddle boarder myself."

"Hm?"

"Haven't been able to get out much since training."

"Hm."

"D'you get out much?"

"Mm-mm."

The conversation continued in this fashion, with the doctor asking Andy whether he'd ever visited this place or that, with some significant variation in the volume of his hummed utterances, until finally his shoulder was the right shape again and his arm was in a sling.

"Cheers." He let go of a massive sigh.

"No problem," the doctor said. "Mind if I take a look?" He nodded at Andy's surfboard bag.

"Be my guest."

The doctor unzipped the case. "Wow. Nice! Expensive?"

"Not really. There's plenty of guys who'll do you a custom board for pretty much the same price as a branded one. I've had that for years, but the dude who made it is still in business. I'll give you his number."

Andy couldn't reach his phone, as the radiographer had put it in his right pocket. The doctor gave him a hand and saved the number to his contacts list.

"Thanks," he said. "Your shoulder should heal perfectly. There's no serious damage to the surrounding tissue, so keep the sling on for two weeks, avoid physical activity and no lifting for a month or so. And definitely no surfing."

Andy laughed dryly. "There's not much danger of that."

"You'll be back to normal in a few weeks. I'll just get a physio booklet and sort out your pain relief, then you're good to go."

Similarly, once Dan had been X-rayed, and they'd given him the all-clear on fractures, they were more than happy to release him into the care of a responsible adult. To that end, they were awaiting the arrival of Len and their mother, although both brothers were adamant they were staying until they knew what was going on with Josh and, more importantly, George.

Josh's x-rays had also come back clear, so the pain in his chest was down to bruising, not that he cared one way or the other, even though it still hurt to breathe. He was having more of a problem with one of the nursing staff, who came to take his blood pressure and refused to put the cuff over his shirt sleeve. She returned to the workstation in the centre of A&E and was currently loudly complaining that the patient in cubicle three was being rude and obstructive. Another nurse came in and tried to reason with him.

"I'm sorry, Mr. Sandison-Morley, but the machine won't measure accurately through your clothes."

"You're wrong."

"Really."

"Yes. The practice is outdated. Modern machines will work through thin fabrics, and it's a cotton shirt."

The nurse breathed out through her nose. "Wouldn't it be easier if you just let me do it?"

"Wouldn't it be easier if you just wrote 'patient refused treatment' on my notes?"

"Are you refusing treatment?"

"No. I'm refusing to roll my sleeve up."

"Why?"

"Because I don't want to."

"Is there any particular reason?"

"Yes. And it's very personal."

"Fine."

The nurse walked out and yanked the curtain shut. A couple of minutes later, she returned with the doctor who had just been treating Andy.

"Hi there," he smiled.

"Hi," Josh responded guardedly.

"OK, I can take it from here," the doctor told the nurse. She left. "I've had a look over your clinical record," he said to Josh.

"My full clinical record?"

"No, although I'm going to assume I'd find in it the reason why you are refusing to have your blood pressure taken."

Josh tutted in exasperation. "I'm not."

"So you won't mind me taking it for you?"

"Through my sleeve."

The doctor nodded once. "I'd be happy to do that, except I'd be opening the hospital trust up to litigation, should it later transpire we'd discharged you with a life-threatening condition."

"I'll sign a disclaimer."

The doctor examined him closely. He nodded again and wheeled the blood pressure monitor across. "How about this. I'll show you how to put the cuff on—"

"I know how to put the cuff on."

The doctor laughed. "You really are obstructive."

"I know, and I apologise. Compliance isn't my strong point."

"All right. I'm going to leave you to do it yourself, without the sleeve. Call me when you're done."

"Thanks."

Josh waited for the curtain to shut and cautiously freed his arm from his sleeve. He'd had his blood pressure taken often enough to know how, although it was difficult to fasten the cuff one-handed, and he was getting frustrated. He pushed the button on the machine, and the cuff started to tighten, then popped open. He switched off the machine and pulled the cuff from his arm. He tried again.

Pop.

"Doctor?"

"Yes?" The doctor came in and closed the curtain behind him.

Josh's arm was still inside his shirt but out of the sleeve. "You've got quite a career ahead of you, I hope you realise," he said.

The young doctor raised an eyebrow. "Do you want me to help you, or shall we skip straight to the insults?"

"I'd like some help."

The doctor approached, and Josh reluctantly bared his arm. A push of a button and a minute's wait later, it was all over. The doctor put the cuff back on the trolley and switched off the machine.

"Perfectly fine," he reported.

"Thanks," Josh said.

"No problem." He smiled, no comment on the scars. No staring, either, which set him apart from almost every healthcare professional Josh had previously encountered. "George is in a side room," the doctor said. "Would you like to go and sit with him?"

"Please."

"OK. I'll sort that out for you. Won't be long." He left.

Josh put his arm back in his sleeve and waited. The doctor returned and beckoned him to follow.

"There's no change, I'm afraid. He's still unconscious, although there's no reason why he should be."

Josh walked alongside and listened in silence to the explanation of the tests that had been conducted, including a head CT and an ECG—all normal. They arrived at George's room and went inside. A nurse was checking readings on the machines, and were it not for those, George could have been sleeping.

The doctor placed a chair next to the bed and moved aside so Josh could sit down. He flinched.

"Have you had any pain relief?"

Josh shook his head.

"I'll write you up for some."

Josh watched him leave. He was an interesting character. He sort of floated about the place, with his head tilted to the side, staring up into the air, but his 'bedside manner' was impeccable. The fact that he'd got Josh to do what was being asked of him was a small wonder in itself, and even now, he could be heard cheerfully acknowledging everyone he passed in the corridor. Josh tuned out and turned his attention to George, who was propped up on pillows, with the barriers extended on both sides of the bed, his raised left leg braced from ankle to knee. The doctor returned and handed Josh some pills and a cup of water.

"Caroline's going to bring you a hot drink. I assumed you were a coffee man."

"I am. Thank you."

The doctor glanced at George. "Are you married or related?"

"Married. Just."

"Congratulations."

"Thanks. We were on our way back from our honeymoon."

"Oh. Bad luck."

Josh paused to take the pills. "We had a fabulous time. It was a surprise."

"A surprise honeymoon?"

Josh nodded. "Our friend, Andy, with the dislocated shoulder? He organised it."

"Did he send you to a surf resort?"

"How did you know?" They both laughed. Josh grimaced.

"You take it easy, all right? I'll come and check on George in a little while."

The doctor left again; the nurse had also gone, so now it was just him and George, who still wasn't responding. Maybe talking to him would help. It was worth a try.

"I wonder how Blue's doing?" Josh began. "That woman who took him to the vet was awesome. I hope the police can tell us who she is. We should get her a gift of some sort, to thank her for what she did." He looked up at George: not a flicker. He ran his thumb over the back of George's hand. "Ellie and Sean are on their way. I'm not sure what we're going to do if you…" He breathed out shakily. "You need to wake up now, George. I don't want to go home and leave you here."

There was a knock at the door, followed by the appearance of the nurse who had attempted to take Josh's blood pressure earlier. She was carrying a cup.

"Coffee," she said curtly and placed it on the edge of a steel trolley.

"Thanks," Josh replied. "I'm really sorry I was rude to you before."

She nodded in acceptance, but she was very cool with him. "Your friends said to let you know they've gone to get food." She left again.

Josh rubbed his eyes and took a deep breath, immediately wishing he hadn't.

"Ow." He tried again, inhaling more slowly and inflating his lungs as fully as he could. He picked up the coffee and sipped at it, keeping hold of George's hand. Another knock at the door. He watched wearily as it opened.

"Hey, you!" Eleanor came in, followed by Sean. She walked over and gently put her arms around him. "Wow! How blonde is your hair? You OK?"

"Just bruised and a bit shaken." He fought the impulse to cry. "And George…" He turned to look at him. "He won't wake up." The tears slowly trickled down his cheeks.

Eleanor took his hand. "What have the doctors said?"

Josh shrugged. "There's no reason. Everything checked out."

Sean had taken George's chart from the end of the bed and was reading through it, a frown furrowing his brow. He rubbed his chin and hummed, nodding complacently.

"It's another attack," he said. He put the papers back in the clip and returned them to the tray. Josh looked at him, not understanding. "Dissociative," Sean clarified.

Josh shook his head in disbelief. "Of course. How stupid of me. And we'd only been talking about it the other day. How did I not realise?"

"You've had one hell of a shock," Sean consoled. "It's not surprising."

"I'd best let the doctor know." Josh braced himself and stood up. He was feeling very wobbly.

"I'll go and find him for you," Eleanor said. She kissed his cheek. "Thank God you're all still alive." She turned away quickly and headed for the door. Josh and Sean watched her leave.

"I'm not sure God had much to do with it," Sean said.

"I prayed, you know." Josh sat down again and busied himself with extricating the plastic hospital band from the friendship bracelet around his wrist. "When we were trapped in the back of the car. I found myself praying. Utterly, bloody ridiculous."

"No. It's not." Sean moved closer and leaned against the wall. "When you're desperate, you'll try anything."

"How long do you think he'll be out of it?"

"Impossible to say. He's likely aware of everything that's going on."

"But this is different from the other times. He had full-blown seizures. This is more like a trance. What makes you think it's dissociative?"

"The lack of physiological aetiology. It's one of those conditions at the juxtaposition between mind and brain. It's almost certainly neurological, but virtually impossible to detect using current technology."

"He also has this aphasia," Josh said. "In response to specific emotional triggers. It came to me the other day that it was linked to the seizures, almost as if his brain overloads if he can't express how he's feeling."

"Give me an example."

"His vows. He couldn't say them until he used the visual analogy of a painting. Then I asked him about his dad, who he's never been able to talk about, and he described him as the Pacific garbage patch."

"Not the closest father-son relationship, I assume?"

Josh smiled. "No. The ranch was his inheritance, but he never saw his dad again after he walked out on them. I think George pretty much looked after his mum from there on. She took it very badly."

"That explains a lot about the kind of person he is."

"And on the whole, he's very resilient. There again, his mum's tough, too. But it was a lot of responsibility for him when he was so young, which is why I need to have a chat with you about getting this thing of mine back in order. He's been carrying other people around all of his life."

"How old was he when his dad left?" Sean asked.

"I'm not sure. Eight, I think."

"Seven."

The sudden involuntarily gasp nearly had Josh doubled over in pain.

"Hi, Sean," George mumbled through dry lips.

"Hello there." Sean smiled at him. "Had a good sleep?"

George smiled back. He was fighting to keep his eyes open. "Hi," he said to Josh.

"Hi, yourself. Are you…" He didn't get any further with the question of whether George was OK, because the sobbing—born of relief—completely took him over, and it hurt. A lot.

"Hey, come on," George comforted. He reached across and tugged at Josh's arm.

"Ouch," Josh sobbed, laughing a little at the same time. "Ow. Oh, I can't breathe."

"Ah, excellent," the doctor said, as he came into the room, followed by Eleanor. "How are you feeling, George?"

"Um, a bit confused, but OK."

"Goodo. I might as well do your obs while I'm here. Save the nurses some legwork." He waited for Eleanor to shuffle to one side so he could get around the bed. She stepped back so she was out of the way, and watched him, astounded. From the looks of him, he wasn't long out of college.

"I think I've entered the twilight zone," Sean said. "A doctor offering to help the nurses out? I never thought I'd see the day."

The doctor laughed. "The nurses here are superb. We get a higher than average number of RTAs, due to being so close to a major motorway, and there's a real team spirit evolved."

"I'm sure a senior manager will have that sorted for you in no time," Sean remarked.

"Oh, believe me, they've tried often enough." The doctor paused to check George's pupil response. "All looks good. Are you comfortable?"

"Yeah. What've I done?"

"Fractured fibula from the central pillar impact. It's stable, so should heal quickly. You'll also need to visit your local outpatients department in a few days to have the wound redressed and then to have the stitches removed."

"OK." George shuffled himself into a more upright position. "You had lunch yet?" he asked Josh.

"Lunch? It's nearly five o'clock!"

"That'll explain it, then."

"Let me guess. You're starving?"

"Yeah." George grinned. Now he knew Josh was OK, he wasn't worried, because Sean was right. He'd been aware of everything going on around him, but he'd felt detached from it, like he was on the other side of a thick glass screen. At the time, it had terrified him, and he'd begun to wonder if he was dying. But they were all alive. And he felt all right. Other than the broken leg. And the hunger.

"I can try to get dinner brought down for you," the doctor said. "Although it might be better if I go to the canteen and get it myself."

Eleanor moved towards the door and glanced back at Josh. "I'll go, and you and Sean can explain to Doctor McAvoy what you were talking about before." Without further ado, she left.

The doctor looked from Josh to Sean in anticipation.

"OK, so," Sean said. "I'll start by telling you I'm a clinical psychologist, and Josh here is a psychologist also."

"That's useful to know," the doctor said. He shook Sean by the hand. "Rab McAvoy," he formally introduced himself. "I'm specialising in neurology."

"Sean Tierney," Sean said. "I think you'll be very interested to hear what I have to say."

"Go for it."

"George had a couple of dissociative seizures last year, following extreme emotional trauma. He also experiences brief episodes of transient aphasia."

"Hmm." Doctor McAvoy frowned as he pondered. "George, do you have any recollection of the seizures?"

"None."

"And what about today? Were you aware of what was happening?"

"Sort of. It was kind of muffled and far away."

"What about the aphasia? What happens with that?"

"What's aphasia?"

"Loss of language."

"You mean when I can't find the words for what I want to say?"

"That's right."

"Erm, well, it's when I try to explain certain things. It's like there's some kind of blockage between my brain and my mouth, because the words are all there, they just won't come out. And then I start to panic because people are listening and waiting, and my mind goes blank."

"And how do you feel when it's happening."

"Kind of like when you get angry, you know? Racing heart, sweaty palms, that kind of thing."

"OK. And today, did you get any of those sensations?"

"Yeah. Before the paramedics arrived, I was trying to tell Josh I was all right, but I couldn't get my mouth to work, and I started to stress out, then it all went fuzzy."

Josh added, "But when we were in Cornwall, we discovered that if George uses visual imagery, he can bypass the aphasia."

Sean shook his head. "I think you'll find what's happening there is you're distracting him, and it's helping him to manage the attack."

"I disagree."

"I probably need to hear it for myself, admittedly—"

"Yes, you do," Josh snapped.

George and Doctor McAvoy made eye contact.

"As George said," Sean continued, "it's when he's put on the spot to speak. Surely that in itself would be sufficient to trigger an episode?"

"Dissociative attacks don't necessarily need a trigger."

"True enough, but in George's case…"

George put his head back and closed his eyes. He was too tired to deal with the pair of them fighting over what he said, or what they thought he said, and if they were right, it might set him off again. He briefly glanced up at the doctor and sighed. "They'll stop in a minute."

The doctor smiled and continued to listen to them. It was an intriguing argument, for it was entirely academic and grounded in research evidence, interspersed with anecdotes.

Eleanor came back into the room and paused a moment to watch the battle of intellects taking place, though it was not novel to her. She rolled her eyes and stepped past to deliver George's sandwich to him. "Sorry. There wasn't much to choose from, unless you fancied goulash in a plastic cup."

"This is great, thanks."

"All right, George," Doctor McAvoy said. "I'm going to get your paperwork together and sort out some crutches."

"OK. Thanks, Doctor. Can I ask you about something?"

"Of course."

"I also get out of control rages. They don't happen very often, but I've tried using anger management techniques, and they don't work. Could they be part of this dissociative thing?"

"Are you conscious of your actions when they happen?"

"Sort of. I know what I'm doing, but it's almost as if someone's taken control of my body."

"It's certainly possible. If it's OK with you, I'd like to refer you to a psychologist in the first instance, although by the looks of it, you've already got access to more than your fair share."

"Yeah." George laughed and nodded in Eleanor's direction. "And Ellie's a GP."

Doctor McAvoy turned to her. "Really? Where did you train?"

"Newcastle."

"Me, too. Come with me while I get these crutches, and we can compare notes."

Eleanor followed him out of the room, the pair of them now sharing memories of their college days. George switched his attention back to Josh and Sean. He stared at Josh until he became aware of it and turned around.

"Sorry," he said guiltily. "Got a bit carried away."

"It's fine. I just want to make sure Blue's all right and go home."

"OK." Josh gave him a kiss and went to see what he could discover.

***

58

Dan and Andy had already been to the local police station and found out which vet Blue had been taken to. He'd been sedated and was all bandaged up, looking very sorry for himself, although they did get a little wag of the tail by way of a greeting.

Now Blue was lying in the back of Len's SUV, in the emergency-purchase dog crate they'd picked up from a local pet superstore—local being ten miles away, but the vet said he needed 'crate rest', and even if he already had his own crate, Andy thought he might yet find a use for it.

They arrived back at the A&E department as Josh came out to the reception desk.

"Alright?" Dan asked.

"Yes, thanks. Just a bit bruised. You?"

"I'll get back to you on that one when the concussion wears off. How's George?"

"He's OK. Broken leg, but conscious and otherwise uninjured. What about Andy?"

"Dislocated shoulder. Perforated ear drum."

"And Blue?" Josh almost didn't dare ask.

"Dislocated shoulder. Pointy ears in perfect working order. He's in Len's car. And I gave the vet your contact details to pass on to that woman."

Josh followed Dan outside, and Len opened up the back of the enormous BMW, before retreating to his seat behind the wheel.

"Oh, poor boy," Josh said. He opened the crate and gently stroked Blue's head. The dog slow-wagged his tail in response. Josh leaned his forearm against the car and fell apart. Dan tapped him on the shoulder, and he turned to find that Dan was also crying. They put their arms around each other and hugged, sobbing for several minutes more before Dan regrouped and stepped away.

"Would you look at the pair of us," he said.

Josh sniffed and laughed—carefully. "Who'd have thought it?"

"Yeah. I tell you what, though. We were bloody lucky today."

Josh shook his head. "Not luck. Excellent driving and damned fast reflexes, I'd say."

"Well, cheers," Dan accepted humbly. "We all lived to tell the tale. That's what matters. I'll see you back home, yeah?"

"You will."

Josh waved them off and returned inside, in time to be met by George hopping towards him with the aid of a pair of brand new NHS best tubular steel crutches. Josh fell in step beside him, and they followed Sean and Eleanor out to her car.

"Testing those vows already, huh?" George said, as he clumsily shuffled himself closer and backed up to the car.

"Yes, you are. And this time, I promise there won't be a snowman in sight."

Then
Early July, 32 years ago

"Hello, Albert." Alice poked her little fingertip between the bars of the budgerigar's cage and gently tickled his chest. He cooed in response. She turned her ear in the direction of the bedroom, whence she could hear much banging of drawers.

"Neil?" The banging continued. Alice retracted her finger and went to the kitchenette of their tiny flat to deposit the groceries. "I picked up some socks for you on the way home."

Still no response. She topped up the kettle and lit the gas ring beneath it, returning to the sofa to collect her bag. Albert twittered as she passed by. She smiled. He was a dear little thing—she'd never imagined herself becoming attached to a bird, particularly one so messy and noisy. Even so, to have abandoned him like that was despicable, and when Neil first brought him home, it looked unlikely the poor bird would survive the night, but three years on, there he was. She paused to check he had seed before continuing on her way. As she reached the bedroom door, it opened.

"Neil?"

"Alice." Neil smiled nervously. Her eyes fell on the rucksack slung over his shoulder. He stepped towards her. She backed away. "Alice?" She shook her head, backing off further, his regret registering as a dark green-black halo.

"Where are you going?" she asked, although she doubted both that he would tell her and that she really wanted to know. However, it seemed right to ask, for he was most certainly leaving. "I bought you socks." She held the brown paper bag before her as evidence.

"Thank you," he said, taking the bag from her. "I'm so sorry."

***

"Before you are joined in matrimony here today, I have to remind you both of the solemn and binding character of the vows you are about to make. Marriage, according to the law of this country, is the union of one man with one woman, voluntarily entered into for life, to the exclusion of all others.

"Alistair, will you take Jennifer to be your wedded wife, to share your life with her, to love, support and comfort her, whatever the future may bring?"

"I will."

"Jennifer, will you take Alistair to be your wedded husband, to share your life with him, to love, support and comfort him, whatever the future may bring?"

"I will."

"Repeat after me…"

***

The kettle whistled still, but each time Alice considered attending to it, her mind wandered, and she temporarily became oblivious to her surroundings. Neil did not intend to return anytime soon; this much she had been able to tell from his demeanour, although he had promised to write whenever he arrived at wherever it was he was going. Their time together had sometimes been wonderful, always an adventure. But this was the end of them. She could sense it in every part of her being.

The shrill of the kettle came into focus again, and she pushed herself up from the sofa. Albert chirruped softly at his reflection, seemingly unperturbed by the whistling. Alice lifted the kettle off the stove and removed the lid from the teapot, not that tea for one required such a vessel. It was only as the stream of steaming hot water began that she saw what was concealed inside.

***

"The exchanging of rings is the traditional way of sealing the contract that you have just made. It is an unbroken circle, symbolising unending and everlasting love, and is the outward sign of the lifelong promise that you have made to each other.

"Alistair and Jennifer, you have both made the declarations prescribed by law and have made a solemn and binding contract with each other in the presence of the witnesses here assembled. It therefore gives me the greatest honour and privilege to announce that you are now husband and wife together."

***

Alice looked over the array of items, now laid side by side across the table. She had been here before so many times during the eight years of life they had shared together, and yet she knew this would be the last for a long, long time. One by one, she picked up the objects and adorned herself with them: his grandmother's fob watch; his mother's engagement ring with its tiny glistening ruby nestled in the thinnest band of softest gold; his sister's cameo pendant.

"One day," he had said, "you will leave me, just like they did."

Now
Sunday 2nd–Monday 3rd July

"Hello, Alice."

She glanced over the man standing on her doorstep, a dishevelled hobo reeking of cheap cider, his filthy clothes hanging drab and loose on gaunt, grey limbs, his odour so overpowering that she instinctively put her sleeved arm to her nose. Only then, when she had diluted the smell, did she recognise him.

"Neil?"

"You look well, Alice."

The same could not be said for him.

"May I come in?"

She shook her head, fearful.

"Come now, Alice. Surely you are not afraid of me? I am the same man I always was."

"The smell. I can't stand it."

Neil looked down at his clothes and sighed. "But that I could have prepared myself for this visit. If I might avail myself of your bathroom, I would gladly do so."

Alice reluctantly stepped aside and allowed him entry. He closed the door behind him and followed her up the stairs, to the bathroom, where she laid out towels and set the shower running slightly hotter than usual.

"I'll make a pot of tea. You do still drink tea?" she said, retreating down the stairs.

"I would love to drink your tea, Alice. You have no idea how much I have missed it."

"Leave your clothes outside and I will launder them."

"You don't need to do that."

"On the contrary, Neil. It is entirely necessary."

"Then thank you, Alice."

She turned back and smiled nervously, pausing to watch him close the door. She made the tea, the cups rattling against the saucers, the biscuits impossible to extract. They tumbled onto the plate in a chaotic, crumbled heap. Back up the stairs to find some items of clothing that he might wear, she peered into the spare room, wondering what he would think to discover she had kept his belongings, although it was not for any reason of sentimentality. She knew that one day he would return for them; she always knew, just as he had known that one day she would leave him. The sound of the bolt on the bathroom door being eased back returned her. Neil exited in a waft of aromatic steam—not quite enough cleansing to completely remove the dreadful odour of street-sleeping, but certainly a significant improvement.

"I hope that you are not," she said.

"I am not what?"

"The man you were." She indicated the wardrobe. "Your old clothes are in here. I daresay they are rather dated, but an improvement, nonetheless." She held her handkerchief to her nose and scooped up the clothes he had discarded before his shower, scurrying them away down the stairs, straight into the machine and on with the hottest wash she judged they would withstand.

Five minutes later, Neil appeared before her once more, dressed in the jeans and shirt she had favoured in their youth. He looked ridiculous, but she could not even bear to crack a smile. The budgie chirped, and Neil spun to face it.

"The Albert you brought into my life was the first of many," Alice explained, observing him approach her small feathery companion who surprised her each morning simply by being alive; he was positively ancient. She poured the tea. "Your Albert outlasted you by almost two years."

Neil was enthralled; so, too, was Albert. They cooed at each other through the bars long enough for the tea to cool in the cups. Alice sipped hers, trying to find the will to tell him that he must leave. She could not have him stay.

As if sensing her thoughts were on him, Neil about-turned and smiled. It was as perfectly enchanting as ever. "How have you been, Alice?" he asked.

"Very well, thank you."

"And your parents?"

"Dead."

"Oh. I'm sorry."

"I am fifty-six years old, Neil. It is to be expected that my parents would be either dead or dying. That is nothing for you to be sorry about. They stayed with me well into adulthood."

"Do you have a husband?"

"No."

"Did you ever marry?"

"No."

"Children?"

"One."

"Not mine?"

"Indeed not."

"His?"

"Yes." Alice put down her cup and rose to her feet. "It was long after you were gone—I ought not feel obliged to explain. And what about you? Did you marry?"

"Yes. She divorced me. Took our children with her."

"Did you desert her too?"

"I am ashamed to admit it, but yes, I did."

"Before she left you."

"And I returned, only for her to do it anyway. I have been a drunken wreck ever since."

"You were never anything but." Alice walked past him and opened Albert's cage, tickling the little bird under his beak. He warbled in pleasure. "You should drink your tea and leave."

"My clothes?"

Alice closed her eyes. It was at her insistence that they were now in a spin cycle; her own fault that there was to be a delay. "When they are dry. You must leave. I cannot have you here, Neil. Not again."

"Tell me," he said.

She continued to attend to Albert.

"Tell me of your life without me. I am eager to hear what adventures you have had."

"None so great as yours, I envisage."

66

"Still, I would like to listen to you. Your voice fills me with such peace. Please? Sit with me. Tell me your story."

Alice sighed. His scent was beginning to bring her comfort. His proximity, she had missed it, for it was easy. She returned to the sofa. He followed and sat beside her.

"The day you left was the day he married her. The love of his life. Oh, and how he loved her. And she, him. It was right that they should be together, and that they remain so in the hereafter."

"He is dead?"

"Nineteen months ago. Murdered, in his own boardroom."

"Murder? This is surely the greatest of adventures!"

"Neil." Alice looked him in the eye. "The death of an innocent man is not a thing of joy. Are you very drunk?"

"I am less drunk than when I was swaying in your shower. I'm afraid I may have pulled down the curtain. But I will leave all as it was, I promise you."

Alice turned away and picked up her tea. Neil copied her actions.

"Eat a biscuit or two," she directed. He did so, vociferously. She waited until he was done. "Eat more. Eat them all, if you wish."

"I wish only to eat up your words. Please, Alice, start with the beginning, not the end. Once upon a time..." He took her hand in his, pressed his thumb to the ruby red, locked minds with her. She inhaled deeply, held the breath, the aroma of him, slowly released it, and with it, she set free her story.

"Once upon a time..."

***

"Good morning, Alice." Alistair came striding towards her, his briefcase swinging carefree, dangling from a single finger and as empty as the coffee cup he placed before her.

"Good morning, Mr. Campion." She smiled back at him. He abandoned the briefcase and pulled up a plastic crate of papers, ready for filing in the strongroom. He sat on it and leaned in towards her.

"I did it," he whispered.

"What did you do, Mr. Campion?"

"I married her."

"You…" Alice stared in disbelief into his joyous, smiling face.

"That's right. Jenny and I eloped over the weekend."

"Mr. Campion! I…I don't know what to say." Even in her anguish, she found a smile for him. "Congratulations. To you both."

"Thank you, Alice. I knew you would understand." He patted her hand and squeezed it. Her fingers remained limp and unresponsive. "I can heartily recommend it. You and Neil should follow our example. No need for the fuss of parental approval, expense of wedding receptions. Just harness a couple of witnesses and head off for a romantic location. I imagine Bill would do the deed for you, too."

"Yes, I daresay you are right." Alice's smile faded, but she quickly reinstated it. "Where did you marry? Was it beautiful?"

"Stratford-upon-Avon. It was exceedingly beautiful, Alice. The register office was as they all are, of course, but afterwards, we walked along the bank of the river, shared a bottle of wine and a picnic, stayed the night in an ancient boarding house. It was wonderful."

"And what did Jenny wear? Was she in white?"

"Yes. A white dress. I think it was satin, or lace. I don't quite know."

"Oh, you! How can you not know the difference between satin and lace?"

"Is there a difference, Alice?"

"Well, yes. Satin is smooth and finely woven. Lace is loosely woven and full of holes."

"Ah. Then it was satin."

"Or was it silk?"

"Alice, please don't confuse me further. And how was your weekend? Was there music?"

"No, alas. There was not." Alice bowed her head.

"Alice?" His voice softened. "What is the matter?"

"The matter?" She laughed sadly. "Neil is gone."

"Gone?"

"I don't know where, or why."

"He has left you?"

"He has left. I don't think he meant to leave me specifically. He just had to go."

"All his talk of fame?"

"It went with him." Alice sniffed.

Alistair gifted her his newly pressed handkerchief. "He has always been a dreamer."

"And a drunk, and a liar."

"Perhaps he is touring."

"Perhaps he has fallen out of favour with the landlord of The Bell."

"He may be searching for a new place for you to share your life together."

"Or searching for a new place to buy his ale, where they don't yet know of his poor credit."

"Has he really gone, Alice?"

"Yes, Mr. Campion. He has really gone."

"Oh, Alice. I'm so sorry."

***

"Good morning, Mr. Campion." Alice typed as he sauntered past, his briefcase today laden heavy with documents, his coffee cup absent. "Mr. Campion?"

He had already passed her desk. He stopped and turned around. "Good morning, Alice. How are you, my dear?"

She did not answer. She watched him, the swirling mist of blue obscuring his face, his eyes. She got up, walked towards him. "Mr. Campion? Whatever is wrong?"

He attempted a smile and retreated to his office, leaving her standing in the middle of the floor, alone and unable to decide how best to proceed. Should she follow? Should she return to her desk?

"Hello, Alice."

She spun on the spot. "Oh, good morning, Mr. Meyer."

"Is he in?"

"Yes. Only just. There is something very…" She stopped. *Personal assistant. Confidante.*

"Wrong?" Bill Meyer completed her sentence. He, too, passed her by, knocked on Campion's office door, waited for the holler of 'Come!' and went inside. Alice went back to her typing.

*****

"Sorry to keep you so late, Alice."

"Oh, it's perfectly all right, Mr. Campion. I have nowhere else to be."

"It shouldn't take much longer. If we can just check over the accounts one more time, then, perhaps, get something to eat."

"Mrs. Campion is not expecting you to visit?"

Alistair shook his head. "She is quite exhausted, but optimistic that she will be well enough to come home again by next weekend."

"Have they been able to establish a cause yet?"

"I believe so. They say it is multiple sclerosis, but she may stabilise and improve a little in time."

*****

Alice unlocked the door and stepped into the draughty hallway, feeling around for the light switch. It was a dreary day and she was not looking forward to delivering wage packets in the rain, but it was Friday; there was nothing else for it, and it was always a joy to see the men at work, so courteous and protective of her. And those boys, bless them, barely fully grown and toiling so hard, so eager to please. She checked again that she had her umbrella, continued on her journey, her low-heeled shoes click-clacking against the parquet as she marched toward her office.

Campion Cables was, these days, more a home than home, but for Albert II—green, unlike his predecessor, and much quieter. She missed little blue Albert. She missed Neil. Still. Four years, and every day, in some way, the memory of him would return. Sometimes it was no more than a fleeting recollection of a moment spent together. It could even, on occasion, make her laugh or smile, such as the day she came home from work to find him songwriting in the nude for the first time.

I was lying in bed and inspiration overwhelmed me, he said.
"Could you not have paused to put on a pair of pants?"

70

"I didn't think to. I just grabbed my guitar and…"

He peeled the back of the instrument away from his abdomen, where it had stuck and left an imprint of itself.

Alice giggled. "Oh, Neil. Go and get dressed. I will make us some supper."

***

"I am glad that I am part of your story," said the Neil of the here and now.

***

"Alice, I need to speak with you."

"One moment, Mr. Campion."

The documents were not heavy, but holding them against the upturned crook of her right arm was making it ache. She pushed the top drawer closed, opened the next one down, found the appropriate divider, shuffled the papers back, deposited new ones, closed the drawer, next one down, more papers placed, up a drawer again, and down, and up again.

"Alice, it is quite important."

"All right, Mr. Campion." She sighed, placed the remaining documents on her desk for later filing and went to his office.

He paced back and forth behind his desk. Back and forth. Back. And forth.

"Mr. Campion?"

"Alice."

"What was it you needed?"

"Sit down, please, Alice."

She did as he asked, shorthand notebook perched on knee, and watched him expectantly.

He stopped pacing, observed life outside the tiny window. "Alice."

"Yes, Mr. Campion?"

"Why do you never call me by my first name?"

"You are my employer. It would be inappropriate."

"But we have known each other for ten years."

"Even so…"

"Should I have been calling you Miss Friar all this time?"

71

"I do not know, Mr. Campion. Which would you prefer?"

"Would you consider calling me Alistair?"

"I would consider it," she said. She was unhappy he was asking her to. "It is too familiar."

"Then perhaps it is best that I do not say what is in my mind to say."

"Mr. Campion?"

He turned to her and smiled.

"Has something happened?" she asked.

"Yes, Alice, I'm afraid it has. And it is so terribly wrong, but I can do nothing about it. Are you available to work this evening?"

She had intended to visit her mother, but it could be postponed. "I am available, yes."

"Good. I won't keep you any longer. I'm sure you have much to do." He turned away again. Not a further word.

***

"I should like us to share a working dinner," Alistair explained as he watched her lock up the offices. "After all, there is no need for us to remain here and pay out to heat and light an entire building when we can enjoy heat and light at someone else's expense."

Alice put away her keys and buttoned her coat. "Your logic is flawed, Mr. Campion."

"How so?"

"Unless you are intending to flee the moment we have eaten, you will be paying for the privilege of using someone else's heat and light."

Alistair laughed. It was a deep and glorious sound that began in his belly and worked its way up, slowly blooming into a vast round balloon of happiness that floated high above their heads. She had not seen him look so happy in a very long time, perhaps even as much as five years.

They continued on foot to a small restaurant quite close by, where they sold good, basic, British dishes: steak and kidney pudding, shepherd's pie, fish and chips, cauliflower cheese; Alice selected the cauliflower cheese, Alistair the steak and kidney pudding. Once they were well settled into enjoying their meals, Alistair began in earnest.

"I am going to build Campion Cables into something great," he whispered across their candlelit table. His eyes shone with excitement, and she chewed quickly so that she might swallow her food and respond.

"It is already something great," she said.

"But it will be much more. I want to do so many things, good things, Alice, to help others. And I want you to be there, by my side, to see us achieve our dreams." He reached across the table and took her hand. She was so surprised she dropped her fork, and it clattered against the plate as it landed. He laughed again. "I'm so sorry, my dear. I didn't mean to startle you."

"*Our* dreams, Mr. Campion?"

"Please. If only for this night, call me by my first name."

She took a deep breath in preparation and repeated the question. "Our dreams, Alistair?"

He smiled and squeezed her hand. "Yes, Alice, our dreams. I have seen how much you care for those boys, for that is what they are. Straight out of school and into the big wide world of work. And they are the fortunate ones. Imagine all that we could do to help those less fortunate, if Campion Cables were bigger, more competitive. I know I am little more than a humble engineer with grand ideas, and I chase foolish notions too often, but with your support, and Bill's steadying influence, I truly believe we can do this."

He released her, for now, so that they could finish their main course. For dessert, she chose a lemon cheesecake, he a slice of apple pie with custard, followed by coffee, for him, and tea for her.

"What do you think of jazz music, Alice?"

"I have never really listened to it."

"I should like to take you to see a jazz band sometime, if you will permit me."

Alice set down her cup and observed him momentarily. She was going to have to ask the question, and be quite frank with him. She spent a couple of minutes in quiet consideration; it was going to be quite a speech.

"Alistair," she said. He was deep in thought, sipping his coffee, but she had drawn his attention. "When you married Jenny, I thought that it would bring an end to this, and yet here we are. And what is this jazz nonsense? In the ten years I have worked for you and, I believed, *known* you, I have heard no mention of jazz music. I must, therefore, ask you to explain yourself. Why this working dinner? Why suddenly are these 'our dreams'? Why, after all this time, are you asking for my company? I chose to keep my life with Neil. You chose to begin yours with Jenny. What has changed?"

Now he, too, had to think and prepare. Truths were always so much more difficult to share.

"There are many reasons, Alice. To begin with the easiest of them: the jazz, I discovered whilst pursuing a trail. I confess, I was hoping that, at the end of the trail, I would find Neil, persuade him to return to you and make you happy once more. It fills me with sorrow to see you so alone. Still, the passage of time has proved itself of moderate purpose in healing your wounds.

"I did not find Neil, of course. Some of his associates claim he has left the country. Others contend he has a wife and child. A more common and realistic notion is he is in prison.

"So I did not find him, but I found jazz music. It stilled my soul, brought me peace, took away my loneliness, in part. Did you think in choosing to remain with Neil you could stop me from loving you? For you could not, but you are right. I made a life with Jenny, and I love her. She has told me I must pursue my own dreams now, but how can I do that? I can't leave her, though she says that I should. She is trying to be selfless. Is it conceited of me to believe she cannot live without me?"

Alice took his hand. "No, it is not. You're a good man, and you must know that I also love you. However, as you say, Jenny will not survive without you."

"Then there is no future for us." He sagged, as if the life were being sucked from him. Alice took hold of his other hand and shook it gently.

"There is a future for us, Alistair, but it is in your business, and *your* dreams. I would be honoured if you allow me to continue at your side, for a personal assistant is a wife, of sorts, is she not?"

74

"Yes, my dear, sweet Alice, she is."

***

"Mr. Campion." She waited for him to look up from his paper. "I need to ask a favour of you."

"Of course."

"I require an extended leave of absence."

"For how long?"

"It is quite a long time."

"Days? Weeks?"

"Six months."

Alistair could think of no reply. Six months? How was he to cope without her for so long?

"It's for, err…" she stammered over the lie she had concocted, rehearsed. She swallowed. "Neil," she said.

"Has something happened to him?"

"No, no. Nothing like that."

"What, then? He has asked you to accompany him on a tour?"

Alice smiled and tried not to cry. She sat on the chair, folded her hands in her lap and studied them. She looked up. She didn't know how to tell him, and the pause her silence created was so massive that neither could find a means to end it. "I am expecting a baby," she said.

She got up again.

"I'm sorry."

***

Alistair parked his car in the viewing spot overlooking the valley, from where, in daylight, he would have been able to see the river flowing gently through fields and onwards, eventually to the sea. Along the horizon, fir trees stretched their spindly backs high into the navy sky, obscuring the view of the town, in front of them the railway bridge, where presently a freight train trundled its last journey through the autumn night, delivering unknown cargo to an unknown destination.

Unknown cargo.

He had not heard from Alice since her request for leave, and he missed her dreadfully. The days in the office dragged on and

75

on, indistinguishably, relentlessly sliding one into the next in an evermore miserable cycle of loneliness. The evenings, when Jenny slept, he spent there, too, trying to occupy his mind with tasks that Alice would have completed in half the time. He could have done them more quickly himself, had he not been trying to fill a chasm.

At least his sentence was almost served. Six months, she had asked for. The time was almost done, although even with his lack of experience in matters of childbirth, he was aware that these things did not work to exact schedules. She may, or may not, have given birth already, and he wondered also about what would happen then. Surely she would wish to remain at home with her child? In which case, her request for six months was a means of breaking the news. She was going to leave him. He did not think he could bear to go on if she left him. But what was he to do?

He considered driving to her house, where he might find her reclined on the sofa, her legs across Neil's as he rubbed her dainty feet, sang her a love song, or a lullaby for their unborn child. Was that worse than facing another night without seeing her?

No.

It was not.

But then, was he so lacking in pride? Alice was his personal assistant; she was Neil's lover.

These were his thoughts as he slowly turned the car to face the way he had come and drove back down the hill, following the dark roads through villages, past schools, and church halls filled with children, and gardens and parks, daytimes populated by families. That was all that he had wanted. He had dreamed of it with Jenny, and with Alice. And been denied it. Now Neil was to have what he could not, and he was almost overwhelmed with sadness and regret, but not jealousy. He was happy for them, for Alice and for Neil.

But what if Neil left her again? How terrible if she had to bring up their child as a single mother.

He drew up outside and watched the lighted curtain billowing slightly with the breeze entering through the open window, though it was a chilly evening. He wound down the car window, turned off the engine, turned an ear toward the house, and listened.

Voices: one belonging to Alice, most certainly. The other? Perhaps his ears were deceiving him. Now the voices fell silent, and he found that he was holding his breath as he waited for them to speak again. A shadowy outline advanced, and the curtain was pulled back. He had been discovered.

***

Alice watched him for a long time, uncertain how to proceed. Should she invite him in? Did he already suspect? She had missed him so much. Oh, how often she had wished that things could be the way they were, before Neil left, before Alistair married Jenny.

Before *this*.

Her eyes became accustomed to the darkness of the street outside; he was still watching her, and she, him. She smiled. He smiled back. She would invite him in. A nod signalled her decision.

***

He locked the car, felt his heartbeat speed up a little as he walked up the path, faster still as he neared her door. Through the frosted glass, he saw her silhouette—undeniable, regardless of the vastness of her pregnancy. She reached the door at the same moment as he, pulled as he pushed, back-stepped as he led and spun her around and around in her hallway, looking upon her in wonder.

"Alice, my dear. I have missed you so." He found guilt was insufficient to stop him wrapping her in his arms, drawing her close. He looked down into her face. There were tears. So many tears. He longed to kiss them away. He longed for it too much. He could not resist.

"And I have missed you," she cried. She lifted her face to his, closed her eyes, fell into his kisses, let him dry her tears. He could hear the voices from within, knew now that it was not Neil and understood the truth that she could not tell him. And he could not rip himself from her; just to have this moment, with her in his arms again. The man's voice grew louder. A door opened. Alistair slowly stepped away, but he did not release Alice, not for a single second.

"Hello, Bill," he greeted the man standing not six feet from him. His best man, his business partner, his oldest friend.

"What the devil are you doing here, Al?"

"I'm afraid I could not stay away."

The men had no more words to exchange and remained standing as they were, petrified by the realisation of all that was unfolding that night. It was, finally, Alice who intervened.

"You'd better come and sit down," she said. "There are things I must tell you, and I'm afraid you will not like them."

Alistair nodded dumbly and followed her to the lounge, where Bill had now taken his previous position alongside his wife. Alice indicated an armchair; Alistair waited for her to sit, but she remained standing. He took the armchair.

"The baby," he uttered. "It is mine."

"Yes," she confirmed.

"Neil did not return."

"No."

He looked up at her, met her gaze, passed into it the message in his heart.

I love you. I wish we could be together, in love as we are in labour. It is not to be; we must continue with our tragedy. And though tonight, you gift our child to Bill and Emma, I know, as I have always known, that we still have each other.

"We still have each other." He repeated the thought out loud. Alice went to him, his cheek nestled as close as could be to his unborn child. And to his child, he spoke these words: "Never believe we abandoned you, that we did not want you, for we wanted you so much we created you when we should not have done."

Alice groaned, her knees flexing of their own accord. She glanced up at the clock, transformed her breaths into long, deep, concentrated inhalations, exhalations. Alistair held her hand. The moment passed.

"May I stay with you?" he asked.

"Yes." It was a gasp of desperation, of pain.

All the way to the hospital, the tears spilled down her cheeks, pooling momentarily on her fundus before running away. The night was colder, and she shivered as she puffed and panted her way through another contraction. Still she kept her hold on Alistair's hand. When this one had passed, she asked the question.

"How is Jenny?"

"Quite unwell. Some days she improves a little. Others she slips away." The thought flashed through his mind, and he was not quick enough to dismiss it.

Alice squeezed his hand. "You must not think it."

He did not speak it, but there was little he could do to take back the thought. He was torn asunder.

"Where does she believe you are this evening?"

"At the office."

"When must you leave?"

"When I have seen our child come into the world, bid welcome, and farewell."

***

The labour was mercifully short, the delivery uncomplicated, the child a healthy baby boy. Alice held him, felt the tug of the maternal bonds as they unfurled and wrapped themselves around her and the newborn infant in her arms, around his father, too.

Bill and Emma entered the room yet stayed their distance, waiting out the time. As the minutes were about to turn to hours, Alice beckoned Emma close, shifted her arms so that her son's mother could take him. Emma's eyes welled and spilled over. Her wish was coming true, and the cost, though it was great, was one that she could afford. A baby. She had a baby.

"Would you like to name him?" she asked Alice.

Alice shook her head. She dared not open her mouth, for fear of the wailing that would erupt from it.

***

Alice stopped speaking and sat quietly, with her hands resting in her lap, the sodden cotton handkerchief scrunched within them. She sighed and looked up, gave him the most fleeting of smiles, tried to rally.

"Where is Neil now?" Sean asked. "Has he gone again?"

"Yes, I think that is probably what he has done," she replied, the nod of her head transforming from a very assured affirmation to a slight shaking from side to side. "No. He hasn't. It's these old bones." She lifted her hands as evidence, extending as best she could the crooked little fingers, the knobbled knuckles whose daily aching served as a constant reminder of her years at Campion's. "We are both getting long in the tooth, Doctor Tierney, and life on the street is hard."

"True, but from what you tell me, it was his choice to leave. You don't have to allow him back into your life."

"It has been a long time, certainly long enough to have put it all behind us. It ended amicably, all things considered."

Sean stood and stretched. "I'm going to make more tea, Alice. Won't be long."

"Thank you, Doctor Tierney."

He collected their empty mugs and left her alone in his office.

It was a pleasant little room, full of things. Books and other publications filled the shelves, with still more stacked on either end of the desk, in between them a selection of markers, ballpoint pens, and a fountain pen. She could smell the ink. She could even have speculated with some accuracy on the brand, for it appeared to be the same as that which she used herself.

He returned, set the full mugs down in the midst of everything else and resumed his position in his chair. The phone rang.

"Hello, Doctor Tierney here." He paused to listen. "No. I'm afraid Doctor Morris isn't in today." He paused again. "Sure." He picked up the fountain pen, removing the lid with his teeth at the same time holding the phone receiver between his chin and shoulder and grabbing a block of paper with his other hand. "Go ahead." They talked; he scribbled. "OK. Got it." A final pause. "Will do. Bye." He put the receiver down. "Sorry about that."

"It's quite all right, Doctor Tierney. This is not your office?"

"It's mine when I'm here. The rest of the time it is possessed by Doctor Morris." He opened the desk drawer and took out a photo frame, which he passed across to her. "Young upstart full of big ideas and plans for world domination."

She examined the photo of the man and woman in an intimate embrace, set against a backdrop of anonymous hills, knowing from the scent of the room that it was he, not she, with whom Doctor Tierney reluctantly shared his space. She passed it back.

"I empathise entirely," she said. "My desk was always out in the open, although back in the days of Campion Cables, there was only Alistair, Bill and myself in the building for much of the time. After the company went public, there were many more staff."

"That must have been a difficult transition."

"Yes, it was."

She blushed and smiled but didn't say out loud what thought had flitted into her mind to initiate such a response. In any case, it was not necessary. Sean knew about the stolen kisses in stock cupboards and brief embraces in coffee rooms. Alistair had confided in him often during their mutual time at the hospice—a period spanning more than five years. Indeed, it was this confidence that meant he had known about Jason long before he became a suspect in his father's murder. Alas, it had not afforded any insight as regards the identity of the man who had killed Alistair, and it was for this reason that Neil's sudden reappearance troubled Sean.

Alice now interrupted his thoughts as if she had read them. "Neil is a gentle, spiritual soul who could not intentionally hurt anyone, however much he has been hurt himself, and he has known pain, Doctor Tierney. He, his mother and sister lived with his grandmother, a woman who was cruel beyond belief, and it was his desperation to escape her that led us to moving in with each other at sixteen.

"She died soon after, and one might think his mother would have rejoiced in her liberation by reuniting with her son, but she did not. She took her daughter and emigrated without so much as a farewell. The first Neil knew of it was when he attempted to secure a grant to study at university, and the local authority claimed he had given false information. New tenants had moved in by the time he found the courage to visit. All they could offer was a box of trinkets that had been left in the hallway."

Alice paused momentarily to show Sean the ring that had belonged to Neil's mother, with the tiny ruby set in its thin, gold band.

"He wanted to marry me, but he could not afford an engagement ring and didn't understand why I would not wear his mother's. He is such a forgiving man. He said I should forgive her, too, but I could not. The day he left, I tried to follow his example. I put on their jewellery and it burned into my flesh, filling me with hatred, not forgiveness. I considered selling it so that it could be melted down, destroyed, but found I could not do that, either. So I kept it and locked it away, until the time came when I finally understood: sometimes the best you can do for your child is leave them in the care of someone who loves them." Alice closed her eyes and whispered. "And I forgave her."

She returned the ring to her finger and opened her eyes again. "We had been together for four years when I started work at Campion's, when Cupid aimed his blasted arrow in Alistair's and my direction. Neil sensed that I was leaving him, in mind if not in body, and he fled. His return is coincidental. I believe that most sincerely. He needs a boarding house, a place to warm up and dry out. I am quite glad of his company, for however long it lasts.

"As to the man who murdered Alistair: he took him from me just months before we would have been together. Thirty-four years we waited for that time to come, gave up our lives and our child, for a murderer to shatter our dream in an instant. And I have thought about little else since. I loved Alistair with all my heart, and he loved me. You are right, Doctor Tierney. Justice must be served, so I will testify, but only when I have made my peace with my son."

The Full Monty
Tuesday 4th July

"Iris?"

"What, love?"

"Could you, erm…"

Josh stood in the doorway, frozen by fear, his gaze fixed directly ahead, trying not to make eye contact with his terrifying yet surprisingly small nemesis.

"Out!" Iris shouted. Monty snarled and slinked off, grumbling and grizzling all the way to the kitchen. "Pack it in!" she called after him. He gave her a backwards glance, accompanied by a final growl of protest, and disappeared into the garden. "Mouthy little fucker," she said. She tutted at Josh.

"Thanks." He gave her a quick, embarrassed smile.

"Just tell 'im. It's my room, shift your arse. You gotta show 'em who's boss, love."

"Easy for you to say!"

"You tellin' me you can control an Alsatian but you're frightened to death of a bloody Westie?"

"I don't control Blue. George does. I just live here."

Iris eyed him carefully, as if to test his argument, and nodded. "Aye, mebbe," she said. "Anyhow, you'll have the house to yourselves again tomorra." She waddled back to the kitchen. "If you're sure you can cope."

"We'll be fine now, I think." He followed her out. "We wouldn't have managed without you this past week, though."

"Aye, well, I couldn't very well leave you strugglin', and besides I had nothin' in at home. Looks like me magic fridge fairy packed in the job when you was on your 'oneymoon."

Josh gazed blankly out of the kitchen window, pretending to feign ignorance. Iris waited until he looked her way again. She folded her arms, keeping her face completely straight as she spoke.

"Nice, them TV dinners. You ever tried 'em?"

"Erm, a few times, yes."

"Aye. Bung 'em in the microwave a minute or two, eat 'em out the tray. Convenient, when you're on your own and gettin' on a bit."

She tried to stare him down, but he refused to break eye contact and started to laugh. She grinned back and patted him on the arm but didn't say anything else about her fridge 'magically' restocking itself with ready meals each week.

Of course, she'd always known it was him. It was an act derived from his own experience of how difficult it was to muster enthusiasm for cooking a nutritious meal for one, having chosen instead to spend fifteen years living mostly on junk food and fresh air. Back when he was at university, he'd occasionally thrown together a shepherd's pie, but Sean did nearly all the cooking. And he made a mean Ulster fry—or 'full English', as Josh would torment. Sean would always point out that a 'full English'—aside from being stolen from the Irish—didn't include soda farl, or potato bread, or vegetable roll. And he made the most delicious raisin soda bread. It was soft and light, and beautiful eaten still warm with butter.

So Josh understood completely why Iris didn't bother to eat, and also how George had come to be such an excellent cook, although cooking for his mother was more of a trial than cooking for Josh. At least he'd try things he wouldn't have chosen for himself, whereas Iris refused flat out. She was face-spitingly stubborn when it came to accepting help from her son, and George couldn't be bothered with the aggravation of fighting her.

She had, however, met her match in Josh, for as much as he was terrified of Monty, he had the same knack with people as George had with animals. Slowly, slowly; build their trust; give them no choice but to do what you expect of them, until they finally realise that it's for their own good. Even so, he wouldn't be seeing her up to the flat when he dropped her off later and she discovered that her fridge was not only fully stocked, but had also 'magically' transformed into a brand new, fully functioning, frost-free fridge freezer. Pauline had phoned earlier to confirm it had been delivered and set up, and they'd even taken the old one away with them.

And so to the final challenge of the day: Sophie's appointment was an hour ago; she and George would be back soon. The time was now.

"Cup of tea, Iris?" Josh asked.

"Aye, go on then."

He filled the kettle, using the time it took to boil to make himself a cappuccino. Iris went outside to smoke. Monty stood at the back door, watching Josh. They both wanted to be friends, but neither was quite sure how to achieve it. If Blue wasn't on crate rest, he'd have probably united them in seconds. Maybe he was trying too hard. The kettle boiled, and Josh made the tea. Iris returned.

"I like a nice garden," she said. "Our first place had one. Long time since we was livin' there, mind."

"Why don't we sit outside?" Josh suggested. Iris took her tea from him and followed him back out. "The chairs are a bit rickety," he warned.

"Aye. I sat on one the other day and nearly went arse over tit." She put her tea down and spread the spindly plastic legs of the chair before she sat. It worked a treat. She got out another cigarette, lit it, and picked up her tea, casting a critical eye over her surroundings.

Josh sipped his coffee. He caught a whiff of her cigarette; every so often they smelled wonderful and he got a craving, but he had no intention of doing anything about it. The breeze blew the tempting smoke away again and caught the wind chimes next door.

Iris glanced over and nodded. "I tell yer what, I feel like takin' a pair of scissors to them friggin' things."

Josh snorted into his coffee and the foam puffed up into his face. "I wouldn't tell anyone if you did," he said, wiping the bubbly milk off his nose with his sleeve. She smiled at him.

"You and me are a lot alike, eh?"

He nodded. "We are." He reached down under his chair to retrieve a small box and put it on the table. "Which is why I know you'll understand why I'm giving you this."

She looked over the box, one eyebrow arching slightly as she considered the object before her.

"It's a good make and model," he said, "but you don't need to worry about all the extra stuff it does, unless you want to, in which case I'll show you how it works."

Still not a word passed her lips.

"For emergencies," he added.

She took another draw on her cigarette. "When did you pack in the cigs?"

"Two years ago."

"Was it 'ard?"

"Not as hard as I thought it would be."

"Did you do it for Georgie?"

"No, but I've stayed off them for him."

"Right." She put out the cigarette and picked up the box, squinting to read the text on the side. "I'm not thinkin' of stoppin', in case you was wonderin'. I was just curious, as I saw you watchin'."

"I see."

"So what d'you want me to do with it?" She nodded at the box.

"Keep it charged, make sure you always have it with you, answer it if it rings. That's basically it. If you want to make calls on it instead of going to the phone box, then you can. You've got three hundred minutes a month free."

"It's not free, though, is it? How much is it costin' you?"

"Not much. And it's worth it, to know we can get hold of you if we need to."

Iris put down the box and lit another cigarette.

"You don't half smoke a lot," Josh chanced.

"Shut it," she said.

***

"Hi," George called. They heard his crutches clicking as he hopped along the hallway.

"Hi," Josh called back. "We're in the garden."

George came out and stopped dead, his eyes widening in amazement.

"Eh, that's fuckin' clever, that is," Iris said. She pushed the screen on the phone—much harder than she needed to—and noise started coming from it. "Look at this." She beckoned George closer.

He hopped across and peered at the screen. "*Rising Damp*?"

"Aye. On a phone!"

George glanced at Josh and shrugged by way of asking how he'd done it.

"And this, too. Only for fun, mind." She closed the TV player and pressed hard on one of the icons. "Bingo," she said. "And if Paul sticks it on hers, we can both play at the same time. Good, eh?"

"Err, yeah." George was still somewhat stunned by what he was seeing. "I thought you hated mobile phones, Mam."

"I do, but as Josh says, they're 'andy for emergencies and whatnot. And that bloody phone box is always gettin' kicked in. Anyhow, everythin' all right with the babby?"

"Yep." George struggled into a chair and pulled a roll of paper from his jacket pocket. "How good is this?" He passed the paper to his mum.

"Oh, here we go again." Josh sighed.

Iris looked over the sheet of paper, nodded, and passed it across to Josh.

"Three-D ultrasound," George explained. "It's so cool. The sonographer said he was asleep, which was a shame, although we could see him twitching while he was dreaming, and it was absolutely amazing, and then the next minute his little arm went up and he rubbed his eyes. So cute."

"You still don't know it's a 'he'," Josh pointed out.

"I do. I told you!"

"Give us that a minute," Iris said. Josh passed back the image from the 3D scan. Iris examined it and tutted. She returned it to George. "That's the umbilical cord, you daft bat."

"I know!" He huffed. "I really hate you two sometimes." He got up and hopped back inside. "How do you know it's a 'he', George? That's the umbilical cord, George. It's not your baby, George." He continued babbling away as he disappeared from view. Josh giggled.

"Think we might've upset him a bit, love," Iris said. She was poking at her phone. She squinted at the screen, pressed a button and put the phone to her ear. "Put kettle on, love, ta." She hung up and grinned at Josh.

"So you've mastered that, have you?"

"Aye. Dead easy. Right, now if I want to send one of them texts, I go in here…" She continued to talk, instructing herself as she went through to the text message screen, frowning in concentration. A couple of minutes later, she put the phone down on the table. "I think that worked. How long do they take?"

"Usually straight away."

"What, like, right now?"

"That's what straight away means."

"Fuckin' funny, you."

Josh smiled sweetly. "Who did you send a message to?"

George reappeared in the doorway. "Can you come and get these mugs?"

Josh followed him back inside. His phone vibrated in his pocket. He took it out, unlocked the screen and started to laugh. He glanced through the window at Iris. She was sitting with her arms folded, a determined expression on her face.

"What is it?" George asked.

"Text from your mum." He passed his phone over.

George read the message. "'Bring me them bloody scissors'? I don't get it."

"No, but next door's wind chimes are about to." Josh opened the drawer and went to grab the scissors.

"Don't!" George hopped across to block him. They were both laughing. "Seriously. She'll do it."

"That's what I'm banking on."

***

Later that evening, as they were on their way to Dan and Adele's for her 'at home' to celebrate her thirty-ninth birthday, Josh received another text message from Iris. It was blank. He put his phone away and forgot all about it. Half an hour later, he got another one. It was a picture message, with an upside-down photo of a fridge, underneath it two words, in capital letters:

YOU FUCKER

More Than Words
Friday 7th July

Heatwaves are dreamed about by the English, conjured by the imagination into some wonderful, much-sought-after rarity of childhood. Most recall a time from their youth when it was 'so hot' that a blanket hosepipe ban was set in place, but 'isn't it worth it' for a few glorious days of Mediterranean sunshine, for evenings spent sitting in the open air, for the tennis not to be rained off?

"Ah, the scent of summer," Krissi said, arriving home from work at a little after nine in the evening to find Jason in the communal garden. The aroma of multiple barbecues—lit, spent or drenched in too much lighting fluid—filled the air, and he was sitting against the back fence in the only spot untouched by the spill of the low evening sun, his laptop perched on the outskirts of his lap, a pencil clenched between his teeth, a heap of papers weighted down by half a house brick on the floor to his right, a can of Dr Pepper to his left. Krissi conducted a panoramic scan of the expanse of slightly too long—where it wasn't bald—yellowed lawn, pausing to watch the couple from the flat downstairs attempt to establish whether their sausages were 'cooked enough', their children batting a sponge ball with plastic racquets across the midsection, finally settling her gaze on her friend. "How come you're sitting out here?"

"Wimbledon."

"There's more than one TV channel, you know."

"And they're all either showing tennis, or going on about it at every given opportunity."

"Even *Kerrang*?"

"Especially *Kerrang*."

"Dear me. Well, I'm going for a shower. The air conditioning packed up this afternoon, and it was mad busy for some reason. You'd think parents would want to take their kids somewhere out in the open, not spend the day sitting in a boiling hot pizza restaurant, complaining about melting ice cream."

"You coming back out?"

"I can do. Why?"

"Could do with your thoughts on my shortlisting."

"OK. Won't be long."

Krissi left. Jason reopened the online chat window, read the message and typed: *So you still didn't ask her.*

The response came back: *Nope. Didn't get a chance. Mental all day.*

Jason shook his head. Excuses, excuses. He picked up the papers and thumbed through them, pausing every so often to type into a text document onscreen. He switched back to the chat window and typed one-handed: *Swap shifts with Lyn so you're off on the same day.*

– Nah man.

He put the papers down again and quickly repositioned the half brick before they blew away. *Why not?*

– She can't handle it. Not on a Sunday.

It's dead!

– Not always it ain't.

Krissi poked her head out of the window. "You need another drink?"

"Please," Jason said. She nodded in confirmation and disappeared from view. *Got to go,* he typed. *We'll talk more.*

– Ha yeah. Alright mate. See ya.

Jason closed the chat window.

"There you go, Gothboy." Krissi passed over the unopened and very cold can and sat next to him, cross-legged. "They the applications?" She indicated with her head to the pile of papers.

"Yeah. I know which ones I want to shortlist, but I've not put them in order, so you can tell me what you think without being influenced." He shoved the brick away with his foot and passed her the application forms. His apprentice, miserable and useless as he was, had done the decent thing and resigned just under a month ago. Today was the advertised closing date for the post of 'assistant sound engineer and studio technician', and there had been twelve applications in all, out of which only four came anywhere near meeting Jason's exacting standards.

"Right, what have we here?" Krissi read over the front page of the first application. She glanced at the very brief personal statement on page two and shook her head. "Definitely not." She flipped it and plonked it face down on the grass: the foundation of her rejections pile. It fluttered, threatening to take off, and she tucked it under her left knee. She shrugged at the second application; that became the first 'maybe', which she placed under her right knee. The third was another outright rejection, as was the fourth, the fifth a maybe, the sixth showed promise. Seven was appalling.

"He can't even write."

"She."

"That's what I mean. What does that say?"

"Roxanne. With three 'x's."

"No way are you employing someone called Roxanne with three 'x's."

"You can't reject her because of her name."

"No, but I can reject her for starting her personal statement with, 'I would like *too* work for *you're* company because...' And what's this? She actually *chose* that name. She probably misspelled it on the deed poll form. Nope!" Krissi slammed the application on the rejections pile. "Next!"

Eight was another maybe, nine was excellent, if not a little over-experienced.

"This guy worked in Abbey Road," Krissi said.

"Yeah, but what's he been doing for the last two years?"

"He's been on the road, it says here."

"On the dole, more like."

"Yeah, but Abbey Road, Jay."

"Look, if he's so experienced, why is he applying for a job as an *assistant* engineer at Black Hole? It's not exactly, erm, well, Abbey Road, is it?"

"He does say that he's moving back up from London due to family commitments."

"He's nearly as old as my dad. How the hell's he gonna cope with dubstep and new metal?"

"Let's be honest, he can't make it sound any worse."

"Dubstep's awesome if it's done well."

"I hope you're joking."

"I heard an amazing Skrillex-Slipknot mashup the other day."

"The word 'amazing' has no place in that sentence."

"Don't knock it till you've heard it. In fact…" Jason opened the music player on his laptop and loaded up the remix in question.

Krissi listened for as long as she could—less than ten seconds—reached over and muted the sound. "That's terrible."

"In *your* opinion."

"Which you value tremendously." She grinned at him and put the Abbey Road engineer on the shortlist pile, now numbering two and only three more applications to go.

The next one had been completed in text message shorthand and even that was a waste of letters; it immediately joined the rejects. Number eleven had potential, although the personal statement was quite long and presented in the smallest handwriting, whereas all but the Abbey Road guy had typed theirs. That said, the writing was neat and legible, so she kept hold of it to return to after she'd checked out the last form. It was OK—nothing particularly dynamic about the applicant, but it seemed like she could do the job. She joined the shortlist. Back to number eleven, then. Krissi moved the page closer to her face. She frowned and sniffed it.

"Smells like disinfectant."

"Yeah. I noticed that."

She read aloud: "Since attending the launch night at Black Hole Studios, I have been intending to write to ask whether you would consider offering me some work experience. I saw this post advertised and decided to put in an application. If I am not successful, I would still very much like the chance to gain some experience working with you on a voluntary basis.

"I do have a little unofficial experience, as I spent a lot of time at school in our music studio, assisting the teacher when pupils were recording and mixing their compositions for coursework. I also helped out at school concerts, cabling the sound desk and live mixing.

"Unfortunately, I was unable to complete my schooling, as I went 'off the rails'. However, I have worked hard to improve myself, and can provide you with excellent references from the psychologist who worked with me in prison…oh!" Krissi stopped reading and looked up from the application form.

"Yeah."

"Well, it doesn't mean we have to dismiss him outright."

"The mobile studio?"

"You or Stu could run it."

She continued to read the rest of the statement in her head. It outlined cleaning duties, responsibilities given in prison, and so on, but it was the last section that got her attention. Out of the twelve applicants, he was the only one whose passion for music truly shone through, and it was all in his final paragraph. He wrote, played, sang, listened to, lived and breathed it. It was his reason for living, the thing that got him through his time in prison. He wanted to learn to read music, to play a guitar properly, to work with other musicians. He wanted to be a part of making music in whatever way he could, however big or small his contribution might be.

Krissi turned to Jason and nodded. "He's the one."

"Yeah."

"OK, so what've we got?" She picked up her shortlist pile and read out the names. They matched up exactly to Jason's list.

"Are you up for interviewing?"

"I know nothing about sound engineering."

"But you know *everything* about me, and I need someone I can get along with."

"Stu knows you, too."

Jason scowled. She huffed. He pretended to cry.

"Oh, all right! I'm off on Wednesday."

"Awesome. Wednesday it is."

Behind Blue Eyes
Wednesday 12th July

Interview day: of the four shortlisted candidates, one pulled out, and they had already seen the only female applicant to make it through. She'd studied the same music technology course as Jason, although at a different university, and knew what she was talking about, but she seemed more intent on demonstrating her knowledge through indiscriminate overuse of jargon than showing how she would undertake the job.

Stu didn't like her. He didn't say as much, but once he'd got the introductory pleasantries and the tour out of the way, that's exactly where he stayed—out of the way—'clearing the stage', he said, but it was merely a means of not being upstairs with her. So that was pretty much the end of the only female shortlisted candidate.

Next, they saw the guy who'd worked at Abbey Road. He arrived ten minutes late, armed with apologies involving not knowing the layout of the estate, which was a valid consideration, given he'd lived out of the area for thirty-plus years and the estate was a recent addition. He was dressed in a charity shop suit and crumpled shirt, his hair partly knotted into dreadlocks and hastily combed flat on top. He was clearly very uncomfortable in what he was wearing, and Krissi was so distracted by the fact he was wearing flip-flops that she hadn't heard anything he'd said so far, all of it spoken in a gentle and eloquent mix of received pronunciation and long-term marijuana use.

Along with the apologies for tardiness, he arrived with a stack of highly impressive references, all from rock 'n' roll legends, detailing in slack English what a great job he'd done on this album or that.

It was clear to Jason that he was talking to an experienced professional who was something of a frustrated rock star himself, but then most engineers were. And so, to the question of why Black Hole, which the man greeted with a smile and the gentlest of laughs.

"I have heard much about your work here, Mr. Meyer," he said, "and you do yourself a great disservice by asking that question. It's true, I've worked with some of the biggest names in the business. I've worked at Abbey Road. Excellent credentials, I grant you, but I am long out of the womb. At my age, there are few who would appoint me for fear that nothing more strenuous than repositioning a mic stand will have me dropping down dead on them. You have a groove going on here. It's got a good vibe to it. So my question to you is, why not Black Hole?"

Jason nodded graciously. "Thank you for the compliment. And how do you feel about dubstep?"

Krissi hid behind her tablet and turned the laugh into a faked sneeze.

"Bless you," Jason said, deadpan.

The man smiled, having noticed the joke passing between them, but he still answered the question.

"I've worked with a good few artists in that genre, and it's interesting. They know their way around, so it's more of a partnership than with other folks, who just want to record the stuff and let you work your magic. So yeah, it's cool—not to everyone's taste, but that doesn't matter. Rock, reggae, trance, dubstep—it's all the same job."

"Very true," Jason agreed. "Did you have any more questions, Krissi?" She shook her head. He turned his attention back to the Abbey Road guy. "Is there anything else you'd like to ask us?"

"No. I don't think so."

"OK. Well, thanks for coming in. We've got one more candidate to see, so we'll be in touch, probably before the end of the week." Jason shook the man's hand and followed him downstairs and out of the building, crossing paths with Stu, returning from his break with three fruit yoghurt crushes. He handed the peach one to Jason and the blueberry one to Krissi.

"Cheers," she said. "What d'you reckon, Stu? Fancy working with the granddaddy of dubstep?"

"Seems a decent bloke. Bet he's stoned most of the time, though."

"Yeah. I thought that. Did you see his flip-flops?"

"Can't say as I did, I'm glad to say. Men in flip-flops." He wrinkled his nose in disgust. Krissi laughed. Jason remained serious and thoughtful.

"What's up?" Krissi asked.

"Nothing, really. If this last one turns out to be no good, I could probably go with him, but he won't stay for long. He's a wanderer."

"Those flip-flops made for walking, huh?" Stu joked.

Jason raised an eyebrow. "They'll have to go, even if I've got to buy him a pair of shoes myself. Health and safety. Right. Gonna go and sort out the studio for Matt and the guys."

"I'll give you a hand," Stu offered. Jason shrugged his consent.

Krissi didn't bother following the two men up the stairs to the recording studio, which was booked out to Gods of War—a local death metal band—for the evening. They were due to arrive at five-thirty and the last interview was at five. It was now almost quarter to; she decided to pop outside and find a spot in the shade of the warehouse to sit and 'drink' her crush in peace. It wasn't the easiest thing to achieve, as the sun was high in the sky, leaving only a thin band of shade at one end of the building. She took it, sliding down the wall and sitting with her knees up, slurping at her straw and watching a forklift carrying lengths of timber around the perimeter of the next warehouse along.

This wasn't quite how she'd intended spending her day off. She'd planned to visit Andy and Jess, to see if they needed any help. She got the feeling the seriousness of the accident was being downplayed by all concerned, particularly as Andy was being far less resistant to accepting help than usual—he'd even let her mum do the shopping for him over the weekend. Krissi decided to pop round after the interview, providing the guy turned up. In fact, it looked like this was him now. She watched on as he walked along the pavement, staring directly ahead of him until he reached the open gates, where he performed a ninety-degree turn to the right and marched towards the door. She got up and walked over to intercept.

"Hi," she called. "Are you Hadyn?"

"Yes. I am." He smiled nervously. She smiled back.

"I'm Krissi." She held out her hand. He hesitated a little and then shook it very quickly. "I don't actually work here," she said, "but I'm going to be in on your interview with Jason Meyer. He owns Black Hole."

"OK." Hadyn offered another brief, nervous smile. "The studio's great. I came for the launch gig and I really enjoyed it. I was going to talk to Mr. Meyer about it at the time, but he was busy, and then I lost my nerve. I hope he doesn't think I'm not interested."

"Don't worry, Hadyn. Your application was excellent. Anyway, come in and meet Jay and Stu—he's the other engineer, and he's really down-to-earth."

She went in, glancing back to check he was following, which he was.

"You mentioned on your form you write songs," she said, genuinely interested.

"Yeah. I try to, anyway."

"What sort of stuff d'you write?"

"I suppose it's a bit indie. Not sure really."

"Cool. How long have you been songwriting?"

"Since I started high school, so eleven years now."

"Wow. Bet you've got loads of songbooks."

"Most of them got, err, lost."

"That's a shame."

"I can still remember the songs, though, and I've started writing them down again."

They reached the control room and could see Jason and Stu through the window. They were chatting, and Jason was positioning microphone stands, whilst Stu was setting up the drum kit.

Hadyn seemed a little less anxious now than he had outside, which was good. Krissi had taken an instant shine to him and hoped the others would, too. He had that same kind of vulnerability she had seen in Jason back in school—a quiet, creative sensitivity that coloured the way he viewed the world around him.

She kept her gaze focused on the activities in the studio, watching Hadyn out of the corner of her eye. He was fidgeting a little, rubbing his hands together. She stepped forward and knocked on the window. Both men turned to look over and abandoned what they were doing.

***

"Hi." Jason came out into the control room first. "I'm Jason Meyer—Jay." He shook Hadyn's hand.

"Nice to meet you."

"This is Stu. He's our full-time sound engineer. And I see you've already met Krissi."

"Yes," Hadyn confirmed, turning to Krissi and smiling.

"Would you like a drink of something, Hadyn?" she asked.

He glanced around him, trying to judge whether the place was clean enough for him to cope with drinking out of their cups. It was pristine.

"Yes, please."

"We've got coffee, tea, hot chocolate and soup. It's from the vending machine downstairs. Or we've got a soft drinks machine. Not sure what's in it, though."

"Coke, Dr Pepper, Fanta and water," Jason said.

"Err, hot chocolate, please." Hadyn was shaking with nerves.

"Coming right up." Krissi patted his shoulder. "Chill."

He nodded at her and tried to do as she suggested.

Jason pulled a chair out from under the console. "Have a seat, Hadyn." Jason sat on the swivel chair and wheeled himself closer. Stu reached past him and switched on the computer.

"Did they need keys, Jay?"

"No. Just the kit. They're bringing everything else."

Stu nodded his understanding and disappeared through the door, reappearing on the other side of the glass screen.

Hadyn spent a moment watching him, although he wasn't entirely paying attention, as he was having to focus hard on keeping his hands still, his palms pressed to his thighs, fighting the urge to apply alcohol rub. The effort was making his heart pound, and he was starting to sweat.

"Are you all right?" Jason asked.

"Yes, thanks. I, err…" Hadyn swallowed, trying to decide whether he should tell Jason the truth and get it over with. He'd told him about everything else, so he had nothing to lose. "I have obsessive compulsive disorder," he said. "It makes me panic if I can't keep my hands clean."

"OK. You know studios are pretty dusty?"

"This one's very clean."

"Yes, it is, but how will you cope if you're lugging other people's kit around? Like, for instance, the band we've got coming in after your interview. They bring their own amps and—ah crap. Hold on a sec." Jason got up and went through to see Stu. A minute or so later, he returned. "Sorry about that. I just remembered they'd asked to use our double bass pedal. Where were we?"

"My OCD. I was going to say I'm all right if I wear gloves, but I thought it'd be weird if I turned up for an interview wearing them. And I'm receiving treatment, so it's getting better."

Krissi returned with the hot chocolate. "There you go, Hadyn." She passed it to him.

"Thanks, Krissi." He smiled at her again. She made him feel calmer somehow, and he was glad she was staying.

"Did you need to wash them now?" Jason asked.

"No, thank you." Hadyn held the cup by its rim and carefully repositioned it so he didn't burn himself. He wanted to put it down somewhere, but the only surface was next to the mixing desk, and that wouldn't do at all.

"Here." Jason extended a slide-out shelf from under the desk. Hadyn put his drink down.

"Thanks."

"So you mentioned you came to the launch night?"

"Yes, that's right. I did. It was a really good night."

"Glad you enjoyed it. We did, too, though we were knackered. Didn't get home till about three in the morning."

"Closer to four," Krissi interjected.

"It wasn't. It was ten past three," Jason argued.

"No way was it ten past three. It was half past when we got out of the taxi."

"Whatever." Jason glowered at Krissi and turned back to Hadyn. "We're planning on having more nights like that in future, maybe once every couple of months. How would you feel about running the desk?"

"Great. I loved doing that at school. Back when I was in Year Ten, we had a rock concert, and the music teacher put me in charge of the sound. I knew how to work that desk, though. It was old, and channels kept cutting out, so I had to swap cables in the middle of songs and stuff. It was a bit hairy, but I really enjoyed doing it. 'Course, I'd need to train on your system and stuff, but that'd be awesome. I love live music. And nights like that get loads of new bands coming in, I guess?"

"They do. We've been pretty much booked solid since the start, contrary to *some people's* reservations." Jason glowered at Krissi again, and she folded her arms. "So, yeah. That's one of the things we're looking at doing. The other thing we've been talking about is setting up a mobile studio to go into schools and stuff, which obviously you couldn't do, but it would mean probably Stu going out, and you and me working here on those days."

"OK."

"And sometimes you'd be working on your own, although you'd receive full training before we did that. We would also pay for you to undertake the diploma in audio engineering and production, which would mean going to college one day a week. What d'you think?"

"That would be really good, yeah."

"Obviously, we'd need you to work a probationary period first, make sure you're going to stick around long enough, but we'll come back to that later. Tell me a bit about why you're interested in the job."

"Mostly, as I said on my application form, because I love music. I've always listened to it a lot, and I've played guitar since I was eleven. And I write a bit. Music's the thing that keeps me sane. I had a bit of a rough time at home, and it was music that got me through it. It's important, you know? Musicians need to be given the chance to play, to get good at what they do, and I like the idea of being part of that."

"That's what we're about, here at Black Hole," Jason said. "We keep our charges low so that young bands can afford to hire the space. I should tell you a bit about the business, I suppose. The studios are part of a community trust, so we're non-profit, although we are making a profit at the moment, which is why we're looking into the mobile studio. We also want to be able to offer opportunities to people like you, who've had a bad start and are trying to get back on their feet.

"That comes from the ethos of the community trust, continuing the work that a local businessman used to do, rehabilitating young offenders. The trust has several other projects on the go, including Milky's—the milk bar in the town centre—and we're working with some local residents to help them set up a housing association. The job you've applied for is just working for the studio, though, so I'll say no more on the rest of it."

Jason went on to outline the duties involved and the kind of hours that Hadyn would be expected to work. He would need to be quite flexible, and in the past, it would have worried him, because part of his OCD was about keeping to a routine. However, he was so excited at the possibilities that he didn't even think about that side of things.

Jason finished explaining the hours, pay, holidays and the like. "Did you want to ask anything?"

"Err…" Hadyn tried to get the barrage of questions forming in his mind into some kind of sensible order. "Yeah," he said cautiously, "but I think a lot of it can probably wait and I would only need to ask if I got the job. But I was wondering if it would be good for me to stay around and help out with the recording session this evening, so you can see what I'm like?"

Jason shrugged and looked at Krissi.

"I can't stay, Jay," she said.

"No problem." He turned back to Hadyn and nodded. "That's a great idea. The band coming in played at the launch. Gods of War?"

"Oh yeah. They were the extreme metal band?"

"Yeah," Jason laughed. "Extreme to the extreme. They're all uni students and dead quiet when they're offstage. Seriously, you wouldn't think they were the same people."

"OK, Jay, I'm going," Krissi said. She got up to hug him, and shook Hadyn's hand. "Nice to meet you."

"You, too," he said. "Hopefully, I'll see you again."

"I have a feeling you might." She grinned at him. "See you later." She waved to Stu in the other room and left.

"The band'll be here any minute," Jason said, "but we've probably got time for a quick tour, if you'd like?"

Hadyn got up and followed Jason from the room, down the stairs and back through the foyer, into the large studio where the launch concert had been held, empty now other than a few odds and ends of cable, and appearing much bigger for the lack of people and equipment. The two men paused in the middle of the dead, silent, black room.

"The lighting is all DMX," Jason explained, pointing up at the bar hanging a few feet in front of the stage.

"OK. I'm not sure what that means, but I learn quickly."

"It's mostly pre-programmed, as we don't need to do anything especially showy with it, but the manuals are under the desk, if you ever get bored." As soon as he said it, he realised that he'd effectively told Hadyn he'd got the job, which was the case, so long as his references panned out. "The sound desk is over here."

They walked together to the desk, and Hadyn eyed it in wonder. He could barely believe he was going to get the chance to do this.

"Would you mind me asking," Jason said carefully. "What were you in prison for?"

"No. I don't mind you asking. I was in for assault occasioning actual bodily harm. I attacked a debt collector who came to our house. He tried to push his way in, and I freaked out and threw a plant pot at him. It broke his nose and cut his cheek open."

"Oh. You don't seem an especially angry person."

"No. I'm loads better now than I was. It's the OCD that does it. I used to think people were getting in my face on purpose, so

feeling he needed to exert his masculinity in the motoring stakes, but he did it anyway.

"Of course," he said, "if this was my car, I'd have gone for the two-litre diesel edition."

"That big, huh?" Jess smiled. "Haven't you heard what they say about men with big, fast cars?"

"Now then, Jessie. Don't be pitting those Jeffries boys against me. You know they're no match." He helped her into the passenger seat and gave her a saucy wink. She rolled her eyes and waited for him to shut the door before she took a deep breath and carefully shuffled around so she could fasten her seat belt. She was feeling quite poorly today.

They spent the journey to the hospice chatting about the facilities, which included a relaxation suite, swimming pool, Jacuzzi and café, Sean citing all of it as evidence that hospices were not just for people on the brink of death. It was something he found himself having to do quite frequently; with medical advancement came longer life expectancy, and whilst much of what the hospice did was end-of-life care, it wasn't all that they offered. However, he had more chance of winning the lottery jackpot than altering Jess's perception and knew she'd agreed to the visit for everyone else's benefit rather than her own, which was a shame. It was a beautiful place—his work there was what made him happiest—and it could really be of benefit to someone like her.

They turned into the long lawn-edged drive and slowly rolled up to the front of the ancient building, architecturally similar to Andy and Dan's mother's house, both buildings having been constructed around the same period in the late-nineteenth century. This one was set in traditional gardens, shady and peaceful with all their flowering shrubbery and ancient oak and elm trees. Jess examined them whilst Sean reversed into a space. He stopped the engine and waited for her to look his way.

"What?" she asked. He shrugged. "You're going to insist on a wheelchair, aren't you?"

"Not at all, lovely. You're a big girl. I'm sure if you need a chair, you'll ask for one."

She tried not to snarl; he knew her too well.

"Shall we?" he said.

When she didn't answer, he relaxed into his seat to indicate there was no rush; whenever she was ready. She continued to observe her surroundings.

"It must cost a lot to keep this place ticking over," she said.

"Yeah, it does. They're always fundraising."

More thoughtful silence ensued.

"I suppose they receive quite a bit from legacies."

"Indeed they do."

"Did Campion leave a legacy?"

"I believe so. The short-stay wing is named after his wife."

Jess nodded. "And they must draw some income from invested assets."

"Probably. Psychologists tend not to be so good with the accounts."

"Although, the market being what it is…" She trailed off thoughtfully. "They get government funding, don't they?"

"About a third of what they need."

"Really? So little?"

The silence resumed. Jess watched a woman with no hair get out of her car and wait for a little boy—her son, presumably—to take a wheelchair from the back, struggling to unfold it and hold it steady for his mother. He couldn't have been more than nine or ten years old. The woman eased herself into the chair, and the little boy took her up to the front door of the building, where another woman in everyday clothes greeted them with a smile and ruffled the little boy's hair. All three disappeared inside the building, but Jess continued to watch the door.

"I'd like a wheelchair, please," she said.

Sean reached across and gently squeezed her hand. "I'll be right back." He got out of the car and strode away, heading down the side of the big house. She watched until he disappeared from view.

So, this was where she was now: sitting in a car outside the mansion of the damned, trying to calculate how much it would take to save them. A soul? A hundred souls? A thousand? She could bequeath every single last penny, and it would make no difference. She returned her gaze to the vast green shrub at the edge of the drive and wound down the window, inhaling deeply.

"Rhododendron," she said to herself, recalling the heady scent of her grandmother's garden from years ago. This particular variety was late flowering, bearing masses of white perfumy blooms throughout the summer months. She tried to cling to the good memories accompanying that scent, but they were being violently trampled by images of this place, in a future where it had for decades been abandoned and neglected, the ivy strangling the tumbledown walls of the old house, the rhododendron straggly and flowerless, the driveway snaked with weeds. Indeed, the illusion, or delusion, was so complete, so consuming, that Sean's return startled her, and the sudden movement made her cry out with the pain.

"Dare to lie to me again, Jessie, and I'll…" He stood by, waiting for her to transfer herself from the car to the chair.

"You'll what? Kill me?"

"In my job, those kinds of statements tend not to accidentally roll off the tongue." He closed the car and locked it. "I was trying to find a suitably punitive measure for you." He started pushing.

"You don't scare me, Tierney," she said. "You're all fecking mouth." She grinned up at him, and he did his best to laugh. The word sounded ridiculous in her very formal accent.

"Well, anyway, first stop: a nurse to sort out that pain relief, then we'll do the tour."

"I'll cope."

"No doubt, but why should you?"

"Because…" She had no defence. Because she wanted her mind to stop fuzzing over? Because she was becoming tolerant and it would cease to be effective in the longer term? What difference did any of it make?

"Here we are," Sean said, once again returning her to the reality she was trying to avoid. He stepped past her and opened the door, whereby another member of staff came over, all smiles and joy, nothing at all like an angel of death. She held the door so Sean could push Jess and the chair inside. Jess managed a smile.

109

"Hi," the woman said cheerily.

"Hello," Jess mumbled in response.

"You must be Jess?"

"That's right," she confirmed suspiciously.

"Sean mentioned he was bringing you to have a look around. Just give me a call if you need anything. I'm in the duty office."

Great, Jess thought. *How am I supposed to 'give her a call' when I don't even know where that is?* Nonetheless, she gave the woman a courteous nod as she and Sean passed by, heading for the light, airy corridor ahead.

"You'll find the call buttons dotted all around the place," Sean explained in a matter-of-fact tone with the slightest hint of smugness. Jess breathed out hard through her nose. She'd forgotten how much she hated it when he did that—letting her make a fool of herself and then correcting her.

They continued along the corridor a little further and detoured diagonally across a square expanse with vast panoramic windows looking down on the gardens that were below their present height due to the lay of the land. They stopped outside a closed door and Sean knocked.

"Come in," the voice called.

Sean opened the door.

"Don't you ever take a day off?" the same voice asked. It belonged to a woman who looked to be in her late-fifties, her face softly crinkled around keen hazel eyes. She spoke with a lilting Welsh accent that Jess immediately recognised.

"This is Cerys," Sean introduced.

Jess and Cerys watched each other from across the room, both of their faces slowly transforming into smiles.

"Jessica Lambert," Cerys said at last. She went over and gave her a gentle hug. "Gracious, it's been a long time."

"You're not kidding!" Jess replied.

An oddly protracted conversation followed, in that Cerys didn't ask how Jess was, as she could see the answer right in front of her, and when Jess asked the question of Cerys, she quickly changed the subject to how lovely the hospice was.

Sean observed they were struggling with the small talk and intervened. "OK, so, how do you know each other?"

"Jess was at the same school as my four," Cerys explained.

"Yeah, and they were a pain in the ass," Jess said jokingly, although it was true. Ethan and Niall Evans, the eldest set of Cerys's twins, were in the year below Jess at Parkside Primary and followed her to high school. If there was trouble to be got into, Ethan and Niall would be in the thick of it. Jess didn't know the younger twins, as they'd started school after she'd left, but she'd heard it said in the Davenport household that they were even worse, where Luke's friendship with them was the source of much irritation to Eleanor's mother, as 'a friend for tea' always meant two extra mouths to feed on top of the five Davenport children.

For all of her complaining, Mrs. Davenport still went on to have two more, and yet their house never felt overcrowded. Jess loved being there, because at home there was just Mum, Dad and her, and it was too quiet. She and Eleanor would argue it out on a daily basis; Jess wanted the houseful of people as much as Eleanor wanted the peace. Over time, they made new friends, and the visits to each other's houses dwindled; Eleanor and Josh became close; Jess started dating boys. She didn't regret that they had drifted apart, not even now, because they were still friends. Maybe not as close as they were pre-adolescence, but friends nonetheless, who knew each other almost too well.

Jess became aware that her thoughts had taken her on a nostalgic voyage, and tuned in to Sean and Cerys chatting around her, occasionally glancing in her direction. Sean noticed she was back. She smiled apologetically.

"OK," Cerys said, "I'll check that syringe driver for you and sort you out some pills."

"Not pills." Even the thought made her bawk. She wasn't good at swallowing tablets before all of this and was only keeping the ones she'd been prescribed so she could throw them at people who annoyed her.

Cerys shrugged. "No problem."

Unbelievable, Jess thought. When she'd had her appendix out, she'd had to fight for pain relief. Now, all any of them worried about was keeping her as pain-free as possible. Dangerous side effects: death. Not exactly something she needed to worry about.

"Are we ready?" Sean asked.

"Hmm?" She'd wandered off in her mind again but found the energy to give him a nod.

"You're off your face," he whispered into her ear as he steered her back onto the corridor. She giggled.

"Yeah. It is a nice place."

He shook his head in mild exasperation. "OK, this is the visitors' suite." He slowed to a stop in an area decorated and furnished in the style of an enormous modern lounge. "And over there is a kitchen and shower room." He wheeled her onwards. "My office—" he indicated to the left "—and the staffroom—" to the right, and then through to the leisure suite.

"I don't wish to be overly critical, Doctor Tierney, but why bother showing me all of this? It's not like I'll be able to use it."

"Fair comment, but you never know."

As they approached the swimming pool, the mother and son she had seen earlier came towards them, apparently having just been for a swim as they were both wet. Jess tried not to stare at the woman's bald head, but with the overhead lights reflecting off the shiny surface, she couldn't help it. The woman drew level in her wheelchair and smiled at Jess.

"I don't even need a swimming cap," she said. "It's brilliant!"

Jess returned the smile uneasily and glanced up at the little boy. He was smiling, too, and yet here they were in the hospice. His mum was dying. Why was everyone so damned happy?

"I was thinking," the woman said quietly to Jess as if sharing some great and important secret, "I might get some rubber flowers to stick up there, you know?" She looked up towards her dripping wet scalp. "Like those swimming hats the old ladies used to wear?"

Jess managed to squeeze out a laugh as the woman and her son continued past.

"You ready to move on?" Sean asked.

"Yeah," she confirmed hazily.

Next stop: the massage and relaxation therapy room, which was in use so they could only view it through the window.

"They're married." Sean nodded at the couple lying one each on the massage beds, their faces turned towards each other.

"Good," Jess said flatly.

Sean sighed but didn't respond, not yet. He was saving it until they were away from everyone else. "I'll show you what the rooms are like, and then we'll head back to the café, grab a drink. How does that sound?"

She shrugged. Up in the lift they went, to the closest vacant room. She glanced around and nodded, unimpressed. She'd seen enough.

"Can we go?" she asked as they descended once more to ground level. "And get coffee somewhere else?"

"Sure," Sean agreed and obediently took her straight back to the car, where he left her and returned the wheelchair, neither of them speaking until he was behind the wheel and they had reached the end of the driveway. Sean indicated and Jess began to speak.

"Thanks for showing me around."

"No problem."

"It's very nice."

He didn't comment.

"It *is* very nice. Lovely, in fact, but it's not for me."

"Why not?"

"It's too—"

"Full of people embracing what's left of their lives?" Sean questioned. He was trying not to get angry with her, knowing it wouldn't help, but it was so difficult to stay detached. She'd gone to the hospice with a very clear idea of what she'd find, and when she was presented with something entirely at odds with her preconception, she'd found another reason to dismiss it.

"I didn't mean that," she said, sensing his change in mood.

"What did you mean, Jessie? Would you have been happier if it was all dull and grey and full of grim scenes of death and dying?"

"No, obviously not. Well…" She turned to look out of the window. "Yes, I would, actually." She sighed. "I don't want to go there, Sean."

"And nobody's going to make you."

"I just feel like…oh…like if I admit I was wrong I'll have nothing to fight with. Do you understand what I mean?"

"I do."

"You don't."

"Yes. I do. The only right way to do this is the right way for you. For Ella—the woman with the son—it's about making sure he has happy memories of his mum."

"That freaked me out. The whole swimming hat thing."

"It's her way of accepting it."

"Each to their own. Am I selfish? To have opted not to have chemo?"

"Do you believe you did it for selfish reasons?"

"Don't humanist me!"

Sean smiled. "Sorry. Force of habit, although you can still give me an answer to help me understand."

"Yeah. I think I did. It made me so sick, but I was already stressing about losing my hair. Stupid, isn't it? I'd rather keep my hair than live a bit longer."

They parked up outside a coffee shop, and Sean left answering the question until they were settled on a sofa with their drinks. Then he answered it with another question.

"Imagine now, if you'd carried on with the chemo, and we were sitting here, chatting about Christmas…"

"OK."

"How does it feel?"

"Hmm?"

"Did you hear what I said?"

"I heard the first part, then I got distracted thinking about how hard it must be, coping with everyone staring at you because you're bald and puffed up."

Sean laughed and patted her arm. "That's my girl."

"It sounds shallow, but it's not. In my work, appearance is everything. I've got to feel one hundred percent confident, convincing, or I can't do it. And my looks are so important to me. They made me what I am."

"No. Your brains made you what you are. Your looks were the supporting cast." He glanced down at her, still managing to appreciate her ample breasts even if the rest of her was decidedly waif-like these days. "And they're some supporting cast," he said with a hint of a grin. She rolled her eyes but quickly became serious again.

"I always said if I ever got breast cancer and needed a mastectomy, I'd probably kill myself."

Sean's stomach turned over, and he picked up his coffee to try to conceal the impact of her statement. She waited until he settled back in his seat and took hold of his free hand.

"Even knowing what I know," she said, looking him right in the eye. "Now I'm here, and I've accepted it, but other people—my mum, mainly—are getting through each day, hoping that a miracle will come along and save me. If I take my life now, they'll always be living with that 'what if', and I won't do that to them." She squeezed his hand. "I promise."

"Thanks, Jessie." He spent a moment just holding her hand and appreciating her company, ignoring the fact that she was dying. "Crazy, isn't it? Being here again, like this."

She smiled. "Yeah. Crazy in a good way, though." She released his hand to pick up her drink. "Can I ask you to do me a huge favour? And it's OK if you want to say no outright, or if it'll cause you problems later."

"Oh, you've got me intrigued."

"It's a really strange request."

"Go on."

"Will you kiss me?"

Sean didn't answer. He just smoothed his hand over his chin and smiled. He put down his coffee, took her coffee from her and put that down, too. Then he leaned in towards her, gently pressing his lips to hers, waiting to see where she took it, because clarifying whether she meant a friendly peck or a full-on Frenchy would have ruined it. It turned out to be somewhere between the two. When the kiss was over, she slowly moved away, her eyes still closed, a smile of contentment slowly blooming upwards from her mouth and lighting up her whole face. She opened her eyes again.

"Thank you," she said.

He put his hand in his pocket and adjusted himself. "The pleasure was mine," he muttered, and her innocent smile transformed into a cheeky grin.

"You don't need a big fast car."

"How nice of you to say so."

"There's no boot space for a pram for starters."

He laughed. "That's what I love about you, Jessie. You're so practical and sensible." He lifted her chin with his finger and kissed her once more for good measure. "And beautiful and brave."

"Don't go soft on me, Tierney."

"Not much danger of that just now, is there?" He released her, and she took his hand once more.

"Thank you for today, Sean. Really. I appreciate it. Promise me, whatever the future holds, whether I end up bald, or bloated and jaundiced—yes, I've read up—just, please, please remember the girl you knew. The real me."

"I don't want to hear talk like that. It does nobody any good. But I promise I'll do my best."

"What more could a girl ask?" She smiled at him, but then frowned and put up her finger. "Actually, there is just one more thing I want to ask of you."

"You always were so damned demanding," he joked nervously, because he could tell whatever was coming was a big ask. "OK. Go on," he relented. "But this is it. Your last request." He winced as soon as he'd said it. "Ah, shit. I was lying, wasn't I? About slips of the tongue. Anyway, go on."

She slowly eased herself around to face him and kissed him once, on the cheek, before she looked deep into his eyes, and said, "Be happy."

LEO

The sign of Leo is the sign of fire.
Hatred we hate: but no man should desire
A heart too cold to flame with righteous ire.

The Legend Of Shabina
Saturday 29th July

"Bored already?" Josh glanced through the lounge door as he came in, his one remaining Saturday morning appointment done for another week. It wasn't yet eleven o'clock, and George was lying on the sofa, playing *Ocarina of Time*, his still-healing leg propped on a cushion.

"Yep," he replied and grunted in frustration. "I can't get past this bit, either." He'd been stuck on the same part of the game for most of the week.

"Do you want me to do it for you?" Josh called back on his way to the kitchen to make a coffee.

"Nope." George paused the game and followed on his crutches.

"Are you sure?"

"Yep."

"How about a hint?"

"Nope. I told you. Even if I end up smashing the controller to pieces in the process, I *will* complete that game, by myself, without your interference, or 'assistance' as you like to call it, thank you very much."

"It would help if you didn't throw the controller across the room. Maybe you should just stick to playing *Crash*."

"On my own? It's a bit too much like, um, self-pleasuring." Josh laughed, and George grinned. "How was work?"

"OK. She still won't agree to move her appointment from a Saturday, though."

"What you gonna do?"

"I don't know. She's probably nearing the end of her treatment anyway, so I might just have to finish it off here. It's that or see if Zsa Zsa can take her on."

"I don't know whether to feel more sorry for us or your client."

This was all part of the grand plan. Come a week on Monday, Josh would officially be an employee of the university. As such, he had given notice on the lease for his surgery, which he needed to vacate by the end of August, and he was trying not to think about it. It had been his second home for the past thirteen years. Indeed, he'd spent more time there than anywhere else, and it was impossible to imagine not being there.

He'd almost considered putting in an offer to buy the place so that he could rent it to someone else rather than letting it go, but as George had rightly pointed out, he'd get over it quickly enough. So the best thing to do was crack on with moving out and moving on, particularly as all but his Saturday client had now either agreed to move their appointments to Fridays or found themselves another therapist. However, Josh's usual firm of removal specialists—Jeffries and Associates—were still working at half-strength, and with George out of action, he'd had to delay making a start. For now, that suited him just fine.

The coffee machine ready indicator illuminated, and Josh withdrew the cappuccino. "I'm just going to drink this, then take Blue out."

"OK," George sighed.

"Hey. It won't be long now," Josh consoled. The doctor had told George that the best gauge of healing with a fractured fibula was pain; if it didn't hurt, it was all right for him to do it. So far, that limited his options to walking from the lounge to the kitchen, possibly doing the washing up or a bit of cooking, followed by resting up for a couple of hours before he could put any weight on his leg again. That was all well and good until he needed the toilet and hopping wasn't an option.

He wasn't even convinced it was the fracture causing him pain, but he was a patient patient and was doing as he was told, even though five weeks of being more or less completely housebound meant he'd put on at least a stone in weight, knew the daytime TV schedule off by heart and had ploughed through a good tenth of Josh's extensive library of not-very-interesting psychology books, never mind that his mother appeared to have settled into the habit of coming round for Sunday dinner *and* 'bobbing in' with Pauline 'of a Wednesday morning' for tea and cake.

Bored? The word didn't even come close. On the plus side, he'd had plenty of time to work on his painting, and he was kind of happy with how it was turning out, when he wasn't being moody and self-critical, like now.

"Tell you what," Josh said, interrupting his thoughts. "After I've taken Blue for his five minutes up and down the road, how about we go somewhere in the car. We could go and eat ice cream. That always cheers you up."

George shrugged. "I dunno. At the moment, it'll probably make me even more miserable." He sighed again.

"You really are very fed up, aren't you?"

"Yeah. Sorry."

Josh put his arms around him. "It's OK."

"It's not. The baby's due in less than four weeks, if Soph doesn't go into labour before then, and I'm still stuck on these damned crutches. What am I gonna do if he comes early, and I can't drive, and she ends up giving birth in the back of a taxi, or on the bus, or—"

"Whoa!" Josh put his hand over George's mouth. "Stop panicking a minute and listen. Can you do that?"

"Mmm-mm," George sounded.

"I'm going to move my hand, OK?"

"Mmm-mm."

Josh freed him, and he took a breath ready to start again.

"Shush!" Josh said. George did as he was told. "First up, if you are still on crutches when Sophie goes into labour, I'll drive. In fact, I'll drive whatever happens."

"But what if you're at work?"

"I'll put my foot down."

"Or if there's a traffic jam."

"How often does that happen?"

"But it could."

"It could, but even in heavy traffic, we'll be at the hospital in less than thirty minutes." George still looked dubious. "Really. It'll all be fine. I promise."

"OK," he said. "You'll keep your phone on?"

"I'll keep my phone on."

"And make sure there's plenty of petrol in the car?"

"I always do."

"But what if—"

"George! I'll keep my phone on, with the volume up full, and make sure the car has petrol, water, oil, brake fluid and screen wash. I'll also avoid alcohol, drugs, sick people, thunderstorms—whatever it takes."

George continued to frown a little longer while he got it all straightened out in his mind. The frown faded and he nodded. "OK. Thank you. Let's do what you said and go get ice cream."

"We don't have to if you don't want to."

"I know, but I need to get out and stop moping."

Josh watched him trying to perk up and smiled. "You are so wonderful. I hope you know that."

"I'm so grumpy, and I need to pack it in."

"All right, we won't be long." Josh attached the lead to Blue's collar, and they left. It was only during the past week that the dog had been allowed to start walking outside of the house again, and he seemed to be healing well, but he would always be at risk of dislocation now, so they were following the vet's advice to the letter. It was a very strange concept for Josh—doing as medical practitioners advised.

By the time they returned from their slow stroll to the other end of the terrace and back, George had hobbled his way up the stairs to put on a pair of slip-on canvas shoes—the only ones he could wear at the moment—and was ready to go, although still not entirely in the mood for it. Josh settled Blue in his crate, and soon after, they were in the car, heading for The Pizza Place. It wasn't yet lunchtime, so they were able to park right outside. Josh went to get a ticket from the pay-and-display machine, leaving George to struggle out of the car independently, as was his wont.

"I've paid for three hours, in case you wanted to go anywhere else," Josh told him.

"Like where?"

"I don't know. Maybe have a peruse of the local shops."

"Shopping?"

"Why not? You like shopping."

"But you don't."

"Will it make you happy?"

122

"Happier."

"That's OK, then."

The restaurant was cool and dark, compared to the outside world. Krissi was behind the counter, her tablet in her hand and a frown on her face as she examined the space underneath the coffee machine, trying to calculate how many replacement cups she needed to order on a regular basis to combat 'natural wastage', which was the polite way of saying clumsy staff. She turned and smiled.

"Good morning! Fancy seeing you here! I've already had Mum and Kris in. They came to borrow my house key. Kris lost his in the woods and went to the salon to get Mum's, but she'd left hers at home."

"Did it fall through the hole in his pocket, by any chance?" George asked.

Krissi grinned. "However did you guess?"

"Every Saturday, that happens. I even offered to sew up the hole for him."

"Yeah, well, they went back and tried to get the dog to seek it out, but he was more interested in chasing squirrels."

George smiled, although he had a distant look in his eyes. He was missing the Saturday morning walks, as was Blue.

"Anyway," Josh said, spotting George going downhill again, "we came to eat ice cream."

"You've come to the right place. We've just had a delivery. *And* we've got a new dessert menu. I'll bring it over for you. By the way, Andy's over there." Krissi indicated to the back left corner, where, sure enough, Andy was sitting on his own, chatting on his phone, a laptop on the table in front of him. Josh and George looked at each other and frowned. "He's fine. It's so he can keep out of the way, but he might like the company."

They went over.

"Hi, Andy," George greeted. He passed Josh his crutches and slid along the seat opposite.

"Alright, mate! How you doing?"

"Not so bad. You?"

"Yeah. Pretty good." Andy shut his laptop and moved it to one side. "Alright, Josh?"

123

"Yes, thanks." He leaned the crutches against the end of the seat and sat down next to George. "How's the shoulder and everything?"

"Shoulder's not so bad," Andy replied, being deliberately evasive. Josh nodded in understanding.

Krissi brought over the dessert menu. "OK, it's all a bit experimental, but it's dead exciting. Wotto's been asked by HQ to design the menu for the whole chain."

"That's awesome!" George said.

"I know. I'm so proud." Krissi beamed. Andy gave her a subtle, knowing smile; she gave him the slightest of winks in response. "It kind of came about because of the milk bar. One of the two women who run it used to work for The Pizza Place main branch, and they came in here a few weeks ago, spying."

"I thought the milk bar was part of Campion Community Trust," Josh said.

"It is, and I know what you're thinking, but Jay has nothing to do with the day-to-day running of the projects. Well, other than the studio, which Stu was supposed to be in charge of, but that was never gonna happen. So anyway, Wotto returned the favour and went on a reconnaissance mission. They've started selling ice cream sundaes in all these mad flavours. And get this. They're doing a white chocolate orange one. Not that I'm saying they nicked the idea, but…"

"They nicked the idea," Josh finished.

"Yeah." Krissi opened the menu and passed it to him, pointing at the item at the top of the right side of the gatefold.

Josh read the name of the dessert, then the description, and started to laugh. He passed the menu to George. "You're famous," he said.

George frowned as he read. "A very adult dessert, with creamy white chocolate ice cream, fresh orange sorbet and a dash of—"

"Look what it's called," Josh prompted.

"Pure Bliss?" George grinned. "Cool. Do I get royalties?"

Krissi laughed. "All the others got their names the same way. That's always been the good thing about The Pizza Place. They've got their standard menu, but the chefs are allowed to get creative if they want to, although most of them aren't that great with desserts."

"But Wotto is."

"His desserts are amazing," Krissi gushed.

Andy rolled his eyes. "I tried the Cherry Precious last Saturday. It's quite possibly the sexiest dessert ever made. By a man." He coughed into his hand.

Josh shrugged. "Why 'by a man'?"

"Because dessert's supposed to be a woman's thing."

"You're clearly spending too much time with your brother."

"Yeah. You might have a point there." Much as Andy and Dan were alike, Dan was always the more stereotypically masculine of the two, and whilst neither was overtly sexist, unless it came to women and football, that was a typical 'Dan' thing to say.

"Mmm. That does sound good," George said. He'd been reading the description of the Cherry Precious. "Sweet morello cherry purée, with whole morello cherries, swirled with almond milk ice cream and topped with amaretto crumble and roasted almonds."

"Almond milk?" Josh queried.

"Yeah," Krissi confirmed. "That's a vegan, dairy-free and gluten-free dessert. We've also got a couple that are guaranteed nut-free, including the Pure Bliss. It's causing a few problems between Wotto and Lyn, though—she's the other full-time chef. She's really good at her job, but he's reorganised the kitchen to avoid cross-contamination, and it's taking her a while to get used to where everything goes." In fact, Lyn didn't get it at all, but Krissi was too professional to say that. "Anyway, he's doing a taster platter while he gets everything right, so if you like, you can choose five desserts and have a little of each."

"Result!" George said. He closed the menu. "I'll go with chef's choice."

"Sounds good to me," Josh agreed.

"OK." Krissi took back the menus. "I'll make sure you get a bit of all of them between you. I can't wait to hear what you think." She bounced off towards the kitchen to place their order.

Josh turned his attention back to Andy. "Is this your Saturday hangout?"

"It sure is. Krissi's been looking after me."

"Her mother's daughter."

"Ha. Yeah." Andy glanced cagily at George.

"It's OK. He knows," Josh said.

George had been deep in thought and only just noticed they were both looking at him. "What?"

"You know," Andy said.

"Do I?"

Josh tutted. "Yes, you do."

"Oh." George nodded at Andy. "I do, apparently."

Andy smiled.

Krissi backed out of the kitchen. She was giggling, and her cheeks were flushed pink. She grinned at Andy as she passed by.

"It would seem it's mutual," Josh observed.

"What, the attraction, or the looking after each other?"

"Both?"

"Yeah, maybe." Andy leaned in closer and said quietly, "Jay's been trying to get them together for weeks, and they won't take the same day off, because they don't trust anyone else to look after the place."

Josh frowned thoughtfully. "I don't know Lyn, but if Krissi appointed her, she must be all right, and Karen always does a great job."

"I know that. You know that—" Andy paused, whilst Krissi walked past on her way back to the kitchen "—but the pair of them are control freaks."

"That's very true. Still, if it's meant to be then it'll be."

"Like you two, you mean?"

"Yes, like us, *too*."

George was playing with the bowl of sugar packets, spinning it from side to side and listening to the swoosh of the granules inside the packets, paying no attention whatsoever to the conversation. However, he was immediately attentive when Krissi arrived back at their table with two large rectangular plates. Wotto was a couple of steps behind her.

"Alright?" he grinned. He shook Josh's hand.

"Hey, Wotto." Josh smiled back, for what it was worth, as Wotto was watching George, who was staring in mute wonder at his plate of desserts. George picked up his spoon and dug into a creamy heap speckled with what looked like pieces of mango and chunks of biscuit.

"I only added that one yesterday," Wotto explained, "so it's not on the menu yet."

"Mmm. What is it? Cheesecake?" George took another spoonful.

"Yeah. It's called 'The Legend of Shabina'."

"Shabina?" Josh and George exclaimed together.

"It's a very sad story."

"Not *the* Shabina?" Josh asked.

"As in the MD's future daughter-in-law?"

They all laughed.

"Yeah," Wotto continued. "Mr. Brown came in with Ollie yesterday. He's finished school for the summer, and he was well upset, poor little guy. So I got him to come help with the cheesecake base, thinking it might cheer him up, and he's going, 'Shabina's skin is like that colour,' when we were pouring the caramel sauce, then, 'Mangos are Shabina's favourite thing to eat,' and, 'I got to have all the chocolate on my own now Shabina's gone.'"

"Bless," Josh said. "I suppose six weeks is a long time when you're four."

"Nearly five," Wotto corrected with a grin. "So there it is. The Legend of Shabina. A mango and caramel cheesecake, except we had to break up the base and stir it in, 'Cos Shabina likes it when it's all crunchy and mixed up.'"

"Right." Josh picked up his spoon, optimistically, but George really didn't want to share.

"Anyway, gonna leave you to it," Wotto said. "Tell Krissi what you think, especially of the Cherry Precious. I think it might need something else, dunno what. In a bit." Wotto nodded, his massive cap following his head movement a split second after the event, and returned to his kitchen.

Josh quickly swiped the last of The Legend of Shabina cheesecake.

"Hey!" George scowled.

"Sharing. That's what we were supposed to be doing. You know, what's mine is yours, what's yours is mine?"

"Except dessert." George pulled his plate closer to him.

"Oh, but look!" Josh pointed to his own plate. "I've got the Pure Bliss *and* the Cherry Precious."

Andy laughed and shook his head. He listened to them squabbling over sharing their desserts for a little longer and reopened his laptop. He wasn't working on anything of great importance, but he didn't want to watch them eat. Instead, he replied to the email from Michal, to tell him how great the photos of the Nepal bakery were and promising to visit him and Zuza in Poland once things had settled down. After that, he sent Charlie a message just for the sake of it. She was online and responded straight away. He told her what he was up to and with whom.

"Charlie says hi."

"Hi back," Josh said. "How's her new job going?"

"It isn't."

"Oh?"

"She's been laid off again. Company went under."

"What a shame. She's only been there, what? Three months?"

"Yeah. It was three months exactly when the receivers came in last Monday. The boss fucked off and left her to deal with them."

"Nice! So she's looking for a new job again?"

"She's got something lined up already. Working for Len."

"Really? Doing what?"

"Creative accounting," George mumbled through a mouthful of Juicy Lemon Heads—'a sweet yet tangy and refreshing lemon ganache formed into tiny lemon-shaped tarts'—with smiley faces.

"Pretty much," Andy confirmed. "Although he does have a legitimate side to his business as well."

"What does he do?" Josh asked.

"Imports and exports cars."

"Ah! Hence the real 'my other car is a Ferrari'."

"Yep. My mum's on about her tenth car since they got married. She's had a Carrera, a Vanquish, three or four Audis, including the current one—I think she even had a Bentley for a while."

"I know where I'm getting my next car from."

"I'll let you into a little secret," Andy said, leaning in close. "I pick up my new car this week. Well, I say new—" He stopped. He hadn't intended to tell anyone about it, but he was far too excited, and now he had Josh teetering on the edge of his seat, too.

"What is it?" Josh asked.

Andy leaned across and whispered into Josh's ear.

"Wow! Sounds fabulous."

"Just wait till you see it. He'd do you a great deal on part-ex, you know."

"You're not gonna get a sports car," George said to Josh in disbelief.

"Why not?"

"I'm not saying you can't. Just that…well, it's a bit, um…"

"Spontaneous?"

"Yeah. You gonna eat any of those desserts?"

"Yes. I am." Josh took a quick scoop of the Cherry Precious so that he could at least report back to Wotto, and turned his plate so George could eat the rest of it. "Mmm. That's gorgeous." He spun the plate back and took another spoonful. George glared at him.

"So," Andy continued, "Len's said if Charlie can give his company a more professional profile, he'll source her the 1985 Golf GTi convertible she's always going on about."

"He looks like he's doing more than all right already."

"He is, but he also wants to work with insurance companies. Like with Dan's four-by-four, he can't officially provide him with a replacement car, because of his firm's bad reputation."

"Ah, I see. So Charlotte would be doing all the PR and paperwork side of things."

"That's right."

"Good stuff. And is Dan going for another four-by-four?"

"Depends on whether he can convince Adele that he really, *really* needs a convertible."

"Don't they do convertible four-by-fours?"

"There's a couple out there, but they're ugly as sin."

"That's a shame. It'd be a good compromise."

"Dan's idea of a compromise is a five-seater cabriolet, like the one that hit us on the motorway? He wants one of those."

Josh was taking it all in. The marriage guidance idea hadn't come to anything yet, because of the accident. For now, the little niggles in life were meaningless and invisible, but he knew it was only a matter of time, and it wouldn't hurt to go onto the field with a good idea of each side's game plan.

"Vanilla," George said.

"Pardon?"

"Vanilla is what it needs. The Cherry Precious. The cherry and almond is fantastic, but it's not quite round enough."

"OK. If you say so."

"I do." He took an enormous spoonful of the Pure Bliss and put it in his mouth, slowly withdrew the spoon and slithered down his seat. "Oh, man."

"Still as blissful as ever?"

"Totally, although you never forget your first time." He tried for a second spoonful, and Josh blocked his hand. George scowled, but he had to relent, as he'd already eaten most of the desserts. "Speaking of which," he said, "I'd like to pop and see Ollie and Toby on the way home, if they're in."

"OK. I'll text Ellie now and see." Josh took out his phone. "You got any plans for the rest of the day?" he asked Andy and typed at the same time.

"Nah. Gonna stay here till this evening, then watch a film. The grass needs cutting, but the physio told me I wasn't allowed to. I'm gutted, obviously."

"Oh, obviously," Josh repeated with a laugh. The response came from Eleanor. "They're out," he told George, "but she said they'll call round to us later, if that's easier."

"Yeah, OK. Tell her to do that, and we can go for a quick browse around the shops."

Josh responded to Eleanor accordingly and went to pay Krissi for their desserts.

"They're all fabulous," he said.

"So no improvements?"

"George said the Cherry Precious needs vanilla."

"Vanilla!" Wotto was standing behind him. "I'm so dense sometimes. Nice one, mate," he said to George and disappeared back inside his kitchen.

"How much do we owe you?" Josh asked Krissi.

"On the house."

"Don't be silly."

"Don't *you* be silly. Wotto's been driving himself nuts trying to figure out what to do with that dessert, so believe me, it's worth it. Besides, I just know you'll be back for more."

"Hell, yeah!" George said, hopping towards the door. "Thanks, Missy." He gave her a big hug on his way past.

"What did I do?"

"Made him happy. And that's quite an achievement at the moment, believe me. See you soon."

***

"Hel-lo-o," Eleanor called, opening the door and letting herself in, as per the text message instruction. No response. She glanced into the lounge. It was empty. She looked down at Oliver and frowned.

He shrugged. "They in the garden?"

"Probably. Let's go see." As she spoke, there was the sound of a deep 'woof' and Blue came through the kitchen to greet them.

"Hello, Blue," Oliver said, patting him on the head. The dog was nearly as tall as Oliver was himself, but even in full health, he was very gentle. He wagged his tail, turned and walked back the way he had come, peering behind him to make sure they were following. At the back door, they both stopped in their tracks. Eleanor scanned the lawn, her mouth opening wider and wider as she took in the scene before her.

"What in God's name are you doing?"

Josh was kneeling on the grass, in amidst a mass of teak-stained wood of various lengths and shapes, with several cereal bowls full of screws, nuts and bolts positioned in close proximity. He set down a sheet of paper and weighted it with one of the bowls.

"Putting together patio furniture, allegedly." He got up and went over to hug her. "You all right, Ollie?"

Oliver nodded, still staring at all of the wood; to a small child, it was like a giant construction toy, and he was itching to 'help'.

"Where's George?" Eleanor asked.

"Next door but one. Sean got called into work and asked George to keep an eye on Sophie. She only came round for a cup of tea."

"Bless her. I bet she doesn't get a minute."

"I go see Dorge?" Oliver asked. Eleanor nodded.

"I suppose that'd be all right. Straight there, OK?"

"OK."

Oliver ran back through the house, and Eleanor screwed her eyes shut in preparation for the bang of the front door slamming shut. "Why can't children close doors quietly?"

Josh laughed. "Would you like a drink?"

"Please. A cold one, if you've got it."

"Frappuccino?"

"Yeah. Why not?"

"Coming right up. While I'm making it, you can solve my enormous jigsaw puzzle."

"Hmm." She stepped over the pieces of wood and freed the instructions, examining the bits Josh had put together so far.

"I think they've mixed up two kits," Josh called from the back door.

Eleanor frowned and turned her head to one side. "No, they haven't. You've used the wrong piece here." She tapped the part-construction with her toe and looked at the instructions again. "And here."

"Ah." Josh disappeared from view again.

Eleanor picked up a screwdriver and started to unscrew the bit he'd already done. By the time he came out with the drinks, she'd swapped the wrong pieces for the right ones. There wasn't much difference between them, other than the holes that had been drilled to attach the support struts for the table.

"That should work now," she said, putting the screwdriver down so she could take the glass. "Thanks." She sucked the straw. "Ooh, that's good. Does your machine make these?"

"No. It's espresso, milk and ice cream."

"It works, whatever." They went over to the patio and sat on the plastic chairs of the retiring furniture. The legs creaked and swayed with their weight, despite neither being especially heavy. "I can see why you wanted new stuff now," she said.

"Yes. This is bloody awful, and I've been trying to convince George for months that we should replace it."

"How did you persuade him in the end?"

"I got him this morning, when he was tanked up on sugar."

"Very cunning!"

"I thought so. Wotto's desserts are out of this world."

"Tell me about it. Did you know James asked him to transfer to HQ?"

Josh shook his head. "Krissi said he'd been asked to put together the new menu, but she didn't say anything about that."

"He wants him on the board of directors, but Wotto's not having any of it. The Pizza Place is a really good company, and they reward hard work. That's how James ended up where he is. They spot potential and do all they can to keep it. Krissi was offered promotion at the beginning of the year, and she declined, too. I don't really understand it."

"Maybe they're happy where they are. After all, how many times were you offered promotion?"

"I suppose, but I don't think it does either of them any good knowing James the way they do. I get the feeling they're worried it looks like favouritism—far from it. If anything, James is harder on the people he considers friends."

Josh sucked on his straw, taking the moment to ponder. "It's a bit more personal than that," he said.

"In what way?"

"I think they want to stay together. Anyway, I've said enough."

Eleanor would have pushed for more information, but George and Oliver's return stopped her from doing so.

"Hi, Ellie." George smiled and leaned down to give her a hug, taking a sideways glance at the still unconstructed new furniture. "You not made much progress?" he asked Josh.

"No. I have no idea what I'm doing, and the bit I'd done was all wrong."

"I thought you were clever."

"Hmm."

"I'll give you a hand," Eleanor offered. "We'll have it together in no time. Then you can make me another of these fantastic frappuccinos."

"You're on," Josh said. They put down their still half-full glasses and returned to the lawn. He passed her the instruction sheet.

"You not brought my godson with you?" George asked.

"He was asleep. James is going to come with him later, if we're still here."

"Oh." George looked disappointed. He'd hardly seen anyone since the accident, and he was missing Toby especially.

Josh and Eleanor watched him trying to be cheerful for Oliver. They exchanged glances.

"How about I cook dinner for us all?" Josh suggested. Eleanor nodded in agreement.

"Sounds like a great idea to me," she said. George wasn't really listening.

"It won't be anything fancy," Josh said. "Just a salad and stuff. It's a shame we don't have a barbecue really, although I suppose I could pop out and *buy one*."

George heard that.

"What you buying now?"

"A barbecue."

"Really?"

"No. I was trying to get your attention. Ellie, James and the boys are staying for dinner."

"You want me to cook?"

"I'll cook. You can keep the children entertained."

"Yeah," George sighed. "OK." He was sliding again.

"How's Sophie, George?" Eleanor asked, hoping to distract him.

"Not too bad. She's fed up, and she's got a stinking cold."

"How long's she got left?"

"Three weeks, five days."

"Poor thing. I don't envy her. The last few weeks go on forever."

"I bet. I hope I don't let her down." He sighed again.

"How is it? Is it feeling any better?"

"It's getting there—killing me this afternoon after traipsing round the shops earlier."

Eleanor smiled sympathetically. She'd figured out the instructions now and was ready to begin. "Right, we need parts E and F, and eight of screw A-one." She looked at Josh expectantly.

He gave her the screws. "You'd be better finding parts E and F for yourself," he advised.

She tutted and started scanning the garden, comparing the pieces to the picture. "Can you bring my drink over, please, honey?" she asked Oliver, who was sitting on the floor a few feet from the outgoing patio table.

Oliver did as requested and then called Blue to him, coaxing him inside the house. Josh watched them disappear from view.

"Here, hold that end up for me," Eleanor said. Josh did as instructed. "So, are you doing your exercises?" she asked without looking up, although the question was obviously aimed at George.

"Yep. As much as I can. The doctor said don't do it if it hurts, the physio said I need to keep at it to get my muscle strength back. It'd be great if they'd actually talk to each other every now and then."

"It'd be great if there was time and means to do so," Eleanor griped. She'd found the two parts she needed and moved them into position.

Josh stood nearby, not sure what he could do to help. He glanced George's way. "Do you need anything?"

"No, I'm fine, although I might go and take some pills, if I can be bothered to get up."

"I'll get them," Josh offered. It was an excuse to leave.

He found Oliver sitting on the bottom stair, the dog lying at his feet.

"Hey, Ollie. Are you OK?"

Oliver nodded and wiped his nose with the heel of his hand.

Josh crouched down and peered into his face. "Are you sad?"

Oliver nodded again.

"Oh dear." Josh moved to his side and sat next to him. "What's wrong?"

Oliver sniffed and shrugged.

"Do you know why you're feeling sad?"

Oliver started fiddling with the carpet grip. "Are you sad, Josh?"

"Sometimes, but not today."

"You not sad about Jess?"

135

"Ah. Well, I am sad about that, but not all the time, because there're still lots of other good things happening that make me happy."

"I got a new car and I still sad."

"You got a new car? That's exciting. What's it like?"

"It's red and it's got shiny wheels and yellow fire on the sides."

"Wow!"

"And you pull it back like this—" Oliver demonstrated against his thigh "—and it goes very faster, but it falled off the table into the mopping bucket. Ellna said to wash it and to leave it at home so it can dry. I show you if you want, next time you come with Dorge."

"That'd be awesome."

Oliver became quiet again. Josh waited, watching the little boy prepare to tell him what was upsetting him.

"I sad about Dorge," he said. His lip started to quiver.

"Why are you sad about George?"

"Cos he got a sore leg and it not getting better."

"Oh, I see."

"And he said, like with Jess and the cancer, that the bad cells, they stop the good ones and then the doctors can't make you better." Oliver started crying. "I don't want Dorge to get the cancer. I his best man. I miss him if he die."

Josh gently lifted Oliver onto his lap and hugged him tightly, aware that his own tears threatening weren't going to help much just at this moment. He blinked them back.

"George isn't going to die, Ollie. He'll be all fixed again soon, I promise."

"He not got the cancer, like Jess?"

"No. He just broke a bone, like you did. But when you're little, you get better much faster than when you're all grown up and old and grumpy, like George." Josh made his voice a little deeper. "Oh, man, it's so unfair," he said grumpily.

Oliver giggled. "I cheer him up. I tell him about my new car and that he can play with it."

Josh waited for Oliver to slide off his knee before he got up.

Oliver took hold of his hand and pulled. "You very clever, Josh. You get Ellna to do all the hard work."

136

Josh laughed. "Thanks, Ollie, but I'm definitely not as clever as you."

They set off towards the garden.

"Shabina is very, very, very, very clever. She can do the times tables."

"Can she?"

"Her mummy teached her how they go. She said she tell me them in September." He sighed loudly in exasperation. "I think they too hard for me."

Josh stopped in the kitchen. "I've got to get George's medicine, OK?"

Oliver waited next to him, rotating on the spot. "Your kitchen is very little," he said.

"It is, you're right. We're getting it made bigger soon."

"When?"

"Erm…" Josh stumbled, trying to think of a good answer.

"It's OK," Oliver told him. "I know you all busy looking after Jess."

Josh examined Oliver, both of them holding eye contact for several seconds. "I think you are probably even as clever as Shabina," Josh said.

"I can get some of the sweeties with the words on them for her, to say thank you for the times tables, like you and Dorge. Where you buy those?"

"From the newspaper shop by the park, or the supermarket."

Oliver nodded. "You give Dorge his medicine and we go to the shop, pleeeaaase?" He blinked at him with big brown pleading eyes.

Josh smiled "Yes, OK. Let's tell George and Eleanor we're going first, though, or they might wonder what's happened to us."

Outside, the random planks of wood were starting to shape up nicely into a picnic table. Josh gave Eleanor a hug.

"Sorry I abandoned you."

"Don't worry. George went to get his pills himself in the end and overheard. Everything all right?"

"I think so. We're going to the shop to buy sweets for Shabina."

"What a surprise! I've never known anyone so besotted—actually that's an outright lie." Eleanor looked meaningfully from Josh to George.

Josh grinned. "Come on, Ollie."

Oliver followed him back inside and took his hand. "We get some sweeties for Dorge?"

"Yes, Ollie. He'll like that."

"We get him the sweeties with the words on, too?"

"If you want to."

"He not like them?"

"He likes them a lot. When George and I were little, we used to play a game with the sweeties with words."

"You can tell me on the way to the shop, and I can play it with Shabina?"

"Erm, maybe."

"She is my best friend in the whole whole world."

Josh glanced down at the little boy marching along beside him. Oliver looked up and gave him his best grin. "Pleeeaaase?"

"OK. But it's a very special game, and it's only for best friends."

"In the whole whole world?"

"Yes." Josh smiled. "Best friends in the whole whole world."

Haze
Thursday 3rd August

Shaunna slumped sleepily down the stairs, her cotton dressing gown billowing behind her and revealing her summer pyjamas: a plain pink vest top and white shorts printed with cherries. It was only just after eight in the morning and already uncomfortably hot. She closed the curtains in the lounge to keep out as much of the morning sun as possible, went through to the kitchen and switched on the kettle, fetched a mug and a teabag, all without properly opening her eyes.

Casper leapt up barking and ran to the front door; a moment later, the letterbox flipped open. Shaunna squinted down the hallway, to where the dog was now standing over the post and slow-wagging his tail, as if he expected the singular white envelope to suddenly jump to life and run away. She watched a moment longer, yawned and made her tea. Now she was ready to go and investigate.

It was from Andy. She probably could have guessed that much from a distance, if her brain had been working; the post rarely arrived this early. So, three months till Krissi's twenty-fourth birthday, and he was still intent on 'paying his debt'. She sighed in exasperation, stooped to collect the envelope, scuffed her way back to the kitchen and flopped wearily into a chair.

It had been so warm during the night, she felt like she'd hardly slept at all. Fortunately, it was her day off from the salon. It had been almost too hot to cope this week, and today was forecast to be the hottest day of the year so far. By the feel of it, it was already well on its way there. She picked up the envelope and started fanning herself with it. The flap came open. She stopped.

"That's not money," she said to herself, or the dog, possibly, because no-one else was home. She pulled the sheet of paper free and unfolded it. It was a letter, handwritten, and surprisingly neat, given that it was definitely written by Andy. It almost filled both sides of the sheet of paper. She picked up her tea, sat back and began to read.

Hi Shaunna,

I don't know if you'll read this letter straight away, but if you do, I'm sitting outside your house in my new car – a 1969 Ford Mustang convertible in a nice inconspicuous candyapple red. She's been completely refurbished, with red and black interior, gorgeous alloys and a reconditioned V8 engine. She roars like an untamed lioness and totally turns heads. A lot like you, I guess.

Shaunna put her tea down and walked back along the hallway, still reading the letter and only pausing to open the front door. She could see the car and the driver in her peripheral vision, but continued to read without looking up.

And I got to thinking, what better way to test out this baby than to take a hot girl on a romantic picnic? Well, you know me, ever the optimist – I've got the hamper all packed up in the back seat. Cheese sandwiches, hard-boiled eggs, fresh fruit, traditional lemonade. And I got you some Skips too.

Shaunna glanced across the road. Andy was fiddling with the car radio and pretending not to have noticed her.

So there it is. No strings, just a quiet picnic for two, somewhere in the countryside. What do you think? Of course, if you don't open this letter until later, then my plans will be ruined, but the offer is open. I can wait.

R.S.V.P. the sad lonely guy in the red Mustang across the street.

Shaunna folded the letter in half and waited for Andy to look up. He smiled, and she smiled back.

"You'd better come in," she called over. "I've still got to shower." She returned inside; Andy followed a minute later. He hovered in the kitchen doorway, watching her. She had her back to him, making him a cup of tea, as was her way.

"Sit," she told him. He did so. "That's not what I expected to find in that envelope."

"Yeah. I did wonder, actually. I was going to send a text, but it would've taken about twenty messages, and I didn't think it'd have the same impact."

Shaunna put the tea in front of him. "You got that right." She laughed. "I won't be long." With that, she disappeared upstairs, leaving him with Casper for company. She returned in cropped jeans and a vest top, a white shirt draped over her arm. She picked up a bottle of sun cream and handed it to Andy.

"Can you put some of this on my shoulders and back?" she asked, lifting her hair and turning away from him.

He popped the cap off and squeezed some of the cream onto his palm, standing so he could reach her shoulders, the perfume of her hair and her freshly showered body almost overpowering him.

"Thanks." She released her hair, and it tumbled down over her shoulders. She turned around to face him. "That's what I like about you," she said. "The way you don't hide your appreciation. It makes a woman feel really good about herself."

He smiled. "Glad to oblige. But so you know, however hot you are, I said no strings, and I really do mean it. I'm looking forward to spending some time with you that, with any luck, we'll both remember."

"Yeah. That'd make a nice change, wouldn't it? Well, I'm ready if you are."

Andy nodded and tugged his key free from his pocket, twirling it on its ring around his finger as they made their way outside.

"When did you get the car?" Shaunna asked as she locked the door behind her.

"Last week, but I only picked it up yesterday. Took it round to show Dan and Adele last night. He turned green."

"I bet he did. What did Adele have to say? Anything?"

"Nothing very nice. She was too busy trying to convince Dan he wasn't missing out by getting another nice, sensible four-by-four, which he isn't, really." They crossed the road, and Andy followed Shaunna around to the nearside. "It won't be as sexy as this, obviously."

"No, it won't," Shaunna agreed, lightly running her fingers along the top of the passenger door. Andy reached past and opened it for her.

"Thanks," she said, with a half-curtsy, and stepped over the sill into the car. It really was sexy, although the seats were already hot, and she had to ease herself against the backrest very carefully.

Andy waited for her to fasten her seat belt and turned the ignition. The engine roared to life, and he revved a couple of times.

"Wow!" Shaunna's lips parted in a wide smile. She put on her sunglasses, and off they went, heading straight out of town for the nearest long, winding country lane. It was the one where Andy had nearly died in his Audi three years previously, but he wasn't going to think about that just now. He was taking it at a leisurely pace—no need to rush, after all. Shaunna seemed quite content, watching the world watching them pass by, her hair flowing out behind her like a glorious trail of flames.

They continued out of town for an hour or so, passing through a couple of small villages, and soon arriving at a National Trust park, with protected meadows and red deer roaming free. Andy checked the position of the sun in relation to where they parked, so that the car would be in the shade when they returned later, and took the picnic hamper from the back seat.

"Now why would you own one of those?" Shaunna asked. "When you said 'hamper', I thought you probably meant 'tatty old rucksack' with a plastic bag of squashed sandwiches."

"Because I'm romantic," Andy protested.

"Of course you are!"

Andy pretended to be offended, but then he grinned. "I bought it yesterday, when I decided I was going to ask you on a picnic date, but I actually am quite romantic. Me and Jess always used to…" He couldn't go any further.

Shaunna squeezed his hand. There was nothing to be said that would make things any less painful than they were, so neither of them tried. The feeling would pass again in a little while. Shaunna took the blanket from the back of the car.

"Come on, Mr. Romance. Let's go find a nice spot." She looped her arm through his, and they began to walk, although it was so warm that their arms gradually slipped apart, and neither attempted to fight it.

"Here looks good," Andy suggested, pointing to a grassy area under a sycamore tree.

Shaunna spread the blanket on the ground. "You do realise it's only ten o'clock?"

"So?"

"So it's very early to be out for a picnic."

"Which means we've got a whole day to do it, if that's what we decide."

"OK."

"To be honest, I thought you'd probably want to be home before Kris got back from work."

"He won't be back until at least six."

"Awesome. That's another eight hours of your wonderful, sober company."

Shaunna laughed. "I bet you get bored by, ohhh, I give it till about eleven."

"Hey! I resent that! Even I can last longer than an hour."

"That wasn't quite what I meant."

"I know." Andy put the picnic hamper down on the corner of the blanket and unbuckled the two straps. He flipped the lid open. "However, I must tell you that I have been known to stick at a single activity for several minutes at a time." He took out two plastic tumblers, then a flask, which he duly opened, decanting the cloudy liquid into the tumblers. He handed one to her.

"Whole minutes, eh? I'm impressed. Cheers!" She banged her drink against his and took a sip. It was cold and sweet, with a sharp edge to it. "Mmm. That's nice."

"I made it myself. With real lemons."

"Really? You're full of surprises."

"Also…" Andy delved into the hamper again and extracted a small, plastic box. He popped the lid, and she glanced inside. "I made these, too. Kind of."

"Lemon curd tarts. Excellent. I love lemon curd tarts."

"Yeah. I remembered that from way back, although I wasn't sure you still did."

"I still do," Shaunna confirmed. She sat down and patted the blanket. He accepted her invitation but was careful to keep space between them, for he genuinely had no ulterior motive. Life was complicated enough at the moment without the added challenge of trying anything on. Besides, she'd said she didn't want a relationship.

"What did you mean about getting home before Kris?" she asked, as if she had read his mind.

"I don't want to cause any more trouble between you."

Shaunna studied the plastic box with the tarts in it. "We've never talked about it, have we?"

"We might've done," Andy said with a grin.

"All right, I'll rephrase that. I don't remember us ever talking about it. Maybe we should get it out of the way now, so we can enjoy our picnic."

Andy shrugged. "Sounds good to me."

"Anyway, you can only cause more trouble if you caused some to begin with, and you didn't."

He gave her a doleful look.

"Don't take this the wrong way, but if it hadn't been you, it would've been someone else. Kris knows that as well as you do."

"Maybe you're right," he said, frowning thoughtfully. "Were you really getting laid that much?"

She slapped his arm, playfully, although she was horrified by the question. Nobody had ever been bold enough to ask it before, but the truth was she had been 'getting laid that much', and she wasn't proud of herself. There again, she was no longer ashamed. After a few minutes of silence, she answered him.

"Yeah, I was."

He nodded, just the once and only the slightest movement of his head.

She nudged him. "Jealous?"

"Very." He opened his mouth a couple of times, kind of goldfish style, as he rephrased what he wanted to say. On the third try, he got it right, he hoped. "Not of the other lads, or a bit of the other lads, but that you were getting it and I wasn't!"

"That's a damned good answer!" She picked up one of the lemon curd tarts and passed it to him, selecting another for herself.

"The thing with Kris is…" Andy began. "I don't know. We've been friends a long time, but we weren't that close. When we were at school, he and Dan were thick as thieves, and I can appreciate why."

"Do you know why?"

"Yep. You know he used to come round to our house all the time?"

"Sort of. He's not said much about it."

"Well, he did. We were at the same nursery, and then his parents put him in that posh school. He had a massive tantrum over that. It went on for weeks."

"I can quite believe it. He's still like that now!"

"I reckon the only reason they let him go to our high school was for some peace and quiet."

Shaunna laughed. "You might be right about that. I always thought you got on all right, though."

"He was Dan's mate, not mine. And when I overheard Mum telling Dad what had gone on…"

"Ah!" So Andy *did* know the 'real' reason Kris and Dan became best friends.

"Obviously, it's not something we've ever discussed, but it makes sense that they're so close. Anyway, I didn't invite you on a picnic to talk about Dan, or Kris."

"And I can totally get why you wouldn't want to."

"What d'you mean?"

Shaunna raised an eyebrow. "Well, he did try to kill you."

"True, he did. And weirdly, I'm fine about it. I never thought I would be, but once I discovered why and spoke to you… You're pretty amazing, Shaunna."

"Here," she said, passing him another tart, "stick that in your mush, before you say something you'll regret."

He took her advice, but it didn't stop his mind from spinning along. She had a knack for saying it how it was, and it was both refreshing and comforting. When he'd told her that he was the one at the party, her response about being an easy lay effectively let him off the hook. It was his own stubbornness that stopped him from swimming away.

***

They'd been sitting talking for almost two hours, about everything and nothing, while the sun slowly tracked the sky until it shone down on over half of their picnic blanket. They got up, shuffled the blanket around by forty-five degrees and back a couple of feet. They sat down again. Andy passed Shaunna a packet of Skips.

"Thanks," she said, gently tugging them open. Several of the lightweight discs erupted from the top of the bag, and one rolled on its edge towards Andy. He picked it up and ate it.

"I thought you got these for me!" Shaunna pretended to complain. He took one from the bag and fed it to her. She kept it on her stuck-out tongue and waited for it to begin to melt.

"How long d'you think you can keep it there?" he asked.

"Ugh, ugh." Shaunna shrugged and started to giggle, a dribble of saliva escaping from her lower lip. She flipped the Skip into her mouth and sucked her lip. Andy laughed and continued watching her closely. "So, tell me why you remember that I like Skips," she said.

"I think it was when we were in sixth form, and you used to come up to meet Kris for lunch. The permanent packet on top of the pram maybe gave you away."

"Oh, yeah. I remember that now. That was before he found out he was allergic."

Andy took an unopened packet from the hamper and read the back. "Let's see. Tapioca starch, sunflower oil, maize flour, prawn cocktail flavour, sugar, salt…" He scanned through the rest of the ingredients. "No shellfish in these babies."

"Yeah, yeah. I've been through this hundreds of times. And what about the lemon curd tarts?"

"None in them, either." He grinned. She tutted. "It's a bit embarrassing, to be honest," he confessed.

She studied him, intrigued.

"I'll tell you about it another time."

"Why not now?"

"Because it isn't right," he said earnestly.

She was still curious, but she let it go. They both fell silent, each following their own train of thought in relation to all that had gone before, and to being there, together.

***

Shaunna lay on her front, her bare feet kicking up into the cool air under the shade of the tree. The sun had moved around quite a bit, and it was time for them to adjust their position once more, just as soon as they could be bothered, or the heat became intolerable. She lifted on her elbows and picked absentmindedly at a bobble on the blanket.

Andy was lying on his back, propped on his forearms, fascinated by the sparkling nail polish on her toes as it reflected the dappled sunlight sneaking through the canopy above.

"What're you thinking about?" Shaunna asked without shifting her position.

"Your toes."

"What?"

"Your toes," he repeated. "You've got very pretty toes."

She rolled onto her side and frowned in bemusement. "Pretty toes?"

"Yeah." Andy turned and grinned at her.

"You're bonkers."

"Probably, but purple glittery toenails catch my attention."

"Right." Shaunna laughed self-consciously and pulled up into a sitting position. She held out her hands for him to inspect her matching manicure.

He took one hand and lifted it closer to his face, tilting it from side to side while he investigated it closely.

"Now what're you doing?"

"It changes colour," he observed. "Your nail varnish. If I tip your hand this way—" he turned it slightly to the left "—then it's

147

pink." He tilted it back to the right. "This way it's purple. Pink. Purple." He repeated the action a couple more times. "That's cool." He nodded.

She rolled her eyes and gently pulled her hand away. "Iridescent, they call it, like the paint job on Dan's old convertible."

"Ah, yeah. That's right." Andy blushed. She'd found him out. Of course he knew what iridescence looked like. What petrolhead didn't?

Shaunna rubbed her shoulder; it was starting to burn, in spite of the sunblock he'd applied for her earlier.

"Shall we shuffle?" he asked, standing up, ready to shift the blanket along again. She followed his lead, and they moved back into the welcome shade of the sycamore, the leafy canopy like a thousand mini parasols. They settled again. Shaunna was sitting closer to the edge of the blanket this time, and plucked a daisy out of the grass.

"You want some more of that sun cream?" he asked.

"If you wouldn't mind."

He reached behind him and passed her bag across. She unzipped it and handed him the bottle, turning to the side. She picked another daisy.

"It's cold," he warned, getting ready to place the palmful of cream on her sun-pinked shoulder. She braced, although his hand was hot, so it wasn't anywhere near as much of a shock as she'd anticipated. He gently lifted her hair away and smoothed the cream over the crest of her shoulder.

"I wish I had olive skin, like you and Dan," she said. "Or even if it was only as dark as George's, that'd be all right." She slit the stem of one daisy, threaded the other through it, picked another and added it to the chain.

"So you don't burn, you mean?"

"Yeah."

"You'd sacrifice your colouring for a suntan?"

"Ginger and freckly? Not much of a sacrifice, is it?"

He pushed her strap back in place and shifted across to the other shoulder. "It's not just ginger," he said, examining her hair up close. "It's got all different shades of red and orange in it. Iridescent. Can you have iridescent hair?"

"They make iridescent hair dye."

"Do they?" He dropped the other shoulder strap and applied the cream—a little more hastily this time, and it made her shiver. "Sorry."

"It's OK."

"And for the record, your freckles are beautiful, too," he said, pointing some of them out with his finger. He closed the bottle and put it to one side. She shifted around slightly, just enough to not have her back to him, yet still be able to reach the daisies. The chain was now six flowers long. He settled back on his elbows once more and crossed his ankles. Shaunna glanced at him, and he smiled.

"I haven't been on a picnic since Krissi was young," she told him. He didn't say anything, but his eyebrows rose slightly. "I think she was about six or seven, and we went up to the lakes for the day, with Mum and Dad. Of course, she wanted to go on the boats, so we didn't picnic for very long."

"She never used to stop running around," Andy thought aloud, remembering back to the occasions he had been home in between his travels, and watched on in awe, as Shaunna and Kris—so young themselves—doted over their incredibly active and curious daughter.

"Nope. Always too much to see and do." She faced him and made eye contact. "I can't think where she got that from, can you?"

"Err…" Andy smiled coyly.

Shaunna shook her head. "I've never told you this…" She paused. He waited, not wishing to prompt her, unsure of whether he would like what she was about to say. She'd turned away again and picked another flower for her daisy chain. "I was pleased it was you," she stated, finally. "At The Party," she added. He nodded to indicate he understood what she meant. "I'm glad you're Krissi's dad."

He lay down flat and put his hands behind his head. "I don't want you to take this the wrong way," he said carefully, "but I'm not."

She got up and brushed the grass from her lap. When she sat down again, she was facing him, with her legs crossed. "Why?"

"Because—it's awful."

She took a deep breath, getting set to blast him, but he sensed it and intercepted.

"Not that Krissi is my daughter, but that I missed out on all of it. You were stuck at home, being a mum, struggling to make ends meet, and where was I? Going wherever I liked, doing whatever I wanted."

Shaunna let the breath go again.

"I couldn't have done it, what you and Kris did. I know that, but I had no right to put you in that situation, drunk or not. It was irresponsible. Stupid."

"Hey, what happened to 'no regrets'?"

"Just let me have this one. I regret nothing else that I've done in my life. Failing my exams? If I hadn't, I'd have never got to be part of our friendship group and probably would've ended up in jail. Scraping through uni? I had serious fun. It was awesome. Travelling the world with next to nothing? Bloody incredible. You really appreciate what you have got when you've experienced what it's like to have nothing, to meet other people with even less. So, no regrets, except for that one."

He looked like he was about to say more, and Shaunna leaned over and looked him straight in the eye. He shrugged.

"OK, maybe three, but the other two are both the same, so technically only two."

"You lost me," she said.

Andy held her gaze. "I spent the night with the most beautiful woman on Earth and I can't remember. That's not just regrettable. It's a fucking tragedy."

She had nothing to say to that, or not that she should say. She glanced up the path towards the car park and spotted the ice cream van. "You want a 99?"

"Sure. I'll go." He moved to get up, but she pushed on his chest and he fell down again.

She took her purse from her bag and hopped to her feet. "Be right back," she said.

Andy lay there, watching her almost skip away, bare-footed, through the meadow, and continued to watch until she reached the ice cream van. He rolled onto his back and looked up at the sky through the leafy branches above. It was such a glorious day, and he was enjoying himself even more than he'd imagined.

His eyes closed and his mind drifted, to thoughts of Dan and Kris, and what they had been through when they were younger. Sometimes, when he was too young and naïve to know any better, he'd wondered if it had been the reason for Kris's sexuality. Of course, if that were true, Dan would also have been gay or bisexual. The thought slowly transmuted into how their parents would have reacted if one of them was gay. Maybe that was what was up with Michael? Living in the closet would certainly explain why he was always angry and miserable.

He was brought back to the moment by a blob of ice cream landing on his lips, and he opened his eyes, squinting up at Shaunna leaning over him and smiling. He sat up and took the rapidly melting ice cream from her, quickly licking off the drips before they ran down to his hand.

"Penny for them?" Shaunna asked.

"I was just wondering if Mike's gay," he said.

"Seriously?"

"Yeah. Well, no. I don't suppose he is. But you never can tell, can you?"

"You can!" Shaunna said. "And he's not."

"How d'you know?"

"I don't know. It's just a vibe. I can't explain it. Like when Kris asked me to marry him? I said to him I guess I'll have to, seeing as I turned you straight, and he just laughed it off, but I knew."

"Except he's not gay."

"No, but he's more into men than women."

"And what about George?"

"You mean you can't see it?"

Andy frowned. "To be honest, I never gave it any thought. I don't ever remember thinking he was one thing or another. He's just George."

"And Josh?" Shaunna asked.

"You knew Josh was gay?"

"Yep."

"No way! I don't believe you!"

"I always knew. Since we were in Mrs. Kinkade's class."

"How?"

"You remember at their wedding, George thanked her for not judging them? They used to hold hands in the reading corner."

"Did they?" Andy crunched on his cone and a drip of ice cream ran down his chin. Shaunna caught it with her finger. He gave her a funny look. She shrugged and put her finger in her mouth. "So, are you saying that they would have known they were gay when they were eight?"

"I'm not so sure about that. Did you know what you were when you were eight?"

"Kind of. But when you're straight, there's no need to question it, is there? You feel the way everyone assumes you will."

"This is a bit deep," Shaunna said.

They both fell silent, other than the occasional slurp as they endeavoured to eat their ice creams before they became entirely liquid. Shaunna crunched the last of her cone and waited for Andy to finish his. It was taking him longer because he was still pondering over their conversation.

"That's quite cute, though," he said, picking up right where they'd left off, "that they used to hold hands when they were little."

"Yeah, well…" Shaunna lay down and stretched her back. "It's really no different from me and Adele holding hands, so I don't think it was much to do with being gay."

"You and Adele, huh?" Andy grinned cheekily and lay down next to her. She gave him a warning poke in the ribs.

"Don't even go there!" she said. "Or I'll tell Dan what you said."

"I bet he'd be up for some of that."

"Both of you at the same time? Now that really is kinky." This time, she was the one grinning.

Andy shook his head and pointed up at a little white cloud, just visible between the branches. "Looks like a sheep."

"All clouds look like sheep."

"Or do all sheep look like clouds?"

"Hmm. You may have a point there."

"That one—" Andy squinted at a more angular cloud floating into view "—looks like a t-rex."

152

Shaunna studied it and nodded. "Yeah, I suppose. Though it's more like a dragon than a t-rex. That bit's the fire coming out of its mouth."

"Or maybe it's the tail of a tiny dinosaur it's just eaten?"

"How gruesome!" Shaunna lifted her legs, pointing her toes into the air.

"What're you doing?"

"Skiing." She beckoned him closer, so he had the same viewpoint as she did. He laughed. From where she was lying, her feet were resting on two streaks of cloud that bore a passing resemblance to a pair of skis. Their faces were very close together, and Andy had to battle with himself to move away. He could feel her breath disturbing his hair. She reached up and flicked his earring. He backed off and turned on his side, propping on one elbow.

"Are you hungry?" he asked. It was supposed to have been a means of distraction, to ease the tension.

"A little. What you got?"

Oh, what he wanted to answer to that!

"Sandwiches. Cheese and pickle. Egg mayo."

"Cheese and pickle," she said. He reached inside the hamper, lifting out a small plastic box.

"You know, you're very well tamed."

"For a straight man?"

"If you like." She sat up and took a sandwich. They were cut into triangles. She nibbled off a point. "Mmm. That's really nice cheese. What is it?"

"Cheddar?" Andy guessed. She laughed. He poured some more lemonade for them both, and they sat in silence for a while, eating their sandwiches and sipping at their tumblers.

It was well into the afternoon and getting too warm, even in the shade, but they were both on the same wavelength of wanting to make the day last a little longer, as now Shaunna resumed her previous position, lying on her back, her shirt serving as a pillow under her head. Andy lay on his front, leaning on his forearms.

"I need to tell you something," she said. He turned to face her. She looked up through the branches and studied the sky. "Kris and I are getting back together."

"Oh." He turned away again, unable to think of anything else to say, and not because he was disappointed, or frustrated, even though he was both of those things. More than that, he didn't think it was right for them, but who was he to make such a judgement?

"I know what you're thinking," Shaunna said. "And I think it, too. But he won't let go."

Andy examined her face. She had her hands behind her head, and a strand of hair had strayed onto her chin. She tried to blow it out of the way. Andy reached across and brushed it back, continuing to play with her hair.

"Why won't *you* let go?" he asked.

"Because I don't know how. He cheated on me, and it hurt, but I always knew I couldn't give him everything he needs."

"And nothing's changed."

"Oh, it has," she said assuredly. "I know that's how things are now, and I accept it. He's all I've ever known, and unless he leaves me for good, I…" She smiled sadly. "I can't let go. You understand?"

Andy nodded. "Shall we make a move?"

"Yeah, I suppose we should, really." Shaunna got up, and together they put everything back in the picnic hamper.

"Thank you for today," Andy said, as they started the walk back to the car park. "I've really enjoyed it."

Shaunna took hold of his hand. "No. Thank *you*. It's been lovely. We should do it again, soon."

He glanced down at their hands and secured their fingers together.

"Yeah," he said. "I'd like that a lot."

One
Sunday 6th August

The Browns' back garden looked like a church summer fête, with balloons and bunting adorning the three sides of fencing and suspended from the back of the house in drooping arches. A baby bouncy castle took up the extent of the bottom left corner; the barbecue was cordoned off in the top right corner; a miniature motorised train on a tiny circular track took up the very centre of the lawn, and the rest of it was slowly filling with temporary bubbles and slightly more permanent balloon animals.

"Do you think this might be overkill, Mum?" Krissi asked, watching Wotto tie off an elongated white balloon.

"It's not every day I get to celebrate my godson's first birthday."

"I know, but seriously. He's one. He won't even remember it. Besides, you never did all this for my first birthday."

"How d'you know if you can't remember?"

Krissi blew a raspberry at her mother. Shaunna stuck out her tongue in response and went off to check on the other aspects of the craziest first birthday party in the world. It wasn't all her fault. Really. It was George's, too.

"So, what is it?" Wotto asked. He and Krissi had been playing that game since they arrived and he began making balloon animals. They were brilliant, but she'd yet to guess one correctly.

"A snake," she said.

"Ain't finished yet!" He bent the front up to form a head with a little bubble on either side.

"A snake with ears?"

He ignored her. She shifted her attention to her mother again, now carrying a massive speaker, Kris trailing behind with a second one.

"I didn't know they were bringing down half the studio with them. Let's hope one-year-olds like death metal."

Jason and Hadyn appeared next, armed with a desk and an amp.

"You got a Sharpie there, mate?" Wotto called across to Jay. Hadyn got there first and chucked one over. Wotto caught it. "Cheers," he said. The two men exchanged nods, and Hadyn went back to setting up the sound equipment.

"Why?" Krissi asked, the question directed at Josh, who had just arrived with George. She knew he'd be on her side. He stopped, looked around him and blinked a few times.

"Good grief. Are we in the right place? I'm looking for Toby Brown's birthday party. He's about this big…" Josh held his hand a couple of feet or so above the floor to indicate.

"It's mental, isn't it?" Krissi asked rhetorically. She cringed at the squeaking of marker pen against rubber and turned around. "A zebra!" She grinned. Wotto grinned back, although there was no way she could possibly have got it wrong this time. "I think you should make a whole herd. That'd be way cool. Maybe a balloon animal safari park. It could go over there, between the bouncy castle and the…puppet show?" She shook her head in disbelief. "I'm gonna go see if Ellie needs any help before I get sucked into the explosion of fun." She went inside. Wotto watched her all the way.

"I thought you two were like weather people in a clock," Josh remarked. Wotto looked confused. "Only one of you is allowed out at a time?"

"Oh, yeah, well, when the big boss mentions that he'd like balloon animals for his son, when he knows that you can make 'em…"

"Yes, that'd do it."

"What the…?" Andy had just arrived, without Jess today. She'd deteriorated quite rapidly over the past couple of weeks and wasn't up to leaving the house. He looked around him in astonishment.

"That's exactly what I did." Josh laughed. George had gone off to find his fellow godparent and check what else needed doing.

"Dan not here yet?" Andy asked.

Josh shook his head. "I've not seen him."

Andy frowned. "Hmm. Wonder how they're getting here?"

"Has he sorted out a car?"

"He's got a hire car off the insurance while they sort out the claim. Might see if he wants a lift so he can have a drink."

"And how's your new car?"

"Fucking awesome," Andy gushed and then covered his mouth, although there were currently no children around to hear it. He leaned closer. "I took her out for a spin in the countryside the other day. Gonna pass on the, err, speed limiter for now, if you follow my drift. See if I can stay within the law without it. Right, I'll give Dan a call, see if they want picking up."

Andy wandered back towards the house, crossing paths with Eleanor. She grinned at Josh and shrugged.

"I have absolutely sweet FA to do," she said.

"Impressive."

"I'd like to say it was me, but it's not, and the party doesn't officially start for another hour, so I think we should go to the pub."

"You're kidding."

"Just for one. What d'you reckon?"

"Erm, yes, I guess." Josh frowned. "Are you feeling all right? Only I thought you just suggested we left all of these people unsupervised in your house."

Eleanor laughed. "I'm fine, but I've got Luke, Kaz and their two staying here, Teddy's watching cricket in the lounge, Tilly's taken all the kids to the park, and Hennessy Sandison-Morley Entertainment and Catering Inc have taken over my kitchen."

"Ah."

"Yes, you may well say 'ah'. So how about it?"

"Sure. I'll just let George know."

"Don't make it obvious, though."

"OK."

George was on his way back out with a tower of multicoloured bowls. Eleanor watched Josh approach and talk quietly into his ear. George looked concerned but nodded his consent. He said something in response, and Josh came back over to her.

"I'm not allowed to drink anything," he said.

"Not even one pint?"

"Nope. I've just been reminded by 'The Birth Partner' that I promised, but no matter. I'll have a Coke or something. Come on." He held out his arm to her, and they walked together through the house and took a left away from the park, in the direction of the nearest pub, which was new and brassy, but only five minutes up the road.

"You'll never guess who else is coming to the party," Eleanor said.

"Who?"

"Guess."

"I'd rather you just tell me."

"Not going to."

"Fine. I'm not going to play either."

"Suit yourself."

"Ellie?"

"No."

He turned and watched her, but she was getting too good at blocking his radar, or he needed to retune it a little, because there was no way at all he could discern who the mystery party guest was. He racked his brains, thinking of interesting or controversial people who would want to attend a one-year-old's birthday, or mutual acquaintances who might have been invited but she'd not yet mentioned, and drew a blank.

"I can't even think of anyone to guess," he said eventually. They'd arrived at the pub.

"No-one at all?"

"No. What are you having?"

"Wine. Rosé for a change, I think, thanks."

He ordered their drinks and paid for them, still deep in thought. They sat out in the beer garden, where he intermittently frowned and sipped. He shrugged. "I give in."

"Nope." Eleanor grinned. She was having immense fun tormenting him, although she'd perhaps built it into something far more exciting than it really was. "You'll have to wait and see now."

"You're so mean."

"OK. Tell you what. We'll do an information exchange."

He studied her through narrowed eyes. "Depends on what it is you want to know."

"How you and George finally sorted things out."

"I thought once we were together, people would stop interrogating us, but you've all found new things to do it with instead."

"Why? Who else has been asking for intel?"

"I couldn't possibly tell you, but you're not the only one, let's put it that way."

"So how about it?"

"Mostly it's not very interesting and far too personal to share."

"Josh, it's me. Your best friend, remember?"

He griped and grumbled under his breath and took out his phone. "OK. I'll trade you on the bit I'm prepared to tell you, and you can decide if the price I've paid is high enough. How about that?"

Eleanor thought about it for two or three seconds at most, because either way she was going to come out on top. "OK. So, what gives?"

"Well, obviously you know about Kris kissing George at the reunion."

"Yeah."

"And after that, we weren't speaking to each other."

"Yeah. I know all this bit."

"Patience, dear best friend. I'm getting to it." He took out his phone and loaded it up, ready for the appropriate juncture in the story. "So, he decided to stay at his mum's to keep out of the way, but that meant sleeping on the sofa, and he ended up staying with Kris and Shaunna for a night."

"Oh, nice move, George! Weren't you jealous?"

"I didn't know at the time. I thought he was still at his mum's, and he bunked in with Shaunna, so it was all entirely innocent. The day of your hen party, I decided enough was enough, but I had to find a way to get him to come back so I could talk to him. So, I sent him a text." He passed across his phone. "Two, in fact."

Eleanor read the text messages and smiled. "Oh, Josh, that's so sweet." She handed him his phone back. "It's still really weird, though."

"Why?"

"Because you've always been so aloof, until last September. Back then, there is no way I could have imagined you sending someone a text message to tell them you loved them. Now it doesn't surprise me in the slightest."

"Should I take that as a compliment?"

"I think so, although you've kind of gone totally the other way. These days, you're actually worse than Adele for bursting into tears at the slightest little thing."

"Hey, you might want to consider the context a little!"

Eleanor laughed. She was tormenting him, although they both had an equally valid point. So far this year, Josh had dealt with his grandmother's stroke, Jess's illness, the massive bust-up with Eleanor, getting married and being in a near-fatal car crash, not to mention George's arrest, or the acute bipolar episode, or all the other little things she didn't know about that involved various members of their friendship group. That said, the years preceding it hadn't been a whole lot lower down the emotional trauma scale, and he'd kept it together through all of that.

And once again, here was a perfect opportunity to tell one of their friends about his diagnosis, but of all of them, Eleanor was the one he feared telling the most, not least because her medical training put her in the enemy camp when it came to trying to live a normal life without interference in the face of possessing a psychiatric condition. Having one herself made no difference, given that she considered it to be 'in remission', which was a wonderful notion, but he knew better. Remission was the ideal; getting a disorder back 'in order' was more readily achievable, yet at odds with the system, which was why he did everything he could to keep away from mental health professionals and fought them all the way when he did come into contact with them.

So, he didn't tell Eleanor about the bipolar disorder. He sat, patiently waiting to see if she deemed what he had told her worthy of the trade.

"Well?" he prompted, once she'd drunk her wine, visited the pub toilet and had a chat with a woman eating lunch at the next table about 'how nice the Caesar salad is here'.

"I'll tell you the initials," she said. "S.K."

"S.K.?" He frowned in puzzlement. They began the walk back. "S.K.?" he repeated. "Who do I know whose name begins with S? Sean, Shaunna, oh!" He stopped walking as a sudden and awful thought came into his head. "Please, God, don't let it be Suzie Tyler."

"How could it be?"

"Her married name might begin with a K. It's not her, is it? Please, please tell me it's not."

Eleanor laughed loudly. "Like I'd be inviting Suzie Tyler to my son's first birthday. No, it's not."

He caught up with her, and they continued walking. "I have no idea."

"Well, it looks like you're about to find out." Eleanor nodded in the direction of the car parked up outside the house. A woman climbed out of the driver's door and spent a moment observing her location, checking she was in the right place. She was dressed in a gorgeous pink dip-dyed silk trouser suit, with deep-pink trousers and a long tunic graduating from the same deep pink to pale rose at the top. Her hair was dead straight and darkest brown-black, flowing like warm treacle right down past her waist.

Her appearance was somewhat at odds with her car, though, which was an old and tatty hatchback with a lopsided number plate, the back windscreen wiper mechanism hanging free and minus the wiper blade. She swooped elegantly to open the rear door. A moment later, a miniature version of the woman jumped down onto the pavement and stood quietly, waiting for the woman—her mother, Josh presumed—to lift the loose door back into place and lock the car.

"Is that…" he began.

"None other than Miss Shabina Kapoor," Eleanor confirmed.

"Wow!"

"Wow, indeed." Eleanor had only seen her in the class photo that Oliver carried everywhere with him, and was as stunned as Josh by the beauty of both mother and child.

"Does Oliver know she's coming?"

"He asked us if she could, but we told him it was unlikely, which we honestly thought would be the case. However, James phoned Mrs. Kapoor, and she was absolutely delighted. She's on her own, as far as I can tell, and they've moved around a lot, so they don't have many friends."

They reached the house half a minute after the Kapoors had gone inside, and James was still doing the introductions. Oliver was in the garden, helping George, or rather, trailing around after him as if joined by a piece of elastic, so he was unaware of Shabina's arrival. Eleanor was now tied up with greeting Mrs. Kapoor—Anushka, or Anu for short—so Josh went to get Oliver.

"You might want to come, too," he said to George.

George passed the bottles of beer he'd been distributing to Andy and followed Josh inside, intrigued.

As soon as Oliver saw Shabina, he did exactly what everyone expected. He became very quiet and sidestepped, hiding behind James's leg. But then Shabina smiled and held up a parcel wrapped in metallic blue paper.

"I got a present for your little brother," she said.

Oliver stepped forward again and took the present from her. "Thank you very much, Shabina. I show you my friends now?"

"OK."

He passed the present to Eleanor and grabbed Shabina by the hand. Anu leaned across to speak to Eleanor.

162

"I might finally get some peace and quiet for five minutes," she said. "All I hear is 'Oliver said such-and-such', 'Oliver did this', 'Oliver likes these things'…"

Eleanor laughed. "Yeah, tell us about it."

"Toby is having a nap. I show you him when he wakes up," Oliver said, leading Shabina outside to introduce her to the other children, a process that consisted of repeating names—'and this is Ben, and this is Ashleigh'—and so on around his seven cousins, and onto little Shaunna, who also got a story involving how she was special because she had been 'born too little, which is why she is called Little Shaunna'. He finished up with all the adults, aunts, uncles, grandparents and parents' friends. Wotto also got special mention, because of his 'best lollipops, ever!'

"Right," George said, "back to it." He was almost at the door when Oliver brought Shabina back inside to finish his introductions, and he looked at George sternly. George gulped and stayed right where he was.

"And this is Ellna. She is my stepmum, and she is Toby's mummy, and this is my dad, and this is my Aunty Charlotte. She is very, very good at football. And this is Josh. He is very clever and makes your brain better when it broken, and this is Dorge. He is the one I told you about."

Oliver cupped his hands around Shabina's ear and whispered. She frowned and shrugged at him. He sighed in exasperation and tried again. She still didn't get it. Oliver let out another very loud sigh.

"I trying to tell you his name is George really, but when I was little I say Dorge, so I call him that, cos it's nicer, and he likes it."

Shabina looked totally bewildered and was standing so close to George that she had to bend her head right back to see him. He crouched down and held out his hand.

"Hi, Shabina." He smiled. She smiled back and put her hand in his. He shook it. "It's very nice to meet you. Are you OK?" She nodded dumbly. "I like your shoes," he said. It was an icebreaker, but he paid proper attention to them. "They're very pretty and sparkly." They were pink glitter-covered canvas pumps.

"I got them for my birthday from the polices."

"Oh, OK," George said.

"My daddy was a policeman. He died fighting a robber."

"Oh dear," George said sympathetically, although he didn't know what else to say. With adults, it was easier to tell how they were feeling about the loss of someone close to them. With four-year-olds it was impossible, and he felt he should come up with something more meaningful than his usual 'I'm sorry, but I don't know what to say'. Shabina rescued him.

"It's OK. I was only very little." She turned to Oliver. "We play with the cousins?"

"Um, OK," he said, and off they went, hand in hand. George stood up straight again and smiled at Anu.

"It's nowhere near as heroic as it sounds," she said. "But it's still far too complicated and painful to talk about with her."

George nodded in understanding. "I'm sorry to have inadvertently brought it up. I was aiming for a nice innocent compliment, and it totally backfired." He blushed guiltily.

Anu reached out and gently squeezed his arm. "Don't worry, George. It's lovely to meet you. I've heard so much about you." She released him and paused to take in her surroundings. "Your house is gorgeous, Eleanor."

The conversation moved on. George returned to his godfatherly duties in the garden, and Josh chatted to Anu and Eleanor, who had instantly clicked. Anu was elegant and beautiful, so well-spoken and intelligent, but every so often her accent slipped, and Josh observed that she was having to consciously think about how she was speaking. He let his gaze fall from her face to her outfit. She wore very little jewellery, yet the trouser suit looked expensive, and Shabina was also dressed beautifully, in the same fabric as the trouser suit, he now realised, as she and Oliver ran past en route to Oliver's bedroom. Josh turned his attention back to the woman before him, taking in the absence of wedding ring, the delicate gold bangle encircling her wrist—

"Joshua!" Eleanor said sharply to attract his attention. He looked up and blushed. Caught out again.

"Sorry." He smiled at Anu. "I was admiring your outfit."

"Do you like it?" she asked.

"I do. It's absolutely stunning."

"Thanks. I made it myself. There's a wonderful little shop not far from the…err, where we live that sells all kinds of silk, and saris. Mind you, I haven't worn a sari since I got married, though some of them are just gorgeous."

Josh smiled to show he was still listening, although he had regressed into his thoughts slightly, speculating on why she had edited mid-sentence. She was doing a George.

"Sorry?" he said, having missed the last part.

"Congratulations," she repeated.

"Thanks."

"On your marriage," she clarified for him.

"Oh!" He blushed again. "Thank you."

Eleanor tutted. "Josh is a psychotherapist," she explained. "He gets so tied up in trying to figure people out that he sometimes forgets to listen to the words."

Anu laughed, and Josh nodded.

"Yes, that's true," he admitted apologetically. Oliver and Shabina ran past them again, back outside. "I suppose I'd better see if I'm needed." He followed the children out and went in search of George.

"Shall we go and find a seat?" Eleanor suggested. They, too, went into the garden, although there was absolutely nowhere to sit. Toby was on James's lap, half awake, rubbing his eyes and looking a little overwhelmed by all the strange people and things in his garden. The other chairs were occupied by the grandparents, with James's father sitting furthest from the joyous commotion, hands resting on his knees as he solemnly surveyed the frivolities.

At the far end of the garden, Charlotte and Shaunna were playing musical statues with the rest of the children; Hadyn and Jason had set up the equipment, instructed Shaunna on how to use it, and quickly left her to it. Wotto was still making balloon animals, on request, with a dozen or more currently bobbing ownerless around the lawn. The rest of the adults were standing wherever they could, in between puppet show staging areas, model trains and bouncy castles, desperate to have a go themselves, but trying their best to be grown-ups.

The game of musical statues came to an end with young Ben declared the winner. All the children got a little prize for taking part and scattered to undertake the various other fun activities available.

"Did you organise all this on your own?" Anu asked.

Eleanor smiled and shook her head. "No. I had nothing to do with it. It's all the godparents' doing." She nodded in Shaunna's direction. "Shaunna, and George."

Shaunna saw them looking her way and headed over. "Hiya. You OK, hun?"

"I'm just perfect." Ellie grinned. "This is Anu—Shabina's mum."

"Hi." Shaunna gave her a brief hug. "I'm Shaunna, Toby's godmum."

"This is a great party," Anu said.

"Err, thanks, though I think my daughter might've been right about us going overboard."

Eleanor tutted. "She's far too sensible these days. I think it's brilliant."

"How old's your daughter, Shaunna?" Anu asked.

"Twenty-four in October."

"Wow! You honestly don't look old enough."

"Thanks. I was very young when I had her, and she's always been too grown up for her own good. Still, the kids are enjoying themselves, and that's all that matters. Now, where's that godson of mine?" She spotted him and went over, babytalking to him. He grinned at her and pushed back coyly against James's chest. She reached out her arms, and Toby went to her to be carried off down the garden so she could show him around all the things she and George had arranged, just for him.

Josh stepped back to get out of their way and nearly jumped out of his skin. "Oops!" He eyed the deceased balloon animal lying at his feet and moved to hide it.

"Josh!"

Oliver suddenly appeared next to him and beckoned him close. Josh crouched down for Oliver to whisper, miraculously hearing him first time.

"Show me," Josh said. Oliver held out his hand. Josh examined what he was holding and whispered in his ear. Oliver grinned.

"Thanks," he said and ran off again.

Andy was standing next to Josh and had watched the whole interchange. "What was that about?" he asked.

"Oh, he just needed my help with something."

"They start young these days."

"They certainly do."

Shaunna wandered back past, still carrying Toby. She smiled at Josh, and then at Andy. He blushed. Josh pretended not to notice, looking away to give Andy time to recompose. He scanned the perimeter, pausing to absorb a little of each interaction—Charlotte and Dan were discussing the start of the football season, arguing over the sensibility of signings and taunting each other with insults of their team's players. Josh was impressed with himself for recognising a couple of the names, but otherwise, it was a dull discussion as far as he was concerned. He moved on.

Tilly and Ashleigh were having an argument for real. Ashleigh was going to high school in September and appeared to be making a head start on the teenage attitude problem, currently lamenting the unfairness of not being allowed to go on holiday with one of her friends. Tilly was having none of it and in the end told her to go and ask her father what he thought. Ashleigh stormed off across the garden to her dad and patiently recommenced the whole explanation part over again.

"Alright, mate?" Dan came over.

"Yes, thanks. You?"

"Yeah. Is it me, or is this a bit OTT for a baby's first birthday?"

"It's a bit OTT," Josh and Andy responded together.

The three men watched a chain of little people conga past, led by Kris. Dan shook his head. "Going for more beer. You want?"

"I'll come with you," Andy said, finishing the last of the green liquid in his glass.

"What the hell's that?" Dan asked as they headed back for the house.

"Cream soda."

"Nice."

"Hey, Josh," Adele called over. "You OK?"

"Yes, thanks. You?"

She nodded and continued with telling Jo about the college course she wanted to do, and that she was probably going to miss the enrolment day. Jo asked why, and Adele made excuses about work and childcare.

"Hi." George spoke close to Josh's ear.

"Hi, yourself." He smiled and kissed him.

"Whatcha doing?"

"The usual. You?"

"Having a rest. My leg's sore."

"Why don't you sit down for a while?"

"I'm OK for now." He shifted his weight onto his right leg and leaned against Josh. Oliver came running over and reached up with his hand. George crouched down, and Oliver put something in his mouth then ran off again. George moved it around on his tongue until he identified what it was. "Love Heart," he said. He stuck out his tongue, and Josh squinted to read.

"WICKED."

George nodded and crunched the sweet. No more than thirty seconds later, Oliver came over again. George took the sweet from him. "COOL DUDE." He nodded. "Yep, that's me."

Josh laughed. "I don't think the messages are directed at you, somehow."

"Why? What's he doing?"

Josh nodded to indicate the back corner of the garden, behind the bouncy castle, where Oliver and Shabina were sitting, cross-legged and close together, their heads bowed. They had their backs to everyone else, and as George watched, he saw Shabina plant a kiss on Oliver's cheek so quickly that a blink would have concealed it from history. Oliver rubbed at his cheek with his hand, and the two children giggled.

"You taught him the Love Hearts game?" George asked incredulously.

"What else could I do? Shabina's his best friend in the *whole whole* world!"

"Oh, well I guess you had no choice then, although I think they've just rewritten the rules."

"Yes." Josh grinned. "Say it, do it, Dorge it."

George rolled his eyes, although he was laughing. "I'm going to get you for this, Joshua."

"Says you!"

"What d'you mean, says me? I will. You know I will." George kissed him and drew in a breath through his teeth. "I'm gonna get some painkillers off Ellie. See you later." As he limped away, Oliver came running over again. He stopped in front of Josh and frowned.

"You can give it to me if you like," Josh offered.

"You give it to Dorge for me when he comes back, please?"

"Of course."

He put the sweet in Josh's hand. "You can have it if you want," he said. "I too little to say it to Shabina, but I can tell Dorge, cos I love him lots and lots." He turned away, paused and turned back. "I love you lots, too," he added as an afterthought.

He ran off again. Josh looked at the sweet and smiled, his eyes filling with tears. He sniffed.

"See? Told you," Eleanor said, coming up alongside him. "What's up? Someone drop an ice cube or something?"

"H-ha. You're hilarious," he said dryly. "Ollie asked me to give this to George, because he loves him lots and lots." He showed her the sweet. She read it and smiled.

"OK. I'll give you that one. They're about to light the candle on the cake. You coming?" She turned and headed back the way she had come without waiting for an answer.

Josh put the sweet in his pocket and added it to his ever-growing mental list of things to do.

Someone Else's Arms
Monday 7th August

It was never going to be easy. He'd known that. Saying goodbye was one of the most difficult things a person ever had to do, and there was much to be said for not dragging it out, but what choice did he have? One little hatchback could only carry so much at a time, and whilst the cardiovascular exercise was undoubtedly doing him a world of good, the thought of having to go up or down those bloody stairs ever again was making the whole prospect of parting with his surgery a lot less difficult to face. Still, only the bottom desk drawer to empty, and then it was just the bookshelf.

"Just the bookshelf," Josh said glumly and sighed, all to himself, because he was waiting for his 'client' to arrive and had received an apologetic text message to say they were running fifteen minutes late, along with a suggestion to reschedule, or better still, forget the whole thing. He'd sent back to say it was fine; he was there anyway. After all, it had taken six months to get this far, even if rescheduling would have given him a welcome excuse to go home and forget all about the bookshelf and the bottom drawer. But he'd only be delaying the inevitable.

The bottom drawer. He lowered his chair to better reach the lock, poked the key in and gave it a wiggle up and to the right. It had always been a bit temperamental, which was why he rarely used it, and in fact couldn't remember the last time he'd had to go in there, since he kept his case notes at home, always used the same pen, and his only other stationery requirements consisted of the occasional paper clip or staple, both of which fitted in the top drawer with oodles of room to spare.

The bottom drawer. The place for the safe-keeping of objects too important to throw away, too dangerous to easily access. He tugged at the drawer handle; it was still locked.

That was typical, of course, because he had piqued his own curiosity, and now the key was stuck at a jaunty angle, clearly not engaged in the mechanism, but would the damned thing budge? He wheeled his chair back and gave the key a kick. Sometimes it worked, sometimes it didn't. Today fell into the latter category, but he was not going to be outdone by a tiny scrap of brass. He frowned and considered his options. Ten minutes was what he had—not really long enough to go out and buy oil. He could leave it until later.

Or not.

He gave the key another kick.

"Bugger."

Well, it served him right, he supposed, for being impatient.

He picked up the half a key from the floor and put it on the desk, thoroughly annoyed with himself, and went to make coffee instead. That took almost the entire ten minutes, because he'd unplugged the kettle to plug in the vacuum cleaner and forgotten to reconnect it to the socket. Seven minutes into pondering on the mysteries of The Bottom Drawer, he realised he'd been standing waiting for, well, seven minutes, and dealt with it, which gave him just enough time to stir his coffee and rinse the spoon before he heard the door at the bottom of the stairs open, followed by the *clunk-clunk* of heavy boots thudding their way upwards.

"Hi, Josh."

"Jason. Glad you made it."

"Yeah."

Josh indicated for Jason to follow him through to his room. "Would you like a coffee, or tea?"

"No, thanks."

"Please, sit down and make yourself comfortable."

Jason looked far from comfortable. He propped himself at one end of the sofa, squashed up against the arm as if he were sharing the seat with many other people, his slight build hardly taking up a cushion. He'd lost weight—quite a lot of weight—since the studio opened, which was the reason Krissi had given when she made the appointment on his behalf—with his consent—although Josh had a feeling that it was only a very small part of the story, if it was even part of the story at all.

"So, Jason, I'm not going to do this formally, unless you would like me to, because I can see you're quite anxious. You mustn't feel under any pressure to say or do anything you don't want to, OK?"

Jason nodded, and his hair fell over his face. Josh raised an eyebrow, recognising the signal. He knew it well, and on a very personal level, as since George pointed out that it was something he did himself, he'd become acutely aware of just how often he did it.

"What did she say?" Jason asked. His face was downturned, his head moving slightly, following the motion of his hand as he smoothed the pile on the arm of the sofa with his fingers, leaving dark trails in the plush fabric and then reversing the process to erase them.

"Are you talking about Krissi?"

"Yeah."

"She said she'd been worried about you for a while."

"Because I'm not eating."

"Yes, she mentioned that."

Jason nodded but didn't speak for a couple of minutes. Josh sipped his coffee. Still too hot.

"It's not true," Jason said. He pushed his hair behind his ear and made eye contact. "I mean, I don't eat, but I haven't got an eating disorder or anything. I just forget to, because I don't feel hungry, or I'm working, or whatever."

"Or whatever?" Josh asked.

Jason averted his eyes again. Yes, the 'whatever' was significant. He wasn't ready to talk about it, but it was he who had brought up the issue of food, and he who had mentioned the 'whatever'.

"I can imagine it's quite difficult to find time to eat when you're working in the studio," Josh tried as a means of at least establishing a dialogue. Jason seemed to relax a little.

"Yeah. Especially with not eating meat. Stu usually goes to the café on the estate, and they do serve veggie stuff, but they prepare and cook it all in the same place."

"They're not supposed to do that, are they?" Josh knew the answer was 'no', but he assumed it would be something Jason knew about and would, therefore, pass control of the conversation back to him.

"No." He sighed, clearly irritated by this state of affairs. "They're not. I s'pose I should do like Hadyn does and make a packed lunch, but I'm crap at getting out of bed and never think to do it the night before."

Not a very common name, Hadyn. Coincidence? Josh pushed the question away for the time being. Whilst it was potentially important in a broader sense, it wasn't in terms of what he was hoping to achieve with Jason.

"Can I ask, why are you vegetarian?"

"I hate meat."

"OK. Not for any animal welfare reason?"

"Well, yeah, a bit. But it's disgusting. It smells horrible, even when it doesn't taste of anything, and the texture, ugh." Jason shuddered, and it wasn't an act.

Josh laughed quietly to respond to his reaction without mocking or trivialising it, although it was tangential.

"I bet there's stuff you feel like that about," Jason speculated.

Josh nodded. "Yes. Quite a few things, as a matter of fact. Foodwise, anything that squeaks when you eat it, and I don't mean in an 'it's still alive' way."

Now Jason laughed. "You mean like green beans?"

"Oh, they're one of the worst culprits. And halloumi. That's terrible for it."

"It tastes nice, though."

"Very true. It does. And pickled onions." Now Josh shuddered.

"Yeah."

The conversation reached a natural pause. Josh watched and waited. Jason fiddled with his ear. He was frowning heavily, thinking, trying to find the courage to open up. He'd always been a very quiet and private person—moody, as Shaunna used to describe him, arty, Kris would contend. Gothboy. That was what Krissi called him. Or sometimes Emokid. That was a terrible fashion; it brought far too much work Josh's way.

Jason was wondering if it would have been easier with someone he didn't know, not that he and Josh knew each other especially well, but they'd seen each other in passing many times over the years, at birthdays, weddings and the like, through their mutual acquaintance with the Johanssons. So what did Josh know about him? Did he know he was adopted? Probably. Krissi's mum knew, and they were all close friends, so he'd also know who his biological parents were, not that any of it mattered. Sure, it had been a shock, but it didn't really bother him that much, so he could maybe safely talk about that.

"You know I'm adopted?" he asked.

Josh nodded. "Yes, I do know that."

Jason hooked his hair behind his ear again. Josh observed that it was his earring he'd been fiddling with before, because he was doing it again, pushing it round and round through the hole.

"And you know who my biological parents are?"

Josh nodded again. "Yes."

"It's crazy. All those times I used to go to work with my dad, and I didn't know it was them." The earring spinning paused. "Did they know who I was?"

"I've no idea."

The spinning recommenced.

"Mum and Dad don't want to talk about it. They'll answer my questions, but they get really hacked off that I'm asking them, so I don't. At least they know how I feel now."

"In what respect?"

"Back in school. Mum'd interrogate me every night. She was worried about me. I get that. But I didn't want to talk about it. There's no point. No-one understands. They think they do, but they don't, and then they judge you."

OK, Josh thought, *scrap the eating disorder theory, and the abandonment issues. What are we dealing with here? Bullying?* He was going to have to wait and see, because Jason had regressed into his thoughts and would benefit from a little time to explore them before they moved forward. *Time to think: that's what the new therapies lack. There might be a paper in there somewhere.*

"Krissi was the first one to ever treat me like a normal human being."

There we go: worth the wait. Josh picked up his coffee and adjusted himself into a position that indicated he was listening and had all the time in the world. Relaxed, receptive, attentive.

"Being epileptic," Jason spoke into his lap, "it's shit. Not because of the seizures. I can cope with them. I mean, they're horrible, and they're embarrassing, but they don't happen often these days. I haven't had one now for—" he paused to think "—about nine months, maybe a bit longer, because Krissi's really good at reminding me to take my pills and stuff, making sure I go to bed at a sensible time, feeding me." He tutted. "She drives me mental, but I do feel bad about it, when she's been working in the restaurant all day and ends up cooking for me and it's dead late, and I tell her not to, but she worries."

Jason shook his head so that his hair fell forward again. Under the fringe, Josh saw the guilt.

"You know, if she wasn't worrying about you not eating, she'd just find something else to worry about? She and her mum are exactly the same. They like looking after people. It's what they do best, and it gives them a great sense of well-being."

Jason nodded, still with his hair over his eyes. "Yeah, I know. I was really good for a while, eating properly and stuff, and she started on about me obsessing over the studio instead. Stu, my engineer, is awesome, and I trust him, totally, but a band would come in for a session, and he'd say, 'Don't worry, Jay. Leave that lot till tomorrow,' then go home, which is fair enough when it's, like, half ten at night, but I couldn't deal with having to put mics and cables away first thing in the morning, so I'd stay on my own and clear up."

"I take it you've resolved that issue now?" Josh asked, noting the switch in tense.

"Yeah. Hadyn. He does it, and I don't even need to ask. He's got OCD, so it's kind of not through choice that he's always tidying the place, but it actually makes him better at his job, so I'm cool with it."

So it *was* the same Hadyn, unless this was the most remarkable set of coincidences in the history of mankind, which in any case was true. Impressive also was the fact that Jason saw right past the diagnosis and focused on its positive qualities. If only there were more employers like him, although it was perhaps the burden of his own label of 'epileptic' that was behind it. From what he said next, it appeared Jason had picked up on Josh's line of reasoning.

"It helps when you know how it feels to be treated differently because of your disability or whatever you want to call it. Like with me and Krissi—when we first became friends, she talked to my mum about what my fits were like, and got advice off Eleanor on what she should do, then she just kind of forgot about it, unless I have a seizure, then she does what she needs to.

"So she kind of treats me differently, but in a good way, and I try to do that with Hadyn. If he's stressing, I pull him to one side and find out what the problem is. Sometimes it's nothing, just his OCD playing up. Sometimes it's because of what happened to him when he was younger. I s'pose I can tell you, it's not like it'll go any further. His stepdad abused him. He beat him up, all the time, called him names, locked him in his room, refused to let him go to the toilet, stuff like that. Total scumbag. Hadyn says the OCD thing is because he's trying to wash him off."

That made a lot of sense to Josh. He wondered if Sean knew, not that they would be having a conversation about it. Respect. Integrity. The rules of their profession.

"And I realised, listening to Hadyn," Jason continued, "that's part of why people don't get it. They look at me and they think, 'Oh, he's all right. His parents are well off, he gets everything he wants, they love him to bits, so what's he got to be miserable about?' And they're right. Maybe if I'd known I was adopted, or they'd kept me locked up because of the epilepsy, or abused me… But they've never even smacked me, not even when I was being an ungrateful little fuck-up."

Jason fell silent again, now completely engulfed by remorse. Josh tried to gauge whether he should attempt to address the self-deprecation, because Jason had been starting to relax; now he was wound tighter than when he arrived. He was right, though; he'd had an excellent upbringing, because clearly the only thing stopping him from getting up and walking out was good manners.

"You're not alone."

Josh gasped in horror. He hadn't meant to say that. OK, maybe he would've said it anyway, but it hadn't been a measured, professional response rooted in consideration of what he had seen and heard. It had been a call from a long-buried part of his psyche that had unconsciously understood, empathised, reached out in desperation. *You are not alone. I'm there, too.* Josh swallowed and turned his attention back to Jason. "Would you mind if I go and make another coffee?" he asked. He wouldn't normally do that, but he needed to escape, to try to reinstate his objectivity. Competence. Rules of the profession.

"Sure," Jason said. He put his head back, shook his hair from his face and gave Josh the briefest, saddest of smiles.

"Won't be a moment." Josh left the room and made a dart for the sanctuary of the kitchen, finally letting go of the rest of the breath he'd been holding since he'd said what he'd said. His hands were shaking, he noticed, as he tried to spoon coffee into the mug, and he was sweating. And that ache in his belly. He hadn't felt that in a long, long time.

What was the best strategy? Let it out and hold it up before him, so he could examine it, consider it, get control of it? It was a slippery fiend, and he might lose his grasp, but it was a thing of the past, and he needed to put it back there, lock it down again. On the other hand, he could use it as a tool. Like Sean said, accept that some things you cannot change—it applied as much to the present as it did to the past, but the future? That was still up for grabs. Mostly. The kettle clicked off. He made his coffee and returned to Jason, who was staring across the room at the half a key on the desk.

"I broke it just before you arrived," Josh explained.

"That sucks."

"It does. Luckily, it's only for the bottom drawer of the desk, and there's nothing in it that I need urgently."

Jason leaned to the side so he could see the locks on the drawers. "They're dead easy to spring," he said. "My dad had a bureau with the same locks, where he kept his spare keys. Brilliant, eh? The key for the safe and everything in a cabinet you can open with a paper clip."

"Really?"

"Yeah. Do you want me to have a go for you?"

"If you wouldn't mind."

Josh unfolded the top of the box into which he had earlier emptied the top drawer and extracted a paper clip. He passed it to Jason and watched in fascination as he unbent then re-bent it to resemble the outline of a key.

"The other half of the key is still in there," Josh said.

"No problem."

Jason knelt down and gripped the jagged metal with his nails—kept long for guitar picking. It took him just a few seconds to remove it and then in with the paper clip. Less than a minute later, he tugged gently on the drawer handle to check he had succeeded. He gave Josh a nod.

"Wow! Thanks!" Josh smiled, suitably impressed. "You're a star." He waited for Jason to move away before he opened the drawer. "There's something I want to show you," he said, keeping his eyes downturned, although he wasn't properly looking at the contents of the drawer. It was a means to avoid eye contact. "I can't swear you to secrecy. It wouldn't be fair or professional to ask that of you. However, I'm not doing it as a therapist." He looked up. "I'm doing it as a friend." He pushed the drawer shut, catching a glimpse of the topmost object within. He wondered where he'd put that. It must have been the last time he went in there, when George 'analysed' his dream and doodled all over his notebook. He made a mental note to remember to take the notebook home and sat down again.

Jason watched on in a half-interested daze. He wasn't feeling mentally well enough to be fully intrigued, but he was a little curious as to why Josh was now slowly unbuttoning his shirt cuff, because he had a good idea that he already knew and was having some trouble believing it. *Josh?* He was always so stable, a bit cool and distant, but—*ah, yeah.*

Jason Meyer—he's a good guy, a bit cool and distant, but…

Josh closed his eyes and kept his arm turned inward as he began to roll up his sleeve. He didn't know if this was the right thing to do, but he'd yet to find a right thing for this situation. He'd counselled many young people from a position of distant, rational objectivity, knowing that his words would not break through.

Now, his cuff was up as far as his elbow, and he wasn't going to take it any further, but he was having something of a problem opening his eyes again and was starting to regret his actions. *Too late for that, really.* He inhaled deeply and opened his eyes to find Jason studying his hands, occasionally glancing up to see if Josh was ready.

Slowly, Josh turned his arm over. "The other one looks the same as this," he said.

Jason examined the flesh, identifying the cause of each pockmark and gash by sight and experience. His expression remained unchanged, other than a slight twitch in his right eye.

"You tried to kill yourself." His voice was flat, emotionless.

Josh nodded. "Twice. That was the second attempt and honestly, I shouldn't be here now. But that's a different epoch."

"How did you know?"

"I'm not entirely sure. I just…" He shrugged. "I picked up on something in the way you were acting. The things you were saying about nobody understanding and being judged for it."

"Yeah. It sucks. And I went to school with all the emos."

"In my time, it was heroin chic. Unbelievable, isn't it? Who on earth decided drug addiction and self-harm were cool?"

"Can I show you?"

"Only if you want to."

Jason stood up and unfastened his belt. "I only did it once on my arm, and my mum saw it." He pulled his jeans down to his knees. "Sorry about the dodgy boxers. Christmas present."

Josh frowned in puzzlement, until he realised what they were and started to laugh. All those scars on his thighs, and Jason was more worried that he was wearing *Transformers* underpants.

"So, yeah," he said, pulling his jeans up again, "a compass through the trouser leg does wonders when you feel like your head's gonna explode. I used to write with it and get all excited about going home, just to see if I could still read it. What a total nut job."

"Have you stopped doing it now?" Josh asked.

"Mostly." Jason sat down and sighed to give himself time to correct the lie. "I kind of replaced it with not eating and not taking my tablets, but the effect isn't immediate enough." He screwed his eyes tight shut and bit hard on his lip. "Why does it hurt so much less when I do it?"

"Well, as a therapist, I'll tell you it's because you use it to create a sense of detachment, or for the feel-good chemicals your body produces in response to the physical pain. As someone who's been there? I was trying to outdo the pain inside, and I didn't stop until I'd achieved that, but the mental pain just got worse, because I didn't deal with it."

"Which is why you attempted suicide."

"Eventually. I suppose that would be a fair assertion. However, self-injury is about trying to cope; suicide is when you give up trying."

Jason nodded to show he understood. "Krissi knows," he said. "She thinks it was just a phase I went through when I was younger. How old were you?"

"I started when I was fourteen and did it continually until I was about twenty-two."

"And you still do it now?"

"Not with blades or anything of that nature. That's what the bottom drawer is about, and I'm finally dealing with all the stuff in my head, because it's the only way to properly diminish the pain: face up to what's causing it."

"This is where I start talking," Jason said reluctantly.

"You don't have to. Not today. You got here, and that's a tremendous achievement."

"Thanks. And thanks for sharing."

"No problem. It helps me, too. As I say, I'm only just starting to face up to it. Maybe you'll be all done and dusted by the time you're thirty-eight."

Jason wasn't too optimistic, but Josh's openness had inspired him a little towards self-help instead of self-harm, so he tentatively pushed on.

"Break-dancing," he said. "That's what they used to call it. 'Do some of your break-dancing for us.' And I'd laugh about it. I didn't think it got to me that much. My dad told me to ignore them and they'd stop, but they didn't, so I thought, fine. If you're gonna treat me like I'm different, I'm gonna be really different, and I got into listening to punk and metal, dying my hair, wearing the t-shirts and hoodies. And the more 'different' I became, the more they bullied me. The more they bullied me, the more I hurt myself. Why did you do it?"

So this was how they were to play it. Honest exchanges of information. Definitely not very professional.

"I felt like I was being bullied for being different, too, because of my sexuality," Josh said.

"For being gay?"

"For being asexual. The bullying wasn't deliberate, but if you're put in a situation where you feel threatened and you can't stand up for yourself, it's still bullying, and it still hurts."

"Krissi told me her mum and Kris got bullied. Did it happen a lot when you were at school?"

"Not really. I don't suppose it was any worse than now, and any school that claims to have no bullying is lying. It happens in every school."

"And in the workplace."

"Yes, unfortunately. Often the boss is to blame for most of it." Jason had disappeared behind his hair again.

"I don't think that's going to be a problem with you at the top," Josh said, trying to keep the lines of communication open. He got the feeling there was a little bit more ground they needed to cover before they called it a day. He was right.

"Alistair Campion was being bullied," Jason blurted.

He was watching Josh through his hair. Josh nodded to show he was listening but didn't say anything.

"I don't know if that's the right word for it, but blackmail sounds too strong and a bit racist."

Josh had his own thoughts on what he saw as a bit of political correctness gone mad. Blackboards were black; black sheep were black; blackmail—that one was maybe a bit trickier and Jason had a point, although whether the use of black and white to denote ethnicity was relevant to the use of 'black' as lesser in relation to the origin of the term 'blackmail' was questionable. And now his brain had gone off theorising. He hauled it back, realised Jason hadn't spoken for a couple of minutes and prompted.

"What makes you think he was being bullied?"

"Extorted? Is that a word?"

"Yes, it is." Josh felt himself shuffling forward on his seat.

"Yeah. Not bullied, extorted from, or by. Whatever. He asked me to have a look at the video link on the screen in the conference room, because my dad told him I knew about these things, which I kind of do, I s'pose. So I connected it to the network and went back to my dad's office to access it remotely, see if I could troubleshoot the problem from there."

He was shaking and twitching, and Josh started to panic a little, although he wasn't sure why. He knew what to do if someone had a seizure, but he didn't think that was what was happening necessarily, because along with the twitching, Jason was rubbing hard at his thigh.

"Jason, you can stop if this is too painful for you," he said gently.

"No. I need to tell someone. It's been eating at me for nearly two years." He pushed his hair back from his face and sighed. "I saw it, on my laptop, when I was connected to the conference room screen. I saw it all."

Josh felt his heart pounding, but he didn't want to jump to conclusions.

"What did you see, Jason?"

Jason closed his eyes, as if to try and call up the image in his mind. He opened them again and looked right at Josh. "I saw Alistair Campion's murder."

Short Circuit
Thursday 10th August

A day to transfer the books to the university, followed by a morning spent manhandling his desk downstairs for Charlotte to take to her new 'office'—her old bedroom at her parents' house. For all of his procrastinating, Josh was nearly done, and his surgery now contained the absolute bare essentials required for him to function: sofa, chair, clock, kettle, coffee.

It was disconcerting, possibly even depressing, but he was determined to use the place to its fullest until the end of the month, which was why he'd suggested having the meeting there. No distractions or unnecessary clutter; no clutter at all, in fact. And it was neutral territory. He sighed and checked the clock. Twenty minutes to four. Sean was due ten minutes ago, which meant that this was him opening the downstairs door. He listened to him whistling as he made his way up.

"Chris de Burgh? Really?"

"What's wrong with Chris de Burgh?"

"Nothing in general. Dare I ask why the 'Lady in Red' is in your head?"

"It's not for the reason you think, Joshy, that's for sure. Anyway, what's the plan? Do we have one?"

"No. That's why I asked you to get here at half past, so we could have a quick chat, before they arrive."

"All right, so. They both wanted this meeting, which means we can be totally open on that score."

"Hmm. I get the feeling he is less enthusiastic for the idea than she is. He doesn't want to cause any upset."

"Understandably, although given what she's told me, I think she'll have already done some groundwork."

Josh got up from his chair. "I'm going to get the kettle on. What are you on? Tea?"

"In the absence of anything stronger, that'll do nicely."

"Like that today, is it?"

"Like that every day at the moment, to be quite honest with you."

"Well, I'm currently transferring my books and journals to my all-new wall-to-wall bookshelves, and you're more than welcome to come and stick your big Irish nose in if you're at a loose end. I'm only using this place because I can."

Sean nodded a grateful acknowledgement. He was missing their weekly planning meetings and popping in to see each other. Last summer, he'd still been drinking, and they were cool and professional, with the occasional good-natured jibe thrown in for good measure. Over Christmas, they'd been in and out of each other's houses. Now, with Josh getting himself settled in at the university, George supporting Sophie and working light duties at the farm, plus their shifts with Jess, he rarely got to see Josh at all. Sphinx had always been good company, of course, but sometimes he needed a little more interaction than a cat could realistically provide.

"And how is the new office looking?" Sean asked, following Josh through to the kitchen. He stood in the doorway while Josh made their drinks.

"A mess. The IT people came to put an internet socket in and ripped the skirting board off. The maintenance team came to put it back and cracked the cover on the internet socket. The IT people came back to replace the cover and gouged the wall with a screwdriver. The maintenance people said it wasn't urgent, so I hit it with a paperweight until it was. Now I have a jagged triangular hole in the plaster and a pile of plaster dust that replenishes itself if I so much as breathe. The bookshelves are bloody awesome, though, and the chair is superb—nearly as comfy as the one at home."

"Not regretting the decision then, no?"

"Not yet. Ask me again in October, when I've got undergraduates knocking at my door from dawn till dusk."

"That's optimistic of you—to think they stop when the sun goes down."

"I thought they adjourned to the SU."

"Pah! I've paid me money, Doctor Tierney, now where's my degree?"

"Is it really that bad?"

"Not if you take them in hand. I'm sure you'll be just fine."

Josh tutted. There was no way he was going to be standing for any of that. He passed Sean his tea and ushered him back to the consultation room, where he sat down and swapped his coffee for his notebook—on the floor on account of the lack of desk. "I'm going to Jess's straight from here, if you want to tag along."

Sean nodded. "Yeah, I think I will." He frowned, deep in thought. "Listen, you know this ridiculous insistence of ours on professionalism? D'you think we could breach a few confidences here? There're some things it might be useful for you to know before they arrive."

Josh didn't answer for a while, instead rubbing his chin with his thumb as he considered the proposal. Obviously, most of what Jason had talked about could go no further without his express permission and in any case wasn't relevant, but Sean was right. There were facts they needed to get out in the open. He nodded, reluctantly.

"Yes. OK."

"Good," Sean said. "Let's start with Hadyn."

"OCD guy?"

"The very fellow."

"Is working at the studio," Josh stated.

"Ah, right. So you know about that. Also, Neil went for the same job."

"Neil?"

"Alice's live-in lover from when she was first employed at Campion's."

"I don't know anything about a Neil."

185

"It might not be important, but he left over thirty years ago, and she hadn't heard from him since. All of a sudden, Callaghan's dead and Neil's back on the scene. Warning bells. That's what I hear. OK. So. I think that makes it your turn?"

"I'm done."

"Is that so?" Sean eyed him suspiciously.

"I only had Hadyn."

"Right," Sean said, clearly not believing a word of it.

Josh pushed his hair back and kept hold of it, trying to decide if he should say anything about what Jason had seen, because if he was telling the truth—and there was no reason for him to lie about it—then it was the singular most important piece of evidence that could lead to the reopening of the investigation.

Jason saw the murder, therefore he saw the murderer. However, he'd also stood up to police interrogation and continued to maintain the secret for two years, which not only put Josh in a massive dilemma as regards sharing this information with Sean, but also suggested that Jason would readily and convincingly deny that he'd seen anything, if put under duress.

Much as Josh wanted to keep it to himself, he could feel Sean's eyes burning into him, waiting for him to divulge what he knew.

"Come on now, Joshy," Sean cajoled. "I'm doing all the giving here."

Josh sighed. "OK. I'll tell you, but, Sean, this has got to stay between you and me."

"Absolutely. You have my word."

That was all he needed to hear.

"Jason says he witnessed the murder."

"Oh." Sean nodded a couple of times, palpably shocked.

Five minutes on, they were still sitting in silence, and it was almost time for Jason and Alice to arrive.

"What are you thinking?" Josh asked.

Sean shrugged. "I'm still trying to fathom why Neil's back."

Josh blinked slowly and rubbed his forehead, hamming up his disbelief. "Does nothing else about all of this strike you as a little odd?"

"Like what?"

"OK, Tierney, let me start from the top, because much as I'm fairly certain you are nowhere near as stupid as you're making out right at this moment, I'm going to assume you really can't see the startlingly obvious."

Sean smiled and sat back, resting his tea on his belly, ready to be entertained. He loved it when Josh caught the tail end of an idea and went chasing around after it, like a small boy trying to reel in an enormous kite before he was forced to surrender it to the power of nature, or the National Grid, whichever got there first.

"So," Josh began, "arriving in less than two minutes, we have Alice Friar and also Jason Meyer, the only witness to the murder of Alistair Campion, who happened to be a close business associate of Dan, whose daughter is looked after by Alice, whose previous employment was personal assistant to the aforementioned murder victim. The prime suspect in the original investigation of that murder was Ellie's then future husband, whose name was cleared, only for her ex-husband to plead guilty and end up in prison, where he met a young guy with OCD, who now works for Shaunna and Andy's daughter's best friend, Jason Meyer, who happens to be the biological son of Alice Friar and the late, murdered Alistair Campion."

"Hmm," Sean said, nodding slowly, then, "Yes," drawing the word out as long as he could. His eyes twinkled, and a smile creased the corners of his mouth.

"Well?" Josh said brusquely.

"I see your point."

Josh huffed in exasperation and picked up his coffee.

"It certainly is a bit of a coincidence—"

"Oh, fuck off!" Josh snapped.

Sean laughed. "I'm just joshing with you, Joshy."

"You don't say!"

Sean gave him a mischievous wink. The door at the bottom of the stairs opened. "When I get a chance," he said quickly, "I'll fill you in on the rest of the Alistair and Alice love story. It's beautiful and will move you to tears, and it'll also give you something to think about over the coming weeks. A bit of distraction therapy can go a long, long way, I've found. Alice. A good afternoon to you." Sean rose to his feet and smiled warmly, giving the new arrivals each a courteous nod. "Jason. Good to meet you," he said to the young man loitering in the doorway.

"Good afternoon, Doctor Tierney," Alice responded coolly. "And also to you, Mr. Sandison."

"Hi, Alice. How are you?" Josh glanced at Jason, and they briefly met each other's gaze—a message that conveyed Jason's surprise at how bare the room was compared to his previous visit only three days ago.

"I'm very well, thank you for asking," Alice replied. She watched him carefully, her expression softening a little as she took in what she saw.

"I'm glad to hear it. Please do sit down. Would you like a drink?"

"Oh. A cup of tea would be lovely, thank you," she smiled at him.

"Coming right up. White, no sugar?"

"Yes, that's right." She perched on the end of the sofa. Jason followed Josh from the room.

"She knows," he hissed in Josh's ear.

Josh continued with the process of topping up the kettle and switching it on, acting as if the voice he had heard was imagined. He prepared a cup. "Do you want a drink of something?" he asked.

"No, thanks."

Josh turned to face him. Jason immediately put his head down, his hair obscuring much of his face.

"What does she know?" Josh asked quietly.

Jason put his hand in his pocket, fished around for a few seconds, and then pulled out a small object. He held it up for Josh to see.

"Your earring?"

"The other one to this." Jason lifted his hair to show the one in his ear.

"OK. Explain."

Jason flicked his hair back and moved closer, looking Josh right in the eye. "When I went to look at the video screen, I must've somehow knocked my earring out." He held up the one in his hand again. "The other one is Krissi's. She gave it to me when she realised I'd lost mine, but Alice found it and hid it from the police."

"Oh. I see. She covered for you."

"Yeah. So she must've known who I am, mustn't she?"

Josh nodded. Yes, it stood to reason. The more pertinent question was whether she knew what he'd seen, and that was going to be much harder to discern. The kettle clicked off, and Josh continued their hushed conversation while he made Alice's cup of tea.

"How did she get the earring back to you?"

"She just came up to me, at Dan and Adele's engagement last year, and put it in my hand. At the time, I wasn't sure if it was her. I mean, I did know who she was, but…" He was becoming distressed. "She said she knew I was there, she saw me. But no-one else was there, only me and Mr. Campion, and then I was in my dad's office. How could she have seen me?"

"I think I know," Josh said. He picked up the tea. "You need to try to stay calm. I'm not going to put you on the spot, OK?"

Jason took a couple of deep breaths. "OK."

"Good. Now, I appreciate you've only just met Sean—Doctor Tierney—and you don't really know Alice, but do you trust them?"

"I, err…"

"Just tell me. Gut instinct."

"Yeah." Jason nodded. "Yes, I trust them. Weirdly." He looked somewhat surprised by his admission. Josh didn't explain; trick of the trade.

"I'm not going to tell them about the thing we have in common, obviously, but we need to be open about the rest of it. What do you think?"

Jason closed his eyes for a few seconds and then nodded again. "All right," he agreed.

"Good man." Josh led the way back into his consultation room. "There you are, Alice."

"Thank you, Mr. Sandison." She smiled at him and peered into the cup. He hoped it was up to scratch, but he wasn't a tea drinker, so he never could tell. She gasped and covered her mouth. He flinched, waiting for the criticism, because Alice, he had observed, was quite brutal with the truth. "Oh. It's not anymore, is it? It's Mr. Sandison-Morley. I'm so sorry."

Josh smiled, relieved. "That's quite all right, Alice. But please just call me Josh. I'm not one for formal address."

"Likewise," Sean said. "I much prefer Sean to Doctor Tierney."

Alice shrugged. "Josh and Sean it is." She sipped carefully at her tea; Josh watched, waiting for the look of displeasure. There wasn't one, and he was pleased, although he found he couldn't help but continue to stare at her. He wasn't quite sure what it was that intrigued him the most. He was aware that the reason she didn't maintain eye contact was the synaesthesia, flitting as she did between looking at and around him, as if a swarm of bees had descended upon him. He wanted to ask her what it was like—what it looked like, how much she could tell about a person by the colour of their scent.

And then there was the confidence. She was, in manner, a typical timid, late-middle-aged spinster, but so self-assured that he could well imagine any gang of malcontents who ran up against her getting a lot more than they bargained for. Added to this was Sean's tantalising taster of a clandestine romance, which required a passion he couldn't quite imagine her possessing, and then the concealing of evidence to protect her son—an act born of maternal instinct, or something more sinister? It was absolutely fascinating, and he was doing a shockingly poor job of disguising his curiosity, to the extent that Sean coughed loudly to gain his attention. Josh shook himself out of it. Alice narrowed her eyes.

"All right, so," Sean said, smiling warmly at Alice and Jason, who were sitting at opposite ends of the sofa. Jason had his body turned away from Alice as much as it was possible to do so and still be facing forwards. Alice was balanced bolt upright on the edge of the cushion. Sean kept his smile as he examined them both. "We maybe need to loosen up a little first," he suggested. "Alice, can I ask you to tell Jason a bit about your synaesthesia?"

"Certainly," she agreed, although she was frowning in consideration of what she perceived to be a very strange request. She turned slightly, waiting for Jason to glance her way, and it was no more than a fleeting glance. She smiled at him, and he just about forced out a smile for her. "I've had synaesthesia all my life," she said. "My sense of smell is processed as colour, and it's very sensitive. It can be extremely overwhelming, even in a low-key situation like this." She shuddered. "Your coffee, for instance, Josh, is so strong there's a brown fog hovering right across the room."

"Oh, Alice. I'm so sorry." He swigged back his coffee all in one go and took the cup away. He returned and sat down again. She nodded subtly at him; he couldn't tell if it was meant as a simple thank-you or confirmation that she'd cottoned on to what he was doing. For now, she continued with her explanation.

"When I look at people, Jason," she said. He turned to look at her as she said his name, but then looked away again. "I can see how they feel, which is due to the combination of my heightened sense of smell and the scent being transformed into colours and patterns. And it is often the case, I've found, that the more chaotic a person's state of mind, the more fluid and disorganised the colours and patterns appear to me." She glanced at Josh and Sean and raised an eyebrow.

Sean smiled, a little nervously, although he, too, was seriously considering asking her to analyse his colour-smell when they were done here.

Jason tucked his hair behind his ear and shuffled around so he could see her properly. "That's cool," he said. "I sometimes see music in colour. That's not normal, is it?" He was asking Sean and Josh.

"Normal?" Josh's tone was flippant. "No such thing! But it's not something everyone experiences, if that's what you mean."

Jason almost smiled. He shuffled around a little more. "Can you see people's scent after they're gone? Like a sort of echo?"

"Yes, indeed I can. I can also see them before they arrive."

"That's like being psychic. Way cool."

Alice laughed. "I suppose it is. Although it's more like a pet dog sees the world, from what the doctors tell me."

"So, do different moods have different colours? You know, like black for depressed, and red for embarrassed, and things like that?"

"Up to a point, yes, but it's always tinted by that person's own scent."

Jason nodded to show his understanding, which he had derived by employing the analogy of music and how the same solo played by different guitarists sounded almost like an entirely new composition.

"What colour's my scent?"

Alice held his gaze and smiled. "I don't sense your scent in the same way as everyone else's. If I had not always known that you were my son, I would still have recognised you by that fact."

Jason put his head down, his hair flopping forward with the motion. Josh glanced subtly at Sean.

"Did you know my mum and dad before I was born?" Jason asked. Alice nodded, although he couldn't see it.

"Yes," she confirmed. "I knew Bill—your dad. He was Alistair's business partner from the very beginning, even before I started working for him."

"For *him*?" Jason queried.

Josh was impressed; he, too, had picked up on the contradiction in Alice's statement.

She acknowledged her mistake but didn't try to correct it, for she could see no point in doing so. "That's right. For him, officially. Bill was always the silent partner, because Alistair's parents were very critical and judgemental. He could never do right by them. His company was already a success before his father died, but it wasn't enough. They didn't approve of his friends, or Jenny, and

192

they hated Bill even though he was a wonderful friend to us both, and remains so to me."

Jason folded his arms and frowned beneath his hair. At least now he understood his father's obsession with the company. Before Campion's death and the building burning to the ground, if his dad wasn't at the office, he was at a meeting, or playing golf with business associates. Even on the rare occasions he was at home, he was always doing the accounts, or on the phone rambling about figures and sales targets. It had been his life. But then the fire happened, and all of a sudden, literally overnight, he retired. No working from home, no office, nothing but the occasional game of golf for the sake of it, and lots and lots of gardening.

"Why didn't my dad take over?" Jason thought aloud, then, realising what he'd done, turned and looked directly at Alice. "Do you know?"

"No. I'm afraid I don't. He should have done. Alistair always contended it was written into his will."

"But it wasn't. He left everything to his wife."

"And she died too soon to inherit, which is why it came to you," Alice said. "Eventually."

"So it should all be my dad's," Jason mused. He sighed and started chewing his sleeve, his arm jolting away from him as he pulled it clear of his teeth. That movement became more pronounced and was joined by a jiggling of his left leg, only slightly at first, but by the time Josh understood what was happening, Jason was fully convulsing, and Alice had already sprung into action.

Jason was rigid as a board and shaking violently, and Alice put herself between him and the floor, slowly guiding him down as he slid from the sofa. The seizure lasted no more than a minute, and as the convulsions slowed, his body became limp, and his breathing started again. Alice gently shifted her legs away and moved him into the recovery position. She pushed his hair from his eyes and stayed where she was, glancing up to Josh and Sean, an admirably calm smile on her face. She placed her hand on top of Jason's so that he'd know he was not alone when he came to.

"There are very few people that I can stand to have in close proximity," she said, "and physical touch is almost always unbearable."

A couple of minutes of silence followed before Jason regained consciousness, with Alice quietly explaining where he was and what had happened, reassuring him that he was safe.

Jason thanked her, and though his brain was slow with exhaustion and it took great effort to form the words, he began to pour out his soul to her, telling her about the teasing and the bullying and how much distress it had caused him.

Across the room, Josh had resorted to scanning through his notebook, and Sean was scrolling up and down a list of search results on his phone. Both activities were entirely pointless and served only to distance them from the interaction happening of its own accord; they were not needed. Josh glanced up and caught Sean's eye. He looked towards the door. Sean nodded, and they both slowly got up, the words of explanation ready on their lips, but Alice and Jason were no longer conscious of their presence.

"We're in the kitchen," Josh said quietly as he left the room, "if you need us." He stepped outside. "Or notice that we've left at any point ever." He dodged into the kitchen and shrugged at Sean. "OK. Now what?"

"We wait."

"For?"

"Them to finish getting acquainted."

"We might be here a while."

"I'm sure he'll be back to full speed soon enough. Tell you what: you get that kettle on again, and I'll tell you a little story."

Josh accepted Sean's suggestion, this time preparing tea for both of them, whilst Sean talked, recounting the tale of Alice and Alistair: how they had fallen in love even though Alice was with Neil, and how, eventually Alistair had given up waiting for her and married Jenny on the very same day Neil left Alice because he knew she was in love with Alistair. It was some years later that Alice gave birth to Jason, and the affair continued to a lesser extent afterwards. Alice was Alistair's right-hand woman, his wife in the workplace, and for all that they felt their choices had kept them apart, they had, in reality, spent more time together than most married couples.

And so, it would seem, both parents were aware of the identity of their son, and were able to keep a close watch on him as he grew up in the care of their mutual friend, Bill Meyer—Jason's adoptive father and Alistair's 'voice of reason'. For where Alistair provided the engineering expertise, Bill was the financial know-how, which was why he had assumed the role of Chair of the board of directors after Alistair's death, and why he should have inherited Alistair's share of Campion Holdings PLC, along with his other remaining assets.

"That bodes well for Jason," Josh said, once Sean finished his story, as always told with Tierney flourish, but without any added garnish for once; it had enough of its own.

"In what way?" he asked.

"Whatever had happened with Campion's business, Jason would have inherited it, which lets him off the hook as a suspect."

"I see where you're coming from. However, there's still a murderer on the loose, and if the motive was financial, Jason's a potential target."

"True." Josh sipped his tea and grimaced.

"That bad?"

"It's tea."

"And very considerate of you. I'm sure Alice wouldn't have minded."

"Probably not, but there are questions to be asked, and I'm rather hoping to have successfully established a little mutual give and take."

"Ah."

"Yes," Josh said. "Here's another little snippet for you to mull over: Alice found Jason's earring at the scene of the crime and removed it."

"Concealed evidence from the police? Mothers will go to extraordinary lengths."

"So it would seem."

Both men fell silent, following the same train of thought, and it was downhill all the way. Steph was barely coping with the burden of her daughter's care, but Jess was adamant she wanted to stay at home. There was nothing they could do, other than keep taking their turns in the unofficial rota and try to support the Lamberts—and Shaunna, who had, in reality, taken most of the load.

"I think it would be best if we take this one step at a time," Josh suggested. Sean nodded.

"I was thinking the same myself. Let's make sure Alice and Jason are on the right track, and leave the rest of it for later."

"Agreed."

'Later' was as close as either of them could get to saying 'until after Jess has died', but they each knew that's what it meant. They returned to the consultation room, where Jason was sitting on the sofa once more and Alice was right next to him, still holding his hand and listening to him as he told her about the studio. It was several minutes more before they acknowledged Josh and Sean.

"Thank you for arranging this meeting for us," Alice said.

"Yeah, thanks," Jason echoed apologetically.

"No problem at all," Sean assured him. "How are you feeling now?"

"OK." Forward came the hair.

Sean smiled. "It sounds like you're getting along famously."

"Oh, yes." Alice turned to Jason. "I should very much like to visit your studio, if that would be all right?"

"Cool," he said. A car horn sounded outside. "That'll be Stu."

Alice took a small notepad from her bag and wrote her phone number and address on it. She passed it over. "It has been so wonderful to talk to you today," she said.

Jason was already struggling to his feet, getting ready to go, as he had a studio booking to prepare for. He staggered.

"Are you sure you're all right?" she asked.

"Yeah. Shattered. I'll be OK. Think I might get Stu and Hadyn to run the recording session tonight, though." He gave her a smile and stepped towards her, holding out his hand. "Thanks," he said sincerely.

She shook the offered hand, keeping hold of it as she stood to briefly embrace him, raising an eyebrow in Josh and Sean's direction. She'd registered the name, and her reaction suggested she'd also realised it was the same Hadyn who had been at the 'case conference' a few months ago, but for now was choosing to keep it to herself.

"I hope I see you very soon," she said. Jason nodded and shook hands with Sean and Josh, giving them a quick smile of thanks.

Alice watched Jason all the way down the stairs and then turned back to Sean and Josh. "I agree with your decision."

It was a statement that made them both feel like they were naughty schoolboys caught doing something they shouldn't.

"It is a terrible thing that you are going through," she said sympathetically. "So very tragic. And that is your priority for now. Go and be with your friend. Finding Alistair's murderer will wait, but thank you for making this possible today. It means so much." She left without another word.

"Oh," Sean sighed, disappointed. "I wanted to ask her what colour I was."

"Yes. Me, too, although George said I was all the colours of the rainbow."

"You got a crock of gold to go with that?"

Josh laughed. "Alas, not." He yawned. "I vote we leave Jess's until later and go home for coffee."

"A splendid idea." Sean followed Josh down the stairs and out to the car. "Shall we pick up some cake?"

Josh nodded. "Fine by me." He waited for Sean to belt up, and pulled away. "And then you can explain the 'Lady in Red'."

"Never miss a trick, do you, Joshy?"

"Not often. Still, in two weeks or thereabouts, you won't have time to ogle loose women."

"True enough."

They stopped off at the bakery just up the road from Josh's surgery, bought the last four cream cakes in the shop, and continued towards home, pulling up behind Sophie's car.

"Your place or mine?" Josh asked.

"Yours. It's quicker to the coffee."

Josh opened the front door to the sound of laughter and glanced into the living room, where George and Sophie were watching a film together.

"Hey," he said. "Ah."

"Hi, Josh," Sophie called.

"Nice dress."

"Thanks. I figured, seeing as people keep staring at me anyway, I might as well make the most of it and wear something bright and cheerful."

"Yeah," George said. "Which one did we decide you were? Po, was it?"

Sophie slapped him on the thigh, hard.

"Po?" Josh asked.

Sean laughed and whispered, "The red Teletubby."

"I heard that," Sophie shouted. George had the giggles. Sophie slapped him again.

Josh shook his head and moved off towards the kitchen. Sean followed.

"The sun is setting in the sky..." they heard George say.

"Piss off!" Sophie shouted.

"Teletubbies say—"

Slap!

"Ouch!"

Josh frowned. "That doesn't even rhyme."

"Must be the remix," Sean joked.

Josh raised an eyebrow. "Yep. Chris de Burgh was definitely safer."

Starlight
Thursday 17th August

"Thanks for this, Steph." Andy stepped aside to let Jess's mum pass. She wouldn't use the front door key if he was in the house.

"No problem." She gave him a quick smile and turned away.

A bad day, Andy acknowledged in his mind. They all got them; some days were OK, some not. It was a situation they dealt with best by not dealing with it at all. Passing ships in a storm. They'd been here many times before, and they'd be here again a good few more before the storm subsided. If they were lucky, they might even find sunshine and clear blue skies at the other side.

Andy returned to the kitchen, where he'd been sitting at the breakfast bar, eating cornflakes. He quickly scooped the last of the cereal onto his spoon, chewing and simultaneously washing his bowl. Adele had sent a text to say they were on their way. All being well, they'd be in London by around midday, with time for a bit of sightseeing before the dinner this evening—the reason for the early changeover. The rest of the thought process was conducted aloud.

"Shaunna's gonna be here around six, Steph."

"Okey-dokey."

"And Josh can stay as long as you like tomorrow."

"That's great, Andy, thanks." She smiled again.

A really bad day, but not much he could do. After all, it was not every day a company like Jeffries and Associates was shortlisted for an industry award for excellence. Both brothers were somewhat bemused by the whole affair, because they just did what they did, but mix that Jeffries competitive streak with Dan's need to achieve and Andy's refusal to lose a challenge…the result was a logistics system that was fast, reliable and frequently achieved the seemingly impossible.

The toot of a car horn outside brought Andy back. "See you tomorrow evening." He gave Steph a quick hug.

She reached up and kissed him on the cheek. "Go and enjoy yourselves. Good luck."

"Thanks." He considered shouting up to Jess, but she'd been awake half the night, and was fast asleep when he'd checked in on her half an hour ago, so he decided not to. Steph watched from the doorstep as he threw his bag into the boot and climbed into the back of the large saloon idling outside. It was a hire car; Dan was still waiting on his insurance to pay out, but it was a decent make and model, so it wouldn't hold them up.

"Alright?" Andy nodded in greeting. He gave Steph a quick wave. She waved back and closed the door.

"Yeah," Dan confirmed. "You?"

"Yeah." He fastened his seat belt and glanced at Charlotte, who was sitting behind Dan, earphones tinkling away, her tablet in her hands. Andy leaned over and peered at the screen. She looked his way and removed an earplug. "Morning," he said.

"Hi," she replied, and promptly shoved her earplug back in, turning her attention back to the screen.

Dan pulled away from the kerb. "I dunno. She nominates us for an award and can't even be arsed to talk to us," he joked. "What's she doing?"

Andy looked across again. "Watching the financial news. You OK, Adele?"

"Yep," she answered distractedly. She, too, was preoccupied with her tablet, although she was playing a game. Dan and Andy made eye contact in the rear-view mirror.

"How's Jess?" Dan asked.

"Not so good."

"In a lot of pain?"

"No, I don't think it's that, to be honest. The stuff she's on now usually knocks her out, but she's been up and down all night."

"She must be feeling terrible," Adele said.

"Well, fancy that!" Dan sniped.

Andy spotted his brother's disdainful frown and sighed. Not even five minutes, and they were at it already.

Adele ignored Dan and finished the current level of her game. She paused it and turned in her seat to face Andy. "You know what day it is, don't you?"

"No. What?"

"The anniversary of Daisy's death."

"Ah. Fuck."

***

"Hi," Shaunna called, letting herself in.

Steph stepped into the kitchen doorway. "Oh, hi, Shaunna. I wasn't expecting you until this evening."

"I know. I'm just off to do the shopping, so I thought I'd pop in and see if you needed anything and I'll bring it back with me later."

"That's very kind of you. I've got a list here somewhere." Steph moved away and picked up a notepad from the breakfast bar. "Let's see." The list was penned partly by Andy, partly by Jess, with a few items Steph had added herself, and she was struggling to read it. "OK. Washing-up liquid, bread, teabags, cornflakes, erm, I think that says cheese, and..." She moved the page away from her and slowly brought it back towards her face, trying to get the letters into focus. "No idea." She passed it to Shaunna, who spent a while trying to read it and then shook her head and laughed.

"Nope. Not a clue."

"Well, I'm sure none of it's urgent, anyway. Have you got time for a cuppa? I was about to have one."

"That'd be wonderful." Shaunna knew what day it was, and although she really was on her way to the supermarket, it was an excellent excuse to stop in and make sure they were coping. She hadn't yet decided if they were. "Is Jess awake?" she asked. Steph had set out three mugs and nodded to confirm that she was.

"She said she was coming down, but that was a while ago. I'll go and check if she wants it up there." As she said it, there was a shuffling above, followed by the sound of gentle footfalls on the stairs. Jess came into view. She looked dreadful.

"Morning, hun." Shaunna smiled at her.

"Good morning," she said solemnly, heading straight for the lounge. Shaunna looked back at Steph, but she had turned away.

The kettle came to the boil. Shaunna sighed quietly and filled the three mugs. Steph stepped outside.

"Here you go, hun." Shaunna walked across the lounge and put the tea down on the table in front of the sofa.

"Thanks."

"I called in on my way to the shops, do you—"

"Yes. I heard," Jess snapped wearily. Shaunna tried not to take it to heart.

"Sorry if I disturbed you. Is there anything you need?"

"A life? Check the reduced-to-clear shelves. You might get one with a short expiration date. Oh, hang on, I've already got one of those."

Shaunna studied her friend for a moment, waiting for the outburst to be followed by an apology, or tears, or more of the same, but there was nothing. She turned and walked towards the door. "Would you like some breakfast?"

"It's almost eleven. A bit late for breakfast, don't you think?"

"Fine." She left the room without another word. Through the open back door, she could see Steph, leaning against the patio table and taking long, slow draws on her cigarette, gazing vacantly across the garden. Shaunna collected her tea and perched on a stool. Lucky it was her day off, really; the shopping was going to have to wait.

***

Once they'd booked in and deposited their bags, they returned to the bar, as arranged, Andy first, then Charlotte. Now to wait for Dan and, more to the point, Adele. Charlotte brought their drinks over.

"I've checked with reception, and the dinner is a half-seven start, for eight o'clock sit down. The awards are at nine-thirty."

"Cool."

"You're up against some big names, you know."

"Yeah. I had a look on the institute's website."

"Even getting this far is a major achievement."

"You don't need to convince me."

"I'm just saying."

Andy took a thirsty glug of his beer and set it down again, rubbing at the brand logo etched into the glass, deep in thought. "Wish I'd known," he said.

"About?"

"Daisy."

"Ah."

"I should've stayed."

"They'll be OK."

"Shaunna's gonna be there tonight. She's been bloody wonderful."

"Then you've got nothing to worry about," Charlotte said. He sighed, and she gave his hand a squeeze. "What shall we do this afternoon? Something touristy?" She was trying to distract him, and he gave it his best effort.

"Like what? The Tower?" Andy suggested.

"Nah. Been there loads of times already."

"The zoo?"

"Maybe. If we take Dan with us, they'll think one of the gorillas has escaped."

Andy managed a laugh. "We could just about make it to the whitewater centre."

"And do what?"

"Hydrospeeding."

"Is your shoulder up to it?"

"I reckon."

Charlotte looked doubtful.

"It's that, or head up the West End and watch Adele shop till she drops."

"OK. I'm sold."

"When d'you wanna leave?"

Dan and Adele stepped out of the lift, bickering. Dan shrugged and hissed something angrily at Adele, and she gave him a sugary smile.

"The sooner the better," Charlotte muttered out of the side of her mouth.

"Yeah," Andy agreed in the same fashion. "Alright, bro?"

"Hmph."

"Me and Charlie were talking about getting the train out to the whitewater adventure park, unless you had something planned that involved us?"

"Erm." Dan looked at Adele.

"We'll come with you," she said.

"What?" Dan could hardly believe what he was hearing.

"Don't you want to go shopping?" she asked.

"What do you think?" he retorted sarcastically.

"Well then."

"Fine." Dan didn't know what else to say to that, but he was instantly suspicious of her motives. A trip to London, with an entire afternoon clear for traipsing around over-priced designer shops, and she was suggesting they went to an adventure sports park? There was something sorely amiss.

"Awesome," Andy said. "You wanna go by car, or get the train?"

"We can go in the car, if you like. How far is it?"

"Twenty minutes around the M25."

Dan shrugged in agreement, and as soon as Charlotte and Andy had finished their drinks, they left.

As always with the M25, it took a little longer than twenty minutes, although they still arrived well before one o'clock. Andy and Charlotte completed the health checks for hydrospeeding—a whitewater version of bodyboarding that involved a foam board not dissimilar to the floats used when learning to swim—with Andy conveniently forgetting to mention his dislocated shoulder in the process.

Meanwhile, Adele was browsing the information leaflets in the reception area.

"What would you like to do?" she asked Dan.

"Dunno yet."

"Did you want to go with Charlotte and Andy?"

"Not really." He picked up one of the leaflets and flicked through the pages. "Golf," he said, indicating at the page with a nod of his head.

"OK," Adele agreed immediately.

"You want a game of golf?"

"If you do."

"What's going on?"

"What d'you mean?"

"You pass on an afternoon in Knightsbridge to come here, now you want to play golf."

"Yes, and?"

"Are you feeling all right?"

"What *are* you talking about?" Adele tried to look puzzled, but it wasn't working.

Dan continued to watch her. "OK. We'll go play golf," he relented. She gave him a toothy smile and tottered over to Andy to let him know what they were doing.

"Golf?" he said incredulously. She shrieked.

"What's wrong with me wanting to play golf?"

"Err…" He glanced at his brother. Dan shrugged. "Nothing. See you later. Have fun, playing golf." He watched them leave and shook his head. "Mental."

***

Shaunna put the lawnmower back in the shed. It was something to do, to pass the hours, knowing that she couldn't leave Jess and Steph on their own. The atmosphere in the house was horrendous, which was why she was trying to find excuses to stay outside. Steph's present state reminded her of the slender white cat figurine that her mum had kept for many years, even though it was broken in three, the pieces precariously perched on top of each other so that it looked perfect, even close up. Dusting the windowsill involved carefully deconstructing the mosaic, laying it on a cushion, then reconstructing it again afterwards, and there was a definite art to it, which her mother had, but she and her dad did not.

"It's the way you hold your mouth," her mum would say with a smile, as she repositioned the third and final piece, stepping back to admire the sleek porcelain creature. Whole again and yet not, all at the same time.

As for Jess: she was mostly pretending to be asleep, punctuated with heavy, exasperated sighs that served as a constant warning that getting too close was likely to result in a venomous attack. Her mother had been edging closer as the day progressed. Now they were only feet apart, the shattered cat and the dying

205

rattlesnake, and Shaunna was standing in the kitchen, listening as they hissed and rattled.

Fight or flee? Attack, or surrender?

The hisses and rattles became louder, and she retreated once more to the garden, but it didn't grant sufficient distance to blot out the battle cries. Such cruel things, words, when there was nothing left but pain and loss. She listened as they rose against each other, and fell, swiping and scratching and biting and tearing, receding away only to rise again, and again, wailing, shrieking banshees lost in time. She couldn't let them do this to each other, for it would be a fight to the death. She marched back inside, straight along the hallway and into the lounge.

"Stop!" she said.

They didn't.

She took a big breath and yelled at the top of her voice. "Stop it now! Both of you!"

Immediate silence.

The two women turned their angry glares on Shaunna, who stood her ground, her weeping granting her a strength that they did not yet possess: the strength of truth. Steph fled the room, ran up the stairs and locked herself away. Jess reached for the remote control. Shaunna intervened and snatched it out of arm's reach.

"No," she said, shaking her head, the tears flying from her cheeks in little arcs and landing like the first drops of the most soothing summer rain shower. "No, Jess. Please. No more."

"No more? OK. I'll just stop dying right now, shall I? You're all as bad as each other, trying to do the right thing, all sweetness and light. Let me help you with this, let me help you with that. And for what? So you can feel better in the end. Well, at least we made her days more comfortable, did everything we could.

"*She's* here today, all full of woe for the Perfect Daughter—'Oh, please understand how hard this is for me, Jess.' Hard, Mother? I'll tell you what's fucking hard! Trying to live up to your vision of Daisy. What would she have been, do you think? A doctor? A lawyer? A mother? Would she have given you the grandchild you wanted? Married the perfect man and lived in a perfect bloody castle of sparkling perfection? Unlike this failure, this loser who never quite got her career right, never found the perfect man, never had children. Because of Daisy. Always because of fucking Daisy."

Jess had nothing to throw, so she banged her head back into the sofa and ground her fists against each other.

Shaunna watched through tear-blurred eyes, every in-breath a constrained sob. "You're being a selfish cow," she said. She walked out of the room and slammed the door as hard as she could.

***

"Not the best idea I've ever had," Andy said, giving his shoulder a stretch and wincing at the same time. They'd been back at the hotel just long enough for him to shower and send Charlotte a text message asking her to come to his room.

"It was a lot of fun, though." She squeezed a dollop of the pain relief gel onto her palm and smeared it over his shoulder; he cursed at the coldness. "Sorry," she said, not sounding very apologetic. "I wonder how much hydrospeed boards cost?"

"Dunno. Probably not much more than bodyboards, but you're right. They're way more fun. And those loops were insane. I got pulled under on both of them."

"You should've gone wide. Right, there you go." She patted his shoulder. It was still sticky. "I'll see you downstairs."

"Cheers, Charlie," he called after her. He got up, took some painkillers and began the painful process of putting on his clothes.

In the room next door but one, Dan was sitting on the bed, prodding at his phone and waiting for Adele to finish in the bathroom. The round of golf had gone well, in that they hadn't killed each other or anyone else and had finished the course without cheating, for the most part. However, he still hadn't got to the bottom of Adele's weirdness. He got up and walked over to the bathroom, banging on the door.

"Aren't you finished yet?"

"Won't be a minute, sweetie."

He snarled under his breath. "It's nearly six o'clock."

"So?"

"So I want to go and get a couple of pints in before dinner."

"OK, OK!" The door opened, and Adele exited in a waft of perfumed steam, her hair wrapped in a towel and another towel around her body. She smiled at him, and he instantly melted.

"I'm happy to pass on the beer, though," he said, pulling her close.

"I thought you needed a shower," she murmured around his kisses.

"I do, but if I go in there and leave you out here, you'll be all dressed up when I come out."

Adele had no intention of doing any such thing and back-stepped, taking him into the bathroom with her, setting the shower running and shaking herself free of the towel, whilst he hastily removed his clothes. He stepped into the jets of water, reaching across to pull the towel from her head, her wet hair tumbling down onto her shoulders. He drew her to him, groaning at the softness of her naked breasts pressing against his chest—such a rare pleasure to be together like this, free from the threat of constant interruption from their daughter, and they both gave themselves to it. He gently lifted her and she hooked her legs around his hips, allowing him to take her weight and push deep into her.

They moved together in that familiar, wondrous rhythm, their lips connecting then breaking apart to explore each other's bare skin, licking and kissing and sucking ever more urgently, the water cascading down between them and aiding their slip, slide and thrust. She almost lost her grip; he tightened his. He pushed her back against the wall, and she arched away from the coldness of the tiles, digging her fingers into his shoulder muscles, her heels into his buttocks, urging him closer, deeper, faster, until at last, he caught her gasp with his open mouth, held onto her so tightly that she fought for breath, his legs almost giving way to the pulsating thrust together, the momentum carrying them up and beyond. She released her grip, and he gently eased himself away, still taking her weight until she was standing once again.

"It's been a long time since we did that," Adele said breathlessly. She stepped out of the bath so that he could shower for real.

"Yeah, and you're still as beautiful as ever." Dan reluctantly released her trailing hand. She bent down to retrieve the smaller towel and spoke as she wrapped it around her hair. "Would now be a good time to tell you I've enrolled on a college course?"

"So that's what this has all been about."

"Not *all*, Dan." She smiled and blew him a kiss. "But I don't mind telling you, I hate golf. It's really bloody boring."

"And the sex? What was that? To soften the blow?" She giggled at the innuendo. He missed it.

"No, sweetie," she said. She moved away towards the door. "That was to say I've stopped taking my pill. Now hurry up and get showered. We can talk about the rest of it later. After all, this might be my last night of being able to get drunk for a while."

***

"OK, Shaunna?" Sean spoke to announce his presence, and it was as well. She'd been sitting at the patio table with her head in her hands for the best part of an hour, her mind very much elsewhere. He sat next to her and gently took her hand. "Steph's gone home," he explained. "They've cleared the air a little."

"Is she all right? Steph, I mean?"

"As all right as she's going to be. She and Dave need to have a good long chat. They're very rocky, but I shouldn't be telling you that. Anyway, Jess would like to see you, when you're ready."

Shaunna closed her eyes and shook her head. "I don't think I want to talk to her—not because I'm angry with her. I accept everything she said, and she's right. Why do we all do this? It *is* about making ourselves feel better. It's just nicer to think that you're doing it for them. When my mum…" She didn't get any further than that, because she finally, totally, fell apart, her whole body heaving with the pain, of losing her mum, of her sense of powerlessness now as she watched her dad slip away with dementia, and of knowing that she was losing Jess.

Sean put his arms around her, stroking her hair and shushing her gently. He didn't speak. He didn't tell her it would be all right, or ask her to pull herself together. He let her cry.

Eventually—she couldn't even have estimated how long it had been—she lifted her head from his chest and coughed in an attempt to clear her mucus-clogged throat, sniffing against the resistance. He passed her the tissues he kept in his trouser pocket at all times; in his job they were an essential piece of kit.

"How's Sophie?" she asked.

He raised an eyebrow. "I will answer that, and tell you that she's fine, other than being thirty-nine weeks pregnant and very irritable on account of the lack of sleep, back pain, heartburn and aching joints, not to mention being a hormonal old goat at the best of times. But don't feel obliged to ask. There's no payback required. We're friends, aren't we?"

Shaunna nodded.

"And if we weren't," Sean continued, "I'd still be doing this in my professional capacity. You did the right thing calling me. I'm here for you, lovely. Whatever you need, if I can give it to you, I will. That's a promise."

Shaunna took a deep and very shaky breath and attempted a smile. "Thanks, Sean. I'm so grateful to you."

"I'm glad to be here, if you get my drift. And I disagree. I think there is something inherently selfless about the human species. We risk our lives to save others. We take care of our sick. Not all of it is about the feel-good factor, or appeasing our guilt."

"I told Jess she was being selfish."

"And she was, so."

"I shouldn't have said it. Today of all days. I shouldn't have said it, but I did. And I'm truly sorry for that."

"Did you mean it?"

"Yes."

"And you accept it as the truth?"

"Yes, but—"

"Would you have told her if she wasn't sick?"

"Well, yes, of course I would."

"She asked that we treat her the same as always."

Shaunna sighed and tried to adjust her thoughts to bring them in line with what Sean was saying. He laughed gently and kissed her on the head paternally.

"I've said it before, but I'll say it again. You're quite a woman, Shaunna, and needing support is not a sign of weakness."

"I'm trying."

"You're doing grand. So, this college course you've enrolled on?"

"Open University. Psychology."

He laughed again. "Thought so. You're a natural. And a beautiful one at that."

She smiled at the compliment and got up in readiness to go and face Jess. "I'll also try not to cry all over your shirt next time," she said.

"Oh, I don't mind the wet shirt so much, but if you can try not to rip out half my chest hair that would be fantastic."

"Oops!" She blushed. "Sorry."

"I'm tormenting. Are you ready?"

She nodded and followed him inside.

*****

"Couscous? At a logistics and haulage institute dinner?" Dan pushed it around with his fork and grimaced.

"You like couscous," Adele said.

"Do I? I don't ever remember seeing the stuff before."

"So how did you know what it was?"

"Jamie Oliver. In fact, this is *exactly* the sort of truckie dinner he'd come up with. Your traditional meat and two veg, but let's dispense with the spuds and gravy and have a nice bit of Moroccan spiced crap and a fruit sauce instead. I mean, what the hell is that?"

"It's called jus, bro," Andy told him with a grin.

For all his complaining, Dan was still eating it, although he did have a point. The chefs had clearly gone for variations on the theme of transport café staples, with their starter of poached eggs on French toast, the braised beef main course, and for dessert, pancakes, or 'crêpes', with cherries and crème fraîche, perhaps to cater for the international nominees, even if their representatives were all typical British lorry driver types. On the plus side, the after-dinner coffee was excellent, and the complementary wine was going down a treat.

And so to the awards. This was no BAFTA ceremony, that was for sure. There were eight awards in all, and Jeffries and Associates had been nominated for two: 'Supply Chain Best

Practice' and 'Information Management', although they'd only made the shortlist for the former, and the closer they edged to the announcement of that award, the more their hopes dwindled, as nearly all of the other finalists were big names in the transport industry.

"How about, 'Jeffries and Associates, finalists for…'?" Andy suggested. They'd spent the interval playing the game of how best to utilise their failure, and the supply chain award was next.

"I doubt the people we deal with give a shit anyway, bro," Dan asserted. He'd had a little too much to drink, spurred on by his confusion as regards Adele's mixed news.

"Thanks, Dan!" Charlotte said, disgruntled by his seeming ingratitude for her efforts. Of course, she knew he was wrong. People *were* influenced by phrases like 'industry leaders', or 'winners of the award for…', but she also knew he was downplaying what he saw as their likely 'failure' because she was just the same herself. Victory was a clear win; top of the league; taking the cup home. Everything else was defeat.

The man announcing the awards was now back at the podium, tapping at the microphone and making the speakers feed back. He cleared his throat, and a hush gradually fell over the room. He was a big, surly bloke with a broad London accent, and looked and sounded like he'd spent a few years too many on the road, smoking forty a day and sampling the 'finest' transport café breakfasts in the land.

"Before we crack on, I'd like to thank your good selves for the exceptional turnout, as always. It's fantastic to see so many of the old faces here, and a few new ones besides. Accordingly, we move on now to the award for Best Practice in Supply Chain Management, where we have three companies all new to these awards. I'd like to ask Cyril Johnson, founder and CEO of Johnson Logistics, PLC, to come and tell us about this award."

A round of applause sounded as the man in question made his way over to the podium.

"This award was introduced back in 1998, as a way of recognising the extraordinary achievements that companies were making, in light of rapid technological advances. The business of logistics has never been an easy one, and in many respects, technology has made it more complex, with greater customer control and fiercer competition. The most successful logistics firms are those with robust yet fluid, dynamic systems…"

"I reckon he must've had the same lecturer as me at uni," Dan whispered to Andy. "We all called him Pete, cos his surname was Stuyvesant. He used to chat all this bullshit."

Andy laughed quietly, and they both tuned back in again.

"…is far greater than getting the goods from A to B, and involves seeing the bigger picture, monitoring the flow throughout the chain and responding quickly to any potential blockages in that flow to ensure that the ultimate customer gets their goods in a timely and economically efficient manner. To this end, bigger is not always better, and our nominees tonight include two companies whose mottos could well be 'quality, not quantity'."

At this point, someone from a table across the room shouted out, "Never mind the quality," and one of his tablemates added, "Feel the width," to finish the line. The whole room broke into raucous laughter.

Dan and Andy exchanged glances. Now they were hoping they wouldn't win the award at all. It was beginning to feel like aiming for the speed boat and going away with a dart-toting toy bull.

The other finalists were a hospital trust and, as mentioned, a small company—though significantly bigger than they were—whose work consisted of providing ready meals to one of the largest pub chains in the UK. In both cases, the summary of their outstanding work in their respective fields made the Jeffries brothers feel like complete amateurs, that is, until Cyril read out the blurb for their company, as written by one Charlotte Davenport on the initial nomination form. Until now, they'd had no idea what it said.

"Our third finalists for this award are what we might call a bespoke logistics company, run by two brothers, between them almost forty years' experience in the fields of technological innovation and construction."

"I never thought of it like that," Andy whispered.

"And it is this expertise that has given them extraordinary insight and great clarity when it comes to seeing that bigger picture. To give detailed examples of the kind of work they undertake would, quite frankly, take more time than we have this evening. Suffice to say, that from shifting catering ovens from the USA to charities working in remote villages in the mountains of Nepal, to delivering thousands of tons of steel components to top English football stadia, never mind shipping the fibre optic infrastructure for an entire Dubai complex from the UK in very difficult circumstances, Jeffries and Associates are the go-to guys for those seemingly impossible jobs, big and small."

"Blimey, Charlotte. We sound bloody amazing," Dan said.

"Because you are bloody amazing," she told him.

"And the winner of the award for Best Practice in Supply Chain Management is…"

They'd realised during the course of the evening that the haulage and logistics business, however unglamorous, still liked to build a little suspense into their awards proceedings, so the pause was mandatory, and there was no predicting which way it would go. Any one of the three companies could rightfully get the award, and because Dan and Andy had gone through wanting it and being convinced they didn't stand a chance, to not wanting it because it seemed a bit of a booby prize, back to wanting it again, they almost didn't care one way or the other by this point. Good old Cyril Johnson was really milking it, and people were starting to fidget.

"…is Jeffries and Associates."

The room filled with applause. Dan and Andy looked at each other, so completely shocked that it took quite a bit of prompting and prodding from Adele and Charlotte before they mustered the wherewithal to get out of their seats and collect their award. In a daze of applause, they walked across to the podium, Andy slightly in front of Dan, who now realised once again they had both opted for the same style of smart yet casual evening wear. He tapped his brother on the shoulder and said, "I'm gonna knock out the first person who says it."

***

"I'm so sorry, Jess." Shaunna slowly edged her way around the bed to get to her friend. Both of them were crying inconsolably.

214

Jess reached up, and Shaunna went into her arms. "I am so, so sorry."

"Don't be. You were totally right. I was being a selfish cow, and it should be me apologising to you, not the other way around."

"With what you're going through, you've got every right to be selfish."

"No, I haven't." Jess withdrew and wiped her eyes, waiting for Shaunna to sit down.

Sean was standing just the other side of the door, listening, all set to intervene if necessary, but he could tell already that he wouldn't be needed. Still, he stayed.

Jess took Shaunna's hand and massaged it lovingly. "What a wonderful friend you are. How could I have not known this until now, when it's too late?"

"It's not too late."

"But we could've had so much fun together."

"Jess, we *have* had so much fun together, and I'm not talking to a ghost, am I?"

Jess laughed ruefully and shook her head. "No. Not yet."

"So please don't feel bad. That was just a bit of a tiff this afternoon. Today's a crappy day. Tomorrow will be better."

"Yeah, I know. It's always a bit of a toughy to get through, but…" Jess paused and held her breath, waiting for the wave of pain to pass.

Shaunna frowned. "That shouldn't happen." She picked up the syringe driver and examined it. The 'error' light was illuminated. "I'll give the nurse a call. Won't be long." She got as far as the door.

"I'll do it," Sean offered. He went downstairs to make the call.

Shaunna returned to Jess's side. "OK?"

Jess smiled and took her hand again. She was absolutely exhausted; mentally, physically, mortally.

"I'm glad you're here tonight," she said.

"Me, too. Can I get you anything?"

Jess shook her head, fighting to keep her eyes open, in spite of the pain. "Just stay with me?"

"Of course."

"Sean sent Mum home, told her to go and spend some time with Dad. He's doing so much overtime at the moment, to cover her salary. They need a break. At their age, they should be slowing down. It's just not fair."

Shaunna shrugged. "Being a mum doesn't stop because your kids hit twenty-one."

"But it should get easier."

"Yeah, right!" They both laughed, but then became quiet again as they individually reminisced. It was coming up to three years since Krissi turned twenty-one, and Jess called to mind a conversation she'd had with Josh around that time, about feeling stuck in a rut and not moving forward. *Careful what you wish for.*

"How's Krissi doing?" she asked. "I haven't seen her in a while."

"She's doing really well. Busy, with the restaurant and helping Jason out, but she's loving every minute."

"You must be so proud."

"Yeah, I am. Although I'm not happy that she hasn't been to see you."

"She's a career girl. That's what we do."

"Even so, family and friends come first. I'll be having words."

"Don't be too hard on her."

They heard voices downstairs. Shortly after, the district nurse walked into the room.

"OK, Jess?" she asked. Jess shifted herself up the bed and nodded, trying to hide how much pain she was in. The nurse came over and picked up the syringe driver. "Didn't the alarm go off?"

"Yeah, this morning."

"You should've called me straight away. No wonder you're struggling. Right. Let's get that sorted for you."

Shaunna got up from the bed, but Jess's eyes implored her to stay, so she stood in the corner of the room, keeping out of the way.

The nurse reset the syringe driver and checked everything was working correctly again. "I'm going to give you a boost, to tide you over the next few hours, all right, my darling?"

"Thanks." Jess rolled onto her side, and the nurse gave her a diamorphine injection.

"There you go. All done. I think we need to review where we're up to, Jess, so I'll be back tomorrow morning."

"OK. Sorry for bothering you."

"Don't you worry about it." The nurse smiled and turned to Shaunna. "If the alarm goes off, make sure you call straight away."

"Will do."

"Good. See you tomorrow."

Sean saw the nurse out, and Shaunna listened to their brief conversation at the door. So, Jess hadn't been selfish at all. She'd been without pain relief all day, knowing it would have stopped Andy from going to London and caused her mum further upset if she'd said anything. Sean brought them cups of tea. Shaunna smiled at him in thanks. He winked back and left again. The injection was taking effect, and Jess was starting to drift a little. She sipped clumsily at the tea and passed the cup back to Shaunna.

"All my life my parents have done everything to encourage me to be the best I can be," she said, her words slurred, but the morphine was making her talkative. "My degree cost them a fortune. They used all of their savings to pay for it, and I was so excited that I was going to university. I don't even remember saying thank you. When I graduated, I promised I'd repay them, make sure they never went without, look after them in their old age." She smiled. "My dad said, 'Well what d'you think we did it for?' and we went on the best holiday to Mauritius, just the three of us, to celebrate.

"My mum—you know, sometimes I catch her staring off into space, and she doesn't know I'm watching her, and I can see it and feel it. That sadness, that Daisy-shaped hole in her life. When I was about fourteen, maybe fifteen, we had a massive row—nothing serious really, not in the grand scheme of things, but spiteful and hurtful, because I was a teenager, and, well, I'm me, and sometimes I can be so horrible—and I was screaming at her that she didn't care about me, that all she cared about was her dead baby. *Her dead baby*. What a total bitch I am.

"When I told Ellie, she said, 'If I'd said that to my mum, she'd have kicked me into orbit, and then some.' But d'you know what my mum did? She took me shopping. We spent a whole day wandering around posh shops, went for lunch in a trendy restaurant and got the train home, laughing at other passengers with their grumpy work faces, sneezing because we were covered in all those stinky perfumes they used to get you with in department stores, feeling fat because we'd eaten too much. We had the best day, the best time, and when we got home, my dad just made his own tea and sat there eating it on his own, smiling at us like a total loon, because all he ever wants is for us to be happy, and we were. Just for a few hours.

"And not once have they taken out their grief on me, or made comparisons between my successes, my failures, and what Daisy might have been. Not even once. All that poison that poured out of my mouth earlier was the stuff I created in my head—my own grief." She closed her eyes and gulped, trying to swallow the tears. "My own guilt, because I've failed them, Shaunna. They lost their daughter, and I'm about to take away their other one."

Now the drug was fully working, Jess could barely lift her arms, and from her current position, sitting on the edge of the bed, Shaunna couldn't get any closer. She walked around to the other side and lay down beside Jess, wiping her tears and gently rubbing her hand. She felt something vibrate against her leg and glanced down. It was Jess's phone. She picked it up and unlocked the screen: a text message.

"What is it?" Jess asked, so drowsy she was almost unconscious.

"Text from Andy. You want me to read it?"

"Please."

Shaunna opened the message and smiled. "They won."

"Oh, wow. Tell him…" Pain-free for the first time in more than twelve hours, Jess drifted off to sleep.

Shaunna typed, "Congratulations. All OK here. x." She hit the send button, and then slowly withdrew her hand and left the room before she tumbled, headfirst, into the Jess-shaped hole.

Mistakes Like These
Sunday 20th August

Sean was there to greet them, as promised, on their arrival at the hospice, even though he didn't work Sundays, but he knew how important it was for Jess to see a friendly face.

Although she was feeling very weak and unwell, she faked a smile in an attempt to conceal her anxiety from the others. Both Andy and Shaunna had come with her, the latter at Jess's insistence. She was the one keeping her afloat.

"OK, Jessie," Sean smiled, "I'm not sure who it'll be, but someone will come and get you booked in soon. I'll take you to your room. It's got a fantastic view of the woodland, and it's lovely and quiet."

Sean continued his gentle chatter as they made their way through the reception area and along to the short-stay wing.

Shaunna looked around her in wonder, taking in the ambience created by the pale, sunlit walls, the multitude of leafy plants and gentle watercolour prints, lending a calmness to the place that would have made caring for her mum all those years ago so much easier to cope with. But then, she, too, had wanted to stay at home, the difference being that her carers were tied by blood and marriage, as well as love.

The room resembled a good hotel room, with little in the way of overtly medical equipment. There was a generous single bed, topped by a thick mattress and light, plush bedding. There was also an en-suite bathroom, TV with the full complement of digital channels, and a phone. The view Sean had mentioned was a stunning vista, visible through a floor-to-ceiling seated bay window, plain net curtains turning it slightly opaque as they billowed in the gentle breeze. Jess shivered.

"Let me shut that for you." Sean reached up and pulled the vent to a close. He turned back and indicated the armchair—the sort one might find in a living room, rather than the standard hospital wing chair. "Make yourself at home," he invited.

Andy and Shaunna stood near the door, watching Jess struggle out of the wheelchair independently and ease herself into the soft armchair. She was trying to maintain a sense of the everyday, even though all three of them were acutely aware of their surroundings and what her decision to stay here meant, albeit for respite only. Her mum and dad were going away for a few days, before their marriage fell to pieces around the imminent demise of their only surviving daughter.

They hadn't said as much, but Sean knew. It was his job to know, or rather, it shouldn't have been his job, because he should have told the district nurse that he was personally acquainted with Jess, which would have seen her case being passed to another member of the palliative care team, and that really couldn't happen. Put simply—and this was no display of the usual Tierney arrogance— if he hadn't been on the team, Jess would have fought them to the end, but he could talk her round better than almost anyone.

Now to the matter of her two friends, still loitering at the portal, ensnared in the hospice limbo field.

"Once you're a little more settled, Jessie, I'll show Andy and Shaunna the visitors' suite for future reference. What d'you say?" He was really asking for permission to be excused, on their behalf.

"Sure," she said vacantly, but somehow clicked back with their reality again. "Yes, sorry. Of course, you both need a rest. Go and have a cup of tea or something. I'm OK." She smiled at them. Andy didn't look too sure. "Go," she told him.

"We'll come back in a little while," Shaunna said.

Sean nodded to Jess and escorted them to the visitors' suite: three connecting rooms, with a small kitchen, shower room and lounge area, and access to a balcony.

"This isn't at all what I expected." Shaunna glanced out of the French doors. The balcony overlooked the grounds, where there was a Monet inspired wooden arched bridge crossing a pond, the large white and gold fish within it visible from her location. Beyond that was an expanse of smooth lawn, edged by well-maintained borders; further on again was the woodland that wrapped around two sides of the hospice. She turned back, glancing at Andy, shattered and collapsed into a sofa, and made eye contact with Sean. He gave her the slightest of winks and a smile.

"It's a beautiful place. Lovely to work in, too. The café should still be open for another half hour or so, but if you need anything, just ask me, OK? I've got coffee and tea in my office, and if you want to head out for a while, that's no problem. I'm going to stay with Jess today, give you a break. How does that sound?"

"Wonderful. Thanks, Sean," Shaunna said.

Andy had his eyes shut, his head resting on his hand. He nodded. "Yeah, thanks, mate."

Shaunna and Sean exchanged looks.

"All right, then. I'll see you both later." Sean left.

Shaunna opened the door onto the balcony. The fresh air was very welcome; even though the hospice was light and airy, there was still something about these kinds of places—hospitals, schools, dentists—that somehow seemed to drain the oxygen away. She stepped outside and inhaled deeply. *How long? How much more to endure?*

She thought back to her mum's last few months, when she had wondered if it would help to have an exact timescale to work to, a lot like being in labour. The pain was truly too much to take, but having some sense of when it would end somehow made it more bearable, and in many respects, waiting for the beginning of a life was no different to waiting for the end, not that she had been aware of that when she was expecting Krissi.

The person she was, at fifteen, ceased to exist the moment that tiny baby entered the world. She was a new person, a mother, a grown-up. What had once been so important to her—going out with friends, buying clothes, listening to music—became inconsequential, replaced by trying to get enough sleep, buying nappies and baby clothes, remembering to register for preschool, tracing fingers across reading books, signing homework diaries, washing PE kits, enforcing revision regimes, fixing scuffed knees and broken hearts—the never-ending round of duties and joys of motherhood. RIP, Shaunna Hennessy. Welcome, Krissi's mum.

But then, knowing when it would end could be so stressful, for there was an urgency to everything that must be done. In her mum's final days, she'd checked through her will, life insurance policies and so on, to make sure they were in order, and tried to do things that she insisted she'd always wanted to do yet never got around to. Shaunna spent hours calling old friends, giving the same speech over and over again, of how her mum had been asking to see them, often having to tell them bluntly: *the end is nigh, so you'd better get your skates on.*

The prospect of having to do that again, for Jess, was not one Shaunna relished, but like everything she had done so far, she would, if she had to, because she was strong. She'd lost her mum, her true best friend, and nothing hurt more. Well, there was one thing, and as the thought filled her mind, uninvited and stubbornly refusing to be overridden by any other thing she could imagine, she fell to her knees and succumbed yet again to the deep well of grief.

She couldn't hear him. She was too far gone, and his pleas for her to get up fizzled away into the deafening bubble of peace surrounding that place. He knelt behind her, his arms around her shoulders, his lips nestled gently in her hair as she grasped at his arms, trying to still the quaking, so delicate, so fragile. He could fight this no longer. He needed her, and she needed him, if only for this moment, and it gave him strength.

They stayed that way long enough for his feet to have numbed, and he tried to shift his weight, toppling backwards as he did so. She fell with him, and they sprawled on the deck, suddenly laughing at their dreadful predicament.

"The café will have shut now," he said.

"What do you want to do?"

"Go somewhere and talk."

She glanced past him, into the visitors' lounge, where they had company, of sorts. "We could go and find a pub or something?"

He nodded his agreement, and they helped each other up from the floor, continuing to hold on. He used the momentum of the upwards thrust to draw her in so close that his stubble rasped against her cheek as she lifted her face to his.

"Andy, I—"

"I know." He swallowed and shook his head. "I can't fight it."

Sean's voice, some distance away, but coming closer, spoke kind words to those he passed on his journey through. Andy backed off.

"You two are still here?" Sean said, appearing alongside them.

"Yeah," Shaunna confirmed unnecessarily. "We're just going to head out now, find somewhere to get a bite to eat, I think."

"All right. Jessie's settled well. The doctor's written her up for antidepressants. In fact, why don't you come and see her now before you go? It'll give you some peace of mind, and then you can leave for real."

They followed Sean back to Jess's room, where she was lying in the bed, looking very comfortable in amongst the downy duvet and well-placed pillows. She was watching TV when they came in—something she'd been unable to do for a few weeks, finding it impossible to concentrate or stay in one place for long enough. She muted the sound and smiled at them.

"Hi."

"Hiya, hun. You look like the queen of the castle."

"I feel like the queen of the castle. This pressure mattress is bloody wonderful, I can tell you." She patted the bed, and they heard air escaping, a motor whirring gently and keeping the mattress inflated to the optimum level. "I thought you'd both gone home."

"We're going now," Andy said. "Just wanted to make sure you hadn't changed your mind about staying."

"No fear of that!" She held out her hands for them to take, and they did so. "Thank you." She looked from one to the other and smiled. There was no need to say anything more; they both understood implicitly. Shaunna broke free and gave her a hug.

"See you tomorrow. Have a good night."

"I will. You, too."

Shaunna stepped back and watched Andy lean down to Jess, tenderly kissing her cheek and rubbing his nose against hers. They held eye contact for several seconds, and Jess nodded and smiled.

"Time to prepare for your next big adventure."

He smiled back. "Maybe. I'll see you tomorrow." He kissed her again and turned to Shaunna. "Ready?"

She followed him to the door. "Are we still on for lunch, Sean?" she called.

"Absolutely. I'll get the milkshakes in," he said with a grin. He saw them out. "OK—" he turned back to Jess, sitting himself in the armchair "—what load of old nonsense are we watching here?"

***

The nearest pub was only a short walk away, but Andy felt it would be taking liberties to leave the car where it was, even though it probably would have been safer than the pub car park, which was so vast that the walk back was longer than if they had left the Mustang at the hospice. He took hold of Shaunna's hand. She tried not to smile.

"What's funny?" he asked.

"I'm your next big adventure?"

He felt his cheeks start to burn.

"So this…" She lifted their hands. "It's with Jess's blessing?"

"I s'pose that's one way of putting it."

They reached the pub and broke apart to order drinks and find a quiet place to sit, right next to each other, not even tissue-paper space between them. Andy laced his fingers through hers and rubbed her thumb with his.

"So, what, then?" she asked.

"What then what?"

"You said that's one way of putting it. Does Jess know?"

"I haven't told her, if that's what you mean."

"But she knows how you feel?"

"About you?"

"Yeah." Shaunna shifted slightly so she could look at him. "Is this a good idea? Our lives are so complicated already."

"Are you saying you don't want to?"

"No, not at all. I want to." Now she blushed. "I *really* want to, but—damn, this is so much harder when we're sober."

Andy laughed. "You can say that again." He picked up his drink, intermittently sipping and taking slow, deep breaths, each slightly less shaky than the last, as he fought and won over the urge to suggest they went somewhere more private, knowing that they'd likely get no further than the back seat of the Mustang.

"We'll get busted in that car," she said, as if she had read his mind exactly.

"Sorry?"

"The pap. They're still tailing Kris, and if they see his 'secret wife' getting into a Mustang with a sexy hunk, they'll bust us before we even get up to any shenanigans. I'm surprised we're not in *Heat* magazine already."

"A sexy hunk, huh?"

"Don't fish." She returned to her original position and leaned her head on his shoulder. "So we'll have to be careful."

Andy shook his head and laughed quietly. "I can't believe we're having this conversation."

"Why?"

"Planning an affair. It's a bit—"

"Mad?" she suggested.

"And dangerous."

"OK. What are the options?"

"We don't do it."

"Can you handle that?"

"If I never, ever, *ever* see you again."

"So that's out of the question. And if we don't plan it, you know what'll happen, don't you?"

"I'm having quite a lot of fun imagining, actually." Andy grinned.

"Hmm." Shaunna dug her fingernails into the back of his hand.

"Ouch!"

"Look, I know it somewhat ruins the spontaneity of the whole thing, but we can't risk snatching moments in the backs of cars, or up against walls in dark alleys."

"Fun killer."

"In case you've forgotten, which is highly unlikely, my husband already tried to kill you once."

"Fair comment."

"Of course, there is one other alternative." She paused, waiting for him to say something. In turn, he was waiting for her to continue. "We get Kris's blessing first."

She felt his grip tighten around her hand. It was an unconscious response.

"You don't like that idea?"

"It's too fucking weird."

"It's not really. He can't stay faithful, so it would be a bit unfair of him to expect it from me."

"Yeah, but…" Andy sighed and shook his head. "I'm sorry, Shaunna, I can't do it."

"But you can if it's a secret? Why? Because it's exciting?"

"No, that's not it at all." Andy pulled his hand free and rubbed his temples. "I know whichever way this happens, I'm sharing you with Kris, and I don't like it, if I'm honest, but I want you so badly." He closed his eyes and breathed out slowly. "I'll just have to find a way to get my head around it. But telling him feels a bit like…" He paused again, because he sort of wanted to laugh. "It feels like swinging."

Shaunna managed to hold back her own laughter for all of five seconds before it burst from her, and Andy couldn't help but join in.

"Swinging? Oh my word!"

"D'you know what I mean?"

"Yeah, I do. I guess sharing the house with Kris and Ade for so long, I've kind of adjusted my understanding of 'normal'."

"But you weren't having, err, marital relations then, were you?"

"No. And we still aren't."

"OK, now I'm confused. Are you back together?"

"Yes, sort of. We're still working it out."

226

Andy frowned. He took her hand again and examined her ring finger, still bearing the faint impression of her wedding band, even though he'd noticed its absence almost a year ago, when they were in Wales. She sensed he was waiting to say something and turned towards him, granting him permission. He took it.

"Can I ask a personal question?"

"Go on."

"Can he actually, you know—get it up for you?"

"Whoa. That really is personal." Shaunna was taken aback.

"I'm just curious," Andy said. "The thing is, well, you know me, I'll try anything once, and there was this guy in New York picked me up."

"You? Really?"

"Yeah, cheers for that!"

Shaunna laughed at his faked modesty. "What I mean is you scream 'straight'."

"But I was in a gay bar at the time. Anyway, I went back to his apartment."

"Right?"

"You can work out the rest, can't you?"

"Yeah, but…" Shaunna smiled and bit her lip.

"No way does this turn you on!"

She looked away across the pub.

"So that's why you didn't have a problem with Kris and Ade?"

"Err, no. That's not the same. They're gay. Well, Ade's gay."

"But a straight guy getting it on with another guy?"

"Hell, yeah!"

"OK. I'll remember that next time I get an ear-bashing for saying girl-on-girl action is hot."

"So, you went back to his apartment?"

"Yeah. And guys know what guys like, so it was good, you know?"

"Good as in?"

"Oh, Shaunna, Shaunna, Shaunna." He shook his head in mock dismay.

"Oh, Andy, Andy, Andy. Just tell me, goddamnit."

He laughed. "We had an awesome night," he said.

227

"Did you…" She whispered in his ear. He nodded. "Oh really? And did you…" She whispered again.

"Twice."

"No way! And did you let him…" She whispered one last thing.

"Ah, now that was the point of my story. No. And he suggested that I erm, well…"

"Top him."

"Ahem. Yeah." Andy picked up his drink, embarrassed.

"But you couldn't get it up for him."

"And he was a really good-looking guy."

"Yes," she said. "In answer to your question. He can."

"Right. OK."

"Because he's bisexual, and you're not."

"Yeah, got that."

"Would you do it again? With a guy?"

"Probably not. As I say, I'll try anything once. Sometimes twice, just to make sure, but I'm pretty sure on that one."

"Which brings us back to us. Maybe we should have a think about it for a while."

"OK." Andy drank some more of his drink. "Thought about it. Still wanna do it."

"And where do you propose we go, smart ass?"

"American cars have pretty big seats."

"Andy."

"Or there's a nice secluded alley at the back of the pub."

"Andy!"

"I'm kidding!" She moved their hands into his lap and glanced up at him. "Yeah, the intention's there," he confirmed. "But as you say, we have to be careful. For now."

"Can you handle it?"

"The lust, maybe. The rest of it? I'll get back to you."

Milk, Genes And Kidney Beans
Monday 21st August

"Good afternoon, lovely."

Sean smiled as he approached. The milk bar was positively heaving, and Shaunna had been there an hour already, waiting for the trespassers to leave 'their' table and claiming it the second they did.

"Hi," she replied, attempting to return the smile.

He saw right through it. "I'll get us a drink. What are you on today?"

"This? It's fruit yoghurt crush."

"What flavour?"

"Dunno. Pink?"

Sean tutted.

She held up the glass to him. "What does it smell like?"

He attempted a sniff and shrugged. "No idea. I can never smell a thing. I'll ask at the counter. They'll know." He left her alone temporarily.

He returned with the drinks. "Cherry," he confirmed.

She nodded and took the glass from him. "Thanks." She sucked the straw. Pointless.

"You got here early. No work this morning?"

"Yeah. Well, supposedly, but actually not." She sighed; still no eye contact. "George and I were talking about this the other day. What is it with bosses around these parts?"

"Why?"

"This morning. I tried to resign, and Hayley looked at me like I was talking in Japanese."

"You resigned from your job?"

"No. That's just it. She wouldn't bloody well let me. She said—" Shaunna affected a gushy voice and fluttered her eyelashes, all part of her impersonation of her boss "—'You take some time off, sweedie, have a good think, and we'll have a nice liddle chaddy-chad soon. OK? OK? Ba-bye now.' And then she turned her back on me and carried on sticking Agnes's rollers in, acting like I wasn't even there, chattering on about Marvin's bloody gallstones!"

"Marvin?"

"Her husband. He's repulsive. He comes into the salon with flowers and 'choc-chocs' and they get all kissy and ugh!"

Sean started to laugh, which prompted Shaunna to continue, because this was the lighter end of the spectrum of her day.

"And he has to bend to reach her over his belly. The size of her, too. She's only like a size eight or something, and her neck's starting to look like a turkey's. I tell you, if they ever outlaw sunbeds, she's going to die of withdrawal."

"She sounds great fun."

"Oh, she's a real sweedie!" Shaunna rolled her eyes, but smiled nonetheless. "She actually is very good to me, but George had the exact same problem when he tried to leave so Jake could get someone to replace him at the farm. Jake was having none of it."

"They obviously both know when they're on to a good thing."

"Yeah, maybe."

"So. Why were you resigning?"

"Because I'm about to run out of holidays, and when Jess goes back home, she'll need a lot more care."

"The hospice-at-home service will be going in during the day."

"And then there's college."

"It's part-time, distance learning."

"Mine is, but Adele's isn't, plus we didn't get to do the whole student thing when we were younger."

"I understand."

"I don't."

Sean raised an eyebrow. Shaunna tried her drink again. A cherry got stuck on the scoop end of the straw. She extracted it and sucked the cherry free.

"I chose that course so I could stay on at the salon."

"Do you want to?"

"Yes." She chewed the cherry and shook her head.

"No," Sean confirmed for her.

"But it's the only normal thing in my life. I went to see my dad before work, and we had the same conversation three times in the space of five minutes. 'Can you pop in some shower gel on your way home, love?' 'Yes, Dad, but you don't need any. You've got two full bottles, look.' 'Oh, so I have. Never mind.' 'See you later, Dad.' 'Have a good day, love. Can you pop in some shower gel on your way home?' Agh!"

"Oh. That's tough."

Shaunna made fleeting eye contact—the first since Sean had arrived—and then studied the ceiling for a few seconds. She closed her eyes, breathing in and out, slowly and heavily. "I'm OK," she said.

Sean picked up his drink and scooped at the fruit, covertly watching her try to keep it together.

"I'm OK," she repeated, her voice squeaking slightly with the pressure of holding back the tears. "Damn it." She covered her eyes with her hand.

Sean put his drink down and reached across the table, resting his hand on her arm. "You're not," he said gently, "and that's OK."

She gulped a couple of times and covered it with a laugh. "No way am I going to break down in Milky's. I'd be so ashamed."

"Do you want to go somewhere we can talk?"

"That's what he said."

Sean ignored that, because her posture dictated it, but he understood it was a confession of sorts. Quite a dilemma, too. "I was going to propose the university, although we'll most likely bump into Josh."

"No, thanks."

"Or we could try the hospice."

Shaunna shook her head. "Ellie's visiting this afternoon."

"And Soph's at mine. I'd suggest your place, but I was trying to come up with somewhere neutral."

"Milky's has gone into profit, Krissi was telling me."

"Ah."

"And the studio is fully booked through to the end of September."

It was, he supposed, somewhere neutral. All right, so she wanted distraction. He could go with that for now.

"That's good news," he said. "And the offer still stands."

She smiled in thanks. "Jason's got a new guy working at the studio."

Interesting she should mention that. If they'd been playing the avoidance game by his rules rather than hers, he'd have been telling her the exact same news, except his take on it was a little less celebratory, more laced with unsolved mystery, but he let her continue with her side of the story.

"He's called Hadyn, and he's about their age. He and Jason get on brilliantly, Krissi said. They're like two peas in a pod."

"That's great to hear."

"Yeah. It's keeping them all busy, but as I said to Krissi on Saturday, she needs to watch that it doesn't take over. She hasn't been to see Jess in a while, and—"

The rest of the sentence lingered between them, unsaid, unspeakable. *Time is running out.*

"Have you met Hadyn?" Sean asked.

"In passing. He seems nice enough. A bit odd, but so is Jason."

"In what way?"

"A little too intense, fussy. He's a hell of a lot like Alice, actually."

"Are we talking about Jason here?"

"Yeah. Sorry. My brain's flitting about all over the place today."

"No need to apologise. You've a lot on your mind."

"Always," Shaunna said dolefully. She'd pulled herself together again, but couldn't handle a return to the previous trajectory of their conversation.

Reading her as accurately as ever, Sean continued with the current theme. "I read a research report a while back into the genetic link between synaesthesia and epilepsy."

232

"What did it say?"

"Not to get too technical, the same chromosomal regions are involved in both, and the brain pathways are denser, thus potentially overactive in synaesthetes."

"'Not to get too technical,' he says and then bamboozles me."

"OK. You know that messages are passed around the brain via electrical impulses?"

"I do now."

"They're orderly, following set pathways."

"OK."

"Now, if you think of an epileptic seizure as being like a lightning storm, with lightning strikes hitting randomly—"

"And it overloads the power grid."

"A very useful analogy."

"I think I see. So, in synaesthesia, the pathways get mixed up. Like with Alice seeing smells instead of smelling them?"

"Precisely."

"Cool. I get that."

"We'll make a neuroscientist of you yet."

"A scientist?"

"What is psychology if not a science?"

"That's one of the things on the course topic list. But anyway, you're saying that Alice's synaesthesia and Jason's epilepsy are caused by the same genetic thingy?"

"Possibly. You have to watch out for them, you know, those genetic thingies. Very tricky, they are." Sean winked at her, and she smiled.

"Speaking of genetic thingies, I had the weirdest conversation with Andy yesterday."

"About Krissi?"

"No, Kris." Shaunna blushed just thinking about it, and she certainly wasn't going to be setting it fully in context. "He asked me if Kris was sexually aroused by me."

"Why is that weird?"

"It's what followed it. Andy spent the night with a man and said he enjoyed it but wouldn't do it again. How on earth can he say that if he's just confessed to enjoying sex with a man?"

"I see what you mean, but try looking at it a different way. Are there any foods you really hate?"

"Chilli con carne."

"How d'you know you hate it?"

"Because I tried it once. It was the kidney beans that put me off. They're vile."

"Did you eat it?"

"Most of it. It was quite tasty, apart from the kidney beans, but I wouldn't choose to eat it again. Oh. I kind of get what you mean, but Kris has had years of people not believing he's bisexual, telling him he's a coward for not coming out as gay, or to stop being greedy, like it's his choice to be that way and either he's trying to blend in or double the pleasure possibilities, but it's double the pain. He loves me, and wants to be with me, but I will never be enough."

"Are you worried Andy's bi as well?"

"No." She answered too quickly and grabbed her drink. It was completely melted and getting the cherries to stay on the scoop was proving difficult, but she couldn't risk making eye contact again. Not with Sean.

"My mum's bisexual," he said.

She nodded into her drink, shocked by his revelation and aware that he was only telling her to let her off the hook.

"She's more your serial monogamist, though. She left Dad for Aunty Aileen, then left Aunty Aileen for Cian, and now she's with Dermot the Dreary."

"Dermot the Dreary?"

"Yeah. He's one of those droning miserable feckers who complain about everything. Feckin' sun's too bright, too hot, rain's too feckin' wet, my tea needs more feckin' sugar, oh, now I'm going to get feckin' diabetes and feckin' die."

Shaunna laughed, although Sean was looking serious and thoughtful. He stayed quiet for a while afterwards, trying to fish the strawberries from the bottom of his glass. They were very lively.

"What are you thinking about?" she asked.

"What I said all along. Honesty is a good thing in a relationship. Like the whole Kris and Ade situation. What actually went wrong?"

"Ade wanted children."

"No. That's where it ended. Where it began was that you and Kris still wanted to be together, but Kris also wanted to be with Ade."

Shaunna started playing with her hair.

"And you still haven't talked about it properly, because you keep telling yourselves it's morally reprehensible. But is it really? We get all caught up on this monogamy nonsense, and why? Take children out of the equation, and it serves no purpose whatsoever, although I, personally, am quite satisfied with only one woman in my life. In fact, just now that's one too many."

"Which is why you're looking after Jess and me, and obsessing over Alice and Jason."

"That's a little harsh, but it's the truth, I must admit. I should be doting on Soph. However, me and my thrice daily threatened testicles are more than delighted George is her birth partner. If we're lucky, we might just see out the week together. Me and the boys, that is, not me and Soph."

"Do you think you'll get things sorted? You and Soph, I mean, not you and err…" She nodded in the general direction of Sean's 'boys'. He laughed.

"I'm hopeful we will, but I have no idea how I feel about the baby, or how it will affect 'us', and I won't know until it's here, so it's pointless to speculate or try to make any arrangements before then. Still, we have at least established an honest dialogue, and I can wholly recommend it. I'm not saying it's easy. Far from it. Lying is much easier, but it saves a lot of heartache in the long run."

"Oh, such wisdom!"

"Quite, although I'm not about to ruin my plagiarism-free career and claim it as my own. You need look no further than the Sandison-Morleys. Their lies rode them to hell and back, and once again you have made me say too much, but while we're trundling along in the honesty wagon, for the record, I don't think they're Andy's thing, either."

"Huh?"

"Kidney beans."

VIRGO

Mysterious symbol, words are all in vain
To tell the secret power by which you reign.
The more we love, the less we can explain.

Crying In The Rain
Wednesday 23rd August

Stuffy, hot underground station, people marching past, rain-soaked clothes, the stench of damp. Kris crammed himself inside the carriage along with the rush hour commuters. He was used to trains, but what a luxury their trains back home were by comparison; not that his work had ever required him to travel in rush hour. He could have avoided it now, if he'd thought ahead, instead of agreeing to Ade's suggestion that they meet at five in King's Cross. A couple of hours would have made little difference.

The place they were meeting was a bar of the stars. Upstairs was the public room, an upmarket yet typical wine bar, with black leather high stools and too much steel. It was cold and clinical and all about the wine, of which he knew nothing. Red, white, rosé, Champagne, and that Prosecco stuff Adele had taken to drinking when they went out anywhere as a foursome, which they didn't do anywhere near as much these days.

He missed it. Back before the separation, the four of them would have dinner at least once a month. It could be a lot of fun, particularly in the days when little Shaunna was just an occasional twinkle in Dan's eye. Some of those girlfriends, though... Adele could be ditzy, shallow, conceited, but underneath, she was one of the most lovely people Kris knew. She adored Shaunna—both of them, in fact—and he'd taken a few cuts from that tongue over the years, usually when she'd decided his behaviour towards grown-up Shaunna was unacceptable.

So, upstairs was the public wine bar. Downstairs was a basement that looked like a cave, extending into an old subway, arch-shaped with exposed stonework and dark secluded alcoves hewn from a boudoir and furnished with scarlet sofas. It was a place where famous people came to socialise—of hissed conversations and secret rendezvous, where journalists dared not tread. Watertight. What happened in here didn't 'leak' out, though it was at Ade's insistence that they were meeting here. Kris didn't care about the photographers, or the snooping journos. He had no secrets. Not anymore. The constant bombardment of headlines had seen to that...

Johansson – How I Raised Another Man's Child
My Nervous Breakdown Hell
Pissed Up and Pregnant At 14! Shaunna Johansson Tells All!

Except she didn't. They used to call the house, until the number was changed. They'd grab a few soundbites, lash them somewhere in the article to give it credibility in the face of legal challenge, move on and destroy someone else's life. No. No secrets. Well, just the one. The stabbing would never make it into the public domain.

"Kris! Fancy seeing you in here."

He glanced over in time to see the man heading his way. He recognised him, like he recognised them all—an actor from some show or another. He tried to place him, thinking quickly. *Nope.*

"Hi, there. How are you?" he asked, winging it.

"I'm great, thanks. You?"

"Very well, thank you for asking." *Still no idea.*

"You meeting someone, Kris?"

"Yeah." He was calling him Kris. If they didn't know him, they called him Kristian. "I'm meeting Ade."

"Ade who?"

"Simmons."

"Ah, yes...that's right." Now the stranger was winging it, too.

"Anyway, it's good to see you," Kris said. He smiled politely as he dodged past and went to the bar. Ade was standing at the other end. He hadn't seen him.

"What can I get you?"

"Lager, thanks."

"Pint?"

"Sure."

Kris turned his attention from the barman to Ade, watching him flicking his thumb across the screen of his phone, frowning at what was displayed. The frown turned to a smile and then a laugh. He typed something, glanced up and smiled for real. Kris paid for his drink and strolled over, casual. He was hoping to look casual.

"Hey," he said.

"Hey." Ade looked awkward. They were both tactile people, but their last encounter had made the insignificant significant. "How have you been?"

"Not too bad. You?"

"Same."

"Good, good." Kris glanced around him. "Shall we go and sit down?"

They found an unsullied alcove and slid into the sofa, one at each end and a great gaping canyon of history between.

"You're looking great." This was Kris.

"Thanks, so are you," came Ade's response. Protracted, artificial, how long would they play at this before one of them said why they had really agreed to meet?

"I saw Silhouetto were on the Pride ents lineup," Kris said.

"Yes. London, Manchester and Liverpool," Ade confirmed.

"That's fab."

"They're doing so well. We're all knackered, though. Been touring for nearly five months solid."

"That's hard going."

"And what about you? Are you filming season two now?"

"Yep. Started a couple of weeks back."

"I loved it."

"Did you?"

"You were wonderful."

"Thanks."

Drink drinks, adjust positions, check phones, sigh.

"I've missed you, Kris."

Nod.

"I keep waking up, thinking today will be the day I start feeling better."

"I've missed you, too."

"I met this guy the other week, at the studio where he works, and they had pictures of A-Ha on the walls, and I remembered Shaunna telling me how she thought you looked like Morten Harket, and I kept looking at those photos, thinking, yes, you do a bit."

Kris turned in his seat and crossed his ankle over his knee. "D'you think so, really?"

"A little, but personally? I'd choose you over Morten any day."

"Thanks. That's so nice of you to say."

"Your eyes are more blue than his, and your chin is more delicate, and…" Ade sighed. "I cried for days, Kris. I don't know why I asked you to meet me here. I should've just walked away, and kept walking."

"No."

Ade turned in his seat, crossed his ankle over his knee.

"No, Ade. I'm sorry. It was me, not you, and I do love you, but Shaunna—she and Krissi are my life. I don't exist outside of them. I needed to tell you, because we should be together, you and me. I *do* love you."

"But you love Shaunna more."

"I love Shaunna *too*."

"Is it a bi thing?"

"I thought you of all—"

"No, no, I didn't mean that." Ade laughed, part in nervousness, part because he was entertained by the notion that he was calling Kris greedy. He was hungry, not greedy. Hungry for attention, for success, and yes, for love. "Is it that she can't give you the one thing I can?"

"The love of a man?"

"The love of a man."

Kris moved closer, until their circumflex knees touched. The contact was for comfort only.

"Tell me about it," Ade said. "The difference. What is it?"

"There's something more honest, more natural, straightforward. With you, I don't have to think about whether I'm being too—manly, I guess. Or not manly enough. I am who I am. With Shaunna, there's always the difference. A woman and a man. And she is *everything* a woman can be. Beautiful, curvaceous, soft, feminine, maternal, emotional, sensitive, sensible, intelligent, beguiling. After we told everyone we'd separated, she grew. She had always been the same woman, but I constricted her, stopped her from fully being."

"But isn't that because you were together for so long? When I was with the ex, that was how I felt, like he was stopping me from being myself, and he apparently felt the same way, or else why did he go off with someone else?"

"Maybe." Kris considered. "The only comparison I can make is to my relationship with George."

"Relationship?"

"Friendship." Kris laughed. "Had you guessing there, did I?"

"Well, I saw those photos…"

"Yes, and they were very telling. I love George so much. He and Josh got married, did you know?"

"I saw online that his name had changed. That's sweet."

"They *are* sweet. It makes me sick."

"Oh don't be a bitch."

"I'm not! It makes me sick with jealousy, because it's easy for them. Now it is, anyway. They are totally in love. But I feel just the same with George. Other than his blatant refusal to accept that I'm bi, we are so honest, so open. Dog people."

Ade looked horrified. "Please tell me that has nothing to do with a very unsavoury practice with a similar name."

"God, no!"

"Phew."

They both laughed and moved closer. It was a strange old dance they were dancing.

"Would you like another drink, Ade?"

"Yes, I think I would."

Ade watched Kris all the way to the bar. He was still in love with *her*, so why had he come? No, that was too cruel a way to think, because he liked Shaunna. She had been an incredible friend, and sharing the house had been almost too perfect. They liked the same music, the same TV programmes and films, drank *way too much* tea. Then there was Casper. He missed him, too. And Krissi. And the thing was, he'd have shared Kris with Shaunna—with them all—if he'd been allowed to do that much.

Kris returned with their drinks.

"Thanks."

And the coolness. That was back also.

"So what was that dog people thing?"

"Oh. Josh said it. When we walked the dogs together the Saturday we got snapped, he picked up on how genuine dog owners are."

"Chicken or egg."

"What do you mean?"

"Do open, honest people choose dogs as pets, or do dogs make them that way?"

"I've no idea. I'm just an actor with no brains."

"I hope you're joking."

"I'm not. I love intelligent people, but I'm not one of them. Shaunna is. Josh is. George is, and you. Shaunna's going to uni in September, to study psychology."

"Is she?"

"She made friends with this psychologist guy. That's all she's gone on about ever since."

"And you're not bothered? That she's friends with a guy?"

"Nope. I trust her. If there was anything going on, she'd tell me."

"Are you sure about that?"

"Absolutely. But did you ask me here to talk about Shaunna all night?"

"Honestly, Kris, I don't care what we talk about, as long as you're here. Like I said, I've missed you."

"I'm sorry, Ade. You were right. I did push you away, and I kept you away from my friends."

"Yes, you did. I thought it was me, that I couldn't figure out what they wanted from me, if there was some kind of hazing I had to go through to be accepted."

"You only needed to be who you are. It was me who kept you out."

Maybe one day he'd be able to tell Ade why. *Honesty.* That's what Sean had told him. It was a good thing. So, should he come clean and ask Shaunna for what he really wanted? Or should he just settle for the same as before? The compromise that he couldn't keep. It was that or lose her, and he'd die if that happened.

"How are you at one-night stands?"

"Shit."

"Yeah. Me, too." *Stupid idea, Kris.*

"Was it still raining when you arrived?"

"I think so."

"Good."

"Why?"

"Because walking out of here without you will break my heart again."

"Then don't." *Stupid, stupid.*

"Will you tell her?"

"Tell her?"

"If we sleep together."

"Is that what you want?"

"Is that what *you* want?"

"I don't want to hurt you any more than I have done. If I could find a way to give us a chance, I'd take it, but not if it hurts you."

They slid together, the space diminishing to nothing in less than two seconds, falling into the great gaping canyon of history between. They kissed. It wasn't a hungry kiss. It bore nothing more than what it was: a moment shared by two people in love, with nothing and yet everything to lose.

"I've missed your lips." This was Kris.

"I've missed yours too," came Ade's response. Protracted, artificial, how long would they play at this before one of them said why they had really agreed to meet?

Labour Of Love
Thursday 24th August

"George."

"Sleeping."

"George. Your phone is ringing."

"It's not."

"It's muted."

George heard movement in the dark. The light shone through his eyelids, and he pulled the covers over his head.

"Hey, Sophie. Yes. He's already…OK, I'll—yes. Where are… All right. We'll be— Ten minutes, yes! Bye." Josh put the phone down and watched the blur of motion as George went tearing from the room. "Sophie's gone into labour," he shouted.

"I gathered." The toilet flushed, and George came racing back. "I didn't honestly think she'd give birth exactly on her due date. How likely is that?"

"About point zero four, although you need to factor in—"

"Joshua!"

He grinned. "She still might not. However, I now know why you get on so well. She'd give your mother a run for her money with that mouth."

George was trying to put his jeans on and stand at the same time. He staggered and fell against the bed.

"Take it easy!" Josh warned.

"No time."

"You'll set your leg off again."

"You said you'd drive."

"Yes."

"You gonna get dressed?"

"I'll go as I am."

"You're joking, right?"

247

"Did you want me to stay?"

"Well, I was kinda hoping…"

"Fine." Josh got out of bed. He stuck a shirt over his t-shirt, pulled on his socks, trousers and shoes and was waiting by the front door whilst George was still banging around upstairs. "What are you doing up there?"

"Trying to find the name book."

"Not your baby."

"Soph still hasn't decided."

"Use the internet."

More thuds back and forth along the landing.

"George!"

"All right!" He came downstairs, puffing, panting and flustered.

"Slow, deep breaths," Josh instructed.

George nodded and followed him out to the car. "Where is she? At home?"

"Yes. She said she'd been having occasional contractions since late evening, but they'd only just started properly, luckily for her, seeing as her birth partner's flapping like a haddock."

"A haddock?"

"Or any other fish, really." Josh glanced across. "Calm down!"

"I am calm."

"If you say so."

"I do. She swore at you, then?"

"A little bit, yes. Accordingly, the edited version is that she'd phoned you six times already and wondered if you'd taken a knock to the head in the crash."

"Sounds like I'm in for an enjoyable night."

"Do you really want me to stay?" Josh asked, sneaking a glance sideways and seeing the answer in that scowl. "OK. Just checking."

They drove on in silence. George wasn't usually very good at the middle of the night, but he was wide awake now—now being 4:25 a.m. and the roads were deserted. All his worries about Josh being at work and traffic jams, and here they were, sailing right through every set of traffic lights: green, green, green all the way. They arrived at Sophie's.

"I'll wait here," Josh whispered.

"Why're you whispering?" George asked.

Josh shrugged. "It seems the right thing to do."

George shook his head and got out of the car, closing the door as quietly as he could. He got as far as the garden gate before the front door of the house opened. He paused, waiting to see what was required of him, trying to gauge the danger level before he went any closer. Sophie glowered. He smiled—nervous but hoping he was affecting calm and in control convincingly—and walked up the path.

"OK, Soph, where are we up to?"

"Not bloody far enough to go to the hospital, apparently."

"You having contractions?"

"No, George. I'm just standing on my doorstep at four-thirty in the morning for the fun of it!" She closed her eyes and started taking deep breaths.

"Sorry. Stupid question. What do you want to do?"

She shook her head and carried on breathing through the contraction. George waited. Josh watched from the car.

"I want to go to the hospital and take whatever drugs they'll give me. They have a different idea, so if I give birth in the car, it'll be their fucking fault, not mine, tell him." She nodded at Josh, and he swiftly looked away.

"What have they said?" George asked.

"Wait until the contractions are five minutes apart."

"And what are they now?"

"Eight minutes."

"OK, so do you want to go back inside, or sit in the car, go to ours—"

"Get a takeaway."

"Really?"

"I want a whopping big burger and a milkshake. I don't give a toss whether it makes me throw up later. They're not gonna feed me when I get there. Drive-thru, now!"

She shoved him to one side and waddled off down the path. He watched her, momentarily stunned by her request, picked up her bag from the doorway and followed. He put it in the boot and waited for Josh to let him in on his side.

"What are we doing?"

"Drive-thru," George said.

"Right you are." Josh was going to do exactly as he was told tonight. It was too dangerous not to. He drove to the nearest drive-thru.

"Not this one," Sophie snarled impatiently. "Do I look like I want fried fucking chicken?" She started slow-breathing again. George took his phone out and checked the time: seven minutes since the last contraction.

"How long had they been eight minutes apart?" he asked.

"How the hell should I know?" Sophie puffed in between breaths. "Drive, for Christ's sake!"

Josh turned the car around, even though he was in the one-way lane leading up to the drive-thru, headed back the way he had come and on to the burger place. He pulled up at the window.

"Can I take your order, please?" The girl behind the counter smiled into the car.

Sophie smiled back. "Hi," she said sweetly across Josh. "Can I have two double cheeseburger meals with strawberry milkshakes, large, please."

The girl nodded, and Sophie passed the money over. Josh moved on to the next window and collected the food. He passed it to Sophie. She groaned and stuffed her mouth full of fries, trying to breathe at the same time. George checked his phone again. Six minutes. He made a judgement call.

"You'll have to eat on the way to the hospital," he said.

Sophie grunted and tore a huge piece from one of the cheeseburgers with her teeth.

Josh pulled back out onto the road. They were only half a mile from the hospital, and he didn't know whether he should drive slowly to give the pregnant velociraptor in his passenger seat time to devour her kill before they arrived, or put his foot down so he could get her out of the car as quickly as possible. He went with the first option, stopping outside the delivery suite as the next contraction started. George checked the time. Six minutes again.

"Have you phoned Sean?" he asked Sophie once her breathing returned to normal.

"No."

"I'll do that," Josh suggested.

"No, you bloody won't!" she growled.

Josh looked straight ahead and decided to keep his mouth shut. He *would* phone Sean, but he was going to wait until the she-beast was safely ensconced in the labour ward. It was quite incredible to see her like this, because she was normally so polite, reasonable—she was one of those people you would describe as 'nice' on first meeting, and 'lovely' once you got to know her—and Josh had thought George was exaggerating when he'd said how horrid she had been. Evidently not.

She'd eaten both of the burgers now and finished one of the milkshakes but decided she felt too sick to drink the other one. She left it in the cup holder and got out of the car. George shuffled across the backseat. She slammed the passenger door shut. He sighed and looked at Josh.

"I hope this is quick. I want the old Soph back. You know, the one that wasn't a psycho?"

Josh laughed. "D'you remember Ellie threatening to impale me on a bollard?"

"Hmm. This must be my payback for thinking it was funny." He pushed the passenger seat forward and got out of the car. Sophie smiled at him.

"I'm sorry, George. I don't mean to be horrible."

"It's OK. I knew what I was signing up to."

"Thank you. You're the best."

George smiled and hugged her gently. "You want to go in?"

"Yeah." She started walking but then stopped again, gripping onto his arm. Josh had gone to park the car, and he returned to find them exactly where he'd left them.

"Still six minutes," George reported. They stepped off once more.

It took a few minutes for someone to come to the door, as there were no free staff around. Eventually, a midwife came over and smiled warmly at Sophie.

"Just wait in here, and I'll get someone to come and see you. Won't be long."

She bustled off again. A second midwife arrived, and Josh left the room. The midwife started to examine Sophie, pausing to wait for another contraction to end.

251

"Heartbeat's nice and strong," she said. "And the contractions are six minutes apart and regular?"

"Yeah."

"You're only two centimetres dilated, Sophie. It's going to be a while yet, my love. Let's see if they settle down. You might need to go home and come back later."

The midwife left. Josh came back in.

"I'm not going any-bloody-where," Sophie shrieked at George. He hadn't said a word. She sat up and tried to move a pillow into the exaggerated arch of her lower back. George gave her a hand. She sighed heavily. "Well, this is shit."

"Do you need anything?"

"No. I'm fine." She pulled her knees up and tried to reach her foot to scratch an itch but couldn't. George scratched it for her, and she laughed. "Don't remember that one in the antenatal classes."

"Nope." He turned to Josh. "You OK?"

"Don't worry about me."

"Do you want to go home?"

"I don't mind either way. If you want me to stay, I'll stay. If you need me to leave, just say so."

George glanced up at the clock. It was nearly quarter past five. "What time are you in today?"

"Nine-thirty, but I'll call and tell them I'm working from home. I've got my tablet in the car, and I can do what I need to do here as well as I can do it anywhere."

Sophie was half listening to their conversation and tried to join in. "Sean says you're writing another paper together." She wasn't interested, and Josh knew it, but she was also starting with her next contraction, so he responded and watched her at the same time.

"Yes, we are. It's a critical review of contemporary approaches to psychotherapy."

"Sounds interesting," she said, grabbing at the sheet on the bed. "Fucking hell! Tell them I want drugs." George obediently left the room. She breathed through to the end of the contraction, exhaled slowly and smiled at Josh. "I tell you what, this is not an experience you'd enjoy."

"No, I imagine not."

"How was Ellie's birthday? Did it go OK?"

"Yes, it was fine, thanks, if not a little strange." The previous evening, they'd all crowded into Jess's room at the hospice to eat takeaway and birthday cake, washed down with a variety of non-alcoholic beverages. Very odd. Lots of pretence and meaningless conversation, no silence left unfilled.

"Have you phoned Sean yet?"

"Erm, no." Josh looked a little flustered.

"I know you're going to."

"I have to, Soph."

"Yeah. I know. It really is OK, whatever else I tell you when the contractions are happening."

George came back in, looking very reticent. "They said they'll come and sort something out for you in a minute."

"Thanks."

The waiting game commenced. The midwife brought in gas and air for Sophie, a cup of tea for George and a smile of curiosity for Josh. He went to the vending machine by the hospital canteen and got his own coffee, trying to phone Sean on his way there and back, detouring via the car park to pick up his tablet. It was coming up to six a.m., and full daylight, although the sky was overcast. Josh paused outside for a few minutes and drank his coffee. He yawned, returned to the vending machine to restock, and went back to the labour ward. Sophie was mid-contraction when he arrived, but she was coping much better now she had the Entonox and was managing to snatch a couple of minutes' nap between contractions. So many weeks of sleeping poorly; she was shattered.

Quarter past six: a midwife came and examined her.

"Three centimetres," she said. "It's quiet this morning." She left again, as if that statement explained everything. The time plodded on, punctuated every six minutes by Sophie grabbing the mouthpiece and puffing and panting for sixty seconds, then back to the silence. George sat by her side, like a faithful hound dog. Josh went and got him more tea, and more coffee for himself. Sophie didn't throw up, even though they'd warned her that she probably would if she overate when in labour.

Quarter past seven: three centimetres; six minutes. All progressing slowly, but well.

"Looks like the babies decided to wait for the sunshine to come out again," this midwife said. "Very quiet this morning. Only you and one other lady. Do you want to stay here, or go home?"

"How long do you think I'll be?"

"I can't say, but it's likely going to be at least another five hours." Sophie looked to George to see what he thought.

He shrugged. "It's up to you."

"Can we go back to your place? It's more relaxing there."

"Yeah, I guess." George turned to Josh to check that was OK with him. "You can go to work if you want."

"As I say, I can work wherever today."

Off they went, back home, where George made Sophie some toast and hot chocolate and set her up with the remote control, a game controller and a magazine, after which he went up for a quick shower. Josh stayed with her for those three minutes, and on George's return took Blue for a walk. He stopped at Sean's on his way back and knocked on the door. No response. He knocked again and stepped away to look up at the bedroom window. The curtains were open. He'd obviously stayed out all night. Josh went back home.

"I'm in my office if you need me," he said, taking a cappuccino upstairs with him. He sat down and switched on the computer, chewing his lip thoughtfully and trying to think where Sean might be. He worked regular office hours, unless he was called in to deal with an emergency, but even then, he'd have been home at some point during the night, and he'd have had his phone with him, whatever. He tried calling him again: straight to voicemail.

Just before twelve o'clock, a taxi pulled up outside the house, and Sean staggered from it. Josh was watching through his bedroom window.

"Ah, crap," he said. He closed his eyes and sighed. He went downstairs. "Just popping out," he called.

Josh saw him on the stairs through the obscure glass and knocked. Sean backtracked and opened the door.

"Morning," Josh said, taking in Sean's dishevelled appearance, his tangled mess of hair, bloodshot eyes, crumpled shirt, unbuckled belt. He hadn't shaved, and by the looks of it hadn't slept or eaten, either, in days.

"I'm going to bed," Sean slurred.

Josh nodded once. He sniffed. Sean shook his head.

"No, Joshy, I haven't. I've been at the hospice all night."

Josh started to panic. "Jess?"

"She's fine, which is to say she's no worse than when you saw her last."

Josh looked relieved, but then it came to him. How had he not realised before? Twenty years. That's how long he'd known Sean Tierney, and he'd seen Sean go through some really difficult times. He'd been responsible for a lot of them himself. Yet it had never even occurred to him, because what they'd had seemed so inconsequential against the backdrop of everything else.

Sean turned away. Josh stepped into the hall and closed the door.

"I'll make us a coffee," he said.

Sean didn't protest. He went and sat down.

"Does this cat need food?" Josh shouted.

"Yes, he will do." Sean got up again and trudged to the kitchen. "I'll do it," he said. Sphinx prowled around his legs and then jumped up onto the worktop, meowing loudly and getting in the way. Sean pushed him to one side and spooned cat food into a bowl. The cat started eating it immediately; Sean left the bowl where it was. He leaned against the cupboard, rubbing his eyes and trying to stay in the here and now.

"She's totally out of it, of course," he said.

Josh continued with the task of making the coffee. He'd never used a real cappuccino machine before and wasn't entirely sure he was doing it right, although he'd watched others often enough, and whatever he was doing seemed to be working.

Sean carried on, oblivious to Josh's efforts. "The antidepressants kicked in fully yesterday afternoon, and I'll admit I've never been so glad of the things."

Sphinx finished eating and sat to clean his face with his paws. Josh carefully poured the frothed milk on top of the espresso and passed it to Sean.

"Thanks," he said. He sipped at it and sighed. It was a sigh of sadness, not contentment, and Josh fought his disappointment at Sean being in no fit state to admire his first attempt at a cappuccino. It looked awesome! Given the circumstances, he let it pass and went on with making one for himself.

"Don't get me wrong," Sean said, staring into the mid-distance. He took another mouthful of coffee. "I'm not in love with her, or anything like that. But going through what we did together, there's a connection between us that I severely underestimated when we were younger."

Josh cleaned the coffee machine, and they retired to the lounge. Sean sat on his end of the sofa with his leg underneath him.

"By now you've no doubt figured it out. The reason I took the job here? Yes, it was to be near her—not because I was under some romantic delusion that we had any kind of future together, though maybe there was always a tiny bit of hope hanging on in there. The possibility. And I kept putting off doing anything about it. After this conference. When I go back on earlies. Just as soon as I get that paper sent off. What was the rush? We were young, weren't we? We're still young. I thought we had years in us yet, time to get that career bug out of our systems, and then, who knows what?

"So I wasn't in love with her, and I don't suppose I am now, if I think on, look at the whole bloody mess rationally. I'm doing my usual trick of wanting, *needing* it because it's transient, no chance to get tied up or bogged down. Chasing the thing I can't have. What chance does someone like me stand, realistically, against someone like your man Andy? What she sees—what they all see—is that happy-go-lucky little Irish feller who works up at that there university, not a lonely middle-aged fool. I know in my heart it would never have come to anything, but will my damned head hear a word of it?"

Josh had listened without comment. Much of this he'd heard before, or variations on the same theme of Sean's lack of confidence and belief in himself. He was a convincing actor, playing the part of the intelligent academic, and he could pick up women without really trying, but, as he said, he pursued temporary, short-term relationships and despatched any that looked set to become more as quickly as he could. He wanted to be happy, to be liked, to be loved. His career afforded those privileges to a greater extent, and he had made it his life, because he was afraid, not of commitment, but that he'd get rumbled.

What didn't fit was that Sophie had seen the real Sean Tierney and accepted him for who he was. He most certainly loved her and didn't talk about 'them' in the past tense. So where had all these feelings for Jess suddenly come from? Usually, Josh wouldn't have needed to ask that question out loud, because Sean would have pre-empted it with the answer. Today, however, he was off with the leprechauns.

"So, you're not in love with Jess, but you're beating yourself up about not pursuing a relationship with her, and meanwhile the mother of your yet-to-be-born child is sitting next door but one, having contractions every six minutes."

"Soph's in labour?"

"Yes, but there's no rush. Talk to me, Tierney. What the hell's up with you? And before you say it, I know Jess is dying, but why are you so bothered if you're not in love with her?"

"Because…" Sean covered his eyes, unable to go on. Josh had never seen him quite like this before, and he was at something of a loss how to help. He went over and sat next to him on the sofa. Sean let out a noise that was somewhere between a sob and a laugh.

"Sean?" Josh put his arm around him. "What's the matter?"

He was crying quite hard and couldn't possibly answer the question yet, but he'd decided that once the tears stopped, he would answer Josh truthfully. They'd known each other far too long to do otherwise.

Josh stayed where he was, patiently offering comfort, thinking how strange it was to be doing it, and yet it didn't feel unnatural. Sean had saved his life. He should consider him one of his closest friends, and sitting there with him as he dissolved into inconsolable grief, Josh realised that was exactly how he thought about Sean. Or maybe more like a brother, because he could be unbelievably infuriating, and they argued constantly, but Josh knew for sure that if he was in the firing line, Sean would take the bullet for him, and the feeling was mutual.

When Sean finally pulled himself together—he still couldn't really speak because of his blocked sinuses—he grabbed the fluorescent blotter pad that he kept next to the phone and wrote:

I TOOK THE PSYCH JOB...

His writing, in large, scrawly capital letters, only allowed for that much on a page, and he held up his hand, trying to sniff through his completely obstructed nostrils, as he continued onto the next sheet.

...TO BE NEAR YOU AND JESS

"OK." Josh frowned in puzzlement.

NOT GOOD AT MAKING FRIENDS

"You are winding me up, aren't you?"
Sean shook his head and poised the pen over the sheet of paper.

FEEL LIKE BOB BLOODY DYLAN!

Josh laughed. "Let this be a lesson to you, Tierney. Get those sinuses flushed!"

NOT A

He held the page and attempted a smile as he scribbled on the next one:

CHANCE

He caught his breath and sighed all in one go. "Joshy." He smiled, and his eyes filled with tears again.
"Take your time," Josh said. "I'm here, and I'll still be here tomorrow, and the day after that, which is Saturday, and Jess

will be home again, so you can have a day off. We'll go and do something fun."

"Fun?"

"Visit a library, or something." Josh grinned at him. Sean managed a laugh. "Do you want to go and see how Sophie's getting on?"

"In a little while. Have I got long enough to shower, do you think?"

"I'd say you've probably got long enough to shower, shave and—"

"Shoot some pool?" Sean interrupted.

Josh laughed. "You took the words right out of my mouth!"

It was an old joke from their university days; even before Josh created his own living nightmare when it came to bathtime, he wasn't a quick in-and-out-of-the-bathroom kind of guy, which had prompted Sean to ask him once, 'What the feck do you do in there?' Josh had coyly replied, 'The three 'S's.' Sean's comeback: 'What? Shower, shave and shoot a few frames of pool?'

Whilst Sean was upstairs, Josh sent George a text message to make sure everything was OK and got, as a response, a singular emoticon with its mouth wide open. Excited? In shock? Screaming for his life? That was exactly why Josh hated text-based communication. He didn't have the first idea what a little yellow face with its mouth wide open was meant to signify, but on a related note, he decided it was about time he did the decent thing and added Ray Jackson as a 'friend' online, now that he actually knew what he looked like. The fact Ray had flown four and a half thousand miles to attend their wedding said much about his and George's friendship, and if they were that important to each other, then Ray was a friend of his, too.

That done, he waited out the rest of the time in the kitchen, topping up his caffeine. When Sean returned, he looked a million times better. Josh passed him the just-made cappuccino.

"Thanks," he said. "For everything."

Josh squeezed Sean's shoulder. "No need. How's your nose? Any better?"

"A little. I've taken some decongestants."

"That's good. All is well next door, I think. Unless I misinterpreted George's text."

"Why? What's it say?"

Josh took his phone out and showed Sean. He looked at it and nodded.

"Drink up, Joshy." He knocked back his coffee in one go and slammed the cup down. Josh followed suit and had to run after him to catch up.

"Took your time!" George snapped.

He was standing on the pavement next to the car, the keys were in the ignition and Sophie was sitting in the passenger seat making the most inhuman grunting noise.

"Sorry." Josh let George and Sean into the back. "Your text wasn't very clear."

"'Contractions three minutes apart, need to go now!' isn't exactly ambiguous."

"Ah, I didn't see that one." Josh glanced at Sean in the rearview mirror. "I wondered how you'd got that from a smiley with its mouth open."

"I did," Sean protested.

"Sure, you did!"

Five minutes later, Josh pulled up outside the hospital and let George out. Sophie was past the swearing stage now, having to concentrate so hard on getting through the contractions that she wasn't even able to speak. George had been timing them in the car, and she was now getting them every two and a half minutes, each one lasting ninety seconds. She speed-waddled off towards the labour ward, with George going ahead to open doors, dropping back to walk next to her, or pause and grimace at the pain of her iron grip on his shoulders as she battled through. Josh went to park the car.

"How are you feeling?" he asked Sean as they walked back together.

"About Soph and the baby, or all the other nonsense?"

"Soph and the baby."

"I don't know. Kind of excited, I think. My head's too far up my backside to make much sense of it. But I meant what I said. Before I met Soph, you and Jess were my only friends, and even

260

Jessie was by proxy. I thought I'd made a friend in Shaunna, all by myself and independently of you, but guess what? She's your friend, too!"

"That doesn't mean she's not your friend, Sean!"

"You know what I mean, though, don't you?"

"And there's George."

"He's Soph's friend, not mine."

"I disagree," Josh said, momentarily distracted by his phone vibrating. He took it out and read the newly arrived, unread message. It was the one George had sent earlier. "Would you believe it?" he muttered under his breath. So Sean had correctly interpreted the emoticon. Clever, clever man.

"As I was saying, George doesn't just see you as Sophie's partner. He considers you a friend, or did I imagine the wedding reception where he thanked you *both* for being there for us? And what about Ellie?"

"*Your* friend again."

"Sean! Get a grip! If I listed all my friends, they would be exactly the same as George's, Ellie's, Shaunna's, Jess's—in fact, you looked like you were getting on pretty well with the husband-ex-husband from where I was sitting. If anyone should be feeling anxious about the security of their friendships, it's me."

"So why aren't you?"

"Because—I can't even believe we're having this conversation. How old are you? Five?" Josh paused and pressed the buzzer for access to the labour ward. "OK, Tierney, I'm going to say this once, so listen up. I love you. You are one of my best friends, and you are most welcome to share my friends, because as grown-ups, we can actually be friends with more than one person at a time. Do you understand?"

"Yes."

"Praise be!"

Sean laughed and gave Josh a hug. "Thanks, Joshy. As I said to George last year, you're more than a friend to me. I love you like a brother."

"Interesting. I was thinking the same thing about you before."

The midwife opened the door for them.

"An eejit little brother who breaks all your toys," Sean added as they went inside.

"Ha!" Josh was still trying to think of a clever comeback when George emerged from a door to their left, a huge grin on his face.

"She hasn't given birth already?" Josh asked in disbelief.

"She most certainly has. She only just made it onto the bed."

"What is it?"

"A baby," George said, still grinning so broadly his mouth nearly extended ear-to-ear. Josh rolled his eyes.

"Can I go in?" Sean asked.

George nodded. "I came out to find you. Sophie's desperate for you to meet your SON." The last word was directed at Josh.

"I have a son?" Sean was completely overwhelmed by the news.

"Come on." George beckoned and held the door open so Sean could enter the room. He and Josh stayed back, watching the parents reunite around their 6lbs 10oz son; name: to be confirmed. George released the door with him and Josh on the outside.

"Congratulations, Birth Partner," Josh said. He kissed him, in a maternity ward buzzing with people, but George was far too happy to care and kept the proximity, continuing to grin and return excited little pecks.

"It's so amazing," he said, in between all the kisses. "He's all warm and soft and covered in this white stuff, and I got to cut the umbilical cord. And his hair—there's loads of it, and his little nails, he's got these teeny-weeny feet and—"

"Not your baby," Josh interrupted the gush, although he was only tormenting and laughing at the same time.

"Can we have one?"

Josh carried on laughing, hoping it was solely down to the temporary euphoria.

George picked up on his unease. "Or can we talk about it sometime, at least?"

"Yes, we can talk about it."

"Thank you. Come and meet him."

George took Josh's hand and led him inside. Sean was holding his son, and Sophie was watching them and smiling, her eyes filled with love for them both.

A midwife was just leaving with a trolley loaded with green paper sheets soaked with all manner of body fluids.

"You missed a treat there, George, for sure," Sean joked, nodding after the trolley. Josh frowned.

"The placenta," George explained. Josh inflated his cheeks as if about to throw up. Sophie laughed at him; he went over to her.

"Congratulations, Sophie. You look fabulous." He gave her a hug and kissed her cheek. "And he's beautiful."

"Thanks. I feel fabulous. No backache, heartburn, swearing…" She glanced at George, and they exchanged smiles. "You are one in a billion, billion," she said.

George went over to give her a big hug, and they stayed together, watching Sean and the baby. "Have you decided?" he asked.

"Yes, I think we're going with Dylan Robert."

"Fancy that," Josh mused.

"Don't you like it? We wanted the Irish and English in there, and when we saw him, it felt exactly right."

Josh peered inside the blanket at the tiny crinkled grumpy face. He nodded. "It's perfect, not that it matters what I think."

"Oh, it does," Sean said, "more than you know." He looked into Josh's eyes, once again fighting the tears, but this time of joy. Baby Dylan started to make the tiniest creaking sound. Sean was unsure what to do.

"He's probably hungry after his epic journey," Sophie said, holding out her arms. Sean passed him back to her and stood nearby, watching as she tried to position him on her breast. "The midwife is coming back to help me," she explained.

"I'll go find her, Soph," George said and did so. He was back within a minute. The midwife looked at the three men—a far from subtle hint that at least one of them might want to leave.

"I'll go and get a coffee," Josh suggested, slowly back-stepping.

Normally, it would have been the case that he actually wanted coffee, but on this occasion, he didn't want it at all. He wanted to stay. There was something so incredible about being there, with Sophie, Sean and their baby—or should that be Sophie, George and their baby? He couldn't quite decide. Maybe they could work out a timeshare. For now, though, a certain little chap was getting fractious, and the audience wasn't helping his mummy much, so Josh tore himself away.

He quietly closed the door and stood alone in the corridor outside the room, immediately lost. He wanted to tell everyone about the baby, but who did he know that would care? It wasn't his place to inform the counselling course students. Sophie and Sean would want to tell their parents themselves. Jess was doped up and probably too near the end of her own life to celebrate the beginning of another, but he wanted to talk to her. He missed that—popping in to see each other under some pretext or other when really all they wanted was a gossip and each other's company.

"I'm just passing the time, you know?" she said self-consciously.

"Yes, I figured that much out for myself. And since when did you need an excuse to come and visit? Fashion advice? I mean!"

"Don't you feel that life is kind of beginning to pass us by?"

He brought up her number. It rang on and on, and went to voicemail. He hung up and tried again.

A drowsy voice answered. "Hey, you."

"Hey. Hope I didn't wake you."

"No. I'm just kind of—floating." She laughed sleepily. "Drifting, that's what I mean."

"Same thing. I'm phoning to say Sophie's had the baby."

"Oh, that's brilliant news. How is everyone?"

"They're great, Jess. Sean's so happy."

"Is he? I'm really glad. I've been worried about him."

"Me, too. I think he's going to be just fine."

He stayed quiet, not trusting himself to speak further. He wanted to tell her what Sean had said, how much she meant to him. *But break, my heart, for I must hold my tongue!* He coughed to clear his throat, a cloak to choke the cry of pain, whistling up through his oesophagus like a bitter winter blast. A beginning and an end. *No.* He shook his head. *NO! NO!* Anyone watching would think he was indeed as mad as the Prince of Denmark. *The observ'd of all observers, quite, quite down.*

"I'll come up to see you when we're done here."

"I'll look forward to it. Give everyone my love. See you later."

He ended the call and studied his phone. Now what? He glanced back at the door, listening to the voices from within; laughter, words of encouragement. He was trying not to feel rejected; he was just the driver, after all, so why this urge to share how overjoyed he was? It was ridiculous, and it was irrepressible.

There were perhaps another two people who may be interested, might even care half as much as he did, and that would be enough to fill an ocean. He unlocked his screen and typed the message:

> Sophie's had a baby boy: Dylan Robert, 6lbs 10oz born today at 13:36. Mum, Dad, Baby and Birth Partner all doing well. x

He sent it to Shaunna and Andy.
Within seconds, he got a reply from Shaunna:

> Aww. Give them my love and congratulations. I've let Kris and Ellie know. Have you told Jess? Is there anyone else you need me to tell? x

Josh was about to press the 'reply' button as another message came in:

> Awesome! Congrats to all. You want me to tell the others? x

Tell *the others*? Josh felt like he should be rubbing his eyes in disbelief, and he was already getting some strange looks from passers-by. He realised he was crying. Not the silent, don't bring attention to yourself sort of crying either. Properly sobbing.

"Are you all right?" A midwife stopped and put her hand on his arm.

"Oh. Yes, thanks. I'm OK. Just delivering the good news."
She smiled in understanding and trotted off.
The others.
What he'd said to Sean was true, of course, but he'd thought he was probably overstating the case a little, about them being his

friends, too, and he completely understood why he would want them as friends. They were good people.

No.

They were wonderful people.

"The others." He smiled and started to recite in his head as he sauntered off in the direction of the vending machine.

> *Friends, you and me.*
> *You brought another friend,*
> *And then there were three.*
>
> *We started our group,*
> *Our circle of friends,*
> *And like that circle –*

He stopped in front of the machine, reached into his pocket.

"There is no beginning or end," he finished aloud. He flipped the coin, watched it spin through the air, and caught it.

For whilst a circle may contract and may even at times constrict, it can also expand, accommodate, embrace.

And it is always whole; eternal.

Poison
Wednesday 30th August

This was not meant to happen. They had done everything they could to avoid this, but still, here they were, in this most dangerous of situations. She went straight up the stairs, glanced into the room: deep, unstirring sleep. She delayed, in the doorway, biting her lip, fighting to retain what little remained of her rationality. She could almost feel them on her shoulders—that angel and devil, digging and kicking at her skin, scratching at her face, pulling her hair, their screeched stereo argument ringing in her ears to the banging bloody rhythm of her ever-quickening pulse, that primal drum, goading, taunting. *You can't fight this. You want it too much.*

As if she had been lassoed about the waist, she felt the tug, back down the stairs. Down she went, fighting it all the way. *No, don't take me, don't make me go in there. Please, let me go!*

"Morning," he said, clutching at his belly, the pain distorting and warping those perfectly chiselled cheekbones, that glorious square chin. She'd always wondered what it would be like, just to touch the very tip of her tongue to that cleft.

"Are you sick?"

"Excuse me."

He ran past her, up the stairs she had just descended. The door slammed. The retching commenced.

Twenty-four-hour thing, caught from his niece. Twenty-four hours' grace. He wiped his mouth, brushed his teeth again and waited. This bout was done with, back down he went, to the kitchen, to the danger zone.

"Got a bug," he muttered, heading for the sink. *Water.*

"Oh dear," she said, rubbing his back. *Motherly.*

"Wouldn't get too close, if I were you."

"OK." She backed off. "Go to bed."

"Can't sleep here."

"Go to your mum's?"

"Yeah. Is that OK?"

"Go."

"Thanks." He turned, trying not to look but couldn't stop himself. Her eyes burned into his. "You don't want this thing."

"The bug? No."

His eyes burned into hers.

"I'll see you tomorrow."

"Yeah."

She reached out and grabbed his arm, pulling him back. "Get well soon."

"Thanks. I'll try."

Front door. Closed. Another day won.

Lips Of An Angel
Wednesday 6th September

"Hello?"

"Hi."

"Hi. What you up to?"

"Couldn't sleep."

"Same. You home alone tonight?"

"No. He's gone to bed."

"Yeah, well, it is twenty to three in the morning."

"True. Is everything OK?"

"She's comfortable, but I'll have to keep my voice down. Very restless."

"Yeah. I've got to stay quiet, too. Shh." The dog had different ideas.

"I wish you were here."

"That wouldn't work very well, would it?"

"You know what I mean."

"You want me to come round?"

"What will you tell him?"

"That she needs me."

"I need you."

"OK. That *you* need me."

"He won't know?"

"No. He won't know."

"You shouldn't."

"You sure about that?"

"Fuck, Shaunna, don't do this to me."

"Sorry."

"Have you had a drink?"

"A couple of glasses of wine, yeah. Why?"

He paused and rested the phone on his leg. He put it back to his ear. "Go to bed."

"Here, or…?"

He laughed. "Yeah. There. Don't you dare come round when you've had a drink."

"Fine. I'm going. See you later."

"Ten-thirty, yeah?"

"I'll be there. Good night."

"Night. I miss you."

She closed her eyes and felt her heart flutter a little. "I miss you, too," she whispered.

***

"Good morning."

Shaunna bounced past him, as if the phone call had never happened. She was wearing *that dress* again. The one that made him want to lift her onto the kitchen worktop, hitch it up, past her knees, up her thighs… He watched her fill the kettle, humming to herself.

"What're you singing?"

"'Mustang Sally'."

"Why did I ask?" He laughed and sighed all at once. Shaunna smiled at him and bounced past again, pausing to pirouette, brushing a finger across his chin.

She ran up the stairs and looked in on Jess. "Hiya," she said, suddenly much quieter, less full of the vibrancy of life, of desire, even though she was aching. *Aching.*

"Hi," Jess replied sleepily.

"I'm just making a cup of tea, and I'll be right back, hun. You want anything?"

"No, thanks." Drifting, listless, heavy-eyed.

"OK. Won't be long." She ran down the stairs. Andy was at the sink, with his back to her. She hopped up onto the cupboard next to him. "What time are you back?"

"About twelve. Maybe before that." He was trying not to look at her offering him his fantasy. *Does she know? Can she see into my head?*

"Okey-dokey. I'm in no rush."

He turned away from her. His jeans were stretched tight.

"Are you avoiding me, Andy?"

"Yeah."

"Why? Did I upset you?"

"In what sense?"

"Drinking wine and phoning to tell you I was thinking about you."

"No." He shook his head to confirm it. "God, no, you didn't. I was thinking about you, too."

"Were you?"

"That's all I think about." He took a breath in preparation and turned to face her. "I could take you right now, in that dress, right there." She looked down, saw the bulge and smiled. He closed his eyes. "It's almost more than I can do to stay away." He moved back to the sink, leaning against it for safety. The kettle came to the boil.

She slid down from her seat; her skirt caught on the drawer handle behind and on his thigh in front. He was shaking with the effort to restrain himself.

"Is it any wonder we have a child?" he asked.

She smiled again. "It's a miracle we don't have a whole gang of them." She reached up and brushed her fingers across his lips, pausing long enough to feel his hot breath against her fingertips.

"I've got to go," he said.

He tried to turn quickly, to pass her by, but she blocked him, pressing herself against him. He ran his hands up her sides and pulled her closer still. A will of steel. It had brought him through many more treacherous moments than this, and yet they all paled to nothing, with her body against his and her arms around his neck.

He took one final, massive breath and kissed her on the head, blocking his sense of smell so that he would not be tempted by the glorious aroma of her hair. "I've got to go," he repeated.

She nodded, sad, disappointed, relieved, and listened to the door close behind him.

***

"What's that you're watching?"

Jess fished around blindly for the remote control and pressed the button. It was easier than speaking.

"*Truly, Madly, Deeply*. A beautiful film." Shaunna lay on the bed beside her and took her hand. "Alan Rickman is an amazing actor."

They lay there, holding hands, for a long time, no movement, no words, just that contact as they watched the ghost on film fulfil his destiny.

When it was over, Jess rolled onto her side, still holding Shaunna's hand. "I'm tired."

"I know, hun."

"You'll look after him?"

"I will. I promise."

"And Josh?"

"And Josh."

"He's not as strong as you think."

"I know. He hides it well."

"Is Kris coming round later?"

Shaunna nodded, not trusting herself to answer. She knew what this was. She'd been here before. "Yes," she uttered finally.

"That's good. When does season two start? Is it soon?"

"End of the month, I think." Shaunna swallowed, hoping Jess couldn't hear the fizzing in her ears.

"Hey," Jess prompted wearily. She lifted a heavy hand to Shaunna's cheek. "You have made my life so wonderful these last few weeks. Please don't be sad."

Shaunna started to cry. "I'm sorry, Jess, I can't help it." She sobbed. Jess lifted her thumb and wiped away the tears. "I love

272

you, and I'm going to miss you so much, and I know it's nearly time, but I don't want it to be. It's not fair." She broke down. "It's just not fair. And I'm so sorry."

"It's OK. It's all going to be OK." Jess tugged at Shaunna's hand to keep her near.

***

The front door opened on a silent house, and it filled him with dread. This was the point they had reached now, when noise at least signified that life continued to exist within, and his voyage up the stairs was one fuelled by the fear of what he might find. He steadied himself before walking into the room, his heart still pounding furiously. He stepped inside, looked at the two of them, lying face-to-face, arms entwined, and smiled in relief.

He returned downstairs and made tea, for three, taking the time to consider the women in his life that he truly loved. They totalled only four. His mum, of course, for few sons do not love their mothers. Sometimes she had been his mortal enemy, a screaming, angry monster demanding and impatient. But she had also been his champion. When he thought about the times he had hurt himself—playing football, climbing mountains, the malaria—it was his mum who had looked after him, brought him tomato soup and soft bread rolls, changed his sodden bed sheets in night fevers.

And finally, she seemed to have found happiness with the right man, someone who loved her and respected her as a person, rather than merely desiring her, because, they all said, she was a beautiful woman. *Too right!* She'd always be beautiful to him.

Then there was Jess, who had nursed his heart often, because, as he'd told Shaunna, he was romantic and prone to leaping into these things without looking first, falling fast and deep, only to find he needed to start climbing out before he was anywhere near the bottom.

Jess, too, had been his enemy on occasion. Last year, with Rob, was the worst time of all, and he'd had word that the bastard was back in town. Were it not for his desire to ensure that *he* never

273

got to say goodbye, he'd have gone round there to kick him from here to however far he got before Dan or someone pulled him off.

But what point was there to retaliation? It wouldn't stop him losing her, although, as she kept telling him, they had the memories of their time together. They'd spent hours talking about uneventful days at the beach, remembering strange little conversations they'd shared about people they thought were hot, and then there were the more private moments. They'd done incredible things together, in incredible places. She was right; all of those memories would still be his, wherever they were.

And Krissi: she was too wonderful for words. The love and strength she had given him over the last few months—he simply couldn't have made it through without her. She truly was her mother's daughter, and he was so proud of her. It made his heart leap and swell whenever he thought about her, and he realised that this was what it felt like to be a dad. He didn't envy Kris for having that privilege. It was because he had done such an outstanding job of it that she was who she was. And she'd told him straight: she wasn't his mistake. She just wasn't planned, which, to be fair, was how he lived the rest of his life, so why should his daughter's conception be any different?

Finally, there was Shaunna. He remembered the first time he saw her *in that way*—no more the skipping, annoying little girl in his brother's year who whined on and on about not being allowed to play on the football team, but a gorgeous girl he wanted to talk to, hold hands with, touch her hair. *Her hair*. If all he'd ever got to do was run his fingers through her hair, entangle them in those curls, then he would have been the happiest boy on earth.

So, he'd have been maybe twelve or thirteen—possibly as much as twenty-eight years ago—and all that had changed was now he'd be the happiest man. Even before she had been here, day in, day out, for Jess and for him, he knew he was in love with her. The thing that he had stopped Dan from saying last year, when they were in Nepal, when they'd still believed she and Kris were OK, was this thing that was happening to them now, this desperate need to hold her, to kiss and caress her, make love to her. And how!

He had been so engrossed in his thoughts of the four beautiful angels in his life that he had neither seen nor heard her approach, but he sensed her behind him now, and that she was not quite so fiery with passion as she had been earlier, which was a good thing. If he'd stayed, he'd have taken her, and she'd have let him, like she had before, and that was not how it was meant to be. He wanted more than a quick fuck against a wall, although he wanted that, too.

So she was here. And he was here. And the world had stopped turning, if only for a few seconds. He moved closer. She watched through eyes still reddened by grief, gazing up into his face, now only inches away. He took her in his arms, slowly, gently. She closed her eyes. He pressed his lips to one eyelid, then the other.

"The lust," he said, "I can handle. The rest I can't. I love you. I want to make love to you. I want to take you far away from here, from all of this, and make love to you over and over again. I want to show you all of the things I have seen, take you high into the mountains, flying through the sky. And I want you to show me what life is about. I want another baby, with you, and I want the chance to be a father, to get it right. I know I shouldn't be telling you all of this, any of this, but I can't help myself. I love you, Shaunna."

She lowered her eyes and turned her face away from his.

"I promised her," she said. She looked up again and cupped his cheek with her palm. "I promised her I would look after you, and I will, but I don't know if I can be all the things you want me to be. I spent a long time on Kris's pedestal, and I'm not about to climb onto yours." She blushed and giggled. "Your pedestal, I mean."

He laughed, too, but then became serious once more. "Will you let me love you?" he asked.

She nodded. "Yes. But you need to know that the end is nearly here. We have to get through this first."

"How long?"

She shrugged. "My mum was a few weeks, maybe two or three."

He nodded to show his understanding and began to move away from her, but she cupped his face again, with both hands now, and stood on tiptoes to kiss his cheeks, his nose, his chin.

***

She rested her lips against that cleft, so desperate to lift them to meet his, but such uncertainty filled her now. He loved her too much, and she did not know if she loved him enough, but she *did* love him.

That much she knew to be true.

Tipping The Scales
Saturday 16th September

"What in hell's name are you doing here?"

He stood at the threshold, a vast, insincere smile prefixed to his face, unflickering in spite of the hostile reception. Or maybe it was sincere, but it was hard to interpret it as such after all that had gone before.

"I was requested."

"Who by?"

"May I come in?"

George shook his head. "No, you damn well may not."

The smile wavered a little. He adjusted his stance. "She asked me to come."

"How?"

He took a breath, preparing to answer, but George went on.

"And when? How and when?" Anger was threatening to get the better of him. He knew because the words weren't there. That couldn't happen.

"She called Lois a couple of weeks ago, asked if she'd seen or heard from me."

"A couple?"

"A month or so. I don't recall. I was coming back this way, so I thought I'd drop by and say hi."

George was rooted to the spot in disbelief, both at what he was hearing and that Rob had the nerve to turn up here at all. What if Andy had been home?

"Are you going to let me in?" Rob asked, then added a smarmy, "Please?" and laughed.

George flew, slammed right into him and shoved him to the ground.

Rob's motorcycle helmet hit the concrete path with an almighty bang—loud enough for Adele to have heard and come running out to investigate. She froze in the doorway, in shock, trying to figure out what was going on, continuing to delay once she'd realised, because Rob deserved everything he got.

George got hold of the helmet and raised it above his head. Adele screamed out as it came down once, twice. She grabbed George's arm as it rose a third time and held on with all her might.

"Stop it. Stop it! GEORGE! STOP IT!"

He was still fighting to free his arm, and she had both of her hands around his wrist, using her entire body weight to pull back. She'd had to do the same thing with Dan once, when he went for someone who'd literally picked her up at a bar and moved her to one side so he could push in, and she knew she couldn't release him, not until he stopped fighting her.

Curtains were twitching up and down the street, and the woman across the way was out of her door. Still Adele clung on for dear life—not her own—waiting for a signal that it was safe to let go. Rob was covered in blood and wheezing, struggling to catch his breath with George's knees on his chest. *It isn't Dan,* Adele reminded herself. *It's George. He doesn't do things like this.* She slowly moved her hand from his wrist and put her arm around his chest.

"Come on," she goaded gently, quietly. "Go inside. I'll deal with *this*." She glared down at Rob, her eyes full of hatred. George was seething, snarling. "George. Go back inside," she repeated calmly.

He got up. Just to make sure, she stepped between him and Rob, still lying on his back on the path, and watched until George had gone in. She took out her phone.

"Josh? Hi, everything's fine, but can you come round to Jess's, please?" He started to reply, but she cut him off. "Now would be really great. Bye." She hung up. Rob moved to roll onto his side, and she put her foot on his chest, pushing him back to the floor again. "Not so fast," she said. He sneered at her. "You want to take me on, do you? Go for it. Let's see…" She lifted her phone and ran her thumb down the screen, squinting as if reading it, although it was locked and the screen was dark. "Who shall I call? Andy? Dan? Or both? How about it, Rob? Want to take them on, too?" She removed her foot and stepped back, keeping her glare fixed on him.

Cautiously, he sat up and wiped his mouth with the side of his hand, checking for blood. He coughed and more blood came up with the phlegm. "I came to see Jess."

"Obviously."

"She asked me to."

"Is that right?"

"Yeah. So you gonna let me do that, or do you want to call in the apes and explain to her why I didn't make it?"

Adele ran her tongue over her teeth, an action she had honed so well it could be highly seductive, or signal she was ready to kill. Rob stayed still and tried not to provoke her further, which suited her perfectly; she wanted to keep him there until Josh arrived. She lifted her hand and started inspecting her cuticles, watching Rob out of the corner of her eye. He moved; she glowered; he stayed put; she continued with the faked cuticle inspection.

In her peripheral vision, she saw Josh pull up, pausing to assess the situation before he got out of the car. He walked up the path, his eyes on Rob all the way, until he was close enough to read Adele. She granted him access.

***

George was sitting in the garden, shaking so violently the chair was shaking with him. Josh went over, sat on the chair opposite and waited. George didn't even look up; no eye contact, no attempt at a smile, just the shaking and staring directly ahead.

Josh took hold of his hand and squeezed it. He got no response. He looked around for something to use as a distraction, as per the research Sean had been reading. There was a little plastic windmill stuck in a plant pot; it would have to do. He reached across and plucked it free, holding it up between them. He blew on it.

"Isn't it fascinating the way it looks completely white when it's spinning?" he said, not even remotely fascinated and knowing

279

precisely why. "And yet it's made of several different colours. What you're going to do, George, is focus on separating those colours." Josh blew on it again. George blinked rapidly, but still continued to stare past the windmill. Josh persevered. "You're safe here. Just you and me, and the windmill. Watch." He set it spinning.

George's eyes flickered and he blinked again, like he was trying to push out a piece of grit.

"See as it slows down? What colour is it making now? I'd say it was peach. What do you think?"

"Fuckwit," George said. Josh stopped talking about windmills and looked at him. George made eye contact, of sorts. "Not you," he clarified. Josh smiled. The windmill spun in the wind and George watched it. "Orange."

"What's that in the paint palette?"

"Orange," George repeated.

"Just orange?"

He made eye contact properly and smiled a little. "Just orange."

"Not burnt orange, or raw orange?"

"Nope. Just orange."

Josh nodded and took his hand again. "That's boring. It should be called, I don't know, vibrant orange or something like that."

"Yeah."

Josh kept going with the paint topic, offering further random and often ridiculous names for colours. The key, Sean said, was for George to focus on something outside of himself, and, of course, the smug know-it-all had been right again. It forced George to concentrate on describing what he saw, whether in reality or in his mind's eye, rather than getting caught up in the panic of not being able to get his mind and body to work in tandem. It was a distraction, pure and simple, however beautiful the end result might be.

Now George was more or less back in the real world, Josh needed to address the issue of what had happened with Rob, because as far as he knew, Adele still had him pinned to the path with fear.

"Why is he a fuckwit? On this occasion?"

"Jess asked after him a month ago, and it's taken him this long to come and see her."

"Who did she ask?"

"Lois. He just thought he'd casually drop by to say hi. Fucking idiot."

"I think we should let him see her," Josh said. George gave him a look. "And I'll tell you why. If he's got any heart, seeing her as she is now will hurt him more than you, Andy or Dan ever could."

"If he's got a heart at all. He hasn't got a frigging spine, that's for sure."

George didn't swear, or very rarely. It was only when he was in this kind of state that he opened his mouth and his mother's voice spilled from it. She'd taught him well.

"What do you think?" Josh prompted.

George shrugged. "You've got to get past Adele first."

"I'm prepared to give it a shot, but only if you think it's a good idea."

"What do I know?"

"A lot more than I do in situations like this. And you know Rob."

George nodded. "Take him to her. Let the bastard suffer."

"OK. Won't be long. Here." Josh gave George the windmill and stood up.

"What's this for?"

"Distraction. If you start feeling weird, just focus on the colours."

"Seriously?"

"Sean's idea, not mine. I'll get Adele to come and keep you company. It'll stop the pair of you getting into any more trouble!"

Josh went back through the house and found Adele and Rob exactly where he'd left them.

"Can you go and look after George for me?" he asked Adele. She nodded and went.

Josh turned to Rob. "Get up," he said coldly. Rob did as he was told. "She's upstairs, in bed. You know she's sick, I presume?"

"Lois mentioned it, yeah. Cancer, she said."

"That's right." Josh signalled for Rob to go inside. "Up the stairs and to the left. Oh, but you know that, don't you? From when you fucked her to get at her money."

"It wasn't like that."

"Surprising as it may seem, I don't care." Josh waited for Rob to start climbing the stairs before he said anything else. "Her dad's sitting with her. Nice guy, Dave, unless you cross him. Then he makes Andy look like a pussycat."

Rob stopped. He was warming to the possibility that this wasn't a good idea, but Josh wasn't going to let him leave.

"Of course," Josh smiled, "you're lucky he doesn't know what you did yet." He nodded to push Rob on.

At the top of the stairs, Rob stopped and glared at Josh. "I didn't have you down as one of them."

"One of?"

"A queer."

"Oh. I thought you meant someone with just enough psychopathic tendency to have no qualms about pushing you down the stairs and claiming you lost your footing. Chop-chop, Rob!"

"If you're trying to scare me, it's not working."

"I see. So, my husband nearly clubs you to death with your own helmet and has to be restrained—"

Rob scoffed. "By a five-foot-nothing bimbo!"

"Five foot two, actually, but that's by the by. Adele saw right through you last year, with your fake reunion, and we didn't believe her. She's a bit annoyed about that, to be honest, Rob. As I was saying, George would've killed you if she hadn't stopped him, and if Andy comes back anytime soon you're dead anyway. But none of this scares you?" Josh shrugged dismissively. "You think you're invincible?"

Rob backed off a little, but he wasn't backing down.

"Anyway, I'll leave you to it." Josh patted him on the shoulder and returned downstairs, where he spent a couple of minutes standing in the hall, calming himself down. It was almost impossible to believe that Rob Simpson-Stone, such a down-to-earth decent lad at school, had turned into this. And that was the problem with being a psychologist—always looking for the reasons why, when maybe it was the case that some people were evil because they chose to be.

In the garden, George and Adele were chatting and giggling. They both stopped when they saw Josh approach.

"He's up there with her now," he said and flopped into a chair.

Adele rubbed his arm. "It's a good thing. Jess needed to see him again, and he needed to see her like that. I only hope Dan and Andy don't get back early."

"Where are they?"

"At Barbara and Len's. They've put in a fitness suite, and Dan and Andy are showing them how to use the machines, not that I can see Barbara and Len using it much."

Josh nodded and yawned at the same time.

"Sorry," George said.

Josh took his hand. "It's fine. I was coming here once I'd had a coffee anyway. Your mum phoned to tell me the 'Paki shop' had been done over." Adele's expression of absolute horror made Josh laugh. "I did suggest to her that she might want to find a more appropriate name for it."

Now George started laughing. "What did she think of that idea?" he asked.

"She, erm, how to put it…" Josh frowned thoughtfully. "She said political correctness was pointless and served no useful purpose."

"Word for word?"

"More or less."

"Uh-huh?" George stared at Josh, waiting for him to elaborate. He sighed and relented.

"Verbatim? She said it was 'a bag of fuckin' shite' and hung up on me." George and Adele started giggling again. "And then Sean came round with Dylan. Honestly, he's driving me up the wall. 'How long do babies sleep?' I've no idea, Sean. 'Should I wake him up?' I've no idea, Sean. 'D'you think this milk is warm enough?' I've not got a bloody clue, Sean!"

Adele looked puzzled. "Why's he asking you?"

"That's a very good question."

"Because he thinks you know better than him," George said.

"About babies?"

"About everything."

"He's delusional. I don't even know what day of the week it is anymore. What is it? Saturday?"

George tutted and turned back to Adele. "Did you tell Josh about your college course?"

"Oh, it's not very exciting," she said.

"Have you enrolled?" Josh asked.

She nodded. "And they're going to do some tests on me in the next couple of weeks." She frowned. "That makes me sound like a guinea pig."

She didn't get any further than that, because they were distracted by the sound of the front door slamming, followed by a motorbike revving loudly and driving off at speed. The three of them went inside to check on Jess and Dave.

"Everything all right?" Josh asked cautiously. Jess was asleep; Dave was reading a paperback.

"Fine," he confirmed. "Rob's just left. I remember Jess talking about him when they were younger. They went to school together, he says."

"That's right."

"Seems a nice guy."

"Erm, yes," Josh agreed. *Best not to spoil the illusion.* "I'm going to make drinks, Dave. Would you like some lunch?"

"I wouldn't mind a sandwich or something, thanks."

Josh nodded and returned downstairs. *No damage done, except, hopefully, to Rob.*

Crossroads
Friday 22th September

Eleanor set the bowl down on the table next to the bed. It was one of those hospital tables that slide over the patient, and it had been a fight to get Jess to accept having it in her room.

Her room.

It was a beautiful, grown-up room, but still feminine; girly. The walls were lilac, with delicate pale-gold swirls around the outer edges; the soft carpet was cream, like the curtains. Eleanor hadn't noticed before that they were covered in tiny flowers, so tiny in fact that she'd always thought they were polka dots, but now she noticed they were forget-me-nots. *Forget me not.* She lifted the soft pink sponge from the soft pink water and squeezed.

"This smells really lovely," she said, watching the water released by the sponge cascade over her fingers, back into the bubbly reservoir below. "I love the smell of lilies. Not real lilies. They're too pungent, but lily-scented toiletries are subtle. Not like lilies at all, really."

She put the sponge back in the water and dried her hands so she could roll back the covers.

"I hope it's not too cool for you." She picked up the sponge again and smoothed it over Jess's cheek, noticing her twitch slightly. "Shaunna's going to come up and help us in a sec, give you a good all-over freshen-up." She saw the goosebumps. "Think we'll turn the heating up a little." She put the sponge back and dried Jess's face. She stepped out of the room. "Can someone turn up the heating?" she called down the stairs.

"Will do," George replied. They'd doubled up on their shifts, for the company.

To ease the waiting.

"Thanks."

She returned to the room, listening to the footsteps on the stairs.

"Hey," Shaunna smiled as she entered. They were well-practised at this now. She stepped to the right of the bed and put her hands on Jess's shoulder and hip, slowly bringing her over onto her side. Jess cried out, a strangled yell of pain. Every movement resulted in the same, though she wasn't entirely conscious.

"I'm so sorry, hun," Shaunna said. "Just try to relax." She held Jess still, waiting for the rapid rattling breaths to slow.

"We'll need to change this nightie, Jess," Eleanor explained, glancing down into the bed and then back at Shaunna.

Shaunna nodded and reached over and slowly eased up the nightie, rolling the soiled parts back on themselves. To the right and to the left again, between them, they removed the nightie, swapped in a new pad, bathed, redressed and caressed their friend.

Eleanor blew her hair out of her face. "I'm bloody roasting," she said.

Shaunna took the spare hair scrunchy from her wrist and walked around the bed, scooping Eleanor's hair and tying it back.

"Thanks."

"You're welcome." Back to her own side. "Has she had anything to drink at all this evening?"

"Not since—" Eleanor thought on it "—a bit before eight o'clock, it must have been, because the carer was still here."

"Should we try, do you think?"

Eleanor shrugged. "Let's see how we go."

"OK. You want some tea?"

"Yes, I will have some this time, thanks."

"Sorry. I just…"

"I know. It's what you do." Eleanor smiled.

Shaunna left.

Eleanor cleared the washbowl and towel away and returned to her seat next to the bed. She set aside the book she had been reading earlier. "So, Jessica Lambert, do you know what's significant about today?" She stayed quiet a moment, as if awaiting a response, and then continued, "It's a year since my hen party, but I'm not going to go on about it." It was a joke-nag, because she *had* gone on about it, even though they'd made up before Christmas, when they'd both had rather too much red wine.

Eleanor laughed now to indicate that she was teasing. However, there was a little more water needed to pass under that bridge before she could leave it behind for good. "I don't know if you're listening, honey. I hope you are, because, well, you know me better than I know myself, I think, so you also know that forgiveness doesn't come easy to me, even though it should, with my beliefs. But—"

She paused so that she could take Jess's hand in her own. It was so cool yet soft, and she bent down to kiss it. "If I never said it before, I forgive you, not that I'm so important as to be granting forgiveness. What I mean is, I'm not angry with you anymore. In fact, the only thing that makes me angry is that Rob treated you so badly, because you didn't deserve that. What matters is you had some good times together before he did what he did, and I'm going to remind myself of that whenever I need to.

"So, a year since my hen party, which means it's also a year since Josh and George finally got it together. I keep probing Josh to see if he'll tell me how it came about, but of course, he won't, although he did show me the text messages he sent to George. I've made up my own little story of what happened next, mostly to appease my curiosity, where Josh comes home from work, and George has made them a romantic, candlelit dinner.

"He'd have had to lock the doors so Josh didn't try and run away, mind you, which kind of ruins the whole romance aspect a bit, but can you see it? The two of them, sitting together, holding hands across the table and telling each other about when they first realised they were in love, feeding each other dessert, and… Yes, you're right, I'm getting carried away. As if they'd have done it the easy way."

They'd talked of all these things before.

"And I don't know if I told you, but I finally got hold of Callum Grady. He's that guy who Kev and I went to uni with, if you recall—the BMA guy. He said to get in touch as soon as things ease off, and he'll come down here so we can meet up for dinner, figure out just what the hell was going on. Sean's offered to show me Kev's psych record from prison, which he really shouldn't have in the first place, but I need to get it straight in my own mind before I read that.

"I think Josh is right, though. Kevin was trying to protect me. I bet you couldn't believe it when you found out it was him. You were so funny, griping about how your hot date wasn't giving out. He was always like that, to be honest. I mean, who could possibly resist? You—" she skipped a beat to rephrase, seeing past the bloating, the jaundice "—*are* gorgeous. So yeah, don't be beating yourself up about it. You haven't lost your allure. He's just a bit of a cold fish."

Eleanor stopped to take her tea from Shaunna. They exchanged smiles; no joy in those.

"You look exhausted," Eleanor observed, and she was right. For weeks, Shaunna had been taking more than her share of Jess's care. Now she was so tired that it was a struggle to stay upright, but she knew if she so much as stopped still she'd probably be asleep in seconds. "Go and have a lie-down," Eleanor advised.

"No, it's OK. I'm fine." Shaunna yawned and laughed a little.

"Go," Eleanor repeated. "I'll shout if I need you."

"All right. I will. Wake me in an hour if I'm still asleep."

***

Shaunna left and went into the room next door, but as was the way of these things, she didn't sleep. She couldn't. It wasn't her bed; Andy's aftershave lingered on the pillow; the sounds were unfamiliar; there were too many people coming and going. Steph arrived and made herself a drink. Josh arrived to collect George, and they left. Andy came home from the gym. He came straight upstairs and into the room, not knowing she was there, creeping around quietly while she kept her eyes shut. He went for his shower...

288

…and returned. She could feel his presence in the silence. She opened her eyes a little, watched him watching her, then opened them fully. He smiled. And there was hope in that smile. She gave up on sleep, shuffled herself up the bed and sat, with her knees up, her arms looped around them. He removed his towel and stood, bold, naked, aroused, at the end of the bed. She felt a stirring within, put her forehead on her knees, squeezed her thighs together, trying not to think about it.

He found his way into some boxer shorts and a pair of jeans. She waited for the sound of the zip before she looked up again and met his gaze, losing it only for as long as it took him to pull a t-shirt over his head, followed it as he came across, sat on the bed beside her and unballed his socks. They heard the front door open and close. Eleanor was in the room next door. Jess was in the room next door. Dying.

"I want you," Shaunna mouthed.

"Hiya, Steph." Adele's voice. A quick, polite exchange. The sound of heels on the stairs, now on the landing, the door to Jess's room, a hushed conversation.

"I want you, too," Andy whispered.

"I noticed."

They both laughed silently. The intensity returned.

He was all about adventure, challenge, risk, yet it was not he who dared to steal that kiss. It was the wrong time, the wrong place. Her pale-pink lips flushed red, her cheeks burned so hot he could feel the heat radiating from them, his heart beat faster as she leaned towards him, closed her eyes, sought out his mouth with hers, slow, soft, gentle, push together, holding so still, so hungry for more, *don't take more, don't take more*, but pull away? Both were afraid to move, not wanting to break the contact, yet knowing that the slightest increase in pressure from either of them would rupture their fragile connection to reality. They were caught in their own trap, frozen in the headlights of their oncoming passion, all set to career wildly off the road. Adele threw them clear.

"Hiya." She announced her arrival with a whispered greeting, stepped over the threshold and stopped dead. They had moved apart, and Andy was putting on his socks, but Adele knew her friend, and she knew her fiancé—not twins, no, but alike enough. She and Shaunna made eye contact, the latter imploring that she forget what she had seen. Adele smiled brightly. "Just thought I'd let you know I was here."

"OK," Shaunna replied. "Thanks."

Adele nodded and left.

Andy ran his hand through his hair and turned to Shaunna. No words spoken. No need. He got up from the bed and waited for her to do the same, pulled her to him, held her close, kissed the top of her head, felt her trembling in his arms though he, too, was shaken to the core by the fury of this thing.

"Too close," he whispered.

"I know."

He sighed to vent his frustration. She lifted her face and looked deeply and lustfully into his eyes. He shook his head. "Fucking hell, Shaunna." She smiled, left the scent of herself on his clothes, left the safety of his embrace.

"I'm going home for a few hours," she said. "I need to sleep."

He watched her leave the room, waited for the swell to recede, and went to see Jess.

The Longest Time
Saturday 23rd September

Andy threw his keys down on the breakfast bar by way of a warning that he was there. Shaunna still jumped and dropped the towel, and she'd only just finished folding it.

"Everything OK?" he asked.

"Yeah. Fine. She's had a wash, and the nurse checked the syringe driver. It was making a really weird noise earlier. Seems to be working OK, though."

"Who's here?"

"Just me and Kris. Steph left about half an hour ago."

"Oh, right."

"How's your mum?" Shaunna asked.

"Surprised to see me on a Saturday. I told her you'd all banished me."

"You needed a break."

"So do you."

She shrugged off his concern. "I'll get through now." The end was near. They could all see it, feel it.

Andy went to the fridge for a bottle of juice—still avoiding alcohol in Shaunna's company. "So, anyway…Mum's buzzing. They're going to Canada next Saturday, apparently."

"Canada?"

"Yeah, for three weeks. They're going to see Len's daughter and grandkids."

"It's all right for some, hey?"

"Well, it's to celebrate their wedding anniversary, so I'll let them off. *And* it was Len who remembered."

"Good for him! Mind you, I've seen your mum in action. I wouldn't want to forget, either."

"She's not that bad if you know how to handle her."

"Ha! Like you, you mean? 'Andrew! If you don't turn that bloody noise off, I'm going to knock you into the middle of next week!'"

Andy laughed at her impersonation. "That was uncanny, although I meant Dan. I've always found it works better to keep my head down and beg for mercy, but she's all mouth, really."

"Just as well, or you'd have lost years!"

Shaunna finished folding the last of the laundry and shifted it all into the basket, ready to take upstairs. She'd have taken it straight up, but Andy was standing between her and the exit, so she left it where it was and filled the kettle instead.

He was watching her every move; she could feel it, even though she had her back to him, and she dared not turn around for fear of making eye contact. Her stomach was churning, and her breathing had become fast and shallow, just with the thought of him being so close. She needed to escape, because if she didn't, she wouldn't be responsible for her actions. This thing was like a raging tempest, tearing up her common sense and her ability to reason. She needed to escape.

The kettle came to the boil, but she abandoned it to the desire to flee and grabbed the basket, stepping off towards the hallway. Her intention in turning sideways had been to keep the basket between them, which worked right up to the point where it caught on the door handle, and the whole thing tipped, sending all the newly folded sheets and towels tumbling to the floor.

"Balls," she said. She put the basket down and sighed.

"I'll give you a hand."

Before she could protest, he was in front of her, and her plastic shield was gone. Nothing between them now but air, and even that seemed in short supply. She tried to take deep breaths; her head was spinning, and she could smell him, the gentle musk of his scent, mingled with cologne and mint. She picked up a towel and tried not to see him, feel him, breathe him, closed her eyes, refused to take in more air, gasped as she felt his finger under her chin, tilting her face upwards. She opened her eyes.

"Just swallowed my gum," he said, taking the towel from her and dropping it into the basket. He moved closer, felt their torsos touch, and at those points a spark, igniting the smallest of flames, radiating outwards like a newborn forest fire.

She gasped again, trying to draw the oxygen away, so futile to fight, too late. He moved closer still; she couldn't back away, their lips almost touching, almost found the will to resist, almost thought the floor had fallen away as his mouth found hers, both so desperate for this kiss and all that it promised, trying to be gentle but overcome by the urgency, the need and the hunger, tasting each other as if for the first time, unable to pull apart now they had come together.

He lifted his hand, combing his fingers through her hair, using it to bring her even closer. Her arms found him, her hand strayed inside his t-shirt, hot palm against the small of his back, pressing him to her, his other arm now behind her doing the same, and all the while the towels and sheets lay crumpled on the floor between them. They couldn't stop—didn't want to stop—yet each knew that they must, and so the kissing slowed, until they found they could uncouple. He gently bit her lip as he tried to depart; she returned the gesture and at last caught her breath. He laughed and bent to rest his forehead against hers, still the sparks falling as kisses.

"Kris is upstairs," she whispered, disbelieving.

"I know," he whispered back. "That's why I did it."

She frowned and stepped away. He moved with her. "Just for the thrill?"

He sighed, humouring her, and kissed her again. "Because it's safer."

She understood now. However much they wanted it, they couldn't go any further with Kris there.

"Bet you'd like that," he said, a smile dancing on his lips.

She stood on tiptoes and ran the tip of her tongue up the cleft in his chin, just as she had always wanted, and kissed him back. "Would you?" she asked, a hint of a dare in the question. He didn't answer. "Of course, you're not really his type. You're too..." Her hand trailed down over his firm pectoral muscles, traced his abs. She inhaled deeply and let go of the breath very slowly, put her head down, fighting herself and the desire within, pushing her towards complete abandon.

Fuck Kris. Just take me here and now. Her mind even fleetingly considered the fortuity of the towels and sheets being so close by, and she could feel him throbbing against her. He didn't seem to care that his state of arousal was so obvious, almost as if he were showing off. *Look what I have for you.* She pushed against him and looked up again. He was smiling.

"Patience, my red hot baby."

"I thought that was the Mustang."

"Jealous?"

"Of a car? Get real!"

"Well, you know how she loves me to gently ease down her top and run my hands over her sexy curves. When she's ready, I just slide right inside, get her started, and we take it nice and slow at first—don't want to rush it when it's that good, then we take it up a gear…"

Shaunna shook her head. "You sound like a complete sleazeball."

"Do I?" Andy pretended to be surprised and hurt. Shaunna laughed, but then they both became quiet again, once more consumed by their desire. She had hooked her fingers through the belt loops of his jeans and used them to pull him to her, stretching up and pushing her mouth against his, forcing her tongue inside. His palms slid up over her hips and under her top, spanning the smooth skin, savouring every inch of contact. His thumbs came up against her bra, and he eased them underneath, but then quickly pulled away from her.

"No," he said, more to himself than to her. He ran his hand through his hair and backed off, studying the floor in an attempt to regain control.

Shaunna, too, was shaking, but she knew he was right. She straightened her top and knelt down to fold the towels back into the basket, glancing up at him every so often as he paced backwards and forwards.

"I'll make that tea for you in a minute," he said, although she was thinking she'd much rather he came close enough for her to grab him by the legs and unzip his jeans. He could sense how dangerous it would be to get any closer and stayed well away.

He flipped the switch on the kettle. "I've paid a deposit on an apartment. It's upstairs from Dan and Adele."

"Why?"

"It's a nice place, and it'll be good to be near them."

"Yeah, but how…" She stopped folding and looked up at him, confused.

"You get caught by a photographer, you're going to see Adele."

"Ah." She smiled. "That's quite clever."

"For me, you mean?"

"You do that a lot."

"What?"

"Fish for compliments."

"How was I?"

"Pointing out that you were cleverer than my comment suggested I thought you were."

"I don't get you."

"Like on the picnic, when I said you were very well tamed, you said, 'For a straight man?' as if I should be surprised that you're domesticated, or romantic, or intelligent."

Andy laughed self-consciously.

"Or is it that you don't believe it yourself?" she speculated. He turned away to make the tea, although it was a means of avoiding looking at her. She finished folding the towels—again—lightly sprung to her feet and walked up behind him, wrapping her arms around his waist.

He turned to face her and kissed her nose. "Or maybe you're just spending too much time with Sean Tierney," he contended.

"Ah, you're right about that, for sure," she said in her best Derry accent, continuing in the same. "But surely a big strong fella like yourself isn't so fussed with cleverness and cuddles?"

Andy laughed. "That was appalling."

"Was it?" Now she pretended to look hurt.

"No, not really. It was very good. So, you had any Irish in you lately?"

"Andy!"

"Oh, sorry, I meant have you got any Irish in you." He grinned mischievously. She play-slapped him on the chest, and they both continued to laugh, but once again, it echoed away to nothing as their lips collided, with him pinned against the cupboard and unable to move away, her pelvis tilted up to maximise the contact.

Her mouth left his, as she dragged her lips down over his day-long stubble, to his neck, kissing and biting, revelling in the sensation of his pulse against her tongue. She brought her hand down to his waist and ran her finger up and down the zip of his jeans, the tip of her nail against the metal teeth making him think she had unzipped them. He waited for the pressure to ease as he was set free, but it didn't.

"You are the most unbelievable tease," he groaned.

She smiled and returned her mouth to his, sucking his bottom lip as they came together again, taking his tongue into her mouth and holding it there with her lips. He pulled out.

"We need to stop."

"OK." She started to unbuckle his belt. His hand shot around from her back and blocked her.

"No!" He shook his head. "I'm already on the edge."

"So am I, so why don't we just—"

"No, Shaunna. Not now."

"And he says I'm a tease?" she muttered.

"But you can't say you're not enjoying it."

"Yeah. I guess 'enjoying' is one way to describe it." Finally, she found the will to back away for real. Knowing he was watching, she bent over to pick up the basket and paused to give him a little longer before she took it upstairs to the airing cupboard.

Kris peered around the door of Jess's room. "You need a hand?" he asked.

"No, I'm fine. Andy's making a cup of tea." She turned and smiled at him. "I'll bring mine up here. You can go home, if you want."

"I do, but—" He glanced back into the room. "I think it might be nearly time to call people."

Shaunna stepped past him and stood still, holding her breath to better hear, and in doing so found herself frozen, motionless, looking upon her friend, lying in the bed, appearing just as if she were asleep, although in Shaunna's mind an image took form, starting out as the memory of waving goodbye to George at the departure gate in the airport. George disappeared, and in his place Jess appeared, happy, waving back. And the tears had dammed themselves. And the tears had dammed themselves.

And that was how she knew.

She turned back to Kris.

"Yes, it's time."

Full Circle
Saturday 23rd–Sunday 24th September

It was a Sunday afternoon, almost twenty-four years ago, when they had first gathered like this, so many of them all trying to crowd into the maternity ward's waiting room, taking it in turns to pace up and down whilst they awaited the news.

The good news.

Baby Krissi's birth had bound them, inextricably, to each other. Nine friends from high school, each part of their own subgroup, now a whole. The Circle. It had been a time of celebration and of revelation, growing into each other, learning how to fit together. In the decades that had since elapsed, they had drifted apart and come back together in endless combinations, like swarming swallows. Jess and Eleanor became Eleanor and Josh; Josh and George became George and Kris; Kris and Dan became Dan and Adele, and so on it went, around and around, ever evolving, never departing.

Twenty-four years.

In many respects, it felt no different, because the last couple of weeks had been so hellish that all of them were experiencing the same mix of guilt and relief that it was almost over. In the armchair, Adele was sitting on Dan's knee, their fingers latticed, eyes part-closed and burning with fatigue. Josh was on the floor in front of the sofa, George sitting behind, massaging Josh's temples to stave off the migraine. Kris sat to George's left, but then he stood and stretched, making eye contact with Adele. They shared a sad smile. He went to make drinks.

The making, like the drinking, was something to do to while away the hours of waiting, waiting. Kris passed Shaunna in the hallway, touched palms together and gently embraced. She was a

297

decathlon athlete at the final event, exhausted yet determined not to let down her team. She and Eleanor were running a perpetual relay up and down the stairs. Presently, Eleanor passed back the baton, and Shaunna went up, to visit the loo and then sit and talk to the Lamberts, or, in reality, talk at the Lamberts, as Jess slowly progressed toward death.

"You OK, Ellie?" Josh asked as she stepped over his legs and collapsed onto the sofa, looping her arm through George's and leaning against his shoulder. George turned and kissed her head—a gesture that meant nothing and everything at once.

"I'm so tired," she admitted, "but I can't grumble. I honestly don't know how Shaunna is still standing."

*

Upstairs, in the other room, Andy was sitting on the end of 'his' bed, with Sean at his side, talking to him very quietly and calmly. He'd earlier overheard a conversation between Adele and Eleanor about Rob's visit and would have lost it completely, were it not for Sean being close enough to also have heard and intervened before he got that far.

"I need to go back in to her," Andy said. Sean nodded.

"When you're ready, Andy."

"There's no time."

He was right about that, Sean had to agree. He left Andy to gather his thoughts and went in to Jess.

*

The carer glanced up from her magazine and gave him a brief smile.

"How're we doing?" he asked as a general question. Jess lifted her fingers slightly, and Sean went over. He took her hand gently in his. "Are you comfy there, my lovely girl?"

Her eyes flickered and opened a fraction of an inch. She attempted to speak; a murmur that failed to make it to her lips.

"Just squeeze my fingers if you are."

She squeezed.

"Good girl." He carefully squeezed back. She drifted away again, and her hand became limp. He placed it back on top of her chest and turned to Steph and Dave. "Do you need anything at all?"

"No, thanks, Sean," Steph said. She sighed a sigh that carried the answer. *We need the pain to end.*

"I'll have a chat with Eleanor when I go down."

Not Jess's pain; theirs. She was twitching again, as she had been intermittently for days. Dave immediately moved over to the bed and laid his hand on her forehead.

"Are you sure she's not suffering?" he asked. He was crumpled, unshaven, his face grey with exhaustion and sorrow.

"It's the side effects of the meds," Sean explained, knowing Eleanor had just told them, and it was a message they had each repeated many times over. Eleanor, too, was struggling to keep her sense of rationality and beginning to question the truth of it. The only thing maintaining it for Sean was how often he had been here before, but never quite like this.

Quietly, he left the room and returned downstairs, stopping at the door of the living room to beckon Eleanor's attention.

"Have we got midazolam here?"

"I did the script earlier. Does she need it?"

"Not so much as her mum and dad, but I think she might be heading that way."

"I'll get it set up."

Eleanor moved towards the stairs. Sean put his hand on her arm. She nodded and continued on her way. Much as it was very useful that they had both been able to help professionally, it was riddled with dilemmas, and Sean understood the stress she was under better than most. During the past week, they had spent hours discussing the advance directive Jess had drawn up months ago, which effectively asked that her life not be artificially extended, and she had made it clear when she was in the hospice that she was hoping someone would make the 'right' decision when the time came.

However, she still had full mental capacity, so unless she specifically requested more pain relief, Eleanor's lasting power of attorney meant nothing. In short, Sean and Eleanor had the legal power to ease Jess's life to an end, but only if she was no longer able to make the decision for herself. Thankfully, the Catholic Church was on their side this time, which had granted Eleanor peace of mind. Her god was with her, guiding her and giving her strength.

Sometimes—the times like this—Sean wished he still believed so he, too, could pray, for mercy, for strength, for a miracle, because right now, that apple looked juicier and more delicious than ever, but it found a temporary guardian in Kris.

"Tea, Sean?"

"That'd be smashing, thanks." He went outside to collect his thoughts.

*

It was a beautiful night, the clear blue-black sky dotted with bright white stars and a blinding cream-white moon, waxing almost full, its opposition lighting up the garden with shadows too sharp for the dead of night. Sean checked his watch: 04:04. The sky would begin to lighten soon—a couple of hours or so—he'd watched it many times of late, here and at home, and not because of Dylan. Sophie had yet to trust him with a lone overnight stay. But sleep wasn't coming easy to him—hadn't done for weeks.

That was how he was. Some people slept when they were trying to cope with stress, others got insomnia. Falling into the latter category was a boon for tonight, at least. And there were no wind chimes here. Small mercy, although the mental battle cared not if there were music to accompany it.

He needed a drink. His brain was so damned insistent, and where at home, there was nothing to tempt, here there was a cabinet loaded with the stuff—whiskey, vodka, gin, rum—he could have provided a full and accurate inventory of the entire stock. Every time he walked through the kitchen, he looked at it, longed to just grab a bottle, slosh a little into a glass. What would it matter, one glass? It was a difficult night. And it didn't mean a thing. Just because he wanted a drink tonight didn't mean he'd want one tomorrow.

300

A one-off.

"Hey."

Josh's friendly call startled him. He glanced over his shoulder, turning away from the house again as he spoke in response.

"What about yer?" he asked.

Josh drew up beside him. "I was about to ask you that."

"I'm OK. Getting a bit of fresh air."

"Is that all?"

"It's all I've taken, but nowhere near enough."

"Sean."

"Will one glass do me any harm?"

"Yes. Total abstinence means *total* abstinence. Not even one glass."

"It's a unique situation."

"And you'll find other equally unique situations to follow if you do this now."

Sean sighed in partial submission, but he was yet to beat it back.

"If not for you, then do it for Shaunna," Josh said.

"Surely, I should be doing it for Soph and Dylan?"

"They're not here now, are they?"

Sean sighed again.

"See? I know you, Tierney. If I'd said do it for Sophie and Dylan, you'd have said—"

"They're not here now, are they?"

"Quite right. And just so as you know, Steph's cigarette packet is on the breakfast bar, and there are seventeen cigarettes in it."

"Ah." Sean extended his arm around Josh. "Then we shall sponsor each other through this godless night." He tilted his head up and squinted at the brightness of the moon. "If I hadn't spent so many hours doing the exact same thing I'm doing now, I'd be telling you what a magnificent sight that is."

"Yes, I know where you're coming from," Josh agreed, although his own insomnia wasn't giving him much trouble; it rarely did. "Makes you wonder, doesn't it? To think men have walked upon it—that those in power were prepared to risk such a dangerous mission, risk lives. Why? What's the point?"

"Adventure," Sean said. "That's why. Exploration and adventure. To boldly go—"

"Fuck off," Josh snapped, although he was smiling as he did so.

"D'yer kiss yer grandma with that filthy gub?"

"Aye, I do," he said. Sean glanced at him. "And if you dare call me a p'tah, I'll lamp yer."

"You coming up with your own language there, Joshy?"

Josh smiled, but the smile quickly faded, and he swallowed hard. "Oh, Sean. How can this be happening? Why? Why? Why…"

The word trailed off into a drawn-out moan as the pain hit him hard and fast in his midriff, sending him to his knees in a protracted collapse, as if he were fighting gravity, although he was too far consumed by his grief to even know down from up.

Sean kept hold, his hands under Josh's arms, hoping he could hold on tight enough to stop him falling through the ground. "All right, now," he soothed, "it's all right."

Josh jerked and jolted violently, his cries nearly howls, so fitting under that almost full moon. He fell against Sean, his legs sliding sideways, exhausted from carrying the weight, the burden of caring for his friends, containing his own sense of loss, and the deathly fear that in letting it drag him down, succumbing to its power, he would be trapped within its cold, clawing hands forever.

Sean knelt beside him on the night-damp grass and allowed Josh's head to come to rest in his lap, continuing to hold him, stroking back his hair as the cries kept coming, wrenching of the soul slowly fading out, out, giving way to coughs, then sniffs, punctuating the still, early morning air. Josh kept his fist clenched and chewed at his knuckle.

"I'm so sorry," he gasped within the after-shocks.

"Don't be."

"I am. I know this is hard for you, too, and I've tried not to…" He took a breath, hoping to purge himself of the sorrow that was crushing him.

"It's OK," Sean comforted. "It's OK to feel like this." He shifted position in an effort to retain the feeling in his feet.

Josh stayed where he was. He couldn't get up; he didn't want to get up.

"This is what loss feels like," Sean continued. "What it does to you. It hurts all the way through, doesn't it?" Josh nodded and started to cry again. "And I know it won't take the pain away, but you mustn't be frightened, my wonderful, brave friend. You have been so strong. You have all been so strong. You've given her so much love, so much of your own life force. But the fight is over for you now. You can start to let go."

"But what if I..." Josh's words came out in stuttered spurts. Sean shushed him, understanding his fear without the need for him to explain.

"I'll be there to stop it, I promise, so let yourself feel."

Josh's breathing had slowed, although it was still rasping. "How are you keeping it together?" he asked.

"I did my falling apart a month ago, remember? And I'll do it again, you can be quite sure of that."

Josh gradually pulled himself up and sat, cross-legged and shivering. "Grass is wet," he observed.

Sean laughed and wriggled uncomfortably against the damp seat of his pants. "Yeah. I kind of noticed already."

*

Adele was sitting with Jess, telling her about a new perfume she'd tested in the department store. It was a one-way conversation, with no response whatsoever from the recipient, but Adele continued, for it was normal, and that was what Jess had requested.

Adele paused only when Andy swapped places with Steph and Dave, turning to smile at him. It was such an innocent, carefree smile, so at odds with the situation, yet it gave him great comfort. He saw through Adele's façade of surgery and peroxide-enhanced blondeness, as did Dan, in reality. He just pretended otherwise, because that was how it had always been.

"Did you need to get some sleep?" he asked.

Adele shook her head. "No. I'm fine. Thank you for asking, though."

303

"You've got little Shaunna and everything else to cope with."

She reached across and took his hand, giving it the gentlest shake. "Andy, I'm fine. Really. Your mum's taking care of Shaunna for us." She looked him in the eye. "This is where we need to be tonight."

He nodded. It was for him that Adele and Dan were here, for whilst they were all part of the same friendship group, they had never been close to Jess. She was too clever, too snooty, too selfish and impulsive. She was all they pretended to be, but were not. Getting close to her showed their deception for what it was, and they chose instead to keep their distance.

So they were here for him, and he couldn't even think how he might convey how grateful he was for that, especially knowing that Adele had taken Rob in hand—the size of her, and the size of him! He was easily over six foot and almost as broad as Dan, but women had a different power beyond the might of physical strength. Andy had seen it time and again—in Adele, in Jess and Steph—in all of the women in his life. He had such respect for them, revered them, though he had often been scolded for doing so. He felt himself smile as he recalled Shaunna's tongue-in-cheek pedestal remark and closed his eyes to relive last night's kisses. He opened them again, and the realisation dawned.

"Where's Shaunna? Downstairs?"

Adele shrugged. "No, she wasn't. She came up here, quite a while ago, actually."

Andy frowned and went to investigate. It was only a two-bedroom house, and he had been in the other room. He checked the toilet first; the door was locked.

"Won't be a minute," George shouted from inside.

"No worries," Andy replied. He pushed the bathroom door open. The room was in darkness, but he could see her outline against the moonlight spilling in. She was sitting on the edge of the bath, her hands on her knees, her head bowed. Andy stepped inside and sat next to her.

"I wondered where you were," he whispered.

She gave him no response. He reached across and took her hand. She allowed it, but she was distant, cut off, like a screen had been erected between them. Before, her passion had been tangible to him. Now, he felt nothing from her at all.

"Can I do anything?" he asked. She shook her head, the movement dispersing her scent. He pulled her to him and nestled his face in her hair, leaving a gentle kiss, desperate to keep hold of her.

She waited a moment and then got up, splashed water in her face and dabbed it dry with the towel.

"Thank you," she said.

She walked out at the same time George exited the toilet, not a word passing between them. George watched her head back for Jess's room. He automatically switched on the bathroom light before he entered. Andy put his hand up to shield his eyes.

"Oh! Sorry." George smiled apologetically and shuffled past to wash his hands. "Are you OK? I mean, I know you're not, but—"

"Yeah, I'm OK, George. You?"

"Yeah, thanks." They exchanged a look of understanding, and both departed, back downstairs. All change.

*

Kris went up to sit with Jess, Shaunna and Adele; Steph and Dave were in the garden with Eleanor, who was explaining what the medication she had just given Jess did; George joined Josh and Sean in the kitchen, which left Dan and Andy on their own in the lounge.

Andy switched on the TV and tuned it to the Extreme Sports channel. It was showing a programme about the environmental threats to top surfing spots, with the usual smug Australian voiceover and footage of sewage and oil spills, melting glaciers and dead whales. Andy switched it off again and flopped back into the sofa.

"Death and destruction everywhere," he said.

Dan rubbed his eyes and pulled his hands down over his face, keeping his fingers pressed to his closed eyelids, wondering how he could be so tired yet still wide awake. He hadn't felt like this since little Shaunna first came home from hospital, and he spent a few minutes thinking back to how hard that had been. They'd taken turns on the nighttime feeds but kept forgetting to switch off the apnoea alarm before lifting her out of her cot, so they were almost always both awake every night. Hopefully, they wouldn't have to go through anything like that with the next one—if there was a next one, as they hadn't had any luck yet. Still, it had only been a month.

Dan's mind started to drift aimlessly, half asleep and vaguely aware of noises around the house. He opened his eyes again. Kris and Adele appeared in the hallway, Adele heading for the kitchen. Kris stood at the door to the lounge.

"Andy," he said, his voice quiet and resigned. He tilted his head towards the stairs.

Andy nodded and got up, suddenly feeling sick, a cold sweat descending over him as he sprinted up to Jess. Steph, Dave and Eleanor arrived a second later and stayed to one side as the procession of others made their way into the room.

Dan took one look, squeezed his brother's arm and fled in tears, back to Kris and Adele, who had remained downstairs, already having said their goodbyes and now sitting at the breakfast bar, waiting out the minutes. The carer was with them, boiling the kettle and setting out many, many mugs in preparation.

Eleanor sidestepped past the others to reach Jess, so still and quiet, no twitching, the rattling breaths now replaced by irregular deep inhalations held for an unnaturally long time.

Shaunna stood in the corner by the window, her eyes trained on the moon, visible through the open curtains, the daylight beginning to spill from above, a bruise-like glow that slowly stole the moon's glory.

She heard Eleanor's breath catch and closed her eyes, listening to the sound of her friends moving around the room. She knew Josh and Sean were there; she could feel them, their presence, their uncontained sorrow. She wanted to haul them to her bosom and cherish them, but she was paralysed, overwhelmed by emotion. Practical support she could do with her eyes shut—she laughed ironically, silently. She felt them depart. George, likewise, said nothing, but he reached out to Shaunna as he left, infusing her with the last of his own strength. She grabbed his hand and clung to it until he was too far away. Eleanor cleared her throat and swallowed hard; Shaunna felt that, too. The air mattress started to re-inflate—she knew—under the weight of Jess and Eleanor's final embrace.

"Good night, God bless, my beautiful friend. I love you."

She listened to Eleanor walk past and leave; she stopped just outside the door.

Now Steph's voice, broken.

"We're here, baby. You just let go now." A pause in speech, filled with the battle of a mother trying not to scream out. *Please don't take my baby. Please, God, let her live.* Steph pulled hard on the air, choking, choking. "Give Daisy the biggest hug for us."

Dave was beyond words.

Shaunna opened her eyes, chanced a glance across the room, saw Steph with her lips to Jess's cheek, Dave clinging to her with one hand, the other grasping at his daughter, trying to drag her from the clutches of the reaper.

She looked to Andy, standing by the door, a statue but for the tears rolling down his cheeks. They met each other's gaze, held it, unblinking, through the sound of the last breath, the release of hysteria mere feet from where they stood in silent communication of nothingness, the beam interrupted as Steph and Dave stumbled from the room, Eleanor's return to declare time of death at 06:31, Josh coming to gather her up from the floor and carry her away to the relative sanctuary of the rooms below.

Still they remained, unable to break free, their ward now deceased, but she alone had died—though she had not died alone.

Eventually, Andy found he could move his feet and stepped tentatively in Shaunna's direction. She closed her eyes again, awaited his arrival and fell against him, her whole being drained of life and love. He held her up, whispered thank-yous over and over, but they were just words. He stepped away again and opened a drawer, extracting from it a small flat box. He held it out to her. She took it from him, searching his face for an explanation.

"She told me I was to give you this straight away," he said, "that you'd need it. I don't know what it is."

Shaunna lifted the lid from the box and unfolded the white tissue paper, making without what was within.

She fell to her knees.

*

Andy reached down and took the box from her, examining the object inside, squinting in the sunrise twilight to read the words painted on the left portion of the plaque; on the right was mounted a shiny silver knife. A butter knife.

And the knight said to the dragon:
This is the most powerful sword in the land,
for it belongs to a maiden with hair of pure fire.

And the dragon looked at the knight and said:
How can you be a knight? You're a girl.

And the knight said:
My teacher said girls can be anything they want to be.
Besides, I am a girl with the most powerful sword in
the land,
and you are just a dragon.

And the dragon got really scared and ran away.

The End.

LIBRA

Examine well the scales with which you weigh;
Let justice rule your conduct every day;
For when you face the Judge you'll need fair play.

Morning Sun
Sunday 24th September

Nine o'clock. The undertakers arrived, performed their business efficiently, deftly; it was just another job. They left. Steph and Dave sat in waking comas at the breakfast bar, trying to find the motivation to get up and go home, if only to shower and change, torn as they were between their desire to sort everything out as soon as possible and their desperate need for sleep. Eleanor had given them both a prescription for sleeping pills. Indeed, she'd never written so many prescriptions for the things in one go.

Kris had fulfilled Shaunna's on the way home. He watched over her as she took them and escorted her to bed. She was sleeping, finally, completely exhausted, the flat black box lying on her upturned palm. He and Casper went for a walk, taking a slightly different route to their usual so they could stop by at Krissi and Jason's flat. It was Krissi's first day off sick from The Pizza Place, and Jason had stayed home with her, leaving Stu and Hadyn in charge of the usual full Sunday of recordings and rehearsals. She was in a terrible state.

Eleanor was wide awake. Toby was at church with his grandparents, and James was on his way to the airport, bound for New York and a meeting that couldn't be postponed—not the first wedding anniversary hoped for, although they'd decided some months ago to delay celebrating until such time as they felt up to it. Charlotte was keeping Eleanor company, which consisted largely of sitting next to her on the sofa and holding her while she cried, interspersed with talking about any old rubbish so Eleanor could get her feelings back in check again. Everything was hollow, blank, numb—all of those and none of them at the same time.

Andy, Dan and Adele were at Barbara and Len's, with Andy employing the self-harm strategy of mental pain management in the new gym, lifting weights so heavy that he was bursting blood vessels in his arms, and eventually, Dan swore at him for being an idiot. Adele and Barbara sat next to the pool; it was getting a little too warm in the conservatory, the sun surprisingly strong for the time of year. Barbara closed some of the blinds and returned to listening to Adele gabble on about potential funeral outfits for Jess. It was something that had been asked of her several weeks ago, and focusing on it was helping Adele to stay just the right side of hysterical.

Josh sat in the armchair, staring into the mid-distance, with George and Sean playing *Crash Team Racing*, as they had been doing since they'd arrived home. It was the only game Sean knew how to play, and Josh was in no fit state to register how their activity connected to the deeper meaning the game had for him and George. Even if it had occurred to him, he wouldn't have cared. It was Sean, after all, and he was getting beaten repeatedly, not that he seemed particularly perturbed.

No, Josh's more pressing concern was the Last Will and Testament of Jessica Lambert, still in the sealed envelope on the table. He knew he was one of the executors; she'd told him back when she first distributed the copies, along with an explicit instruction that they not be opened until she was gone.

She was gone.

The reality washed over him again, his whole body rising with the flood of emotion, and even though he thought he was concealing it well, both Sean and George saw it. George immediately went over.

"Hey," he said gently, taking Josh into his arms and holding him tight. Out of the three of them, it was George who was the most together, as was always true in such situations—when Kevin had Ellie in the car, it was George who had been level-headed enough to formulate a plan, and when Krissi decided to uncover the identity of her father, it was George who came running to Josh's rescue. At his side, as always.

"I love you," Josh sobbed.

"I know," George said, kissing him, "and I love you, even though you've just snotted in my mouth." He pretended to pull away in disgust and wiped his face. Josh laughed in spite of how awfully sad he was.

"Can I join in?" Sean asked from across the room.

"I'm not sharing my snot with you," Josh said.

"I damn well hope not!"

"I love you, too, *Seany*."

"I don't care," Sean replied, as usual. "But the feeling is mutual, *Joshy*." Sean grinned, and Josh stuck out his tongue at him.

"D'you want a game?" George asked.

Josh peered at the paused image onscreen and shook his head. "No. I need to open that." He shifted his eyes in the direction of the will on the table. "I've got to phone the funeral director tomorrow, and I don't know what she wanted." Jess had refused to discuss her funeral arrangements with him. "I wonder if anyone else has looked at it yet?"

"Would you like me to do it?" George asked.

"Yes, please," Josh answered immediately.

George looked at him in resigned disbelief. "You only had to say."

"I didn't want to ruin your game."

"We're just playing for something to do, that's all. Our son's coming round soon."

Josh pulled back so he could look George in the eye, and then glanced over at Sean. "OK. I don't think I want to know any more than that."

George winked at Sean. They were tormenting him, although Dylan's parents were in agreement that George would continue to be a big part of his life, because the attachment was already forming between them, so Josh wasn't a million miles off with his timeshare idea. Now, he watched George peel back the flap of the envelope and extract Jess's will.

"Do you want me to read it out?" George asked.

Josh put a shaky hand on his chest and took a breath in preparation. He nodded to indicate he was ready, or as ready as he was ever going to be.

George cleared his throat. "OK." His voice wavered slightly. "'This is the Last Will and Testament of me Jessica Lambert of...' It's just her address after that. 'One: I revoke all former wills made by me. Two: I appoint Joshua Sandison of...' our address, 'and my husband Andrew Jeffries of...'" George's voice trailed off and he turned, jaw dropped, to Josh, whose eyebrows were drawn so high they had completely disappeared under his hair.

"*Husband* Andrew Jeffries?" Josh repeated. He took the will from George and scanned the first few lines to check for himself. *Yes, that's definitely what it says.* He passed it back and looked at Sean, all set to ask if he knew about it, but he could see from his face he was as shocked as they were.

"I need to call Ellie," he said. "She thought she was the other executor."

"She's on here, too," George confirmed. "After you and Andy. Like a reserve, I think."

"Hmm. She's not going to like that very much." Josh reached into his pocket for his phone. It wasn't there. He left the room to go and check his jacket, calling back as he searched. "Jess told me she didn't want Andy as an executor. She said it would be like giving a five-year-old the keys to a sweet shop." He came back into the room, phoneless. "I think I've left it at Jess's." He sighed. He wasn't ready to return there yet. George took out his own phone and passed it across; he and Sean sat in silence as Josh made the call.

"Hey, George," Ellie answered very wearily.

"It's not, it's Josh. Listen: sorry to jump straight into this, but have you had a chance to look at the will yet?"

"Not yet. Charlotte's running me a bath. I'm freezing. Must be because I'm so tired. Why?"

"Oh, it's not urgent. You enjoy your bath. I'll speak to you later, OK?"

"OK. Love you."

"You, too."

They both hung up. Josh sat down again.

"Shall I go and make coffee?" Sean suggested. He was fidgety with fatigue, but also feeling quite upset. He and Jess had spent a lot of time together, confided in each other, and he was devastated that she hadn't told him about Andy.

He didn't even get as far as the door before the music started: 'Boss of Me'—George's ringtone for Eleanor, which didn't get aired much as his phone was usually set to vibrate only. Sean started to laugh. George passed the phone to Josh, who smiled, pressed the answer button and put it straight on loud speaker.

"*Husband* Andrew Jeffries?" Eleanor shrieked.

***

By the time Kris got back from Krissi and Jason's, Shaunna was awake again, sitting at the kitchen table with a mug of tea in front of her. Casper nudged her hand with his nose, and she absently patted him on the head. Kris watched her for a moment or so and touched his hand to the mug. Lukewarm. He picked it up and tipped it down the sink.

"I'll make you another one," he said.

Shaunna remained still and quiet, which was normal. He'd expected it. She'd been like the same after her mum died, and then she'd suddenly exploded. In fact, he wondered if he should just call Adele now and have her on standby. He made two mugs of tea and sat down opposite, pushing one across so that it was directly in front of her. He took hold of her hands. He didn't speak, for there was nothing to say. All he could do was be there for her and hope she came out of it soon, preferably with as little damage as possible to herself and the house.

He squeezed her hands and she looked up. "Do you want to do something?" he asked. "Go out somewhere, maybe?"

She shook her head. She freed a hand to pick up her mug and sipped carefully.

"OK." Kris mirrored her actions. "I've phoned Barry. He can manage without me until Wednesday, so I'll just do whatever you need."

"Thank you," she said, her voice so quiet it was little more than a whisper.

They continued to sit in silence but for drinking their drinks, still with his hand around hers. He watched her carefully and listened to the sip-gulp-sigh rhythm, her expression unchanged. Over time, his gaze wandered past her, to the flat black box she had brought home from Jess's. He was curious to know what it was, but unsure if he should ask—whether doing so would make things better or worse. He decided to take the chance.

"The box you brought home," he said. She blinked a couple of times, but nothing more than that. "Is it a present, or…?"

She looked up at him again and coughed to ensure her voice would sound. "You can have a look, if you like."

He slowly retracted his hand and got up.

She closed her eyes, knowing he wouldn't understand the significance of what was inside, and she didn't feel like explaining.

Kris opened the box and read the plaque. He laughed gently. "You gave her the butter knife. I wondered where it had gone."

The one mounted on the plaque was a new knife—not the same one she had given to Jess. She turned on her chair, beckoning to him to come back to the table and bring the box with him. He did so, setting it down between them.

"Why did you give her the butter knife?" he asked.

"To fight the dragon."

Kris surmised an answer from hers and hoped it was the right one. He didn't want to probe and cause her more pain.

"I'm so tired," she said.

"It's not surprising, really."

"And I told Steph I'd help Andy clear the house."

"Don't worry about that now."

"I'd rather get it done sooner, but…" She closed her eyes and rubbed them hard. "I'm so tired, Kris." She looked up at him, and he smiled. He took her hands again.

"You are amazing, Shaunna. What you did for Jess, and Andy, was above and beyond, but you need to take a break and look after you for a while."

"I will, when it's all over. I promise I will."

Kris tried to hide his exasperation. Her course started in a couple of weeks, and the way she was talking, she'd be careering headfirst from helping out with the funeral and house clearance right into studying. That was a breakdown in the making.

"OK. I've got an idea," he said. "How about you go and see if you can get a little more sleep, then I'll come back to Jess's with you if that's what you want to do. Or we can go for a walk, or maybe go out for a meal somewhere. We haven't done that in a long, long time."

She thought for a moment and nodded. "Yeah. That sounds really good." She struggled to her feet and tried to blink away the dizziness of sleeping tablets and exhaustion.

Kris saw her sway and was straight at her side. "I'll walk up behind you."

She smiled and kissed his cheek. "Come and lie with me? I don't want to be on my own."

***

Sophie was watching George change Dylan's nappy. It was taking him ages, because Dylan had filled it on the way over, so it had spread everywhere by the time she got him out of the car, and now he was screaming at the top of his voice, his little legs rigid in the air, impatient with hunger. She wriggled uncomfortably and winced.

"Let-down?" Josh asked.

"Yeah!" she said, amazed. "How did you know that?"

"Ellie was breastfeeding until a few months ago. She told me all about it. It sounds terrible."

"It's not, once I get in the right position and he's latched on properly, but he fights me all the way, as you'll see in a minute."

George popped the final popper shut on the Babygro and passed Dylan back to Sophie. She had already unfastened her bra and lifted her t-shirt. Josh watched in fascination as Dylan's scrunched-up little face moved from side to side, his mouth wide open, rooting for her breast, which was still bigger than his head. Sophie lifted her nipple and brushed it on Dylan's lips. He homed in, sucked noisily, and started squawking again. She shifted forward and lifted him up a little. After a couple of false starts, her nipple and all of the dark circle of areola around it disappeared into his tiny mouth.

317

"Wow!" Josh said, still staring in wonder. George had been watching him rather than Sophie, because it didn't feel right to watch a woman breastfeeding, but Josh's curiosity overrode all of that social etiquette nonsense, and he continued to listen and observe as Dylan gulped away at the heavy flow of milk Sophie was now producing. "It's so utterly brilliant, nature, isn't it?"

George tutted and went to dispose of the dirty nappy. He returned to a very critical and rather one-sided discussion of breast milk versus formula, as opposed to breast versus bottle, because Dylan was obviously having to be fed from a bottle when he was with Sean, but it was with expressed breast milk.

"In fact, I'd be expressing now if I was at home," Sophie said.

"You can do it here if you like," Josh suggested.

"Are you sure? It'll mean me sitting here with both boobs out."

"Who will see? George and me. And Sean, when he gets back."

Sophie shrugged with her non-feeding side. "OK. If you're sure you don't mind." She reached down to her bag, still with Dylan attached to her right breast, extracted her breast pump, opened the other side of her bra and positioned the pump—all one-handed, and with Josh still completely enthralled. George shook his head.

"You are…" He didn't finish the sentence, but it probably would have ended with something like 'completely nuts' if Josh hadn't pulled him down into the chair and kissed him.

"What was that for?" George asked, trying to right himself.

"Because I felt like it." Josh grinned. "And because you're all red and flustered."

"Yeah, well."

"Yeah, well, what?"

"Boobs," George said. He got up.

"Boobs?" Josh repeated.

"Yeah." George left the room, and Josh and Sophie looked at each other, mystified.

Josh followed him out to the kitchen and watched him washing his hands, still blushing beetroot red. George didn't really want to explain and had a feeling that Josh would interrogate him until he submitted, but he thought he'd try and get away with it for a while. His luck was in, because Sean chose that moment to return from Jess's, having gone there in Josh's car to get his phone for him. He came in, went straight to the lounge to give Sophie and Dylan a kiss, and then came through to the kitchen.

"There you go." He handed over the phone and car keys.

"Thanks. Everything OK?" Josh asked, surreptitiously sniffing at Sean as he replied.

"Fine. There was nobody there. I'm guessing Andy's at his mum's."

"Yeah, he is," George confirmed, his blush having subsided. He returned to the lounge.

"I didn't," Sean said to Josh as soon as they were alone.

"Didn't what?"

"Touch the stuff."

"Good."

"The urge has passed. How about yours?"

"Same." Josh nodded to confirm it, although he was still struggling. The link to cancer had been quite helpful in keeping him off the cigarettes, but it wasn't doing him a lot of good just now.

"One day at a time," Sean said.

Josh snarled and shook his head in dismay that Sean had seen right through him. Again. They returned to the lounge, where Dylan had finished feeding and was fast asleep in George's arms whilst George grinned down at him, all gooey-eyed.

"Did you tell Soph?" Sean asked Josh.

"Tell her what?"

"About..." He nodded at the envelope on the table.

"Oh. No. Not yet."

"What?" Sophie asked.

"Well," Josh said. He sat down, preparing himself for the story. It was a bit of an act, because it was still less than twelve hours since one of his best and closest friends had passed away, but at least it was an entertaining diversion. "You'll never guess what we discovered in Jess's will..."

***

"Married?" Dan rubbed his ear as if he really did think he'd misheard his brother.

Andy stood nearby, staring down at his feet scuffing the tiles. He'd decided it was better to come clean now rather than wait until Dan discovered it another way.

"When the fuck did you get married?"

"When she found out she was sick."

"Who else knows?"

"No-one."

"What did you do for witnesses? Grab a couple of strangers off the street?"

"Mum and Len did it for us."

Dan glared at his mother incredulously. She refused to make eye contact. He turned back to Andy. "This is fucking mental. After what she did to you last year—"

Andy sighed loudly. He knew it would be like this. However, they hadn't married for love. Jess had always said she was going to give all her money to charity when she died, but she didn't have enough time to set it up without getting hit by the Inland Revenue, so they'd discussed it and agreed that getting married was the easiest way around it. Andy had written off what he'd lost to Rob anyway, aside from which, she'd lent him enough over the years. In essence, all she'd done was pass her assets to him to dispose of in the most efficient way he could. And they did love each other; they'd had a great sex life together once, so it wasn't really a sham marriage, just a marriage that happened a little bit too late. Bolting the stable door, as it were.

"So, what now?" Dan asked.

"I sell the house, pay off her mum and dad's mortgage and other debts—"

"No, I mean what you gonna do now you're a widower?"

"What the fuck are you on about?" Andy was tired and out of patience. "We did it so she didn't end up paying shitloads in tax. Or not her, obviously, but... Why am I even bothering to explain this?"

"Oh!" Dan backed off. The penny had dropped. "It's just to dodge the taxman?"

"Yeah, bro, but it's mostly going to charity. She wanted to split it between the hospice and a cot death charity."

"Right. Gotcha now."

"Thank Christ for that."

"Anyway," Dan said in an entirely different and much gentler tone, "eloping aside, how are you feeling?"

Andy shrugged. "All right, I s'pose, all things considered. I just wanna get hammered and have a good night's kip. You up for it?"

"If Adele doesn't mind."

Adele was at the opposite end of the pool, holding little Shaunna up whilst she 'swam' widths. She was having the time of her life.

"What d'you want?" Adele asked.

"You OK if I have a few with Andy this evening?"

"Why don't you have a drink here?" Barbara suggested. "I'll keep an eye on Shaunna for you." She looked from Dan to Adele as she spoke, to confirm she was more than happy making the offer, and then made eye contact with Andy, holding it until he understood. He attempted a smile.

"Thanks, Mum." He went over and hugged her.

She smoothed his hair. "It's all right, love."

He kept hold, and she put her arms around him, hugging him tightly as he started to cry. Dan turned away, blinking back his own tears.

"Daddy, look!" little Shaunna shouted. "Swim! Swim!" She paddled with her arms, and Adele moved her through the water.

Dan went over and dangled his hand over the edge. "Clever girl."

Her happy smile faded when she saw his tears. She looked at Adele and shook her head. "Daddy hurt?"

Adele nodded. "Yes, Daddy hurt. You give Daddy a big hug to make him better?" She walked over to Dan, and Shaunna reached up and hugged him, drenching him right through.

"Thank you, baby girl." He moved back and wiped the water from his bare forearms. "Oh, no! I'm all wet!"

She giggled and splashed him. "Splash!"

He pretended to be shocked, and she splashed him again, giggling all the while. Adele looked up at him, and he smiled.

"I think," he said, standing up and unfastening his jeans, "I might as well join you, seeing as I'm soaked now anyway." He stripped to his boxers and climbed in beside them, kissing Adele and at the same time taking Shaunna from her. "Right, Madam. Ready?"

"Steadygo!" she said all as one word, and off they went, zooming through the water like a speedboat, with matching sound effects. Adele turned back to Barbara and Andy. He'd recomposed and was sitting on the lounger alongside his mother's.

"When Leonard gets in, I'll get him to sort out the beer. There's a few in the fridge, but probably not enough for you lot."

"Don't worry, Mum. We'll manage."

"Don't *you* worry, son." She brushed his cheek with her hand, which nearly set him off again. "Have a night off, get drunk and forget about everything. D'you know, I haven't seen you drunk since you were about nineteen."

"That's cos I never used to get drunk," Andy joked.

His mother cuffed him playfully around the ear.

"You've got to admit I always hid it well," he said.

"True enough—except for that time you came back from… who was it now? Oh, I can't remember. Someone's eighteenth anyway. It was in the middle of summer, I know that much, because me and your dad had only got back from Tenerife that morning. Bloody terrible, that holiday."

Andy smiled to himself, and not because the trip to Tenerife culminated in their mother kicking their stepdad—'Dad the Second'—out, which in itself was worthy of at least a smile. He knew whose eighteenth it was, and why he was so drunk, and was also very pleased that his mother wasn't going to tell any more of the story, seeing as she'd sat in the bathroom with him for half the night, whilst he threw up and poured his heart out. Incredible, really, that he could remember spending the night with his head in the toilet, but had no idea how he'd got home beforehand. Still, at least he could be sure he'd kept his pants done up on that occasion, because Kris hadn't let the birthday girl out of his sight.

***

"Good evening, both!"

"Good evening." Shaunna stepped over the threshold and kissed Sean on the cheek. Kris followed her in and shook hands with him.

"Now, Kris. The cat's locked away upstairs, but before you come any further, have you got your epi-pen with you?"

Kris smiled. "I have, but I shouldn't need it." He could feel a bit of irritation in his nose and throat, but the desensitisation seemed to have done the trick. Only time would tell.

They'd brought some mocha coffee beans, and a box of chocolates for Sophie, not really sure what she would like, although Shaunna recalled that when she was breastfeeding, she'd had to avoid citrus fruits, because they gave Krissi wind, and so she'd resorted to eating orange and lemon chocolates just to get a taste of the much missed real deal.

"Aww, thanks, Shaunna," Sophie said. "I haven't had oranges for weeks. They make Dylan grouchy."

"Must be quite common, then," Shaunna speculated. They heard the sound of a tiny baby crying.

"Hmm. Not that he isn't grouchy the rest of the time," Sophie grumbled, heading into the lounge. "Takes after his father."

Sean's eyebrow rose, but he didn't take the bait. "Come in, come in," he beckoned.

Shaunna and Kris followed him down the hallway to the kitchen, looking around them and wondering how a house identical in shape and design to Josh and George's could be so very different, not just in décor, but also in the general feel of the place. Next door but one was decorated in light, neutral creams and pastel washes and had a cool, clear-headed sense about it. In complete contrast, Sean liked his bold, dark colours, with burgundy walls in the hallway, oak cabinets and red tile floor in the kitchen, all of it lit with small, bright LEDs. His lounge also had a dark wallpaper, in green, and the carpets were the same deep green with a burgundy speck. It was a little overbearing, but warm and welcoming.

"Wow! That's funky!" Kris said, immediately spotting the enormous chrome coffee machine.

"Thanks," Sean accepted with a smile. "Would you like a drink? I've no alcohol in, I'm afraid, but I could go and buy some beer or something if you like?"

"No, it's fine, Sean, really," Kris assured him. "Coffee would be fab, though."

Sean nodded and set up the espresso. He wasn't sure if Shaunna had told Kris about his drinking problem and was surprised to find that it didn't matter to him whether she had or she hadn't. "All right, so, what d'you fancy? Espresso, cappuccino…"

"I'm going to be awkward and ask for a caramel latte, if that's OK?"

"Coming right up, sir. Shaunna, my lovely? What're you having?"

"I think I'll have a, erm…"

"No yoghurt not-smoothies, unfortunately."

She laughed. "I'll try a caramel latte, too. That's milky, isn't it?"

"Fairly."

"Yeah. I'll go with that. I'm not a big fan of coffee."

"I can make you a pot of tea. Or there's juice in the fridge."

"Tea would be wonderful. I'll make it, though. You get on with your showing off."

Sean rose to the challenge. He steamed the milk and started pouring it from a great height, slowly bringing the jug down, wiggling it from side to side as he filled the cup.

Kris grinned, impressed. "That's very clever," he said, admiring the shamrock on top of his latte.

Sean beamed proudly. "Well, if you can't have a real Irish coffee here…"

"Another enormous poo." Sophie came into the kitchen and stopped next to Kris. She glanced at his coffee. "That's the only latte art he can do."

"Not so," Sean protested. "I can make a heart, and a fern, and—"

Sophie and Shaunna tutted at the same time and then laughed.

"I've made a pot of tea, Sophie," Shaunna said. "Would you like a cup?"

"Oh, yes, please."

And thus, it began.

***

"So," Josh said.

George pulled back the duvet and sat on the edge of the bed, preparing to get in.

"Boobs, then?" Josh prompted.

"Ah, man. I thought you might forget."

"Yes, of course that was going to happen!" He turned and propped himself on his elbow, watching George lie down and pull the duvet right over his face. Josh reached over and pulled it down again so George's eyes were visible. "Windows to the soul."

George frowned.

"Come on, Sandison-Morley." Josh huffed at his own words. Sometimes he wished they'd kept their own surnames—only so he could still use George's the way George and everyone else used 'Joshua'—to exert authority. Jess used to do it all the time. The realisation hit him that he'd made his first past tense recollection. It was the little things that always made the missing harder. He pulled himself back and poked George in the side.

"OK, already!" George sighed. "After the porn incident—"

"The what?"

"Kris—'Do you like all-girl porn, George?'—that one?"

"Oh, right. OK."

"And after Jono, actually, because that was where the conversation started. He says to me, 'Don't you think big boobs are sexy?' And I just looked at him and thought 'what planet is he from?' So then he got all defensive, like I was judging him, which I was, because we were together, and there he was, going on about girls' boobs." George shook his head. "Anyway, I was sitting in the canteen a couple of days later, and he walked past and elbowed me and then started nodding really obviously at this girl—no idea what her name was, but she had massive boobs—and he's nodding away and nudging me, as if to say, 'See? They are sexy.' And she came over and—"

"Tipped your plate into your lap," Josh finished with a giggle. "Petrina Forshaw. I remember that."

"Not funny, Joshua. Those baked beans were really bloody hot! And I wasn't looking at her boobs…well, I was, because you couldn't *not* look at them. But sexy? How, please?"

"You're asking the wrong person. But I suppose they are soft, and round, and probably really nice to cuddle up to—I can see why Kris would—"

"Stop it."

Josh grinned. "They were big, though. Jess says hers make her shoulders ache, and they're nowhere near the size of Petrina's." He stopped to correct himself—"Said. Made. Were."—rolled onto his back and studied the ceiling. "I think we should get some of those glow-in-the-dark stars."

George looked up. "Seriously?"

"Not for us, you goon. For Dylan."

"What made you think of that?"

"The wonder of nature. We came from the stars. We go back to the stars. When I was sitting in Jess's back garden at four o'clock this morning, staring up at the sky, it came to me that it's not death, not in the vast context of the universe. One day, that's where we'll all be. In the stars." Josh turned on his side again. "Talk to me about this baby thing."

"That was quite some change of subject."

"Not really. I was talking about getting stars for Dylan, who, I believe, is one of those baby things. Do you still want one?"

"After that nappy today? No thanks!"

Josh sighed.

"What's the sigh for? You don't want a baby, surely?"

"Well…" Josh frowned. "No. I don't, but I was reading about fostering. We've got a lot to offer."

"And we do, to the children who are already in our lives. Ollie, and Toby, and Dylan."

"And little Shaunna."

George screwed up his nose. "Not so much. I probably need to make more effort."

"She has lots of strong, hunky men in her life already," Josh said. George glanced sideways at him, and Josh blew him a kiss. "You're right. It's better this way." He snuggled up and nibbled George's neck.

He should have seen it coming, really.

***

"Fucked if I know," Andy said, reaching his left leg over Charlotte's right arm and trying to put his foot on the only yellow circle he could find.

"Know what?" she asked.

"How you're supposed to do this without falling over." He tumbled to the ground, taking her with him. They both rolled about, giggling, and started dancing on their backs to 'YMCA', which was playing on the TV and had just reached the chorus.

"I think you're s'posed to play it when you're sober," Eleanor said loudly over the music. She squinted at her glass, trying to remember how many she'd had since she told her sister they should get a taxi and go home.

"That wouldn't be much fun, would it?" Andy pointed out.

"No, I s'pose not."

"I won that one," Dan announced.

"No, you didn't!" Charlotte said.

"You and Andy fell over!"

"Yeah, but—"

"Erm, I'm the referee," Eleanor shouted.

"What am I?" Adele asked.

"You're…Adele." Eleanor grinned at her.

Adele looked down at herself. "Oh yeah. So I am. Why aren't I playing?"

"Cos Dan said you weren't allowed."

"Why not?"

"I…I dunno." Eleanor shrugged, completely befuddled.

"Just in case," Dan told her.

"But I'm drinking."

"Well, you shouldn't. Stop."

"I shouldn't stop?"

"No." Dan stepped off the Twister mat. "Excuse. Need a piss." He stumbled off across the atrium and staggered up the stairs, singing 'YMCA' quite loudly.

His mother stepped out of her room. "Daniel!" she hissed.

"Sorry, Mum." He hugged her drunkenly and continued on his way.

She watched him and shook her head in despair. She'd hoped they would all be too tired, but it was nearly one in the morning, and they were still going strong.

Dan came meandering back again with one eye shut.

"Just try to keep the noise down," she suggested.

He saluted and hugged her again. "I love you, Mummy."

She pushed him away. "Go on with you."

He grinned and returned to the sitting room; they'd been banned from the conservatory for safety reasons.

"I'm going home," Eleanor slurred at him as they met at the door.

"Why?"

"Cos I live there. And I'm drunk."

"So?" Dan tried to shove her through the doorway, and she shoved him back, which normally wouldn't have shifted him as much as an inch, but he was too drunk to keep his balance and fell backwards.

"Charlie?" Eleanor shouted.

"Coming," she said. She wasn't, though. She was sitting on the sofa, where she'd been conversing with Andy, but at some point had switched to talking to the fish in the tank.

"You're very pretty, with your big yellow tail. And you've got a cute black nose like a panda, and you...ugh, you ugly, liddle fishy." She tapped on the side of the tank, and the catfish darted away.

"Charlotte Davenport! Get your pissed-up arse over here!"

"Yes, boss!" Charlotte dragged herself up off the sofa. "Have you rung a taxi?"

"No. I thought you had."

Andy pushed Charlotte back down again. She huffed and took out her phone, squinting at the screen, unable to focus. She held it up to Andy. "Can't do it."

He took the phone from her and somehow managed to make the call. "Thirty minutes," he said.

"Oh, goody. Time for another lager." This time, she got up just fine and went to the fridge, collecting a beer for herself and filling an empty glass with wine. She handed it to Eleanor on the way back.

"What you giving me more for?" Eleanor asked.

"Taxi's not for half an hour. Drink up, sis." She wandered past and returned to the sofa and her conversation with Andy, though neither of them could remember what it was about.

"She's a good little sister," Eleanor said to Dan.

"Yeah," he agreed.

"Are you a good little brother?"

"Dunno. I reckon so."

"And so modest, too." She poked him in the chest with each word. "Gosh, that's very firm." She did it again. He grabbed her hand.

"I work out a lot," he told her, as if she wouldn't know.

"Do you?" she responded, as if she didn't know.

"Yep. Come see the gym." He led her, by the hand, up the corridor and to the room past the conservatory.

"It's very dark," she said.

"It's got lights. Hang on." Dan staggered around, feeling along the wall for the switches. He found them. "There. See? Lights."

"Oh. Yes. Lights. Bikes. And stuff." She nodded and stumbled forwards. Dan caught her. She held onto him with her free hand. "Thanks."

"No problem."

It would be inaccurate to say that they gazed into each other's eyes, because both were too drunk to fix their gaze on anything, but they *were* looking into each other's eyes, and then they were moving closer together, and then they were kissing, and neither could quite comprehend why they were doing it, but they kept doing it, because it felt good. There was no sudden pulling away from each other as they realised; they just continued until they were both sure they'd had enough of the kiss and slowly moved their lips apart.

"Mmm," Eleanor said. "That was nice."

"Yeah," Dan agreed. "What the fuck, though?"

Eleanor shrugged. "Dunno, Dan, mate. Tomorrow, we'll probably be beating ourselves up about it, but today? Oh, hang on, it is tomorrow, except it's today, but—you know what I mean. It's been a horrible day, and we deserve a little treat."

"A *little* treat?"

"Now, now, Daniel." Eleanor giggled. "Let's go back to the others. My taxi'll be here soon, and we can all go to bed with our lovely husbands and girlfriends." She stopped and sighed. "Except Andy." She started to cry.

"Hey," Dan said. "He'll be OK. We all will." He put his arms around her, and she leaned against his chest. Their kissing moment was done—a thing of the past—and this was pure, innocent love and friendship, albeit the most unusual combination. But maybe it was to be expected. The dynamic had changed.

And that change was forever.

Savies
Monday 25th September

It was cold in the house; it was cold out in the garden, too. He wished he'd waited and not come alone, yet somehow, he'd felt compelled to make the trip, hoping that the time of day would afford him the sanctuary of his own company. So, there he was, sitting on the lawn, where he had sat only twenty-four hours before, except now he was staring at a heavy, star-free sky and spinning the cigarette packet between his forefinger and thumb, trying to understand.

Savies.

He couldn't save them all, and he'd tried. How hard he'd tried, for all those years, that it should still come to this? Without thinking, he pulled at the cellophane tab on the cigarette packet and peeled the tape away, freeing the top of the box.

A noise. From inside the house.

No. His imagination playing tricks on him. It was four o'clock in the morning, and the house was empty, so empty, but for the remnants of a life outlived. Dirty sheets, unspent pads and tubes and bags. Nothing. It all meant nothing.

"Without you, we wouldn't be here now, all still friends. Well, I don't mean here, now, obviously. This whole situation is the pits."

Savies.

Brilliant as his mind was, even at times like this when it evaded sleep and skidded like an out-of-control racing car from one side of the track to the other, he still made mistakes. He wasn't too proud to admit it. He missed the obvious, failed to appreciate the salient facts, ignored what was staring him right in the face, followed a trail and got lost along the way, or took a detour into some far-flung notion, forgot to buy matches.

Bloody savies.

That's all it said, on the envelope—the tiniest envelope he'd ever seen, not much more than a special edition postage stamp in surface area—'Savies'. That was all it needed to say for him to understand it was for his eyes only. He reached into his pocket and extracted it, placing it against the cigarette packet, though he could not read the word out here, but it was implanted in his brain so he could still see it, that swirling cursive writing. He turned his head, to put the envelope in his peripheral vision and pick out the contrast of black ink against white. Perhaps he shouldn't open either receptacle, for each contained its own truth that should not be realised.

He held his breath, straining to listen. His imagination? No. More than that. But that he could find the strength to stand, to fight, because he could feel it rising through him. He could clear the house before anyone else was even out of bed. They'd all be at home, warm, safe in the temporary oblivion of sleep. But that he had the strength.

He did not.

She did.

"Josh?"

He felt a shiver run right through him, top to bottom, back to front, every part of him frozen yet still clutching around blindly for a scrap of rationality. It could not be her, for she was gone. So it was an apparition, a figment of his mind, his broken, feeble mind that could not cling to the life he had and sought a truth in the life she did not.

"Josh."

There it was again. How could it be? And closer now. He could not move, dared not move, for fear of…what? That he would chase her away? That he would see her and realise? She was gone. She was not gone.

"Why are you here?"

Icy fingers poked and clawed at his shoulder. He gasped in horror.

"Here. Let me help you up."

She reached over, grasped his hand with her own, deathly white, and pulled. He shook his head, in terror, in denial, in refusal. A futile hope, a wisp of fear.

"You're so cold. Come on inside and get warm."

He allowed himself to be led back into the house by this spectre of his imagination. Was he dreaming? That surely made more sense.

"I couldn't sleep, either." She paused in the middle of the room—a black shadow invisible yet not. She moved away from him, drifting aimlessly into the distance. And then there was light. So much light. He lifted his hands to his face. The pain of that light. Blinding, burning.

"I…" he began, an infant cry.

She was close to him again now, and no longer cold. Her fingers brushed against his arm.

"Did you need a light?"

A light? What was this scorching his eyes if it was not light?

"Here," she said, so matter-of-fact, this other-worldly being.

He moved a hand from his face, slowly lifting his gaze to look upon it. The breath left him all in one go, deflating, collapsing. She caught him.

"Let's get out of here. It's not doing us any good at all."

She tugged at him. He resisted.

"Come on, Josh. Let's go."

So gentle, so comforting, so motherly, so…*impossible.*

Reality returned. He held out the cigarette packet and nodded to her to take it from him. She frowned, puzzled.

"Take it," he pleaded. "Please, take it from me."

She shrugged, took the packet, and along with it the small envelope.

"What's this?" she asked, holding it up and squinting to read the word.

"That's mine." Josh snatched it back possessively. She stepped away from him, hurt and surprised.

"OK, I'm just going to the loo…" she backed out of the kitchen "…then we really must leave." She almost ran up the stairs.

Josh stared at the envelope, his fingers now searching out the flap underneath. He tore it open, pulled the folded square of foiled paper from within, turned it over and unfolded it, looking down on the words. The words from beyond the grave.

> Nought's had, all's spent,
> Where our desire is got without content.
> 'Tis safer to be that which we destroy
> Than by destruction dwell in doubtful joy.

She was returning. He shoved the paper and the envelope in his pocket, tried to slow his pulse and his breathing. He smiled, but she was not fooled. She talked, the apparition. She talked and she talked and he tried to listen, but the words, if they were indeed words, could have been another language, for all the sense they were making. *Go where? Do what? But I have this letter, and she is gone, and you…*

"Shut up!" he yelled. He bent over double, covering his ears. "Please just…"

She came towards him again, and he, in his weakened position, could not repel her.

"I'm sorry," he whispered. "I'm sorry. I'm so sorry." She held him, so gentle, so comforting, so motherly. "Steph, please forgive me. I didn't mean to—"

"Shhh, I know."

"I'm sorry. I'm sorry…"

The whispered apologies, pleas for forgiveness, continued all the way to the car. She seated him, belted him in, closed the door to keep him safe. A noise drew her attention; she turned to see. "You as well?"

Shaunna nodded.

"Will you come with me?"

Silently, Shaunna took her place behind Josh and allowed Steph to secure her, too. And then they drove, to the drive-thru, bought coffee and tea, drove on, through the naked streets, on and on, until they reached that most dreaded and necessary destination. Steph stopped, slowly raised the handbrake and switched off the engine.

"See this place," she said. She reached across with one of the cups, uncurled Josh's fingers and positioned them around it. She repeated the action with Shaunna. "See this place with me."

They looked up, peering through the windscreen at the darkened railings ahead, beyond those a playground, unfamiliar and frightful in its shadowy pre-dawn existence.

"On the day before Daisy died, we came here." The images filled her mind now, not of the five o'clock bleak September morning, but of that summer afternoon, twenty-nine years ago, children squealing with joy, round and round the roundabout, swing-swing on the swings, slide-climb-slide again the slide, her beautiful daughters, so full of life, and she, so happy, so proud.

"Please can I take Daisy on the swing?"
"No, sweetie-pie. She's still too little."
"I'll be very careful and hold on tight."
"No, Jess."
"Then can I take her on the roundabout? We'll only go slowly."
"Jess, she's too small."
"What about the slide. I can—"
"When she's bigger, Jess."
"Promise?"
"I promise."

"We never came back."

Josh reached out and grasped her hand.

She turned and smiled at him. "Your mum died when you were only young, didn't she?"

He nodded.

"Did she ever make you a promise and break it?"

He did not know.

"Only the one," Shaunna said. She leaned forward and placed her hand with theirs.

Steph put her other hand on top of Shaunna's to surround these motherless children in her childless love. "It is the worst thing a mother can do—break a promise to their child. I promise I'll keep you safe and warm. I promise never to leave you. I promise—" She looked away. "I have Daisy's ashes."

Josh closed his eyes but kept hold of Shaunna's hand. Her fingers tensed around his.

"You know what I'm asking of you, don't you?" She looked behind her into steely wet eyes. Shaunna shifted her gaze away from the monochrome playground, her answer within it. Steph offered as much of a smile as she could find.

"Thank you," she said. She turned now to Josh. "And will you?" she asked.

He remained with eyes closed, uncertain that he could fulfil her wish and survive. But what was life without her? A mother's promise. Nothing less.

"Yes," he said. "I will."

Goods And Shackles
Wednesday 27th September

This is the Last Will and Testament of me Jessica Lambert.

1. I revoke all former wills made by me.

2. I appoint Joshua Sandison and my husband Andrew Jeffries to be the Executors and Trustees of this my Will and in case the aforesaid shall die before me or shall refuse or be unable to act in the office of Executor and Trustee then I appoint in the following order of priority Eleanor Davenport and George Morley.

3. My Trustees shall hold the remainder of my estate in trust for sale on the following terms:

3.1 To pay debts and funeral and testamentary expenses;

3.2 To pay inheritance tax in respect of property passing under the Will;

3.3 To pay transfer and assign residue of my estate to my husband Andrew Jeffries for his use absolutely.

4. If the trusts hereinbefore declared concerning the residue of my estate shall fail entirely then from the date of such failure I direct that the residue of my estate shall be held upon trust as to both capital and income for all children present or born within twenty-one (21) years of my death both biological and adopted of the following persons named and with each child receiving an equal share:

4.1 Eleanor Davenport;

4.2 Shaunna Johansson;

4.3 Andrew Jeffries;

4.4 Daniel Jeffries;

4.5 Kristian Johansson;

4.6 George Morley;

4.7 Adele Reeves;

4.8 Joshua Sandison.

5. I declare that in the event…

Josh had read Jess's will twice in its entirety, six pages of rambling legal jargon that he had now committed to memory for the rest of his days—not a choice, as he'd told her; an affliction. As to her funeral preferences? Nothing. His solicitor questioned why he'd thought he would find any such statement in her will. It was a popular misconception, and Jess was a family lawyer, so Josh, too, was questioning why she had told him that's where it would be. The answer, he suspected, was that she had not wished to discuss it with him at all, in which case, the unfinished conversations relating to the same were a nonsense. But why?

Questions; always more bloody questions and no answers, although pondering had got him through a shower without so much as a thought to himself. He wrung the towelling wristbands dry, hung them on the bath taps and returned to the bedroom. 5:30 a.m. Not really enough time spent asleep to decree that he had even been to bed, but when George turned to switch off the alarm, that was the claim Josh made as he straddled him and began to paint a trail with his tongue down George's still-bare chest.

"You're up early," George said, attempting a yawn and a stretch under the rain of kisses.

"Yes," Josh murmured seductively. "I am."

George tried to keep hold of the duvet, but it was too late, and now he felt flesh against flesh.

"You know, I thought once you'd got the whole—" he used his fingers to put the phrase in inverted commas "—'losing your virginity' thing out of the way, you'd stop pestering me. Josh!" He tried to sit up. "I've got to get up for work."

"I'll drive you in." Josh slid up against him and smiled.

George sighed. He didn't want to do this. To him, it was still wrong, regardless of everything they'd talked about on their honeymoon, but last night, he'd submitted, aware they were climbing hypomania hill and hoping it would give him a foothold, remove one of the constant and urgent demands made of him during these episodes. Alas, it would seem hypersexuality was not so easily thwarted, and nor was he winning the battle to stay unresponsive.

"Anyway," Josh continued, "that wasn't a euphemism." He moved back down the bed, taking George's boxers with him.

"No," George said quietly, shaking his head and trying to pull Josh back. "Don't."

"Why? If you think about it, I'm only half done."

He could be so manipulative when he was like this, and it was difficult to negotiate a path across the quicksand, decide where was safe to walk and where not. George started to cry—not a deliberate ploy—just as he had the previous night, when he finally relented and then throughout, the tears falling as Josh revelled in the wonder of 'the ultimate itch'. Erotic? Absolutely not, but they'd made it to the end, and he was assured that he was loved more than ever, for his gift and his sacrifice while Josh repeatedly declared his newfound status, as excited as a child with a new bike.

Now, though, Josh paused and moved away.

"OK," he said brightly. For, even in his current state of mind, it hurt him to see George cry, because George wasn't actually a 'soft shite' at all. True: he was gentle and compassionate, and he loved those children as if they were his own, but on an emotional level, he was tougher than almost everyone they knew, perhaps with the exception of Shaunna.

And whilst Josh was thinking, George was thinking, too.

"All right. Do it," he said.

Josh had rolled onto his own side of the bed and stayed where he was.

"Just get it over with," George told him. "Really. I want you to."

***

"I need to tell you something." Eleanor spoke as she shoved the last of the still-sealed catheter bags into a box. Josh stopped doing the same with the incontinence sheets and waited for her to continue. She blushed and screwed her eyes tightly shut.

"Ohhh." Josh observed her closely. "What've you done?"

"Err, well…" She opened her eyes and half smiled, half grimaced. "It wasn't just me. I mean, I didn't instigate it, I don't think, or maybe I did?" She paused, frowning and biting her lip. "No. It just kind of…happened."

Josh sighed and carried on packing the medical supplies. He picked up a box and headed for the door.

"Me and Dan kissed," she said quickly.

Josh stopped and turned back. "You *what*?"

"We…kissed." She blushed even more.

"You mean actually, properly kissed?"

"Err, yeah."

"Wow!" Josh put the box down. "How did that happen? When did that happen?"

"Sunday night—Monday morning, really. We were all completely out of it and…it just happened. I have no idea why or how. We just…did." She shrugged. He nodded slowly.

"Does anyone else know?"

"No. And please, please don't tell them."

"I'm telling George."

Eleanor huffed and picked up the box, following him from the room. "Why do you always have to tell George everything?"

"Because he's my husband."

"So?"

"Don't you tell James everything? Well, maybe everything other than that you snogged a beefcake the other night."

"He is, isn't he?"

"Yes, but James isn't exactly an eyesore."

"Joshua!"

Josh turned back and grinned at her. They took the boxes to her car.

She stopped and leaned against it, tapping the key on her teeth. "It was a one-off. We both know that, and it was really nice, and everything, but it's Dan, and—"

"Even if he is a beefcake, he's not in your league."

"Yeah. Sounds really snooty, hey?"

"Not really. It's about compatibility. You and James are both extremely intelligent, emotionally deep people. Dan and Adele are very attractive, and while I wouldn't say they were unintelligent—"

"OK, that does sound snooty," Eleanor said.

Josh nodded. "Sorry. You know I adore them, really. So is he a good kisser?"

"Are you going to tell George you asked that question?"

Now it was Josh's turn to blush.

"Thought not." They stepped off again. "And yes, he is."

They returned to the house, taking a quick detour to the kitchen for a drink. The plan was to clear as much as possible before Shaunna and Andy came back tomorrow, to ease the burden a little. Today, Sean, Sophie and Dylan were Shaunna-minding and were out visiting Cordelia's Aquarium, amongst other places, although Shaunna had been sending text messages all morning to remind Josh and Eleanor of things that needed doing that they'd already done. Meanwhile, Dan and Andy were on a 'business' trip that involved visiting a number of licensed premises in Manchester, 'to test the quality of the merchandise'.

"I've got something to tell you, too," Josh said, and carried on talking, because he didn't want Eleanor to look at him as he said it. "I'm not a virgin anymore."

"OK." She kept her back to him. "I didn't know you still were one."

"Well, it's a bit difficult getting down to 'it' when you haven't even kissed anyone before. Oh, and I told him that I accosted you, by the way. He was OK about it."

"That's good. Can we talk about something else?"

"Why?"

"Because we'll end up having a row."

"Why?"

Eleanor turned and examined his face. He blinked innocently, as if he genuinely didn't know why the topic of conversation might lead to an argument.

"Fine," he said. "If you want to be like that. But I didn't tell you to challenge your beliefs. I told you because it's important to me, and I'm really happy about it. I was terrified I'd still be a virgin when I got to forty, and with Jess and everything... Anyway, that's all."

Josh could see Eleanor was feeling extremely uncomfortable, so he left it at that, not that he would have shared the rest. After all, it was a bit difficult to explain to a religiously homophobic best friend how making love to your husband could begin to heal twenty-year-old wounds. There was no possible way she'd understand the emotional significance when she couldn't get past the act itself.

That was why Josh had persevered, because whilst he was hypomanic, he was aware of it and had it contained in the same way he'd always contained it in the past: by focusing on the needs of his friends. Sitting outside the park with Steph in the early hours of Monday morning had brought his self-control mechanism out of hibernation, and he was coping. He had it in order—not entirely, kind of like a box of maggots a fisherman's kept too long, but enough to function, and that would have to do.

"I also have something else to tell you," he said.

"Oh, God." She sighed dramatically and picked up her tea.

"It has nothing to do with God, or Sodom and Gomorrah."

"Get on with it, then," she said impatiently.

"Actually...forget it. It's not important."

Not cold feet this time. He'd just had something of an epiphany. He picked up his coffee and went back upstairs.

***

"I need to tell you something."

Josh lifted the bedding into the plastic bag and waited for Shaunna to look up. She'd arrived half an hour ago, barely five minutes after he'd received a text message from Sean, which read: 'Sorry. I tried my best.' Eleanor had gone to dispose of the medical equipment and supplies, and it was terrible being in Jess's house alone, so Josh was glad of the company, but Shaunna shouldn't have been there; not today.

She continued with the removal of pillow cases, still keeping her eye on him, waiting for him to speak. Something slid down the end of the mattress and fell to the floor with a loud clunk. He frowned and pulled the bed away from the wall.

"OK," he said slowly, stretching to retrieve the object. "Not generally something you'd expect people to keep under their pillow." He held it up for Shaunna to see, and before his eyes she crumpled. He dashed to her side of the bed and put his arms around her.

"It's mine," she sobbed, which explained nothing. She pulled away and fled from the room, he assumed to hide her sorrow, but then she returned and passed him a flat black box. He looked at her questioningly. She nodded to encourage him to open it. He did so, studied the contents for a couple of minutes and sat down, covering his eyes with one hand, continuing to hold the box in the other.

"Our A' Level teacher was always telling her off for that." He sniffled. "She'd say, 'Jessica: your essays are excellent, but would you please write a conclusion rather than leaving the reader dangling?' So Jess'd just stick a one-liner in and write 'The End'."

Shaunna laughed through her tears and came and sat next to him. Josh placed the butter knife and the box in her hand, furling her fingers around them and keeping hold.

"What did you want to tell me?" she asked.

"That you are a beautiful person," he said.

"Thanks."

"I mean it most sincerely, Shaunna."

"I know you do. And the other bit?"

"I have bipolar disorder."

"OK. Did you want me to look after you?"

"Sometimes."

"Like now?"

"Yes, please."

"Up or down?"

"Up."

"Right. You do the wardrobe. I'll instruct and snap my fingers if you go off on one."

He got up and opened the wardrobe. "Shaunna?"

"Mmm?"

"Thank you."

"You're more than welcome. And thank you. I was about to start getting bored."

***

"Cut!"

Kris let his shoulders drop and came out of role.

"That was great. We'll keep that last one," Barry—the director—called, walking across the set to where Kris was currently sitting: in 'DI Lundberg's Office', a small space, consisting of two walls presently adorned with photos of the 'victims' in the overarching storyline for season two of *Shadows*. In front of them was a desk with a computer, a phone and a photo of 'Mrs. Lundberg'.

"Thanks," Kris said. He was feeling quite fragile today and finding some of the more emotional lines particularly difficult to deliver—five takes for a sixty-second phone call to one of the victims' mothers to tell them their daughter was dead. If he didn't know any better, he'd have said they were doing it on purpose.

"So, I think," Barry continued, "on Monday, if we aim to shoot the first pier scene before we lose too much daylight."

"Pier scene?" Kris asked.

"We're bloody tight on time, but if we can box off all the pier stuff by the end of the week—you've had the shooting schedule, I take it?" Barry's tone was matter-of-fact, assuming that Kris both knew what he was talking about and that the answer was in the affirmative.

"Remind me again," Kris said.

"Brighton? The hotel's sorted. I think the train's booked for—"

"Err, my friend's funeral is on Monday," he interrupted.

"Ah." Barry rubbed his chin and clicked his tongue, as was his way when he was pretending to think. "I wonder if we could have a chat with—" He stopped, suddenly realising that even for him, making the suggestion that they employ the might of a TV network as a means of swinging it with the crematorium was a little heartless. He changed tack. "Fine. We'll rejig the schedule for you again, but get down as soon as you can. Right—" He turned and hollered orders at the crew to set up for the next scene, which didn't involve Kris, so he left the set.

"What a fucking joke," he complained quietly to Ade, who was sitting out of shot, watching the filming.

"What did he say?"

"He didn't say it, but it sounded like he was about to suggest rearranging Jess's funeral. It's only a TV show, for Christ's sake. So now, I'll have to race down to Brighton straight after. That's not gonna be well received."

"You're the star. Can't you just flounce and turn up late?"

"With that contract? You must be joking!"

"It's not on, you know. You should have a chat with Equity."

"They've been all right, really. In most jobs, they don't let you take time off when a friend dies, and they rescheduled this week for me."

"And did you tell them that she was more like a sister than a friend?"

Kris looked away, up into the dark rafters of the studio, his eyes filling with tears.

"Oh, hey, I'm sorry, babe." Ade rubbed his arm, trying to comfort him. "Would you like me to come on Monday?"

Kris was too teary to answer, but he also wasn't sure how best *to* answer. If he said no, Ade might think it was because he didn't want him there, which wasn't true. He was worried about how it would be between Ade and the rest of them, given they'd broken up in April and everyone was aware of that, but no-one knew how difficult it had been, or how complicated things were, or that they were effectively back together.

That was the problem with dodging media bullets all the time; it was hard to remember who can and can't be trusted, and Kris had distanced himself from everyone other than Shaunna. They'd been waiting for Jess to pass; now they were waiting for the funeral to be over. Being on location for four weeks was only going to delay them further, and the longer it went on, the more it would look like they'd deliberately stayed quiet.

Ade touched Kris on the arm. "If you don't want me there, just say so. It's fine."

"It's not that. I don't want you to feel awkward, or not a part of it."

"They still don't know about us?"

"Not yet. With Jess, and…"

Now Ade looked away. Kris shook him gently to keep his attention.

"I meant what I said, Ade. I want to do it properly this time. That's the only reason I haven't said anything. You've seen what it's like. It's worse than the Mafia. Well, maybe not. D'you understand what I'm saying, though? There's only been James who's stayed the distance, and that's probably because he's not around much of the time. They are truly the most wonderful friends in the world, and they mean everything to me, but so do you, and somehow I've got to find a way to make us fit."

Ade was getting angry, because that was exactly the problem they'd had to start with. Fitting 'them' into Kris's pre-existing life was like having the last piece of someone else's jigsaw.

"OK, Lundberg conference scene," the director called, "That's scene—" he checked his script "—fourteen. Who the fuck numbered this? Look." He stormed over to one of the writers; there were now four of them, and the *Shadows* creator was executive producer, along with her husband, Barry the director. To say they didn't much like each other was something of an understatement.

Barry slammed the script down in the poor writer's lap, knowing she was little more than a typewriting monkey, doing his wife's bidding. "Eleven, twelve, fourteen. What the hell's happened to thirteen?"

"There isn't one, Barry."

"Why not?"

"Bad luck."

"Fucking bad luck?" He went stomping back the way he had come. "OK, folks, so that's the scene formerly known as fourteen, which is actually scene thirteen."

Kris cringed. "That's going to upset a few people. She's *very* superstitious. You should've seen her freak when I walked under a ladder back in the early days. Now I know better."

Ade laughed. "Hey, you never know. You might have a new director by Monday!"

Kris rolled his eyes. "Yeah, unlikely." He gave Ade a kiss. "We'll talk later," he promised sincerely and then slipped straight back into role. "Now, if you'll excuse me, Mr. Simmons, I've got to brief my team on a couple of matters." He winked and walked back on set.

Ade watched him all the way, and sat down again. Someone nudged him from behind. It was one of the runners from reception.

"Have they just started?" she whispered. Ade nodded. "Will you let Kristian know there's some people downstairs for him. They say they're friends of his? Said to tell him they're not twins."

Ade grinned. "OK. I'll let him know," he whispered. The woman started to walk away. "Actually," he said, "I'll come with you."

***

"Orj! Orj!"

There weren't many people around, but all of them turned to look.

"Oy! Shush!" Adele hissed at her daughter. Little Shaunna completely ignored her.

"Orj!"

Across the paddock, trying to catch a very small and wayward goat, George was oblivious.

"ORJ!"

"Be quiet!" Adele said more loudly. "George is busy."

"Dat?"

"It's a goat."

"Goat."

"That's right! Clever girl." At least there was one word she could say, and say it she did.

"Goat. Goat. Goat. Goat. Goat."

"Yes!" Adele put her head down and hid behind her hair. The few other people—all parents with young children—laughed sympathetically at her most embarrassing plight.

"Goat. Goat. ORJ! GOAT!"

Finally, George spotted them, grinned broadly and headed their way.

"Fancy seeing you two here!" He leaned over the fence to give Adele a kiss on the cheek then crouched down and pinched Shaunna's nose affectionately. "Hiya," he said. She grinned at him coyly and reached through the fence to touch his face.

"I thought I'd come and tell you about college," Adele said. "Although I wish I'd just gone home now!" Shaunna was waving wildly, still shouting 'goat' and paying no attention whatsoever to her mother's frantic attempts to shush her that went as far as turning the pushchair to face the opposite direction. Shaunna twisted back in her seat and carried on shouting. George thought it was hilarious.

"You been to the college today?" he asked.

"Yep. All signed up and ready to start next week."

"Cool. And what were…" George paused, distracted by a woman and her two children laughing as they watched something happening behind him. He turned and saw little Bo dart off again.

"Goat!" little Shaunna declared, pointing.

"Yes. She's a very, very naughty goat," George said.

"I'm guessing she's not meant to be in with the ponies?" Adele speculated.

"Nope. Tell you what. Stay there a sec, and I'll come round."

George jogged across to the stile, cleared it in one jump and made his way around the outside of the paddock. "What were the tests like? Did they go OK?"

"I haven't done the proper ones yet, but I spoke to one of the learning support people. He was so nice, George, and I was really worried, and he kept saying, 'Don't worry, Adele. Lots of people need support.' He said a lot of adults weren't assessed at school, so basically, we muddle through, feeling like we're thick, when actually, we're quite intelligent."

"Well, yeah," George said, like it was the most obvious fact in the world.

For Adele, it was far from it, but she was keeping an open mind, relieved to have someone taking her seriously at last. "I've got to go in tomorrow and do some functional assessments—maths and spelling and stuff—where they figure out what I struggle with the most, then they'll try and get me a mentor, or a computer, or whatever I need. It's so exciting. I can't wait!"

"Goat!" Shaunna said.

George shook his head and laughed. "Can I take her out of the pushchair?"

Adele shrugged. "Be my guest."

George unclipped the straps and lifted Shaunna clear. "Wanna come see the ponies?"

"Ponies!" Shaunna repeated perfectly.

"That's what we've been doing wrong!" Adele said. "All those normal, everyday words, like milk and juice? Not a chance. Show her some farm animals and she's away!"

George smiled. "Come on. Let's go say hi to Dolly."

Shaunna frowned at him, not understanding.

"See there?" George pointed at the Shetland pony in question. "Her name is Dolly."

"Doy-eee!" Shaunna attempted, bouncing up and down in anticipation. They went over, and George reached out his hand, stroking the side of the pony's neck.

"Gently," he said.

"Genkee," Shaunna mimicked, also copying his movement.

"That's it." George smiled. "Dolly likes being stroked, especially just behind her ears." He tickled behind Dolly's ear, and Shaunna did likewise, but then sharply jerked her hand away, pointing into the distance.

"Goat!" she shouted.

George glanced past Dolly and saw Bo, her front legs up on the edge of the ponies' food trough. He sighed.

"Naughty goat," Shaunna said crossly.

"Yes. I'll take you back to Mummy so I can go catch that naughty goat." He carried Shaunna over to Adele. "I'd best get on," he said. "Got to try and get *that*—" he thumbed at the pygmy goat "—back into the enclosure. She's a pain in the you-know-what."

"OK, George. See you soon." Adele gave him a hug and a peck on the cheek. "Once we get next week out the way, you'll have to come round for dinner again."

"Awesome."

"It'll give me a chance to try out some of my new recipes on someone who appreciates them."

George laughed. "Can't wait. Bye-bye, Shu." He waved at Shaunna. She puckered her lips at him, and he leaned across so she could give him one of her best soggy kisses.

"Why did you call her Shu?" Adele asked.

"I don't know. It just kind of came out."

Adele looked perplexed.

"It suits her," George justified.

"Yeah, it does. It's what me and Dan used to call her when she was in hospital."

"Maybe that's where I picked it up from."

Shaunna was still waving at Dolly and saying, "Bye-bye, Doy-ee!" but then all of a sudden she shouted, "Goat!" and started wriggling to be put down—so vigorously, in fact, that Adele couldn't keep hold of her. Before Adele knew it, her daughter was off after Bo, who had squeezed herself back through the gap in the paddock fence and was trotting around like she owned the place.

George was about to chase after the pair of them, but stopped when he saw what was happening, for now Shaunna was running away from Bo and squealing with excitement as the goat trotted after her. Shaunna toddled past him, and he quickly grabbed Bo by the collar.

"Yee-ha!" he said and grinned.

Adele started laughing and clapping. "I see you haven't lost your touch. That was brilliant! Right. Definitely going now." She scooped up her daughter and strapped her back into her pushchair.

George nodded a farewell rather than risk losing his grip on little Bo, waited for Adele and Shaunna to go, and returned the feisty little beast to her pen.

***

"So do you work in the studio?" Dan whispered to Ade. They were standing behind the set, waiting for Kris to finish his final scene of the day.

"No. I only come down here to loiter. I live just up the road." He continued to watch with his chin held high, hoping that he was affecting nonchalance convincingly. Andy was examining the rigging and nodding knowledgeably, not that he knew about set construction; anything for a distraction, really. The director brought the scene to an end and released the cast and crew. Kris came over smiling.

"Hello!" he said. "What on earth are you two doing here?"

"We were, err, working," Dan said, giving Kris a swift embrace.

"Hmm." Kris frowned, getting a whiff of beery breath. "Working your elbows, presumably?"

351

Dan laughed. "Yeah, we've had a couple. Just thought we'd call in while we were down this way."

"You OK, Andy?" Kris asked. Andy was still studying the back of the flats. He nodded vaguely.

"Yeah, not bad. You?"

"I'm fine, thanks. Are you rushing off, or have you got time to get a coffee, or beer, or…?"

"Always time for beer, mate!"

"There's a really nice little pub round the corner," Kris suggested, ushering them on. Dan and Andy moved off, and Kris gave Ade a cautionary glance. He had no idea what he'd said to them but was hoping desperately that it wasn't incriminating, not that he thought for one minute Ade would deliberately have said anything, but they all knew each other too well for casual slips of the tongue to go unnoticed.

It was only a five-minute walk to the pub, which was very small and quiet, with a couple of older men standing at the bar and a very bored-looking barmaid sitting on a stool at the end, drinking Coke through a straw. She immediately perked up when she spotted Dan and Andy.

"Alright, lads? What can I get you?"

"Four pints of lager, cheers," Dan said.

She gave him one of her best and most flirtatious smiles and started pulling their pints. "You not from round here?"

"No." Dan wasn't being intentionally evasive. He'd just seen something out of the corner of his eye that troubled him.

"Oh, right," the barmaid persisted. "I see you're mates with Kris."

"Don't say that like I'm in here all the time," Kris joked, as he did, in fact, go there all the time, though usually just to sit in a quiet corner and learn his lines. The pub was out of the way and frequented by a small number of regulars, all of whom spent Saturday nights sitting at the bar and watching a muted TV that showed sport, and only sport. These days, anonymity was a rare and much-welcomed commodity.

"How's the filming going?" she asked.

"Pretty well. We're on location for the next few weeks, which I could do without."

"Whereabouts is that?"

"I'm afraid if I told you I'd have to wipe your memory afterwards, and I don't have my sunglasses with me today." He tried to maintain a serious expression. She laughed.

"Fair dos," she said. She placed the last of the four full pint glasses on the bar, and Dan paid for them. He'd watched Andy throughout the conversation. Granted, everyone was far from their usual cheery selves at the moment, but this was different. Andy kept switching between staring vacantly at the chasing lights of the fruit machine and watching Kris. No, not watching; glaring, and quite angrily, too, as if at any minute he might suddenly decide to take him out. It was odd, for as much as they weren't close, Andy and Kris had always got on all right. Dan let it go and turned his attention to Ade.

"What are you up to these days?"

"Same as ever, really. Got a new act just started. I think he's going to be a roaring success."

"Yeah?"

The four men walked and talked at the same time, heading for a table in the back corner of the pub. The barmaid returned to looking bored.

"He's a mentalist," Ade explained.

"What's one of those?"

"Tricks of the mind—hypnosis and suggestion and all that jazz."

"Oh, I get you. Like Josh does, you mean?"

"Does he?"

"Well, yeah. Not for entertainment purposes, obviously." Dan stole a glance at his brother—he could do with Josh just now to figure out what the hell was the matter with him.

"Hey—sorry to hear about Jess," Ade said.

"Thanks. We want to put it behind us now. It's been a rough few months."

"I understand."

353

"Do you?"

"Yeah."

Ade didn't want to elaborate, and Dan didn't want to listen, so he took him at his word. He swigged at his lager. "The funeral's on Monday, if you wanted to come and pay your respects, although don't feel obliged. Funny thing, inviting people to funerals." He left it at that, partly because that's the sort of thing he did, but mostly because Andy had walked out. "Won't be a mo," Dan said and followed his brother.

As soon as they were alone, Kris reached across and took Ade's hand.

"Thanks," he said.

"What for?"

"Not dropping us in it."

"Why would I do that?"

"I didn't—" Kris began, but Ade cut him off.

"Yes, it pisses me off that you haven't said anything, but I can see your reasoning. Don't leave it too long, though, will you?"

"No. I'm going to tell them as soon as I get the chance, I promise."

Ade gave him a look of warning. He loved Kris and wanted to be with him, but he could live without him.

"It's going to be after Brighton now." Kris sighed.

"Fine," Ade said, and he meant it. "You don't want to go, do you?"

"No. We all need to be together at the moment, and Shaunna's struggling. It's a shame you and…well, you know the rest."

Ade squeezed his hand. "Let's just see what happens, shall we?"

***

It took Dan a while to work out where Andy was, as he'd stepped into the alley that ran along the side of the pub, and it was only when Dan heard him speaking that he was able to pinpoint his location. However, he couldn't hear what he was saying, as he

354

was talking very quietly into his phone, and as soon as he realised Dan was close by, he said his goodbyes and hung up.

"Alright, bro?" Dan asked.

"Yeah. Just feeling a bit antisocial."

"No problem. We'll have this pint and head home."

***

Josh watched Shaunna all the way back into the room. He hadn't heard a word of the phone call, because she'd locked herself in the toilet, so he'd purposely tuned out. She gave him a brief edgy smile and picked up a bottle of perfume from the dressing table.

"Only the shoes to go now," he said.

Shaunna sidestepped and glanced in the bottom of the wardrobe. "*Only* the shoes?" She spun on the spot, taking in the mass of full plastic bags. So many clothes. It was ridiculous. Some of the outfits were nothing like the stuff Jess wore, in work or casually, and the same was true of the shoes. "Cowboy boots? Do you ever remember her wearing cowboy boots?"

Josh shook his head. "Not even when we were at George's. But, you know, she did have a bit of a shopping addiction."

"I didn't know that, although it doesn't surprise me."

"Does anything surprise you?"

"Not much." She grinned at him and continued with transferring the bottles of perfume from the dressing table to a box. "So, bipolar disorder usually starts when you're quite young, doesn't it?" She carried on with what she was doing, but Josh stopped. "Keep going," she prompted. "Do all the boots, then we'll go and have a drink." He did as instructed.

"Yes, it does," he said. "And yes, mine did."

"I've been reading a lot about mental health."

"For your course?"

"No, for personal interest."

Josh was quite puzzled by that.

"I was looking up what 'normal' meant," she explained, "and got all this stuff about psychological disorders, so I started reading it."

355

"OK. Why were you researching definitions of normality? That must have been for your course, surely?"

"Nope. That was because—" She paused to look at him sternly, as he'd stopped packing again. He blushed and got back to it. "Because of my situation," she finished.

"What do you mean?"

"Relationship-wise. Anyway, I don't want to talk about it, if you don't mind."

"Sorry." Josh carried on packing up the boots into boxes and bags, mulling things over. He was still curious to know what she'd meant, but he wouldn't probe, not even with his stupid flighty, impulsive mind trying to take over.

"OK. I'm done," Shaunna said. "You want me to wait, or go and get the kettle on?"

"You go. I've only a couple more pairs to squeeze into this bag."

Shaunna nodded and went downstairs. By the time Josh was ready to join her, she was sitting at the breakfast bar. She indicated the coffee she had made him.

"Thanks," he said. He picked it up and remained standing, too restless even to stay still, let alone sit down. He sipped at the coffee, watching Shaunna over the lip of the cup as she lifted her hair from her neck and held it up in an attempt to cool herself. She noticed him watching.

"I'm really hot. I wish I'd tied it up this morning now."

He carried on staring. She let go of her hair and it poured down over her shoulders again.

"What?" she asked. He shrugged.

"Liquid fire."

She narrowed her eyes and continued to examine him examining her.

"I was always fascinated by your hair," he said. "When we were in infants. Can I plait it?"

She swivelled around and looked right at him. "Pardon?"

"Oh! I'm sorry. I didn't mean to say it. My brain gets carried away sometimes." He closed his eyes and tried to get his thoughts back in order.

"Do you know how to?"

"Plait hair?"

She nodded to confirm.

"Yes. I do."

"OK." She turned away from him again, flicking her hair back over her shoulders.

He put down his coffee and moved closer, scooping up her thick, warm hair with both hands and inhaling deeply. "It smells almost as beautiful as it looks," he said, gently separating it into three, combing each lock through with his fingers. "What conditioner do you use?"

"This one is shea butter and almond."

"Is it from your salon?"

"Yeah. It might be a bit heavy for your hair, though. There's another one we use that smells even more amazing and is for finer hair. That's got almond in it, too."

"Cool. I might have to pop in and get some."

He continued to plait her hair. It wasn't as long these days as it had been back in primary school, although it still fell almost to her waist when she dried it rather than leaving it to dry naturally. Then it would twist into ringlets that curled around her face in a wonderful glowing halo.

"I remember when your grandma died," Josh said, "and you came into school with your hair untied."

She smiled. "Yeah. And you were so puzzled by it, like you thought it was completely different hair."

Josh laughed, because it was kind of true. He'd never considered before that her hair could be anything other than two neat plaits trailing all the way down her back, each finished with a blue ribbon bow.

"Do you remember what you told me?" he asked.

"About?"

"Why you had no plaits."

"No?"

"Remarkable, isn't it? Something so important to me, so life-changing, and you don't remember."

"I might, if you give me a clue."

"You said sometimes when grown-ups are sad they forget to plait your hair, but it doesn't mean—"

"They don't love you." She finished the sentence and turned slowly so he didn't lose his hold. She looked up at him and smiled. "I do remember." He shooed her and waited until she had her back to him once more before he spoke again.

"After my mum died, even though I didn't really understand what it meant, I knew everything was different. I thought it was because we'd moved to England. Everything was strange, as if we were marking time. Sometimes they'd forget to read to me at bedtime, or even to talk. They'd sit for hours in silence, and then all of a sudden try and make amends and over-indulge me, asking about school, and my friends, and what I'd been learning. And they kept buying me presents—books, games, a bike—I got everything I could have wanted, but it never felt like it belonged to me.

"When you said that, I tried to make sense of the words, but I couldn't, not until my dad died, and one night, I was on my way up to bed and my grandma shouted me back, upset that I hadn't given her a kiss good night. I went back down and climbed onto her knee, cuddling her tight and telling her how much I loved her, and I felt so guilty, because I'd been so caught up in my own little world of missing my dad and wishing I was going up to wait for him to come and read to me, that I'd forgotten to give her a kiss."

Josh became quiet.

"I'm still listening," Shaunna said.

"Have you got a bobble?"

"Nope."

"Oh." He sounded disappointed.

"It'll stay in for a while without."

"OK." He let go of the plait and waited for it to unravel, but she was right. The curl in her hair was enough to keep it secure for now. He nodded, satisfied with a job well done, and sat down next to her.

"You're a good listener," he said.

"Thanks. You're a good talker. I always liked listening to your stories when Miss got you to read them out to us. I thought they were wonderful."

"Thank you." He laughed self-consciously. "Although I hated it. I'd look around the class and think…nobody's listening, why is she making me do this?"

"Well, *I* was listening. My favourite was…" She pretended to ponder, but she already knew. "The one about the little orphan boy who was so poor that he didn't even have a pair of shoes, and he found a magic lasso."

"Oh, good grief." Josh hid behind his hands and giggled with embarrassment.

"And the magic lasso granted him three wishes, but the only thing he wished for was his very own horse, and a kindly, handsome cowboy brought him a magnificent black stallion with a long, sleek tail and mane."

"I'm so ashamed," Josh said. "I can't believe you remember."

"And the little boy rode his magnificent black stallion off into the mountains, where they lived happily ever after."

"The End!" they both said together. Shaunna clapped her hands. "It was a very touching story."

"Erm, yes. When you get to Freud at uni you can revisit that opinion."

"I always thought it was about George."

"You thought right."

"You two were so cute—you still are. I love how you're all kissy and cuddly and…" She went all squishy, and Josh poked her in the side.

"You and Kris used to be like that."

"We did, you're right. And I really miss it. He and Krissi are both very touchy-feely people." She sighed. "Maybe not Krissi so much, but she humours me. Now she's left home, and Kris… well." She shrugged. "I miss it."

"OK, so from here on—" Josh got up as he spoke and beckoned to her to do likewise. He put his arms around her. "We'll have to make sure you don't get neglected."

They continued to hug for a long time after, and were still doing so when Eleanor returned.

"What's up with you two?" she asked.

"Nothing. We're just cuddling," Josh said.

"I can see that, but why?"

"Because we want to."

Eleanor shook her head. "Told you, didn't I? From the sublimely aloof to the ridiculously sentimental. Right, where are we up to? Are the clothes and shoes ready to go?"

"Clothes are. I'm still doing the shoes."

She tutted in disgruntlement and went back up to Jess's room.

Shaunna withdrew slightly. "She doesn't know?"

"No. I decided not to tell her. She won't understand."

"I thought she was your best friend."

Josh nodded. "She was."

Leaf From A Tree
Monday 2nd October

George pinned Josh down by his arms.

"Stay in the bloody bed!" He was laughing as he said it, but there was a serious undertone to his demand; it was gone midnight, and Josh hadn't slept in four days.

"Fine," Josh sighed loudly. George let go of him, and he pretended he was going to get out of bed again, but then rolled back, grinning.

"Seriously, Joshua. I *will* tie you down."

"Ha! As if you would!" Josh tried to lie still, but he couldn't. "Once you're asleep, how are you going to stop me getting up, really?"

"I'll stay awake."

Josh shook his head. "No, you won't."

"Watch me." George sat up and folded his arms. Josh watched him. George started to smile. Josh laughed and pulled himself up so that he was sitting, too.

"Look, I'll try and stay in bed, but I can't promise anything. My brain won't shut down, and I'll get fed up watching TV, it'll be three in the morning, and I'll be sitting here, bored, while you're sleeping—"

"So, wake me up."

"You don't want me to."

"No. I don't, but if it means you stand a chance of getting some sleep..." George turned to face Josh and took his hands, studying them momentarily and then kissing his fingers. "Once today's over, I think you'll be back to normal, but tonight please stay here with me. I don't like waking up to an empty bed."

"OK. Just for you, I'll do it."

***

Shaunna rolled onto her side and squinted in the dark, trying to see the clock. No illuminated numbers, no charge light on her mobile phone, no electricity.

"Balls," she said.

"What's up?"

"What time is it?"

"It's… Ah." Kris reached over and picked up his phone. "Five a.m."

"Ohhhh. Why am I awake?" Shaunna sighed in exasperation, the thoughts of what they had to do today flooding into her mind, uninvited and unstoppable. If she stayed in bed, awake, they would overcome her. "I'm getting up," she said.

Kris groaned. "Don't get up yet." He snuggled close and kissed her neck. "I can give you a reason to stay."

She could almost see him smiling, in the dark, and she smiled, too.

"OK," she consented. She turned to face him and closed her eyes, focusing on the sensation of his gentle kisses trailing down her neck to her breasts, her pyjama top being pushed down, and then her pyjama bottoms, his warm, soft hands behind her, drawing her to him. She rolled with him, slowly working her way down his chest to remove his shorts, and back up again until they were face-to-face, writhing against him until they locked together, his hips rising and falling in time with her own. Only the second time they had done this in almost two years, and yet it felt so familiar, so comforting, so satisfying.

As the motion took them over, they forgot about the day and the other trials that would follow it, just flowing together, feeling each other building towards the climax, matching their speed until they rose together one last time, and fell.

Shaunna stayed where she was for a couple of minutes, fighting the strange emotions flooding her mind; fulfilment was still holding court, but regret and guilt were banging at the door. She rolled onto her side of the bed and quickly got up, pulling on her dressing gown.

"What's wrong?" Kris asked.

"Nothing," she lied. "Just don't want to start wallowing. I'm going for a shower."

***

"Daddy."

Dan opened his eyes: not quite six o'clock. His daughter stood in silhouetted relief at the bedroom door. He stretched.

"Come on, baby girl," he said.

She came running across, and he lifted her into the bed between them. She wriggled, and he felt the wet of her pyjamas. She was only wearing nappies at night now, except for when she decided she didn't need them and took them off herself. He didn't want to get out of bed, but even though it was only 'maiden's water', as his mother called it, he could still smell it and feel it soaking into his t-shirt. He relented.

"Shall we go and have a bath?" he asked.

"Bubblybath," she said. "You Daddy?"

"OK." They got out of bed and left Mummy to sleep a little longer.

***

"Ready? Meeee-aaaaawwww!" Eleanor zoomed the spoonful of cereal down through the air, performing a loop-the-loop before it nosedived into Toby's mouth. He giggled, and half the milky gloop dropped onto his chin. He could feed himself now, but sometimes it was fun to play, and she had time this morning. James was in the shower; the in-laws had offered to collect Oliver from his mother and take him home again later.

It felt odd to Eleanor: still over a week until his fifth birthday, yet he'd asked to come to the funeral; James had said yes without hesitation. And, she supposed, she didn't really have a problem with it, not in principle. It was just that having attended a few open-casket occasions during her own childhood, and eventually reaching a point where she and Ben would compete to be the first to say, 'Oh, look! Another dead body!' it felt forced and meaningless, taking young children to such events.

363

But this was Oliver, the Prince of The Question Why, which was probably what she was dreading most. She could do funerals. She was a hardened Catholic girl. Funerals were what they were good at. Lots of incense swinging, black suits and misery. Except, of course, Jess wasn't a Catholic girl. The only smoke would be coming from the crematorium chimney, and her parents had requested that people wear whatever they felt comfortable in, which was even worse than asking for no black. It would have been better to have said nothing at all.

So: no black, no flowers, no miserable organ music or hymns, but they were to have a wake, and that was the only bit of planning she'd been allowed to do, which suited her just fine, because Jess was her oldest friend, for a long time her best friend.

She put down Toby's spoon and pinched the corners of her eyes, trying to stem the flow of tears, but it was pointless. Toby bashed the side of his bowl with his fist, and it upended, sending soggy wheaty gunk everywhere. Eleanor sobbed over the cereal, over still having to decide what to wear, over answering Oliver's questions all day; for the loss of her friend.

James came into the dining room and leaned down behind her, wrapping her in his arms to keep her as one.

***

"Charlotte's here," Andy's mum shouted over the din of music and his feet pounding to the beat on the treadmill belt.

"Huh?" He pushed the volume control, and the thumping bass receded.

His mother rubbed her ears. "How can you stand that dreadful racket at eight in the morning? Or any other time for that matter? I said, Charlotte's here."

Andy stopped the treadmill. "I didn't think she'd be this early. Just tell her to come through, thanks, Mum."

His mother nodded and left again. Andy wiped his face and neck with a towel.

"Morning." Charlotte smiled at him. She stepped around the treadmill and reached up to kiss his cheek.

364

"I wouldn't do that if I were you," he said. "I've been running since six."

"Still not sleeping?"

"No. Well, kinda. I reckon I got about three hours. You OK?"

"Yep. Just wanted to check in. I'm gonna stick all their stuff in the car before the funeral and go straight to the airport."

"No worries. Can't have them missing their flight when it's already cost them enough to change it. I told them they didn't have to stay for today."

"Yeah, well, I think you've become Number One Son, so just go with it. See you later." She gave him a quick hug and pulled a face at his sweatiness.

"I did warn you," he called after her. She waved, and then she was gone.

***

Steph sat in the kitchen, smoking a cigarette, trying not to hear the sound of the hearse and other cars pull up outside, leaving Dave to greet the funeral directors. She wanted to die. It was only getting through today that was keeping her here, not Dave, not Jess's friends. Nothing. There was nothing left to live for. Twenty-nine years of being torn in two by her grief for Daisy and living for Jess. Nothing left but the hole in her soul that had been killing her for twenty-nine years.

Josh walked past on his way in from the garden, where they were all gathered, waiting out the time before they had to get in *those* cars, and follow *that* hearse carrying *her* coffin. And it was a beautiful coffin. He'd made sure of it. She'd loved the fine things in life; it was right that she should have this one last extravagance. He stopped and laid his hand upon Steph's.

"Just stay for now," he whispered.

She nodded. She could agree to that much.

The others traipsed past, but he remained where he was, exchanging glances with George and Sean, and then with Kris. Dan touched Josh on the shoulder as he passed by, Andy trudging behind him, both brothers unable to make eye contact with anyone. Adele had hooked her arm through Shaunna's and was holding her up, holding her together.

Eleanor had not yet made it from the garden, where she was desperately trying to stop the tears. Her eyes burned with the pain of crying for four hours straight. Josh peered furtively through the open door.

"Go to her," Steph said. "She needs you more than I do."

He doubted that, but Steph looked up at him and smiled the saddest of smiles.

"Go and look after her. She's a mother. This—" she put her palm against her chest, over her heart "—is her pain, too. You need to remind her that she still has Toby. She has to hold on to that thought today and every day."

Josh nodded and left as Dave came through. He held out his hand to his wife, and they came together, holding onto each other, because that was all they had. They drifted away, along the hall and out of the door, down the path, pulled, pulled by that invisible, invincible force of mourning, towards the car, a grey-suit man their guide, their captor, luring and encouraging. His silence respectfully filled the vacuous bubble between their house and the car.

Steph closed her eyes to the coffin that held her baby girl. Her beautiful, wonderful, loving baby girl, so full of life, refusing to keep her pigtails in, shrill squeals of grazed knees, shrieks of fury in skirts too short, sobbing broken teenage heart. Back seat of car, off to university, halls and boys and living on pasta for weeks on end; back seat of car home from graduation, so proud, too tipsy on Champagne, too expensive; back seat of car leaving home, own house, crazy purchases, overspent on credit cards; back seat of car along winding gravel driveway, slow procession on, and on, and on to that place, wondrous and peaceful and nothing, nothing, nothing.

Andy, Dave, Josh and Sean, mismatched men beneath the gleaming white. So beautiful. So this was it. Thirty minutes more to endure of the performance. Thirty minutes sitting before the gleaming white box, first to listen to a man say the words he said over and again each day. Was there a script? A sheet with underscores to 'Insert Name of Deceased Here'? He finished and moved respectfully to one side for the real eulogy to be delivered. Steph shifted her gaze to the ceiling and considered the complexities of the architrave.

Josh rose to his feet and stepped reluctantly, waiting until the very last second to release his grasp on George's hand, afraid that when he did, he would also lose his grasp on his faculties, for they were frail and flitting, and he was glad of the sleep he had secured in the early hours, but oh, to never have had this day.

He walked up to the lectern and looked over the people before him. His first lecture; he'd imagined today would begin with an hour's slog before a hundred undergraduates, not a room full of mourners. To read at a funeral: a dreadful burden yet such a privilege, although he did not need to read—not from paper. It was all in his mind. All in his mind.

"Steph and Dave asked me to say a few words about Jess, and I'm truly honoured." The rest he did not say, for it did not need saying, what a terrible honour it was. "First, I want to explain how I came to know Jess.

"We met at high school, always in the same classes for English and a few other subjects besides, although it was in English that the bond between us developed, particularly in sixth form, when our teacher paired us to work on a text for our exam. That text was *Hamlet*, and my love of it was matched only by Jess's hate for the same. We'd sit together for hours, she constantly griping about how rubbish it was, and me defending The Bard's honour.

"That battle continued into our first days at university, slowly fizzling out as we replaced the knowledge of our adolescence with the grand ideas of our respective academic disciplines. Yet it remained special to us. When Jess told me of her illness, it was, as it had always been in our youth, the words of Ophelia and Hamlet that enabled us to say what needed to be said.

"To try to sum up a life, to explain what someone meant to so many people in the amount of time we are given here to say goodbye, is just not possible. Indeed, if we'd had all the time in the world, it would never, ever be enough." Josh coughed against his fist and attempted to swallow back his tears. He heard George's trembling gasp and lost control...*but*, he reminded himself, *it's OK to feel. It's OK to show other people how you feel*, and they were all feeling as wretched and lost as he.

"Jess would have wanted us to do our best to enjoy today. She'd have demanded it, ticked us off for being overly sentimental, but that was what she was like—always demanding the impossible and being furious when it wasn't delivered.

"Anyway, as cliché as this is, it is absolutely right that on this most awful, unbearable, utterly inconceivable day, I present, in memory of my dear friend, fellow academic and champion, that most famous Shakespearean soliloquy of all. Why? Because it is most apt. And because it would wind her up."

A few people smiled and laughed lightly, but then returned to solemn listening. Josh waited in silence, and as he looked out at those faces, he felt the strength being given to and sapped from him all at once. Their friends; her family. He began.

> *"To be, or not to be, that is the question:*
> *Whether 'tis nobler in the mind to suffer..."*

As he spoke, he let his gaze settle on Steph and Dave, unsure if they were listening or would even comprehend the comfort to be had from these words, if he could deliver them well enough.

> *"To die, to sleep,*
> *No more; and by a sleep, to say we end*
> *The heart-ache, and the thousand natural shocks*
> *That flesh is heir to: 'tis a consummation*
> *Devoutly to be wished..."*

He continued through to the end of the soliloquy—so much effort to walk that line, that precarious path of necessary dislocation from the sea of troubles that he had himself once opposed to end the heartache, trying to keep his head together as best he could, before he delivered his final words. They were the hardest of all.

"All of us go through difficult times, and if we are fortunate, we have people like Jess in our lives, who are there by our side, through the good and the bad, holding our hand and reminding us to just keep on fighting. They're the ones who never judge, or offer placations. They're the ones we can phone in the middle of the night who will lie to us that they weren't sleeping anyway. They're the ones who know when we're lying to them and don't need to ask why. And they're the ones we can never imagine leaving us, because it hurts too much.

"A few months ago, on the day of my marriage to the most amazing, wonderful man in the world, Jess and I shared breakfast together, and I finally found the courage to tell her how much she means to me, not in Shakespeare's words, not through the mouthpiece of Hamlet, but in my own words."

Josh turned now, to look at the coffin, that gleaming white casket, within which lay his beautiful, glorious, slain knight. And he said to her the last words that he had written so long ago.

"Good luck, Jess. You are the best lawyer ever and a truly wonderful friend. Thank you with all my heart."

**

"That was beautiful," Eleanor said, finally, as they walked back to the cars, and quickly stuffed her face in a tissue.

Josh wasn't speaking. He was completely drained, of words, of the energy required to do more than keep walking. All around him, people were holding quiet, meaningless conversations, straight-faced emotionless interchanges, their outlines fuzzy and vague in the aftermath of his performance. Kris caught up with him and pulled him to one side, embracing him. Josh was surprised, even in this situation, but he was grateful, also, and accepted Kris's love.

"I know," Kris spoke close to his ear. "I know what it takes to deliver lines like that with such passion." He moved away. "And I must say I have never heard them delivered so beautifully." He winked a bloodshot eye, and Josh smiled.

"Thanks," he said. "My head is totally fucked."

Kris looped his arm through Josh's to guide him onwards. "Mine's not so great, either, and I've not had to do what you have. I only wish I could stay for the Chinese."

"Have you really got to go today?"

"Yeah. I can't get out of it. I tried. The producer said unless I was sick, and, he said, 'by sick, I mean at death's door yourself...'"

"He actually said that?"

"He actually said that. He's a heartless bastard, and he's the director as well. I'm gonna quit at the end of this series, and only because of him. I got my foot in the door, and I've got other work lined up if I want it, but I can't do *Shadows* anymore."

They drew up alongside George and Oliver, who were standing together, holding hands and looking up at the chimney of the crematorium. Oliver was frowning, deep in thought.

"Is that how they get to heaven?" he asked.

"I guess," George said. He turned to Josh and smiled. "You OK?"

"Josh, why don't you believe in God?"

He gave no answer. He didn't have time to think of one before Oliver continued.

"Ellna said that God loves all of us, and when we die, like Jess, we go to heaven with God, and God makes us better, and then we live for ever and ever."

It would have been a difficult enough conversation to have on a normal day, without the clutter of emotional debris.

"It's hard to explain, Ollie. Can I think about it for now? We can talk about it another time."

"Um, OK."

Josh smiled and affectionately rubbed the little boy's head, still amused and delighted by Oliver having picked up that particular nuance of George's. It was a tiny, shimmering spark of light on this desperately dark day.

"I'm going back to the car," he told George. "Are you coming?"

"Yeah. In a sec."

Josh pulled his jacket tight around him. It wasn't especially cold, but the wind had a bitter edge to it that was all the harder to stand when he was so exhausted. He and Kris returned to the car park, where Shaunna was standing with Steph and Dave. Josh went straight over to them, and they all exchanged hugs. Only then did he notice who else was with them.

"Hey, Ade. I didn't know you were here."

"Hi, Josh." They shook hands. "I'm so sorry about Jess."

"Were you in there for the service?"

"Yes. I was sitting at the back. Your words were so beautiful."

Josh smiled tacit thanks and then stood by in a vacant haze as, car by car, the place began to empty. He, too, wanted to get away, to go and be somewhere—anywhere—else, but George and Oliver were still staring up at the sky, and he didn't want to disturb them. As he watched, Oliver bent down, retrieved something from the floor and reached up to pass whatever it was to George, who was so still, he could have just been turned to stone.

Oliver reached up again and pulled on George's arm. On receiving no response, he tugged even harder, until George crouched down to his level, and Oliver put his arms around George's neck and hugged him tightly. They remained in the same position, with their arms around each other, for several minutes before George slowly rose to his feet.

"Here." Eleanor nudged Josh, interrupting his observation. She gave him Oliver's booster seat and a smile.

"Thanks," he said. She kissed his cheek and left with James and Toby.

Now it was only the three of them. George and Oliver arrived back, sporting tear-streaked cheeks. In George's hand was the object Oliver had given him: a sycamore leaf, tinted orange and red.

"Ollie has a couple more questions for you," he said.

"OK." Josh turned his attention to the very determined looking little boy, hoping they weren't going to be too hard to answer.

"Why do elephants paint their toenails red?" Oliver asked.

"I don't know."

"So they can hide in cherry trees."

Josh smiled, about to praise him for his joke, but Oliver wasn't done yet.

"How do you get an elephant out of a cherry tree?" he asked, still with that same very serious expression.

"I don't know. How do you get an elephant out of a cherry tree?"

"Stand it on a leaf and wait for autumn."

Josh laughed and Oliver smiled up at him. That was what he'd wanted—to make them laugh, because they were both so sad.

"Are you guys ready to go?" Josh asked.

The words left his mouth and were whisked up by a gust that detached many of the leaves from the trees lining the crematorium driveway, creating a soft orange blizzard that fluttered to the ground around them.

Oliver's mouth opened wide in wonder, and he lifted his arms up high in the air, trying to catch the swirling, falling leaves.

"See? I still the best man," he said. "I ask God for fetti for Jess, and look." He smiled up at them both as he ran past and waited by the car door.

Josh looked at George in total wonderment, and George shrugged. He placed the sycamore leaf on Josh's palm, sandwiching it with his own, and they remained completely still, eyes locked, instantly understanding each other's pain, but also sensing hope.

*Life goes on...*although the same could not be said for their silent communication, which was brought to a timely end by a loud tutting from behind Josh, and they swapped their tears for laughter. Oliver suddenly reappeared between them, hands on hips, a stern frown on his face.

"Come on, you two. Stop dawgling or we'll be late for the Chinese foods."

Josh gave George the booster seat and scooped Oliver up in his arms.

"Thanks, Ollie, you're awesome."

"Why?"

"Asking God for fetti."

372

"You don't believe in God," Oliver stated.

"No, but I do believe in Oliver Brown." Josh poked him in the tummy. "Hmm. He seems real." He tickled him, and Oliver giggled. "Yes, I think he probably is."

"You silly, Josh."

"And I'm also very, very hungry. Shall we go and eat foods?"

Oliver nodded. "You still sad?"

"Yes, I am, but you've made me happy, too."

"You can be happy and sad together?"

"You can be happy, and sad, and cross, and everything all at once."

"Oh."

Josh put Oliver down so he could climb into his seat, and reached across to fasten the seat belt.

"I don't like to be growed up. It's too hard."

"Yes, it is," Josh agreed.

"But then it's good as well, cos when I growed up and big, I can marry Shabina, and then we can have fetti leaves at our wedding, and…"

Josh backed out of the car door and looked over the roof at George, both smiling as they listened to Oliver's life plan taking shape in the back seat.

George opened his door and climbed inside. "You OK there, Ollie?"

"Yeah, I'm OK. You OK there, Dorge?"

Josh shook his head and looked up at the leaves still fluttering all around. He caught one and smiled.

"See you in the next one."

Playground In My Mind
Monday 9th October

Shaunna double-checked she'd locked the door and walked down the path towards the car.

"Good afternoon," she said with artificial cheeriness. She climbed into the passenger seat and did her best to ignore the two boxes in the back. Josh stared straight ahead.

"Good afternoon," he replied quietly. He covered his face with his hands. "Oh, I was trying not to do this." He gasped and started blubbering.

Shaunna reached out and took his hand. "Hey, I know this is awful, but we'll get each other through it, OK?"

He nodded and sniffed. "OK."

"I got you some of that conditioner." She held it up as evidence. He turned and saw the enormous bottle.

"Thanks. I won't be needing to buy any more for a while. How much do I owe you?"

"A smile?" Josh smiled, and Shaunna squeezed his hand. "We can do this."

"Yes. We can."

He dried his eyes and set off down to the end of the road, turned left, and left again. He knew the route well, though he'd travelled it just the once and was quite sure this would be the last time he drove there, to that playground.

"I hope there aren't loads of kids about," Shaunna said. "I'll feel really silly if there are."

"Maybe we should've borrowed Toby and Dylan for the day."

"Yeah. Pity we didn't think of that earlier."

Josh continued onwards, staying well under the speed limit, terrified that if he went any faster, he might have to do an emergency stop and tip the ashes all over his car. He was also delaying their arrival, because he was dreading it. He didn't want to do this, but he'd promised. They both had.

In spite of his dangerously hesitant driving, they arrived at the park far too quickly and stopped outside, peering through the railings, trying to see if there was anyone in the playground.

Shaunna got out of the car first and stood on tiptoes. "I can see the swings moving, but not much else," she reported. Josh tipped his seat forward and passed one of the boxes to her. "Hi, Daisy," she greeted it.

Josh grabbed the other box and shut the car door. Shaunna looked at him, then at the box in his hands. "I'm not talking to a boxful of ash," he grumbled.

"Just thought it might help to get into the spirit of things, if you pardon the pun."

He laughed ruefully. "You do the getting-into-the-spirit part, I'll do the cynical, mocking part."

"OK, Mr. Scientist."

They stepped off towards the park entrance, both immediately regressing into their own thoughts. Josh was thinking about the lecture he needed to write for the counselling course tomorrow, but not out of flippant disregard. It was a coping strategy, a way of urging his feet to keep moving, distracting his brain from its desire to turn and run. He stopped and looked behind him.

"Oh, Shaunna!" He walked back and put his free arm around her. She snuggled against his neck and sobbed. They stayed where they were, too upset to pull themselves together, irrespective of the curious looks they were getting from the occasional dog walker or jogger who passed them by. Shaunna's phone beeped; she took it out and frowned at the screen.

"Hope today goes OK. Wish I was there. Have fun," she read aloud. "Have fun? Yes, Kris, of course we will!" She put it back in her pocket. They moved off again. "If there are people here, what do we tell them?"

"The truth."

"It might freak them out."

"See? That's what I mean. Beliefs are supposed to be comforting."

Shaunna didn't comment. She wasn't overtly religious, but she had been brought up Roman Catholic and used to attend church when she was younger. She supposed she did believe in God but didn't agree with much of what the Church said and did. However, today, it was giving her some strength to imagine there was more to this existence than was represented by the box of ash in her hand. Seven weeks old. It didn't bear thinking about, so she pushed the thought away and tried to focus on her surroundings.

They'd never been inside the park before, and it was beautiful; their route was lined with mature oaks, boughs heavy with acorns, and willow trees still clinging to their thin lemony leaves. The flowerbeds were planted with colourful winter pansies, yet the closer they got to the playground, the more gaudy and out of place they seemed, the black marks on their petals transforming into sinister, sneering faces. Shaunna shivered and shifted the box so she could carry it with one hand. She grabbed Josh's hand with the other and held tight.

"Can you feel that, too?" he asked. She nodded. "It's all in our minds. You know that, don't you?" She glanced sideways at him, doubting and admiring him all at once.

They were close enough now to hear the noise of play being caught up in the autumn wind and blown their way.

"It sounds busy," Shaunna said. "Maybe we should come back later."

"When it's dark? There is *no way* I'm doing this in the dark. It's already scary enough."

They walked on along the winding path, turning the final corner, the playground almost in view. Josh pushed the gate and held it open, following Shaunna through. They took a couple of steps forward and stopped to take in the sight before them. The playground was positively teeming with people. All three swings were swaying back and forth, the roundabout was spinning at full throttle, and the slide was barely free of one person before the next came swooshing down. Josh and Shaunna turned to each other and laughed through their tears.

"You know who's to blame for this?" Shaunna asked rhetorically.

Josh looked across to the swings and shouted, "Tierney! What d'you think you're playing at?"

"Swings." Sean grinned back. He waited for his to finish its forward trajectory, dismounted and walked over. "I thought the four of you might appreciate a bit of company."

Josh shook his head, still too astonished to think of a witty retort.

"Come on, bro, shift it!" Andy pushed on Dan's back with his foot until he could no longer hold on and went hurtling down the slide. He got up, waited for his brother to come down and then quickly sat on the end, so that Andy knocked him to the floor.

"Ow. I'm telling Mum," he whined. Andy held out his hand and pulled Dan to his feet. Josh and Shaunna watched on, laughing.

George, Toby, little Shaunna and Adele were on the roundabout, which was going much more slowly than before and with both adults looking decidedly green, whilst Toby bounced up and down on George's knees, his eyes wide and watery, his face glowing with excitement and windchill. Little Shaunna shouted, "Steadygo!!!" but Adele was having too much of a problem with the 'steady' part to go anywhere.

Meanwhile, Eleanor and Lois were competing to see who could get highest on the swings, or, at least, they were until Lois flicked her feet and one of her shoes went spinning through the air, colliding with Dan's head as he reached the bottom of the slide again.

"This is brilliant," Shaunna said.

Sean smiled and put his arms around her; she hugged him back with her free arm.

Josh nodded. "Yes. It is. Thank you." He pushed away the tears and held out his hand to Shaunna. "Come on, let's do it."

Sean released her, and she took Josh's hand, the two of them moving into the midst of their friends, no longer worried that they'd fail Steph in their promise.

First stop: the roundabout. They waited for it to come to a halt and climbed aboard, settling into a segment each, backs against the central pole, legs out in front of them, with Jess and Daisy in the sections between. Josh kept his hand on top of Jess's ashes, and Shaunna's hand was on top of his. The same was repeated on the opposite side of the roundabout, with Shaunna keeping a tight hold on Daisy's ashes. George grabbed one of the guide rails and gave it a gentle push, setting them slowly spinning clockwise.

"I should point out," Josh said, "that I was never keen on roundabouts when I was little."

"No, they're way too much fun," Shaunna teased. He tightened his grip on her hand until she squeaked. "Really, though, did you ever go out to play?"

"Not much. I didn't have anyone to play with, and there were no parks near where we lived."

"Weren't you bored? Or lonely?"

"Sometimes, I guess, but it was normal for me. I saw other children at school and I kind of thought that's all you did, unless you had brothers and sisters."

"Hmm." Shaunna laughed. "That's a bit weird."

"Yes, I agree. Still, I got there in the end." He looked up at George and smiled, watching as he passed from view and turning his head to follow him all around the rotation. On the next pass, George stepped onto the roundabout and slowly worked his way to the middle, exaggerating the fight against the very small amount of centrifugal force. He bent down and kissed Josh gently on the lips.

"You'd best not be smooching back there," Shaunna said, knowing that they were.

Josh crossed his legs so that George could sit down. Next, Sean climbed into the segment with Jess and lifted the box onto his lap. Eleanor did likewise with Daisy. Andy came over and gave the roundabout a spin.

"Faster," Eleanor said. Andy shrugged and gave it another push.

"Faster," George said. Andy obliged yet again.

"Faster! Faster!" Shaunna shouted, smiling up at him as she passed by. He sensed the desire had returned to her and swallowed hard, giving her a subtle, knowing look the next time she came his way.

"OK, I'm starting to feel just a tiny bit sick," Josh complained. "Shall we move on to the slide?"

Shaunna nodded. "Sure."

Andy grabbed the bar of her segment and pulled back on it to slow the roundabout, every so often glancing down at her until it stopped. He held out his hand to help her up, and she bounced to her feet, brushing against him as she jumped down to ground level again. She heard his sudden intake of breath and smiled.

The slide was quite high, and the steps were steep, so Eleanor held the box for Josh whilst he climbed to the top.

"Do you remember when you and Jess tried to make me go down that waterslide?" he asked.

"God, that was a long time ago."

"I haven't forgotten."

"No. Of course you haven't. And we didn't make you. We just suggested you might enjoy it, but you wouldn't even get in the pool."

"I don't like swimming."

"You don't like anything."

"I do! I like reading. And I like playing computer games. And I used to like bike rides."

Shaunna was still waiting at the base of the steps. "Come on!" she urged.

Josh sat down and took the box from Eleanor. "And I'm afraid of heights, but my therapists have been working hard with me. I believe I'm making good progress."

He was doing very well, although the colour had drained from his face, and he was definitely only doing the slide once. He closed his eyes and took a deep breath, preparing to let go.

Shaunna bumped up behind him and gave him a shove. Being as slim as he was, he went tearing down at speed and flew right off the end, landing hard on the muddy patch at the bottom.

"Oops!" Shaunna said. She quickly descended and helped him to his feet. "Sorry!" She winced, trying not to laugh.

"That was a rough landing," he grumbled, rubbing the base of his spine. He'd been so desperate to keep hold of the ashes that he couldn't slow or brace himself on the way down.

"Was it fun, though?"

"That might be asking a bit much."

She grinned and took his hand. "There's only the swings left. Are you ready?"

He nodded.

Everyone else stopped playing and drew closer, watching Josh and Shaunna position themselves on two swings next to each other, their arms looped around the chains so they could hold the boxes. This was the moment they'd been dreading, but it wasn't awful, really. The autumn wind swirled around them, and the playground was so full of life, and love and happiness, that they knew it was the right time. Slowly, using their feet to push off, they moved back together in tandem, settling into the gentle motion of the swings.

"Look," Shaunna whispered, indicating towards the gate with her head.

Josh glanced over and saw Steph and Dave, standing together, clinging to each other and watching them. Josh smiled and began to cry.

Shaunna released one hand from the box and reached across to him. "We can do this."

He squeezed her hand and released it again so he could get a good grip on the box. Together, they started to build height, and Sean and Andy moved behind to give them a little help, pushing them higher and higher until it was almost impossible to hold on.

"Ready?" Shaunna said.

A short distance in front of them, little Shaunna heard her cue and shouted, "Steadygo!"

Josh and Shaunna lifted the lids from the boxes and threw them aside. Loosened by the motion of the roundabout and the slide's descent, the topmost layer of ash was whipped up by the wind and went spiralling through the trees. They watched until it disappeared, and then each took a handful of ash from their boxes and threw it into the air, once again waiting for it to dissipate through the trees and up into the sky. They did it again, and again, until so little remained they couldn't get hold of it, and both jumped from their swings, tipping the last of the ash as they landed. Momentarily, it swirled around them, and then it, too, was gone.

They smiled at each other and hugged tightly as they cried— for Jess and Daisy, for Steph, and for their own mums. When they finally let go, they looked across the park, to where Steph and Dave had been standing before. They'd gone.

Sean came up and put an arm around each of them. "Milk bar blowout?" he proposed. They both nodded.

"Yeah," Shaunna said, wiping her eyes on Sean's jacket. "Good idea."

"Do they sell coffee?" Josh asked as their entire group moved off.

Shaunna shrugged. "Dunno. But they do a mean banoffee hot chocolate."

"Mmm. That sounds awesome."

"The yoghurt fruit crush is good, too."

"It is," Sean agreed. "If you want to give yourself a hernia."

Shaunna held the gate open and waited for everyone else to pass through. She closed it and looked back at the park, watching the leaves being tugged from the trees and pulled up, up and away into the darkening sky.

"I miss you, Mum," she said. She pulled her cardigan tight around her and closed her eyes. "I'll miss you forever." She opened her eyes again to find Josh standing next to her.

He reached out and smoothed her hair back from her face. "She didn't break her promise. She'll always be with you." He touched her forehead with the tip of his finger. "Mr. Scientist says it's all in here." Then he pressed his hand against hers, clasped against her chest. "But this is where you'll find her, whenever you need her."

Hand in hand, they turned and strolled away from the playground, through the smiling winter pansies, past the swooping lemony willows and the acorn-laden oaks. Not a mother's promise broken.

A mother's promise fulfilled.

Fire, Water, Burn
Monday 16th–Thursday 19th October

10:24 Andy [mobile]
Hey rhb. Guess who's home alone? x

10:25 Shaunna [mobile]
Home as in? x

10:25 Andy [mobile]
Mum's. Wanna sleepover? x

10:26 Shaunna [mobile]
I can't. I've got the dog. x

10:27 Andy [mobile]
So? Bring him too. x

Andy opened the front door, and Casper went tearing past, skidding across the marble floor of the atrium, straight up the left staircase, along the landing and down the right staircase, sliding off the bottom and righting himself before racing away in the direction of the conservatory. The dog disappeared from view; Andy turned back to Shaunna and smiled. She was wearing *that* dress. A short cardigan covered her shoulders, and auburn spirals tumbled down loosely from the large sprung clip in her hair.

"Hi," he said.

She smiled back and stepped inside, revelling in his obvious appreciation as he looked her over. His gaze returned to her face to find her staring at him intently, her lips red and full. She was out of breath.

"Did you walk here?" he asked.

"No. Got a taxi."

He nodded. Still, they remained standing in the doorway. The sound of the dog racing around echoed through the atrium.

"Would you like to come in?" Andy suggested.

"OK. But I'll tell you now. Up against the wall, on the kitchen table, in the pool, on that marble floor over there, I don't care where, but I do not want to be loved, or cherished, or treated like a princess. I don't want gently undressing, or cuddling or caressing, or for you to wait for me. Capisce?"

Any control Andy had over the behaviour of certain body parts was well and truly finished by that statement. She noticed the movement in his jeans and laughed. He gave her a coy, sexy smile.

"Do you, err..." he moved closer, "have any preference on the order?"

She shrugged. "Take me anywhere you like, any way you like, just take me."

He needed no further prompting. He pushed her backwards, bringing the door to a slam behind her, and pinned her to it with his body, pressing his mouth hard against hers and thrusting his tongue in between her hot, wet lips. Without stopping, he reached up to unclip her hair, let it flow through his fingers as it tumbled down, and grasped it. His other hand moved to her cardigan, popping open the buttons, one by one.

Releasing her hair, he used both hands to push the cardigan away, revealing her bare shoulders and breaking the kiss to trail his tongue down to her neck, biting and kissing, and sucking, the taste of her perfume tingling on his lips. He hooked an index finger under each shoulder strap of her dress and pulled them down, too, grinding against her as her legs slowly slid apart. She put her hands on either side of his face and pulled him back up to kiss her again.

"Kitchen," he murmured hungrily.

He walked backwards, kissing her all the while, parting just long enough to take off his t-shirt, flinging it to the floor to join her cardigan. She kicked off her shoes and stepped out of her knickers, adding them to the trail of clothing across the atrium floor, like the zoom-in to a Hollywood sex scene, down the corridor to the kitchen, their need so urgent that he hoisted her onto the nearest worktop, and she blindly shoved objects from behind her to clear the space, still kissing and panting for breath, both of them, as he unbuckled his belt and peeled back his jeans. The zip opened itself, and he moved forward, using the flats of his hands to slide the soft fabric of her skirt up until he met with bare thighs. Giving himself a moment to enjoy the sensation of her skin under his fingers, he gripped her hips and pulled her towards him, pushing deep inside.

She gasped in pleasure and leaned back on her palms, lifting her knees so he went deeper still. At first, he moved slowly, easing himself in and out, watching her expression change as he built up speed, thrusting faster, harder, his jeans sliding down and revealing his bulky, defined thighs. He hooked his arms under her knees, and she started to moan, lifting herself from the worktop to push back against him, closer, deeper, the straps of her dress sliding away, down her arms, and taking the bodice with them, revealing her red lacy bra.

He wrapped her legs around his back, freeing his arms so that he could drop down her bra straps, the motion making it impossible to unhook and remove it. As the straps slid down, so, too, did the cups, and he leaned forward to touch his tongue to one nipple then the other. Her moaning became louder, her thrusts against him more urgent. He put his hands under her buttocks and pulled her in tightly. She cried out and kept grinding against him. He tried to hold back.

"Just do it," she urged breathlessly. She lifted herself even higher, meeting each slam of his pelvis as he banged into her, sliding easily against each other. He pushed forward in one final thrust so deep, his climax so massive and so long-awaited that he was seeing flashing lights, and now she was climaxing, her breathing stopped, returning in short, panted gasps for air, her abdomen rising and falling, rising and falling.

He let out a shaky laugh and released his grip around her legs, but he couldn't quite speak yet. She adjusted her position slightly, still with him inside her, enjoying every little post-climax twitch.

"Terrified," he said eventually, missing the rest of the sentence as he tried to make his brain connect back to his mouth.

"Who? You?"

"Yeah." He still didn't move away and was also still fully erect. He pushed gently. She pushed back and smiled.

"What were you terrified of? Or for?"

"It'd be over too quickly."

She glanced up at the wall clock. "We managed just under ten minutes. That's pretty good going when you're sober and super-horny."

"Super super-horny," he said. He started to move in and out again, and she slid forward until she was no longer sitting on top of the kitchen cupboard.

"Let's try a different position," she suggested. She clung to him with her legs, and he carried her across to the table.

"I've never done this before," he said.

"Me neither."

"It's fucking awesome."

"It sure is." She remained sitting on the edge of the table as the rhythm started up again, her bra now removed, her dress pooled around her waist. He ran his hands up her bare back, over her shoulders and down her sides, cupping her breasts and gently squeezing them, pinching her nipples between the thumb and forefinger of each hand. She smiled in delight, and he did it again, pulling her to him so that her breasts were pressed against his chest.

"Oh my god," she uttered, falling backwards. He caught her and eased her down flat against the table, using his body to slide her along the surface until he could climb on top of her. He increased his speed and momentum again, lifting on his arms, but she grabbed him and pulled him back down, biting at his earlobe and holding on to his earring with her teeth. He sounded her name in his throat, and she tugged on the earring. He groaned, which only served to excite them both further. She continued as he bit at her neck, now heading rapidly towards their second climax, and she'd not even been in the house twenty minutes. She put her feet flat against the table and arched her back, lifting him with her body.

"I'm nearly—" he began.

"I told you. Don't wait for me." He didn't need to. Just the thought of his firm, muscular chest pressed against her soft, naked breasts was enough, and she moaned with each exhalation—his cue to take it up a notch. This time, he could give her more, because they'd already done it once, because of the position they were in, and as he thrust deeper and deeper, harder than before, she yelled out for real, entering her climax a little before he did. And then they were once again groaning and panting and saying the words in their head about how good this was, the pleasure escaping from him as grunts with each final thrust.

He didn't stay where he was. He was too far gone to hold himself up, and she wouldn't have been able to breathe pinned underneath him, so he got up and spent a moment just looking down on her sex-exhausted body, trying to fasten his jeans, fumbling with the button. She laughed at him and sat up, fastening it for him, and he pulled her dress up, now the only item of clothing she was wearing.

"Worth the wait, my red hot baby?"

She smiled. "Was it ever!"

"Have you brought any other clothes with you?"

"No. I didn't think I'd be needing them much."

He raised an eyebrow. "There's some of Charlie's stuff here. I'm sure she won't mind."

Shaunna eyed him suspiciously.

"No! I've been waiting for you."

"Hmm." She still didn't believe him.

"D'you want to know how long I've been waiting for you?"

"How long?"

"If we don't count the times we can't remember, twenty-five years."

"That long, huh?" She put her arms around his waist and reeled him in, smiling and kissing him at the same time. "That'd explain your big love."

He didn't comment on her observation, although it was nice to hear, as by her own admission she knew about these things.

"I kinda got that, you know?" she said. "Back in school. You lurked."

"I did not lurk!"

"You did. Everywhere we went, you and your idiot mates were there, lurking."

"Hanging around, not lurking."

"Same difference." She looked up into his eyes. "I really am sorry I turned you down."

"What, now you've realised what you were missing?"

"Always fishing, aren't you?"

"Yeah, but look at it from my point of view. The most beautiful girl in the school, who isn't exactly famed for her shyness, knocks you back for your little brother—"

"That's not what happened. I said it wouldn't be fair."

"Because you fancied Dan, not me."

While Shaunna was trying to think of a suitably soothing response, Casper came waddling in and shook vigorously, completely drenching them.

"Oh-oh! Casper!" Shaunna released Andy, and they both wiped the sprayed droplets of chlorinated water from their bare skin. "No prizes for guessing what he's been up to," she said.

Andy huffed in annoyance, and not because the dog had been in the pool, which meant he was going to be spending hours sieving out the dog hair. He wasn't bothered about that at all, and had a fleeting thought of how much fun it was going to be, playing fetch, with Casper splashing around after his ball. No, Andy was annoyed with himself, for feeling so ridiculously insecure. He was self-assured and confident, and he'd never shied away from a challenge, not since he'd asked her to go out with him and she'd said no. His ego could take quite a battering, but her rebuttal had always smarted.

Shaunna noticed his pensive expression and lightly dropped down to the floor. "I'm going to make a cup of tea, and we're going to discuss this like sensible adults."

She was already filling the kettle. She returned it to its base and turned back. He was propped against the table, his arms folded, chin resting on hand, a sullen expression on his face. She walked over and pulled his arms away, wrapping herself in them and shuffling forward between his thighs. He huffed again and kissed her on the head.

"And after our tea," she said, "you can take me on a tour of the garden, or something." She gently placed her lips on his chin and poked at the cleft with her tongue. He smiled.

"You like doing that, don't you?"

"I've always wanted to do it, like I've always wanted you to slam me up against a wall and do your worst."

"Oh, Jesus!" Andy looked up to the skies and shook his head. "What have I let myself in for?"

"You know you love it," she teased. He couldn't argue with that.

"All through the summer," he confessed, glancing down at her attire, "every time you turned up in that dress, I couldn't get the image out of my head." He blushed at the recollection of his constant fantasy, where he was doing precisely as he had done when she arrived today.

"So we're even on that score," she said. The kettle clicked off, and she went to make the tea.

"I'd like to do it the other way, too," he said.

She spun on her toes, her skirt swirling out around her as she turned to look at him, but he wouldn't look at her. "What? D'you mean—"

"Make love to you. Slowly, gently, on a rug in front of a roaring fire, feed each other marshmallows, whisper sweet nothings. You know, all that mushy stuff?"

Shaunna returned her attention to the tea. "I thought you meant, err…"

Andy laughed and walked up behind her, grabbing her around the middle and nestling his face in her hair. "I know what you thought. You have a very dirty mind, Shaunna Hennessy."

"Want to come in and play?" she asked, turning within his embrace and lifting her chin so they could kiss again.

This time, he pulled back, so that their lips met gently, with less of their prior urgency. "After I've refuelled."

She smiled and pushed his arms away. "Tea." She handed him a cup. He nodded in thanks and sat on a chair at the table. She followed and sat on the table a little way from him.

"They all fancied Dan," he said quietly. "All the girls at school, all my girlfriends. I stopped bringing them home, because I knew as soon as they saw him that'd be the end." He paused, thoughtful for a moment. "All apart from Jess, anyway. She was the only one who didn't fall for it, and I'm not saying he's putting it on—the whole 'angry because underneath I'm vulnerable and in need of love' routine? That is him, but she didn't find it attractive."

"That's not what Adele fell for, either," Shaunna said, "although I must admit that I really like that quality in him. He's like a big angry kid."

"He's more mature than me. Always was."

Shaunna shook her head. "No. Not so. You're the one who's putting it on."

"How?"

"You pretend that you're irresponsible, with your crazy trips and all that mad extreme sports stuff, but you never have been. All you ever want is to make people happy, and while you're off having a wild time, other people *are* happy, living their dreams through you—'Oh, I wish I was brave enough to skydive…' 'Maybe one day I'll go snowboarding…' 'I'm too much of a wimp, but I'd love to go swimming with great whites…'

"So, yeah, you might be doing it to fulfil your need for excitement, but as soon as something you've done makes someone else unhappy, you stop. Like your accident. We were all so worried, and what did you do? You stopped living. No more wild and whacky adventures from now on. You hung up your snowboard and hiking boots and retired. Why?"

Andy shrugged. "I don't know. To be more like Dan, I guess."

"But you're not him, and nor should you try to be."

Andy was so confused. He, like everybody else, admired and respected Dan, for his success in business, with women, how proud their mother was of him. On the surface, he was Mr. Perfect—beautiful girlfriend, beautiful daughter, beautiful apartment, fast cars, good looks. And whilst Andy, as Dan's older brother, had enjoyed a feeling of being superior to him in the past, and knew, as their closest friends did, that Dan was far from perfect, he felt privileged to be his brother, to be counted as one of his closest friends. For all of that, the reason he most aspired to be like Dan was sitting less than two feet away. Shaunna had chosen Dan over him.

"Let me tell you something," she said, shuffling herself along the table so that she was directly in front of him. She put her feet on his thighs and leaned forward so she could look him in the eye. "It wasn't that I liked Dan more than you. It was that I hated your mates. They were horrible, horrible people. They made my life a misery. And not just mine. Kris, Josh, Ellie, Jess—they were terrorised by those idiots you hung around with.

"By the time you got away from them, I had Krissi, and Kris was with me, looking after me, falling in love with me, while I was just trying to be the best mum I could be. And I'd come to sixth form with her, and you'd be there across the common room, watching me. I knew you were always watching me, and I thought…why now, when I can't do anything about it? Now I've messed up, he's finally got his act together."

"You didn't mess up."

"No. I didn't. I made a mistake, and it's the best thing that ever could have happened to me. I grew up and stopped acting like a spoilt, dippy bitch. It was hard. I had to leave it all behind, the old me—the easy lay, the slut—to be a mum. So, you see? I didn't choose Dan over you. I chose my daughter—*our* daughter."

"And yet you like his hidden vulnerability?"

"Yeah, I do. It appeals to my motherly nature."

"Damn! And there was me, trying to come the hard man."

Shaunna sat back and laughed, wagging her finger at him. "That's what I mean. You *are* a hard man, and if you're thinking otherwise, you've fallen for your own performance. You're the hero, the one who comes swashbuckling in to save the day, like you did with Jess. Can you imagine Dan doing that for Adele? And what about when you saved Dan's life?"

"Which time?"

"Exactly! You know what I said when I arrived, about not wanting to be loved and cherished and treated like a princess? That's all well and good, but what about raw passion? No negotiating orgasms or which position works best, just get down to it. Besides, nobody who loves and cherishes a woman is going to have the balls to stand up and fight for her."

"But I do love you."

"Yes, I know. The difference is that with you, it's instinctive, primal. You don't have to think about it, and to be honest, when you do think about it, you make a bloody mess of it, like with Danni, and Rachel, and Bertie…"

"Me and Bertie are still friends," Andy protested.

"But you set out to fill the hole left by your daughter, not to find a girlfriend. It was the same with Danni. As for Rachel—"

"Don't go there."

Shaunna leaned her chin on her hands and blinked rapidly. "Oh, hi, Andy," she said in a bright, high-pitched voice. "Are we going out tonight? Can we meet your friends tonight? I hope they like me. Do you think they'll like me?"

Now Andy laughed and blushed at the same time. "I don't know what I was thinking."

"I do. You were after a bit of fluff, just like Dan's got Adele, but you know as well as I do that she's a whole lot more than a bit of fluff."

Andy nodded. "Yeah. I love her to pieces, which is weird, because she used to really get on my nerves."

"Of course you love her. She makes Dan happy, and she gave you little Shaunna."

Andy smiled and started to melt at the thought of his tiny niece, and how much he loved her.

"As for Charlie," Shaunna interrupted his thoughts, "I can only conclude that you've switched heroes to worship and are looking for an Ellie-alike."

"She's nothing like Ellie, and there's nothing going on between us."

"Really?"

"All right. Let's put it this way. She has a lot more in common with your husband than she does with her big sister."

"She's a famous actor?" Shaunna asked, feigning surprise.

Andy tutted. She grinned at him and moved further forward. "So, anyway," he said philosophically, "even though she has dated guys in the past, she hasn't dated this one. She's a good mate, though. Are you OK with that?"

"Why shouldn't I be? You can be friends with anyone you like. I don't get jealous." She slid off the table onto his lap, her legs spread either side of his. The effect was instant.

"So, as you were saying…?" Andy said.

"What was I saying?" She wriggled herself closer and combed her fingers through his hair.

"The primal thing."

"Oh, yeah." She pushed her lips against his, and he returned the pressure, automatically sliding his hands up under her skirt. "Like that," she said huskily through the kisses, her breath catching at the probing touch of his fingers. She unzipped his jeans and repositioned herself, sliding against him, until he was inside her once more. "Tell me what you want to do."

"Screw you in the pool," he said without thinking. He stopped kissing her immediately and shut his eyes tight. She laughed.

"Just like that." She slid off his lap and took his hand. "Come on, big boy." She pulled him to his feet and led him away.

"To the pool?"

"To the pool."

***

Andy awoke, stretching out his arms right across the bed, taking care not to disturb her, for he hadn't forgotten while he was sleeping that Shaunna was there, in the bed next to him, fast asleep still, with her hair fanned across the pillow and falling gently around her shoulders. He wanted to lift the covers away, and look on her while she slept, but decided it was too creepy, so he turned on his side and settled for watching her face, the delicate arch of her eyebrows, the curl of her eyelashes against her cheeks, that little turn-up at the end of her nose, her soft, rose-pink lips. She started to smile.

"Been watching me long?"

"Just a couple of minutes."

She rubbed her eyes and opened them. "Good morning, sexy," she whispered, and he did look sexy, with his hair all tousled and a shadow of stubble on his chin, that smile… She shuffled closer and kissed it. "What are your plans for today?"

"Well, I'd normally work out, but I think my abs have seen enough action in the past twenty-four hours to last a month."

"You work out every day?"

"I do here."

Her eyebrows rose briefly as she settled on the image in her mind. "I'd like to watch you work out," she said. He nodded once and started to blush. She laughed and glanced under the duvet. "I think you'd like me to watch you work out, too."

He breathed deeply and slithered up against her as she continued to taunt him.

"Thrusting those heavy old dumbbells, your shoulders rippling with the tension, torso gleaming—"

"I usually wear a vest and shorts."

"Meh. Clothes are for losers." She rolled him onto his back and straddled him.

"Hang on, I thought I was doing the taking," he protested.

She eased forward, sliding back gently, because yesterday had been something of a marathon session, and she was feeling a little fragile.

He grabbed her hips and pulled her forward again then pushed her back. "But I'm easy," he said, feeling her warmth completely envelop him.

"So I heard."

"Hmm. I won't state the obvious." He groaned as she increased her speed, torn between keeping hold of her hips and trying to control the action, or caressing her breasts and going with it. She sat up and shook her hair loose so that it tumbled down around her shoulders, her nipples peeping through between the curls. Decision made. He shifted his hands up over her stomach and covered her breasts, focusing on the sensation of her nipples against his palms as she swayed back and forth, up and down. She was having to work quite hard to last out; he could see it on her face.

"Don't wait," he said. "Just do it."

On hearing her own words being said back to her, she smiled and did as he suggested, lifting as far as her legs would allow. She pushed down onto him, marvelling at the feeling of him deep inside her, the pressure of his hands on her breasts, the tickling of his hair against her buttocks. Her mind flashed back to the workout conversation, and there was nothing she could do to stop herself. She fell forward, burying her face in the crook of his neck and shoulder, pressing her lips to his skin to mute her cries. Now he was moving with her.

"Oh, fuck," she said, feeling herself being pushed further up the bed, teetering on the edge for the briefest moment before once more they climaxed together and collapsed, panting and kissing and laughing to cover their bashfulness at being caught by each other again.

"See?" he said. "This is easy. You and me."

With a bit of a struggle, she lifted herself and leaned on one elbow, putting her finger to his lips. "Shhh." He frowned, and she shook her head. "Don't speak." She moved to get off, but he rolled with her, lying on his side and watching her, as the emotions accompanying her thoughts flickered across her face. He reached over and pushed her hair away, twirling it around his fingers.

"What's wrong?" he asked.

She shook her head again and attempted a smile. "Nothing's wrong. In fact, everything is right. *You're* right. Being here with you is so easy, and that's what makes it so hard."

"No, it isn't." He cupped her face with his hand. "Look at me." She wouldn't. "Shaunna, look at me, please?" She glanced at him briefly but then lowered her eyes. "Hey," he prompted, and she held his gaze. "Once I move into the apartment, you can come round anytime you want, with Casper or on your own, I don't care. And when we're together, we'll hump like rabbits, and then you can go back to being loved and cherished, until the next time."

"It's not fair."

"Maybe not, but…" He tried to look serious. "Making love to a beautiful woman is a lot like surfing."

"Oh, no!" She laughed. "Don't start that again."

He laughed, too. "Seriously, though, when I'm out there riding a wave, or bombing it down a mountain at forty miles an hour, I'm not thinking, 'Ah, crap. What am I gonna do when this is over?' I'm just living it, buzzing at how awesome it is. And we're here together now. Let's just enjoy it and have fun."

She nodded. "Yeah." She moved closer. "I sometimes forget you've got a brain in there," she teased. "You know, with your whole big himbo meathead routine."

His mouth dropped open in horror, but there was still laughter in his eyes. She grinned and pushed his chin up, lingering a moment to kiss it, before flicking all the way up the cleft with the tip of her tongue.

"Right, my red hot baby, I'm going for a shower. Wanna come?"

"So soon?"

He rolled his eyes and got out of bed, taking a moment to stretch his back and shoulders. "I'm glad we've got no work on at the minute, or I'd be having to pull a sicky."

"That's very irresponsible."

"Yeah, it is a bit. Speaking of being irresponsible, or not, as the case may be, do you, we, whatever, need to take Casper for a walk?"

"Yeah. Why?"

"There's two acres of woodland at the bottom of the garden. I thought it might be nice to go for a wander."

"You're a freak."

"Why?"

"Thinking about walking the dog while you're standing there stark naked."

"Clothes are for losers." He grinned at her, and she tutted. "I'm just trying to be sensible and responsible."

"What, like checking you weren't going to impregnate me again before you spent a whole day filling me with your seed, you mean?"

"Ah, see, now I did think of that."

"Did you really?"

"Yeah. I figured you'd probably take care of it."

"How is that being responsible?"

"Because I don't care if you get pregnant, and actually, I'd be chuffed if you did. But if you don't want to, it's up to you to do something to stop that."

"Are you deliberately trying to sound like a misogynistic shit?"

"No. I'm telling you that I want you to have my baby, even if I end up a single parent, bringing her or him up on my own." He leaned over the bed and kissed her on the nose. "Now I'm going to run away, before you lose your temper completely and knock my teeth down my throat." He kissed her again. "Love you," he said, and then he was gone, leaving her lying in the middle of the vast messy bed with her vast messy thoughts.

***

He sat on the edge of the bath, watching her wash her hair and waiting for her to open her eyes before they continued their conversation. It was better to think of it that way, because it was still about his comments the previous morning, and how he had left the birth control decision with her.

OK, so it was more of an argument, because they were both hot-headed, and he couldn't see what her problem was. After all, he wanted another child, and she wasn't saying she didn't, not that any of that had stopped them from continuing to throw each other against the closest surface and get down to business. In fact, their disagreement had taken it to a whole new level, as if they were trying to outdo each other on the fantasy front. She opened her eyes and scowled at him.

"Look. If I say I'm sorry and you're right, will that do?"

"Are you?" she asked. "Am I?"

"Well, I'm sorry I upset you."

"But you still think I'm making a big fuss about nothing?"

He took a breath to respond, but she continued before he had the chance.

"Do you really think it's acceptable to have sex with a woman without sorting out contraception first?"

"No. I'm usually the one who sees to it."

"So it's just me you're neglecting?"

"It's just *you* I want to get pregnant, or not even that. I… Ah! I don't know how to explain it. You're the only one I've never used a condom with."

"And that makes it acceptable?" She put her head under the water, so there was no point in him answering the question. By the time she emerged again, though, what he'd just said had filtered through. "The only one?" she asked.

"The only one."

"Not even Jess?"

"Nope."

"Oh."

"Does that make a difference?"

"Yeah." She stepped out of the bath and into the towel he held out for her. He wrapped it around her and pulled her close.

"Are we done now?" he asked wearily.

"With?"

"Fighting."

"I suppose. I was rather enjoying it." He looked at her questioningly. "Nobody argues in my house. Not since Krissi was a teenager. I tell a lie. We've had one argument since then—when she wanted a DNA sample from me for the paternity tests, so that was your fault, too."

"You can't blame me when I wasn't even there!"

"See, now who's starting an argument?"

He frowned and let it go. He didn't like fighting, but he had to admit it was kind of fun. However, he also had to agree that she was right, because as much as he wanted another child, it was something they needed to discuss, rather than creating one by accident—again—regardless of how much the idea excited him.

***

They were in the pool, naked and kissing, but no more than that, because they'd not long finished, when Andy's phone started ringing. He stretched an arm out of the water—pointlessly, as his phone was on the table six feet away from them.

"Can't reach," he said and got straight back to kissing. His phone stopped ringing. Then it started up again. He ignored it. It rang again. "For fuck's sake." He got out of the pool and checked the missed calls. "Dan."

Shaunna nodded once and took the opportunity to re-secure her hair. The spring in her clip wasn't quite so springy as it had been on Monday, on account of the number of times it had been pulled out.

Andy put his phone down on the table. He got as far as the edge of the pool when it started ringing again. "Hello?" he answered.

"Alright, bro? Are you in?"

"Yeah. Why?"

"The door won't open."

"The door?"

"The front door? My key's getting stuck halfway."

Andy ran his hand through his hair and mouthed, "Oh, shit!" Shaunna frowned and shrugged in query.

"I'll come and let you in," he said. He hung up. "He's at the front door."

"What? Oh God!" Shaunna got out of the pool and grabbed the bathrobe—Barbara's bathrobe. "I, err…" She didn't know what to do and looked around her in panic.

"Hide upstairs," Andy suggested.

"The dog?"

"Agh. Fuck. Summerhouse."

Shaunna nodded and called Casper to her in a hissed whisper. For once he did as he was told, and she grabbed his collar, leading him out of the back of the conservatory and down to the summerhouse, her bare feet squelching in the wet grass. She stepped inside, quietly closed the door and shivered. "Summerhouse," she said. "Pfft!"

***

Andy unlocked the front door. "Alright? What're you doing here?"

"Hadn't heard from you since Sunday. Thought I'd come check you were still alive." As soon as the words left Dan's mouth he wished they hadn't.

Andy watched him cringe and smiled. "No worries, bro. I'm fine."

"Were you in the pool?"

"Err, yeah."

Dan nodded. "You gonna let me in, or…?"

"Oh, yeah. Sorry." Andy stepped to one side.

Dan came in and shut the door. He turned around and sniffed. He frowned.

"What?"

"Smells like wet dog."

"Does it?"

"Yeah."

Andy felt the blood rush to his cheeks. He was about to claim he didn't know why, but Dan had moved on already.

"Got any beer in?" he asked, striding across the atrium, towards the conservatory.

"Err, I...yeah. Probably. I dunno." Andy followed, his heart thumping faster the closer they got. Dan stopped at the fridge behind the bar and took out two beers, passing one to his brother.

"You sure you're all right? You look a bit peaky. Not sleeping too well?"

"Just had a, err, busy few days, that's all."

"Yeah?" Dan swigged his beer. "Doing?"

"Oh, you know. This and that." He was sure Dan was never this chatty.

"You should get out a bit, bro. All work, and all that."

"Yeah. You're probably right." Andy felt his towel start to slip and put his beer down to secure it.

"You been skinny-dipping while the house is empty?"

"Yeah. Might as well hang loose while you can."

This was awful. He didn't know what to say to make Dan go away. He'd have usually taken the hint, realised Andy didn't want the company, downed his beer and left.

***

Meanwhile in the summerhouse, Shaunna was doing star jumps in an attempt to stay warm, but only succeeding in keeping Casper entertained, or that's how it worked for the first ten minutes. She pulled the sleeves of the bathrobe over her hands and sat down, trying to tuck her bare legs inside it.

"If I lose consciousness," she said to the dog, "you pretend you're Lassie and go for help, OK?"

He came over and snuggled up to her for a minute or so, although he was soaking wet and it only served to make her colder still. She shivered, and Casper darted off towards the door again.

"Come back here," she called.

He came over, went around in circles a couple of times, and back to the door, scratching to be let out.

"No, Casper! Come here!"

He ignored her and carried on scratching.

"Casper!"

He jumped up at the door.

"Come here!" she shouted, but it was all too late. Casper's front right paw pressed down on the handle, and the door started to open. Shaunna leapt to her feet and ran after him, skidded, lost her balance and landed on her front, righting herself in time to see the Labrador's waggy tail follow the rest of him into the conservatory.

***

Andy heard the sound of claws on non-slip tiles first, which gave him around two seconds to come up with a convincing story for why the Johanssons' Labrador was in his mother's house. Casper came bounding over and shoved his nose in Dan's hand.

"Hello, mutt!" Dan stroked the very wet dog, even more puzzled than ever. "Bro?" He gave Andy a 'what the fuck?' look.

"Shaunna's gone away for a couple of days," Andy said quickly, thinking on his feet, which wasn't his strong point at the best of times and was certainly made no easier by half a week of nonstop sex on top of several months of sleep deprivation.

"And you agreed to look after the dog for her?"

"Yeah. I was thinking of getting one and thought it'd be like a trial run, you know?"

"You? Get a dog? Where did that come from?"

"When we went down to get Josh and George." That bit was true, and Andy relaxed into the lie a little. "I was talking to Josh about it."

"What kind of dog were you thinking of getting?"

"I dunno. I hadn't got that far."

"And what about when you're away on business?"

"I'll stick it in kennels, or get someone to come and look after it. As I say, I was only thinking about it. I haven't actually done anything yet."

"What's the verdict?"

"Huh?"

"After spending the week with the loony Labrador."

401

Andy nodded. "Yeah. I've enjoyed it."

"That's good." Dan was still doubtful about the credibility of the story. "Where's Shaunna gone?"

"To see Kris." It was the first thing that came into his head.

"Oh?" Dan frowned. "He didn't mention it this morning."

"Didn't he?"

"No. He called for a chat. He's really pissed off."

"That's probably why she's gone, then, to surprise him." Could this get any worse?

Not long after, he discovered that the answer was yes, it could.

⁂

"I can't believe you've done this."

Shaunna continued to mutter as she marched up and down, her arms folded, her bare feet slapping loudly against the cool marble floor as she stomped, a furious expression fixed on her face.

"Sorry," he said. Again.

"Why couldn't you have told him I'd gone to see my aunty or something? Anyone other than Kris. For Christ's sake, Andy. They talk to each other. Almost every day!"

"How was I to know?"

"You know what I'm going to have to do now, don't you? Get on the next bloody train down there. I was supposed to have started my course last week and I haven't even picked up a bloody book yet!"

"Ask Josh to give you some tuition. Or Sean."

Shaunna spun around and glared at him. "What the hell's that supposed to mean?"

"Nothing." Andy tried not to shout back. He'd never seen her angry before, and she was scary. Very scary. "I'll just tell Dan I got it wrong. That you've gone to see your aunty, like you said."

"Brilliant!" she spat sarcastically. "And you think that won't make him even more suspicious?"

"Or I could tell him—" Andy stopped to prepare himself for the potential explosion.

"Tell him what?"

"The truth."

"You're joking, right?"

"No. I'm not. He knows how I feel about you. He's always known. He won't say anything."

"So, to dig yourself out of a hole, you're going to burden your brother with the knowledge that we're having an affair, when he lives with my best friend and his best friend is my husband. Are you off your rocker?"

"It's not just my back I'm covering here."

"But we didn't have to get into this mess in the first place. If you'd let me tell Kris—"

"Oh, great. Now it's my fault."

"But no," she continued in a mocking tone, "it's too much like swinging, he said." Her clip fell out of her hair and clattered to the floor. She picked it up and threw it across the atrium. "And now I can't even put my hair up!" She burst into tears and flopped down on the stairs.

Andy watched her for a moment and approached, carefully. "Tell me what you want me to do." He put his hand on her arm. She didn't hit him, so he rubbed her shoulder. She sighed, though not in submission. She was too angry to do anything else.

"I don't know," she said.

"Do you want me to drive you down there?"

"To Brighton?"

"Yeah."

"All the way to Brighton?"

"Yeah."

"And then what?"

"I'll turn round and come back again."

"With Casper."

"Well, yeah. I'm dogsitting, remember?"

She bit her lip thoughtfully. "You'd actually drive all the way to Brighton?"

"It's not that far. It'll only take about five hours at this time of day."

"For me?"

"I got you into this mess—"

"No." She shook her head. "No. *We* got *us* into this mess." She kissed him. "Thanks." She kissed him again. "I'm not letting you drive me all the way to Brighton, but you can take me to the train station."

"OK, are you sure? I really don't mind."

"I'm sure, Andy."

"When d'you want to go?"

"Once you've apologised properly." She looked up and gave him a wicked grin. He pushed her backwards onto the stairs and tugged at the belt of her bathrobe. He flung it wide open and looked down on her nakedness.

"I take it you mean this kind of apology?" He whipped the towel away from around his waist.

"Less talk, more action," she said, holding onto the stair as he came down on top of her, easing her legs apart with his hips and thrusting into her.

"How big an apology do you want?" he asked.

The front door swung open.

"I just had a thought, bro. D'you want to— Ah."

In The Shadows
Friday 20th October

A text message.

Sent you an email. Text me when you get it. x

Josh deleted the message and opened another essay on his computer. He was at the bottom of the first page before he realised he hadn't absorbed a single word. He sighed and started over.

> This essay will compare and contrast the biological and social explanations for gender differences in levels of empathy.

"Awesome." He minimised the essay and brought up the email again. Two sentences. *Unbelievable. Is that all I'm worth? Two measly sentences.* He closed the email and returned to the essay.

> Whilst biological explanations centre on the evolutionary potential of higher levels of empathy within the female population, some social psychologists suggest that this may be a learned response, conditioned by…

A knock at the door. He made a mental note to comment that this wasn't *entirely* accurate and prepared himself for yet another intrusion into his so-called admin day.

"Come in."

The door handle slowly turned, and the door opened a few inches. A young male student peered through the gap.

"Hi. Sorry to bother you, but I wondered if I could speak to you about the presentation?"

"Which one?"

"Ethics."

"You're a third year?"

"Yeah. Sorry. I should've said." The student edged nervously into the room.

"What is it you want to ask? For an extension? Or to get out of it completely?" It was said as a joke but not received as one.

"Oh, no! I just wanted to know if we should refer to anything other than the BPS and APA. Only, I was looking through the Canadian Psychological Association guidelines, and although they're more or less the same, I noticed that there were a couple of—"

Josh raised his hand to interrupt the long and winding explanation. "Just stick with the UK and US."

"Right. Thanks." The student turned and opened the door again. "I read that paper you and Sean Tierney wrote last year."

Josh nodded.

"It was very thought-provoking, and I'd really appreciate some advice about doing something with the negotiation of consent for my Master's, when you've got the time. Should I—"

"Book an appointment through the VLE," Josh said dismissively.

"Will do. Thanks again." The student stepped outside.

"Hey," Josh called after him. He turned back. "What's your name again?"

"Gerry." He sagged in disappointment. "Gerry Berry."

Josh nodded and tried not to giggle. "Drop me an email when you're ready to discuss your Master's, OK, Gerry?"

"That's great. Thanks, Josh." He smiled and left, quietly closing the door behind him.

Josh chuckled to himself. "Gerry Berry. Poor guy." He turned back to his computer and started once more on the essay, determined to make it to the end, and it wasn't that bad a piece of work really. It was just that he hadn't quite stepped off the emotional roller coaster, and then *that* email suddenly appears in his inbox—it was hardly surprising he couldn't concentrate. Nonetheless, he made it to the conclusion before the next text message came in.

Hasn't it arrived yet? x

He threw his phone down on the desk and put his hands behind his head, studying the corner of the room. He wasn't going to text her back. No way. He picked up his phone again and deleted the text message as another came in.

Josh? Please? x

He held his finger over the delete button and started counting down.

"Five, four, three, two—"

His phone started to vibrate in his hand.

"One. Hello," he answered wearily.

"Hey."

He said nothing. She hesitated.

"You got the email, I take it?"

"Yes."

"OK." Another pause. "I'm sorry." And another. "I didn't know how else to do it."

He opened the email and read aloud into the phone.

"Hi, Josh, I just wanted to let you know that James, Toby and I are moving to Birmingham. I'll explain when I see you next. Love Ellie."

She stayed silent. He waited. The seconds dragged on.

"So what?" he asked.

"What d'you mean?"

"What is there to explain?"

"Well, I thought you'd want to know why."

"I know why. You can't afford the lease on your surgery and don't want the hassle of subletting, plus James is commuting pretty much every day, and Oliver's there. It makes perfect sense."

"Yeah," she said obstinately. "It does."

407

"So there's no need for you to explain, is there?"

"Then why do I get the feeling you're still expecting me to?"

"Do you?"

He was contemplating just hanging up on her. There was nothing left to say, because her decision said it all.

"What time are you home from work?" she asked.

"Three. Maybe. Four. I don't know yet."

"Oh, stop being so damned awkward!"

"I'm not! I've got a mountain of marking to get through, and people keep interrupting me with text messages and stupid bloody emails that they shouldn't have sent to begin with, but they didn't have the balls to tell me to my face."

"That's not it at all," she said. He could hear the commencement of tears in her voice, but he wasn't going to play it her way.

"Fine. I'll make sure I'm home by three, but I've got plans for this evening, so can you try to be on time, please? I'll see you later."

He hung up.

***

"Hey." Her tone was light-hearted and insincere. He stepped aside. She came in and followed him into the lounge. She was on time. That was something.

"Coffee?"

"Please."

He indicated the chair. She sat down. He left the room and put the kettle on. Just at the moment, he didn't like her enough to make her anything more fancy than instant. He popped upstairs to use the bathroom whilst the kettle boiled, refusing to look into the lounge on his way past in either direction, made the coffee, took it in, and sat at the far end of the sofa.

"OK. Go," he said.

She frowned.

"Say what you need to say."

"Why are you being so horrible about this?"

"I'm not."

"Then what's with the attitude problem?"

408

"I don't have one."

"You know how hard it's been for James to—"

"Let me stop you right there." He sat forward and put down his coffee. "It's always been difficult for James to commute back and forth to head office. Oliver has always lived down there. And the cost of the lease hasn't suddenly doubled overnight, has it? It's been a burden for six months."

"Which is why it makes sense."

"I'm not disputing that. But it made sense six months ago. Two years ago. And yet *now* you decide that you need to move."

"I was waiting for Jess to—"

"No, you weren't."

"I beg your pardon?"

"You weren't waiting for Jess to die. You could've put the house on the market before now and stayed with your mum and dad if that was all it was. This has nothing to do with Jess, or, at least, it's not *just* to do with Jess."

"OK, why do you think it is?"

"I know why it is, as well as you do. All those reasons were never enough, never so important that you were prepared to leave your friends behind, until now. We've become secondary in your life, and you know what? That's fine. Really, it's not a problem, because you found the right person and made a new life with them. What is a problem is that you can't be honest enough to admit that. You think you can sit there, lying to me. *To me*! How long have we been friends? Yet you would rather feed me bullshit, knowing I can see straight through it, than tell me the truth." He shook his head. "You've changed, Ellie."

Although he was angry, he had delivered the words calmly and rationally, fighting and winning the battle to keep control, which only served to fuel her fury further. She slammed down her cup and turned on him, eyes blazing.

"I've changed?" she shouted. "Take a look in the mirror, Josh!"

Now she was up on her feet, getting ready to depart once she'd said her piece. He stayed where he was, watching her, coolly, calmly. She laughed; it was bitter and joyless.

"All those years of being the go-between, wishing you and George would stop being such a pair of fucking idiots—I thought it'd be the best thing that ever happened to you. Far from it! And before you say it, I'm not jealous of George, nor do I feel pushed out, even though I'd have every right to, because he's the only one you've got time for these days.

"And now you're just trying to mess with my head—what's this? See this unflappable, distant Josh in front of me? That's who I've always known, but it's not you anymore. You've turned into some crazy, overly emotional drama queen. You were never like that, with your hugging, and kissing, telling me you've lost your virginity. What made you think I'd want to know? It's private, and I'm not even going to start on the wrongness of it, but you know my beliefs, which makes it even more absurd that you told me. Were you trying to shock me? I'm not shocked. I don't actually care what you choose to get up to. However, I do care when you push it down my throat, and you know that, so why do it?"

She stopped for breath, fastening the coat she hadn't taken off since she'd arrived.

"So you're right. It's not just because of James, or Oliver, or the lease on the surgery. Everything's different now. But it's not me who's changed. It's you. And it's not a good thing. I love you, and I want you to be happy, but not at everyone else's expense. And definitely not at mine."

She moved towards the door, hesitating a little, because she was expecting him to respond. Indeed, she was hoping for an apology, or even one of his ridiculous emotional outbursts as he was hit by a sudden realisation that she was right. He gave her nothing.

"We need to fix things a bit before we move," she said. "We're going to have to stay on speaking terms, for the sake of the boys, but we're done, Josh. And I'm sorry, but I think you'd probably figured it out already."

She let herself out, passing George on the doorstep. She gave him a courteous nod and no more.

He watched her get into her car and crank up the stereo before she tore off down the road, slowing only to clear the speed bumps. He waited until she was out of sight, giving himself time to prepare to go inside, because the windows, well, they needed replacing and they weren't much of a sound barrier. Now he had to try to stay calm, because Josh was going to be wild.

Stay calm.

Tall order.

***

Ticking time bomb. They'd eaten, walked the dog, showered, and now they were on the sofa. George lay with his head in Josh's lap, watching his face as he artificially attended to the news and pretended not to know that he was being watched. He continued for ten minutes or so before he glanced down at George and gave him a watery smile.

"I can't talk about it," he said.

"OK."

Return to the news, then the weather, then coming up next; it could have been anything. George didn't hear the announcement, listening instead to Josh take in air a couple of times before he finally pushed the words out.

"She doesn't know me at all."

Music was playing. Josh watched through glazed eyes as the titles slid off the top of the screen. It was just noise and motion.

"How can we have been friends for so long and she still not know the real me?"

He was unconsciously jiggling his leg. George sat up.

"Where are you going?"

"Nowhere. I was getting seasick."

Josh smiled and took his hand. "I'm really angry."

"I know."

"I want to hit something. Smash stuff up."

He released George's hand. George watched the movement out of the corner of his eye, the skin-pinching through the sleeve. He reached across and stilled it. The leg jiggling became more pronounced.

"Talk to me," George said.

"I can't. I'll lose it."

George shrugged. "Define 'lose it', because screaming and shouting and crying is a lot less damaging than the alternative."

Josh got up and paced the room. He couldn't even put into words how upset he was about what the move meant for George and Toby's relationship; nor would what he had to say help George in dealing with it, so he decided to stick with venting the 'easier' reasons for his rage.

"I wouldn't mind, but she's the one who kept abandoning me. What's she talking about, I've only got time for you? Where was she, when I was slumped half-dead in a bath? Where was she when you walked away? And all through looking after Jess? She only wafted in at the end—trust me, I'm a doctor. Go fuck yourself, you self-obsessed bitch." Josh stopped pacing and looked at George. "Just don't listen, all right?"

George laughed. "Carry on."

"Overly emotional drama queen. Overly emotional drama queen? What the hell is she talking about? She doesn't know the half of it. Last year—can you imagine her doing what Sean did for us? She's jealous of him, did I tell you that? Yet every time she could have proved her mettle she kept out of the fucking way instead. It's all about her, assuming that I choose to tell her the things I do because it has some bearing on her well-being, or lack thereof. Or maybe, Ellie, it's because I need someone to listen!"

Josh went back over to the couch and flopped down so hard that George was pushed upwards by the momentum. He waited a short while, listening to Josh's breathing slow and become less shaky, and then turned sideways, crossing his legs and taking Josh's hand again.

"Tell her."

"Why?"

"Because she needs to know. It doesn't matter what she thinks, or what she says, but she needs to know that you've kept it from her."

Josh frowned. George squeezed his hand.

"She's an intelligent adult—"

"Allegedly."

412

"What I was gonna say is that it takes her a little time to digest things, but once she realises you've been keeping this from her, she'll end up going round and round in circles trying to work out why."

Josh turned and looked at George, incredulous and amused. "You've got a really vicious streak."

George grinned and gave him a wink. "I'm my mother's son," he said. He got up and headed for the door. "I'm in the mood for some nuts." He left the room. Josh listened to the sound of drawers and cupboard doors being opened and shut in the kitchen. George returned with a bowl and a pair of nutcrackers.

"There ya go," he said, handing over the nutcrackers. "Smash in a few brazil nuts. It'll make you feel better." He resumed his position with his head in Josh's lap. "Feed me," he commanded. Josh rolled his eyes and picked out a nut.

"Time to settle back into your sofas with an Americano, double shot, to go," the continuity announcer's voice broke through. "Live on tonight's *Elliot Sanchez Show*, Elliot talks frankly with *Shadows* star Kristian Johansson, there's music from…"

"Do they really do the show live?" Josh asked.

"Yeah, but they have a few seconds' delay in case someone in the audience strips off or something."

"I'd be terrified."

"Of someone stripping off?"

Josh tutted. "You know what I mean."

George grinned up at him. "Kris said he's a bit nervous. He got the questions a couple of days ago, but Elliot Sanchez springs things on you, apparently."

The theme music started up, and Elliot Sanchez appeared on-screen to enthusiastic applause from the studio audience. He was a really odd character of Mediterranean appearance, yet he spoke with a lilting Welsh accent. He always wore outrageous suits, and tonight's mustard yellow pinstripe with red shirt was no exception, his jokes about his own outfit serving as the perfect lead-in to announcing his star guest.

"DI Lundberg might be famed for his smart tailored sensible attire, but the same certainly isn't true of the actor who plays him."

413

The view switched to a shot of the green room, where Kris was chatting with the other guests and turned to smile at the camera.

"See what I mean?" Elliot asked of the studio audience. They laughed. So did George and Josh.

"It looks like the old BBC test card," George said in reference to the shirt Kris was wearing.

Josh nodded. "It does, too. I think I might empty these nuts out of the bowl so I've got something to throw up in when they're both on-screen together."

First, though, they had to sit through Elliot intimidating the other two guests—a Bollywood actress, who was an upcoming star, by all accounts, and exceptionally beautiful. She wasn't dissimilar to Shabina's mother in both looks and demeanour, although she spoke with a definite Indian accent, as opposed to Anu's mix of RP and Brummie.

After the actress came a top-flight professional footballer outed as a member of the English Defence League a couple of weeks previously, who was booed loudly by the audience and sneered at them as he came on set. Elliot made no secret of his loathing of his guest in his body language, although the questioning remained light and impartial. The footballer wasn't an especially interesting person, other than the hate he spat with every word that came out of his mouth.

George glanced up at Josh. "You OK?"

"Hmm. Just..." He shook the nutcrackers at the screen. "Couldn't you..." He huffed and puffed. "It's not even worth wasting words on, is it?"

They continued listening to the man drone on about the purity of 'the English game', glad when he finally left, to be followed by a musical interlude from the in-house band, and, at last, the reason they were watching a chat show they usually avoided at all costs.

"...Kristian Johansson," Elliot announced. The studio audience applauded loudly and whistled as Kris came on. He and Elliot shook hands and embraced, taking their seats as the applause died away. Someone in the audience called out in Swedish. Kris smiled. He put his hand up to shield his eyes from the lights and replied in the same. A few people—the Swedish speakers, presumably—laughed.

"Wonder what they said?" George asked.

"It was rude, whatever it was," Josh observed.

"Kristian Johansson," Elliot said. "You prefer Kris?"

"That's right," Kris confirmed. There was a little round table between the host and guest armchairs, on which was a jug of water and glasses. Kris poured some water into a glass, calmly picked it up and sipped.

"Bless, he's so nervous," Josh said. George watched and frowned. Kris's hand wasn't shaking or anything else obvious. "He's doing that jaw-rotating thing," Josh explained.

"What jaw-rotating thing?"

"Watch."

George watched, but he still couldn't see it. He let it go and settled for listening to the words, like normal people.

"Doesn't he look like him? Doesn't he?" Elliot asked the audience. There was a mixture of clapping, whistles and whoops.

Kris kept his smile. It was getting a bit tedious, but even he admitted that he bore more than a passing resemblance to Morten Harket, though he was slighter in build than the Norwegian pop star and had a much lighter complexion.

"Thanks for joining me tonight, Kris. It's a real pleasure to get you on the show at last."

"Thanks for asking me."

"We had Morten on a few weeks ago, did you see?" Elliot asked.

"Yeah. He did a great interview, really laid-back, funny guy."

"You're a bit of an A-Ha fan yourself?"

"I like their music—"

"But it's your wife that's the fan."

"Err, yeah."

"I'm all right to mention her?"

Kris shrugged. "You just did."

The audience laughed.

"Let's talk about *Shadows* for a bit. So, last Saturday was episode three of season two, is that right?"

"Yeah," Kris answered vaguely. "We're a few weeks ahead of that with the filming, so I'm never totally sure where we're up to."

"And you're currently on location?"

Kris nodded. "We've got another week in Brighton, after which we're back in the studio."

The usual chitchat followed, about how much of the filming took place in and around Manchester's gay village, with Kris attempting yet again to quash unsubstantiated rumours that they were moving the show to London.

Josh slid down the sofa. "God, this is boring."

"Yeah," George agreed. "Same old questions. How long d'you reckon before Elliot asks if he's getting it on with DI Summers for real?"

"I don't think he will."

"Why not?"

"He's setting him up. Mentioning Shaunna before? He's going to hit him with a load of personal questions."

Josh was right. A few more questions followed of trying to get Kris to reveal the storyline, which were always met with the same jokey responses about waking up to find it was all a dream and clichés like that, and then one final statement that had Josh totally dumbstruck.

"It's a great show to work on. Brilliant people," Kris gushed, "which I think is why it's been such a hit. There's a real chemistry going on, and we've just signed the contracts for a third season…"

Josh examined the screen, and turned to George.

"I know nothing," George said. "He told me he was quitting, too."

Josh shook his head, still amazed. "They must've offered him seriously big bucks."

He tuned back in to Kris's performance and had to admit it was very convincing. There was no way anyone would know how much he hated playing DI Lundberg, the way he was enthusing about the cast and crew and the challenge of the role. And it *was* a challenging role, but not in a good way, which was where the host was leading the questions—right into the convergence between

Kris's real life and the life he portrayed onscreen. It was about to get very personal.

"Now," Elliot began, "Lundberg is, of course, one of very few openly bisexual male characters on British TV."

"That's right," Kris confirmed, "along with Captain Jack Harkness from *Doctor Who* and *Torchwood*."

"What makes Lundberg different, do you think?"

"Well, as in those series, we try to portray diverse sexuality without drawing attention to it, just a part of the rich tapestry."

"Surely the revelation of Lundberg's secret history in season one did the opposite?"

"Not really. That came from the reviews rather than the story itself. It was the press who overplayed the fact that the murder victim was a man, but the point was meant to be that he was the victim of the serial killer Lundberg was trying to hunt down, and his feelings for the victim added a personal edge to that."

"Right. I see what you mean. Speaking of a personal edge, you got quite a lot of hassle from the press when they discovered you're bisexual yourself, didn't you?"

"I did, although I think we're making progress in the UK as a whole. When I was younger, some people found it very difficult to accept when I came out. In school, I was open about not being straight, but everyone assumes that means gay, so when you end up in a relationship with someone of the opposite sex, it's as if you've been lying about who you are, and those closest to you can feel very betrayed.

"It's more accepted now, but a lot of people still see it as an experimental phase that you go through while you figure out whether you're gay or straight, and I admire the *Shadows* writers for how they tackle misconceptions in a subtle, indirect way, for instance, by not only showing the effect that Aaron Devling's murder had on my character, but also depicting his emotional and sexual connection to DI Summers, and to his ex-wife."

George had been making a big deal of removing bits of brazil nut from his teeth, knowing that Kris was talking about him.

Josh gave him a nudge. "He's back to his script now. I think you'll be safe."

"Not straight," George repeated. He sat up and chewed on his thumb thoughtfully. "He's a lying toad. I was just trying to work out if I'd concocted it and he'd not actually said that he was gay."

"No. You didn't."

Elliot pressed on. There wasn't much of the programme left, and this was the final round of interrogation. "You still live with your ex-wife?" he asked.

"I still live with my *wife*, yeah. We're separated."

"That's unconventional."

"We love our house, and we're best friends, so it works for us. It might not work for everyone."

"It must be a bit tricky bringing new love interests into the equation."

"No, it's absolutely fine. As I say, we're best friends, and she and my partner have so much in common, it's actually me who gets left out."

"Partner?" George questioned aloud.

A member of crew passed Elliot a card, and he took a moment to read it. "It says here you've just been appointed patron of the hospice in your hometown."

"I think he's back with Ade," Josh said.

"Yeah, I have," Kris confirmed. "It's a very special place, and I'm honoured to be able to give something back."

"Since when?" George asked. "Ade, I mean, not the hospice thing."

"A few weeks ago," Kris continued, "a very close friend of mine lost her battle against cancer, and the hospice staff were fantastic. They offered so much love and support to her and to us—her family and friends. We wouldn't have got through without them. I want to say a huge thank you to all of the staff at Victoria Hospice, and also much love to Steph and Dave, and my friends."

"Not sure," Josh said. "I think—"

Before he got any further in voicing his conjecture, Kris confirmed it, live, on TV, in front of millions of viewers.

"Unfortunately, I had to leave for filming straight after the funeral, so I haven't seen anyone since, and I hope they know how much I miss them and wish I could've been there. Ade—my partner—has been wonderful this past couple of months, but I can't wait to get home to everyone."

The studio audience made lots of sympathetic noise. Elliot patted Kris on the arm.

"Thanks for coming on tonight's show. Kristian Johansson, everybody."

The audience erupted into applause once more, and Elliot and Kris embraced.

"Well," Josh said philosophically, "I suppose that was one way of telling us."

The chat show went into its final segment, and George's phone vibrated. He picked it up, knowing it would be a text message from Kris.

I'm sorry. I love you. x

He showed it to Josh, who read it and smiled.

"Seriously," George said, "who needs enemies?"

Short Back And Sides
Monday 23rd October

"No ham and tomato," Shaunna called as she came through the back door into the salon stockroom. Her boss Hayley was heading through to the front of the shop.

"Not to worry, sweedie," she said. "You eat yours now. I'll go finish this cut and blow."

Shaunna opened her own sandwich and nibbled a corner from it, chewing unenthusiastically with her incisors. She wasn't feeling even slightly hungry; she hadn't got her appetite back since looking after Jess, but that wasn't the reason. She knew this feeling, the one where you'd swear your heart was missing beats, where the heat races up through you like the sensation of sinking into a deep, hot bath, and you have to think to breathe, and find yourself staring off into space for minutes at a time, to be brought back to reality with an embarrassing thump by whoever you were meant to be conversing with when you drifted off in the first place.

Oh, yes, she knew this feeling. It was infatuation, love, lust—call it what you will—and it was ridiculous. A teenage crush, at her age. She took another bite of the sandwich, forcing herself to chew and swallow. She wrapped the rest back up and put it in her bag for later. Ridiculous.

"Yah, that colour is beaudiful on you," Hayley was saying to the customer seated in front of her, in between puffing at the vast bouffant of platinum highlights with an industrial-size can of super-firm-hold hairspray. She glanced at Shaunna and frowned. "Done so soon?"

"Yeah," Shaunna responded hazily. She perched on the stool behind the counter while Hayley finished dealing with her

420

customer, although she was neither watching nor listening to their superficial chattering. Her mind had drifted off again, to the kisses in the kitchen the night before Jess passed, to the picnic under the tree in the heat of midsummer, and to last week: four wonderful days of sex, sex and more sex. God, she was missing it. Him. Both. A noise broke through and tore her from the blissful daydream.

"Hmm?" she said, feeling herself blush.

"I'm going for my lunch, sweedie," Hayley called back and disappeared from view.

"OK," Shaunna shouted after the fact. She looked around her for something to do. The capes were all hanging neatly; there was no hair on the floor; all but one chair was tidily tucked away along the edge of the room. She got up and straightened the offender, returned to her stool, leaned on her elbow and sighed. She took out her phone. No calls or messages since Thursday, when Dan walked in and caught them. They'd waited so long, wanting each other, teasing and tantalising, all for it to end up being the shortest affair ever. Four days—not even that much, but what an affair!

She kept reminding herself of what he'd said, about living for the moment rather than being sad about it being over, but that was when there was to be a next time. Instead, they'd ended it, deciding it was better to stay out of each other's way completely and cool off. Fat chance of that.

She checked her phone again—still nothing—and plopped open the hairdressing magazine on the counter, flicking over the pages without looking, although she was trying so hard to focus. She'd brought her study books in with her; Monday afternoons were quiet, and she was only there because she didn't want to be home alone. But if she couldn't even pay attention to a glossy magazine, what hope was there for making sense of personality theory? Maybe she should just withdraw from the course now, or defer until some distant time in the future when she got her head back together.

"Afternoon. I wondered if you could fit me in for a quick trim."

She jumped so violently that she ripped the corner off the page she was holding, and her heart immediately set off at a gallop of about two hundred beats per minute.

"Dan!" She leapt to her feet and knocked the stool flying.

"Shaunna," he replied calmly. He watched her fighting to right the stool, clearly flustered. He shouldn't have come unannounced, but it was the only way he could think to do it.

She stood up and smiled, nervously straightening her tunic. "A trim?"

"Yeah. Couldn't get an appointment at my usual place. So, can you?"

"Can I what?"

"Fit me in?"

"Oh!" She didn't think it was possible to blush any more than she was doing, because her face was absolutely burning. "Yes. Now?"

"That'd be great." Dan waited for her to lead the way over to where she wanted him to sit, although the prospect of having those shaking hands bringing a pair of scissors anywhere near his head was starting to worry him.

"I'll just go, err…" Shaunna waved at the rack of black capes and wandered over to get one, only realising when she got there that she hadn't taken his jacket, or even noticed whether he was wearing one. She glanced back and found he wasn't, pulled a cape free from a hanger and returned.

Dan watched her in the mirror as she fiddled with the Velcro, trying to make it stick. She looked up and met his gaze. He smiled, and she tried to smile back, her expression like someone who's had a really bad face lift. She looked away again and went to pull her scissors from the pocket of her tunic, but her fingers felt as if they belonged to someone else and she dropped the scissors. They fell with a noisy clatter and spun across the floor.

"Ah," she said, scurrying away to retrieve them. She came back again and let out a very shaky breath.

Dan reached over his shoulder and took the scissors from her. "I think it'll be safer all round if you just go through the motions of weighing me up for a cut while I talk, don't you?"

She nodded gratefully and moved her dithering hands up to his head, lifting the tiniest, shortest wisps of hair around his ears and pretending to examine them.

"I'm really sorry about…the other day," he said. "If I'd known…" He made eye contact briefly; she lowered her eyes and focused on his hair. "I should've realised, to be honest, when the dog suddenly appeared from nowhere, and with Andy acting so strangely."

"It's OK," Shaunna said lightly.

He continued to watch her reflection, the shimmer of the salon lights on her smooth eyelids, her perfect skin flushed pink. She looked so young, with her hair up in a ponytail, just a few curls hanging down around her face, framing those rosy plump cheeks, her arched brows squeezed in a frown, her long eyelashes curving gracefully as she blinked.

She peered up at him again, and he stared deep into her eyes, an inquisitive look on his face. "What?" she asked.

"I always thought your eyes were green."

"They are. These are contacts."

"Why would you wear contacts when you have such lovely eyes?"

She shrugged self-consciously. "Just for a change, I guess."

He nodded. "I've never looked at you properly before, I mean as a woman. You're Adele's friend, Krissi's mum, Kris's wife, but I've never considered how beautiful you are."

"Thanks," Shaunna smiled—still blushing furiously, but feeling a little less uneasy now.

"Look, I…" Now Dan looked away. He wasn't good with this kind of interaction and was finding it hard to get the right words. "I wanted to reassure you. I'm not gonna say anything about what's going on."

"Was."

"What d'you mean?"

423

"There's nothing going on, Dan, and that's the truth."

He swivelled around to face her. "Why?"

"Because it's not fair. On you, or Adele, or anyone else who gets caught up in it."

"It's not fair on the both of you if you end it."

Shaunna shook her head sadly. "We can't let it continue, however much we want to. We talked about it, after…when you left." She turned him away from her again and met his gaze in the mirror. "We ended it, because it's not fair. And he deserves better."

"Better than the woman he's in love with?"

"I was a challenge to be won. Nothing more. Now he can move on."

"Shaunna—"

"No," she interrupted.

Dan watched her, his breath held, along with the rest of what he'd been about to say. She leaned forward to take her scissors back from him, and he released both them and the breath.

"OK. I promise this is the last time I'll mention it, but whatever happens, my lips are sealed. You have my word."

She put her hands on either side of his head and positioned him so he was facing forward. "Did you have a particular style in mind, or is it just a trim you're after?"

"Just a trim," he said. And that was all.

SCORPIO

There's not a creature in the realm of night
But has the wish to live, likewise the right:
Don't tread upon the scorpion, or he'll fight.

Paint, Balls, Warfare
Tuesday 24th October

"What we doin'?" Iris asked, groaning as she eased herself into the front seat of the car.

"Err, hospital, then housing office, then back to ours for dinner?"

"Dinner? Since when is it fuckin' dinner?"

"All right. Tea!" George tutted and fastened his seat belt.

"I could've got the bus, y'know." She was still struggling to fasten her own seat belt.

"Here." George went to assist.

"I can manage, ta very much." She slapped his hand away and scowled at him.

"Great. The two of you in a foul mood. My day off keeps getting better and better."

"I'm not in a foul mood. I'm…" She ummed and sucked air in as if inhaling from a cigarette. "I'm a bit worried about this anaesthetic and whatnot."

"Why? You've had operations before."

"A long bloody time ago!"

"So, it's safer these days."

"I've seen it on the telly, that MRSA doodah. It can kill yer. Did you know that?"

"Mum—"

"And choppin' off the wrong bits."

"Mum! Stop worrying. You're not gonna get MRSA and no-one's gonna be chopping off the wrong bits. It's a straightforward operation."

"Says you. And I'll be stuck indoors with that bloody idiot."

"Who? Monty?"

"No. The feller next door. Bangin' around all day, music blarin'. It's no bloody wonder his missus fucked off with the postie. I'll end up killin''im before the year's out."

"Come and stay with us."

"Don't be daft."

"What's daft about it? If the lift packs up, you've had it anyway, and I can take you to bingo."

"And what about Josh? Dun't he get a say?"

"We can ask him when we get back." He glanced across at her; she still looked frightened to death. She'd already cancelled the appointment for her bunion surgery three times, so getting her this far was quite an achievement, not that it had anything to do with George, although it *was* why he was taking her rather than letting her get the bus. "You know it'll be worth it," he comforted. "Just think. A few weeks from now you'll be able to put your high heels on."

"Oh, aye," she said dryly. "Can't you just see me clip-cloppin' down the school corridor in them bloody things?"

"I didn't mean for work. When you go anywhere posh."

"What? Like your place, you mean?"

He ignored her and concentrated on dodging around the potholes in the road. It wasn't far to the hospital, and his mum didn't say anything else until they got there. Today's appointment was only the pre-operative assessment, and if all was well, she was in for the surgery in two weeks' time. George dropped her at the main entrance and went to park up, giving her a chance to have a smoke before they went inside.

"So what's up with Josh, then?" she asked as they made their way down the hospital's long and noisy corridor.

"It's a bit complicated."

She tutted at him.

"Well, it is!" he protested. "I'm sure he'll tell you all about it later."

They arrived in the waiting room, where Iris gave the receptionist her details and sat down. There was no-one else waiting, and it couldn't have been any more than a minute later when a nurse called her name. George moved to go with her, but she gave him a look that told him to stay right where he was. He

428

picked up a magazine to pass the time. His phone vibrated in his pocket.

Can you get teabags?

No 'please', no 'thank you' and no 'x'. He typed back:

Will do. xxxxx. X

He waited with his phone in his hand for a full five minutes before he gave up on getting a response. Maybe it wasn't such a good idea to suggest his mother came to stay after all. He returned to skimming through the pages of the magazine, stopping to read an article entitled 'Star Cooks', with celebrities sharing their favourite meals. Accordingly, Kristian Johansson liked nothing better than a good traditional fry-up—sausages, bacon, eggs sunny side up—the full works.

"At least he didn't lie about that," George muttered to himself. His phone vibrated again.

Sorry. x

He smiled. His mother waddled in front of him.

"You look a right bloody barmpot, sittin' there, grinnin' to yourself."

George got up and put his phone away. "Everything OK?"

"So they say."

She looped her arm through his as they walked back along the corridor and out of the main entrance, where she stopped next to a 'no smoking' sign and lit a cigarette, blowing the smoke towards the automatic doors.

"That's what I think of your suggestion, interferin' arse'oles."

George looked down at the floor and acted like she wasn't with him. When she was about halfway done with the cigarette, she started walking slowly in the general direction of the car park.

"I'll go get the car," George offered. "I had to park right at the back." He jogged off without waiting for a response, because she'd have insisted on paying the parking fee, which would escalate into an argument that inevitably he'd lose. By the time he returned with the car, she'd finished smoking and got in beside him.

"You can leave the housin'," she said. "It's not so cold yet. I'll manage without the fire for now."

He took a deep breath and let it go as slowly and quietly as he could. She turned and glared at him.

"It's nowt to do with you!" she snapped.

"No. It's not."

"Right then."

Now, where he would normally have kept his 'gob' shut and let her have her own way, he was suddenly feeling very brave, or stupid, he hadn't quite worked out which, but it was about time she started listening to what he had to say. He was forty next year, for goodness' sake, and he had her best interests at heart.

"Actually, Mam," he began firmly, "it is to do with me. I worry about you all the time in that flat. The wiring's dangerous. It's cold and damp, and when the lift packs up you have to climb all those stairs, then end up crippled for days after. Pauline said if you move, she'll come with you, so you need to stop being so damned stubborn and tell the council."

He stopped at the traffic lights and turned away from her, expecting a massive, sweary rant.

"Aye, alright," she mumbled.

He turned back to look at her, but she wasn't facing his way.

"You only had to say," she said, then, "Lights have changed."

George shook himself out of it and moved off, desperately fighting the urge to tell her that he had said it many, many times before. Maybe he'd just caught her off-guard, because she wasn't acting much like the feisty mother he knew and loved.

They journeyed on in silence, parked in the town centre and walked through to the housing office, where she sat, quiet and subdued, whilst the housing officer filled out the form for rehousing and showed her the map, indicating where the one-bedroom flats were situated. George asked what they'd need to do if she and Pauline wanted to share somewhere; the housing officer went to see what he could find out, returning a couple of minutes later with his manager, who scrolled through the completed form on the computer.

"Paul was saying the other day," Iris said quietly to George, "we should get one of them reclinin' chairs. They had 'em in that place what does all the stuff on credit. Ten pound a bloody week, it was! You'd be dead before you was done payin' for it. Where the hell does she think we're gonna find a tenner a week for a reclinin' chair?"

"I bet you could pick one up at the recycling centre for not much," George said. "I might pop in and—"

"We'll manage with the couch, ta."

"You'll be in a nice new flat, though. Wouldn't it be good to have new stuff to go with it?"

"What for? Paul's just got a new cooker, and I've only had that fridge freezer a couple of months. We don't need owt else. Waste of money, love." She sat back and watched the woman tip-tapping on the keyboard with her long fingernails. "I might shell out for some of them earmuffs, though."

"Earmuffs?"

"Aye. She snores worse than the dog."

"Earplugs."

"You know what a mean."

The woman cleared her throat.

"OK. Just check that through for me," she said to her subordinate. He did as he was told. She gave Iris a fake smile and peered down at her over the top of her glasses. "You don't share a tenancy with your *friend* at the moment, Mrs. Morley?"

"No."

"And *she* has her own tenancy?"

"That's right."

"In the same block?"

"Correct."

The woman nodded and pushed her glasses back up her nose. She looked at the screen again, and back at Iris. "So you'll be wanting to apply for a two-bedroom property?"

"Obviously."

"You do realise that you could lose some of your benefits if, in future, you are deemed to have a spare room?"

"Well we won't have, will we? There's two of us and we're askin' for two rooms." Iris looked puzzled by the questioning.

431

"Mrs. Morley," the woman said in a condescending tone. She pulled out the chair opposite and sat down. "Be assured that we operate a very effective equal opportunities policy in this local authority, but I do understand how difficult it is for people of your age to accept, never mind admit to being in, shall we say, an unconventional relationship—"

Iris laughed loudly. George blushed. He could have predicted, more or less word for word, what his mother said next.

"We're not lezzers, love. We just go the bingo together, watch a bit of Saturday night telly, mebbe share dinner on special occasions, wear a natty 'at at Christmas and all that."

The woman looked quite taken aback, but rallied quickly.

"I don't appreciate your choice of language, Mrs. Morley. I apologise if I offended you, but there's really no need—"

"Oh, you didn't offend me at all, love," Iris interrupted. "See, the thing is, there's a difference between sayin' it and thinkin' it. I'm not clever like you lot, with your bits of paper and qualifications. I don't get me words right sometimes, but I've got nothin' against anyone. Live and let live, I say."

"Ignorance is no defence, Mrs. Morley."

"No, love, it's not."

The woman smiled that fake smile again and turned to her colleague. "I'll take it from here," she said. The man nodded and moved towards the door. "All right, Mrs. Morley, can I please take your *friend's* name?"

"It's—" Iris began, but George cut her off.

"Excuse me for butting in," he said, addressing the woman, "my mum might not be offended, but I am."

The male housing officer had his hand on the door handle and didn't know whether to stay or run away as fast as he could.

"Why's that, Mr. Morley?" the woman asked, turning her smarmy smile on George instead.

"My mum's been a council tenant for more than thirty years and has never missed a single rent payment. Even though she's got next to nothing, she'd rather go without food than get into debt. She gets a piddling little bit of housing benefit and that's all, because she's too honest for her own good. She's sixty-three years old and should be looking forward to being happily retired.

Instead, she's cancelled having an operation she needs three times, just so she doesn't have to claim more benefits, and is probably going to end up working until she drops dead. Does she really sound like the sort of person who would lie to get an extra bedroom?"

The woman waited a few seconds to see if he was finished and then took off her glasses. She set them down on the table, drawing out the motion, presumably to try to intimidate him.

"I totally understand where you're coming from, Mr. Morley," she said. "If only everyone were as honest as your mother." She turned back to Iris. "I'm very sorry, but your application will go through much more quickly if all the details are correct to begin with, which is why I'm such a stickler for detail."

"And," George continued, as if she hadn't said anything at all, "I take exception to *your* choice of language. Unconventional relationship? Is it any wonder people aren't truthful when they come here?"

"I'm quite sure that members of the gay community would rather be referred to as unconventional than by terms like the one your mother used, Mr. Morley."

"Is that right?"

"Were you to be on the receiving end yourself, you'd no doubt feel very differently about it, but I've taken your comments on board. Now, we have a housing application to finish. Shall we?" The woman turned back to Iris and smiled that dreadful smile again.

George listened and silently seethed, desperate to get out of there as quickly as possible and glad that less than ten minutes later they were all done.

"OK, Mrs. Morley," the woman said, logging out of the computer. "One of our inspectors will be in touch to arrange a visit to assess your current accommodation. However, we won't be able to fully process your application until your friend has completed her part of the form. Any questions?"

"No, I don't think so, ta, love," Iris said.

The woman was already moving towards the door, by way of prompting them to do likewise.

433

"Mr. Morley," she said, giving George one final, highly exaggerated, teeth-on-display smile.

He smiled right back at her. "It's Mr. *Sandison*-Morley, actually. Sandison is my husband's name, and I think I speak for both of us when I say we would rather be called poofters by someone like my mum than have someone like you call our relationship unconventional. Thanks for your help." He smiled again and ushered his mother out of the door, leaving the woman dumbfounded and looking somewhat less smug than before.

"Fuckin'ell, Georgie," Iris said when they eventually got back to the car.

"What?" he snapped.

She smiled and put her hand on his. "You gave her what for, eh?" He glanced across at her. "I'm bloody proud of you, lad, for stickin' up for your poor ole mam. Ta for that."

He huffed and started the car.

"And for tellin' her I was sixty-fuckin'-three. I was hopin' to pass for fifty, with that young feller there."

George felt himself smiling. "You didn't think he was good-looking, did you, Mam?"

She laughed. "Did I hell as like. And she was no friggin' oil paintin' either."

"Oh, I don't know. She could probably give *The Ugly Duchess* a run for her money."

"Aye, fuck. She was one ugly old trout." They both chuckled at that. Back in sixth form, George had been on a school trip to an art gallery and had come home with a set of postcards that included one of the painting by Matsys. He kept leaving it around the flat, which prompted many a discussion of whether the person in the portrait ever found a suitor, and also lots of threats from his mother that she would set fire to it if he didn't put it away somewhere so she didn't have to keep looking at it, because it was one of those pictures that you keep revisiting, just to revel in its ugliness.

"Speaking of paintings," George hedged nervously, "I want to show you one I've been working on, when we get back to ours."

"Oh aye?"

"Yeah. So you can tell me what you think. If it's any good."

Iris didn't respond in words, because she was very moved by his request. She covered it with a change of subject. "So what we havin' for tea?"

"Dunno. What d'you fancy?"

"Anythin'. I'm not fussed. So long as it's none of that fancy shite with garlic and a load of other crap in it."

"D'you know, you and Josh should've got married. You could've moaned at each other over a nice bowl of gruel every night."

Iris moved her mouth as if repeating his words, and George grinned at her.

When they parked up outside the house, Iris took off her seat belt, but stayed where she was.

"What's up?" George asked.

"Just thinkin' about that council woman."

"Don't let her get to you. She's not worth it."

"I know, love." She patted his arm. "But it's not like you to get all het up like that."

"She just caught me on the wrong day. Come on." He got out of the car, and she followed him up the path.

"Why, has someone else upset you?"

"Not me, no," he said. "Are you ready for it?" He pushed open the door and braced himself. "Hi," he called. No response. He beckoned to his mother to step inside and closed the door, listening to the music coming from upstairs. It was much quieter than when he'd left.

Blue came trotting down, wagging his tail, very pleased to see Iris. He stopped to have his ears rubbed and then went off towards the kitchen, asking to be let outside. George followed him through and spotted the empty, open container on the side.

"Ah, hell. I forgot teabags. I'll have to pop back out and get some." He opened the back door for Blue. "I'll just tell Josh we're back," he said as he passed his mum in the hallway and ran upstairs, where he found Josh exactly where he'd left him: sitting at his computer, watching music videos.

Josh turned and attempted a smile. "Hey," he said quietly.

"Hey, yourself. I forgot teabags. I'm going back out for them. Mum's downstairs."

"OK."

"You OK?"

"Hm."

"Won't be long." George gave him a kiss and returned downstairs, repeating the line for his mother's benefit.

Josh waited for the front door to close before he went down. He heard the flick of a lighter from the garden and went out to join her.

"Hello, Iris. How did you get on today?"

"Alright, ta, love. I've put me name down for a flat transfer."

"Have you? That's great news."

"Aye. Not sure how long it'll take to go through. And I'm fit enough for me op an' all, so they tell me."

"Good stuff." Josh was saying the right words, but they were lacking in sentiment, and he looked miserable.

"What's to do, love?" Iris asked.

He shrugged. "Feeling a bit down."

"I can see that."

"Did George tell you about Ellie?"

"No. Why, what's she done this time?"

"She's moving to Birmingham."

"Right. For her hubby's work?"

"Yes. Mostly." Josh took a deep breath and looked longingly at Iris's cigarette. She had one last drag on it and quickly put it out.

"Why else?" she asked.

"She says there's no reason for her to stay here now, with Jess gone, and…" He closed his eyes, hoping to contain the temper trying to resurface.

"You've fell out again?" Iris stated. He nodded. "Over her bein' a bigot?"

His lack of response said it all.

"Well, forget about it, love. She'll realise soon enough, and if she doesn't, what've you lost, really? Eh?"

Josh nodded again. "Yes, I suppose you're right." They went back inside, and Josh filled the kettle.

"Anyhow," Iris said, "this'll cheer you up. When we was at the housin', this woman thought me and Pauline was havin' it off with each other and started on about us tryin' to get a bigger flat than we needed. And Georgie proper flew at her. It were fuckin' brilliant."

"Really? What did he say?"

"Well, she got the right arse cos I said somert that offended her, dunno what it was, mind—"

"Lezzers," George said, coming into the kitchen and now armed with a box of teabags.

Josh laughed. "You know that conversation we had about political correctness, Iris?"

"Aye, fuckin' load of shite, that is. So she says to me how she understands it's hard for women of my age to admit to bein'… lezzers." Josh and George both covered their eyes at the same time. "What the fuck am a s'posed to call 'em?"

"Lesbians?" George suggested.

"Gay women?" Josh offered.

"Lezzers," Iris said. "There's nowt wrong with that. Better than her and her fuckin' whatsit unconventionals, eh, Georgie?"

Josh looked confused.

"She referred to gay relationships as unconventional," George explained. "Then, surprise, surprise, she assumed I was straight."

"You soon put her right, though, din't yer, son?"

"What?" Josh was incredulous.

"Well, I'm sick of it. All that crap Kris was spouting on Friday—*that's* unconventional. And then bloody Ellie." He acted all prim and proper, doing a very insulting impersonation of Eleanor. "Oh, Josh, I've got nothing against homosexuality, but… You know the Bible says don't lie with another man, Josh… You've changed, Josh, since you turned gay… Ooh, don't be shoving that gay sex down my throat, Josh, it's disgusting…"

Iris and Josh both turned away and tried not to laugh, but they couldn't help it, and the laughter exploded from them so loudly that the dog came tearing in from the garden to see what all the fuss was about. George glared for a moment and then grinned.

"Right, Mam, this way," he said. She nodded and followed.

"Where are you going?" Josh called after them.

"None of your business," George shouted from halfway up the stairs. Iris looked back at him and shrugged, following George up to the office. He pushed the button on the remote control for the loft stairs, and she watched on, her eyebrows going up as the staircase descended.

"I'm not fuckin' goin' up there," she said.

"Fine. Wait here." George ran up into the loft and switched on the light. Iris looked up, her eyes following the sound of his footsteps across the ceiling above, and back again. He eased himself sideways through the hatch and carefully came down, carrying a vast canvas draped in a white, paint-smeared sheet. He took a deep breath.

"OK," he said, hands shaking with nerves. He was terrified she'd think the painting was awful, but then, that's why he was asking her. He knew she'd be brutally honest, and much as he was dreading her reaction, he wanted the truth. He'd lost all sense of objectivity during the four months he'd spent on the portrait; to him, it was perfect, but he needed a second opinion, and she was the only person he trusted to offer it. He balanced the canvas on the office chair, slowly pulled away the sheet and stepped back, turning away so he didn't see her initial reaction. The silence filled the room, and he could hear his own breathing, fast and shallow. Still, she said nothing. Slowly he turned to face her.

"So what—" He didn't get any further than that, because he saw exactly what she thought, in her expression and the tears rolling down her cheeks.

"Why the fuck are you wastin' your time workin' as a bloody farm hand?" She shook her head. "Come 'ere." She pulled him into her arms and kissed his cheek. "That's a masterpiece, that is." She peered around him to look at the painting again.

"Do you like it?" he asked.

"What do you think? You daft bat!"

She stepped back and continued to stare at the painting, shaking her head slowly, her hand over her mouth. It was utterly beautiful in every sense. From the way George had captured the light and the position of the 'model', she knew it was a memento of their honeymoon. In the painting, a warm orange glow of sunlight beamed down from the right, lighting up one side of the bed, catching the crumpled sheets, accented so perfectly by shadows that it was almost photographic.

And on those sheets, with his legs crossed, one arm hanging loose and relaxed in his lap, the other flung lazily behind his head, sat Josh, his blonde hair falling gently across his face, a smile teasing his lips, his cheeks flushed peach and his eyes bright blue and glistening with the joy of life. His part-unbuttoned shirt fell open, revealing a bare shoulder and a little of his chest, and the sleeve of the arm behind his head had slipped down, revealing more milky-white smooth skin. It was a stunning likeness.

"Has he not seen it yet?" Iris asked. George shook his head. "Was you savin' it for Christmas or somert?" George shook his head again. "Just bein' a soft shite?" He nodded. "Well get him up 'ere!" she ordered. George looked panic-stricken. His mother turned towards the door, and shouted, "Josh!"

"Yes, Iris?"

"Get yer arse upstairs, lad." She waited until she heard the sound of footsteps on the stairs. "Right. Just bobbin' to the little girls' room," she said and made a hasty exit, passing Josh on the landing.

"What did you—" He frowned at her. She scurried into the bathroom and locked the door. Josh scratched his head and glanced into the office, where George was standing with his back to him, the painting still on the chair. Josh cautiously stepped into the room and gasped.

"Is that me?" he whispered in disbelief. He gazed at the painting, then at George nodding dumbly, then back at the painting, examining it in detail. The light was so warm and vibrant, and real, that it immediately put him back in their room in Cornwall, sitting on the bed, with the sunset pouring through the open balcony doors. He laughed breathlessly. "Wow!"

He moved closer, running his fingers over the sheet, as if to check that it really was just a painting. "How did you…where are…" He turned to George again. "Is that really how you see me?"

"Yeah. It is," George managed to utter. They heard the toilet flush and the taps run. Iris emerged. She smiled at Josh.

"What d'you think, then?" she asked.

He shook his head and shrugged, his mouth still wide open in surprise—and delight. What was it George had said? *I'll paint you, and then you'll see.*

"Damn. I'm fine!" He grinned at Iris.

She rolled her eyes and laughed. "I'll be downstairs, makin' me own tea." Off she went.

Josh moved closer to George and took his hands. "You did that from memory?"

George nodded. "Our last night. Well, our second-to-last night."

"I remember." He glanced back at the painting. "It's amazing. It truly is."

"Do you think so? Really?"

"George! Can't you tell by my reaction? I love it. It's…amazing. Wonderful. Fabulous. Beautiful. I love it. I really do." He kissed him. "Almost as much as I love you." He kissed him again and put his arms around him. "I love you, ma moitié."

George smiled and pulled Josh closer. "I love you, too," he said.

"Where are we going to hang it? Where would you like to hang it?"

"I don't care. I painted it for you, so you decide."

"I want to show it to everyone, but I want to look at it all the time myself, which would mean leaving it in here. Oh, I don't know. I'll ask your mum, see what she thinks." He withdrew from their embrace and took George's hand, leading him from the room. As he reached the door, he looked back at the portrait. "Can I just ask one question? It's not a criticism or anything."

"What's that?"

"Where are my scars?"

George shrugged and smiled. "I don't see them."

Therapy
Monday 23rd–Thursday 26th October

Monday afternoon: Sean sat alone with no more than a hot chocolate for company, and it was proving to be nowhere near as tasty without her. She'd stood him up. It was the first time ever that she had stood him up. She'd been late, she'd been early, she'd asked in advance to rearrange, but she'd never stood him up. He attempted to call, left several voicemails and sent enough text messages to put him in the league of stalker, but got nothing in response. He went home and tried to get on with some work, pausing every so often to try her phone again, on the off chance that it had been out of range or turned off earlier. He went to bed.

***

Tuesday morning: he tried calling again—still no answer—and decided that it would be best to go to the hairdressing salon after work and catch her there.

He was on foot and turned into the road as the lights went off inside the shop. He jogged across. "Hi," he said, coming up behind the woman locking the door.

"Jeez!" She dropped the massive bunch of keys and spun around to face him, fists already balled and set to give her assailant a good duffing.

"Sorry." Sean quickly raised his hands and backed off. "I was looking for Shaunna Hennessy."

She squinted at him, like a biologist examining something unidentifiable and unexpected in a Petri dish. "Who are you?"

"I'm a friend. Sean."

"The psychiadrist?"

"Yeah, something like that. Has she left already?"

"No, sweedie. She, err, hmm." The woman smacked her lips together and rolled her eyes very slowly from side to side as she considered how to respond. Whilst she was pondering, Sean was reading her and had more or less worked it out for himself.

"Has she resigned?" he asked.

"Yah, doll, but, you know, if you catch up with her, tell her I'm delaying gedding a replacement, won't you?"

"I will. Thanks for your help." Sean turned and started walking away.

"Ba-bye now." The woman gave him a little wave with the very tips of her fingers. He turned back, gave her a swift nod, and continued on his way.

So, she hadn't turned up at the milk bar, and she hadn't been into work. He could try calling her again, but it was a pointless exercise. She was clearly avoiding company, and he could understand why she'd want to. It had been a hectic few months, with little time to themselves, and he was feeling the pinch on his own sanity, although he was surprised to find that whenever he started looking forward to his own company, it transformed into a desire to be with his son.

That was what he'd be doing this evening, as Sophie was meeting an old school friend at the station and bringing her back to the house. Interestingly, she was also called Hayley, although it was safe to say it was the only thing she had in common with Shaunna's boss. For a start, Sophie's friend was known as 'Hay' and was an earth mother, feminist and a vegan. She wore only naturally dyed clothes and no bra, which was something Sean had tried not to notice, but she was a large-breasted woman, and gravity hadn't done her any favours.

Once he'd got past the 42FFs dangling down to her midriff and the constant angry ranting about the state of the planet and how it was all the fault of patriarchy, he'd found that Hay was a good, honest person and a loving mother, as well as being a veterinary nurse and a volunteer at her children's school in her 'spare' time. Sophie was godmother to Hay's seven-year-old triplets, or maybe goddessmother would be more apt, as it had been a wiccaning ceremony, but whatever, the two women were very close, and Hay had yet to meet Dylan.

The problem with all of that, of course, was that even though Sean was now on his way to Shaunna's, should he find her there and in need of comfort, if he couldn't cajole her into leaving the house, he'd have to abandon her to her solitude, or loneliness. He'd make a judgement on which it was, once he'd had an opportunity to assess the situation, and it was a very strange one to be in, because she was an independent, responsible, sensible adult with so many potentially good reasons for why she hadn't met up with him yesterday, the simplest being that she'd forgotten.

Or perhaps she'd got stuck into her studies and was so absorbed in reading classic psychology experiments that she couldn't bear to be away from them, not even for a blueberry yoghurt not-smoothie. His gut instinct wasn't having any of it, though, and by the time he arrived at her very-much-in-darkness house, he was starting to worry. He knocked, waited for the dog to quieten down, and listened closely for any signs of human life within. Not a peep. He frowned and rubbed his chin.

"OK," he said to himself. "Once more with feeling." He banged on the door again, hard. Casper went crazy, but that was all he got: a lunatic Labrador flinging himself at the other side of the door and a couple of twitching curtains from the neighbours. If he didn't leave now, he'd be late for Sophie, and that wasn't a viable option. He patted his pockets until he found a pen, and then rummaged around for a scrap of paper. Typically, today was one of the days where he hadn't accidentally stolen the admin clerk's sticky notes, an unconscious act that amused him almost as much as it annoyed her.

He glanced around, in the unlikely event that there might be a fortuitous scrap of paper on which to leave a message, and spotted a corner of an envelope jutting out of the letterbox, which worried him all the more. If the post was uncollected, either she hadn't been home at all today, or she was inside and something had happened to her. He dismissed that thought for now. After all, it had only been twenty-four hours. With the intention to graffiti it, he tugged at the corner of envelope. It easily came free, revealing itself to be a remnant of old post, the rest of which had no doubt been 'retrieved' by the dog at some point in the past. Sean scribbled in the dark what he hoped was a legible 'Call me. S x' and used spit to stick the gum edge to the door. It was the best he could do.

He returned home and spent the evening sitting at his computer, sometimes with Dylan on his knee, sometimes with Sphinx, whilst Sophie drank too much scrumpy for someone who was breastfeeding and Hay drank too much scrumpy for anyone who intended to see the morning after from a perpendicular perspective. They talked and talked, Hay fussed over Dylan and Sphinx interchangeably, Sophie cried with laughter at Hay's stories, Hay did likewise for Sophie's, and all the while Sean worried about Shaunna.

"Doesn't time fly?" Sophie slurred at him at the end of the evening, with Hay flat out on the sofa, the cat draped around her neck, and Dylan tucked up in his cot.

"Yeah," Sean agreed indifferently; it hadn't for him.

***

Wednesday morning: instead of going to the hospice, Sean went straight to Shaunna's again, immediately relieved to find that his tiny triangular note had gone. It was only just nine o'clock, but hopefully late enough for her to be up and out. She might even have decided to go into work today. These were his thoughts as he tried to explain the absence of an answer to his knocking. He couldn't walk away again. He stepped onto the grass next to the path and peered up close through the window, squinting to see through the net curtains.

"There she is."

And there she was, sitting on the sofa with her legs bent up, her head resting on her knees. He tapped lightly on the window. She didn't even flinch. He tapped again, a little harder, and saw a slight movement. She must have seen him, but still she didn't get up. Sean stepped back onto the path and scratched his head.

"What to do," he wondered aloud. He took out his phone and tried calling her. He could hear her phone ringing, but it went to voicemail. He called Josh instead.

"Sorry to be a pain. I know you're about to go and teach, but, well, I'm at Shaunna's, outside, and she's inside, so I'm just, oh I don't know. She's kind of, well, catatonic."

"Can you start again?" Josh said, his confusion apparent in his tone.

"Err, yeah, sorry. She didn't meet me on Monday, and she didn't go into work yesterday. She's sitting on her sofa and not answering the door or phone. Ideas?"

"Ring Adele."

"Adele?"

"She'll sort her out."

"We are talking about the same person here? Short with blonde hair and the IQ of a peach?"

"Just ring Adele. Bye." Josh hung up.

Sean stared at his phone. "Ring Adele, he says."

That was all well and good, but he didn't have Adele's number. His phone vibrated, and he tutted.

"I guess now I do." He called Adele.

"Hello?"

"Hi, Adele?"

"Yes?"

"It's Sean here."

"Oh! Hi, Sean. How are you? Are you OK?"

"Yeah, I'm fine, but…I'm at Shaunna's and, erm…"

"I'm on my way." Adele hung up.

Sean rubbed his eyes and looked at his phone again. It was all a bit too much to take in. He sat on the step and leaned back against the door, letting his thoughts roam free. So, this was what it was like to have friends? You call someone and don't even need to ask for their help. They implicitly know and offer it without prompting. Phenomenal. He'd never experienced anything like it before, and part of him was instantly suspicious. All of his life, all the people he'd been acquainted with…they weren't like that. Sure, they'd come running, but there was always an ulterior

445

motive, and if it wasn't preloaded, then sooner or later they'd be seeking payback. Thus, much as he was trying to accept that Adele was acting out of the goodness of her heart, and kept reminding himself of what he'd said to Shaunna about altruism, he was still thinking that at some point in the future he would be made to pay.

Not long after, Adele jogged to a stop at Shaunna's gate and pulled her earphones out of her ears.

"Hi," she said with a smile.

"Hi," he replied. "You were quick."

"Yeah. I only live ten minutes' walk away, and I ran most of it."

Sean noticed she was wearing exercise gear.

"Don't worry." She smiled again as she stepped around him.

Taking a key from her pocket, she opened the door and fought her way past Casper. Sean followed her and stood in the hallway.

"Hiya, sweetie," Adele called through the lounge door.

Shaunna was still sitting with her legs up and her back to them. She stayed as she was.

"I'll put the kettle on," Adele said. She continued through to the kitchen, leaving Sean standing, stunned, both by the scene before him and Adele's lack of reaction to it. The lounge was completely trashed. The table was on its side, plants were lying limp, the soil spread across the carpet, shattered bowls spilled potpourri in a colourful chaos around the TV, facedown on the floor, with DVDs, some in cases, some not, splayed underneath. Somehow, Sean got his legs working again and followed Adele through to the kitchen. She turned and saw his expression.

"It's OK," she whispered. "She does this." Sean nodded. "She'll be fine, don't you worry."

She continued making the tea around him. When she was done, she passed him a mug and indicated for him to sit at the kitchen table. He did so, not really knowing what else to do.

Adele took the other two mugs through to the lounge, stooping to deposit them on the floor whilst she righted the table. She brushed the soil from it, transferred the mugs, and sat next to Shaunna.

446

"I've made you tea," she said. She wasn't expecting a response, which was as well, because she didn't get one. "And I've left Sean in the kitchen. I don't know if he's staying, but I'm here now. I'm supposed to be in college this afternoon. It won't matter if I'm not, though." Cruel as it sounded, Adele knew her friend. Shaunna needed a deadline on her misery. She sniffed. "You don't need to tell me what's wrong, sweetie, but if you want to…"

Shaunna shook her head.

"That's fine." Adele picked up one of the cups of tea and moved in front of Shaunna, placing it in her hands. "You drink that while I get this mess tidied." She moved away and started clearing the devastation, singing quietly to herself.

Shaunna sipped at her tea, gradually tuning in to Adele's activities. It didn't take long to get the room back to normal, although the carpet was going to need a good clean to get the compost out of it. Adele checked it was as good as she could get it and sat down again.

"When you've finished, you can go and have a shower, and I'll dry your hair for you, if you like."

Shaunna nodded.

"And I'll have to do something about Sean. He looks a bit lost, sitting out there. Have you drunk your tea?" She peered into Shaunna's mug. "OK. Shower." She took the mug from Shaunna's hand and waited…and then gave her a nudge. Shaunna got up. She sat down again. "What is it, sweetie?" Adele asked, knowing that she wouldn't get an answer.

Shaunna sighed and got up again, this time making it upstairs and into the shower. Adele took the cups through to the kitchen, pretending she wasn't aware of Sean watching her every move as she rinsed them and put them in the drainer. She checked the washing machine was empty and gave the cupboard a quick wipe, turning to look at him once she was done.

"Are you all right, Sean?"

"Yeah. Thanks," he murmured. He was frowning heavily and seemed shocked.

"Are you sure?"

He nodded and took a breath to speak. Adele blinked attentively. He let the breath go and took another one. "Do you know how many years I went to university?"

Adele shook her head.

"And how much studying I have to do to keep my knowledge up to date?"

She shrugged.

"Feckin' loads!"

"That much?" she said and giggled. He smiled.

"I was listening to you getting Shaunna back together, and it made me realise how utterly useless qualifications are."

"Oh, don't be silly. I've known Shaunna nearly all of my life."

"And that was just what she needed."

He got up and hugged her. She found it a little strange, because in her head he was of the same ilk as Josh, which wasn't so in reality, but she didn't know him well enough yet to know any better. She hugged him back and stepped away.

"I can take it from here, you know, if you need to go to work."

"Yeah, I do, but I'm going to stay a little bit longer, if you think that's OK?"

"I'd say so, but what do I know? I'll be upstairs."

She left him again, and he put the kettle on to make more tea. This was the first time he'd been inside Shaunna's house, and other than the wreck of a lounge that had greeted him, it was a wonderful place, full of so many interesting objects. It felt warm and welcoming, and even with his lousy sense of smell, he could pick up a hint of vanilla and spices. The only thing that didn't impress him was the sound of the wind chimes emanating from the garden, although there were far fewer than his next door neighbour possessed, and they were quite tuneful.

He heard conversation from upstairs, followed by the buzz of a hairdryer. He sat down with his cup of tea and checked through his email on his phone. Most of it was junk—book recommendations, discount vouchers for things he'd never buy— but there was one that wasn't junk, and he paused with his finger over it for several minutes, trying to decide if he should read it or delete it outright. *Damned curiosity.*

Hi Sean,

I trust that all is well with you. I thought I should update you on what's happening with me, but I can't do it via email. Can you give me a call sometime? You have my mobile number still, don't you?

Hope everything is progressing well with Marigold.

DS

Sean read the email several times, closed it, opened it again and read it once more, just to make sure.

"Marigold?" he questioned aloud. "Why Marigold?" At their first meeting, Hadyn said Diane Sheridan *always* called him by his name. Sean immediately went to his address book and checked he still had her number, because she'd got his attention, which was precisely why she'd done it. He *would* call her later, but for now, he was brought back to his surroundings by the vision of beauty before him.

"Hello there, lovely." He smiled and stood up to greet her.

Shaunna went into his arms and wept for a long time. When she was done, she opened her bag, took out a psychology textbook and put it down on the table.

He frowned and picked it up. "I don't think I've ever seen anyone cry over research methods before."

She managed a teary laugh. "Can you help me? I'm so far behind with my studies."

"Of course." He glanced up at the clock. He was late for work.

"I don't mean right now," she clarified.

"How does first thing tomorrow sound? I'll bring the breakfast and the highlighters, and you can make the tea."

"That'd be awesome." She was fighting the tears again.

"Come here." He beckoned gently. She did so and cried some more.

"Did you watch Kris on Elliot Sanchez?" she asked through the tears.

"No, but I heard about it. Did you know?"

449

"I knew they were back together." She pulled away again and wiped her eyes, flicking her hair over her shoulders. That was all the crying she was going to do. "So, breakfast tomorrow then?"

Sean smiled and kissed her gently on the cheek. She didn't want to talk about it. That was fine, for she'd told him enough already.

"Breakfast tomorrow then," he repeated. He left soon after.

Shaunna and Adele ate lunch, and walked up to the college together, where Adele went to her English class and Shaunna returned home via the salon, her intention being to officially and calmly resign for real. Hayley told her to go away and think about it.

***

Thursday morning: Sean arrived a little after nine-thirty, armed with two bacon rolls and a massive bag of pick 'n' mix sweets, which he placed in the middle of the table as soon as they'd eaten their breakfast. He waited for Shaunna to settle into the chair opposite and ready her pen over her pad. And then he began to teach her, watching her all the while, as she asked questions, made notes, listened intently, delighted in understanding, laughed at his jokes, frowned in confusion when he failed to adequately explain what he meant, and tormented him for stating the obvious.

Early afternoon: they paused for lunch, and Casper wandered up and down the hallway, wagging his tail and looking up at them expectantly. They took him to the park and played Frisbee, chatting all the while about the morning's lesson, interspersed with comfortable silences, and then back home for another cup of tea. They were done for today, and once again, Sean made her promise to call if she needed him. Shaunna assured him she'd be fine, and he said goodbye.

She wasn't OK, not yet, and that was OK. The last few months had knocked her sideways, but she was on the mend, slowly on her way back to normal. Whatever that was.

What's Wrong with This Picture?
Monday 30th October

First-year undergraduates could be so needy, and it wasn't even a module Josh was responsible for.

"Do a guest lecture, she says," he muttered under his breath as he marched back to his office, 'she' being the professor on whose module he had just given a lecture on the history of psychoanalysis. "It'll be straightforward, only take an hour... Ha!" It was almost eleven o'clock, and the lecture had started at nine, with many of the students arriving late and appearing to believe it was entirely acceptable. It was as well it wasn't his module, or they'd have lost about fifty percent of their intake by now. A month into their degree and already thinking they could turn up when they liked.

Sean had been right, as-bloody-usual, although neither of them ever had a problem with students turning up late, not without prior permission. Still, it was over now—until the next time the hapless professor wanted her undergrads taking in hand—and Josh stopped by the café to pick up a takeaway cappuccino in celebration of that fact. It was lukewarm, and he'd drunk it before he got to his floor, which was probably a good thing, as he wasn't looking where he was going and almost walked straight into Dan.

"Whoa! Alright, mate?" Dan said.

"Hello!" Josh replied, recovering slightly. "What are you doing here?" He unlocked his office door and went inside. Dan followed.

"Thought I'd stop by and give your new place a bit of a gander."

"OK." Josh frowned at him, intrigued. "Did you get my message?"

"Yeah," Dan responded distractedly. He was examining the expanse of bookshelves along the far wall. He nodded at them. "Good bit of craftsmanship, that."

Josh tutted. "Only you would notice the shelves instead of the books. Did you want a coffee? I'm just about to make one."

Dan turned back and examined the empty coffee cup still in Josh's hand.

"I drank it on the way up," he explained. He put the cup in the bin and switched on the kettle, assuming that the answer was 'yes'.

"So, yeah," Dan said, "I'm a bit confused by it, to be honest."

"Why's that?"

"Are you sure you're all right?"

"Well, I've got a meeting with a student at one, but I'm fine until then."

"That wasn't what I meant."

"Oh." Josh continued with making the coffee whilst Dan stood, arms folded, scanning the room.

"It's just that, erm, well." He cleared his throat. "It was all the missed calls."

"Ah, I see." Josh smiled to himself and turned to face Dan. "Sorry about that. I didn't realise how early it was."

"Yeah. You not sleeping?"

"On and off. Last night was the first really bad night since Jess." The kettle boiled, and Josh filled the cups, passing one across.

"Cheers." Dan sat with his thighs spread wide, one ankle resting on the other knee. He noticed Josh analysing his posture. "I must remember to give George a ring later, actually. Me and Andy were talking to the landlord at your local before the summer. He wants to set up a footy team."

"Oh, right. OK." Josh suddenly understood what this visit was really about, and it had nothing whatsoever to do with pub football. He was overwhelmed and tried to cover it with a quick smile of reassurance. "I'm fine, really. Just not sleeping, but whatever, I think George might be up for a bit of that." He blushed. Dan studied him for a moment and decided he believed him.

"What would that make you? A HAB?"

"A what?"

"Husbands and boyfriends."

452

Josh laughed. "Think I might try to steer clear of the WAGs if I do come and watch. Anyway, enough of this nonsense, I did want to talk to you about something, which is why I was calling you at whatever ungodly hour—"

"Ten to four onwards."

"Sorry."

"Don't worry about it. My daughter got me up for real at five. She's decided that now she's three, she's a big girl and doesn't need a nappy anymore. I don't think I've changed a bed as many times in my life as I have during the past month."

"And you still want another one?"

"Yeah."

"Are you mad?"

"Quite possibly. Friday's the day. Again." That was when Adele's period would officially be late; they were quite regular, and usually fell somewhere between twenty-five and twenty-nine days apart. Friday would be day thirty of attempt number three. "Cheers, by the way," Dan said.

"For?"

"Having a word with Adele."

"I didn't."

"Oh. I thought…" Dan brushed imaginary dust from his trousers. "Never mind."

"OK," Josh said, steering them back on track. "I've been trying to get something straight in my mind, and I wanted to see what you knew before I went any further."

"Right?"

"Andy and Jess."

"Yeah?"

"Did he tell you what date they got married?"

Dan shook his head. "No. I think he just said it was when she found out she was sick."

Josh chewed the inside of his cheek in contemplation. "It doesn't fit."

"What d'you mean?"

"The letter she gave us." He went to his desk and opened the drawer, removing a pile of documents, including the envelope

453

containing his card with the print on the front of *The Enchanted Garden*. He passed it across to Dan and gave him a couple of minutes to read over it. Dan shrugged.

"You're gonna have to explain, mate."

"The dates on there: she went to the hospital on Monday the twentieth of March, and she showed me that letter on Friday of the same week."

"OK."

"Then she gave us all copies of that letter and her will the following week, which would have been Tuesday the twenty-eighth."

"And?"

"How much notice do you need to give to get married?"

"Sixteen days…ah!"

"Ah, indeed."

"So…what? You think Andy's lying?"

"That sounds appalling, doesn't it? But, well, yes. I can't think of any other explanation."

Dan rubbed his chin. "I s'pose it is the kind of thing they'd do. Run off and get married, but then, he said my mum and Len witnessed for them, and Mum's not gonna lie. In fact—" he took his phone out "—I'll ask her."

"Why don't you just ask Andy?"

"I could do that, but, err…" Dan couldn't think of a reason quickly enough, because the truth was he hadn't spoken to his brother much since he'd caught him and Shaunna together, and it was both his fortune and misfortune to be dumbstruck in the present company. Whilst Josh wouldn't push him to explain, he'd know there was something going on.

"I agree your mum is probably better. It's amazing to think it's only four weeks today since the funeral."

Dan nodded, although it was in gratitude for Josh hoisting him out of the hole they'd dug between them rather than in agreement with the statement. He made the call. No answer. "What now?"

"I don't know." Josh rubbed his eyes and yawned.

"Tired?"

"Yes. And feeling a bit stressed." He picked up the letter again. "When did Andy go down to Reading?"

"Did he?"

"He did. Jess told me he took her out for pizza when she was working with the Shipleys."

"Did she?"

Josh laughed at Dan's puzzled expression. "Yes, he did, she did—whoever did whatever. So, if I remember correctly, that was the end of January, and she was still down there for my birthday, although she knew there was something wrong before she went."

"Did she?"

"When we went out for the Chinese on Kris's birthday—she knew then, but she was in denial."

"Was she?"

"Would you stop doing that?"

"Sorry, mate. Just ignore me. I'm kind of... I'm really struggling here. Did she tell you she was sick?"

"Not in so many words."

"But you think she might've told Andy?"

"Honestly? I don't know. Before I realised it didn't add up, I'd have said no. She always kept things to herself, but if she was going to tell anyone, and I know this sounds conceited, but—"

"She'd have told you," Dan finished. Josh nodded. "That's not conceited. It's the truth. It's what we've all always done."

"However, given that her will refers to him as her husband, and we've had it since the twenty-eighth of March, I can't think of any other explanation."

"OK, so let's assume that they got married in, what? February?"

"Yes. It'd have to be, and it must have been after my birthday, because he put the loft stairs in."

"OK. So the fifteenth or thereabouts." Dan tried to think back to whether Andy had been away during that period. "I'll try my mum again." He pressed the call button; this time, she answered straight away.

"Hi, Mum. Quick question. When did Andy and Jess get married?"

"Hello, Daniel. I'm fine, thanks for asking."

455

"Sorry. It's important."

"It was a Thursday..." Dan could hear the sound of pages turning in the background and knew she'd be checking her diary. "Yeah. It was the eighteenth."

"Thursday the eighteenth," Dan repeated back.

Josh shook his head. "Can't have been. My birthday was a Tuesday."

Dan frowned. "This year, Mum?"

"Of course this year! When else would it've been? Honest to God, you do something for one son and get the bloody third degree off the others. I'd have thought by now you'd have all grown out of that."

"OK, Mother! I was just checking!"

"Well, when did you think it was?"

"It's...oh, it doesn't matter. So, you're sure it was the eighteenth of February?"

"May."

"What?"

"Not February, May. Thursday, the eighteenth of May."

"And you're absolutely sure about that?"

"Oh, now let me see. My son got married, could I be mistaken?" Her tone was very sarcastic.

"Yeah, all right. I'll be round later. I'll explain then, OK?"

"Fine. I'll let to get on."

"Thanks, Mum. Bye." He ended the call and shrugged at Josh, who had heard her repeat the date and looked as flabbergasted as Dan felt. "I don't know what to think," Dan said.

"No. Me neither, although that date rings a bell for some reason."

They both sat in silence for a while, sipping at the last of their almost cold coffee.

"Could she have replaced the wills?" Dan suggested. Josh looked at him in disbelief. "Yeah, stupid suggestion. Or maybe they planned it in advance?"

Josh shrugged. "Maybe." He drummed his fingers on his chin. "That date—I was trying to recall if it was somebody's birthday or…I don't know. Well, I suppose there's no point in blindly speculating. Do you want me to talk to Andy?"

"Nah, it's all right. I'll catch up with him later and see what he says." Dan got up and passed his empty cup back to Josh. "I'll give you a call and let you know."

"OK. Good luck."

"Cheers."

Josh waited until Dan reached the door. "Dan?"

"Yeah, mate?"

"Thanks."

"No problem."

***

In the office two doors down the corridor, Sean was trying to make sense of an entirely different mystery, and he was more than a little bit angry.

"OK," he said, "to recap, you were approached by a high-ranking police officer who told you to arrange to send Hadyn to me, and you didn't say anything about it."

Diane nodded and examined her shoe.

"Why?"

"I wasn't allowed to."

"No, I got that. But why send Hadyn to me?"

"They didn't say."

Sean sat back and rubbed his eyes. "Why do you think it is?"

Diane looked up from her shoes and shrugged. "I don't know, but…can I talk off the record?"

"Sure."

"I mean totally off the record, Sean. This goes no further than these four walls."

"Did I tell anyone that you gave me Kevin Callaghan's files?"

"Not to my knowledge."

"All right, I'll be up-front with you, Diane. I told Josh, because I trust him completely. There's something very odd going on here, I'm sure you'll agree, and there's a lot more to it than you are perhaps aware of. People's lives could be in danger, so I really need to know what you know, and I swear on my son's life that I will tell no-one but Josh whatever you choose to divulge now."

Diane examined Sean's face, and he held her gaze. "I trust you," she said. "I do. I trust you absolutely, but I've lost everything, Sean. My job, my house, my career. I've been expelled from the BPS. It sounds melodramatic, I know, but the only thing I've got left is my liberty, and I can't lose that. I've seen it destroy countless lives. I'd end up taking Callaghan's route."

Sean laughed dryly. "I'd like to be able to reassure you and say you *are* being melodramatic, but I'm not so sure."

It didn't comfort her much to hear that, but it did make her mind up.

"Hadyn shouldn't have been released when he was. When I said he took Kevin's death badly, I mean really badly. He attacked a prison officer, and they cancelled his parole. Don't get me wrong, he didn't do him any serious harm, and I spoke to him before his release. I believe him when he says it was because the officer got too close, and in general he was very stable, but he should have served his full sentence on the basis of that incident. Then, all of a sudden, this police superintendent's on the scene, Hadyn's being released, and I'm being 'advised' to persuade you to take him on."

Sean was stunned, utterly speechless. He rubbed his head, he folded his arms, he sat forward, then back again, pinched his nose between his forefingers, all of it without a word. Finally, after many minutes of trying to make sense of what he'd just heard, he collated the evidence and presented his findings.

"He's an informant."

"Yes," Diane agreed. "It certainly looks that way to me."

"Which means the police know Callaghan was innocent."

"So it would seem."

Sean exhaled heavily and scratched his head. "Oh, Jesus. What the hell am I to do with this?"

Hurlyburly
Tuesday 31st October

"Read this."

Josh shoved the folded scrap of paper into Sean's hand. He glanced down at it, and then back at Josh.

"Why?"

"Just read it and tell me what you think."

Sean blinked a couple of times and looked at it again, squinting to focus on the small, swirly writing.

> Nought's had, all's spent,
> Where our desire is got without content.
> 'Tis safer to be that which we destroy
> Than by destruction dwell in doubtful joy.

"OK, I've read it, so?"

"Well?"

"Well what? What do you want me to say? It's Shakespeare."

"Well spotted!"

"Can you give me a clue?"

"Do you recognise anything else about it?"

Sean shrugged. "It's Jessie's handwriting?"

"OK. Now we're getting somewhere."

"You know, I've got a banging headache, and Soph's bringing Dylan within the hour, so if you wouldn't mind just getting on with it."

Josh huffed. Since yesterday, he'd had what he considered to be a very good night's sleep and was once again firing on all cylinders. As such, he'd been able to think things through with a little more clarity and had reached a number of startling conclusions. First and foremost, Dan's mother was right; Jess and Andy had got married on Thursday the eighteenth of May. He'd checked the public records, not because he didn't believe Barbara; he just needed to see it with his own eyes.

Secondly, having discussed it with George, he now knew that the date had stood out because it was the first slot they'd been offered for their own wedding, which suggested that Jess and Andy had booked theirs around the same time, in which case they must have discussed their intentions before Jess distributed the wills—either that or she performed some kind of magic trick to swap all eight copies after the event. He'd yet to hear from Dan on that score, but the will was dated March the twenty-second so there was no other explanation for it.

Lastly, the 'Savies' note, as Sean had pointed out, was Shakespearean in origin, but it wasn't right. However, Josh didn't want to lead the witness, which was why he was being so cagey and obscure.

"Jess left me that note, in a place only I would find it."

"You mean she left it for you to find after she'd gone?"

"Yes."

"Interesting. Why do you think that is?"

"I've no idea, which is why I'm showing it to you. Do you recognise where it's from?"

Sean rubbed his eyes and looked at the note again. "*Hamlet*, presumably?"

"What makes you think that?"

"What you said in your eulogy. That you and she used that play as a means of communicating complex emotions, which is wonderfully poetic, if not a little bizarre, or perhaps not—for you two."

"What are you trying to say? That Jess and I had trouble communicating our emotional state?"

Sean shrugged smugly and laughed at Josh's affronted expression, quickly discovering that laughing really, *really* hurt. He screwed up his eyes.

"Is your headache that bad?" Josh asked.

"Yeah."

"Can't you ask Sophie to swap nights?"

"She's got a meeting with her supervisor. I'm sure it'll pass."

"Take a painkiller."

Sean raised his eyebrow—unintentionally, because that hurt, too. Josh knew there would be no painkillers in the house; it was another lasting legacy.

"I'll pop home and get some if you like," he offered.

"I'm fine, for now."

"Or we can babysit for you."

"You're offering to babysit?"

"Yes!" Josh tried to look outraged, but failed. He grinned. "George will be home in an hour."

Sean made a conscious effort not to roll his eyes. "Thanks, but I think I'll be all right. I've got to keep in mind that if I was doing the parenting on my own, I'd have no choice."

"Well, the offer stands."

"It's OK. Really. Anyway, this verse."

"Hm. It's not *Hamlet*. It's *Macbeth*."

"It's still a tragedy."

"True. But it's still *Macbeth*. Specifically, these are lines delivered by Lady Macbeth after her husband kills Duncan. They're about regret and fear."

"They're common emotions when you're facing death."

"I'm not disputing that, but there are plenty of passages she could have extracted from *Hamlet* that would have conveyed the same message."

"No," Sean said, shaking his head and very quickly wishing he hadn't. "Not so." He winced and closed his eyes. "I might take you up on your first offer."

Josh nodded and got up. "Won't be long."

Sean sat back and rubbed his temples. He was going to have to do something about his sinuses. The headaches were becoming far too frequent, but he hated going to the doctor. Of course, having to work through what Diane Sheridan had told him wasn't helping matters at all, because he couldn't think of a way to frame it so Josh didn't immediately act on it. If Hadyn was an informant and had deliberately positioned himself in Black Hole Studios, then there was something going on with Jason. Oh, for a common or garden ethical dilemma instead of this crazy crime drama romping through his poor addled brain.

Josh returned with the painkillers and brought Sean some water. He swallowed both pills in one go.

"So what were you saying?" Josh prompted.

"Err…" Sean had to work hard to think what he'd been saying. "Yeah. Hamlet. His intentions are honourable, and his counterpart, Ophelia, is good and pure. In contrast, Macbeth is potentially innocent but is seduced by greed, which is how Lady Macbeth is able to coerce him into killing the king."

"And there I was, thinking you only knew about Maslow and Rogers."

Sean smiled wryly. "You said you and Jessie used the lines of Hamlet and Ophelia in character, so it stands to reason she was using the lines of Macbeth and Lady Macbeth in the same way."

"She put herself in the role of Lady Macbeth?"

"I'd say so."

"Which means she's asking me to do something I consider morally reprehensible."

"Possibly."

"Like what?"

Sean wasn't sure he should answer that question. It was a good few months ago now, that he and Jess had spoken about it, but she was gone, so what did it matter?

"Look, Sean," Josh appealed, "the note you have in your hand was meant for my eyes only. I trust you."

"I know you do, Joshy." Sean rubbed his head with the flat of his hand, trying to ease the throbbing within. Somehow the words 'I trust you' didn't sound quite so soothing just at this moment. "OK, I'll tell you, but you're not to go beating yourself up about it." He paused, giving both of them time to prepare for what he was about to reveal. "I think she was hoping you'd assist her to end her life."

Josh registered the words, but they didn't sink in properly for a good few seconds, and when they did, they brought with them the realisation of what that meant. "Why would she do that?" he asked, even though he knew the answer.

"For that reason, yes," Sean said gently, "but she also loved and trusted you to do what was right for her and make sure no-one found out about it."

Josh folded his arms and stared across the room, trying to think. It still didn't make sense. She'd had an advance directive in place; Sean or Eleanor could have done what she'd been asking, if that was, indeed, what she'd been asking. He carried on gazing into the mid-distance as he spoke.

"You smoked when you were at school, didn't you?"

"I did," Sean confirmed.

"Did you have savies?"

"You mean where you share a cigarette with someone else?" Josh nodded.

"Yeah, we did."

"Jess and I used to do savies, but it became more than saving the second half of the cigarette for each other. We'd buy a packet between us and leave it in a secret place—our 'Savies' place. That was how the *Hamlet* stuff started. I forgot to leave the cigarettes for her one time, and she was a bit cross about it, as you can imagine, so the next packet I bought, I opened out the foil in the top and wrote on it, 'The fair Ophelia: Nymph, in thy orisons Be all my sins remember'd.'"

Sean glanced down at the small square of foiled paper, understanding now why she had chosen that medium.

Josh continued. "She didn't say anything about it, and I thought she hadn't seen it. Then, a few months later, we'd had an argument and we weren't talking, but she must have known I'd look in Savies, and she'd left a note for me: 'My lord, I have remembrances of yours, That I have longed long to re-deliver; I pray you, now receive them.'

"I was bloody furious. You know how it is—returning belongings to someone is basically saying it's over. So I went straight round to her house to have it out with her, which is exactly what she'd played for. We screamed and shouted and got it out of our system, and then we made up."

"Why did you fall out?" Sean asked.

"I don't remember."

Sean looked at him dubiously.

"Oh, all right. It wasn't anything exciting. She and Rob had just started seeing each other, and she kept abandoning me during our study sessions, which I assumed was so she could spend time with Rob, but then he had a go at me, about keeping his girlfriend away from him. It turned out she was seeing someone else behind his back. I liked him, so I stood up for him. She told me to stop interfering, and it escalated from there."

"God, she was such a floozy."

"She was, too. There's only George and me in our friendship group that she didn't make a move on, although I think she tried a few times and didn't get anywhere."

"You're joking me."

"Out of the men, I mean."

"I gathered that much, but Dan and Kris as well?"

"Yes. Kris was a bit of a non-starter. The only woman he's ever had eyes for is Shaunna." Josh sensed Sean tense at the mention of her name. "Maybe we won't go there for now."

"No, best not," Sean agreed.

"Is she coping?"

"I think so. She did that hair flicking thing."

"She's fine, then. See, that's what I mean about Jess. She never changed. She was always a floozy; she always confided in me, and she always quoted Ophelia back at me, not Desdemona, or Juliet, or Lady Macbeth. Ophelia. And nor would I have found the note before she died, not where she left it."

"Which was?"

"Under a loose flag in the churchyard." Josh put his head forward, hiding behind his hair.

Sean leaned over a little, trying to peer underneath the shield. "What's so bad about that?"

464

"It's embarrassing."

"Why? Most kids have a secret place, or, at least, somewhere they think is secret till they grow up and discover it was nothing of the sort."

Josh sighed. "I suppose you're right."

"So why are you embarrassed?"

"Because…" Josh lifted his head but still kept his hair over his eyes. "Because we promised that when one of us died, we'd come back and meet each other there."

"And that's what Savies is."

Josh nodded. "Which is why she'd have known that if I did go there at all, it would only be after she was gone." He shrugged. "None of it makes sense. She married Andy after she'd referred to him as her husband in her will, and she's quoting the wrong play at me. There's something amiss."

"I'm sure it'll sort itself out soon," Sean said, distracted by the sound of his front door opening. A moment later, Sophie came into view, carrying Dylan's car seat, with Dylan sitting in it. Sean was immediately on his feet and went over to his son, who was wide awake and kicking his legs.

"Hello, little feller," Sean cooed. Dylan smiled up at him.

"Guess who laughed for the first time today?" Sophie said in a babytalk voice.

"Did ya?" Sean asked. He unfastened the straps and lifted Dylan clear. "Did you laugh at your mummy? She makes me laugh, too. Yes, she does." He rubbed noses with Dylan, and gave Sophie a kiss. "Everything all right?"

"Yeah, fine. And it was at George, actually. We went up to the café at the farm this afternoon."

"That's early."

"It was almost three o'clock."

"I meant for Dylan to start laughing," Sean clarified.

Sophie grinned at him. She'd known that's what he'd meant all along, and he was right. Dylan was just coming up to ten weeks old, so it was quite young for him to be laughing, although Hay said one of hers had laughed around that age and then hadn't done it again until the other two were doing it all the time. Still, every parent likes to think their child is advanced beyond their age, and Sophie wasn't about to spoil the illusion for Sean.

"You OK?" she asked. "You're a bit pale."

"Headache. Otherwise, I'm fine, too. What time are you back?"

"How d'you fancy an overnighter?"

Sean's eyes lit up at the prospect, in spite of his headache. Dylan had only stayed with him overnight twice, both times with Sophie also staying.

"Is that a yes?"

"Of course!"

"Cool. I'll be here between eight-thirty and nine in the morning, if that's all right?"

"Perfect."

"Right, I'm outta here. Got a man to see about a paper on toddler-centred rational emotive therapy. Bye, Josh."

"See you, Sophie."

She gave Dylan a kiss and left.

"I'm going, too," Josh said. "I agreed to cook dinner. Not sure what, although fillet of a fenny snake with a dash of eye of newt would seem most apt."

"Sounds delightful. Us guys might pop round later, see if you've further unravelled your latest great mystery and maybe I'll share one of my own that I've been brewing, just for you."

"Fun, isn't it?"

"It certainly doesn't leave much room for boredom, I'll give you that." He saw Josh to the door and closed it behind him. "Right, Mister." Dylan went glassy-eyed and started to grunt. "Ah. Not so much of a mystery what you're up to, now, is there?"

And so began Sean's first night of flying solo.

Sleepless And Unsettled
Wednesday 1st November

Sean waved Sophie and Dylan off and went straight upstairs for a shower. He had a whole day at the hospice ahead of him, and he'd had next to no sleep, but it was nothing to do with his son. Dylan had been an absolute gem, waking up just the once, a little after three, for a feed and a nappy change. And it was whilst Sean sat, cuddling his baby and being grateful that the headache had gone, that he finally started to get his thoughts straightened out.

Soon after, father and son fell asleep together on the sofa, with the TV quietly mumbling away in the background; every so often Sean would half awaken, give his neck a bit of a stretch, look down at Dylan in his arms and be overwhelmed by the rush of love and protectiveness he felt towards him. It was a truly astonishing feeling, and he shed a tear or two along the way.

His thoughts, then, were thus: of Josh. He was obsessing over Jess's death, as was his way, looking for answers where there were no questions, chasing after ghosts. Telling Josh what Diane had said may even serve as a useful distraction, give him something else to obsess over. But was it simply a case of sharing the burden? Sean had promised not to act on what he knew; he would be asking the same of Josh, therefore, what point was there to knowing? Hadyn was a plant, although to what end it was impossible to say. Did the police believe Jason was guilty after all? Or did they know the identity of the real murderer and were trying to keep Jason safe?

Our police protectors.

Sean had never been enamoured of the work of the boys in blue, not growing up where he did, living in the shadows of injustice, where civil liberties were systematically abused in the name of peace. Granted, his dealings with the police since moving to England had always been positive, but he still couldn't bring himself to trust them, not to protect the innocent, if the innocent were deemed worthless. Kevin Callaghan was a doctor, a respected member of the community, not a disaffected twenty-three-year-old with no qualifications and a criminal record, and if they'd let Callaghan take the fall, they'd have no qualms whatsoever about letting Hadyn tumble.

Still, there was a possibility that he would provide them with whatever it was they needed, and then he would be set free for real.

Aye, there's the rub.

For the love he'd felt for the sweet, innocent bundle sleeping in his arms, had imparted a wisdom that could not be procured from books and years of study. Krissi Johansson: the girl with nine parents. If any one of the surviving eight found out that she was in danger, even by the proxy of her friendship with Jason, they would be bound to act upon it.

Which was why Sean wasn't going to tell Josh about Hadyn.

Not this Time
Thursday 2nd November

"Think of it this way," Adele said, "you get another month of lots and lots of sex."

Dan scowled and heaved the last of the bags of shopping out of the boot.

"It's not my fault!" Adele snapped.

"I didn't say it was."

"So stop acting like it is."

He ignored her and took the bags inside.

"I know why you're being so vile about it." She followed him into the kitchen.

"Because I'm disappointed."

"It's because of that car."

"It's got nothing to do with the car."

"You were fine before we left."

"I'm fine now!"

"You're not!"

"And even if I'm not, how is that anything to do with the car? Maybe it's the shopping."

"It's not. It's the car."

"There's nothing wrong with the car!" Dan started slamming things inside cupboards.

"Here, give me that," Adele said, shoving him to one side. He backed off with his arms raised. Adele continued to speak as she took over putting the groceries away. "Do you like that car?"

"It's decent enough. Economical, comfortable, lots of boot space."

Adele stopped and glowered at him. "That's not what I asked."

"No. I bloody hate it. I want a convertible."

"So get one."

"Don't be stupid. We won't fit child seats—"

"Dan." She said his name quietly, slowly moving towards him. "What if it never happens?" She reached up and put her arms around his neck. "What if we don't get pregnant again?"

"We will," he said, smoothing her hair.

"But if we don't you're going to hold it against me, because of the car."

Dan laughed.

"You know it's true. You'll say it was all a waste of time and complain forever about driving around in a comfortable, economical saloon for no reason. And I can't be bothered with all of that. Life's too short to listen to you harping on about cars. So, I've got a proposal for you."

"I'm listening."

"Talk to Len about getting the car you want."

"What's in it for you?"

"I want you to stop calling me stupid."

"That sounds too easy. I'm missing something here."

"That's all."

He eyed her suspiciously. "What about having another baby?"

"What about it?" She stood on tiptoes and nipped his chin with her teeth. "We'll just have to keep practising till we get it right."

Dogged Determination
Saturday 4th November

"I'm so excited!" Josh was almost skipping down the road. "I've wanted to do this for months."

George tutted. "Why didn't you say something?" He was having a little more trouble than usual keeping Blue calm because of Josh's excitement at going walking together in the woods.

"I didn't want to be in the way. The Saturday morning walk is your time together."

"Hmm, we'll see about that." George hadn't spoken to Kris since his appearance on the *Elliot Sanchez Show* two weeks previously, when he'd announced to the world, and his closest friends, that he was back with Ade.

Kris had got home from Brighton last weekend, and where Josh would normally have pushed George to contact him and sort things out, this time he hadn't, partly so he got the opportunity to do the Saturday morning walk in the woods, but mostly because the fallout with Eleanor had cast a new and most elucidating light on their entire situation.

She was right, he accepted. Their relationship had changed, and it was part of a ripple effect spreading through their group. Losing Jess had dramatically shifted the dynamics, with people realigning themselves, much as they had in the years after they left school.

Yet he and Eleanor had been the constant in 'The Circle', the firm friendship around which the others revolved. They were the bearings, stabilising and steering the others back on track, now seemingly unable and unwilling to do anything but watch as they rolled away from each other. Maybe it was his doing to a certain extent, but she also had to take responsibility, and she wasn't prepared to do that. It was he who had changed; that's what she believed, and if he could change, then he could unchange, if their friendship mattered to him at all.

The situation with George and Kris was no different, in that they hadn't changed either, but the bisexuality issue had always been something George struggled with, so they'd left it alone, both afraid to poke at the wasps' nest. Kris's interview had been the metaphorical equivalent of charging full-speed ahead with a big pointy stick.

So, their plans for the morning weren't set in stone, but Shaunna, Kris and Casper were meeting them at the gate to the woods as usual, apart from their expansion in number, and then they'd walk, and they'd talk. It wasn't a location that guaranteed protection from the prying eyes of the media. Indeed, this was where the photos published earlier in the year had been taken, but photos told only part of the story, and it was a story that was now in the public eye.

To the woods, then. Neutral territory: the realm of the Dog People.

"Good morning." Kris smiled nervously.

"Good morning," George replied with not a trace of good humour. "You OK?"

"Yeah, thanks. You?"

"Fine."

They released the dogs. Shaunna and Josh glanced at each other and fell in behind the two friends so recently yet devastatingly estranged. The dogs tore off through the trees, a flash of black pursuing yellow, then yellow tearing after black, in and out, in and out, weaving through the thick dark trunks, scuffing up the fallen leaves with their game of chase.

"How are you doing?" Shaunna asked so quietly that it was only Josh who heard her.

"I'm much better, thank you."

"That's good."

"And you? Are you all right?" The rest of the words weren't needed to qualify the myriad reasons she might not be.

472

"I am. Sean helped me catch up with my studies. I hadn't realised how stressed I was about being behind. Now we've just got to sort this mess out." She nodded towards George and Kris a long way ahead of them, still not talking and with three feet of space between them.

"They'll get there," Josh comforted. "It's not like they've never fallen out before, is it?"

"True. So, have you spoken to Ellie since—"

"No. Next question."

"Sorry."

"It's OK. I've calmed down a bit, but I wonder what's becoming of us all. Why can't we talk to each other anymore?"

"It's that weird post-bereavement thing," Shaunna said knowledgeably.

"What do you mean?"

"Everyone's hypersensitive, trying too hard not to say or do anything that might upset someone else and then ending up doing it anyway. Like after my mum died, I had this conversation with my aunty. She phoned me, and she was just rambling on about the roses in her garden. They are lovely and everything, but it was so random that I didn't know what to say, so I said nothing, and she made some snide comment about how selfish I was being, then hung up on me. It turned out my cousin was pregnant, and I only found out six months later, when I got a card with a photo of the baby inside. My aunty had phoned to tell me but couldn't find a way to do it without upsetting me."

Josh nodded. "I understand now. This is the first death I've had to deal with as an adult, and it's making a mockery of everything I've said to clients over the years. I feel like such a fraud. This guy who comes to see me lost his wife in a car accident. He's been coming now for almost nine months, and the first thing he told me was that he sees ghosts. I thought once we started making progress with his counselling, it would stop the erm…"

"Hallucinations?" Shaunna suggested with the slightest hint of mischief.

"That's exactly what I was getting at. I've been treating him as if he's completely bonkers, but now I'm not so sure, not that I'm

473

seeing ghosts or anything like that, but—oh, I don't know. This stuff with Jess's will is mind-boggling. I need answers so I can put it behind me."

"Hey, maybe you could ask your client to have a chat with her," Shaunna suggested. Josh turned and looked at her. She grinned.

"Am I seeing things that aren't there?"

She shrugged. It wasn't an intentionally dismissive gesture, but he got the feeling she did think he was making more of it than he ought.

"Yes, all right," he said. "I'm going to catch up with Andy this week, and then I'm going to let it go. Has he said anything to you about it?"

"I, err, I haven't seen him for a while." She gave him a quick smile.

He acknowledged her response with no more than a nod, but it was enough to reassure her that he wasn't going to ask any more questions. Nonetheless, it created a moment of tension between them, and she looped her arm through his.

"How good is this?"

Josh smiled and squeezed her hand. "I know!"

"Why haven't we done this before?"

"Because it's not ours to have."

"I suppose not. We're just the referees?"

"Mediators."

"Same difference, isn't it?"

"More or less. Referees sounds too sporty. We're academic."

"Ha-ha! *We* are, aren't we?"

"So what have you been learning?"

"Not much really. I know what the key features of an experiment are, and that friendships are built on the potential for intimacy and trust…"

*

Several feet in front of them, the silence was about to be bravely breached.

"I'm not going to wade through a ton of crap to get to this," Kris said. "I'm going to get straight to the point, if that's OK with you, because I can't take this silence."

"OK." George continued to look directly ahead, but he was listening.

"I am truly, truly sorry for what I said. I meant every word of it, but I should've talked to you before I went on TV. I love you so much, and it kills me that you can't understand what it's like to be me, because you know me better than anyone, and if you don't understand me, then no-one will."

"So help me out a little," George said. Kris looked across at him; George still refused to make eye contact.

"Help you how?"

"To understand. Because it's not that I don't want to. I can't."

"Have you ever tried?" Kris asked. George opened his mouth to reply, but Kris carried on speaking. "I mean *really* tried? Or did you get so caught up in feeling betrayed that you couldn't see the, err, woods for the trees?"

George managed to squeeze out a laugh. Casper came into view, paused on the path ahead of them to stare up into the branches of a tree, and then started running around it in circles.

"Squirrel!" George and Kris said in unison, watching as the giddy Labrador bounced up and down at the base of the tree, his tail wagging frantically. Blue appeared, took one look at Casper, and returned to his humans, specifically George, plodding along sensibly at his side.

*

"That is one well-behaved dog," Shaunna remarked to Josh. "How does he do it? Do you know the secret?"

"Not a clue, I'm afraid. I wish I did. Monty's coming to stay on Monday. He's George's mum's dog, and he's almost as terrifying as she is."

"What is he?"

"He's a, erm…" Josh sighed. "He's a West Highland terrier."

Shaunna burst out laughing. "I thought you were going to say a Doberman or something. A Westie?" She carried on laughing.

"Right, Hennessy, you are officially invited round for dinner one evening, then let's see who's laughing."

"Accepted!"

They passed Casper, still fixated on the squirrel in the tree, and Shaunna whistled him. Josh rubbed his ear.

"Sorry." She grinned. She had quite a whistle on her, which was no bad thing, as it had got Casper's attention. He was now walking in front of her, backwards, waiting for his Frisbee to be thrown, but she didn't have it. "Kris!" she shouted. He turned, saw the dog and did the necessary with the Frisbee.

*

"You were saying," George prompted.

"Actually, I asked you a question."

"Ah, yeah. So you did." He didn't want to answer it, but Kris had been brave enough to speak out, so maybe he owed him that much. "You're right. I didn't try, because I did feel very betrayed." He waited for Kris to throw the Frisbee again. "You kept on and on about how hiding the truth was the same as lying, and how we were paving a future for other pupils, but I didn't want to pave the future. I wanted to get through school without always feeling like I was gonna get my head kicked in. You were braver than me. I admired that, and I know it made a difference, but being your friend was hard. Everyone assumed they knew me, and I ended up caught between lying or coming out, when I didn't want to do either. So I stayed quiet and let them assume what they liked."

"That *was* brave, George," Kris said.

"How? How was it brave?"

"Do you remember the fight before Jono?"

"Which one?"

"Hey, it wasn't that bad!"

"Really? Are you talking about the one where you couldn't understand why I didn't get turned on by girly pictures, or the one where you screamed 'two-timing shit' at me across the school field, or the one—"

Kris interrupted angrily, "The one where you said you wished you were bisexual so you'd never have to worry about being

476

labelled 'the gay striker' because you could pretend to be straight, too."

Shaunna and Josh had heard every word of their interchange and slowed to a halt to put some space between them.

Kris launched the Frisbee and sent it flying at speed into a tree. It stuck. "Fuck." He started to walk over, but George put Kris's hand on his arm.

"I'll get it." George shinned up the first couple of feet and reached across, stretching his fingers as far as he could and just about making contact with the disc. It fell to the floor, and Casper scooped it up, taking it to Shaunna. George returned to Kris, and they carried on walking.

"Sorry," Kris mumbled.

"OK."

"I'm still not over the Jono situation."

"I figured."

"You know what got me about it the most?"

"Aside from you getting caught up on the whole stupid thing of him being 'gifted', you mean?"

Kris managed a smile. "Yeah, aside from that."

They were coming up on the stream now, where they would soon be joined by Phyllis and her two spaniels. They needed to reach a truce before that happened.

"It was the fact that he wasn't gay," Kris explained in a quiet voice, and not out of fear of being overheard. It had never stopped hurting.

"You said that at the time, and I still don't get why it mattered. We'd broken up."

"Sort of."

"We had broken up, I promise. I wouldn't have two-timed you, however much you hurt me, and you did, but it wasn't about you being bi. It was the fact that you'd been there at my side all through high school, and the more I watched you and listened to what you were saying, the more I believed you were right. I was ready to tell everyone, and then suddenly you weren't gay anymore, and I couldn't do it on my own.

"Then we were back together, but you couldn't stop talking about Shaunna, and I could see it was real, the way you felt about her. I don't understand it, how you can be sexually attracted to her and to Ade, and I don't care about that, by the way. It's been the worst year ever, and I'm really happy for you and Ade. We can work that bit out later, but why go on TV and tell the world that people were hurt because they assumed that you were gay when you weren't? You made a liar of me, Kris. On live TV!"

"I know. It was unforgivable," he said, ashamed. "That's why I need to explain." He spotted the spaniels heading their way. "I got asked to go on a schools tour. It's part of an LGBT anti-bullying campaign, and the organisers want to keep the message as straightforward as possible. I'm sorry I didn't explain first. I didn't have time."

Phyllis came into view and waved. George and Kris waved back.

"Be yourself," George said. "What's more straightforward than that?"

"Good morning!" Phyllis greeted them.

"Hi, Phyllis." George smiled. Kris nodded solemnly and tried to pull himself together.

"We've missed you these past few weeks, Kris." She put her hand up to shield herself from the splashing. "How was Brighton?"

"Not as bad as I thought it would be."

"That's good." She peered along the spring to where Josh and Shaunna were standing together, deep in conversation. "A family outing?"

George laughed. "Yeah, something like that."

"Incidentally, you might like to know that there's a photographer sitting in a car at the gate. I noticed him arrive as I did." It had become a weekly game since the photos appeared in the magazine, and Phyllis was very good at spotting the paparazzi.

"Thanks for the warning," Kris said. "I'll make sure I'm on my best behaviour." He smiled innocently, and she chuckled.

"I imagine they'd still manage to snatch an incriminating shot of you even if you were."

Josh and Shaunna were walking over.

478

"Hey, Phyllis." Josh smiled and shook her hand.

"Hello, Josh. Lovely to see you again. Congratulations on your marriage."

"Thanks. Wow, it seems so long ago."

Shaunna and Phyllis were watching the dogs and occasionally sneaking glances at each other, hoping someone might think to introduce them. It wasn't looking likely, so Phyllis opted for small talk instead.

"George tells me you went to Cornwall for your honeymoon, Josh. What a beautiful place it is. We used to go there all the time when I was a child."

"Yes. It is beautiful. We had a lovely time."

The Frisbee relay was about to commence, with Casper watching and waiting for someone to throw it, so he could complete the first leg.

Kris paused, shaking his head at Casper seesawing with excitement. The disc spun off along the path, and Casper went tearing after it, picked it up and promptly dropped it into the spring, where Blue was already in position and went charging through the water to retrieve it. He grabbed it and cleared the bank in one leap, dropping the Frisbee at Kris's feet.

"What the…?" Shaunna began. She watched, stunned, as the game was repeated, and then again. She started to laugh. "I would never have believed it if I hadn't seen it with my own eyes. I'm totally going to train him to help with the washing when we get home."

Phyllis frowned and looked from Kris to Shaunna and back again.

Shaunna stepped towards her and held out her hand. "Seeing as this lot are too rude, I'll introduce myself. I'm Shaunna—Kris's wife-ex-wife." She gave Kris a smile.

"Wife-ex-wife?"

"Well, we're separated, but we still share a house."

"Oh, yes. I recall you telling Elliot Sanchez that now," Phyllis said to Kris. "What an appalling little man he is."

"He's not so bad off-camera," Kris defended, "and he did apologise after. Most people think we're freaks."

"Not at all! It seems very sensible to me," Phyllis said. "If you get along with each other, why give up what you've worked so hard to build in the first place?"

"Our sentiments exactly," Shaunna agreed.

"On the other hand, if I could get my lump of a husband to find his own place, I'd be utterly delighted."

*

Whilst the conversation had been taking place, Josh and George had wandered up ahead and were now stopped midway across the arched bridge, leaning on the rail and looking down on the dogs splashing in the stream below. George hooked his fingers through Josh's.

"Are you OK?" Josh asked.

George nodded.

"Brain still connected to mouth?"

George nodded again.

"Prove it."

George smiled. "I love you."

"You pass. I love you, too, but what's this?" He tilted his head at their hands.

"I promised you on our honeymoon that I was going to try and be more out for you, but I haven't."

"You told that council woman, didn't you?"

"Yeah, but…" George frowned. "Kris just explained why he said what he said, and I told him to be himself, then realised how hypocritical it was, saying that to him, and telling you that you needed to open up to everyone. And it messed up your friendship with Ellie, while I'm carrying on as always, letting people make up their own minds about me."

"That doesn't make you a hypocrite. You don't lie about it, do you? If someone asks you directly, you tell them the truth."

"But if they get it wrong, and they usually do if you're not with me, then I let them carry on believing whatever they like."

"Except the council woman."

"I think I was feeling brave because I had my mum there."
George shifted so he could look properly at Josh. "I'm going to
join the pub football team with Dan and Andy."

"Are you?"

"Yeah. And I'm gonna tell everyone from the outset, because I
want you to come and watch the games."

Josh smiled. "Is that so?"

"Uh-huh." George moved closer.

"You're going to kiss me up here on this bridge when the
paparazzi are parked outside?"

"Well, it seems public announcements are all the rage." George
leaned in and kissed Josh, slowly bringing him into his arms. He
didn't release him for a very long time.

*

Down on the bank of the spring, Phyllis noticed them and
smiled. "I don't know why I thought you and George were
together," she said to Kris.

He looked up and tutted. "Yeah. They're perfect, aren't they?"
he muttered. He didn't mean it as a jibe, but that's how it came
across.

"Time to move on," Phyllis said. "Lovely to meet you,
Shaunna."

"You, too."

They waved and watched Phyllis head off. Her two spaniels
stopped on the bank to shake and followed obediently.

"Did you explain?" Shaunna asked Kris once they were alone.

"Yeah, but I don't know if it made any difference." He turned
away from her.

"Hey," she said gently. She turned him back again and put her
arms around him. He cried quietly.

"I'm fucking everything up."

"No, you're not."

"I am. I'm trying to get it right."

"And you are."

"I'm sorry."

"What for?"

"For asking you to stay with me."

"Is it what you want?"

"Yes."

"Then don't be sorry." She pulled away and took a tissue from her pocket, lifting his face to dab gently at the tears. "But you have to promise me that you'll quit *Shadows*. It's making you ill."

"I know. I want to go back to the radio stuff. Get my life back. Our life."

"We will. Come on. Let's go and collect love's middle-aged dream and get out of the way of prying cameras."

Kris sniffed and laughed. "They're really sicky."

"Vomit inducingly so, but so are we."

Shaunna did one of her loud whistles with her fingers and made Josh and George jump.

"Fuck, that's loud!" Josh said.

"You ready?" Shaunna called.

They nodded and made their way over, and the six of them sauntered back through the woods. George still held Josh's hand initially, but then broke away so he could join Kris. Shaunna dropped back and walked with Josh again.

"Hey," George said quietly. Kris looked at him and tried to smile. "You been crying?"

"Yeah."

"Why?"

"Because I hurt you, and I hurt Ade, and Shaunna, and I never wanted to hurt anyone. I was trying to make things right, and... I'm sorry, George." He started to cry again.

George stopped walking and put his arms around him.

"What are you doing?" Kris asked through the sobs.

"Hugging a friend who's sad and in need of some love."

"But the pap are lurking."

"Sod them. Let them lurk. Unless, of course, you like the burden of protecting me?"

"Sorry?"

"Never mind. We've all been getting on with trying to get over Jess and you've been on your own. And before you say it, I know Ade was with you, thank God, or else I might not be able to do this now." He kissed Kris on the cheek. "I love you, too, in case you didn't know. Now stop being soppy."

Kris smiled and exhaled shakily. "Thank you so much."

"Seriously, man. Enough of the waterworks already. You'll have people thinking you're one of them homos." George winked and released him, but they kept their arms around each other as they strolled along the path, chatting about nothing in particular and exchanging greetings with dogs and their owners.

When they eventually made it back to the gate, Shaunna and Josh had already connected the dogs' leads and were leaning on a gatepost each, pretending to be asleep.

Kris tutted as he walked between them, pausing to take a quick glance up and down the street. He frowned. "I recognise that bike," he said, trying not to look too obviously at the motorbike parked twenty yards or so from where they were standing. "Oh, well. He'll have got plenty of shots today. Can't you see it now? '*Shadows* star's forest lovefest' or some other hilariously gripping and witty headline."

Josh and Shaunna laughed wryly, but George was watching the car that had been parked behind the bike when they first came out onto the road, now slowly reversing and turning to face the opposite direction, before it headed away from them.

"What is it?" Josh asked.

George shook his head, still watching the car. "I don't think it's paparazzi."

"Why not?"

He nodded after the back end of the saloon as it disappeared around a corner. "It's an unmarked police car."

"How do you know?"

"Because DS Farrar is behind the wheel."

The J-Word
Tuesday 7th November

"Right, I'll see ya later, love," Pauline called, grabbing her coat and heading straight for the door. Josh had just come in from work, and he eyed her in bewilderment. She leaned in close. "Good luck," she whispered, his entrance and her exit one and the same. He braced for impact.

"Evening, Iris," he called.

"Aright," she said. Josh glanced into the lounge, where Iris was sitting on the sofa with her feet up on the stool, her arms folded and the grumpiest scowl on her face.

"What's up?" he asked.

"Fuckin' bored to fuck."

"Oh. That's not good," he said, somewhat distracted by the sound of snarling behind him. Blue had gone to the farm with George, so it could only be the ferocious beast. Josh swallowed hard.

"Mont! Get yer arse in 'ere!" Iris shouted. The dog immediately complied. Josh exhaled in relief. Iris shook her head in disdain. "And I want a cig, but I can't get off the friggin' couch, can I?"

"Is it hurting that much?"

"No, love. It doesn't hurt at all." She gave him a sarcastic smile. "They've hacked half a bloody inch of bone off me feet. Of course it hurts that fuckin' much." She sighed, immediately repentant. "Sorry, love. Not your fault."

"It's all right, Iris. How about—" Josh paused, because he knew George wouldn't be happy with him making the offer, and he wasn't entirely happy with it himself, but he couldn't watch her suffer. "How about we open the window and you have a cigarette in here?"

"Don't be daft."

"Why is it daft? You need a cigarette and you can't get up."

"Well, I'm gonna have to go for a piss soon anyhow. I'll manage, love, but ta." She returned to scowling at the TV. *Ah*, Josh mused, *that familiar Morley stubbornness.*

"I'm making coffee. Do you want one?"

"Go on then. One of them—what did you say they was called?"

"Latte?"

"Aye. One of them, ta."

Josh nodded and went through to the kitchen. "When are you next due painkillers?" he called back.

"Dunno, love."

"When did you last take some?"

"Dinner time."

That meant lunchtime in Josh's world. "OK. I'll get you some."

"They don't fuckin' work."

Josh made their coffees and returned to the lounge. Iris kept hold of Monty until Josh had set the cups down on the table and got himself safely settled in the chair. He took out his phone and made a call. No answer. He opened up text messaging.

Post bunion op pain relief for Iris – paracetamol and ibuprofen not working. Thoughts? x

He watched the TV whilst he waited for a reply. It was a dreadful film made for television, with an unconvincing set and appalling acting, if it could even be called that.

"What are you watching?" he asked.

"Not a bloody clue. I just turned the thing on."

"You can change channels, you know. See this?" He reached over and picked up the remote control. "You point it at the TV and press the buttons. It's like magic."

Iris glowered at him. He pretended not to notice and carried on watching TV. His phone vibrated.

17:01, Ellie

Will send a prescription through to your local pharmacy. Give it an hour.

So, emoticons were a foreign language to him, but a missed 'x' from the end of a text message? He understood that one, no problem at all. He threw his phone down on the table and returned to watching the terrible film.

"Ellie's sorting out some stronger pills for you," he said, still artificially focused on the TV.

"Oh, right. Ta," Iris replied. She, too, continued to watch TV and glance at him every so often. He sat forward and picked up his coffee, bowing his head so that his eyes were hidden by his hair. He drained his cup and got up.

"Do you need anything?" he asked.

"No. I'm alright, love."

"Are you going up to the loo?"

"In a bit. You go and have your shower."

He nodded and went upstairs. Iris waited until she heard the bolt on the bathroom door, carefully put her feet on the floor and slowly, painfully shuffled her way along the sofa.

***

By the time Josh had showered, she was sitting outside and smoking.

"So you made it?"

"Aye. Mind over matter, love."

It was cold in the garden, but Josh still went out and joined her.

"You know this thing of Jess and Andy getting married?" he said, trying to sound casual. She wasn't looking at him, but he could tell she was listening, so he continued. "What do you think about it?"

"What d'you mean?"

"Am I obsessing over it?"

"You are, love, but that's what you do, in't it? You think too bloody much about everythin', you do."

"That's what George said, too."

"There's nowt wrong with it, mind. Everybody has their own way of copin'. Yours is ruminatin' and cogitatin' until you get it sorted in your 'ead." She shifted position and winced. "Fuckin'ell this is a bastard."

"I'll go to the chemist in a minute, see if your prescription's ready."

"Ta, love." She put out her cigarette in the ashtray Josh had bought especially for when she and Pauline visited. "I'm gonna have another while I'm here."

"You don't have to justify it to me, Iris."

"No. I s'pose not." She took a long draw on the virgin cigarette and blew the smoke away from him. "When I heard Jack was dead, I didn't know what to do with meself. I'd always thought I'd be wantin' to go and dance on the fucker's grave."

Josh didn't comment. It was only the second time he'd ever heard her mention George's dad, and the first time she'd referred to him by name.

"It were months before I got the sound of his smarmy fuckin' whinin' out me 'ead. Like he'd come back to haunt me, givin' Georgie the ranch. I never asked about her—the one he married over there. I'm not fuckin' interested, to tell you the truth, but I did wonder if he kept his kex on for her."

Still Josh remained quiet, for Iris didn't talk openly, and he was humbled by the love and trust she was extending to him. He shivered, and not just because of the chilly autumn evening.

"Georgie says he met her son. Joe, is it?"

Josh nodded.

"Aye. Said he was a good-lookin' lad. His mam's one of them red injuns."

That broke the moment. Josh tried not to laugh and ended up snorting instead.

"What did I say now?" Iris asked innocently.

487

Josh giggled. "I think the term you're looking for is Native American or American Indian, Iris."

"Ee God. There's no bloody 'ope for me, is there, lad?" She chuckled and carried on smoking in silence for a while and then said, "So anyhow, don't you be frettin' about what other people think. Do it your way and fuck the lot of 'em." She stubbed out the cigarette and pulled herself forward, taking deep breaths in preparation. "I'm off for that piss."

"I'll follow you," Josh said.

"You don't need to do that, love."

"Yes, Iris, I do."

"Well, ta, love. I'm grateful."

"Anytime."

Dot
Wednesday 8th November

Sean rubbed his temples with his thumb and forefinger, not because he had another headache, although it was a surprise he didn't. He'd only popped in to Dan and Adele's on the off chance of catching Alice but was waylaid by a fair damsel requesting his help. His task: to feed the different coloured blocks into holes of the right shape.

"Dis!" Little Shaunna grinned up at him, crashing the star-shaped and square-shaped blocks together right in front of his face. He backed off slightly and took the blocks from her.

"Did you say you wanted sugar, dear?" Alice called through from the kitchen.

"No, thanks." Sean took the star-shaped block and tried to push it through the circular hole, as little Shaunna had shown him, just so she could say, "Nooooo!" and do it the right way. He was learning quickly.

"Here we are." Alice placed his tea on a coaster on the nearest surface.

"Thanks, Alice," Sean said, continuing with his game. He was actually having rather a lot of fun—and it was good practice, so he didn't really mind—but he'd had a thought on his way home from work, which was why he'd got off the bus before the end of his journey, and he'd not yet found a chance to act on it.

"I'm pleased you called in," Alice said. "I wanted to ask your advice on something."

"OK."

"Dis!" little Shaunna squealed.

"Well done," Sean said as if he were acknowledging an undergraduate who had extrapolated a complicated theory rather than a three-year-old who had successfully pushed a triangular block into a bucket.

"It's Jason's birthday next week," Alice continued, "and I was considering purchasing him a survival bracelet. I noticed he wears a lot of hemp bracelets, and the one I have in mind is of a similar design, but it would explain to emergency services that he has epilepsy."

Sean's lap was now loaded with dollies, all in various states of undress, and he had a new mission. He picked up the tiniest red sweater and frowned in puzzlement. Little Shaunna helped him out by passing him the correct dolly. "I tell you what. Three-year-olds are damned clever," he said. Alice laughed. "Sorry." He shook his head in order to refocus on her question. "Yes, that sounds like a great idea."

"That's all I needed to know. Thank you." Alice picked up her teacup; Sean followed her lead. "And what was it you wanted, dear?"

"A couple of questions, if I may?"

She nodded her consent.

"I wondered if you'd got around to visiting the studio?"

"Oh, yes. I've visited several times. I must say, some of those young people are marvellous musicians."

"Are they now?" Sean was quite surprised to hear Alice describe the musicians who used Black Hole in that way, as Shaunna had also been down there once or twice and described the experience as like listening to a rhino repeatedly charging a dustbin.

"Not my cup of tea, of course, but I can still appreciate their talent."

"Fair enough. Did you happen to see Hadyn while you were there?"

"Yes. He's always been there whenever I have."

"And what do you think?"

"He's a lovely boy. Troubled, but he carries it well. He's very much like Jason, and they really do bounce off each other." She smiled to herself and sighed. "It reminds me a little of Alistair and

Bill in their younger days. I think the word you psychologists use for it is synergy."

"That would be a good word for it," Sean agreed. He didn't need to ask anything else about Hadyn, as it had merely been a means to establish whether he was still working at the studio. However, there was one other thing he'd wanted to ask since the case conference back in February, and it had played on his mind a great deal over the last week, usually in the middle of the night.

Whilst he wasn't a light sleeper as such, at the moment, those wind chimes were driving him insane, so he'd taken the opportunity to start putting together what he knew about Campion's murder, which wasn't very much at all, like a half-finished game of Cluedo: 'in the boardroom with a fishing knife', along with a list of suspects and their possible motives.

First on that list was Jason Meyer: son of the victim, but unaware of it at the time of his father's death. Jason would have inherited the business even if it had gone to his adoptive father, as Alice claimed it should have. Next, therefore, was Bill Meyer: Jason's adoptive father and Alistair's 'secret' business partner. Financially, he had everything to gain from Alistair's death, but he owned the most shares in the company after Alistair himself.

Based on everything Alice had said about the relationship between the two men, it seemed unlikely he would have killed his best friend, and in any case, he had a rock-solid alibi, as he'd been on holiday at the time of the murder and had to be called back for the emergency board meeting.

Of course, as all of the information was being corroborated by Alice, she had to be suspect number three. She stood to gain nothing directly from Alistair's death but had believed that Bill would have inherited everything and it would, therefore, have gone to her son eventually. That knowledge meant she could also have questioned the details of the will, on top of which, she was the spurned woman. Of the three of them, she was the one with the most motive, but Sean couldn't see it. Whether it was his own sexism that led him to deny the possibility a woman could have murdered a good, innocent man, he didn't know, but he had a strong gut feeling it wasn't her.

And so to the men the police had favoured for it: Kevin Callaghan, a GP with a psychotic disorder, who held his ex-wife at knifepoint in the back of his car, 'for her own safety'. He was certainly unstable enough to do it, motive or not, but he had no reason to be in Campion Holdings, nor did anyone see him there. If it was simply a random attack by a lunatic with a knife, then it could have happened anywhere and to anyone, so why Campion?

There was also James Brown, the prime suspect in the initial inquiry, close friend of the victim and, coincidentally perhaps, the present husband of Callaghan's ex-wife. In light of everything Sean knew, he could only conclude the police had suspected him purely because he had been a petty juvenile offender and he was black. No surprises there, and Diane Sheridan had been able to confirm Callaghan had no visitors at all during his time in prison, so his claim that James had been to see him was part of his psychosis. However, there was still the small matter of a single eyewitness who identified James as the man who stole his fishing knife, which was what Sean wanted to ask Alice about.

Finally, there was the mystery man Alice and James had suspected all along: one Anders Folden. The investigating officers of the original case were of the opinion that he was a figment of Alice's imagination—understandably, as there was no-one by that name in Campion's personnel records—although if she had imagined him, so, too, had James; the descriptions each gave were of one and the same individual.

Accordingly, Anders Folden was four years younger than James, around six foot in height and slightly stocky, with straight blonde hair. Campion had taken him under his wing when, barely turned eighteen, Folden moved from Norway to live with his aunt in England. His parents were at their wits' end, for he was constantly in trouble with the police, and at first, it seemed he had failed to make a fresh start, as by the time he was twenty-one he was serving a two-year custodial sentence for selling counterfeit passports.

Folden began studying whilst in prison, completing his degree at university after his release, and the last time James had spoken to him, he'd said he'd turned over a new leaf. Unfortunately, no-one had seen him since, although Alice had observed his body odour, a spectrum shedding light on time in all its stages, on the morning of Campion's murder.

All the while Sean had been thinking and absentmindedly dressing dollies, Alice had been sipping her tea and watching him. He'd been aware of it and didn't mind at all, but he was still curious and wanted to understand her experience.

"Will you describe it for me?" he asked. "What you see when you look at me. I'd love to know."

Alice set down her teacup and folded her hands together, studying him a moment longer.

"It is very much like the dissipation of paint in shallow water. Imagine pushing a brush loaded with red paint against the centre of a wet plate. The colour spreads unevenly outwards, slowly bleeding into the surrounding water, the same way our scent spreads and fills the air around us. Now imagine taking a different brush, perhaps with blue paint, and, dotting it in the centre of the red. What happens? The blue spreads, turning some of the red to purple whilst leaving the outer edges untouched and a little of the blue at its point of origin."

"Am I red and blue?"

"You are today, dear. Other days you are less blue. The colours do not necessarily reflect moods in the expected sense, however. Red does not mean you are angry, nor blue sorrowful. But it does tell me that you are not your usual self."

Sean nodded to confirm she was right. "That would be very useful in my line of work."

"You understand people well enough without it."

"Thanks."

"It's not a compliment. It's the truth. Nonetheless, I will tell you that your purple hue, on this occasion, suggests there is still more you wish to say."

Sean smiled. "There's no getting past you, is there, Alice?"

"Very few do."

"All right, so, I wanted to ask you what you can remember about the eyewitness who identified James."

"Davey Price? He was very unusual—all kinds of earthy colours but angular shapes. Had his story been credible, I would have remained certain he was lying. He had a particularly distinctive body odour, too; metallic."

"Do you have any thoughts on why he lied to the police?"

"Someone bribed him to do it?"

"Anders Folden?"

"That would be my guess, yes."

Sean rubbed his chin thoughtfully. Little Shaunna paused from dolly dressing to watch him and copy the motion. He smiled at her, and she thrust the dolly at him.

"You like your dollies, don't you, Princess?"

"Want toyet," she said and toddled off towards the bathroom with Alice in hot pursuit, as the little girl didn't give much notice, thus didn't always make it, as was the case on this occasion.

Sean was still deep in thought when they returned. He shrugged at Alice. "I don't know where to go from here."

"You need to track down Davey Price."

"But how?"

"Dan has a friend in the police. He was forthcoming with information at the time of Alistair's murder. Perhaps he will be able to help."

"And if I do track him down, what am I to say to the man? He's hardly going to tell me the truth, is he?"

"I'm sure you'll find a way to get it out of him." She gave him an encouraging smile.

"Well, I'd best be off, Alice. Thanks for the tea."

"Oh, that's quite all right, dear. I should be thanking you, for entertaining Shaunna awhile, and also for your efforts to keep my son safe."

"I'll do everything I can. You have my word." Sean got to his feet, ready to depart.

"I know you will. Now, if you just wait there a moment, I have something you may find useful."

Alice darted off towards the dining room, lifting a vast handbag onto the table. Sean watched on, smiling to himself. Why did women of a certain age insist on having such enormous handbags? It would be fascinating to do a *Through The Key Hole* kind of analysis: 'Who owns a handbag like this?'

Alice trotted back across to him, in her hand a small brown envelope. She held it out, and he took it, glancing inside.

"You see, Doctor Tierney, there are personnel files," she said, "and there are personnel files."

"Alice, you are unbelievable." He turned to go for real this time.

***

On his way home, Sean stopped at The Pizza Place, as he was alone for the evening. He was getting better at buying proper food when Soph and Dylan were over, but he really was going to have to kick the takeaways into touch. He arrived home and automatically went to his phone, playing back the messages as he booted up his computer, at the same time extracting a slice of very hot pizza from the box and cursing under his breath.

"Welcome to your messaging service. You have one new message. Message received today at 18:38."

Sean checked his watch: 18:44. He'd only just missed the call.

"Alright, Sean? It's Dan. I had a word with my mate about that Price bloke, and he said he can't give out his home address, obviously, but he did happen to let slip that he's a welder by trade. Hope that helps. Catch you later."

"End of messages."

Hard On The Knees
Thursday 9th November

"Aww! He's such a cutie!" Shaunna gushed, scratching the belly of the upended Westie in her lap. "I might get a small dog next."

"Not one of them fuckin' yappin' little rats, though, eh, love?" Iris said.

"A Chihuahua, you mean? No. I was thinking something more like Monty, or a Cairn terrier. I like them."

"Aye. We had one of them, din't we, Georgie?"

He delivered their drinks and was on his way back to the door. "What's that, Mam?"

"A Cairn terrier."

"Oh, God, don't remind me!" He left the room.

Iris laughed. "He was a narky little fucker. He'd have yer as soon as look at yer."

"D'you know the worst thing about it, though, Shaunna?" George called back from the kitchen.

"What's that?"

Iris tutted. "There was nowt wrong with it. It suited him."

George reappeared in the doorway with a tea towel in his hand. "Nero," he said. "That's what his name was."

"That's what you called him, but it wasn't his name. I mean. What kind of name is that for a Scotch dog?"

"Scottish."

"Scotch, Scottish, same bloody difference."

"What was his name, actually?" Shaunna asked.

"I'll give you a clue," George said. "It sounds like Nero."

"He was fuckin' black!" Iris protested.

"Ohhh." Shaunna stopped stroking Monty to remove a dog hair from her mouth. He remained upside down in her lap and patted at her with his paw to prompt her to continue.

"OK." Josh paused in the doorway. "The potatoes are on," he informed George.

"Righteo."

"I'm going to drink this while they boil." He stepped into the room, coffee in hand. Monty immediately shot to his feet and started growling. "See? I didn't do anything!"

Shaunna laughed. "Other than be afraid." She got up. "I'm gonna pop round and see Sean before we eat." She stepped past Monty and peered out of the front door to check Sean's lights were on; they were. "Won't be long."

The conversation faded behind her as she headed next door but one. She knocked and waited, listening to the sound of a radio playing from somewhere within. No answer: she tried again. The radio momentarily became louder and then stopped altogether. Still no other signs of life, though. She knocked once more, waited for ten seconds and turned to walk away. The door opened. She turned back.

"Oh! Hi!"

Andy stared back at her.

"I, err, I was…" she stumbled over the words, watching him push his hair back from his face, still staring at her. She averted her eyes, looking down at his feet, following up from the baseball boots to the tapered jeans ripped at the knees, the denim taut on his thighs, the inch of boxers showing above the waistband slung low on his hips, and his t-shirt, damp with sweat and clinging to his torso, showing off his muscles. With great effort, she looked back at his face and smiled quickly. "I was looking for Sean."

"He's gone to get takeaway."

"Right."

Now he was trying not to look at her.

"So you're…?" She shrugged.

"Sorting out his loft."

"Right."

"Yeah. The stairs are done. I'm fitting the skylight."

"Right." She mentally kicked herself for not being able to find anything else to say. He didn't seem to have noticed. In fact, he

497

didn't appear to be having anywhere near as much of a problem as she was with suddenly finding themselves face-to-face for the first time since they got caught out. If anything, he looked angry.

"What's up?" she asked.

"Nothing. Why?"

"Just that…forget it. Can you let Sean know I called round?"

"Will do."

"Thanks." She turned away and started to move off, glancing back as the door closed and his outline retreated upstairs.

She walked slowly, trying to get her head back together. Three weeks; she'd been doing OK, too, filling her time with studying, and a girly shopping trip with Adele to celebrate Krissi and little Shaunna's birthdays. They'd spent the day at the big out-of-town shopping mall, the four of them, gossiping and trying on clothes and shoes, followed by dinner—just her and Krissi—and it was lovely to be with her grown-up daughter, chatting about the everyday, uncomplicated things in life. Now Kris was back, and Ade was moving in at the weekend, and she thought she'd nailed it. The fling with Andy was a brief interlude in the insanity that had been caring and grieving for Jess, nothing more.

Nothing more than deceiving herself.

She returned to Josh and George's house, where dinner was about to be served, on knees in the lounge as they had yet to extend their kitchen, and the closet of a room next to it was a useless space for dining purposes but was also currently entirely taken up by a single bed for their temporary, post-operative lodger. Their guests didn't care; Iris was trying to keep her feet up and out of the way of accidental knocks, and Shaunna was preoccupied with her thoughts but doing her best to hide it.

"Did you see Sean?" Josh asked.

"No. He wasn't there."

"Oh." He frowned. "I didn't think he was going anywhere this evening. Isn't Andy working on the loft?"

"Yeah. Sean had gone for takeaway."

"Ah, I see."

End of conversation. Shaunna kept her face downturned as she ate, forcing herself to chew and swallow each mouthful, furious that she was letting the infatuation knock her over once again.

The evening passed pleasantly enough. After she helped George wash up, she watched TV with Iris for a while, laughing at her biting commentary of whatever was showing, but her mind kept drifting, and then she'd shake herself out of it to find Josh examining her out of the corner of his eye.

"I haven't shown you my painting yet," he said the next time she caught him watching her.

"What painting?"

"It's still up in my office, because I don't know where to put it. Come and see!"

"Not very original, that," Iris said without taking her eyes off the TV. "Come up and see me etchin's."

"Have you met my hilarious mother-in-law?" Josh muttered to Shaunna. They both glanced back at Iris; she pretended not to notice.

"What's it a painting of?" Shaunna asked on the way upstairs.

"You'll have to wait and see."

"Is it one you bought?"

"I'm not telling you anything else till you've seen it."

"Oh, Josh!"

"We're here now. Stop moaning!" He opened the door.

"I'm not. It's just all this myst—" She stepped into the office and was instantly rendered speechless. Several minutes forward, she uttered a breathless, "Wow!"

"Do you like it?" Josh asked.

"It's beautiful." She stepped closer and turned her head to the side. "Is it a computerised thing?"

"A what?"

"You know, where you take a photo and add effects so it looks like it was painted."

Josh laughed. "No. It's a real painting."

"That's brilliant. It's so lifelike."

"Do you think so?"

"Yeah. Definitely. Your hair's not that blonde now, but that's exactly what you looked like when you got back from your honeymoon, all kind of sunned up and dreamy."

Josh blushed.

"Who painted it?" she asked, moving closer still to read the signature. "No way!" She turned to Josh, staring at him in disbelief. "Did you know he could paint like that?"

"I kind of had an idea. You saw the sketch in the hallway?"

"Of the horse? Is that his? Oh my word! He should think about doing commissions."

"Tell him." Josh indicated behind Shaunna, where George had been listening to their conversation. His expression was deadly serious.

"George! It's so beautiful."

"Thank you."

"You should totally do it for a living, you know."

George frowned as if weighing up the idea, and then brought out a sketchbook from behind his back. Shaunna took it from him and flicked through the pages, hardly able to believe what she was seeing.

"The dragon," she whispered. "You really do tell each other everything, don't you?"

George nodded. "Yep. I've already started painting it, but I wanted to make sure you were OK with my ideas before I did any more."

She looked down again at the line drawing of the dragon. "Yeah," she said quietly. She smiled. "I can't wait!" She gave him the sketchbook back and hugged him. "That's so exciting!"

George returned downstairs, and she heard a conversation start up between him and his mother about getting the kettle on.

"Feeling any better?" Josh asked. Shaunna hugged him, too.

"A lot, thank you," she said. "I keep thinking I'm OK, then I start sliding again, and everything gets too much to cope with."

"It's not been that long. Just give it time."

She snuggled against his shoulder and sighed, wishing she could confide in him. He must have sensed what she was thinking.

"Do you want to talk about it?" he asked.

She nodded. "But I can't."

"Why? Is it too painful?"

"It wouldn't be fair."

"On who?"

"On you."

He examined her for a moment, wondering if it was worth trying to persuade her. She closed her eyes to block him out.

"OK," he said. "I won't ask any more questions, but I'm here if you need me, even if it's to sit in silence, or watch rubbish on TV, or talk about experimental design."

"Thank you. You're a wonderful friend." She kissed his cheek. "And sassy, too. Look at you!" She nodded at the painting, and he blushed again. She laughed. "I'd best get going or I'll miss the bus."

"I'll give you a lift if you like."

"No, it's fine. Honestly, I'd rather have the thinking time."

They went downstairs again. Shaunna put on her coat and said her goodbyes. She leaned over to give Iris a hug.

"Thanks for cheering me up tonight."

"Anytime, love," Iris said. "Don't let the fuckers grind you down."

"I won't. Night." She gave the dogs a pat on the head each, and did the same with George. He blinked in surprise, and she grinned. Josh saw her to the door.

"I've had a lovely evening," she said. "Now, remember: you big strong human, he tiny fluffy dog."

Josh smiled. "I'll try. See you soon."

She waved and walked down to the kerb to wait for the bus. Josh watched until it arrived and she was safely on board before he went back inside.

"I'll be havin' words," Iris said, hobbling past and drawing breath sharply through her teeth with each step. "It's not right, what he's doin'. Not right at all."

"Who?" Josh asked.

"Kris, of course."

"Why, what's he doing?"

"Movin' in with that feller of his. It's her house when all's said and done."

"It's *their* house, Iris."

"If there's a woman, it's hers."

"And if there's not?"

"Don't fuckin' start." She stepped outside.

George came up behind Josh and laughed in his ear. "That's you told," he said.

***

Shaunna doodled in the condensation on the bus window, replaying in her mind the way Andy had been with her. Maybe it was just that she'd made him come all the way down to answer the door and then asked to see Sean. Yes, that would be it. After all, he'd made the occasional jokey jibe about her and Sean spending time together, so that on its own would probably be enough, without the fact that she'd disturbed him when he was working.

She switched back to her surroundings and sighed despairingly when she saw she'd doodled a heart. She rubbed it out with her sleeve and peered into the darkness beyond in time to see a motorbike tear past. The bus driver slammed on the brakes.

"Bloody idiot!" he shouted. He glanced at his passengers through his rear-view mirror. "Sorry about that. Everyone all right?"

Shaunna and the other two passengers confirmed they were and listened as the bus driver muttered on about irresponsible boy racers who shouldn't be allowed to ride bikes. Shaunna tuned out again until she reached her stop, where Kris was waiting with Casper.

"Hi," she said, giving them both a kiss.

"Hi," Kris replied. "Have you had a nice evening?"

"I have. Just wait till you see the painting George has done of Josh. It's absolutely brilliant. And Iris's dog is so sweet. Plus, we had the most gorgeous mash."

"Sounds fab!"

"It was. What've you been up to? Anything?"

"Nope. Waiting for you."

"Is that all?" She looped her arm through his as they started the short walk home.

"It is. What would you like to do with the rest of the evening?"

"I thought perhaps we could have a bath and then—"

"Early night?"

"Great minds."

To Dot
Monday 13th November

Sharston Strang and Partners had the appearance of the typical English law firm, with drab offices fronted by lettered sash windows draped in grey vertical blinds, behind those the usual timeless mix of modern equipment, teak panelling and over-waxed parquet. The woman at the reception desk peered over her spectacles, rather than put to use the black cord tidily tucked under the collar of her blue-and-white-striped blouse. Josh resorted to examining the ceiling.

"Mr. Sandison-Morley," a woman called from a door to his right. He got up. "Mr. Strang will see you now."

Josh nodded and followed her along a corridor coated in more teak, to a frosted-glass-paned door. She knocked. A voice from within called, "Enter." She opened the door.

"Mr. Sandison-Morley for you, Mr. Strang."

"Thanks." Alan Strang, barrister, stood and extended his lengthy arm across the vast oak desk, his shirt sleeve sliding back with the motion. "Mr. Sandison-Morley," he greeted. Josh shook the offered hand. "Alan Strang. Take a seat." Josh did as instructed. "How can I help you, Mr. San—"

"Josh, please."

"All right. What can I do for you, Josh?"

So this was him. The senior partner who'd lost Jess the best job of her career, because he couldn't keep his pants up. Interesting. Or, in fact, not interesting at all. He had an exaggerated air of self-importance and evidently considered himself to be a handsome and charming man, but Josh had yet to identify anything about him that was remotely attractive, with his expensive boring navy blue suit, handmade brogues and extraordinarily obvious hair piece. And that smile! How did juries fall for that?

Josh's analysis had taken him less than three seconds, so the delay in his response was barely discernible. He smiled back and took Jess's will out of his file.

"Thanks for agreeing to see me, Alan. Jess spoke very highly of you." If highly included how far into space she wanted to send him on the end of a pointy-toed stiletto.

"How very kind of you to say. I'm sorry for your loss. You were close friends."

"We were."

Alan shuffled his cufflinked sleeves down a little. Josh observed the wedding ring; heavy gold, set with a disgustingly oversized black onyx. Alan's hands were ultra-clean.

"I wondered if I could ask you to take a look over Jess's will with me. I am one of the executors, as I'm sure you're aware, and there are several points we would like to clarify, if that would be acceptable?"

"Of course."

Josh had made two copies and left the original at home. He passed one across the desk. "The first point is the date, which I just need to confirm as correct." He paused to give Alan Strang a chance to look over the papers. He nodded as he read.

"That seems to be in order. I recall Miss Lambert visiting the offices earlier this year. I can check the exact dates for you. One moment." He picked up his desk phone and called through to his secretary. "Hi, Sarah. When you have a moment, can you bring up the files for Jessica Lambert?"

"Certainly, Alan."

"Confirm dates for appointments and pull out her will, please." He put the phone down and smiled again, his perfectly straight white teeth fully on display.

Josh felt like he was being weighed up by a shark to see if he'd make a decent aperitif. A knock came at the door, and the woman who had brought him to the office entered carrying a very thin brown foolscap envelope. She placed it on the desk in front of Strang.

"Thanks, Sarah. That's all."

She nodded and left. Strang picked up the envelope and removed the contents. He scanned through the multiple pages—

504

far more than were in the will but still nowhere near what Josh had expected of a lawyer's legal file.

Strang raised an eyebrow. "Yes. It would appear that Jess made quite a few changes to her will on March the twenty-second this year, prior to which she amended it in October of last year, and then two years before that."

"Is that standard practice?" Josh asked. "I mean for lawyers? I have a will, but I've only ever changed it once."

"We are perhaps more concerned with ensuring all is current and correct, yes."

Well played, Josh thought, *to cast the seed of doubt so deftly*. He knew he'd be checking his own will when he got home to make sure it was 'current and correct'. Onwards.

"The second thing I wanted to check was the use of the term 'husband'. Could this apply to common-law spouses?"

"It could, potentially. However, there would be no tax incentive to be gained by doing so, and it leaves the estate vulnerable to legal challenge. The law would still treat a common-law marriage as cohabitation rather than marriage."

"In other words," Josh stated rather than asked, "unless the beneficiary is married to the deceased, they'll have to pay inheritance tax."

"That's right."

"And what would happen if, for instance, Jess had made her husband the sole beneficiary, but there was no husband?"

"She would have died intestate."

So that was all of his theories shot to pieces.

"However," Strang said, a hint of that smile and a tip of the eyebrows as he spoke, "she was married, was she not?"

"Yes, she was when she died."

Josh could feel himself being mind-probed and blocked it too late, although he also caught the tail end of something from Alan Strang and decided to try his luck, because he'd spotted the certificate poking out of the papers in the barrister's hand.

"Of course, she married in secret, so we're not quite sure how long ago that was. Would that, perhaps, be something she would have kept in her legal files?"

"It is not unusual for people to store their documents with their lawyer, if that's what you're asking, Mr. Sandison-Morley."

Ah, the formal address. He'd been duly rattled.

"And did Jess utilise this facility?"

"I'm afraid I can't share that information."

And now he was lying, or at the very least being evasive. If Sharston Strang and Partners held any documents of Jess's, they now belonged to her estate, so therefore to Andy.

"That's fine, Mr. Strang, I totally understand," Josh said.

"Will that be all?"

"I do have just one more question regarding the witnesses. I see that one is Mrs. Angela Sharston, the widow of your deceased partner, Charles Sharston, which doesn't seem at odds, given that she and Jess were well acquainted. However, I was wondering about the other witness. I don't recall Jess ever mentioning anyone called Simon Yarrow. Is he one of your staff?"

"He is a partner here, yes."

"Right, that makes perfect sense." Josh smiled and made a big deal of returning Jess's will to his file. Alan Strang called through to his secretary to escort Josh back to the reception area. "Many thanks for your assistance."

"No problem at all. Do make another appointment, should you require any further advice, or perhaps to check that all is in order with your own arrangements."

"I might just do that." Josh stood and shook hands, glancing down at the documents as he did so. *Yes, definitely a marriage certificate.* The secretary arrived. Josh gave the smarmy lawyer one final smile. "And I'll be sure to let Jess's widower know he needs to formally claim his property from you. Good afternoon, Mr. Strang."

***

Shaunna's phone was on the kitchen table, and she had her hands in a sinkful of hot, bubbly water. She tried to ignore the text message alert, but curiosity got the better of her. She wiped her hands dry and picked up her phone. One message:

17:35, Andy [mobile]
WE NEED TO TALK

Her pulse quickened. All of a sudden, clear, rational thinking was an ungraspable concept, and she put her phone down, returning to the washing up, commanding herself to finish it before she took action, allow some time to pass in the hope that she'd find the willpower to tell him.

No.

We don't.

She dropped a glass, and it hit the edge of the sink, a piece falling into the sud-obscured water and, knowing the consequence, she still mindlessly fished around for the missing fragment.

"Yeah," she said resignedly, withdrawing her bleeding hand and watching the red spill across her wet skin. She dabbed it dry with a paper towel. It wasn't a bad cut. She finished the washing up one-handed—left-handed and clumsy—emptied the sink and found a plaster. She picked up her phone again.

17:35, Andy [mobile]
WE NEED TO TALK

The message hadn't changed.

They'd agreed they weren't going to do this. It was one of those things. However much they wanted it, and how they wanted it, it was not to be.

Where are you?

"Shit," she said, as soon as she'd pressed send. The angel and devil were back whispering in her ears and she'd not heard a word they'd said.

17:47, Andy [mobile]
NEW PLACE

***

She arrived in the lobby and glanced at the stairs and lift; it was a big building, and other than 'upstairs from Dan and Adele', she didn't know where his apartment was, or even what number. She stepped back outside, trying to think. The simplest way, of course, was to send a text message or call and ask, but her brain wasn't playing things simply today. She spotted Andy's car in the car park and slowly wandered over. She smiled.

"Awesome," she said. "And really, really stupid."

The parking spaces were reserved, one for each apartment, and they were numbered, which meant that anyone casing the joint had a ready reckoner of which properties were vacant. All right, they'd have needed to get in the gate first, but that wasn't difficult. Just say 'taxi for number x' into the intercom—they didn't even bother checking. So, number sixteen, then.

As she approached the door, she started to have second thoughts. This was a bad idea. Before Dan caught them, being in the same place at the same time left them unable to resist acting on their impulses. They'd seen each other once since, and the exchange had not been a good one. This was a bad idea. She rang the bell. The door opened.

"Hi, Shaunna!" Charlotte's face smiled back at her.

"Hi." She couldn't think of anything else to say, dumbstruck once again by the unexpected.

"Come in," Charlotte prompted, looking both bemused and amused by Shaunna's statuesque appearance.

"Err, thanks." She stepped inside.

"Where did you say this lamp should—" Andy stopped dead, a standard lamp in his hand. He stared at Shaunna.

For a long time, nobody moved, nobody spoke; everything stopped. Push play.

"I'll take that," Charlotte said, taking the lamp. She disappeared into the lounge and closed the door.

"What are you, err…" Andy paused. He didn't want to ask her that question. "Hi," he said instead.

"Hi."

"Did you…" He scratched his head. "Sorry. You, err…" He laughed at himself. "Surprised," he said. He shrugged.

"Confused!" she replied. He shrugged again. "You sent me a text."

He shook his head, looking horrified by the suggestion.

"You did! It's here. Look." She took her phone out and showed him the messages. "If I'd known Charlotte would be here—why ask me to come when she is? Ah." Now she saw. He was trying to clear the air, but there was safety in numbers. "Chaperone," she said, nodding knowingly. Andy kept right on shaking his head.

"I didn't send those. Not me."

She frowned. This was so confusing. "OK." She turned and walked back to the door. "Sorry." She gave the hallway a cursory glance. "Nice place." She left and closed the door behind her.

***

Page three of the search results for 'Simon Yarrow barrister' with the appropriate quotation marks to avoid the usual Boolean search nightmare, thus only another two pages to go.

Josh took his glasses off and rubbed his eyes. He had a lecture to plan, essays to mark and a treatment programme to write up, and here he was, scrolling through business profiles, yearbooks and citations, none of which were telling him anything useful, not that he was sure what would constitute useful, but there was something about this that continued to bother him.

He took Jess's will downstairs with him, reading over it again as he waited for his coffee, even though he knew it word for word, but maybe he'd missed something. He checked his phone to see if Andy had responded about going to see Alan Strang, but he hadn't, and that was the other problem. It was only he who was obsessing over the will. Everyone else was trying to get back to normal, and he knew they thought this was his way of coping, but there was more to it. Or maybe there wasn't. He just didn't know anymore. He took his coffee back upstairs.

"Right. I'll get through these, then do some proper work." Glasses back on, scrolling down, next page, scrolling down, down—

"Hm." He moved in closer to read the ellipsis-littered summary in the search results: "Newcastle Coroner's Court... Simon Yarrow, barrister... GMC investigating..." He clicked the link.

A lawyer who advised a doctor to let his patient die gave evidence yesterday at Newcastle Coroner's Court.

The motor neurone patient, who cannot be named for legal reasons, had been seriously ill for two years and had an advance directive in place, asking they not be provided with any treatment that might prolong dying.

However, the patient's general practitioner disregarded the advance directive and resuscitated the patient following a choking incident. The patient later died in hospital.

Simon Yarrow, barrister, acting on behalf of the patient's family, said, "Doctors are legally bound to obey a valid advance directive explicitly laying out their patient's wishes, which is the case with our client."

The General Medical Council (GMC) is now investigating the conduct of the patient's GP, who may be charged with assault and struck off the medical register if it is found he ignored an advance directive.

The coroner recorded a verdict of death by natural causes.

Josh scrolled back to the top of the newspaper report and checked the date the patient died: December the sixteenth three years previously.

"That fits," he said. The dog lifted his head and looked at him. "It does, Blue. It fits. You know what that means, don't you?" Josh sighed and took out his phone. It rang out twice and went to voicemail.

"Hey, Ellie. Hope you're OK. Can you give me a call when you get a chance? Thanks. Bye."

He ended the call and put his phone back in his pocket.

***

Shaunna was almost back home when her phone sounded.

18:11, Andy [mobile]
Come back. Please? x

She let herself into the house, and Casper went crazy, because she'd only been back from work for twenty minutes when she left him alone the first time, although Kris would be home soon, so she didn't feel quite so bad about leaving the dog again—or not for that reason. She fed him, made a cup of tea and sat, sipping rapidly at the hot liquid and scalding her mouth a little in the process, until she could take it no longer. She tipped the remaining half a cup down the sink, wrote a note on the kitchen table jotter pad—*gone to Adele's*—and left, wondering all the way there why she was doing it.

Eight minutes of whirling thoughts later, she ran up the two flights of stairs to the first floor and drew to a halt outside number sixteen; her common sense arrived a split second later.

"Why am I here?" she asked, pushing the button. The bell made a loud *ding-dong* inside the apartment. She focused on its fading resonance until it was overpowered by the thumping in her ears. The door opened, and he stood before her, socked feet, ridiculous knee-length shorts, vest top, stubble, messy, messy hair. *So long, good intentions.*

"Hi," she said. He was staring deep into her eyes, his expression serious and still angry.

"Hi," he said. "Come in."

She did.

"Charlotte's gone home?" she asked, still in the hallway.

"Yeah." He motioned for her to go through to the lounge—the lounge she had not yet seen.

"Wow! This is…empty?" She turned back and frowned in query but refused to look at him properly.

"I need to buy a sofa."

"No TV?"

"In the bedroom. I don't have anywhere else to sit."

"A sofa."

"I need a woman's touch, Charlie said. I declined."

Shaunna nodded and patted the carpet with her foot. "New carpets. Very soft."

"Yeah," he agreed.

"We do need to talk."

"About?"

"Why you're angry with me."

He didn't deny it.

"Is it because of Sean?"

"No."

"Because I made you come all the way down from the loft to open the door?"

"No."

"So why?"

"Can we, err, do this over a drink, maybe?"

"Fine. A glass of wine?"

"A cup of tea."

She smiled and nodded. "A cup of tea. Thanks."

He walked away across the room, towards the kitchen, she knew, as the layout of the apartment was the same as Dan and Adele's, but the lounge was a massive expanse of carpeted desert without sofas and dining tables and koi carp. She trudged across the plush cream sands and made it to the oasis.

"This is OK," she said, taking in the layout of the cupboards, all white doors and brushed steel. She ran her palm over the smooth, cold, empty black granite worktop. "You really do need a woman's touch in here."

He swallowed hard and filled the kettle. *Not a woman's touch; this woman's touch...* But she had pushed him away, made her excuses, made it impossible. Still, she wanted to talk. He made the tea.

They adjourned to the lounge and sat on the carpet, she cross-legged, he against the wall. She looked up above, at the bald light bulb.

"No lampshade."

"No."

"When did you move in?"

"Last weekend."

She raised an eyebrow.

"I know. I'm still living like a bachelor boy in his mother's house. Bedroom, kitchen, bathroom. I don't even need this room."

"So, the text messages," she said, sipping her tea.

"I don't know, honestly. I only sent you the one, half an hour ago."

Shaunna set her cup down and took her phone from her pocket. She loaded the messages. "It's definitely your number." She passed him the phone. Their fingers made contact. The embers caught light.

"I wouldn't...shouting?" he struggled to explain.

She put her phone away to hide her shaking hands and left her tea right where it was. "So, again, why are you angry with me? What have I done?"

"You led me on."

"I'm sorry?"

"It was just a bit of fun."

"What was?"

"That week at my mum's. You know, if you were only up for a few days of uncomplicated sex, you should've said."

"Huh?"

"I told you. I couldn't stop myself, whether I wanted more or not. But as I say, if all you wanted—"

"I don't know what you're talking about."

"Let's put it this way, if Dan hadn't caught us, it'd have all been over soon enough. He saved you the trouble."

"Saved me the trouble?"

"Yeah. Of telling me that you didn't want it to carry on. Instead, you let me believe the lie."

"Andy..." She was getting angry herself now. "What lie are you referring to? I'd never lie to you."

"About you and Kris."

"What about me and Kris?"

"That you were trying to work things out."

"OK. Tell me how that makes any difference to our situation."

"We agreed to finish it because it wasn't fair to put anyone in the position of keeping our secret."

"That's right. We did."

"We don't need to keep it a secret, though, do we? Unless you're ashamed that you're fucking your daughter's father."

Shaunna shook her head. "You've lost me."

"Kris announces on live TV that he's back with his boyfriend, and you still think you can fool me into believing we can't be

513

together because our secret affair would be too much of a burden on our friends."

"Ah."

Now the penny dropped. Not just the penny, but a whole torrent of coins, tumbling and rolling around and around, an avalanche of realisation.

"OK," she said. "I'm going to tell you something, but only you. No-one else must know. Absolutely no-one. Not even Dan or Charlotte."

"Ooh. Sounds like a bi-i-ig secret. Are you sure I'm up to keeping it?"

"Stop being shitty. It doesn't suit you."

Andy sighed and closed his eyes. "I'm having something of a problem here," he said quietly. He took a deep breath and opened his eyes again. She gave him a sultry smile and licked her lips.

"So perhaps we could…"

He was already there, moving her cup out of the way and pushing her down onto the plush, thick cream carpet, pulling off her leggings, their lips now crushed together, her hands up inside his vest, fingernails digging into his shoulders. No slow build this time; he slid straight into her, and she didn't mute her cries for more, for faster, for harder, and what could he do, other than oblige his red hot baby? As they teetered on the brink, the words escaped from him. He couldn't have stopped them if he'd wanted to.

"I love you."

And then they fell to the floor in a panting, untidy embrace.

"I love you," he repeated, kissing her lips, her nose, her cheeks, her eyelids, over and over and over, until not a single spot was left untouched. He rolled onto his side, but she kept her legs clamped around him. His panting slowed, and he smiled at her. "I've got carpet burns."

She laughed. "You think *you've* got carpet burns?"

He reached across a hand and rubbed her bare buttocks, sneaking another kiss.

"The truth?" he murmured. She nodded. They slowly disentangled themselves so they could redress, and then sat, leaning against the wall, his arm around her shoulders, her head on his chest.

"The truth," she repeated, running her fingers up and down his belly as she spoke. "Kris and I are back together."

"But—"

"And," she interrupted, "he is also with Ade."

She gave it a little time to sink in before she said anything else. "So, you see? I didn't lie to you. I just didn't tell you everything."

"Because of the press?"

"Because of our friends."

Andy pondered on that statement for a few seconds. "Fair enough," he said. He could totally understand that. They'd judged him for lesser things in the past. He stayed quiet, inhaling the scent of her hair, appreciating the sensation of her fingers on his skin.

"What are you thinking?" she asked.

"Nothing."

"You must be thinking something."

"See? Too much time with Sean. I wasn't thinking anything at all, although now I'm wondering if he knows."

"I've never told him about what's happening with me and Kris and Ade, but I think he figured it out a long time ago, even before we did. He doesn't know about you and me."

"And does Kris know?"

"No." Shaunna pulled away. "You said you didn't want him to, so he doesn't, and he won't. It's not like that."

A grin crept onto Andy's face.

"And it's not like that, either!" she admonished him. "Ade's gay, and I told you—it's not hot when they're gay. I mean, what would be the point?" She settled back against his chest again. "I thought you wanted to end it, too."

"Why?"

"I was just another challenge."

He stroked her hair back from her face, and she looked up at him. He kissed her.

"No," he said, continuing to run his fingers through her hair. "You are definitely not just another challenge. A challenge, yeah."

She grabbed a few of the curls of hair running up to his belly button and tugged.

"Ow!"

"You're not freaked out?"

"Me? It'd take a lot more than that to freak me out. I still hate sharing you, and it feels even more like swinging than it did before, but I can't change any of that. I want you. I need you. And I love you."

"You don't love me. You love my hair."

"Yeah, you're right." He tangled his fingers in it and used it to pull her face up to his, allowing her tongue into his mouth.

She ran it over his teeth and thrust it as deep as it would go, slowly rising to her knees and wriggling out of her top at the same time. The doorbell sounded. "Balls." She shoved her arms back inside her top but he carried on kissing her. "Aren't you going to answer that?"

"Nah."

"OK." She grinned and grabbed his nipple through his vest. He groaned.

His phone vibrated in his pocket. He reached down and took it out, answering it with her mouth roaming down his neck. "Alright, bro?"

"Yeah. You?"

"Just dandy."

She pinched his nipple.

"Ee-ah!" He shook his head at her, trying not to laugh.

"I've got this fridge for you," Dan said. "Are you gonna open the door?"

"Yeah, I'm just coming," Andy replied. Shaunna dipped her head towards his crotch. He grabbed her hair again to stop her reaching her destination and remembered to push 'end call'. "Stop it!" he hissed.

She grinned at him. "I'll go wait in the bedroom," she said, rubbing herself against him as she departed. He got to his feet and waited a minute, straightening his shorts on the way to the door.

Dan was leaning against the massive fridge and scowling, unimpressed at having to wait.

"Sorry. I was on the loo," Andy said.

Dan nodded and stepped to the side.

"How did you get this up here?"

"The bloke from the flat next to mine let me borrow his trolley."

"Cool. Right, let's get this monster inside."

Between them, they manoeuvred the appliance through the door and across the new carpet, the feet leaving a trail in the pile. They pushed it into position and returned to the lounge. Andy rubbed his foot over the marks.

"It'll brush up fine," Dan said. "Nice bit of carpet, this." He scanned the expanse, nodding. "When you gonna get some furniture in here?"

"This weekend. Might pop up to that place just off the motorway."

"Yeah? They've got some decent stuff in there—it's where I got the dining table. Speaking of which, dinner calls."

"No worries. Cheers for sorting out the fridge."

Dan nodded and walked to the door, turning back as he opened it. "I'll see you tomorrow," he said and stepped outside. "Oh, and bro? Next time, tell Shaunna to take her shoes with her."

***

"Josh." Eleanor gave him a fake smile and moved aside so he could come in. She closed the door behind him.

"Ellie. Thanks for this. I know it's getting a bit late."

"It's not yet nine o'clock."

"True, but you have a young child, and…I was trying to be considerate."

"You were trying to make small talk! Since when did we ever need to? Don't insult me, Josh."

"Sorry."

She waved him on towards the kitchen, where she'd already made a coffee for him and a cup of tea for herself. They were laid out on the table, one either side. Josh took his place.

"You mentioned this is to do with Kevin?" she said, sitting down opposite. Straight to the point. So it really was over.

"Yes. Or, at least, I think it might be."

"OK. Explain."

Josh took Jess's will out of the folder that had become his constant companion over the past couple of weeks. He flicked directly to the last page and pointed to the witness signatures. Eleanor tried not to let her exasperation show, but she'd heard from the others that he was still on some conspiracy theory kick. He'd also heard her sigh.

"Go on," he said. "Tell me I'm being irrational."

"Well, aren't you?"

"I don't think so, but I wouldn't know, would I, if it's true?"

Eleanor sighed again. "Fine. Show me what you want to show me."

His nostrils flared indignantly. He spun the will around to face her, the force crinkling the paper. "Simon Yarrow, barrister." He prodded at the signature in question.

"What about him?"

"Works for Sharston Strang and Partners."

"OK. They were Jess's lawyers. So he witnessed her will. So what?"

Josh pulled out the printed search results from his research earlier in the evening and put them down next to the will.

"Simon Yarrow, barrister," he said again.

Eleanor frowned and flicked to the second page—the article about the coroner's hearing. She reached the bottom, returned to the first page and checked the date of death. Without another word she picked up the phone, watching Josh all the while.

"Hi, Callum?" she spoke into the phone.

"Yes?" a puzzled voice responded at the other end of the line.

"It's Eleanor Davenport here. Sorry to bother you so late." As she spoke, she reached down, turned a couple of pages back in Jess's will, and tapped on the list of their names. Josh scanned over it whilst he listened to the call, now on loud speaker.

"Hi, Eleanor. How are things?"

"Not too bad, thanks, although I am, unfortunately, now in a situation to make arrangements to meet."

"I'm sorry to hear that."

"Thanks. It'd be great if we could catch up properly sometime soon, but for now, I wondered if you'd be able to give me a bit of information about Kevin's case?"

"I will if I can. Let me get the file."

There was the sound of the phone being set down and then receding footsteps. Josh shrugged at her in relation to the names.

"Mine and Shaunna's," she said.

"Hi, Eleanor?"

"Yes, still here."

"OK. I've got my notes in front of me. What is it you'd like to know?"

"I realise you can't give me details of what happened, but can you give me some indication of what the Biddiscombe case was?"

"Sure. It involved a terminal patient and an advance directive."

"And when was that?"

"It was, let me see…" The line went quiet again. "It was December sixteenth."

Eleanor looked at Josh, unsure what she should say. He mouthed, "Ask him questions." She shrugged and pushed a pen and notepad his way.

"Was there anything else?" Callum prompted.

"Err…"

Josh scribbled and shoved the paper towards her.

"Simon Yarrow was the patient's barrister, is that right?"

"I can tell you that without even looking. Yes, he was. He's a very forceful individual."

"In what way?"

"I can't really say much more over the phone. Are you free around the end of next week? I'm on a case not too far from you."

"I can be."

"Good. I'll email you to sort something concrete."

"That's great, thanks, Callum."

"Bye now."

"Bye." She put the phone down and turned back to Josh. "You're not being irrational," she said, then qualified, "about this."

"That's something," he muttered under his breath.

"Pardon?"

"Nothing. So what was this thing about yours and Shaunna's names?"

"Look at what they are."

"Eleanor Davenport and Shaunna Johansson." He shrugged. "What's wrong with—oh! I didn't notice that."

"No. I didn't think anything of it, either, at first, as I just assumed she'd written it prior to last September, but then I realised she must have amended it after she and Andy got married."

"She did amend it after *you* got married, but not since they did."

"So why does it say 'husband'?"

"That's what I've been trying to figure out—you know, all my 'irrational obsessing'? She wrote this will in March, and they got married in May."

"How do you know she wrote it in March?"

"It's dated, you goon."

Eleanor shook her head. "My copy's not." She left the room and came back a moment later with her copy. She was right. There was no date on it.

"This just gets madder and madder," Josh said, still switching between the two versions of the will, identical in all other ways, as far as he could see. "She said she gave us all exactly the same documentation."

"Maybe it was just a copying error," Eleanor suggested. "But whatever, they must've discussed it in advance."

"No. Andy says he can't recall discussing it, although he did say that might be him 'being a man'. However, I went to see that Alan Strang creep today, and there was a marriage certificate in her file. I've been trying to get hold of Andy ever since, so he can go and claim her documents, but he's not answering."

"Can he do that? Claim Jess's records back from her lawyers?"

"Yes, he can. They belong to the estate, but Strang wasn't too eager to hand them over. There's something not right, Ellie, and everyone's treating me like I'm making a big deal out of nothing."

Eleanor shook her head and reached across the table. She squeezed his hand and waited for him to make eye contact. She smiled. "You're not. There is something very wrong with all of this."

He smiled back. "Thank you. That means a lot." He felt his eyes filling with tears. "Bugger," he said. Eleanor laughed and got him a tissue.

"You really need to stop being such a baby," she said. He sniffed and tried to smile. "Shall I make us another drink?"

He nodded. "I'd like that." He blew his nose. She filled the kettle and stayed with it.

"So, what is it?" she asked, studying him intently.

He put his head down and didn't respond.

"Come on, Josh. I know you. There's something really important that you want to tell me, but you're worried about how I'm going to react."

Still, he didn't speak.

She returned to the table and pulled out the chair next to his. She sat down and took both of his hands. "I've found it so hard this last year. I could feel us drifting apart, and it hurt so much, and then losing Jess…" She paused, gently stroking the backs of his hands with her thumbs. "I'm sorry. I shouldn't have said what I did. I was being deliberately hurtful and selfish. And I don't want to leave you all, but I don't know what else to do. It's not fair on James and Oliver for us to stay here, and you were always so important to me. You and Jess were my best friends in the world, and I feel like I've lost you both."

"You haven't." Josh gulped. "I'm still here." Now the tears were flowing freely, unhindered by what stoic best friends might have to say about it. "I'm still the same me I always was, Ellie. I just stopped hiding behind my couch."

She hugged him and felt herself crying too. "That must be pretty scary," she said.

He laughed and cried at the same time. "Yes, it is a bit."

She got up to make their drinks and brought them over, along with the entire box of tissues, and they sat together, talking properly for the first time in a very long time. She told him how devastated she was to find out Kevin had killed himself, and of what a struggle it had been to hide her pain whilst treating Jess, because that was what Jess had asked of her.

All of that had followed on from postnatal depression, where she was fighting the urge to binge at the same time as making sure she was eating enough to breastfeed, and throughout it all she'd felt like she had no-one to turn to, because he and George were making up for all the time they had missed.

For all that she was genuinely happy for them, she desperately needed his friendship. She knew she'd overreacted to their marriage, but once she'd said it, she didn't know how to back down, and then George's mum had offered her a get-out—that she just needed longer to think about it because she was supposedly 'more intelligent', but she didn't feel that way, especially now Shaunna and Adele were studying again. She and Jess were the clever ones out of the girls, and as childish as it sounded, she didn't want someone trying to steal their intellectual spotlight. That jealousy and insecurity also extended to Sophie, which was part of why she felt the way she did about Sean. So, for all of her complaints that Josh was the one being irrational, it was merely a reflection of how she was feeling about herself.

In response, Josh told her about his bipolar disorder, and how he had spent the last year trying to find a middle ground between the complete control he'd had in the past and the emotional roller coaster he'd been on ever since he told George he was in love with him. He also admitted to being scared to tell her, knowing she would try to fix him, for all the right reasons, but it wasn't what he wanted or needed.

He told her about his depression back at university, Jess and Sean getting him through it—though not of the self-harm and suicide attempts—and of the meeting with Jess, when she was refusing to go to the hospital and what she had said about having the old Josh back. He talked about *Hamlet* and Savies, and how he had visited, hoping for her ghost, instead ending up with a passage from *Macbeth*. He explained what had happened to George with Sam, and how painful it had been to work through it together, although he admitted that he had, on occasion, deliberately picked fights with her.

He also confessed to completely adoring Iris. She was the first person he had ever met who wasn't intimidated by his job, and they had so much in common, not least their love for George. Finally, he told her honestly how he felt about her moving away— that it had always been his greatest fear that she would find 'the one' and leave him for good.

"I'm not leaving you," she said when he came to the end. "I'm just moving a couple of hours down the road."

"I know, but that's what it feels like."

"And then there's George and Ollie and Toby. We'll still see a lot of each other."

"I suppose."

"James and I were talking about it a few days ago. We would love it if the boys could come and stay with you sometimes."

"Really?"

"Yes, really."

"That will be so awesome. I can't wait to tell George. Or do you want to tell him?"

"No. You can tell him."

"I will, as soon as I get home. He was a bit cross about what you said to me, you know."

"George? Cross?"

"You don't know the half of it! You heard about him pinning Rob down?"

"Yeah, but I thought the report had been greatly exaggerated."

"It was! *Under*-exaggerated."

"You do surprise me."

"Yes, well he didn't get quite that upset about you, but…" Josh suppressed a laugh at the memory of George's impersonation. "Anyway, he'll be really happy we're friends again. And he's going to be like a kid at Christmas when I tell him about the boys coming to us for little holidays. It'll be amazing."

"Hmm. If you say so, but before we get there, we've got to pack up and move and say our goodbyes. I'm not looking forward to it, I must confess." She became teary again.

"But you're only moving a couple of hours down the road," Josh reminded her with a wink.

"I'm still going to miss you, and my mum." She sniffed back the tears and took a moment to recompose. "So, it looks like we've got ourselves a mystery to solve."

Josh smiled. "Yes. We have. Are you ready to sleuth it out with me, Doctor Brown?"

"I most certainly am, Mr. Sandison-Morley." She suddenly got all excited. "We should get some deerstalker hats."

"Fedoras would be much cooler."

"Yeah!" She opened her laptop. "I think I might go and see how much they are."

"I think I might leave you to it and go home to my husband and mother-in-law. Have you seen the time?"

Eleanor glanced up at the clock. It was almost one in the morning.

"Perhaps I'll leave the fedoras till I've had some sleep."

"Good idea." He got up and held out his hand to her. She took it and allowed him to pull her to her feet. "I'm so glad we've made up," he said. "I've missed you."

"I've missed you, too." She rolled her eyes and tutted. "I guess I'll have to get used to the all-new, old gushy Josh, hey?"

"I guess so." He kissed her on the head. "I'll give you a call if I hear anything. Will you let me know when you're meeting up with Callum? I'd like to come with you."

"Will do." She walked him to the door, and they hugged again. "I love you," she said.

"And I love you," he responded. He stepped outside and waved back as he walked away.

"Incidentally," Eleanor called after him, "that adorable mother-in-law of yours is an interfering old busybody!"

Big Enough
Saturday 18th November

Saturday morning: Kris got back from walking Casper and went straight up to shower.

"What else do you need to pack?" Ade shouted through from the bedroom—his and Kris's, that is.

"Err, change of underwear, blue shirt, antihistamines, phone charger. I'll bring my toothbrush now."

"Blue shirt," Ade repeated to himself, glancing over the array of shirts hanging in the wardrobe, none of which was entirely blue. Blue with orange; blue with pink; blue, black and yellow paisley, but not just blue. Kris came into the room, still dripping wet and wearing only a towel around his waist. "Which one?" Ade asked. Kris left the room again and went next door—his and Shaunna's room—returning a few seconds later.

"This one," he said, holding up a royal-blue silk shirt.

"You might want to specify which wardrobe next time."

Kris smiled apologetically and dried off whilst Ade finished packing his bag for him, for no other reason than it saved time, as they still needed to stop off in Manchester before they got the train to London for the awards ceremony that Kris was presenting. He'd told his agent to start looking for new roles for him, preferably in stuff that didn't end up Saturday prime-time viewing, and was treating this as little more than a networking opportunity.

"So, we need to go to your sister's to pick up your tux," Kris recounted to remind himself, "and we're booked on the 15:55."

"Yes," Ade confirmed. "She said she'd give us a lift to the station. We've got plenty of time."

"OK." Kris relaxed and slowed down a little. They didn't need to get the train that early, but he didn't like rushing around at the last minute, and he was feeling quite positive today. The weekly walk in the woods was back to normal, now he and George had sorted out some of their differences. And he was almost looking forward to this evening.

"Do you want a drink?" Ade asked.

"No. Let's go somewhere and have lunch, then head straight off."

"I thought you'd want to make Shaunna's lunch before we left."

"She's going to her dad's straight from work, she said, and then furniture shopping."

"For her dad?"

"No," Kris laughed. "For Andy. He still hasn't got anything to sit on."

"He'd have been better taking you. That sofa downstairs is, err, well—"

"Excuse me, but *I* chose our sofa!"

"That explains everything." Ade grinned. Kris balled the towel and threw it at him.

***

"Hi there, red hot baby."

Shaunna climbed into the front seat of the Mustang and shut the door. "You know, people will start to think you're a bit nuts if you keep talking to your car like that."

Andy waited for her to fasten her seat belt before he put his foot down. "Did you say you needed to go to your dad's?"

"Yeah. Only for ten minutes or so."

"OK. Direct me."

She did as requested and they pulled up outside. She got out of the car. "Come with me if you want."

"Nah. I'll stay here and give my other girl some of my good, long loving."

"You're so disgusting." She shut the door in his grinning face. When she returned ten minutes later, he was sitting back with his eyes closed, listening to the stereo.

"I thought I'd never have to hear this rubbish again after Krissi left home."

"It's not rubbish. It's—"

"Faith No More," she interrupted. "I know!"

"They're awesome. I saw them in concert three times."

"Did you now?"

"They did the best version ever of 'This Guy's In Love With You'."

"Is that right?"

"Are you taking the piss?"

"Yep."

"Thought so." Andy cranked up the volume and put his arm across the back of her seat. Shaunna smiled to herself and got into the groove.

The furniture warehouse they were going to was about forty minutes' drive away, and they walked across the car park with their arms around each other, safe in the knowledge that no-one they knew would see them.

"Do you have any idea what you want?" Shaunna asked.

"I don't mind, as long as it's big enough for me to lie on, and bouncy enough to, err...play bounce."

She pushed him away as they approached the automatic doors. Once inside, they wandered around, both feeling a little strange. Neither of them had ever done this before. Kris had always bought the furniture, because he had more interior design sense than Shaunna, and Andy had always lived in pre-furnished places—his mother's, the rented house and then with Jess—so it was both novel and exciting to be buying furniture for the first time, and together. They could feel themselves being sucked into an illusory alternate reality, where they were doing this for *their* house, and Shaunna felt a bit wobbly, not for the first time. She reminded herself. She loved him. He loved her. Nothing else mattered.

"What about this one?" Andy said, flopping down in the middle of an enormous sofa. Everything about it was massive— fat cushions, chubby black wooden feet, and the upholstery was jumbo corduroy. Red jumbo corduroy.

"What's with the red thing?" Shaunna asked, sitting down next to him. Andy shrugged.

"It's my favourite colour."

It was a very comfortable sofa, she had to admit. She wriggled around a little, and bounced up and down. Andy raised his eyebrows and fought the urge to smile.

"What d'you think?" he asked.

"Put it on the list," she said. She got up. "That one's nice." She nodded at a sofa that, again, was red, but with a black swirly pattern. She went over and sat on it, patting the seat next to her. Andy joined her.

"Yeah," he agreed. "This one's OK, too."

And so it continued all around the vast shop, until they had tried every sofa that was a three-seater or more, and narrowed it down to five possibilities, in between dodging salespeople who were doing more harm than good. They'd already watched two would-be customers walk out, rather than put up with the constant harassment.

A second round saw them reducing the shortlist further, so that they were left with just the two red sofas and were arguing out the benefits of having wider cushions so they could lie on it together even though Shaunna's feet didn't reach the floor, or the fixed cushions of the red and black swirly sofa that wouldn't slip off if put to the test. A sales assistant loitered nearby, trying to be patient, but they could see he was itching to approach.

"I reckon we get him," Shaunna said.

"How?" Andy asked.

"Follow my lead."

"Hi, do you need any help?" The man swooped in, giving them both his best salesman's smile.

"We're trying to decide between these two," Shaunna said, putting the tip of her finger to her mouth and blinking at him, all wide eyes and pouty lips. "But we just can't agree. Which one do you like the most?"

"Well," he coughed and suddenly his voice was much deeper, "the Lanchester," he pointed to the red corduroy sofa, "is a very popular, hard-wearing design."

"Hard-wearing? Oh, that's just what we need. And does it clean easily?"

"Yes. All our sofas have—"

"I mean, if we were having a little party and the guests got a bit raunchy—I think you know what I'm saying?" She smiled at him and ran her tongue over her teeth.

"Quite, madam." The man blushed. "It will stand up to red wine and all kinds of… things." He gave her a wink. Andy decided he'd just watch and try to enjoy the show.

"And is it well sprung?" she asked. She sat down in the middle of it and bounced up and down with sufficient vigour for her breasts to also bounce up and down. Andy took a deep breath. She smiled up at him and bit her lip. He turned away. The poor sales assistant didn't have the same luxury, and she was being profoundly provocative, albeit in a dreadfully stereotypical way. However, by the time she'd put the red corduroy sofa through its paces, she'd concluded that Andy was right. It was the more comfortable of the two, and she actually rather liked it. The sales assistant looked very relieved when her decision finally released him, and he swiftly scurried away to get his clipboard.

Andy walked back over to Shaunna and put his arms around her. "You are a bad, bad woman. You just terrified that poor bloke to death."

"I was trying to turn you on," she said innocently, reaching up and kissing his chin.

"You did that, all right."

"Was it too much?"

"Not for me."

"Ooh!" she teased. "I sense a challenge coming on."

"I thought I was the one who took the challenges."

She nodded slowly and smiled. "There you go. Can you rise to it, do you think?"

"Stop it." He laughed, although he was having some trouble resisting the urge to abandon the sofa purchase and head for the nearest secluded spot, wherever that happened to be.

"Here we are." The sales assistant returned, and they sat around on the red sofa and its armchair companion whilst Andy's order was written out. He answered yes to whatever he was asked regarding stain protection and extra warranties in order to expedite the process. They booked his delivery in for the first week of December, and that was it. All done. New sofa ordered and paid for and it was still only mid-afternoon.

"What do you want to do now?" Andy asked pointlessly, as he knew exactly what she wanted to do. She grinned at him. He shoved the car in gear and tore out of the car park, getting back to the apartment in under thirty minutes. They just about made it inside the door before she literally ripped off his t-shirt and pushed him backwards, her intention being to walk him to the bedroom, but he stumbled and landed on the floor. She pinned him down by his arms and kissed him, biting at his lips, his chin and all the way down his neck to his chest, losing her grip on him in the process.

He sat up and pulled off her top, reaching behind her to unfasten her bra, pausing only while she removed her pants and his, and there they were again, having sex in the middle of that plush cream carpet, but this time, she was in control, and he let her do just as she wanted.

Afterwards, in the bathroom, Andy stood in front of the mirror while he waited for the shower to warm up. He examined his neck.

"You bit me," he said.

She squinted at the purple mark. "Oops." She grimaced guiltily. "Maybe it'll fade."

They showered, rubbing shower gel over each other and sliding skin against skin, covered in the fragrant lather. He washed her hair and played with it, pulling it down over her breasts and then pushing it back up into curls. Every so often, she'd catch a glimpse of the mark on his neck, which wasn't fading at all. They finished showering and wandered about the place wrapped in towels, and then naked, and she dried her hair as best she could with no hair dryer. Again, he couldn't keep his hands off it.

"I need to go and feed the dog," she said.

She was sitting on the end of the bed, staring out at the darkening sky, and he was sitting behind her, intermittently massaging her back and lifting her hair to kiss her neck. He stopped and put his arms around her, coming up close so that he had completely wrapped her in his body. She held onto his forearms and sighed heavily.

"What's the matter?" he asked.

"Just thinking about Jess. How are you doing?"

He lay down on his side and waited for her to join him before he answered. "It still hurts. It's like the worst bellyache, and every now and then it just hits me."

"Yeah. I know what you mean." She rolled onto her back and studied the ceiling.

He reached over and played with her nipple, purely for contact and comfort. "I started sorting out her accounts last week. I can't make sense of them, so Charlie's taken them."

"Was she loaded?"

"She had quite a lot of money in one account, but there's just so many savings accounts and shares and God knows what else. She probably owes a fortune on credit cards, too. Anyway, I'm more than happy to pay Charlie to do it for me. I want it all finished with now. And someone's made an offer on the house, so hopefully that'll be off my hands before Christmas."

"What're you gonna do with all the money?"

"You mean any that's left after I've paid for all the shoes and shit?"

Shaunna laughed.

"She wanted to give it to charity. And that suits me just fine. I don't want it. I'm not materialistic."

"Other than the 1969 Mustang convertible, and the massive red sofa, and the super-stylish bachelor pad—"

"They're not for me," he said.

She turned her head so she could look at him. "Don't do it for me."

"Why not? It keeps us both happy. Right, RHB, get your kit back on. Let's go feed the mutt."

"I can go on my own."

"No, you can't. It's getting dark."

"So?"

"I won't let you."

She smiled. "See? Instinctive."

***

531

Shaunna was quiet and thoughtful all the way home. Kris and Ade were away overnight, and she wasn't sure what to do for the best. She wanted to stay at Andy's, but she couldn't leave Casper on his own and didn't think it was right to suggest taking him back to the apartment with its very new and very clean carpets. However, Andy had also realised all of that for himself, and he truly didn't care for material things, so he made the offer.

"You know dogs are not clean animals?" Shaunna asked as she let them into the house. As if to prove it, Casper brought Andy the most disgustingly dirty, soggy old rope toy and insisted he took it. Andy screwed up his face and dropped the toy back into the dog's basket on the way through to the kitchen. Shaunna let Casper outside to do his business, filled the kettle and started making the dog's dinner, all in one fluid motion.

"Just watch your jeans when he comes back in. He goes troughing in the plant pots, so his nose will be filthy."

Andy came up behind her and leaned in, kissing her neck. "I don't care," he breathed.

"Also, when he's eaten his dinner—"

"I spent four days with him at Mum's. I know what he's like."

"Yeah. Of course you do." She carried on with making Casper's dinner. The kettle came to the boil, and Andy broke away to make the tea. Shaunna put the dog's bowl down on the floor and straightened up, stretching her shoulders.

"I'm a bit stiff."

"It'll be all that stressing about your doydy dawg," Andy said. He was waiting for the tea to brew. She moved closer to him, standing on tiptoes to kiss him. He pushed against her. "Damn. I was gonna offer you a massage, but I'm a bit stiff myself now."

"Is that so?" She leaned on him and pushed him back until he was rammed up against the cupboard. She started to unfasten his belt, and he grabbed her hand.

"Not here. It's not right."

She stayed where she was, sneaking her hands inside his t-shirt. He breathed out shakily and shook his head.

"OK," she relented. "I'm gonna go and grab my toothbrush and stuff. Won't be a sec." She left and went upstairs.

Andy wriggled to adjust himself and stepped around the dog to reach the cutlery drawer. He fished the teabags out of the cups and stood with them balanced on the end of the teaspoon, frowning as he looked around for the bin. He was still doing that when the front door opened, and Kris came in.

"Hey, Andy," he greeted cheerily. He ran straight up the stairs.

"Alright, mate?" Andy responded, still holding aloft the teaspoon, a puddle of tea on his upturned palm below. He could hear conversation above him, although he couldn't make out the words. Kris returned downstairs and came into the kitchen.

"Cupboard under the sink," he instructed.

"Ah! Cheers." Andy opened the cupboard, revealing a plastic lid and bag attached to the inside of the door. He deposited the teabags. "I thought you were in London."

"I am. Well, I will be." Kris glanced at his phone to check the time. "I forgot to pick up an epi-pen. I probably won't need it, but it's better to be safe. Anyway, we've just missed the train, so we're getting the next one. How did you get on with furniture buying?"

"Yeah. All right. Ordered a sofa. It's bright red."

"What colour's your lounge?"

"Cream."

"That'll be really nice."

"I hope so."

"Can I just, err…" Kris indicated to the wall cupboard behind Andy, advancing on him.

"Oh, yeah. Sorry." Andy stepped to one side.

"Thanks." Kris opened the cupboard and studied the contents. Now the two men were standing so close that their thighs were touching, and Andy was still aroused from before. Kris glanced down.

"That's quite a load you're packing," he said quietly.

Andy tried not to react, but he could feel his pulse quickening. Kris looked up again, making it as obvious as possible that he'd seen the bite on Andy's neck. And for all that he was terrified because he knew what Kris was capable of, Andy felt himself getting hard again. It was freaking him out.

Kris carried on staring at him until he had no choice but to make eye contact. "Tell you what," Kris said, still in the same steady voice, "you don't shove it in my face, and I'll try not to shove it in yours. How about that?" He walked away, deliberately brushing against Andy's crotch with his hip.

Shaunna arrived at the bottom of the stairs at the same time as Kris. He gave her a gentle peck on the lips.

"I'll see you tomorrow night," he said, all sweetness and light.

"OK. Be amazing," she called after him as the front door closed. She returned to the kitchen, the smile fading from her face the instant she saw Andy's expression. "What's wrong?"

"Your husband is the scariest man I have ever met."

"Why?"

"I don't even know what that was." Andy scratched his head and went to sit at the table. He was so unnerved he nearly missed the chair.

"What did he say?"

"He knows, Shaunna."

"How? The love bite?"

"I think that just confirmed it for him."

Shaunna brought their tea over and sat opposite Andy. "So what d'you want to do? Stop?"

"Do you?"

"No."

"Neither do I." He rubbed his eyes. "It's fucking with my head."

"Tell me."

"He noticed I was still…from your antics before he came in. Jesus, can you imagine if we'd been on the table or something? Anyway, he basically told me not to do anything in front of him and he'd pay me the same courtesy."

"That'll explain that stupid little kiss I got on his way out."

Andy was mindlessly spinning the cup of tea between his hands.

Shaunna reached across and rubbed his arm gently. "I'm sorry. I know you didn't want it like this."

"No, I didn't. But it's, err…" He closed his eyes. "So help me, God, I never thought I'd be in this situation."

"What?" She watched him carefully. "It excites you more that he knows we're sleeping together?"

"Yeah, that's it, isn't it?"

"Is it?" she asked. She was still studying his face, trying to interpret his confusion. "Andy. Talk to me."

He shrugged. "It turned me on."

"It turned you on, or *he* turned you on?"

"That's what I mean. I don't know."

"Ohhh." Shaunna sat back and picked up her tea. "OK," she said. She sipped slowly. "That's tricky."

"Tell me about it. What the fuck, Shaunna?"

"Look. Don't worry. It'll only be your latent homosexuality showing through."

"Don't say that!"

She winked at him. "I'm kidding. There's lots of reasons why it aroused you, but it doesn't mean you've suddenly 'caught gay'."

"Like what?"

"OK. Well, given my relationship situation I know quite a lot about this, so if I get a bit carried away just stop me. Firstly, you can't suddenly turn gay or straight, but it isn't entirely fixed. Most people have sexual feelings for people of the same or different genders at some point in their lives. However, I don't think it was sexual, necessarily, although maybe it was a bit."

Andy was watching and listening, but he also had a slight smirk on his face.

"Am I boring you?" she asked. He shook his head.

"No. It's like having a conversation with Josh."

"Hmm. I tell you what. If you saw the painting George did of him, you'd be getting yourself in a right old twist. It's beautiful and it's him, but, phew!" She fanned her face for effect. "My goodness, is it him!"

Andy laughed. "You're like a burning hot ball of passion, Shaunna Hennessy."

"Thanks. You're pretty hot stuff yourself." He smiled properly this time. "Honestly," she continued, "if it was sexual at all, it'll only be because of what I said about two guys together turning me on, but really I think it was just because he scared you, even

though he's a five-foot-eleven streak and you're six two and—"
She eyed him over. "Damn those muscles!" Andy gave her a faked
weary look. She grinned. "It's your love of danger. Nothing more."

"Yeah. Maybe you're right."

"And if I'm not, so what?"

"You don't care?"

"I don't care, though I'm definitely not sharing you with my
husband. He's already got two of us on the go."

"I think he's got a bloody cheek, if I'm honest."

"Not really. He loves Ade, but he needs me. He can't bear the
idea of sharing me any more than you can. He's not saying I can't.
He's just asking me not to advertise it, which works perfectly all
round." She smiled brightly.

Andy nodded. "OK. I can go with that, for now. Shall we
scoot?"

Casper was long since done eating his dinner, and that was all
they'd been waiting for.

"Yeah. Let's do it." She got up and rinsed the cups. When
she was done, she pulled Andy close and traced a path with her
tongue, up his chin, to his lips. "And as I told you. You're not his
type, so you're safe. From him, at least. Let's go, big boy."

She attached Casper's lead to his collar, grabbed Andy by the
hand, and led them both down the garden path.

SAGITTARIUS

Life is an arrow, therefore you must know
What mark to aim at, how to use the bow—
Then draw it to the head and let it go!

The Y-Files
Thursday 23rd–Friday 24th November

"Are you sure you wouldn't rather have cash in hand?" Sean handed over the cheque in payment for the loft conversion.

"Nah. We're all above board. We have to be, with the amount of overseas stuff we do."

"Well, cheers. It's a bloody fine job you've made of it." Sean shook Andy's hand. "I'm still negotiating with Soph on whether I need to be looking at extending upstairs, but I'll come back to you on that one, if you don't mind."

"Sure. I like doing these little construction jobs. It makes a nice change."

"Good to know. So how are you? Better?"

"Yeah." Andy nodded, trying not to smile. "I'm feeling pretty good at the moment, thanks. You?"

"Not so bad at all." Sean was doing an appalling job of sustaining the conversation, for whilst it had not been admitted by either party, he could have guessed with some accuracy as to why Andy was 'feeling pretty good at the moment'. However, it was not Sean's intention to prompt the usual deep discussion against a backdrop of Andy doing jobs around the house. He had a slightly different request to make and decided to go for broke.

"Listen, I wondered if you'd be up for doing another little job for me? It's not construction, but it'll only take a couple of hours of your time. Are you free tomorrow morning?"

"I can be."

"Great stuff. You don't need to bring any tools with you. Just your muscles and your best snarl. What d'you say?"

"OK?" Andy laughed, although he was a little worried.

539

"Don't panic. I only need you to look the part," Sean assured him, but Andy still wasn't convinced. "It'll all make perfect sense, I promise you."

***

"Eleanor! You look fantastic!" The short and rather flamboyant Scotsman threw his arms around her and kissed her, with a loud smacking sound, somewhere around the point where her ear joined her cheek.

"Hello, Callum. It's great to see you." She couldn't return the compliment. His face looked like it could do with a good iron, and his hair had receded to a thin line around the base of his skull, still kept long and scraped back in a straggly ponytail. "This is my friend, Josh. I think you spoke briefly on the phone a while back."

Callum held Josh's hand with both of his to shake it and smiled warmly. "Can I get you two something to drink?"

"Oh, thanks. I'll have a glass of house red," Eleanor responded.

"Just a coffee for me, please," Josh said.

Callum nodded and ordered their drinks.

Eleanor made eye contact with Josh to see what he thought of her old college buddy, although they'd been little more than fellow students. Josh was suitably intrigued.

Callum ushered them towards a table in the corner of the dimly lit gastro pub. "They're going to bring our drinks over. I gathered we'd be wanting to lunch at some point, which is why I chose this place. It serves an incredibly good steak."

He positioned himself in the corner of the bench seat and placed a battered briefcase next to him. Josh examined it.

"It was my grandfather's," Callum explained. "He gave it to me when I graduated, on the very same day he retired from a forty-year career in medicine. Very proud, he was."

Callum became wistful momentarily, and then flicked the catch of the briefcase open. It had a wonderful heavy click to it. Josh smiled, for the tiniest hint of a memory of his dad had popped into his head. Eleanor noticed the smile and frowned at him in query. He subtly shook his head to indicate it wasn't relevant.

Callum lifted a huge red-sheathed sheaf of papers from the case and placed it very carefully on the table. The bartender brought their drinks over. "Thank you," he acknowledged and waited for her to leave before he continued with the matter in hand. "I was dreadfully sorry to hear about what happened to Kevin." He gave Eleanor a smile of genuine sympathy.

"Thanks."

"Such a tragedy. I'm almost certain if he'd turned up to the hearing, the case would have been dismissed more or less outright, and you'll understand why I'm saying that when I show you what I've got." He unfastened the band on the red vellum binding and extracted the top few papers. "This is Patricia Biddiscombe's medical history." He handed the papers over.

Eleanor began reading right away and passed each page to Josh as she finished it, both of them nodding and humming as they read over the initial summary that made clear the article Josh had found online was indeed concerning the death of Patricia Biddiscombe, who had been diagnosed with motor neurone disease at the age of forty-three and died five years later.

The rest of her medical history related to management of the symptoms of her condition and included a note two years prior to her death that she had an advance directive in place. Her GP at that time, as they'd already figured out, was Doctor Kevin Callaghan, and the information he'd recorded was nothing out of the ordinary: the usual date plus a couple of lines of explanatory text for each of his consultations with his patient.

The printout was comprehensive yet succinct, and it took them only a few minutes to read it in its entirety. As Josh came to the bottom of the last page, he reached out and took Eleanor's hand. Kevin had suddenly departed from his previous objective documenting of medical facts and written the last two entries in lengthy, emotional prose. They detailed what Kevin found when he arrived at the scene—family and friends gathered for Patricia's final few hours of life—and it could have been a description of the last night they had spent with Jess.

That was also the point at which things started to make less sense, as Kevin had recorded that the patient was calm and settled, yet the next entry saw him intubating her, after which she was taken to hospital. The GP notes ended there, with the next two pages detailing the consultant's findings: the patient was being ventilated manually on arrival at the hospital; once ventilation ceased, the patient died.

Josh handed the notes back to Callum and took the opportunity to consolidate what he'd just read whilst sipping at his coffee. It was an exceptionally good cup, with a tight foam and a rich, deep flavour and aroma.

"Mmm," he sounded without realising he'd done so. Eleanor peered sideways at him.

Callum laughed. "I've had the coffee here myself, and it's a mighty brew. So, what do you think so far?"

"Not sure," Eleanor said. "Presumably, there's an explanation for why Kevin tried to ventilate a patient with a DNR and, in any case, one with a condition that wouldn't benefit from such a measure."

"Indeed there is." Callum handed her another set of papers: only two or three pages this time, and handwritten by a carer who had witnessed what took place at Patricia's home when Kevin visited that afternoon. The carer noted Kevin often called in after work, out of courtesy and compassion rather than in his professional capacity, as there were private nurses on duty around the clock.

On the day she died, Patricia was in partial respiratory failure but was comfortable otherwise, and it was apparent she was already near the end. Therefore, on first consideration, it seemed odd that Kevin had suddenly intervened and inserted the ventilation tube that meant she had died in hospital in a state of distress, rather than peacefully drifting away in her sleep at home. However, the carer had also listed everyone else who was in the house at the time. Most of those present were family—her stepsister and nieces, her closest friend—and then finally there was that name again.

"I'm guessing Patricia Biddiscombe and Simon Yarrow were friends?" Josh speculated.

Callum shook his head vehemently; his ponytail swung from side to side. "No. They were not, and I say that with some certainty, as both the carers and Kevin mentioned in their formal statements that they had overheard heated discussions between Yarrow and Patricia's stepsister on numerous occasions."

"Is it common practice for a lawyer to be present if there is an advance directive in place?"

"Not unless there are questions raised regarding its validity, and even then, it would be at the physician's request in order to clarify their legal position."

"Validity is determined by mental capacity at the time of signing the advance directive, isn't it?" Josh asked, although he knew it was so. Callum and Eleanor both nodded in confirmation. "Which she drew up two years before she died, and there are no underlying mental health problems detailed in her GP's record."

"I think at this juncture it might be useful for you to see the official statements." Callum was already fishing them out of his file. "Much of what I've got here isn't relevant, I imagine, as it relates to Kevin's professional status—qualifications, character references, and so on—but I'll show you his and the family's statements and also—" he passed the whole pile over "—Yarrow's statement."

Eleanor took the papers and gave half to Josh. He went straight to the one provided by Simon Yarrow.

On Tuesday sixteenth December I attended the home of Patricia Biddiscombe client of Yarrow and Perlett with reference to legal documentation drawn up in consultation with Patricia Biddiscombe during the two previous years specifically an advance directive detailing her request that life-prolonging medical interventions be withheld and the last will and testament of the aforementioned.

In particular on this occasion concerns had been raised by Patricia Biddiscombe's stepsister regarding misplaced documents. I was thus requested to provide a copy of the last will and testament of Patricia Biddiscombe which I duly did.

Patricia Biddiscombe's general practitioner Doctor Kevin Callaghan arrived during my visit and communicated with the nursing and care staff on duty at that time. I was with Mrs. Biddiscombe's stepsister and nieces namely Rebecca Pilkington Jayne Docherty and Sandra Pilkington-Greaves in the downstairs lounge of the property. Upon Doctor Callaghan's arrival Rebecca Pilkington excused herself and went upstairs to her stepsister's bedroom whereby she discovered that Doctor Callaghan had called an ambulance and was in the process of intubating Patricia Biddiscombe in order to manually ventilate her.

The ambulance arrived approximately ten minutes later and Patricia Biddiscombe was taken to Newcastle Hospital. I followed in my car and was present when a doctor informed Patricia Biddiscombe's stepsister and nieces that she had removed the ventilator tube and Patricia Biddiscombe had died soon after.

"I wish lawyers would use bloody punctuation," Josh muttered when he'd finished reading. He rubbed his eyes and blinked a few times.

"Where are your glasses?" Eleanor asked.

"At home," he said cagily. He'd yet to brave wearing them outside of the house, but they were, in fact, in his inside pocket. Eleanor examined his face, and he sighed. "All right. Fine," he relented. He took them out and put them on.

"They suit you," Callum complimented.

Josh gave him a quick smile and picked up Yarrow's statement again. It was much clearer but still lacking commas. "What've you been reading?" he asked Eleanor.

"Rebecca Pilkington's statement."

"Ah, now that's particularly interesting," Callum said, "as you'll notice something of a fabrication in Yarrow's statement when you've read the two in conjunction with what the nurse had to say."

Josh and Eleanor exchanged statements and began to read again.

"I'll go and get a menu," Callum suggested. He left.

"Hm. That is particularly interesting," Josh said in an accent that wasn't dissimilar to Callum's, if not a little exaggerated. He waited until Eleanor was finished with Yarrow's statement. She turned to him and shook her head in disbelief.

"So Kev intubated after Rebecca told him she believed her stepsister's will had been tampered with."

"Looks that way, although she also says that she and Patricia were 'estranged for almost ten years'. I'd have been questioning why she was back on the scene and making a fuss myself." Eleanor swapped Yarrow's statement for that of one of the nieces. It, too, was honest about the estrangement between the two sisters and went on to detail that they had fallen out over Patricia's choice of husband.

Callum returned with the menus. "I also have a copy of a letter from Patricia to Rebecca, which makes clear they made up long before Patricia's death, if that helps to clarify the relationship for you."

Eleanor nodded. "So Kev was acting in the patient's best interests." She leafed through the other statements and located the one given by the nurse; it corroborated what Rebecca Pilkington had said. "Why the hell did you go on the run, you idiot?" she asked of Kevin's spectre in her imagination. "He'd have been cleared just on the basis of these statements."

"Not necessarily," Callum argued. "The legislation and GMC guidance both refer to acting in the patient's best interests in the event that the validity of the AD is called into question, not the validity of the patient's will."

"But you said he'd probably have been cleared."

"Probably, yes. The Mental Capacity Act section 4c states that, I quote, 'an advance decision may not be applicable if there are reasonable grounds for believing that circumstances exist which the patient did not anticipate at the time of the advance decision and which would have affected his decision had he anticipated them.'"

"That only applies to medical circumstances," Eleanor said.

"It does, but the lack of clarity was what we were intending to utilise, and both the stepsister and niece were prepared to testify at the hearing to the effect that Kevin had tried to prolong Patricia's life so that there was time for her will to be investigated. The copy they had in their possession differed to the one they found with the rest of her documents, in which she had left the entire estate to her second husband, who had died several months earlier. There was no provision made in the event of the failure of the will."

"I hear big clanging alarm bells," Josh said. He noticed Eleanor pick up the menu, look over it, and then put it down again. "do you want to eat?" he asked. It was a question with a double meaning, and her answer covered both of them.

"Yes," she said, nodding to confirm it.

"OK. Shall I choose?" he suggested. She nodded again. He went with Callum's recommendation and ordered the steak, after which he continued to read the rest of the statements, all confirming what they had already realised. Simon Yarrow was, at best, giving poor legal advice and more than likely defrauding his clients. The question was not only how he was actually achieving that, but, more importantly, how it came to be that both Patricia Biddiscombe and Jess had the same lawyer. They lived over a hundred miles apart, and there was only one other person connecting them: the late Doctor Kevin Callaghan.

Based on the evidence, it appeared that Kevin *was* acting in Patricia's best interests, which suggested that he was being usurped by Yarrow, rather than being part of any scheme himself. A further question, therefore, was whether he was aware of what was going on and went 'on the run' for that reason.

For now, though, their meals had arrived, and so they put the evidence away to eat and enjoy a bit of socialising, which was to say Eleanor and Callum chatted away about life in uni while Josh watched and listened as and when he was paying attention, but his mind was working overtime. He wasn't especially knowledgeable about inheritance law, although he did know that if a person died intestate, their closest relatives inherited automatically, so if Yarrow was defrauding clients, it needed an extra step beyond simply ensuring they died with no nominated beneficiaries.

Patricia Biddiscombe had living next of kin; even though her husband would have inherited had he still been alive, her stepsister would have been next in line. In Jess's case, in the absence of spouse and offspring, it would have been her parents. However, she'd married Andy, hence it went to him, and Josh couldn't quite put the final stitch in place to see how Yarrow was making anything out of the scam, if, indeed, that was what it was.

They came to the end of their meal, and Josh bought a round of drinks, over which they read Kevin's statement and discussed his mental health. Nothing Callum had to tell them was news, for it played out word for word as per Kevin's letter to Eleanor, up until the end point where he named James as the man she should fear.

Callum explained that Kevin's initial psychotic break happened a few weeks after the Biddiscombe case and before the date of the first hearing of the GMC panel—not surprising, given the stress he was under with his registration suspended and the hearing on hold, never mind the CPR case, or the animosity his father displayed towards him. By the time he'd arrived in Lincoln, Kevin was so ill that Callum suggested he go to the hospital on a voluntary basis. Kevin had refused, insisting that 'they' were after him, with no real explanation for who 'they' might be.

In retrospect, Callum acknowledged that the paranoia was most likely fuelled by Yarrow's threats to take civil action, should the GMC happen to find in Kevin's favour. But the more Josh listened to Callum's account, the more he began to wonder just how psychotic Kevin really was, for the trail began and ended with the same name—evidence enough for someone under significant stress to believe that they were being followed. And that name was Simon Yarrow.

Callum had given them everything he had and was eager to make the next train back to Lincoln, so they said their goodbyes soon after. Josh and Eleanor journeyed home in silence, both pondering over everything they had seen and heard. It had been a very useful meeting in many respects. Eleanor now understood how her peaceable, law-abiding ex-husband could have ended up in the situation he was in and was entirely satisfied that he was innocent of Campion's murder.

Josh had a few more answers to his puzzle over Jess's will, although with those answers came more questions, and he'd fairly worn himself out thinking. He dropped Eleanor off and went straight home, utterly exhausted and glad to be spending the evening in the straightforward company of George and Iris, who accepted that today he didn't want to talk about how the meeting went beyond saying, "It went OK." Tomorrow was another day, and, with any luck, he'd be greeting it after a good night's sleep.

***

"Good morning!" Sean greeted with a certain amount of undisguised surprise at finding both Jeffries brothers on his doorstep.

"I figured," Andy said, "that if it's muscles and snarling you want, then it was worth bringing my big little brother along."

Sean laughed. "A great idea." He glanced past them and eyed the Mustang. "Nice wheels. Interesting choice of colour."

Andy led the way to the car without comment.

"All right, so," Sean began, "this job, then. We're going on an information-gathering mission, but the source might not be too willing to part with that information, which is why I asked for some assistance."

"Would this involve visiting a steel fabricator, by any chance," Dan asked, strapping himself into the passenger seat and getting a whiff of perfume from the seat belt as he did so. Sean got in the back.

"It very well may do." He looked around him admiringly. "Great car, the Mustang. I used to drool over the one in the Bond film. What was it now?"

"A 1971 Mach One," Andy said.

"That's right. That was red, too, wasn't it?"

"Yeah," Andy confirmed absently. "So who is this bloke?"

Sean didn't answer for a good while, because he wasn't sure how far he was prepared to trust Andy and Dan. He barely knew them, but they were part of the phenomenon: this curious bunch of people, all so different and yet so loyal to each other. It hadn't mattered when they were all pulling together for Jess; it shouldn't matter now.

"How's your little fella doing?" Dan asked, as if to help Sean along with the decision.

"Oh, he's smashing, Dan, thanks for asking. He's a really well-behaved baby. I was telling your Andy here that I'm hoping to convince Soph to let me take on a bit more of the parenting. She doesn't trust me to not drop him on his head, or pass out and leave him screaming for food."

Dan frowned sympathetically. "I know what you mean, mate. Adele was exactly the same when we first brought little Shaunna home."

"She's a beauty, for sure. She was born a bit premature, wasn't she?"

"Yeah. A lot prem, actually…"

The conversation continued, and Andy tried to ignore them, but after five minutes of driving and listening to them rambling on about nappy rash and the glorious scent of baby powder, he couldn't take any more.

"Do you think you could pack in with the whole *Daddy Day Care* routine?"

Sean and Dan stopped talking and looked at each other guiltily.

"Right. Somewhere around here, is it?"

Sean scanned the warehouses and spotted the sign for Miller Steel. Andy drove past and parked on the other side of the road.

"OK," Sean said. "So this guy was the eyewitness who identified James Brown."

"Witness?" Andy repeated.

"The fisherman whose knife was the murder weapon," Dan explained.

"Murder weapon? Who got murdered?"

"Campion."

"Oh, right." Andy nodded.

Dan tutted. "You're on another planet, you are."

"Yeah, bro, I was. Planet Dubai, remember?"

"Anyway," Sean interrupted, "Price is on his own on a Friday morning, so I thought we'd drop by and say hello."

Dan and Andy got out of the car and flanked Sean as they walked across to the warehouse. The sound of arc welding came from within, where, sure enough, a lone man was working. Sean waited for him to come to a pause before he approached.

"Davey," he called.

The man took off his welding mask and frowned. "Do I know you?"

"Are you Davey Price?"

"That's right. Who are you?"

Sean smiled. "I want to ask you a couple of questions, if I may."

"Are you police?"

"It'll only take a moment or two of your time."

"What's this about?"

"I've been working on a case for the past couple of years—the murder of Alistair Campion."

"I told you everything I know already." The man kept glancing past Sean, at Dan and Andy, who were both dressed in their usual smart yet casual work attire and looked the part.

"Well, see, the thing is, Davey…" Sean smiled again. "I can call you Davey?"

"Yeah," the man agreed nervously.

"So the thing is, Davey, a little birdie told me that you might have been, let's say, a wee bit off in your description of the man who took your knife."

"I don't know what you mean."

"What I mean, Davey boy, is you lied."

Sean saw the shadows of the two men behind him grow larger. Davey Price backed away, his eyes flitting from one to the other, and back to Sean. Sean nodded slowly, implying that one word from him and his two cronies would rip Price to pieces.

"So, how about we start again, and you tell me the truth this time. What did he look like?"

"I dunno. Tall, fairly well-built, not quite as hefty as the Thompson Twins there." He nodded at Dan and Andy. They snarled. Davey backed off further, now almost up against the workshop wall.

"Can you be a little more specific?" Sean asked.

"He was about six foot, maybe six one, dirty-blonde hair, had a foreign accent. German or something? I dunno."

"Blonde hair?" Sean repeated. Davey nodded. "So he was white?"

"Yeah."

550

"And what did he say, this *white* man?"

"He gave me five hundred quid and a photo to study, said if anyone came asking, that's who took the knife, and if he found out I'd said otherwise, he'd break my legs."

Sean reached inside his jacket. Davey flinched. "Don't worry, pal," Sean said. "I'm not going to shoot yer." He pulled a photo out. "Is this him?"

"Yeah." Davey nodded assuredly. "That's him."

Sean patted him firmly on the shoulder. "Good man," he said. He turned and strolled away very, very slowly.

"Is…is that it?" Davey called after him. Dan and Andy were still standing right in front of him.

Sean looked back and smiled. "For now." He carried on walking.

Davey sneered at Dan. "You heard him, didn't you? Tin Tin's done with me."

Dan grabbed him around the throat and pushed him against the wall. He wasn't holding him particularly tightly, but Davey gasped and nearly choked himself.

"Let me go!" he demanded. Dan's grip tightened, and Davey started to panic. "Please. Let me go. I've done nothing wrong!"

Andy put his hand on Dan's shoulder, and Dan let go. The two brothers turned to leave.

"Fucking psychos," Davey muttered under his breath. Quick as a flash, Dan turned back and grabbed him again. Andy stepped to the side and leaned in so he was right up in the man's face.

"I think what my brother's trying to tell you," he hissed, "is we're not twins." He gave Dan a nudge and once again, he released Davey, who coughed and rubbed his neck, just like he'd seen in the movies. He stayed right where he was, until Dan and Andy were out of sight, and then he locked all the doors.

As soon as they got outside, Dan and Andy high-fived each other.

Sean shook his head. "I bet you two were a complete pain in the arse at school."

"What d'you mean, *were*?" Dan grinned. They returned to the car to head back to Sean's.

"So, who is he?" Andy asked. "The bloke in the photo?"

"Anders Folden."

Dan's teeth clenched.

"He's not German, he's Norwegian," Sean continued. "And he's been living in the UK for the past ten years."

Andy glanced across at his brother, spotting the vein throbbing in his neck. At the next set of lights, he waited a little too long so that Dan would look his way. He gave him a subtle wink; Dan gave a single, barely detectable nod in response.

They arrived back at Sean's and went in, having been promised a cappuccino and a full explanation.

"There we are," Sean said, setting down their cups. "This Folden guy went off the radar a couple of years back, around the time of Campion's murder, interestingly."

"You reckon it's him?" Dan asked.

"It looks likely."

"Presumably, Campion did something to piss him off?" Andy speculated.

"Your guess is as good as mine."

And that was where Sean was having something of a problem, for whilst everything pointed to Folden being the murderer, he'd yet to come up with any plausible reason why, beyond him being a psychopath. Campion gave Folden a chance. He had no obvious motive. The only other lead Sean had he'd been reluctant to follow; now it looked like he had no choice, so when Andy and Dan left, he hitched a lift with them, back to the industrial estate, and to Black Hole Studios.

***

Deceptive: that was the most appropriate, though somewhat understated description of the quietness Sean experienced on his approach, because the noise that hit him when he opened the door was quite something to behold. He stood in the reception area, flinching in pain in time to the rapid bass beat and trying to adapt to the volume before he moved any closer to the source. He reached out and put his hand on the door in front of him, braced for impact and pushed. *Boom!*

The room before him was large, painted entirely black and empty other than for the three people on stage, one behind a drum kit and two armed with guitars. Sean edged closer, squinting to focus on the musicians, smiling when he recognised the guitarists: Jason and Hadyn. They, too, had seen him, and Jason waved his arm at the drummer. It took a few seconds for the signal to register.

Jason jumped down and walked across. "Hi, Sean! What're you doing here?"

"Hello, Jason. That was, err, very—"

"Loud?"

"Yeah. Good, though."

"Thanks. Me, Stu and Hadyn are rehearsing some of Hadyn's songs."

"Good stuff," Sean said, nodding. He wasn't sure what else to say, because he needed to get Jason on his own and couldn't think how best to do it with Hadyn there.

"You want to see the recording studio?" Jason asked, sensing what Sean was trying to do.

"Yeah, I'd like that." Sean followed him out of the room and up the stairs.

"This is the first chance we've had to rehearse in weeks," Jason explained. "And really I should be doing paperwork, but I hate it. I still haven't given up hope of talking my dad into giving me a hand."

"That's a great idea." Sean went with the flow, hoping it would keep things nice and calm. The last thing he wanted was to put Jason under any unnecessary stress.

Jason unlocked the control room and waited for Sean to step inside before he switched on the lights in the recording space.

"This is quite something," Sean said, genuinely impressed by what he was seeing. "I used to play a bit when I was younger, you know."

"Really? What d'you play?"

"The fiddle. I don't suppose I'd remember how now, mind you."

"Cool."

"Yeah, not so cool as bass guitar."

"It's in the ear of the beholder, as I keep telling Krissi. She listens to some terrible music. Whining, miserable indie stuff."

Sean laughed, although he wasn't entirely sure his own music collection was free from 'whining miserable indie stuff'.

"So," Jason continued. "I'm guessing you wanted to talk to me about something?"

"Yeah." Sean took the photo of Anders Folden from his pocket. "I was wondering if you've ever seen this guy before?" He passed the photo across.

Jason examined it and shrugged. "I don't think so." He handed the photo back. No questions about who the man was, or why he was being asked. Sean was getting a strange vibe. Maybe he needed to have another think about how to approach this, to get Jason onside.

"Ah well, not to worry." He put the photo back in his pocket. "I'll let you get on with your rehearsal."

"OK. Sorry I couldn't help."

"That's all right. It was a long shot. But you know, if you ever need a middle-aged fiddler, I'm sure I could give the old girl a dust down."

"I'm gonna hold you to that." Jason followed Sean to the door, but then stopped and retraced his steps, stooping to retrieve something from the floor. "You dropped this," he said.

Sean frowned and looked down at the item Jason had placed in his hand. He looked up again.

"It must have fallen out of your pocket," Jason said meaningfully.

"Thanks." Sean smiled. "I don't know what I'd have done if I'd lost that." He put the memory card in his pocket and returned downstairs, where Hadyn was getting a drink from the vending machine.

"Hi, Sean."

"Hadyn. How are you? I haven't seen you for a while. You getting on OK?"

"Yeah. I'm great. Working here is the best thing that's ever happened to me."

Sean nodded. Again, he was picking up subtext to what was being said, but he couldn't quite figure it out.

"I'm hoping Jay will keep me on when my probationary period is over."

"When does that come to an end?"

"Soon, I hope." Hadyn looked Sean directly in the eye. "It'll be good to be working here as a fully fledged sound engineer."

"It seems to me Jason already sees you as such."

"Yeah. We've got a good, honest working relationship, if you get me?"

"Yes," Sean said, "I do." He lightly squeezed Hadyn's arm. "I'll be on my way. Good to see you."

He left, but he didn't go home. He went straight to the university, where he knew Josh would be working today. Much as Josh loved Iris, she was something of a distraction when it came to getting things done, particularly as the notion of working at home was somewhat lost on her.

As Sean climbed the stairs to the floor where their offices were located, he felt very smug and self-assured. He couldn't wait to show off and tell Josh about his visit to Davey Price. He knocked and pushed on the door handle at the same time. The door stayed where it was.

"Ah, balls," he said.

"Bloody Irish," a voice said behind him.

"I know. You have to nail everything down," said another voice.

Sean swivelled on the spot. "What in God's name are the pair of you wearing?"

"Fedoras," Josh said in a matter-of-fact tone. "Cool, aren't they?"

"Hmm. As a wise man told me not so long ago, 'cool' is in the ear, or in this case, eye of the beholder."

Eleanor tutted. "You're just jealous because you haven't got one."

Sean laughed and shook his head. The two of them looked ridiculous but happy with it. "So are yer gonna open the door, Joshy?"

"I might." A couple of students came past and stared. Josh tilted the brim of his hat at them. They looked terrified. He and Eleanor burst into giggles. "Come on, then. We've got something exciting to tell you." He opened his door, and the three of them went inside. "So yesterday," he said, ready to begin telling the story. He stopped and glared at Eleanor. "Best friend or not, that's still my chair!"

"Has it got your name on it?"

"No, but it's my office, and my desk, ergo *that* is my chair."

"I thought you two had fallen out," Sean said.

"We had," Eleanor confirmed.

"We might again…if somebody doesn't get their backside out of *my* chair!"

Eleanor grinned mischievously and went to sit next to Sean.

"Anyway, you were saying?" Sean prompted.

"Yes. Yesterday we met up with Callum Grady for lunch."

"OK. And?"

"We've found a connection between Jess's will—" Josh stopped speaking because Sean rolled his eyes. "Fine. I won't tell you."

"Ah, come on!"

"Nope."

"All right. I don't want to know."

"Oh, for God's sake!" Eleanor got up and stood between them. "Joshua, tell Sean what we know. Sean, keep your mouth shut."

"I—"

"Uh-uh!" She wagged her finger at him. "Wait your turn."

He scowled.

"Don't make me come back over there."

Sean pinched his lips together with his finger and thumb. Eleanor nodded at Josh. He frowned and folded his arms.

"Joshua!"

"OK," he relented. "Kevin Callaghan's registration was suspended because he ignored a patient's advance directive. The patient's lawyer was also a witness to Jess's will."

"Are you sure?" Sean asked doubtfully.

"Of course we're sure."

"You know more than one person can have the same name?"

"True, but how common a surname is Yarrow?"

"Fair enough." Sean sat back. "Are yer gonna put that kettle on, Joshy?"

"Are you staying?"

"I am. I've got something to tell you, too, once you're done."

"That's all we've found out."

Eleanor sighed loudly.

"Well," Josh backtracked, "almost all."

"We're going to be here all day at this rate," Eleanor snapped. She turned to Sean. "Kev ignored the advance directive to give

556

the woman's relatives time to look into the will, because it had been changed so that her dead husband was named as the sole beneficiary."

"Now you've got my interest," Sean said. He nodded at Josh and tilted his head at the kettle. Josh huffed and got up. Predictably, Eleanor stole his seat.

"Yes, so we've now got two cases where the beneficiary would have been non-existent at the time of death."

"Except that Jessie and Andy married."

"They did. That's true. Even so, Yarrow was a partner in a legal firm in Newcastle, now he works for Sharston Strang. It's more than a coincidence."

"Or not," Sean dismissed. "Is it my turn yet?"

"If you must."

Sean took the photo out of his pocket and put it down in front of Eleanor. She leaned forward and looked at it.

"Snap!" She opened the folder on Josh's desk and took out another photo, laying it next to the one Sean had set down. "Simon Yarrow," she said.

Sean shook his head. "Anders Folden."

"Who's Anders Folden?" Josh asked from across the room.

"That is." Sean tapped on the photo. "I went to see the eyewitness this morning—you know? The fisherman who claimed James took his knife? Turns out Folden bribed him to make the false identification and threatened to do him over if he told anyone."

Josh paused from his coffee making and came to look.

"That's Simon Yarrow," he said. The two photographs were of the same man, but in one, he looked to be in his late-thirties, in the other his mid-twenties.

"How old is James?" Sean asked.

"Thirty-three," Eleanor said. "Why?"

"Alice told me Folden is four years younger than James."

"Is this the guy she and James thought was responsible for murdering Campion?"

"Yeah, and Davey Price told me this morning this is the man who approached him."

557

"He just volunteered that information, did he?" Josh asked dubiously.

"Erm, I may have taken a couple of friends with me, to make sure he was feeling honest."

Eleanor raised her eyebrow at him. "Who, exactly?"

"A couple of…big, burly brothers."

Josh shook his head in disbelief.

"What?" Sean asked innocently.

"Nothing. Welcome to the bloody circle, Tierney."

"Aww, thanks." Sean grinned. "Anyway, there's no way Folden could be a barrister. He's too young, and he's got a criminal record for selling counterfeit passports. In other news, Hadyn's a police informant, and I've got this little—"

"What?" Eleanor and Josh exclaimed in unison.

Sean nodded. "Yeah. I was kind of hoping you'd just let that one go by."

"Oh no," Eleanor said. "He's working with Jay at the studio."

"I know."

"And James is a trustee."

"I know that, too."

"And Jason is Krissi's best friend," Josh added.

"And that, which is why I didn't tell you. We mustn't say a word about it to anyone. I promised."

"Who did you promise?" Eleanor asked.

Josh laughed incredulously. "Vera Bennett?"

Sean tried to cover himself, but it was too late. Josh had rumbled him.

"It's got to stay between the three of us," Sean reiterated, "although I think Hadyn might have told Jason himself."

"That's useful," Eleanor said, "or not."

"I don't think he's there to watch Jason. I think he's there to report back on anything suspicious. Jason was very careful in how he spoke to me, like he was trying not to give anything away, which is why I suspect he knows what Hadyn's up to. I showed him the photo, and he clearly recognised the guy, then he made out I'd dropped this." Sean fished the memory card from his pocket.

"What's on it?" Josh asked.

"Finish making that coffee and I'll show you, assuming one of your gadgets will be able to read it."

"My tablet. In there." He nodded at the bag on the floor behind Eleanor. She took it out and started it up. Josh made the coffee and brought it over.

"Now, I don't know what's on this," Sean said, "so if it turns out to be a nasty virus, I'll pay to get your tablet fixed up." He handed the memory card over, and Josh fed it into the slot. The video player automatically started and the screen filled with the fuzz of white noise, slowly clearing to reveal a boardroom.

Every so often, lines would flicker down the screen and the picture would disappear again, and there was no sound, but there was no mistaking what this was, or who this was. The three of them watched in horror as the two men went from what seemed to be a fairly genial and benign discussion to the taller and younger of the two advancing on the other, who momentarily froze, and then slowly collapsed and slid out of the camera shot. Even with the poor picture quality, it was clear to see the other man smiling down on his victim. And then he walked away. The screen went black.

"We have to tell the police," Eleanor said.

Josh and Sean nodded dumbly in agreement. Eleanor took out her phone. Josh put his hand on her arm.

"Hang on a minute. Let's work this out first."

She sighed in exasperation. "What is there to work out? Simon Yarrow, or Anders whatever his name is, killed Alistair Campion."

"There are people in danger, Ellie."

"And the best way to ensure they're safe is to tell the police."

She was right. Sean could see she was right. He nodded. "OK, but we can't tell them where we got the memory card."

"How did Jason get it?"

"It was…from Campion's," he explained vaguely.

"So what do you suggest we tell them?"

"That it came through the internal post here at the university."

"We can't lie to the police, Sean!"

"I understand what you're saying, Eleanor, but we can't incriminate Jason."

"Why? He's done nothing wrong."

Sean and Josh looked at each other.

"Josh?" she appealed. He put his head down so he couldn't see her.

"Client confidentiality," Sean said.

Eleanor threw her hands in the air. "Just listen to the pair of you! You're psychologists, not bloody priests. Come on. What did he do?"

"He withheld evidence, and so did Alice."

"What? My husband got arrested for this murder. My ex-husband killed himself, because of this murder, and now you're telling me that Jason and Alice had this all along?"

"Alice didn't know who the murderer was, but she knew Jason had something."

Eleanor couldn't believe what she was hearing. "Kevin died in prison, serving a sentence for a crime he didn't commit, and all the while Jason had this video." She couldn't think what else to say to make them see reason. "What do *you* think we should do?"

Sean and Josh remained silent.

"Anyone?"

Still they said nothing.

"Fine. I'll deal with it." She went to grab the tablet, but Josh got there first.

"No," he said. "Leave it with me. I'll get it to Aitch."

Luminosity
Monday 27th–Wednesday 29th November

Monday morning: the traffic from the village was slow-stop all the way into town, with roadworks littering every route, as was usual for the time of year—the start of the Christmas shopping chaos. Josh tapped along on his steering wheel in time with the current song playing on the radio. Sean tried to breathe in loudly through his nose to express his irritation but ended up coughing instead.

"What time's your lecture?" he asked.

"I haven't got one this morning. Why?"

"Do you want to do a quick detour and see what your man Aitch has to say about the video?"

Josh had delivered the memory card on Saturday morning, so Aitch would definitely have had time to look at it by now, and they'd expected to be hauled in for questioning, but they'd heard nothing.

"Yes, let's do that. Then I can get a decent coffee on the way." He turned off and headed across town to the police station.

***

"Have you seen it?" the actor who played DI Louisa Summers asked Kris as she took her seat next to him.

"What?"

"The new contract."

The entire cast and crew were gathered in the studio for a production meeting, and Kris hadn't got as far as looking through his pack yet. He wasn't interested.

"Right, folks," Barry said loudly, sitting on the back of the chair with his feet on the seat so that he had the height advantage.

561

"As you are all no doubt aware by now, someone—" he looked pointedly at Kris as he spoke, as it was Ade he was talking about "—spotted a little hole in the contract. We've had it drawn up again, checked and double-checked, and all seems in order. I'm also very pleased to be able to tell you that after several weeks of pointless talks, we officially have the go ahead to move the show to London."

Kris sighed and closed his eyes. So much for 'unsubstantiated rumours'.

"Copies of the new contract are in your pack, along with the rehearsal and shooting schedule, which we've delayed by a couple of days to give you a chance to get yourselves settled in. We'll be starting next Tuesday. If you've got accommodation, let Clare know, otherwise, it's—oh, I can't remember what the fuck it's called—the shitty place in King's Cross. Any questions, don't bother me with them. See Clare. So, we need to get the last of the Manchester stuff boxed off this week, and I'll expect you all bright-eyed…"

Kris got up and walked out.

***

Tuesday, and the wheels of justice were at a standstill.

Josh was clock-watching. Aitch hadn't been there when he and Sean had stopped by the previous morning, nor when Josh had called later and been advised to try again today. Instead, he'd called Dan for Aitch's mobile number and left him a cryptic voicemail. Now it was almost 12:30, and he was getting impatient. He called the station again.

"No, sir, I'm afraid DI Hartley isn't in today."

"Are you sure? I was told he'd be in after ten o'clock."

"I don't know why you were told that, but he's definitely not in today."

"OK. Thanks." Josh hung up. He waited five minutes and called back again.

"Good afternoon. This is Josh Sandison. Would it be possible to speak to PC Granger, please?"

"One moment, Mr. Sandison." The line went quiet. "I'll just put you through."

"PC Granger speaking. How can I help you, Mr. Sandison?"

***

"Kris." The executive producer strode towards his table at the back of the pub. She was the *Shadows* creator, and Barry's wife. Kris glanced up from his script as she sat down. They'd always had a good working relationship, but he didn't want to talk to her. He didn't want to talk to anyone.

"I'm sorry, Kris. We still hadn't finalised the deal when we last spoke."

"I'm not doing it," he said quietly, but with conviction.

"It's only for a few weeks at a time, you know that, and we've scheduled long weekends, so you can all get—"

"I'm not doing it. I'm not signing the contract. I'm not going to London. I can't do it anymore."

"But without you—"

"There's no *Shadows*? You're the writer. Kill Lundberg off. Bring in a replacement."

"Lundberg is *Shadows*. That's the whole point. He's dark and complicated, intense."

Kris rubbed his forehead. He felt like crap.

"I can try and get you some time out, maybe talk to Fuckface about rewriting Summers in as lead on the investigation for some of it." She smiled hopefully at him.

He smiled back, and even managed a little laugh at Barry being referred to as 'Fuckface', but still, he shook his head. "I'm sorry, Jan, I can't do it. It's making me ill. I'm not signing the contract."

***

Wednesday: waiting for Mr. R. Forster to show and still no word from Aitch. Josh was beginning to wonder if the video was a fake or a figment of his imagination. Maybe he'd ask Mr. Forster if he'd seen Alistair Campion recently.

There was a knock at the door.

"Come in."

The door opened.

"Good afternoon, Mr. Sandison-Morley, I'm—"

"DS Farrar," Josh finished.

"That's right." Farrar nearly frowned but was quick to cover it. "DI Hartley asked me to call in and have a chat with you."

"Is that so?" Josh examined the police officer, who was now sitting down uninvited. He was casual, relaxed, and completely closed off. Josh couldn't see past the shield at all, but he'd learned everything he needed to about DS Graham Farrar at the quiz night all those months ago. Six months. When Jess was still here. He switched back again. "How can I be of assistance?"

"He was curious to know how you came by the memory card."

"It was delivered by hand to my office."

"This one?" Farrar glanced around him as if questioning that it were Josh's office at all.

It's the only one I have," Josh said coolly.

"And when was that?"

"I'm not sure. Some point between Wednesday evening and Friday afternoon, which was when I found it in my pigeonhole."

"Can I ask where you were on Thursday?"

"Why?"

"Are you aware of what is on the memory card, Mr. Sandison-Morley?"

"Yes. I assumed it was a student's work, so I put it in my tablet." He picked up his coffee and took a large glug. It was cold but no-one would have guessed.

Farrar scrutinised Josh's face, seeking evidence that he was lying. Josh was a good liar. He had an excellent memory and complete conscious control of his gestures and expressions. There was no way Farrar was getting through, not with this approach. He changed tack.

"OK. Thanks for your help, and for passing on the memory card." He smiled amiably. "My wife is a student here."

Josh nearly choked on his coffee. "Your *wife*?"

"Yeah." Farrar acted as if he hadn't noticed Josh's reaction. "She's studying history."

"Oh, right." Josh rallied quickly. "That would be on the other side of campus."

Farrar nodded in agreement, confirming for Josh that he, too, was lying; the Humanities Faculty was next door to Social Sciences—the building they were in now.

"She's enjoying the course," Farrar said. He stood up again, and Josh moved to see him to the door. As they got there, Farrar leaned in close and shook Josh's hand. "Just a word of warning for you and your friends, and I've given Doctor Grady the same advice." His tone was firm, but not hostile. "Keep out of it."

***

"Right, Kristian, here's what we're proposing."

It was the big boss's turn to have a go at talking Kris around: the guy from the network that had negotiated with Barry and Jan to get the series. He was slick and smarmy, and Kris could smell his breath and the sushi he'd had for lunch. He backed off.

The man eyed him with disdain—understandably. Barry had sold *Shadows* as a package, DI Lundberg and the rest of the cast included. Now half of them had followed Kris's lead and also refused to sign the new contract.

"We'll kill off Lundberg if you're set on leaving, but there's still time to change your mind. Whatever, we need to make sure the viewers are on board with the new principal, and that's going to take two or three episodes, at least."

Kris studied the pictures on the walls of the room they were sitting in, trying not to swear. He wasn't going to change his mind; he thought he'd made it crystal clear.

The man sat back with folded arms, waiting for a response. "What do you think? Will you do that much for us? Three episodes? You'll be done this side of Christmas."

"Fine." Kris got up. "Sort it out with my agent. I'll see you next Tuesday, aptly."

***

"So I had a visit from DS Farrar this afternoon," Josh told George as they cooked dinner.

"About the memory card?"

"Hmm. His wife's a history student, apparently."

"OK."

"His *wife*, George."

"And?"

"He's gay."

"Is he?"

"The way he hit on you at the quiz night?"

George sighed. They'd had this conversation at least a dozen times already. "He wasn't hitting on me. He was giving me—"

"An update. I know."

"What else did he say?"

"That we're to leave well alone."

Josh attempted to make a heart on top of the latte he was preparing for Iris. It failed. "Damn. Oh, well. The sentiment's there."

George picked it up and took it through to her in the lounge, explaining that the lopsided white blob floating on her coffee was meant to be a heart.

"So he's not gobbed in it, then?" she asked. George tutted loudly and returned to the kitchen.

"Just pretend you're 'arry Potter, love," Iris shouted. "You know, swish 'n' flick."

Josh was still giggling when George returned and asked, "What is she on about?"

"We were watching video clips yesterday, of people creating latte art, and I said mastering *wingardium leviosa* would be easier, and she said something to the effect of, 'I have no idea what you are talking about, Josh.' So I loaded up *Harry Potter and the Philosopher's Stone* for her this morning."

George shook his head. "That's why she's calling Blue 'Fluffy'."

Josh laughed. "That's awesome, unlike this sauce. What have I done wrong?"

George tasted it and grimaced. "Too much salt."

"Oh. Bugger."

"Give me the pan."

"I'll fix it."

"How?"

"Erm…" Josh thought for a moment, but he had no idea how to fix it, or, indeed, if it could be fixed.

George waited for him to move away, but he didn't, so he tickled him and shoved him to one side whilst he was in a weakened state. He tipped the parsley sauce down the sink and started again. "So what else did DS Farrar say?"

"That was it, really, and that Callum Grady had been given the same warning, which was only to make it clear that he knew where Ellie and I were on Thursday."

"Looks like you're gonna have to hang up your fedoras."

"Ha! Not likely. I've already ordered the beige trench coats."

"You know, I'd laugh if I thought you were joking."

Josh grinned and kissed him. "You know me too well."

***

"Hi," Shaunna greeted Kris cheerily. "I thought you were staying till Friday. I wasn't expecting you to be back." She gave him a wide berth.

"I needed to come home."

"OK." She hadn't intended to stay home. "I'm just gonna pop up and shower. Busy day. Won't be long." She dumped her bag on the table and started to walk away.

"I've quit *Shadows*," he called after her.

She backtracked. "You've quit? Completely?"

"Almost. I've got to do the first three episodes of season three so they can bring in Lundberg's replacement. They moved it to London."

"Wow. After telling you all to deny everything. I'm so glad. I need to go shower, but we can continue this conversation when I come back."

He watched her leave, knowing exactly why she was so eager to go and shower. He'd been staying at Ade's old place since Sunday, and he'd missed her. He'd hoped she'd missed him too.

For several minutes, he listened to the sound of the running water above and then took out his phone and typed a text message: *I love you. x*

A short while later, he received a reply: *Uh oh! What've I done? Love you too. Kx*

He responded: *Just needed to tell you. x*
Has something happened? Are you OK? Is Mum OK? Kx
Everything's fine Missy. Be good. x
I will ;) See you soon. Kx

***

"Josh?"

"Yes?"

"You have a visitor."

"I'm in the shower."

"You're not."

Josh huffed. He was *almost* in the shower. He put on his bathrobe and went back downstairs. "Oh!"

"Mr. Sandison. May I come in?"

"Erm. Yes. Sorry. Please do."

PC Granger stepped into the hallway. She wasn't in uniform. Blue watched her from the kitchen doorway, his head cocked to one side. She watched him, too.

"What a beautiful dog," she said. "I used to have one just like her, or him?"

"Him. His name's Blue. You didn't need to call in, you know. I could've come to the station tomorrow."

"I couldn't get your memory card back. Sorry."

He hadn't expected her to. It had merely been a means of attracting her attention, but at the moment, they were still establishing the rules of transaction. He gave her a smile.

"Thanks for trying. I suppose I should've thought ahead, really. Police evidence now, isn't it?"

She looked away.

"You've not come here just to tell me you couldn't get my memory card back."

"No."

"OK. I'll go and put my clothes on. Please—" Josh gestured towards the lounge "—take a seat. I won't be long."

PC Granger nodded and went into the lounge. Iris muttered, "Hello," and carried on watching TV.

"Would you like a drink of anything?" George asked.

"A cup of tea would be lovely. White, one sugar, thanks."

George left the room, crossing his fingers in a vain hope that it would stop his mum from saying anything embarrassing. He filled the kettle and listened; nothing but the sound of the TV in the lounge and wardrobe doors being closed upstairs, followed by Monty scratching at the back door to be let in. The dog wasn't used to having free access to the outside and was making the most of it. George opened the door, and Monty trotted right on past him as if he wasn't even there, straight through to the lounge.

Not long after, Iris shouted, "Mont, pack it in."

George knew what that was about.

"Get here!" Iris hissed, then, "Sorry, love."

"It's OK," PC Granger's said, sounding surprisingly timid. George chuckled to himself.

Josh returned downstairs and paused at the doorway to the lounge, trying to get into the right frame of mind. "Assertive," he whispered. He realised George was watching him.

"That's nothing to do with PC Granger, is it?"

Josh shook his head, took a deep breath and went in.

"Mont! Get back here now!"

George took the cup of tea in, grinning at the pair of them, Josh and PC Granger, both looking as if they'd fallen into the bear pit at the zoo, and Monty sitting in the middle of the sofa, growling and occasionally baring his teeth.

"Come on, Monty," he said. "Let's go for a walk."

The Westie obediently slinked from the room. Blue followed, and soon after, the three of them left.

"I'll be outside, love," Iris said, struggling to her plastered feet and hobbling away on her heels.

Josh waited until he heard the back door open and close again. "So," he said and then nothing else. He was hoping it would prompt an explanation.

PC Granger sipped her tea, keeping the cup in her hands, and her eyes on the TV, as she spoke. "Is that…?" She tilted her head in the direction Iris had just taken.

"My mother-in-law."

"Mm-hm. Mr. Morley's mother?"

"That's right."

She carried on nodding.

"PC Granger, I—"

"Natasha," she interrupted.

"Natasha, I'm not really sure why you're here."

She laughed ruefully. "Neither am I." She made eye contact with him. "You work in a profession where confidentiality is key."

"Yes."

"What I'm going to tell you—" She stopped, giving him an opportunity to reassure her.

"Absolutely," he said.

"I can understand if you have to share, but no-one must know it came from me."

"You have my word."

"Yesterday, after you phoned, I went to see Aitch, err, I mean DI Hartley, but he wasn't in. I was told he'd gone to Cardiff as part of an investigation, but, well, the thing is—"

"You and Aitch are in a relationship."

She nodded. "We've been together for two years—since we worked the Campion case—and he wasn't planning to go to Cardiff when he left for work yesterday morning. I called him, but all he would say is that he was on a case and it was on a need to know." She shrugged. "We don't have that sort of relationship. If he'd not been able to tell me on the phone, he'd have said so, not it's on a 'need to know'.

"And it got me thinking. That memory card you gave him on Saturday—he was really fired up about it, because he'd finally be able to prove he was right that it wasn't Callaghan, and pissed off, too, that he'd have to pull all the files. Then he came home Monday night, and he was quiet and withdrawn—said he had a headache, which isn't like him. He's one of those tough nuts who

570

get on with it, and he kept saying, 'If anyone asks, you haven't seen that video.'

"So I was already starting to wonder what was going on, then you called, and I found out he was in Cardiff. I went to have a look through the files again myself, or I tried to. The physical ones have been archived, and the electronic ones are now restricted, which they weren't a few months ago, but I can't access them anymore. And while I was at the computer, one of CID pulled the plug, I mean literally just pulled the power cable from the socket and then walked off without a word."

"Was it Farrar?" Josh asked.

"How could you possibly know that?"

"He came to see me this afternoon and warned me off."

"Yeah. I can sort of see why, to be fair to him."

"What do you mean?"

"You and your friends are a bit…well, the word vigilante springs to mind." She gave him a wry smile.

Josh laughed. "Yes. We have got a bit of a thing for taking the law into our own hands."

"And you get away with it, because Aitch thinks the world of you all, especially Dan Jeffries and his brother. I'm not kidding, once he starts on about your school football team you can't shut him up, which is why he got George let off when he went for that bloke in the park, and also why I'm telling you all of this. As I say, though, you didn't hear it from me." She paused. George's mum was on her way back.

"Iris won't say anything," Josh assured her. Iris heard him and stopped outside the lounge door.

"It's all right, love, I'll just bob up to the loo on a long job and leave you and 'ermione to it."

Josh hid behind his hair in embarrassment.

PC Granger laughed. "It's not the first time I've been called that."

Iris grinned at her and started her slow, painful and inevitably grunty climb upstairs.

"Hold on," Josh said. He got up.

"I'll manage."

571

He glared at her. She relented and let him walk up the stairs behind her. He waited at the top, until she was steady on her feet, and turned to go back down again. "My computer's still on if you wanted to play solitaire, Iris."

"Ta, love. I might just do that."

"OK. I'll bring you up a cup of tea in a sec." He returned to PC Granger. "Sorry about that. My fault for introducing her to *Harry Potter*."

"Don't worry. She's fun."

"Yes, she is. Very droll sense of humour." He collected the empty cups. "Would you like a refill?"

"That'd be great." She followed him through to the kitchen, surveying her surroundings. "This is a really nice little house."

"Little being the operative word," Josh grumbled. "We're going to extend the back, but I suppose it's big enough for the two of us."

"Iris doesn't live here?"

"No. She's staying while she recovers from her surgery. She lives in that awful tower block. We're waiting on a council transfer—no idea how long that'll take. They didn't even offer an indication, but with the shortage of housing, who knows? It's as well we get on, really."

"It might be quicker than you think," PC Granger said. "They're converting Campion's to flats."

"The council?"

"Sort of. It's a social housing association—part of Campion Community Trust."

"Really? I wasn't aware of that."

"Yeah. Campion owned the land and left it in trust to the local community. I know it's really pathetic that I know all this, but me and Aitch are still a bit obsessed with the Campion case, to be totally honest with you. See, we knew that Brown and Callaghan were both innocent, but we were told to let it ride if one of them confessed. Aitch was pretty sure Jason Meyer had information, and he was making progress, until he was ordered to release him.

"That was only the start of it. He's been under so much stress since his promotion, and it's not the workload. Every big case he gets is passed on to Farrar, like he's being primed for greater things, then nothing comes of it, and the case gets closed or marked as restricted. Like the shoplifter we picked up who—"

"Sorry," Josh interrupted, as she'd lost him at 'left it in trust'. "I was kind of listening, but can you go back to the top? How do you know the land was left in trust?"

"It was written into Campion's will."

"Which you've got a copy of?"

"We have, but it's—"

"In the archives," Josh said at the same time she did. He sighed in frustration at the constant running up against brick walls, although it was probably nothing compared to how PC Granger and Aitch were feeling. "Why are you telling me all this?" he asked. "We didn't exactly hit it off."

"That's one way of putting it." They both laughed lightly at that truth. "I promise you, I'm not always such a hard-nose. That's just me at work."

"And this is?"

"This is me worrying about my other half. I don't know where he is or what he's doing, and we're getting blocked every step of the way." She frowned. "I believe in the police. I wouldn't have joined if I didn't, but I don't know who to turn to, or who I can trust." She looked Josh in the eye. "What I do know is that Aitch trusts you and your friends, and I hear you're a genius."

"Hmm. That's arguable. I've got a good memory, that's all."

"No. It's much more than that. When I interviewed you...I can't even explain it. You started making connections that nobody else had even realised existed, like you had the box with the picture on the lid, while we all just had a couple of pieces of the jigsaw puzzle each."

"That's one awesome analogy, PC Granger."

"Why, thank you, Mr. Sandison."

"Sandison-Morley."

"And pedantic."

"Erm..." Josh pretended to weigh up her description. "Yes, I am, and you're right. I can see what the picture is meant to look like, but it takes me a while to work out how it all fits together. I

573

think it goes with the territory of being a psychologist. Anyway, tell me about Campion's will, and I might be able to help you get a few more of those pieces in place."

"OK. Well, he left almost everything to his wife, other than the land, and a pretty substantial legacy for Victoria Hospice. The only other thing, I think, was his jazz collection, which was to go to James Brown."

"James? I assumed he was one of the witnesses."

"He couldn't be a beneficiary and a witness."

"No, but I didn't know he was a beneficiary. I don't suppose you happen to recall who the witnesses were?"

"Alice Friar was one."

Josh shook his head. "She didn't know what was in it."

"She wouldn't necessarily have needed to. She only had to witness the signature."

"I don't think she did."

PC Granger narrowed her eyes. "Are you saying it's a forgery?"

"I don't know. What do you think?"

"That it's a forgery."

"Who was the other witness?"

"A lawyer from Sharston Strang."

Josh raised an eyebrow. "Fancy that."

"You're about to show off again, aren't you?" PC Granger said. He smiled and nodded. She watched him in anticipation.

"Simon Yarrow," he said. She shook her head. "Alan Strang?" She shook her head again. "OK. You win."

"Jessica Lambert."

High And Low
Friday 1st–Tuesday 5th December

Within the dark of the midwinter morning, the only light was the glow of illuminated numbers, LEDs—the symbols of power being restored, the dim golden haze of a streetlight beyond here, beyond now, this moment in the dark. No light inside.

He watched her sleeping, her hands clasped beneath her cheek, tinged pink even in these bleak early hours, in his mind where he would see her, forever. If she were to leave him right now, he would not sleep until he found a way to get her back. And all he could do was lie here, beside her, and watch her sleep.

Daylight came, bringing with it more tears; relentless sorrow. She made tea around him as he sat at the kitchen table, powerless to do more than follow her with his eyes. She sat opposite, smiling.

"What's the matter?" she asked.

He shook his head. "Nothing." *You.*

"I'm going shopping with Adele after work. I'll be back around seven."

"OK." *Please don't go.*

"But if I'm going to be any longer, I'll give you a call, OK?"

"That's fine." *Please don't go to him.*

"What are you up to today?"

"Not sure." *Tearing myself apart, imagining you with him.* "I think Ade wants to go and see his mum. I might go with him." *What else is there for me to do?*

"Cool."

"He wants me to go there for Christmas." *And I love him. And I love you.*

"Are you going?"

"I don't know." *How can you ask me? What about Krissi? What about us?* "What are we doing? Do we have any firm plans?"

"Adele says she's thinking about having a dinner party and inviting us round. Actually, that might work quite well. If you do go with Ade, I mean. I won't be on my own that way."

You won't be with me. You'll be with him. "I'd quite like to be here." *To be here with you.*

***

She left. He stayed, wandering the house and listening to the echoes of the life they once had. What he'd told Ade—that he had stopped her from fully being—now she was. This was who she was; a woman, and no longer his. He was losing her, and he didn't know what he had to do to keep her, or even if it was too late for that. He returned to their bedroom, lay on her side of the bed, her pillow pressed to his nose, inhaling her scent, drowning in her becoming.

"What are you doing?" She breezed into the room.

Seven o'clock already?

She wafted past, a drift of perfume and musk of sex.

You've had sex with him. Does he love you? Does he love you like I do? Do you know how it feels to love you like I do? Like he does.

"Kris?"

"Sorry. I was thinking."

"About?"

"Us." *The lies we tell when we think of us.*

"What about us?"

"Did you think it would work?"

She sat on the edge of the bed, in the crook of his curled body. "Yes. I did."

But it isn't working. I'm losing you. I'm losing everything.

"I wish we could be honest and open about it, though. It's so hard sometimes to remember that everyone thinks we're still separated."

Does he know?

"They might even be OK about it, now they've got to know Ade, not that I'm suggesting we tell them. It'd weird them out. I mean, George can't even cope with you being bi, so imagine what he'd think of this."

He's known this pain. I wish I could be honest and open about it to him. It's so hard sometimes to remember that he doesn't know. I need someone to know. I need you to know.

"I love you."

She smiled. "I love you, too. Are you sure you're OK?" She leaned down and kissed him.

"Yeah. Just a bit down today."

"Soon it'll be over."

Soon it'll be over. For you. For me, it will never be over.

"Just think, once you get back from London, there will be no more DI Lundberg." She frowned. "That's kind of sad. I'm going to miss watching him."

Are you going to miss me?

***

Another dark morning. She was awake, waiting for the numbers to change from 6:59. He was awake, watching her.

"Can I make love to you? Have you got time?"

The alarm sounded. She stopped it and rolled over to face him, laying her hand on his cheek.

"There's always time to make love." She reached across and kissed him, gently, quietly loving him, like he loved her. They moved together, under the duvet, for the morning was cold as well as dark. They locked together, such a perfect fit it was almost possible to forget that outside of this complete connection they were frayed and he was falling apart.

She climaxed, and he forced himself to do the same, not with fantasies of wild passionate sex, but of them as they had once been.

"I'm going for a shower," she said, leaving him again. He awaited her return, like he would forever.

"Are you coming home after work?" It was more of a plea than a question.

"Why?"

"Just wondering."

"I can do, but I was going to head over to do some of that essay with…"

He tuned out. More lies, by consent. That's what he'd asked for in his silence, but he couldn't do it anymore.

"Can we talk?"

She studied him for a while, looking deep into his eyes, finally acknowledging the pain. "Yeah, we can." She moved closer and waited for him to sit up. "What's wrong?"

"Nothing." He smiled at her, and the tears began again. "Everything."

"Kris?"

He held up his hand to keep her away. "Later. OK?"

"OK." She frowned, worried about leaving him alone now. He wasn't strong. "I'll see you about half two."

He nodded and pulled his knees up to his chest, watching through the tears as she left.

***

She didn't call Andy to explain. She couldn't find the right words. How could she tell him that her husband was breaking down because of what they were doing? And still she couldn't stop—no. She could. But it was the last thing she wanted to do. Last resort.

She arrived home from work to find he'd made it downstairs and also made her a cup of tea. He hadn't made it as far as wearing clothes, still in his sleep boxers and tee. She took him by the hand and led him to the bathroom.

"You need to shower," she said, "to keep going. Where's Ade?"

"Gone."

"What do you mean, 'gone'? Gone where?"

"To his mum's. He said we needed time alone." Kris stood, forlorn.

"Come on, hun."

She jollied him along, pushed him under the shower. He cried, gargling the sobs in the running water. She, too, was fighting the tears, watching him dying inside. He finished washing, for what it was worth, and followed her to their room, taking each item of clothing from her and somehow understanding what to do with it even though he was so disconnected from the world that the garments and their purpose were novel to him. They returned downstairs to the lounge and sat together on the sofa, joined yet separate. The husband-ex-husband and the wife-ex-wife.

"I can take you having sex with him," Kris mumbled through his tears. "I can. It's not that. It's not you coming home smelling of him, of his aftershave, of his…" He stopped and closed his eyes, inhaling deeply to purge the scent that filled his mind. "I can take all of that."

She didn't speak, for to do so would be to confirm or lie by denying that she and Andy were having sex, and it was not to be. Of course Kris knew, but she would not confirm or deny it.

"Come on," he said, his voice a little louder now. "Tell me. Surely you owe me that much?"

Still she would not say it. He'd said he didn't want to know, so why was he pushing her to admit it?

"It's because of Ade, isn't it? That's why."

"No."

"You're telling me that if I'd stayed faithful to you then you'd have stayed faithful to me?"

"I'm fine with you and Ade, and us. If I wasn't, I'd tell you."

"You're lying. And you made a liar of me. Do you know that? I told Ade if there was anything going on between you and Sean, you'd have said something."

"There's nothing going on between me and Sean."

"It's the same principle."

"We're friends."

"Friends who fuck each other."

"We're just friends, Kris."

"I'm not talking about Sean! Are you unhappy?"

"No."

"Are we no longer friends?"

"Of course we're still friends."

"And yet you won't tell me the truth!"

"Why are you doing this?"

"Why won't you talk to me?"

"Kris, please stop."

"Just tell me why you're fucking him!"

"Because we can't help it!"

She put her hand over her mouth too late. It was said. The words had escaped her and instantly crushed his anger with their truth. She had cheated on him with the man he once believed had raped her, the one he had saved her from. It was an appalling betrayal.

They had discussed and talked openly about Ade, in his absence and then in his presence. It was a consensual, negotiated relationship, and it was working perfectly well, or if it wasn't, it had nothing to do with what was going on with Andy. It would have happened one way or another. She'd known that much for a year or more. For Andy's sake, she'd kept it from Kris, and now he knew for certain, but he wasn't angry with her. This was far, far worse.

"I think of you together all the time," he said, now so quiet she had to strain to hear him. "I think of him, fucking you, and what he gives you, what he gave you, turning you into a woman, and your wonderful daughter. And every time he fucks you, he takes a little more of you from me."

Shaunna began to cry. "Please stop using that word. It makes me feel like a dirty slut, and I'm not, Kris, I'm not a slut. Please don't use that word." She was bordering on hysterical. So was he.

"I'm sorry," he said. "I didn't mean to call you that. I just need it to mean less than we do. I'm sorry. I've never thought you were a slut, Shaunna, I swear."

They cried together until they were too exhausted to cry anymore. The dog lay on his bed across the room, looking sorrowful.

Kris groaned; his head was aching. "I'll go and feed him now," he said.

Shaunna nodded and watched him struggle to his feet. "I'll come, too, make some tea."

He held out his hand to her, and she allowed him to pull her up from the sofa.

In the kitchen, around the normality, they resumed their discussion.

"Do you love him?" he asked. She nodded.

"Yes. I do."

"And does he love you?"

She didn't answer. He said he did, but who was she to declare it the truth? She thought he did.

"He does," Kris confirmed. "He always loved you, but you didn't love him. And that was OK. Now it's all different."

"The only thing that's different is that I've told you, but you knew, didn't you?"

"I thought it was lust."

"And lust is better?"

"Lust doesn't tear us apart. Love does."

"You love Ade. That hasn't torn us apart."

"No, because you and Ade are better than me."

They returned to the lounge and clung together on the sofa. Kris continued his terrible analysis.

"What about us?" he asked.

She shrugged. "We're still here now."

"Have we got a future?"

"I don't know."

In his heart, he knew he shouldn't have asked the question, because he had hoped desperately for a different answer to that which she had given. He tried to drink his tea, to swallow back the fresh tears, but he couldn't do either and was about to throw his cup across the room. She caught hold of it just in time and disarmed him. He started to wail like a baby, and she could do nothing, nothing to take away the pain.

"I love you. I messed up, and now he is taking you from me, and taking our life, everything we had together. He gave you what I couldn't give you. And I love her so much. As I lose you, I lose her too. You are my life. Where do I go from here? You are my life."

"No. Listen to me, Kris. Please. Listen to me. You'll never lose Krissi. She is *your* daughter."

As good as blood, this love that filled his heart and kept it beating, but now he could feel it ebbing away, the pulse getting weaker.

"And you'll never lose me, Kris. We will always be—"

Be what? She didn't know. He did.

"If I hadn't screwed up, if I hadn't gone with Jack, if I could've played it straight and you'd been enough, it would still have come to this. He loves you, and I hate him for it. He loves you in a way I never can and I want to, Shaunna. I want to love you. I need to love you. I don't know what else to do."

He was lost. She was lost. She'd seen him break before, and here it was happening again, and though she knew his work was mostly the cause, so, too, was she. He felt like he was losing everything. His job, his life with her, his daughter, his mind. Everything that had made him was now breaking him apart, tearing him into a million pieces that were slipping away with no-one to catch them and stitch them together again.

***

The train was ready to depart. Ade was on it, waiting, watching. Shaunna hugged Kris.

"Two more weeks," she whispered in his ear and kissed his cheek.

"Will you still be here?"

"Yes. I promise."

"I love you." The tears had not stopped for days.

"I love you." She released him. "Go," she said. He nodded but didn't move. "Go, Kris."

***

Living grief. So much worse.

"Hello, lovely," Sean greeted her phone call warmly. She couldn't even draw enough breath to speak. "Are you at home?" he asked.

She nodded and made some kind of guttural, primal sound that he took to be in the affirmative.

"I'm on my way, Shaunna. I'll be there as soon as I can."

She dropped her phone and it fell to the floor, as did she.

The knock at the door came soon after; she was not dwelling in everyday time. She was caught in a nightmare where time could stretch into forever or flash by in less than a blink. She stumbled to her feet and onwards to the door. The dog was happy to see someone familiar because his people were not.

Sean patted Casper on the head and paused to take in the devastation. Not the plant pots and potpourri this time.

"Oh dear, what a hell of a mess."

He leapt the abyss from everyday time, and into her nightmare.

Gumshoon
Wednesday 6th December

The front door opened as Jason was about to walk away. He turned back and did a double take. "Abbey Road guy."

Neil nodded. "Jason. Good to see you."

"What are you…why…" He shrugged, hoping the man before him would rescue him from his confusion-induced speechlessness.

"You'd better come in."

Jason did as suggested, dumbly shadowing Neil into the lounge.

"Why don't you sit down?" Neil waved an arm at the closest chair.

Jason stayed where he was. The room was exactly as he'd expected: floral three-piece suite, budgie chirping away in a cage, nest of mahogany tables, everything dust-free, prim and proper. Except for the acoustic guitar discarded on the sofa, a trail of paper covered in scribbled chord symbols and lyrics, and this shambles of a man who was clearly living here. With Alice.

"I didn't know you knew each other," Jason finally managed to utter.

"Yeah," Neil confirmed lazily. He sounded stoned, although he wasn't, because Alice wouldn't allow marijuana in the house. "We're old friends."

"OK." Jason was still struggling to think what to say. He'd come to see Alice, to talk to her about what was going on. He didn't know who else he could trust.

"By the way," Neil said, "I did work at Abbey Road, and I am a sound engineer."

"I could tell from what you said in your interview. But…" Jason stopped and started over. "OK, I get that you're a sound engineer, and that you're an old friend of Alice's, but how did you end up coming to my studio for an interview? Do you know who I am?"

Neil laughed. "I've heard that question quite a few times over the years, usually from rock stars who think they deserve preferential treatment because they're famous. In your case, I assume you mean do I know you are Alice's son? To which the answer is, of course, yes. As to your other question, she asked me to help her to keep you safe. She's worried that you may be in danger."

"Did you know there's an unmarked police car outside?"

"Yeah. They've been here all week."

"There's also a motorbike tailing me, the studio's under surveillance, and my sound engineer—the guy I gave the job to instead of you—thinks he's some sort of spy. I'm going completely mental."

"No wonder. Why don't you have a beer and chill out here for a while, man? Alice will be home soon."

Jason nodded. "Yeah, I'd like that. Thanks."

**

"How long you goin' to sit lookin' at that?"

"As long as it takes for it to make sense, Iris." Josh rubbed his eyes. He'd had so little sleep over the past week that even he was starting to worry about it, but his mind refused to rest until the mystery was solved, and that wasn't going to happen unless he accepted what was staring him right in the face. Jess had signed Campion's will—the one bearing Alice's signature—and it looked genuine enough, but the rest of it was wrong, all so very wrong, which led to only one conclusion and he refused to so much as consider it. How could he ever believe that his friend of more than a quarter of a century, the one who had stood by him through life-threatening depression and kept his secret safe ever since, was part of a massive scam to defraud people of their inheritance?

It wasn't small fry, either. Patricia Biddiscombe, they now knew, was worth at least as much, if not more than Campion, and there were others. For whilst Aitch was still missing in action, Natasha Granger initially had some success digging through old crime records and came upon a whole string of cases involving Sharston Strang and Partners. Then, all of a sudden, every search for the name of that particular legal firm terminated at a restricted record. Someone in the police knew what she was looking for and was trying to stop her from finding it.

Josh was brought back to the present by the sound of the front door opening and glanced up to see who it was.

"Hey." Eleanor smiled at him.

"Hey. Everything OK?"

"Yeah. Not too bad, other than spending half the day arguing with the removal firm over our postcode. Apparently, our road doesn't exist."

"Maybe the town planners appointed Sharston Strang too."

Eleanor laughed. "Yeah, maybe. I've just dropped Toby at Mum and Dad's for the evening so I could come and lend you a few brain cells."

"Thanks. I need them. Where's James tonight?"

"I left him at home, but he's going to sort the trust accounts at Jay's, I think. I wasn't really paying attention. How are you getting on? Made any progress?"

"If you measure it in gallons of coffee consumed, yes. As for working out how they made any money out of this nonsense?" Josh indicated the pile of papers in front of him and threw his pen down on top of it, temporarily accepting defeat in favour of a shoulder stretch and caffeine top-up.

Eleanor followed him through to the kitchen, catching a glimpse of Iris through the window. "At least she gets to see what you're really like. It never occurred to me before."

"What didn't?"

"The reason why you spend half your time tearing around like a toddler on a trike and the other half hiding from the world."

"I do not!"

"You do!"

585

"See, that's one of the reasons I didn't tell you. I knew you'd start analysing my behaviour."

"I'm not saying there's anything wrong with it, Joshua. Just stating a fact."

"What's that?" Iris asked, hobbling back into the kitchen.

"Josh's interesting…lifestyle."

"Oh, right." She stared very obviously at the two cups he had set out in readiness for when the coffee machine had reached the end of its self-clean cycle.

"Did you want a latte, by any chance?" Josh asked.

"Well, if you're offerin'. That'll be me last one today, mind, or I'll be spendin' the whole bloody night goin' up and down them stairs. Eh, mebbe I should save meself the legwork and go in with Georgie, bein' as how you'll be sat down here with your papers and whatnot."

Iris's eyes twinkled, and Josh saw her wink at Eleanor. They were ganging up on him. As if he *chose* to stay awake all night!

"No. I'm going to bed at a sensible time this evening. I need to at least *try* to get some sleep. I'm knackered and I'm getting nowhere."

They returned to the lounge with their drinks and sat in silence for a while, the TV playing away quietly in the background. Josh was trying not to think about the wills scam, but his mind was a disobedient creature that didn't like to sit still for too long, and as it once again went 'tearing around like a toddler on a trike', something occurred to him. It wasn't even as much as a fully formed thought; just a vague recollection of something he may or may not have heard. He took out his phone and made a call.

"Hi, Natasha? It's Josh."

"Who's Natasha?" Eleanor whispered to Iris.

"That policewoman."

"PC Granger?"

"Aye, that's her."

"Hi, Josh," Natasha Granger responded.

"You know what you said about the shoplifter?"

"What did I say about the shoplifter?"

"Well, nothing, as it happens, but it just dawned on me that it didn't fit. You said that all of the big cases were getting passed to Farrar, and then you mentioned a shoplifter, which doesn't strike me as being 'a big case'."

"No, it's not, in the general course of things, but you cut me off before I got any further. When we brought him in, he had a holdall full of fake IDs, and we passed it up to CID, who were going to pass it on to the fraud unit, but Farrar ended up dealing with it."

"Fake IDs?" Josh repeated. "What, like driving licences and passports?"

"That's right."

He got up and left the house, still with the phone to his ear, and went to Sean's, hammering on the door until Sean came and opened it.

"What the hell? I'd just nodded off there. You frightened the life out of me."

"Anders Folden."

"What about him?"

"You said he had a criminal record."

"Yeah. For selling counterfeit passports. Why?"

That was it. The missing link.

"Natasha, I'll call you back." Josh hung up. "'Tis safer to be that which we destroy," he said, suddenly wide awake again.

"What now?"

"The passage from *Macbeth*. Will you come to the church with me?"

"Confessing your sins, are you, Joshy?"

"No, but I know a woman who is."

***

The house was empty. Alice could tell before she'd even put her key in the lock. And Jason had been there, which meant he was now aware of her deception, because Neil was a wonderful, kind man, but he couldn't keep his mouth shut if his life depended on it. She pushed the key home and stepped into the warm hall, closing the door behind her.

Fear.

She gasped and put her palm against her chest. Now why was she sensing fear? She realised it was her own a split second before the bang on the door behind her, so close and so loud that she staggered, startled, and hit her ankle on the sharp corner of the radiator. She turned back and moved cautiously towards the door, getting just close enough to peer through the spyhole, even though she knew already who was standing outside. She could see his body odour seeping through the letterbox and under the door like a putrid, inky-thick fog.

"Alice," he sang. "Open the door."

"Go away. I'm calling the police."

"Oh, Alice, don't be so silly. You know me. The lost little Scandinavian boy, remember?"

She fumbled around in her bag, trying to find her mobile phone, her hands shaking so much that she dropped it before she could press the 'call' button. She watched it bounce once, twice, on the carpet, and land a few inches from the door.

"I can see you, Alice."

She looked up from her phone to his piercing eyes, staring at her through the letterbox. They were so, so cold and filled with such spite.

"Leave it where it is," he commanded, his accent stronger than she ever recalled it. She tried to breathe silently and crept closer, stretching out her foot in an attempt to reach her phone. Another loud bang on the door. She gasped again, and he heard her.

"Open the door, Alice. We're going on a little trip together." He said the words in that same singsong voice, but there was an impatient edge to it now.

"No! Leave me alone!"

"You will come with me."

"I will not."

"I have Jason."

Alice put her hand over her mouth and tried not to cry out. She took off her shoes and crept towards the door, reaching out a shaking arm to quickly push the handle down, and immediately moved away, standing on her phone in the process.

The door slowly swung open and Anders stood before her, leaning against the frame, smiling calmly. He stepped into the hallway and advanced on her.

"Hello, Alice." He threw his arms around her and left a hard, wet-lipped kiss on her cheek. She almost vomited with the vertigo brought on by the stench of his body and his breath. "It's so good to see you. I missed you."

"What do you want?"

"Only what's mine." Now the smile was gone. "We're going to do this sensibly and not raise the alarm."

"The police are outside."

"Don't worry about them. I'm an old work colleague, and a lawyer."

Alice shook her head in disappointment. "Alistair believed in you. He gave you so many chances. How could you?"

"Now, now, Alice. Don't be like that. Are you ready?"

"Where are you taking me?"

"Inn i det svarte hullet."

"Anders, please."

He laughed manically. "Ingen kan unnslippe det svarte hullet."

"Tell me, or I won't come with you."

"You will."

He gestured towards the door and waited for her to move. When she didn't, he slapped her hard across the face.

"It's quite simple, Alice. Either you come with me or I will kill you, and then I will kill Jason."

He meant it. That much was apparent, and he would likely kill them both whether she went willingly or not. But her fear was being tempered by a mother's desperation to save her child, and she refused to let him make her cry. She swallowed back her tears and walked to the front door, trying not to react to the crunch behind her as he stamped on her phone. It didn't matter. She'd made the call already.

***

589

"I'll be frank with you, Joshy, a derelict church is not my ideal place to be on a dark winter's night."

"Stop being such a wuss, Tierney. What d'you think's going to happen?" Josh led the way down the side of the ancient building, past the vestry and into a small courtyard flanked by overgrown shrubs. He stopped walking and took out his phone, switching on the LED and shining it over one of the uneven flagstones.

"Savies?"

"Yes." Josh held his phone between his teeth and stood on one corner of the flagstone, its diagonal opposite rising a couple of inches. He pushed his fingers underneath and lifted the flagstone clear. Taking his phone out of his mouth, he shone the light into the exposed space below. "Savies Plus."

Sean peered into the hole. It looked like exactly what it was: a sand base compressed by a slab of concrete, with a slight dip to one side where they had once secreted their cigarettes and soliloquies. He watched on as Josh took out his credit card and dragged it through the sand, scraping it back against the edge of the hole. After a minute or so, the card hit resistance. Josh put it away and dug with his fingers, pulling free a flat metal box. Sean was utterly astounded.

The box was slightly distorted by the weight of the stone under which it had been hidden, and it took quite some effort to open it, not that Josh needed to see the contents. He already had an appallingly clear idea of what he'd find inside. He finally managed to get the lid off, the force flinging it from his hand and sending it spinning through the air. It landed several feet away with a noisy clatter.

He took out the documents and examined them one by one before passing them to Sean: a certificate of marriage for Jessica Lambert and Andrew Jeffries, dated three years previously; a passport bearing Jess's photograph and the name 'Jennifer Campion', and last but by no means least, a full written confession naming everyone involved in the fraud scam, including Alan Strang, Charles Sharston and Anders Folden AKA Simon Yarrow.

Josh read until his phone switched itself off, the battery drained by the LED. He was completely devastated, even more so that Rob Simpson-Stone's name was on there, along with all the other fraudsters. So the entire reunion had been an act. Her eight closest friends, and she'd conned them all, pretending Rob had ripped her off to make sure there was no trail for them to follow.

Josh passed the letter to Sean and walked away, leaning against the church wall as he tried to come to terms with what he had discovered. In a way, he wished he'd left it alone and just lived with the suspicion that she was involved, but she'd have known he would never let it rest until he had answers. She knew *him*. He felt numb, other than the pain in his chest that he was sure was his heart breaking. *How could she do this? To me. To us. Was our entire friendship a lie? Just a means of making contact with 'clients' to defraud?* He could feel the migraine oozing its way into the back of his eyes, and for as much as he knew he should fight it, he didn't have the strength. He had nothing left to give and started to slide away.

"No, Joshy. Stay with me," Sean urged. He grabbed Josh by the shoulders and shook him. "The day I took her to the hospice, do you know what she said to me?" Josh refused to look at him, but Sean continued just the same. "She told me to remember the girl I knew—the real her. I thought she was talking about the decimation of her body, but now I understand. This wasn't her. Deep down you know that's true."

Josh struggled to hear Sean's voice over the top of the questions racing around, colliding with each other and with each impact exploding into a hundred more. He put his hands up and covered his ears.

"No!" he shouted. "Stop it!" The voices he heard were all his own, an overload of thoughts trying to escape his mind.

"Josh," Sean said firmly.

"Why tell me this? What's the point? You're dead. Why tell me this when I can't do anything about it?"

591

"Joshua Sandison!" Sean bellowed. Josh snapped out of it immediately and looked at Sean in bewilderment as if he didn't know where he was. "Just stay with me, Joshy, all right?"

Josh nodded.

"Good man." Sean put his arm around him to steer him to the car, and they returned home, taking the box and the documents with them.

George was back from work, and Eleanor had done her best to explain what was going on, but it didn't stop him from panicking when Josh came in and flopped onto the sofa, detached and defeated. Sean put the box on the table, signalling with his eyes that George should open it, and he did so, reading each document and handing it to Eleanor.

"Oh my god," she gasped. She closed her eyes and held out Jess's confession so that George would take it away from her.

Iris had no idea what it was they were reading, but she could see how shocked they all were. She picked up the tin box and examined it.

"There's a bit of a cig packet in the bottom of here," she said. She fished it out and held it at arm's length, trying to read the tiny, swirly writing. "Not a bloody hope!" She gave it to Sean.

"More *Macbeth*?" he asked. Josh looked up, almost too weary to care. Sean passed it to him, and he scanned the four lines of text.

"The not-so-sweet Ophelia has returned from beyond the grave." He screwed the paper into a ball and threw it onto the table.

"What's it say?" Iris asked.

Josh recited it back, word for word: "How should I your true love know From another one? By his cockle hat and staff, And his sandal shoon."

"Well, what're you gettin' het up about then?"

"You don't understand, Iris."

"Don't you dare," she warned, her voice low and threatening. "You think you're all so bloody clever with your big words and your degrees, but there's not an ounce of common fuckin' sense

592

between the lot of you. Can you not see what's goin' on here? Why d'you think she left that for you? Read it again, lad."

"I don't need to. It's in my head."

"So look in yer head, you twerp!"

Josh took a deep breath, getting set to give Iris a mouthful, which wasn't the wisest move, but luckily his sense of reason rescued him, although he still hadn't the faintest idea what she was hearing in those words that he wasn't.

"I'm sorry, Iris. I was out of order, but I don't understand what you mean."

"Is she not tellin' you she's who you always thought she was? Just because she went about things the wrong way—"

"She conned us all!"

"Did she?"

Everyone remained silent, thinking back to the reunion, and all the time they had known Jess.

"No," Eleanor said eventually. "She didn't."

"So there you are, then." Iris nodded smugly. "And I reckon she's hopin' you'll clean up her bloody mess for her an' all, with all that talk of pilgrims."

"Huh?" George was confused.

"Cockle hat, staff and sandal shoon," Josh explained. "The clothes of the pilgrim."

"Oh, OK." George shook his head in a mix of despair and wonder at how clever his husband was, and also what his mother might have made of her life if she'd been offered the chances she'd given him.

"What is there left to do?" Josh asked rhetorically. "She's dead."

"But the rest of them aren't," Sean said. "And if we're looking at corrupt police too, then maybe it's down to us."

"We're not the famous bloody five, Sean!"

"No." George grinned. "We're The Circle."

"The Circle," Josh muttered. "A bunch of intellectuals, construction workers and creatives trying to bring down an organised crime ring. Talk about biting off more than we can chew."

"A Vicious Circle?" Iris suggested. Everyone else laughed. Josh gave up.

"So does that mean the murder mystery's back on?" Eleanor asked. "Because personally I prefer the fedora and trench coat, but if you'd rather the cockle hat…"

She didn't get any further than that, as the sound of a car screeching to a halt outside stole their attention. Josh looked out of the window and frowned.

"Oh God. What now?" He went to the door. "Dan?"

"Alright, mate? We've got a bit of a situation."

In I Svarta Hålet
Wednesday 6th December

"James Brown."

James startled at the sudden appearance of the man in his passenger seat, and it took a moment for him to call to mind who he was. He had met him only once before, and it was more than a year ago. "Robert?"

"That's right. I'm going to give you directions, and you're going to drive and ask no questions."

"Why would I do that?"

"Because I have a gun."

***

"Here we all are," Anders said with a sneer, shoving Alice through the doorway. It was dark, and it took a while for her eyes to adjust and take in who else was present.

"Jason." She hurried across to him. "Are you all right?"

"Yeah, I'm OK. Are you?"

"Such a touching reunion," Anders mocked in that same sickly sweet voice. He slammed the door shut and locked it.

"Hadyn's hurt," Jason said, nodding across the room. "He tried to get out and raise the alarm, and she hit him."

"Who did?"

Jason shrugged. "A tall, older woman, well-spoken—I've never seen her before. I heard her tell the other guy that if he messed up again, she'd kill him. At first, I thought she was just saying it, you know the way people do?"

"There's three of them?"

"No. The other guy left before."

"Where's Neil? Is he not with you?"

"Yeah." Jason's tone was resigned. "He's through there."

Alice looked to where he pointed and quickly turned away so she didn't have to see the limp body, crumpled and bleeding, propped against the wall.

"God save us," she said.

***

Dan played back the voicemail again, but it made no difference. They had listened to the conversation between Alice and Anders until they knew the bits they could understand off by heart, but his answers to her questions remained indecipherable.

"It's got to be Norwegian," Josh said. "If we could even hear it well enough to spell it phonetically we could translate it online."

"Yeah," Dan agreed. "Where's bloody Kris when you need him?"

"He's Swedish," Josh stated.

"Same difference."

"No, it's not!"

"Look," Eleanor interjected as they were starting to get shirty, "we haven't got time to mess around. We don't know what it says, and we're not going to figure it out, so forget it. Where can we think of that he'd take her?"

"Campion's?" George suggested.

Josh nodded. "Natasha said it's a building site at the moment."

"Natasha?" Dan asked.

"PC Granger."

"Ah, gotcha. Aitch's missus."

"That's right."

"We call her Hermione."

"Quelle surprise!" Josh said dryly.

"What's wrong with that?"

"I don't know, *Twinnie*, you tell me."

Dan scowled at him.

"The Norwegian and Swedish languages are similar, aren't they?" Sean asked.

"I don't know," Josh sighed in exasperation. "Are they?"

"Yeah. I think so. What about asking Kris?"

"He's in London."

"So call him up."

596

"Nah," Dan said. "I spoke to him this morning, and he was funny with me. I don't know what's the matter with him."

Sean nodded thoughtfully. "Can I have a word, Dan? In private?"

Dan frowned and followed Sean outside.

"What's that about?" Eleanor asked.

"No idea," Josh said, "but it's nothing to do with us."

"You gonna tell them we can hear them?" George asked, and he was right. Dan and Sean were standing just outside the front door, and the windows still needed replacing. Josh coughed lightly into his hand and went to sit next to Iris. Monty was on her lap and started growling.

"Oh, shut up!" Josh commanded. "I'm trying to listen!"

Monty grumbled at him but he stopped growling.

"Good boy," Josh whispered, glancing at Iris. She gave him a swift nod of approval.

For all that they could hear the two voices coming from outside, they couldn't make out much of their mumbled conversation, and it wasn't long after that Sean and Dan returned.

"I need to use your house phone, mate," Dan said. Josh pointed across the room. "Cheers."

Sean looked around at all the curious expressions and shook his head. "You're nosey feckers, the lot of yer."

"Alright, Kris mate? It's Dan," he said into the phone.

"Hi," Kris said gloomily. He'd been filming all day and had only just got back to the hotel. He was shattered in every way.

"How good's your Norwegian?"

"I understand a fair bit. Why?"

"We need your help with something."

"OK." Kris perked up a little.

"Somebody's kidnapped Alice."

"What? Please tell me I misheard…"

"No. You didn't. We think he told her where he was taking her, but he told her in Norwegian. I'm gonna play you the recording. It's not great quality, though."

"OK. I'm ready."

Dan called up his voicemail and played the message into the phone. Kris listened, but it was very crackly and muffled. He got Dan to play it again, and again.

"Any joy?" Dan asked.

"Kind of. I can't make out the first bit at all, but after that, he says, 'No one can escape…' something. That's not a lot of help, is it? Can I hear it once more?"

"Sure."

Dan played it one final time.

"Yeah. I've got it!" Kris said. "In Swedish, it's 'in i svarta hålet'."

"Meaning?"

"'Into the black hole.' And then, 'No one can escape the black hole.' He's taken her to Jay's studio."

"Kris Johansson, I bloody love you, mate, and don't you ever forget it. We'll go for a pint or ten when you get back, yeah?"

"Definitely! Be careful."

"I will, don't you worry. Bye." Dan hung up. "Black Hole Studios," he announced.

"Nice work!" George said.

"Cheers, although I was only the corresponder." Dan grinned.

As the others were putting on their coats and making their way outside, George tapped Sean on the arm, and the two of them held back until everyone else had gone. "I won't ask you to betray a confidence, Sean, but tell me how I can help him."

"Don't judge him. That's all. Let him know that however he chooses to live his life, and whatever happens, you'll always be his friend."

"Surely he knows that already?"

"Not at the moment, he doesn't."

***

"Alice!" James stumbled, blinking and dazed, into the control room. The door was locked behind him.

"Oh, James." She immediately got to her feet and embraced him, way past being overwhelmed by his or anybody else's scent. "Have you any idea what's going on?"

"None whatsoever, although the man who brought me I have met before. He's an old school friend of Eleanor's. It was he who organised the fake reunion last year."

"Rob Simpson-Stone?" Alice asked. James nodded to confirm she was correct. "I've overheard Adele and Dan speak of him many times. He's part of this thing, with Anders?"

"So it would seem." As James's eyes became accustomed to the dimness, he noticed the other two men, both on the floor. Jason was sitting with his back to the wall, and Hadyn was lying on his side; a gash ran the length of his cheek, and his eye was swollen shut. James returned his puzzled gaze to Alice and noticed her bruises. "You are hurt."

"Anders hit me, but I'm all right, James. Don't worry. Hadyn is very badly injured. That woman smashed him in the face with a microphone stand. And Neil…" She indicated with her hand to the recording room behind them.

James moved closer and squinted through the window. It was too dark to see the man properly, but he wasn't moving. James decided it was best not to say anything; even if Neil was still alive, they couldn't help him. He heard a key turn behind him, and the door opened again. A woman entered the room, Anders a step behind her, a gun in his hand.

"Well, isn't this cosy?" The woman smiled, looking around the people within. "As always, we're having something of a problem getting hold of that one last loose end. Very elusive, is Doctor Tierney. Perhaps you could help expedite proceedings a little, Alice?"

"I don't know you," Alice said, feeling very brave with James at her side and her son to protect. "How dare you call me by my first name."

"Don't be ludicrous, woman! You're being held at gunpoint and nobody knows you're here. Was it not enough to see how we dealt with the poor soul who deserted you, and for what? Your pathetic overture for a man who didn't love you enough to leave his dying wife? I'll assume your silly little outburst is because you're frightened, which means you have no idea where Tierney is. No matter." She turned and walked out of the room. Anders glared at Alice and James and then followed, locking the door behind him.

"Why is she after Doctor Tierney? What has he got to do with anything?" Alice asked.

"I believe," James speculated, "they are trying to remove anyone who was in close contact with Alistair."

Jason nodded in agreement. "Yeah. He was being blackmailed by that guy who was just here. I saw it for myself."

"What did you see, Jason?"

"I was trying to get the video link set up, because my dad told Mr. Campion I'd be able to do it, and I really wanted to. It's the first chance he ever gave me to show him what I'm good at, and I knew I could do it. I connected my laptop to the video screen remotely. They were just chatting about golf and fishing and stuff, and it was helpful because I could tell the sound was working, but I couldn't get audio and video going at the same time. Then I heard him saying to Mr. Campion it was his last chance, in that weird calm voice he's got, and Mr. Campion told him he'd rather die. I lost the sound again, but I got the video back, and I watched him."

"You watched him kill Alistair?" James asked. Jason nodded. "That certainly sheds new light on our situation."

"Indeed," Alice said. "If they've realised we know they killed Alistair, then they'll have no qualms about killing any of us."

"Or all of us," Jason pointed out.

"The fire at Campion's…" Alice thought aloud. "We need to find a way out of here, and quickly."

***

Dan stopped his car around the corner, out of sight of the recording studio. He had brought Eleanor with him. Josh, George and Sean arrived in Josh's car a moment later.

"Shouldn't we have planned what we were going to do before we got here?" Eleanor asked.

"How? We don't know what's going on."

She had to concede that one. They got out of the car. Josh, George and Sean did likewise.

"OK," Josh said. "What's the plan?" Dan looked at him and shrugged.

"We don't have one."

"That's what I was just saying," Eleanor said. "We should have tried to come up with something before we left."

"Like what?" Sean asked.

"How should I know?"

Josh sighed loudly. "Awesome. George?"

"Why me?" Everyone looked at him expectantly. "Seriously? What d'you expect me to do? Go in there brandishing a pitchfork?"

Another car had just parked up opposite. Natasha Granger got out of one side and Aitch the other.

"Thank God," George muttered.

"Alright, Dan?" Aitch said, shaking hands with his friend and clapping him on the back.

"Alright, mate? How's tricks?"

"There's some serious shit going on. Did Tash tell you they sent me off to bloody Wales for the week?"

"I heard."

"Wild goose chase, it was. But I knew you lot'd work it out. I should've come and talked to you about it sooner."

"How did you know we were here?"

"Farrar's got every available officer out patrolling the estate, so we put two and two together and ended up with Black Hole."

"No wonder you failed maths, is it, Aitch?" Dan grinned.

Aitch chuckled. "Anyway, I think we just need to hang fire, see what Farrar's got planned."

"He's bent, though, isn't he?"

"No. He's a good guy. When I got back from Cardiff this morning, I went to see him to demand the truth—I'd have more than gladly beaten it out of him. He said he couldn't tell me anything, that it was a big case and he was working for another department, but they were close to cracking it, and he'd make sure I got to see some of the action, as it was my case originally. He dropped enough hints for me to work out it all goes back to Campion's murder. I want to see those bastards nailed, but they're slippery. I couldn't even get beyond that Sharston and Strang were involved, never mind how the hell Callaghan got caught up in the investigation."

Josh nodded at Natasha. "Did you explain?"

"Yeah, I did."

"Good. I've got a bit more information."

"I'm listening," Aitch said.

"Rob Simpson-Stone and Jess were part of it."

Dan and Aitch both looked at Josh as if they were waiting for him to reveal that it was a sick joke.

"Our Jess? My late sister-in-law?"

"Since when was she your sister-in-law?" Aitch asked.

"Now there's a thing," Josh said. He'd been so caught up in the rest of it, he'd neglected that part of the puzzle, and it still didn't fit. "Why did she marry him? She already had a fake marriage certificate."

"Did she?" Dan asked.

"Don't start that again," Josh warned. "Yes, she did. I found it earlier, along with her full confession." He'd just done a bit of his own mental maths, and realised that the fake certificate was from around the time Andy had his car accident and things weren't looking too favourable. It appeared they weren't even loyal to their own. "You know what I think? Jess married Andy so she didn't get stung herself."

"They'd just take him out too," Aitch said, and then realised what he'd done.

Dan took his phone out. "I need to tell him." He walked off up the road to make the call.

"Nice one, Aitch," Natasha remarked sarcastically.

George tutted. "Your mouth always did get you in trouble."

"This from the man who—"

"Err, yeah. See what I mean?" George interrupted before Aitch went any further. Eleanor and Sean knew nothing about the incident in the park, and George wanted to keep it that way.

During the course of their interchange, a blue van bearing the name of a local plumbers' merchant had drawn up next to them. They stopped talking and watched the passenger door open. DS Graham Farrar got out.

602

"Alright, Aitch? Tash?" He acknowledged the others with a general smile. Natasha Granger gave Farrar a courteous nod, but no more than that.

"Alright, Graham?" Aitch responded. "How's it going?"

"Not great," Farrar admitted. "We're having something of a problem. Our man on the inside's lost contact."

"Hadyn, you mean?" Sean asked, barely concealing his loathing of the police.

Farrar looked him up and down. "Doctor Sean Tierney," he identified. He turned back to Aitch and continued without answering Sean's question. "All the sound equipment's interfering with our surveillance stuff. We can't figure out what's a weapon and what's not."

Dan returned to the gathering and briefly shook hands with Farrar.

"Everything OK?" Josh asked.

Dan nodded. "Yeah. They're safe."

"What a relief."

"Also," Farrar continued with his report, "the IR is lousy. We don't even know how many of them are in there. It's like the whole place has got a shield around it."

"That'll be the soundproofing," Dan said. "Andy dealt with fitting it—I wouldn't have the first clue. However, I do know the acoustic foam is Mylar coated, and the cavity walls are full of fibreglass."

"Bloody hell! Talk about overkill."

"I'm not so sure about that," Sean said. "Have you heard the sort of noise they make in there?"

Farrar smiled to acknowledge Sean's stand-down. "We had the copter out last week, and the place is almost invisible to our systems."

"So it really is a black hole," Josh mused.

"Yeah, pretty much. Anyway, we've got all the information we require now, so our priority is to get everyone out safely, which means we need to get closer without rousing their suspicion. And I'm afraid that's why I'm talking to you."

"What d'you need?" Dan asked.

"Someone to go in with a tap so we can establish the number and location of our targets, who's armed and—"

"OK. I'm up for that."

"Thanks for the offer, Dan, but no can do."

"I'm a trustee. I can say I stopped by to see how things are going."

"That's the problem. You're a trustee, and our intel says they're trying to get everyone involved in Campion Community Trust in one place, then stage an explosion or a fire—make it look like an electrical fault."

"I thought this was just because of the video," Josh said.

Farrar shook his head. "It's much bigger than that. Folden doesn't know Jason Meyer saw him, or he'd have killed him already."

Throughout the discussion, Eleanor had remained quiet, every so often trying to get hold of James by phone, but he wasn't answering, and now the panic was rising.

"Who else is in there?" she asked. "Out of the trust's personnel?"

"We know Jason Meyer was already here, and we saw them bring in Alice Friar, and yes, I'm sorry to say, your husband's in there, too."

Eleanor turned away and walked up the street. She was a strong woman—it was what James said had attracted him in the first place. She was independent and knew her own mind. She'd got through losing Jess and finding out she was part of a massive fraud operation. For the most part, she'd coped with Kevin's suicide, and even before that, when he held her hostage in his car. But this was different. She and James had a child, and so many plans for the future.

Josh watched her in the distance as she tried to keep herself together, understanding everything she was thinking and feeling.

"Is Strang in there?" he asked.

"No. Strang's dead."

Josh nodded. "I'll do it," he said quietly. He looked DS Farrar in the eye. "I'll go in. I'm Jason's counsellor. I've got a valid reason to be here."

"What about Rob?" Dan asked.

"Yeah, he's in there," Farrar confirmed. "But I don't think it'll matter. It's a small town, and people are sometimes going to know each other."

He had faltered mid-sentence, Josh noticed. It was barely anything at all, but it was there, nonetheless. Farrar was still staring at him and he at Farrar, both men aware that the other had received a message, intentionally or otherwise.

Farrar broke away. "I'll get you a vest and transmitter." He returned to the van and opened the side door.

George tugged at Josh's arm to get his attention. "I'm coming with you."

"No, George."

"You can't...you're not...ah, hell!" George took a deep breath. "I can't get it out!" He screwed up his eyes and grunted in frustration.

"Shh. Think." Josh took hold of George's hands and held eye contact with him, to give him a chance to get the words straight in his mind. "OK?" George nodded. "Try again."

"You're not going in there. Not alone."

"I'll be OK. The police are here."

"But what if..." George's eyes filled with tears of desperation. "Please?"

"No, ma moitié. You're already struggling to speak. You'll lose it. You know that."

"Why's that bad?"

"I guess it's not, really, on this occasion, but if something happens to both of us, who's going to look after your mum and Blue?"

"Josh, please?" George was properly crying now, and Josh was having to fight to stay in control of his emotions. He was terrified, but the thought of losing George if only one of them came out of this alive was something he couldn't face.

"How about I go with you?" Sean suggested.

Josh nodded. "Yes, that would work."

Sean smiled at George. "OK?" George sniffed the tears back and nodded gratefully.

Farrar had heard and was already getting a second vest out. He beckoned Josh and Sean over and helped them to put the vests

605

on under their jackets. Once he'd checked they were fastened correctly, he gave Josh a small device that looked like a car key fob.

"This is voice activated and will transmit anything above a whisper, so you'll have to talk at a normal volume. All we need you to do is say what you see."

"Easier said than done."

"I appreciate that. As soon as we know who's in there and where they are, we'll be straight in, so just try to tell us ASAP. Listen, thanks for this."

"I don't have any choice, really, do I? You ready, Tierney?"

Sean shrugged. "As I'll ever be."

Josh returned to George. "I'll be OK. I'm wearing body armour. What can go wrong?"

George tried to smile and gave him a kiss. "I love you."

"I love you too. See you soon."

***

Rob put the gun down and stretched his back. They'd been setting this up for days, and he was tired.

Folden kicked the vending machine. "He hasn't even got the fucking keys with him," he snarled.

"We'll be done soon, and you can go get a beer."

"Any sign of Strang yet?"

"No. Not yet."

"Fucking idiot. How hard is it to track down a psychologist? They don't strike me as especially intelligent."

"Have you ever met one?"

"Yah. I was watching *him*, remember. His fucking cat nearly finished me off. If Callaghan hadn't turned up, I'd have strangled the vicious little shit."

Rob started to laugh, but was silenced by the sound of heels on the stairs. Angela Sharston came into view.

"You'll have to deal with him separately," she told Folden. "We can't wait any longer."

"Should I do it now?"

She picked at her teeth with a fingernail, as if removing meat from between them. "No. Let's get this mess cleaned up first, shall we? Oh!" She stepped closer to the window and watched the two men approaching. She laughed and clapped her hands. "Well, well! If the mountain won't come to Muhammad…" She gave a loud sigh of contentment. "I'll be upstairs," she said and turned on her heel.

Rob frowned. "Josh Sandison? What the hell's he doing here?"

"Who's that?" Folden asked.

"The guy with Tierney. I went to school with him."

"Well, you go away, stay in the big room and I will talk to Sandison."

"You could just tell him to go."

"I could, yah." Folden grinned. He had no intention of letting anyone leave alive. He liked killing people, showing them how strong he was, preferably one-on-one, so he could watch them struggle and fight for that last breath, not like the fire he set back in Campion's, although he did enjoy seeing the flames take control and the efforts of the firefighters, knowing he was the cause of all the commotion. But there was nothing like hearing a man beg for his life, looking into his eyes and seeing the horror, that last spark of hope dwindle to extinction. And then it was time to find a new spider to torment to its twitching death.

Rob stayed back out of sight, but he remained in the reception area, watching from a distance as Folden unlocked the door.

"Hello?" he greeted, his Norwegian accent now covered by the RP he affected in his role of lawyer. "Are you here for the trust meeting?"

"Hi." Josh smiled. "I'm not, actually. I was on my way home and thought I'd pop in to see Jason. Is he about?"

"He's upstairs." Folden beckoned the two men inside.

"I don't want to disturb their meeting."

"Don't worry. They haven't long started."

"I don't think we've met before, have we?" Josh glanced sideways at Sean as they followed Folden up the stairs.

"No, I don't believe so. I'm Simon Yarrow, Mr. Meyer's lawyer."

"I see, yes. That makes sense. And, erm, you're here for the meeting?"

"That's right."

"If you don't mind me saying, you seem very young to be a lawyer."

Folden gave a small, polite laugh in response. "I don't mind you saying at all. It's quite a compliment."

"Is it a full trust meeting? Are there many of them here?"

"Why do you ask? Are you involved in the trust?"

"Oh, no. Just curious. I'm Jason's counsellor, and it's always good to know what's happening in my clients' lives, you know? Helps to frame the work we do in our sessions."

They had reached the top of the stairs now, and Josh shrugged at Sean. He didn't know what else to say.

"Here we are." Folden smiled and turned the key in the outside of the control room door.

"I thought you said they were already in their meeting."

"That's right."

"So why is the door locked?"

"You have a lot of questions, Mr. Sandison."

"I didn't tell you my name."

"No."

"I did," a voice said from behind them. Josh and Sean turned to see who it belonged to.

"Rob?" Josh acted out being surprised very convincingly, although the gun in Rob's hand did have quite a bit to do with that.

"Hello, Josh," Rob replied solemnly.

"Were you downstairs when we came in?"

"Yeah, obviously." He was standing at the top of the staircase.

"I didn't see you, that's all. Or your gun." Josh couldn't keep his eyes from straying to it, and he reminded himself that he was wearing a bulletproof vest. The worst Rob could do, other than shoot him in the head, was no worse than he'd done to himself over the years, and he fought to keep eye contact. He heard a toilet flush and water running behind a door to his left.

"The boss," Rob said.

"Your boss?"

"That's right. You'll meet her soon enough."

"And has she got a gun too?"

"Stop the chitchat already!" Folden snapped, pulling a pistol from inside his jacket. In a flash, Rob was behind them, and Sean instinctively hit out. Rob yanked Sean's arm back hard, and he

608

yelled out in pain. Josh held his breath, trying desperately to conceal how frightened he was.

"For God's sake! We're psychologists, not marines. There really is no need for you to threaten us. Just tell us what you want us to do, and we'll do it."

"Get in," Folden said coldly, jerking his head towards the door, the pistol trained on them all the while. Josh took a step then hesitated.

"Just do as he says," Rob snarled, his face close enough to Sean's for the quiet warning to set Sean's ears ringing. Rob eased off on the arm lock, although Sean could still feel the barrel of the gun pressing into his back. They needed more time.

"Isn't this the control room?" he asked. Rob tightened his grip again, and Sean winced. He kept his gaze on Josh, urging him to keep going. Josh gave him the tiniest, most fleeting acknowledgement.

"I've never been here before. It's big, isn't it?" He addressed Folden now, sensing his pride in his work. "It must take quite a few of you to pull off a job like this."

"We are professionals, Mr. Sandison." The Norwegian accent was back in full force.

"No doubt, no doubt. Still, I can't imagine there's much of great value in a recording studio."

"Do you always talk this much?" Not Folden this time. A female voice.

"Angie?" Sean said. He blinked at her in disbelief.

"Sean, darling!" She smiled back at him with no sincerity whatsoever. "How have you been?"

"Just what the hell's going on here?"

"You know each other?" Josh asked.

"Yes," Angela answered. "Or, should I say, we *did* know each other, because very soon, all of this and you will be no more. Before he got himself embroiled in this Campion nonsense, Sean and I were—"

Now, for as much as Josh was disappointed that she was interrupted precisely at that moment, his minor irritation was alleviated entirely by the sight of armed police officers on the stairs behind her. All of a sudden, there was a frenzy of activity.

Rob charged forward and shoved Josh and Sean into the control room, locking them on the inside, from where the muffled shouts and bangs of people being thrown to the floor outside could be heard. A gun fired, followed by deathly quiet, and then shouting started up again.

Josh and Sean became accustomed to the dim light in the room and noticed the others staring at them in shock. None of them could muster so much as a greeting. As the noise died down, Sean let out a very shaky breath.

"I hope to God that was the sound of law enforcement victory, or we're done for."

They heard the key in the door and slowly backed away, unsure what was on the other side. The door opened. It was DS Farrar, accompanied by a female officer, and Farrar was smiling.

"What a blinder," he said, stepping forward and shaking hands with Josh first, then Sean. "That was one hell of a performance."

"Thanks," Josh muttered. He was ready to collapse but just about holding it together. He turned back to the others and saw Hadyn lying on the floor. Sean went over.

"Hadyn?" He felt for a pulse and found one. "Hadyn? Can you hear me? It's Sean."

Hadyn groaned in pain. "Head," he said, which was sufficient description, given the state of his face.

"It's all right, Hadyn. There's an ambulance on its way." Sean glanced over at Farrar and received a nod of confirmation.

"Is everyone OK?" Farrar asked.

Alice pointed to the recording room, unable to speak; her synaesthesia had already delivered the truth.

"Neil's in there," Jason said.

Farrar removed the keys from the control room door and took them over to unlock the other door. He went inside, and everyone held their breath. He came back out again and shook his head. "I'm sorry, Miss Friar."

She started to cry, and Jason put his arms around her, holding her tightly, crying himself as he tried to comfort her.

"Please tell me this is over," Josh said, addressing Farrar. "That no-one else is going to die."

"Yeah. It's over." As he spoke he glanced past Josh. "Excuse me." He left the control room. Josh watched him reach out a hand to someone and lean in to embrace them. Only then did he see who it was.

"Rob?"

Rob gave Josh a wink and a smile, and mouthed the words, "One minute."

Josh leaned against the wall and rubbed his eyes, listening to the sound of people moving past him in both directions, voices asking questions and giving answers, all blurring into one muddled mass of noise that cyclically rose, peaked and fell away to nothing in the dead room. He had no idea how long he'd been standing there when he felt someone touch his arm and opened his eyes again to Rob's concerned face.

"Alright?" he asked. Josh nodded. "I'll explain everything once we're out of here."

"Undercover," Josh uttered.

"Yeah. It's been a, err…" Rob looked away, close to tears. "I'm sorry. I hope you understand."

"How long?"

"This case? Three years."

"Wow!"

"And before that, five years, and before that?" He shrugged in defeat. "I can't even remember. But I'm done now. No more." He turned back and smiled sadly. "No more."

"I'm really glad," Josh said. "Not that it's over… Hold on." He paused to give himself time to get the words in order. After months of nonstop thinking and surviving on virtually no sleep, his brain was finally shutting down. Worst timing ever. "Let me rephrase that. I'm glad it's over, of course, but I'm also relieved to know this is what you've been doing. I thought I'd got you all wrong."

"You mean you didn't think I was a bad guy?" Rob pretended to be disappointed.

"No."

"Not even when you were threatening to push me down Jess's stairs?"

"Ah." Josh smiled. "I must admit, you had me questioning my conviction at that point. The others will be relieved too."

"Yeah. I'm not looking forward to telling them."

"Do you want me to do it?"

"No. I want to tell them myself. I owe them that much."

"You can get it over and done with now if you like. They're outside."

"Will you vouch for me?"

"Didn't I always?"

Rob nodded. "Yeah, you did. And I appreciate it." He called back to Farrar to let him know what he was doing, pausing for a body bag to be brought through.

"He challenged Folden," Rob said, watching the two men carry Neil's body away. "Got between him and Jason. And Hadyn—he's a brave kid—tried to get help. I couldn't tell him we were on the same side, risk Sharston seeing anything. She took over the operation, and she's damned wily—that's why it's taken us so long. Her husband was a bit of a show-off, which was how we discovered them, but the women—they're dangerous."

"More dangerous than Anders Folden?"

"Without a doubt. Folden's a psycho who doesn't care about getting caught. He's done time before and likes to brag about his crimes. He's reckless and makes mistakes. Sharston and Jess—even getting close to them…" Rob ran his hand over his fuzz of hair and exhaled loudly. "She was quite a piece of work."

"She always was," Josh said.

"Yeah, she was. And Strang's an idiot."

"Aitch says he's dead."

"Doesn't surprise me. His brother got the brains in that family."

"Should you be telling me this?"

Rob smiled. "No, mate, I shouldn't. That's almost the hardest part of all—keeping your mouth shut, standing by and doing nothing when all you want is to stick a gun to the bastards' heads." The stairs were clear now, and they moved off again.

"Almost the hardest part?" Josh asked.

"Leaving Zoë and Lucas and not being able to tell them that I was coming back. It nearly killed me when she filed for divorce."

"Are there people you can talk to about it?"

"Yeah. The support's excellent, and having contact with Farrar over the last few months has been a life-saver, but it's not going to get me back my wife and son."

As they reached the bottom of the stairs and turned the corner, they came face-to-face with George and Dan. Rob held his hands up.

"Friend, not foe," Josh said. "As you were." George and Dan backed off immediately.

"I'm sorry, mate." Rob held out his hand to Dan. "It's shit when you've got to lie to your friends and miss out on all the important events in their lives just to do your job."

Dan continued to stare at the outstretched hand.

"He's in the police," Josh said.

"What, like an undercover cop?"

"That's right," Rob confirmed.

"Sounds glamorous."

"It's not. I can only tell you now because I've jacked it in. I said when we got this lot banged up, that'd be it. It's not worth the aggro."

Dan was still frowning and seemed doubtful about what he was hearing. He looked to Josh for guidance, and Josh nodded in encouragement. Dan shrugged and shook Rob's hand. Rob hauled him in and put his other arm around him, hugging him firmly.

"Jesus, Rob. Get a cold shower!" Dan joked.

Rob released him. "What can I say? It's been a rough ride."

"Still cool, though. Undercover cop."

"Yeah, maybe. I owe your brother a massive apology."

"He's outside."

"I'll go see him in a sec." Rob looked at George. "I tell you what, mate, I have never been so scared in my life."

"Yeah. Sorry about that."

"No need. It's just that I knew about, err, the dog incident? I thought I was a dead man when you had me on the deck. Thank Christ Adele stopped you."

"She's gonna be a bit pissed off," Dan said, a grin creeping onto his face. "She told us you were up to no good, and we weren't having any of it."

Rob laughed. "To be fair, she didn't like me much back in school."

"Mmm, I wouldn't go that far," Dan winked.

"Well, tell her she was kind of right—and she's bloody terrifying, and all! I'm not kidding, I was already crapping myself that day I went to Jess's. First you, George, then Adele, and I'd waited till Andy had gone out, thinking it'd be safer. It was bad enough with her…" He swallowed hard. "It broke my heart, telling her I was sick and then finding out she was dying." He stopped and put his head down, trying to stifle his sobs. The other men looked away while he got it together again; he sniffed and wiped his eyes. "Which is why," he turned to Josh, "I said what I did. I knew you'd see straight through me if I didn't lay it on, and I didn't mean a word of it. Congratulations to you both. It took you bloody long enough, didn't it?"

"Yes. My fault," Josh admitted.

"I've got a little present for you in my digs."

"You didn't need to."

"I did. These guys are, or were, my best mates, and I feel like I screwed you all over. Anyway, it's nothing special, but I missed out on your wedding, and Ellie's wedding, and your engagement, too, Dan. It's the pits. I felt like the kid looking through the sweet shop window." Rob took a deep breath, preparing himself for facing Andy. That was the worst reconciliation of all, because they'd always butted up against each other, in football and in love. Now he was going to add lying through his teeth into the mix.

"You ready?" Dan asked.

Rob nodded and followed him outside, scanning the vicinity and spotting Andy leaning against his car. Dan put his arm around Rob's shoulders, to make it as clear as possible to Andy that Rob was not his enemy. As they got closer, Andy took a step forward, and Shaunna and Eleanor grabbed him.

"It's OK," he said, standing his ground but not advancing any further. "I'm not gonna start anything." The two women released him. He ran his hand down Shaunna's arm and smiled to reassure her as he moved off again.

"I didn't know Andy and Shaunna were together," Rob said.

"They're not," Dan lied. If Josh and George doubted it, they didn't let it show.

"Andy," Rob said, stopping a few feet from him.

Andy glared at him, and then at his brother. "What's going on?"

"Rob's been working undercover, to get the fraud ring Jess was part of."

"What fraud ring?"

Rob answered the question. "The Sharstons, the Strangs, Folden, Perlett and Lambert. That's the top of the food chain, then there's loads of runners, counterfeiters and grunts further down, which is mostly what I've been doing for the past three years—running fake passports up and down the country."

"Then what was all that crap about you conning her last year?"

"A sting operation. We had to wait till you were out of the way for a while, so I could get close to her. That was my cover story to throw her off. The money will go back to her estate now. We were pretty sure they'd use the reunion to poach for business, and we needed to see them in action."

"Surely she knew you were part of the firm?"

"You've got to be kidding. The top brass don't mix with the riff-raff. Aside from which, I was working from Newcastle under an assumed name. I never came into contact with Sharston and Strang, or her, until they upped the ante on their operations here, and my bosses—my real bosses—decided to transfer me and use my connection to her. That was when we set up the reunion."

Andy continued to study Rob for a little longer and decided to accept his version of the truth, although he wasn't ready to back down.

"Right," Dan said, satisfied that the situation had been sufficiently neutralised. "I'm gonna go dump the car back home and head for the pub. Anyone joining me?"

Andy nodded. "Yeah. I will. Rob?"

"I'd love to, but I'm still working."

"No worries. I'll get you one next time."

"Cheers, mate." Rob smiled at him, more grateful than Andy would ever know.

"What about you, Ellie?" Dan asked.

Eleanor ran off without answering. James had been checked over by the paramedics and was on his way out of the building.

"Neil's dead," Dan told Andy.

"Who's Neil?"

"Alice's lover."

"Alice has a lover?"

"Yeah."

Andy threw his hands in the air. "I give up," he said and went back to the car.

Dan turned to Josh and George. "Are you coming for a pint?"

Josh was mid-yawn. "No. I'm ready to drop." He turned to George. "You can go if you want."

George shook his head. "I'm coming home with you." He pulled Josh to him and kissed him. They remained close with their foreheads pressed together, whispering reassurances.

Rob smiled. "At least some things are right with the world. I'm going back inside. I'll catch up with you all soon."

He shook hands with everyone again, and reluctantly trudged back to the studio building, pausing to talk to James on the way.

"Do you think she'll want a lift?" Josh asked generally and in reference to Eleanor. The others understood what he meant.

"If she does, I'll drop her off," Dan offered.

"OK. Tell her we said good night."

"Will do, mate. See you tomorrow, maybe."

"You might, although the way I'm feeling, I'll probably sleep right through it. Night."

Josh and George waved and started walking back to their car.

"I'll see you there," Andy called to Dan.

"OK, bro."

Shaunna got in the Mustang, beside Andy, and they left. Once Dan was sure James and Eleanor had transport home, he left too.

Squared
Wednesday 6th December

"Pain relief and some extra steristrips for you, Hadyn." The nurse passed the items to Sean because Hadyn was very agitated. "Try not to get the wound wet for a couple of days if you can."

"Thanks," Sean said.

"Yeah, thanks," Hadyn mumbled through his severely swollen face. The nurse smiled and left the cubicle curtain open as she exited to signify that they should leave.

"All right now, just take your time." Sean stepped to one side to give Hadyn some space. He dropped down to the floor and moved off carefully.

"Thank you for coming with me," he said.

"Oh, I don't mind at all, Hadyn, although I also wanted to be sure you didn't relapse."

"I did OK?"

"You did grand, young man. Have you thought any more about my offer? It's only a wee room, but the bed is clean and comfy, and I'll even make you a full Irish in the morning."

"I don't want to be a pain."

"If you were, I wouldn't have suggested it. What do you say?"

"OK."

"Great stuff." Sean led the way out.

"Thanks, Sean. I don't deserve it," Hadyn said quietly. Sean stopped and turned back.

"Now you listen here." His voice was kind yet firm. "You have done nothing wrong. Nothing. Do you hear me?"

"I lied to you."

"You omitted some of the details, that's all, because you were told to. Chances are you'd have been assigned to me, whatever,

617

and I'm very glad you were. Think about it this way: you've just completed a very important secret mission. How about that?"

"Yeah, I suppose so."

"More importantly, you stayed strong and confident, so I don't want to hear any of that 'I don't deserve it' rubbish."

"Sorry."

"And you can stop with the feckin' apologies!"

Hadyn opened his mouth, all set to apologise again. He shut it and tried to smile. It hurt.

"That's better," Sean said. "Truth be told, I could do with the company myself. It's been a rough old day all round, and I'm ready for a nice cup of tea and my bed, so let's be having yer."

They headed out to the waiting room, where Sophie was sitting, reading a magazine. Dylan was with his grandparents. She got up and smiled when she saw them.

"Hadyn, this is Sophie," Sean introduced. "Hadyn's going to be staying with me for a few days, Soph."

"Good luck, mate!" She winked at Hadyn. "It's nice to meet you."

***

"Here we are, Alice." Bill stopped his car outside of her house. "Are you sure there's nobody I can call for you?"

"No, thank you, Bill." Alice busied herself with unfastening her seat belt so that she didn't have to look at him. She'd cried so much over the past couple of hours that her sense of smell was out of commission; small consolation.

"At least let me see you inside," Bill suggested, opening the door before she dismissed that offer too. Jason had been in the back and was standing by.

"I really am perfectly fine," Alice said. Nonetheless, she allowed the two men to walk her to her front door. "It was only a little slap." She took her key out and attempted to push it into the lock, but her hands were shaking too much. Jason reached across and held her hand steady, knowing her well enough by now to also know that she hated accepting help from other people. She smiled in thanks and stepped into the hall, immediately coming over light-headed.

"Oh, dear me," she said, holding onto the radiator.

Again, without speaking or taking control, Jason held out his arm for her to take, and she did so. He led her into her lounge and cleared a space for her to sit.

"Neil always makes such a terrible mess when he's writing. He gets carried away and doesn't even stop to eat, drink or sleep. One time, he even…" She couldn't go on. Jason waited for her to sit down, and sat beside her holding her free hand; her other hand clasped a handkerchief to her face. Albert chirruped, and she laughed sorrowfully.

"I'm going to make tea, Alice," Bill said, not knowing what else to do.

"Thank you, Bill. You have been so kind and patient."

He nodded and left the room. Jason's phone rang in his pocket.

"Oasis," Alice said through her sniffling.

"Err, yeah," Jason confirmed, surprised she recognised 'Stand By Me'—the song that was his ring tone for Krissi. He answered his phone. "Whassup, Scene Kid?"

"I'm just closing. Did you want me to pick up a takeaway?"

"No, thanks. I'm not hungry."

"Jay."

"Krissi."

"Have you eaten today?"

"Yes." Jason started playing with the buttons on his jacket, not that Krissi could see, but she could tell he was lying from his tone and the abruptness of his answer. She remained silent and waited for him to revoke it. He sighed. "I'll make some toast when I get home. I'm gonna stay with Alice for a while."

"Should I wait up?"

"Err…"

"You can invite her here," Alice suggested. Jason frowned. "I'd like to meet her properly, and besides, I really don't want to be alone just yet."

"OK," Jason said. "Krissi, Alice said you can come round here."

"Wotto's with me. He says I need an escort."

"That should be all right."

"Don't assume. Ask her!"

He sighed. "Is it all right if she brings her boyfriend?"

"He's not my boyfriend!" Krissi snapped. Jason smirked.

Alice heard her response and laughed, amused by their conversation in spite of everything else. "They're both more than welcome," she confirmed.

***

"Kris?"

"Hi, Jan." Kris moved to the side to grant her access to his and Ade's hotel room, but she stayed where she was.

"Barry's waiting downstairs in the bar. He wants to talk to you."

"Does he now?" Kris shoved his feet into his shoes. "Let's do it."

"Kris!" Ade shouted, but it was too late. He was already halfway down the corridor. Ade and Jan looked at each other in panic, knowing what was coming. They quickly followed.

"What's happened?" Jan asked Ade, as they drew up behind Kris at the lift.

"One of his friends was—"

"Our friends," Kris corrected. Ade smiled.

"One of *our* friends—"

"Two, actually," Kris corrected again.

"Two of our friends—"

"And Jay."

"Do you want to explain?"

The lift doors opened and the three of them got in.

"Long story short, Jan," Kris said, "there was an armed hostage situation at the studio owned by my daughter's flatmate, and the police asked friends of ours to assist in the negotiations."

"Jesus! Is everyone OK?"

"They're fine, but I need to be with them, for my own peace of mind."

"You really do take method acting to a whole new level!" she joked. "Listen, there's no need to explain to me, but Barry might take some convincing."

"With all due respect to you, Jan, your husband can go fuck himself. Family and friends come first."

The lift stopped, and they walked through to the bar, where Barry was openly chatting up the barmaid, and continued to do so, even though he'd clearly seen them arrive. Jan shook her head in disdain.

"You can do better," Kris said.

"I know, I know," she sighed. "And I hate what they're doing with the show already."

"Kristian." Barry faked a smile as they approached. "Can I get you a drink?"

"No, thank you."

"Fair enough. Now, what's this crap I'm hearing about you having the day off? Can't it wait till the weekend? We've got one hell of a—"

"No. I'm afraid it can't."

"So you're just going to get a train home in the middle of filming? What the fuck are we supposed to do in the meantime? Use a bloody mannequin? Mind you, I doubt anyone would—"

"That's it. I'm done." Kris turned to leave. Barry grabbed his arm.

"You're not going anywhere," he snarled.

"Watch me."

"Breach of contract."

Kris glanced down at Barry's hand, still gripping him tightly, and he bruised easily.

"I suggest you let go of me before I have you arrested for assault."

Barry sneered at him. "If you leave us in the shit, I'm gonna make sure you never work again."

"Go for it," Kris challenged, using his 'good eye contact' to full menacing effect. Barry released him, and he walked away. "I'll be back as soon as I can," he called over his shoulder.

"Don't fucking bother," Barry shouted after him.

Kris raised his arm to indicate he'd got the message and would be abiding by it. Jan watched in horror.

"Why did you say that?" she asked.

"Don't worry, he'll be back. He hasn't got the balls to leave."

She continued to watch Kris retreat for a moment, and made her decision. "You know what? I'm done too. I quit."

"Whatever, sweetheart. We have a whole team of writers. No-one's indispensable, not even the series creator."

"And what about wives? Have you got a team of those too, *sweetheart*?"

She picked up the drink he had bought her and calmly poured it over his head. Without another word, she marched to the lift, arriving at the same time as it did. She got in with Kris and Ade, the doors closed, and she clenched her fists and shrieked. Kris and Ade glanced at each other. Jan let out a long, slow breath and smiled.

"Ahhh. Why didn't I do that years ago? Have you bought train tickets yet?"

"No, not yet."

"Well don't. I'll give you a lift, if you can wait till morning?"

"That'd be fab, thanks."

"And on the way, I'll tell you all about the new series I've been writing, if you're interested."

"Will it be primetime?"

"Never."

"Does it involve being in London or Brighton?"

"All set in Manchester and Liverpool."

"Would I need to learn a Liverpool accent?"

"Darling! Only Scousers can speak Scouse." Jan was from Liverpool herself.

Kris nodded. "I'm interested."

"Excellent!" She stuck up her middle finger in the general direction of the bar, which was now several floors below them. "We'll show that fuck'n knob'ead who's boss," she said in a broad Liverpool accent. Both men laughed, and she grinned at them. "Don't suppose you know a decent producer?"

Kris glanced at Ade and winked. "I think I might."

***

"Carl Watkinson!" Alice sprang to her feet and wobbled dizzily. Wotto caught her.

"Miss Friar," he said, grinning that huge toothy grin of his.

"OK." Jason frowned. "I totally didn't see that coming."

Krissi tutted and went straight over to hug him. He stood with his arms hanging limp at his sides. She nudged him. He huffed, pretending it was a terrible effort to hug her back, but did so anyway.

"Are you OK?" she asked.

"Yeah. I feel great. Seeing Anders Folden with a cop's foot on his head, squashing his smarmy face into the carpet, was very cathartic."

"The policewoman who came to tell us what happened said someone died."

"Err, yeah," Jason confirmed cagily. "Abbey Road guy?"

"He was at the studio?"

Jason didn't want to explain now, not with Alice being so upset, although she was still gushing over Wotto, seemingly oblivious to their conversation.

"It's a long story," Jason whispered, "but he was a friend of Alice's."

Krissi mouthed an 'oh' and left it alone for the time being, instead tuning in to Alice and Wotto's conversation, which was very enlightening. He'd just taken off his cap and Alice was inspecting his hair, as always in a fully plucked-out afro, if somewhat flattened by a day in a warm, humid kitchen.

"Yes," she nodded approvingly, "a definite improvement on the dreadlocks. Neil's always smelled dreadful, but then he wasn't the cleanliest of people."

"Mine didn't smell," Wotto said defensively. "But they didn't help much with getting a job, neither, not with my record."

Jason looked at Krissi to see if she reacted to Wotto's statement, as it was news to him, but apparently not to her. She shrugged.

"I was in juvey for robbery," Wotto explained for Jason's benefit. "That's where I started training to be a chef, then I got a kitchen porter job in the staff canteen at Campion's."

"Which is how you and Alice know each other," Jason realised.

"Yeah. Best foster mum in the world, Miss Friar," Wotto said. She smiled fondly at him.

"Speaking of parents…" On those words, Jason left the room. His dad had taken the empty teacups to the kitchen before Krissi and Wotto arrived, and as Jason approached, he could hear him crying quietly. He'd never seen him cry before, which wasn't to say that he didn't, but he certainly didn't in front of his son. Jason opened the door very slowly.

"Hey, Dad," he called through the gap to give him time to recompose, but Bill didn't even try.

"Jason," he said, attempting a smile.

"What's up?"

Bill cleared his throat. "Nothing to worry about. Just the after effects of a very trying day. At least you and Alice are both safe." The words left his mouth at the same time as another strangled sob.

Jason didn't say anything, instead standing close by and waiting for this round of tears to subside.

Bill dried the teacups and passed them to Jason to put away, speaking as he did so. "It was my fault Neil came back," he said. Jason nodded to indicate he was listening. "I tracked him down to a hostel in London. He'd been working as a roadie, and when the tour finished, he had nowhere to go, so he was living on the streets. I told him Alice was in danger."

"Which was true."

"If I hadn't told him, he'd still be alive now."

"He might've died on the streets. There's no point beating yourself up about it, Dad. True, he wouldn't have been at Black Hole if you hadn't told him about Alice, and he might still be alive now, but he got between me and Folden. If he hadn't been there, I'd be dead, not him, and you'd still be blaming yourself. He was telling me earlier about working at Abbey Road, and some of the massive tours he's worked on, and yeah, it's really sad he's gone. I'd have loved to have got to know him better, got him to help out at the studio, because he really knew his sh...stuff."

Jason blushed. Bill raised an eyebrow in disapproval.

"You can only start swearing in front of your father when you've put all that moody teenager silliness behind you once and for all."

Jason laughed. "Well, prepare to be sworn in front of, because I think I might finally have grown up."

Bill nodded. He could see it was true. "Your mother will be very pleased to hear it. You've no idea how many sleepless nights you caused with your silences and locking yourself in your room all the time."

"Glad someone worries about me," Jason said, feigning sulkiness.

Bill managed a smile. "I'm proud of you, Jason. And Al would have been, too."

"Thanks, Dad. Alice said he was your best friend."

"He was. More like a brother. I still miss him very much."

"And she knows Wotto."

"Who?"

"Carl Watkinson?"

"Ah yes," Bill nodded. "Al gave him the job at our place, then had a word with James to see if the pizza chain would take him on as a chef. James didn't hesitate, but Carl said he wanted to get the job on his own merits, and that's just what he did. In the end, all James had to do was approve the appointment at head office, as the old MD had a policy against appointing applicants with a criminal record, regardless of type or how good their credentials. It's all changed now. Not like the old days. These modern companies are no place for dinosaurs like me."

Jason acted out a resigned nod. "That's a pity. I was going to ask you if you'd reconsider being a trustee. James is still going to be involved, but I need someone on hand who knows what they're doing."

"I don't know, son. I'm a bit old to be taking on full-time work, and your mother won't approve. After all, who would water her dahlias, or wash her car, or—"

"How about a job share?"

Bill frowned, still doubtful. "It would have to be somebody I know I can work with."

"Fair enough. Let's see what she thinks, shall we?"

"Who?"

"Alice, of course."

They returned to the lounge, catching the tail end of a conversation that stopped the minute the two men came into view, but it didn't matter. Jason beamed at Krissi. She was blushing furiously, and Wotto had his head down, but they were sitting next to each other on the sofa, holding hands. All those months of failed matchmaking, and Alice had nailed it in less than fifteen minutes. She gave him a wink.

625

"I was just reminiscing with your good friends here about how you came to be conceived, Jason. I fear I may have embarrassed them a little."

"Yeah, well. Serves them right."

"As I told them, love doesn't wait for a perfect moment to occasion." She studied the two of them for a few seconds and nodded in satisfaction. "Yes. The blend is exactly right. Now then." She turned her attention on Jason, or rather, on the air around Jason. He rolled his eyes, and she laughed at him. "What is it you want to ask me, dear?"

***

"So, Shauuuunna," Dan slurred, trying to focus on her face. He grinned.

"Bro," Andy warned.

"I wasn't gonna say anything bad!"

Andy pinched the corners of his eyes. He was still feeling sober, even though he'd had exactly the same number of drinks as his brother and Shaunna. She was quite tipsy, but nowhere near in the state Dan was.

"All I was gonna say was that, err, go get us another one." Dan swigged back the last inch of beer in his glass and pushed it across the table. It toppled, and Andy caught it. Against his better judgement, he went to the bar.

Shaunna watched him from a distance; the bar lights reflected off his earring. "Go on," she said, her gaze still fixed on the earring. Dan didn't say anything, and she turned and looked him in the eye. "Go on!"

He shrugged. "I'm pleased. That's all."

"Right."

"Yeah. You've made him happy."

"OK." She just knew there was more. Andy brought the drinks over. Dan nodded in thanks and took a large gulp. He frowned.

"Doesn't it hurt your back, though? Shagging on the stairs?"

Andy growled. "Shut the fuck up!"

Shaunna giggled and tapped her glass against Dan's. "Cheers."

***

"I'm telling you, Shaunna and Andy are together," George said, shuffling down the bed and fussing with his pillows.

"They're not. It was just the situation." Josh was already settled in bed, lying on his side and watching George struggle to get comfortable. "Did you see what came in the post this morning?"

"Err. Not sure."

"The Christmas card from Puddles and Linzi?" Linzi was the woman who had taken Blue to the vet following the accident on the way home from their honeymoon. Puddles was her German Shepherd dog—a three-year-old bitch born with a congenital bladder condition, hence the name.

"Yeah," George confirmed distractedly. He was still fidgeting. "I love that she addressed it to Blue first."

"I know." Josh laughed sleepily. "I sent one back, anyway, and explained why we'd not kept in touch." He frowned at George. "What's the matter?"

"Dunno. Can't get comfy." He sat up again, lifting his pillows to fluff them and discovering the reason for his discomfort. He grinned. "It's just as well I found that before I went to sleep!" He extracted the small tub of 'Pure Bliss' and popped the lid, scooping some of the ice cream with the little plastic spoon. "Are you OK?" he asked, feeding the first spoonful to Josh.

"Mmm," Josh replied, sucking the cold dessert away from his teeth. "Yes. I'm fine. Are you?"

"Yeah. I think so." George put some of the ice cream in his mouth. "Agh! Brain freeze!" He rubbed his nose until the coldness passed, and then fed some more to Josh, gazing at him. "You were very brave today," he said quietly.

"Don't make me agree with your mother again."

"Huh?"

"About you being a soft shite."

"Well, you were, although I sometimes wonder if you and Sean think being psychologists means you're impervious to bullets."

"Bullets are nothing when you battle with undergraduates daily, believe me."

"I swear it was never this exciting on the ranch. Our lives are too crazy."

"You must have brought the crazy with you. It was pretty quiet here before you came home."

"Fine I'll just go back again, shall I?" George joked.

"Actually, there's an idea."

"Oh, thanks!"

"I don't mean on your own, you goon. I mean we should take Ray up on his offer and go and visit."

"Seriously?"

"Yes. We could do with a proper holiday."

"Cool. I'll have a chat with him after Christmas. We'll need to work around the uni terms, which is tricky, as the farm's pretty quiet until March, but if we only go for a week, we'll have just got there and it'll be time to come back again. Having said that, I could probably get one of the summer staff to cover. And Blue could stay with Shaunna and Kris…"

George stopped, having realised he'd been jabbering unshushed. He quickly finished the rest of the Pure Bliss and turned on his side to watch Josh sleep for a while. He didn't often get the chance, and Josh looked wonderfully content and peaceful, his blonde eyelashes flickering lightly against his pale cheeks, a stray few strands of hair rising and falling with each deep breath that passed his peach-pink lips. George reached across and gently smoothed the hair back from his face.

"Good night, my hero," he whispered. "Sweet dreams." He kissed Josh on the forehead and turned out the light.

Whodunnit Part Two
Monday 11th December

"We do not need a debrief!" Josh shoved the 'invitation' back across his desk.

"Can you not just humour me for once?"

"I humour you all the time."

"Come on," Sean goaded. "It'll be fun. Everyone else is up for it."

"Everyone as in?"

"Everyone! Just say yes."

Josh scowled and put his glasses on, turning to his computer and acting as if Sean wasn't there.

"Joshy, come on. I'll buy the coffee."

"For *everyone*?"

"Sure. And cake too."

Josh took his glasses off again and huffed. Sean continued to stare at him.

"You know you're going to say yes. Just say it. Three little letters. Yes!"

"I've got all of these essays to mark," Josh waved his hand at the computer, "and a stat test to run."

"I'll mark your essays."

"You'll what?"

"And I'll even do your stats, if you insist."

"You'd know all about insistence."

"Ha! If ever the pot called the kettle…"

"Tell me how you know Angela Sharston."

"And there y'are!"

Josh turned back to his computer again.

"Oh, all right! She was a client and…" Sean blushed.

"Oh, Seany!"

"I don't care."

"You slept with a client?"

"She seduced me."

"Interesting." Josh tipped his chair back and spun it from side to side, chewing on the arm of his glasses. "And highly unethical."

"She's a professional. We saw that for ourselves."

"But still."

"But nothing. So the debrief, then?"

"By 'seduced', what exactly—"

"Debrief?"

"I'm intrigued to know how a woman like Angela Sharston was able to seduce the great Doctor Sean Tierney. I thought you preferred the pretty young things."

Sean rolled his eyes. "Debrief?"

"What did she do? Wiggle her—"

"Goddamnit, Joshy! Just say yes!"

"Fine. If it'll shut you up. Yes!"

"Great stuff." Sean grinned and got up to leave. "You know you won't regret it."

"Regretting it already," Josh shouted after him. The door closed, and Josh shook his head. The door opened again.

"How many essays are we talking about?"

"Erm, two?" Josh admitted.

"All that fuss over two essays? Email them to me. I'll get 'em done now."

"And the ANOVA?"

"And the feckin' ANOVA."

"Well, you made the off—"

The door closed again.

"—fer." Josh allowed himself a celebratory little cheer and air-punch. He'd have said yes anyway, but two more lectures and that would be all his work done for the term. He opened up his email, sent the essays and data to Sean, and sighed in satisfaction.

"Bring on the Christmas break!"

***

Sorry.
The aquarium is closed.

"Are you sure this is the right place?" Alice asked.

Jason shrugged. "That's what it says." He unfolded the piece of paper and checked again. "Cordelia's Aquarium."

"Maybe it's just that the sign hasn't been changed today?" Hadyn suggested.

"Or perhaps it's only open for us?" Alice speculated.

"Hmm. I guess there's only one way to find out." Jason pushed the door, and it opened, sounding an old-fashioned shop bell. The three of them stepped into the wide corridor, in darkness but for the vast illuminated fish tanks lining both sides. "I've never been here before."

"Wow!" Hadyn stopped, his eyes wide with wonder at the brightly coloured coral and sea anemone swaying back and forth in the tank running the length of the wall to his left. "This is ace!"

Alice, too, was rather taken with the luminous fish darting around in mini shoals, a dazzling neon-pink blur that scattered as it approached a rock, reformed and shot off in another direction.

"Nor have I visited, to my shame, although I confess I had always worried that the smell would be overwhelming, and it is not. In fact, it's rather comforting."

They slowly continued along the passageway, too enthralled by what they saw to rush. Behind them, the doorbell tinkled, and they turned to see Dan, Adele and little Shaunna come in. All three stopped and looked around, their smiling faces glowing in the light from the tanks.

"Blast from the past!" Adele said.

"Fishes!" little Shaunna shouted, pointing at the nearest tank. She ran over and bashed her palms against it.

"Oh, no, Shu. Don't do that. You'll frighten them."

"Friken!" Shaunna repeated.

"That's right," Dan said. "Remember what Nana told you? Fish have got very, very good hearing. You have to be quiet. Shhh."

She raised her hands in a shrug. "Where ears?"

"Ah, yeah." He frowned, not quite sure how to explain that one. "Shall we go and ask Mrs. Kinkade?"

"Ask Kinkle. Mon Daddy." She grabbed his hand and pulled. He stumbled forward and allowed her to lead him away. The doorbell sounded again; George came into view, followed by Josh and Sean, arguing as usual.

"Hi, Adele." George gave her a hug and paused to look around. "No way! It hasn't changed at all!"

"No. I feel like I'm eight again." Adele nodded at Josh and Sean. "What's up with them?"

"Nothing important. Something to do with Sean doing the wrong maths." Josh and Sean continued past them, still quarrelling. Adele listened in complete bemusement.

"What's multivariate?" she asked. George shrugged, and they followed the warring academics onwards to the café.

Outside, Andy had parked the Mustang some distance away and was watching Shaunna, Kris and Ade cross the street on foot. Shaunna had seen him but was trying not to look too obviously in his direction. It was the first time he and Kris would be in the same place together since Kris challenged him, and he was worried. He didn't think Kris would do anything with other people around, or even without. However, it could get awkward, not for Shaunna or him as such; for Dan and Adele, who both knew what was going on and were openly supportive, even though Kris and Dan were as close as they had always been.

Added to that, Andy and Shaunna hadn't seen each other since the night at Black Hole, and he missed her, but what could he do? He continued to watch as Eleanor, James and Toby met them at the door and shared hugs. It was making him feel very alone. As soon as they were all out of sight, he locked up the Mustang and made a move towards the aquarium, gradually becoming aware of a car kerb-crawling alongside.

"Oy, Jeffries! Get your hair cut!"

Andy grinned at the driver. "Alright, Aitch?"

"Yeah. Not bad." Aitch grinned back. He stopped the car and got out. "You?"

"Pretty good. I see you've brought half the force with you." Andy was referring to the passengers in Aitch's car: Natasha Granger, Graham Farrar and Rob Simpson-Stone.

"Well, we figured that all the troublemakers are here today anyway."

Andy laughed. "You got that right."

Rob got out of the car and came over, offering his hand. Andy shook it.

"Rob," he acknowledged with a nod.

"Andy," Rob responded in kind.

"You OK?"

Rob nodded again. "Getting there."

"Glad to hear it." Andy clapped him on the back.

"D'you know that Tierney bloke well?" Aitch asked.

"Reasonably. Why?"

"He phoned the big boss and got us off duty this afternoon."

"Yeah? I'm not surprised. He can be very persuasive."

"You're not wrong there. If you met mine and Tash's boss you'd know what I mean."

"They're free floaters, are they?" Andy asked, nodding at Rob and Graham.

"Different ACPOs. Rob's Met and Graham's—" Aitch looked at his colleague. "Northumbria, is it Gray?"

"That's right," Graham Farrar answered.

"A Geordie," Andy said.

"Aye, and proud."

"Shall we go in?" Aitch suggested. He led the way through the door, the smell of the heated tanks immediately filling his mind with the memory of the last time he was there, back in second year of junior school on a class trip. He paused and closed his eyes, taking the moment to reminisce, smiling as he recalled jostling with his mates, trying to make the blowfish inflate, Mrs. Kinkade ticking them off… *Good times.*

***

Cordelia crouched down, so that she was closer to little Shaunna's level, and listened carefully.

"Where fishes' ears?" the little girl asked again.

"Mm. That's a very good question!" Cordelia extended to her full, willowy height, and little Shaunna craned her neck to watch. She was already completely taken with the retired school teacher, who hadn't yet got as far as greeting the rest of her 'guests', but, as always, children came first. "Vincent, could you pass me the tuning fork from under the counter, please?"

"Certainly," Vincent replied with a courteous nod. He searched around amongst the pens and pencils and various other odds and ends, just like a teacher's desk drawer, finally laying his fingers on the metal tuning fork. With an artistic flourish, he passed it over.

Cordelia tapped it on the counter, and put it against her skull, behind her ear, to show little Shaunna what she was about to do to her.

"Fish don't have ears like yours and mine. Listen." She set the tuning fork resonating again and touched it to the little girl's head, momentarily startling her with the noise that she could feel rather than hear. Cordelia smiled at her encouragingly. "That is how fish hear."

"No ears," little Shaunna said with a smile, understanding without the words, and went happily toddling off with her newfound knowledge.

"Once a teacher…" Josh remarked. Cordelia laughed.

"Quite right, Joshua." She glanced past him, to where George was trying to walk with little Shaunna attached to one leg and Toby to the other. He made an exaggerated effort to move his feet, making both children giggle excitedly. "I wonder if it will take him another eleven months to make it to the counter?" Cordelia mused.

Josh looked shamefaced. "Sorry, Miss." He shook his head and laughed at his habitual persistence in calling her that. She smiled and took his hands.

"No apology needed, Joshua. What a year you've had!" She didn't get any further than that, as she was distracted by the newest arrivals. "Good heavens! Is that Henry Hartley?"

"It is."

"He polished up nicely," she muttered out of the side of her mouth so no-one but Josh could tell what she was saying. "I must confess, I didn't expect him to."

Aitch, Natasha, Rob and Graham had stopped just inside the door of the aquarium café and were gazing around them in awe, overwhelmed by all of the people gathered within.

"DI Hartley," Sean greeted. "I'm so glad you could make it this afternoon."

"So am I, Doctor Tierney, I think. I was expecting a formal debriefing."

"Ah, yes. I may have slightly mis-sold the proposition to your chief inspector," Sean admitted. "But it is a debriefing, nonetheless, so please do help yourselves to refreshments, mingle and what-have-you." The four police officers nodded and strode off across the room. "And for God's sake, loosen up a little," Sean said to no-one in particular, although Andy had followed them in and heard him.

"They'll be all right, once they get a couple of fairy cakes down them," he said.

"You sound like you could do with a bit of pepping up yourself."

"Hmm?" Andy was distracted by Shaunna's antics, which consisted of nothing more than a whispered conversation with Adele and was entirely normal.

"Are you all right, Andy?"

He shook himself out of it. "Sorry. Just a bit strange being here with, err, everyone." He saw Dan across the room, excused himself and headed straight over. "Alright, bro?"

"Yeah, other than Adele came on over the weekend."

"Damn. Next month, then."

"I wouldn't mind, but we only did it the once to end up with Shu."

"Shu. Haven't heard you call her that in a while."

"No. For some reason, we've started again. Mind you, it saves confusion. I was having a conversation with Kris last week and had to keep stopping to identify which Shaunna I meant."

Andy's eyes glazed over at the sound of her name.

"I s'pose we could always use it as code," Dan suggested, tongue-in-cheek. Andy raised an eyebrow. "He knows, doesn't he?"

"Yeah."

"Thought so. Sean had a word with me about him feeling down."

"Sean doesn't know, though. Does he?" Andy looked worried by the possibility.

"Not as far as I could tell. We only talked about Kris. The thing I don't get is why, if Kris is back with Ade—"

"I'm gonna go say hi to Mrs. K." Andy abruptly cut his brother off, leaving him dangling mid-sentence. It was not a conversation he could have, even if he wanted to. Nor did he get as far as talking to Cordelia, as Josh was introducing her to Alice, although an outsider could be forgiven for assuming that they had known each other for years, the way they were finishing each other's sentences and laughing about it. Andy went to get some food instead, or that was the plan. He scanned the array of sandwiches and cakes and found he had no appetite whatsoever.

"Mmm," Shaunna said, coming up next to him. "Lemon curd tarts." She picked one up and bit it, seductively pushing a stray drip of filling into her mouth with a fingertip. Andy looked away. "I miss you," she whispered.

"I miss you too," he replied, also in a whisper, then, seeing Kris was not far behind her, continued at normal volume. "Are you OK? I haven't seen you at Dan and Adele's lately."

"I'm fine. I've been busy studying."

"Yeah? How's it going?"

"OK. We've been reading about how children learn by imitating adults."

"Oh, right. Sounds interesting."

"It is. What've you been up to?"

"Not much. Took Charlie down south to pick up her new old car."

"What did she get?"

"Golf GTi, 1985 model in black, 1800 cc."

"Sounds sporty."

"It was, back in the day. Nice car." Andy gave Kris a nod of acknowledgement. "You alright, mate?"

"Yeah, thanks," Kris replied, attempting a friendly smile, but the unease between the three of them instantly killed their mindless chatter.

"All right, folks," Sean said loudly. The murmuring of conversations slowly dropped away. He smiled around the room. "Thanks ever so much for all coming down here today, and thanks, also, to Cordelia for allowing us to meet in her excellent establishment. Before you all get too carried away with socialising, there is the small matter of the very real pretext under which I got you here, to which there are two aspects that are, sadly, interconnected.

"Specifically: the activities of our recently deceased good friend, Jessica Lambert, and the murder of Alistair Campion two years since. I'm aware that Detective Sergeant Farrar also needs to formally debrief quite a few of us, and he has agreed to do this while we're here in the company of friends and family.

"To deal first with the easiest of these matters, Andy, if you could come and explain…"

"Cheers, Sean." The two men exchanged places, and Andy took over. "OK, as you know, Jess and I got married in May this year. Sean and Graham are gonna say more about how that fits with everything else in a minute, but whatever, she made me sole beneficiary and asked that pretty much all of her money be given to charity. Well, it turns out she had quite a lot more than any of us realised, I guess because of what she was up to.

"I've talked to a financial advisor and have decided, on Jess's behalf, what to do with her estate. In her will, she said that if all else failed, trusts should be set up for our kids. Therefore—good word for me, that." Andy paused and laughed to himself. He was still feeling quite nervous and needed to get this over and done with; it was the very last duty he had. He glanced at Sean, who gave him a nod of encouragement.

"OK. What I've done is set up a trust fund that will be divvied up on the twenty-fourth of September in twenty-one years' time between however many children we've got by then. I've also made

637

sure that Steph and Dave Lambert have got enough money so that they can retire. They're currently taking a well-earned holiday in Mauritius—"

He paused again, this time interrupted by a quiet gasp from Shaunna.

"—and asked me to wish you all the best for Christmas and the New Year."

Another pause as cups of lemonade, orange squash, tea and coffee were raised in Steph and Dave's absence.

"Now, what Jess said she wanted to do with the rest of the money was split it two ways, between the hospice and a cot death charity, but we think she just felt guilty about bad-mouthing the hospice, so what we've decided—that is, me, Shaunna and Ellie, because we were there with her and know this is something that's desperately needed—what we've decided instead is to pass the money on to Campion Community Trust, who are going to work with Sean to set up a project for children and adults who have lost brothers and sisters through cot death.

"That's all the will stuff out of the way, but I just want to say thanks to all of you for your support. I was too proud to ask for help, and you made sure I didn't have to. Much appreciated."

Andy quickly stepped out of the limelight and went to sit with his niece. Sean waited for the exclamations of sympathy to fade before he picked up again.

"Thanks, Andy. On to the next matter, I must apologise in advance, to Alice, Jason and James in particular, for talking about the people present in the third person, and also for my uncharacteristically dry and humourless delivery, but my esteemed colleague has ordered me not to 'Tiernify' the proceedings, even though I got him cake and coffee—"

"Get on with it, Tierney," Josh said, right on cue. Sean smiled.

"Of course, because I'm a show-off, I can't resist pointing out that if I'd been privy to James's statement to the police at the time, I could've got it discredited in a heartbeat, and I'm somewhat surprised that my genius friend here didn't pick up on it, but anyway, that's by the by."

"No, it's not!" Josh interrupted.

"It's not relevant to this, but you'll figure it out, Joshy. So—" Sean ignored Josh's petulance and carried on "—without further ado, Alistair Campion, the founder of Campion Holdings PLC, was murdered in his boardroom around midday on Thursday the third of December two years ago, whilst preparing for a meeting with overseas investors. Jason Meyer, the adopted son of Bill Meyer, Alistair's close friend and silent business partner, had been asked to set up a video recording of the meeting. In the process of doing so, Jason inadvertently caught the murder on video and also heard the murderer attempting to blackmail Alistair.

"The murderer was one Anders Folden, who moved to the UK from his native Norway at the age of eighteen. As is well known, Alistair worked with young men who were in trouble with the law, and endeavoured to set Folden off on the right footing. Folden failed him—not once, not twice, but three times, and the third was fatal.

"DS Farrar will explain a little more about Folden and the fraud and blackmail ring that he was part of in just a moment, but I want to focus on Alistair and those close to him. There are not many people Alistair trusted. Firstly, there is Alice, the great love of his life who gave birth to their son, Jason.

"Alistair confided in Alice throughout their time together, but he married another woman rather than take Alice away from her lover, Neil, another tragic loss in this terrible saga. Alice has reliably reported that it was Alistair's express intention to make Bill Meyer the sole beneficiary of his estate, as Alistair's wife, Jennifer, was unlikely to outlive him. She had multiple sclerosis and was a long-term resident in Victoria Hospice. It is through my work there that I knew Alistair and was aware he had a son and also that he was being blackmailed, though he did not say by whom.

"The threat transpired to be personal. The blackmailer threatened to inform Jennifer of Jason's existence and therefore of Alistair's lifelong affair with Alice. I imagine Jennifer would've given them her blessing, but both were too, shall we say, 'compassionate' and chose to keep it a secret. Bill Meyer raised their son as his own, and was also aware of the blackmail, which explains his decision to stay silent on all counts. He was protecting his son and his friends.

"As to the matter of how Alistair's will came to name his wife as beneficiary, we now know it was a forgery produced by the late Jessica Lambert, although in her defence, it would appear that it was she who tipped off the police as to Jason's existence, rather than follow through with her false claim to the inheritance by assuming Jennifer's identity. Campion was a very wealthy man and had investments in a number of global companies.

"Suffice to say, he was worth enough for the fraud and blackmail ring to make a second attempt, culminating in the hostage situation at Black Hole Studios Wednesday last. To give you some idea of the kind of people they are, I'll tell you that it was also their intention to make a fraudulent claim on Jessie's estate, but she got wind of it and convinced Andy they should marry in secret so her will passed without legal challenge.

"Finally, there was one other person whom Alistair held dear, the one boy who grasped the second chance afforded him and has gone on to likewise inspire the great things his role model taught him, through his trust, respect and love. That man is James Brown, who was identified by an eyewitness as the man who took his knife—the murder weapon. This witness has since admitted he was bribed and threatened, by Folden, to implicate James.

"It would seem appropriate at this juncture to take the opportunity to say a couple more words about James, for whilst it is sad to be saying goodbye to both him and his lovely wife Eleanor as they embark on their move to Birmingham for James's work, I'm sure you'll appreciate what an indispensable asset he is to the company he runs, and join me in wishing them all the best."

Once again, everyone raised their cups, to wish James and Eleanor luck. As they came to the end of doing so, Eleanor dashed over and spoke into Sean's ear. He nodded.

"Eleanor would also like me to announce that you are cordially invited to the Brown residence for their leaving party on New Year's Eve. And that's me almost done."

Sean stopped and took a swig of his cup of tea, now stone cold, although with his lack of sense of smell he could almost imagine it to be a medicinal whiskey.

"All right, so." He looked around the room and smiled at each person gathered within. When he met Josh's gaze, he saw his concern and gave him a wink to confirm he was OK. "I wanted to organise this today, because I've spent my career telling people going through tough times, especially when they lose those close to them, that the support of family and friends is what gets you through, and I've always truly believed it, but until I met all of you, I'd never really felt it for myself.

"I've known Josh and Jessie for more than twenty years, and we were thick as thieves, so you can probably understand that her death hit me pretty hard, even though it came soon after the birth of my son, Dylan. He means everything to me and has given purpose to my life, but I can honestly say, hand on heart, that if it hadn't been for your love and support, I'd have fallen off the wagon. Feck, I'd have probably fallen under the damned thing and got me stupid self crushed to death.

"Now, I'm not a mushy feller, but I do like to say it how it is. And that's how it is. Thank you to all of you, for being the most fantastic friends, to each other and to me." Sean smiled again and tried to sniff back the tears, but he couldn't, of course, and now they were applauding him, which made it even worse. He moved away to signal that he was done. Josh grabbed him by the arm on the way past and hugged him. He sobbed and coughed against Josh's shoulder.

"Come on, Tierney, man up. There's far too much testosterone in this room to have you bawling like a baby."

Sean tried to laugh.

"Take ten, folks," Graham Farrar said loudly and everyone broke away into their own conversations. He tapped Sean on the shoulder. "Thanks for not mentioning Callaghan."

"No problem, matey."

Graham wandered off again.

"What was that?" Josh asked.

"Farrar's going to push for a formal inquiry into what happened to Kevin."

"Wasn't he part of the operation that told Aitch to let Kev carry the can?"

"What can I say? Guilty conscience got the better of him, maybe?"

"Or was it a certain psychologist with impressive powers of persuasion?"

"I don't know what you mean, Joshy." Sean winked a wet eye. "But anyway, did you work out the little discrepancy?"

"I did, and I'm a bit pissed off that I missed it the first time around."

"Can I ask," George said, "without getting the biggest longwinded explanation in the world, what are you talking about?"

Josh answered, "The police officer who interviewed James about Campion's murder asked him where he was on Thursday, December the fourth, but Thursday was the third."

"How can you even remember that?"

Josh shrugged. "I just can."

"That wouldn't have got him off, though, would it? They'd have re-interviewed him, surely?"

"True, but he'd have had legal representation and wouldn't have incriminated himself by lying. Water under the bridge now, anyway. Speaking of which…"

Rob was on his way over. He smiled and gave Josh and George a warm embrace.

"Your wedding present," he said, handing over a large, book-shaped parcel. "As I say, it's nothing special, but the minute I saw it, I thought it would be perfect for you two." He stayed quiet whilst they opened it, peeling back a taped end each to reveal a writing journal filled with thick, roughly cut pages, and on the front, the words:

You are in every line I have ever read.

"Wow!" Josh smiled. "This really is perfect."

"It's from *Great Expectations*, apparently," Rob said.

Josh nodded. "Yes. It is. Did you know the book was special to us? Only you didn't go to our primary school."

"Yeah, well, err…" Rob rubbed his hand over his head and screwed up his eyes. "I had to fit surveillance equipment in your house last year. Sorry."

Josh felt a little rush of panic. "OK," he said shakily.

"I'm so sorry. I know how much you value your privacy, but we had to be sure you weren't involved, with you being so close to Jess."

"It's all right, Rob. Don't worry."

"Are you OK?"

"No," Josh laughed self-consciously, "but I'll get over it."

"It was only for the week after the reunion, if that makes you feel better."

George covered his face with his hands and blushed. "Of all weeks, it had to be that one."

"How much did you hear, Rob?" Josh asked.

"Not much," he answered quickly, and it was the truth, as Josh and George had spent the better part of that week avoiding each other, or out at stag nights and hen parties. On the Thursday, when they'd had their life-changing discussion, Rob had told the other officer to listen and report back, knowing that to do so himself would be prying.

"Thanks, Rob. For everything, and especially this." Josh indicated the book. "It's very thoughtful and, erm, resourceful."

Rob smiled. "Cheers. I'll catch up with you later." He left them alone again.

Graham Farrar was waiting, ready to begin, and the room once more became quiet.

***

"Thanks, everyone. OK. Where to start?" Tact wasn't part of Farrar's repertoire, but to put it how it really was—that Jessica Lambert had used her friends as well as her natural assets to reel in wealthy clients—seemed even a little too callous for him. "I'm going to keep this as brief as I can, because it's far more fun eating cakes than it is listening to boring police officers drone on.

"We first became aware of the activities of this particular group of lawyers three years ago, when our colleagues in the Metropolitan Police asked us to keep an eye on a new law firm that had set up in Newcastle. The firm was a front for the fraud operation in the area, and was the work of Anders Folden, going under the pseudonym of Simon Yarrow, and Michelle Perlett, both of whom we are now holding in custody, along with Angela Sharston and Terence Strang. The other lawyers involved were Jessica Lambert, Charles Sharston and Alan Strang, all three deceased. The latter was killed when he threatened to shoot a police officer.

"Our colleagues in London had picked up on Folden while he was working in the city with Anthony Adamson, AKA Terence Strang, when they received a complaint from the son of a man with a terminal condition, stating that his solicitor had advised him to write an invalid will. When officers followed up, they discovered that there were many peculiarities in the work of Adamson and Yarrow, not least that the real Simon Yarrow had died some years previously. However, by that time, both men had left the area and moved north.

"Working in collaboration with police in other regions, we were able to establish the link between Sharston Strang and Partners, and Yarrow and Perlett in Newcastle. We know that someone here was feeding information up to the North-East on likely targets for their operation, and we believe that it was Jessica Lambert.

"I know some of you will have realised this means she was utilising knowledge obtained from her associates to identify wealthy, terminally ill people to defraud, but as far as we can tell, she never victimised her friends and did everything she could to cover her tracks so it wouldn't come back to you."

***

Eleanor quickly and quietly left the café. She couldn't bear to hear any more. She stood in the semi-dark corridor, listening instead to the droning of filters and heaters in the tanks, focusing her attention on a stone fish that had scuffed up the sand, startled by her approach. It looked so benign, lurking in amongst the rocks, waiting for unsuspecting prey to come its way, unknowing of the mortal danger that lay ahead. *Just like Jess.*

She'd trusted her, told her things that she shouldn't have, defended her decision in the face of what she perceived to be Josh's paranoia about confidentiality, and his mantra to never share information, not even with friends. But the only connection between Jess and Newcastle was Eleanor. All those times they'd sat together having a cup of tea, and she had chattered on about Kev and his work, she was effectively feeding those poor innocent people into a mincing machine.

The sound of Farrar's voice momentarily became louder than the bubbling filters, and was gone again. She knew who was behind her without the need to look.

"You told me, didn't you?" she said resignedly.

"Yes. I did."

"I feel such a fool. And guilty. What happened to Kev—"

"Wasn't your fault, Ellie."

She turned around. "He confided in me, Josh, and I betrayed his confidence."

"You didn't know who Patricia Biddiscombe was."

"I didn't know her name, but as soon as Callum gave us the case notes, I recognised the medical history. Then you found Jess's confession, and I've been hoping ever since that it wasn't all down to me and my stupid big mouth."

"It wasn't your fault, Ellie," Josh repeated. "Kevin was mentally ill, and he was being followed and threatened, which is ironic, as it led to him wrongly believing he was being followed and threatened. If that hadn't triggered his illness, something else would have done so eventually."

Eleanor looked back into the tank, trying to locate the stone fish, but it had moved on again and was now entirely camouflaged by its surroundings.

"You trusted a friend," Josh said. "What's wrong with that?"

"People died. I understand what you're saying, and that they would've found their victims one way or another. Maybe I'll forgive myself in time, but people died because of me, and I can't do it anymore, Josh. I can't be a doctor."

"This has no bearing on you being a doctor."

"It's the same stresses and dilemmas. I shouldn't have gone back to medicine. I made a mistake."

"Are you sure you're not just thinking that because it was Jess who persuaded you to give it a go?"

"No. I don't think so. I had to try again to be sure. And I'm sure."

"So…what? You go back to managing a pizza restaurant?"

She tutted. "No, Joshua. I'm going to take a leaf out of my husband's and Alistair Campion's book. Anu's involved in a community group for young mums whose partners are in prison, helping them to stay healthy and safe. I can afford to undertake voluntary work, so I'm going to get involved."

"Is it what you want to do?"

"Yeah. It is."

The door opened again, and Dan came through. He stopped and breathed out heavily.

"Fucking hell," he said, shaking his head. "You know I worked with Campion for ten years? I recommended Jess to him."

Josh and Eleanor exchanged knowing glances.

"Been there, done that." Eleanor patted Dan on the arm.

"She set him up. I can't believe it. I mean, obviously, because of the passport, I knew she'd intended to claim Jenny's inheritance—"

"But they already had a man inside Campion's," Josh said. "Anders Folden."

"True enough. I remember Al telling me about him now, one of his waifs and strays who'd graduated with a law degree and needed experience. I wonder if that genius brain of yours can figure out who suggested that he talk to Sharston Strang about getting some."

Josh laughed. "Awesome!"

"You think it's funny?"

"Yes, because it is. She used us, and we're all idiots. But we're idiots together. A circle of idiots, you might call us."

"I bet that's what the police are calling us," Eleanor grumbled.

Once again, the door opened, and Ade came tearing past, straight down the corridor and out onto the street. A moment later, Kris came out, too, and stopped next to the others. Dan raised an eyebrow.

"He went that way," he said.

Kris sighed. "I'm gonna leave him a minute."

"Is he OK?"

"Not really. In between when we split up and got back together, his ex died, and today's his birthday."

"Ah. That's rough."

"Yeah. So, why are you all out here?"

"Guilty conscience," Eleanor explained.

"Same," Dan said.

"Entertainment?" Josh joked.

Kris tried not to smile. "He does go on a bit, that Farrar bloke, doesn't he?"

"Is he still at it?"

"Yep. So much for 'being as brief as I can'!"

"Do you think he's gay?"

Kris shrugged. "No idea."

"He told me he's got a wife."

"Maybe he has. I've got a wife."

"Ex-wife," Dan contended.

"We're still married," Kris argued.

"You know what I mean."

"No way is Farrar married to a woman," Josh interjected.

"He is, you know," Dan said. "She's a mature student."

"It's got to be part of his cover."

"Or you're wrong?" Eleanor suggested.

"I doubt it!" Josh said superciliously. "I'll ask Vincent what he thinks. He'll know."

Now George emerged from the café. "He's done," he said.

"Hurrah! Time to go and eat cake. Did we miss anything?"

"I'm not telling you."

"George."

"Nope."

Josh went to tickle him, and he dodged out of the way. "Please?"

647

George grinned. "Nope."

"I'll make it worth your while."

"Uh-huh?"

"I'll, erm…" Josh couldn't think of a suitable bribe.

George tutted. "I'll tell you this much. Jess knew what she was doing."

"Of course she did. She was highly intelligent."

"Even more of a genius than you?"

"You can't have degrees of genius, George. And I do wish people would stop calling me that."

"But you are clever."

"Good memory."

"For irrelevant information."

"Not so. Anyway, what do you mean, she knew what she was doing?"

"Farrar says she broke into Sharston Strang, cracked their safe and removed every single document relating to her, and nobody even realised she'd done it, until after she and Andy got married for real."

"Strang still had documents of hers."

"See what I mean?"

"What?"

"Irrelevant information."

"It is relevant. Farrar's saying she removed all the documents relating to her, and clearly she didn't."

George gave up arguing. They returned to the café, where the atmosphere was now much more relaxed, with people back to chatting and enjoying each other's company. George nudged Josh and nodded over at Shaunna and Andy. In Kris and Ade's absence, they were standing close together and having what appeared to be a very deep conversation. Shaunna leaned closer, talking into Andy's ear, her fingertips briefly brushing his bare forearm.

"See?" George said. "There's definitely something going on."

"They're just flirting with each other, like always," Josh replied dismissively.

"You're lying to me, Joshua."

"Let it go, George."

George opened his mouth to protest. Josh put his finger under George's chin and pushed his mouth shut.

"For your own sake. Please?" he appealed.

George tried to nod, but couldn't with Josh's finger still under his chin. He shrugged instead.

"OK. Good." Josh released him. "I'm going for a coffee," he said and headed for the counter, and Vincent.

"How about you let it go?" George shouted after him.

Josh waved him away. He didn't know why he was bothered really, other than that he hated not having the answers to everything, and maybe there was a sense of seeking vindication, too, because he hadn't forgotten how he'd felt that night when they were in the pub for the quiz.

"Good afternoon, sir," Vincent greeted crisply.

Josh rolled his eyes. "I've been trying to come over and say hello ever since we arrived. How are you, Vincent?"

"I'm very well, thank you, Josh. And you?"

"I'm very well, too. Did you close up shop especially for us today?"

"Alas, no. Business is very slow, and given that the last customers to visit my establishment on a Monday were you and your husband, I made the strategic decision to stay closed and free up the time for myself."

"Wow! That was…" Josh started to think back, but Vincent beat him to it.

"The fifth of June."

"I was just about to say that."

"And how are your rings?" Vincent's eyes twinkled with mischief. Josh giggled.

"They're holding up well."

"I'm delighted to hear it. Now, what would you like? Coffee?"

"Please. And also to ask you what you think of him." Josh nodded in Graham Farrar's direction. Vincent observed the detective whilst he prepared the coffee. "Well?" Josh prompted.

"I'm far too ancient to become embroiled in the rituals of courtship."

"That answers my question nicely." Josh smiled and took his coffee. "Good day to you, *sir*." He gave Vincent a wink and returned to George's side.

"Why don't you just ask him yourself?" George suggested.

"Because he told me he has a wife. I can hardly go up to him and say, 'Hey, Graham. I know you're married *to a woman*, but are you gay?' can I? Or maybe I could." Josh looked thoughtful.

"No! Don't!" George said, laughing, but not entirely sure that Josh was joking. "I'm gonna go see Hadyn, make sure he's getting on OK. You behave yourself!"

"Of course!" Josh said innocently. "I'll just chat with, hmm… let me see—"

"Seriously, Joshua. Don't do anything you'll regret later." George kissed him and left. Josh glanced around, spotted James sitting with Toby, and went over.

"Everything all right?" he asked.

"Yes, thank you, Josh. I am glad that Alistair's murder is finally solved and Anders is behind bars."

Josh examined him carefully. It was not an answer to the question Josh had asked. James smiled warmly.

"You are too astute, my friend," he said. He leaned in closer. "I fear that Eleanor is struggling with her goodbyes."

Josh watched her circulating and trying to engage in small talk. She felt his eyes on her, and glanced over, smiling tearily. "She'll be OK. She was telling me about her plans before."

"The community project? Yes, indeed. She is very fired up about it, and I am glad. She has not been enjoying her work since Jess passed through."

"Passed through. That is a beautiful way to describe it."

"And not entirely at odds with your own perspective, I envisage."

"Not at all, though I have never been closed off to the possibility of an afterlife. I would be a poor scientist if I were."

"You are an exceptional scientist, however, if there is one small wisdom I may impart, it is that you must learn to look beyond the evidence. It shows only what you wish to believe is real, not what you really wish to believe."

"Are they not one and the same?"

James smiled. "Perhaps, although presently, however much I wish to believe to the contrary, the evidence indicates that my son has filled his nappy. Please excuse us."

As James stood up and carried Toby away to the toilets, Josh caught a whiff. He remained where he was, observing the interactions around him and considering what James had said. It made a sense and a nonsense of the way he lived his life, always unravelling theories, testing predictions, searching for answers. Perhaps sometimes it was not so much that there was no answer, but that the search for it in itself was meaningless.

"Mr. Sandison-Morley. A word, if I may?"

Josh was startled by the interruption of a thought process that was in some abstract form about the very person who had torn him from it.

"Certainly, Mr. Farrar." Obediently, he followed him from the café—into the deserted second corridor and towards the fire exit.

"Please, call me Graham," Farrar said. "We are no longer engaged in official matters." They continued to walk until they were some distance from the café. Over the years, Josh had noticed that there was always one tank in amongst the stunning display of brightly coloured marine life that contained nothing more than murky water, and it was next to such a tank that Graham came to a halt. "Tell me about Rob," he said.

"What do you want to know?"

"What is he like?"

"He's a nice guy. Down-to-earth, honest, got a strong sense of fair play and a great deal of integrity."

"And Aitch?"

"Very similar to Rob, although more competitive, and he would bend the rules if he believed it may prove to be beneficial."

"And Sean Tierney?"

"What's this about?"

"Your ability to read people is extraordinary and fascinating."

"In what sense?"

"You saw through Rob's cover."

"We went to high school together."

651

"So you were merely trying to see the best in him?"

"Quite possibly."

"Don't do yourself a disservice by feigning modesty."

"I'm not. I didn't see through Jess, did I?"

"Because she was your equal. Intelligent, attractive, smart as a whip."

"Yet she got herself involved in an organised crime ring?"

"No. She instigated the crime ring."

"Then why leave Sharston Strang?"

"She used them and moved on."

"And the job at the CPS? A cover? A means of obtaining inside information?"

"Alan Strang was a problem to her. He forgot the rules of engagement."

"So did she. She used her friends."

"She gleaned information from them in specific situations, just like you and Doctor Tierney."

"We only glean information, as you call it, in order to help people. We have integrity and respect. Where was the integrity and respect in what she did?" Josh shook his head. "No. We were not equals."

Graham shrugged. "A ton of rock and a ton of feathers weigh just the same, do they not?"

Josh didn't respond.

"Your friendship preceded all of this and is not worth less because of it. Nor is there any need to distinguish yourself from her in order to reconcile what she did."

Josh turned away and peered into the algae clouded tank. "Eulerian circles," he said. Graham didn't ask the question, but Josh answered it nevertheless. "The intersection of The Ring and The Circle."

"A Venn diagram?"

"Similar. Eulerian circles show only what we know. A Venn diagram seeks to illustrate that which we do not."

Graham nodded. "You're right," he said. Josh turned to face him again. "About me? At first, I thought you'd singled me out."

"Not at all. I do it to everyone, all the time. It's why I became a psychologist."

"Because you were already a psychologist."

"Yes, I suppose that's true."

"You enjoy being an academic?"

"More than being a therapist."

"Would you consider a change of career?"

"Like what?"

"Psychological assessment of targets' characteristics."

"Offender profiling?"

"Suspect profiling. So there is no confusion, though you've likely realised already, I'm headhunting you."

"Erm…" Josh hadn't realised and was taken aback. "Wow! I don't know what to say. I'm flattered, but…I don't know. It's a high-pressure job. I'm not sure I'm up to it."

"You are, believe me."

"Thanks for the vote of confidence." Josh frowned. "You know that I have a long-term mental health condition?"

"As does most of the population these days."

"A valid point." He needed time to think about this conversation, even before he got to considering what was being asked of him.

"Look, Josh, this is between you and me, OK?"

"OK."

"I'm putting together a team for another big case, and I really could do with someone like you on it. You wouldn't be out in the field as such, so we could forego the in-depth screening—I doubt you'd agree to it anyway. You could also continue your work at the university, if you wished, and we would ensure that your employers were suitably supportive."

Josh rubbed his chin thoughtfully.

"I don't need an answer of any sort from you until the new year," Graham assured him. "Not even a tentative maybe."

"All right." Josh nodded. "I'll think about it."

"Great. I have no problem with you discussing it with George or Doctor Tierney in general terms, however, the specifics—"

"George and I have no secrets. Our relationship depends on it, and we've promised that we will tell each other everything."

"Yet you refused to confirm to him that your friends are having an affair?"

Josh flinched as if he had been physically struck.

"You did so for his own good. That much was clear and is no more than we would ask of you. We try not to put anyone in a situation where they have to lie to their family. Anyway, I will say no more on it and we'll talk again in January." Graham stepped away, but didn't leave yet. "Just one more thing," he said. "I'd prefer it if my colleagues didn't know about me."

"It's none of my business, but I understand. The police service is a very traditional, masculine organisation."

"No. You misunderstand. Graham Farrar is a straight detective sergeant from Newcastle. I am not."

"I see," Josh said. "But you are called Graham?"

"You may call me Graham, yes."

Whatever his name or identity, the conversation was over, and he returned to the café, leaving Josh to follow at his leisure. He waited back, staring into the murky tank, now noticing the smallest of creatures squirming about in the gentle flow of bubbles coming from the air stone. He smiled to himself.

"Only what you wish to believe is real, not what you really wish to believe."

Event Horizon
Thursday 21st December

"This is the show flat, or apartment if you like. We're hoping to be ready for people to move in by the end of January."

Lee Johnson stepped to the side so that Iris and Pauline could pass. George waited in the corridor outside.

"George," Lee acknowledged. George nodded once in response, listening to his mum and Pauline inside, planning where they would put their furniture if they moved here. It was already apparent that they really liked the place.

"It's a big flat," George observed.

"Yeah. It's a big building, and there's no point scrimping. It's horrible living in a pokey little place, as well we know."

"True."

"What d'you think of what you've seen?"

"Looks good. What made you set it up?"

Lee shrugged. "I loved our block. It was home, but it was a shithole. I wanted to help the people who made it special for us when we were growing up. I think that was all, really. I was happy there, and I still sort of miss it. Is that weird?"

"No, not at all." George smiled. "It was pretty awesome. I remember when we moved in, you and your mates used to be out playing footy until eleven at night, and I drove my mum up the wall demanding to know why I wasn't allowed to play out when everyone else was."

"Because your mum is…" Lee was lost for a word to describe her. After George left for university, Lee would still go and sit with Iris rather than stay at home. His own mother had eventually died from illnesses relating to her heroin addiction when he was in his mid-twenties, and it had been a relief to be free of his ties to the tower block, but as he said, it was home, and the community that lived there was special. That was why he and a couple of the other younger tenants on the estate had come together to form the social housing association, and here it was, finally taking shape. The prospect of having his 'adopted mum' being one of the first to move in only made it better. Perfect, in fact.

"You do realise," George interrupted Lee's reflecting, "they're never going to give you a minute's peace?" They were currently compiling a list of questions for Lee about water rates, and utility bills, and service charges, and repairs, and the internet, of all things.

Lee laughed. "I'm sure they'll settle down eventually. Dan Jeffries is gonna sort out a wi-fi network for us for the whole building. I'm so excited for this, George. I feel like I'm really achieving something. For the first time ever, I'm doing something with my life."

"What d'you mean, 'first time ever'? You've achieved a lot."

"Nah, not really."

"Yes, really. You looked after your mum, and I saw how hard that was. And you qualified as a mechanic—you know as well as I do how many of the lads from round our way are still on the dole and doing drugs. You could've been like that, but you're not. Even if you hadn't done this, you've got a trade, and a gorgeous wife and beautiful daughters."

"Yeah. I suppose you're right." Lee put his hands in his jeans pockets and shrugged bashfully. He kept his eyes averted as he spoke. "You know, erm, that thing between us?"

George felt his cheeks heat up. Lee glanced at him and smiled. His cheeks were burning too.

"I just wanted to say thank you for being such a good mate. The other stuff sort of got in the way later, made it a bit awkward, and I hoped we could clear the air."

George smiled. "Consider it done." They gave each other a swift embrace. "And the feeling's mutual, by the way." It looked like his mum and Pauline were almost done with their grand tour. "Listen, can you do me a favour?"

"Sure."

He spoke quickly and quietly into Lee's ear, and Lee nodded. "No problem." He gave George a wink.

"Right then, young Jono," Iris said, hobbling across. Pauline was behind her but still looking around the apartment. "End of January, you reckon?"

"Yeah. We might not have all the laundry and internet and things up and running by then, but you'd be able to move in."

"And we're all right havin' a dog here?"

"Need you ask? I had you and your little monsters in mind when we were talking to the landscapers. I'll show you the garden on the way out. It'll be nice in summer."

"And smokin'?"

"It's your flat. If you want to smoke in it, that's up to you."

"Aye. I think we might be puttin' that little terrace to use, eh Paul?"

"What's that, Iris love?"

"Smokin'."

"What about it?"

"Do it outside."

"Do we 'ave to? It can get a bit bloody chilly."

Iris tutted.

"Whatever, love. I s'pose it'll be nice to 'ave the place not gettin' all yellered up an' that."

Iris nodded. "Aye. Put us down on your list, lad, and we can get to arguin' about furniture again."

"Just let me know what you want, and I'll get it ordered for you."

"Is it a furnished flat, then?"

"Err, yeah. Not officially, but we wanted to compensate for the inconvenience of not having everything else sorted for the first people moving in."

Iris studied him for a moment, sure she was missing a trick, but she didn't push him on it.

"And while we're at it," she said, turning to George, "I want one of them paintin's of yours for the front room."

"Um, OK. Of what, Mam?"

"Dunno. I'll leave it up to you, love."

"You paint?" Lee asked.

"Yeah, only as a hobby."

"Have you always done it?"

"Since I was in sixth form, yeah."

"What do you paint?"

George shrugged. "People, horses, I dunno. Whatever I feel like. I just do it."

"Would you paint to order? You know, like, if I wanted a picture of my girls?"

"I guess."

"Nice one. I'll have a chat with you about it at some point, if that's all right? And maybe about getting some in the communal areas here, too."

"OK."

"There you go, Georgie. Your new career." Iris grinned up at him.

He shook his head and sighed. "Come on. I've still got my old career to keep."

They stopped to have a quick look at the garden on their way back to the car. Even in the dead of winter, with lots of building debris littering the place, they could see it was going to be wonderful on warm summer days, with benches and water features and a fenced dog exercise area.

George gave Lee a sneaky thumbs up for his furniture story, and drove home, his mind filling with ideas for the painting for his mum and also those for the apartment block, not that he was seriously thinking about a career change. He loved working at the farm and had no intention of giving it up. It was easy on the mind and kept him physically active. Still, maybe he could try taking on a few commissions and see what happened.

***

"Adele?"

"What?" she snapped. She was in the middle of her fourth attempt at sticking on false eyelashes and once again misaligned them. She shrieked in frustration. Dan appeared at the bedroom door. He was holding a red envelope. "It's a Christmas card," she stated.

"Yeah."

"So open it."

"It's addressed to you."

With a huff, she pulled off the eyelashes and snatched the envelope from him, groaning when she spotted the postmark. She flopped down onto the end of the bed. Dan remained where he was.

"Why has she sent me a Christmas card? She *never* sends me a Christmas card." She turned the envelope over and carelessly tore it open. Little red and gold stars erupted into the air and fluttered down all over the bed and floor. Adele eyed them with contempt.

"I'll get the vacuum out in a minute," Dan said, still watching her.

Adele sneered at the front of the card, emblazoned with the greeting 'Joyeux Noël' and the skinniest, ugliest depiction of Santa Claus she'd ever seen. She flipped the card open and squinted, trying to read the words, but they were written in gold and merged in and out of each other. She started to cry.

"Adele?" Dan's tone was questioning, concerned. She shook her head. He moved closer. She looked up at him and held the card out.

"Will you read it to me?"

He took the card from her and frowned in puzzlement. The writing was neat and legible, the vocabulary not complex, and whilst it wasn't the best news in the world, the message itself wasn't especially upsetting. He cleared his throat and started to read aloud.

"My Dearest Adele. Just a quick note to wish you a wonderful Christmas. I am currently living in Paris, but I'm planning to come back home in the new year. I hope we can meet for lunch sometime and catch up on all the news. Mummy." He stopped reading and closed the card.

"Merde," Adele said. Dan chuckled. "Can we move house?" she asked—a joke and also a further expression of her dismay that her mother was returning.

"That's a bit drastic."

"I hate her."

"I know."

"She's a bitch."

"So tell her you don't want to 'meet for lunch and catch up'."

"She's my mother."

"It doesn't give her the right to walk in and out of your life whenever it suits her."

"I can't say it to her face."

"Write her a letter."

Adele looked down into her lap.

"Or type it," Dan suggested.

Adele started to cry again. "Why am I so stupid?"

"You're not stupid."

"You think I am."

"I don't!"

"I can't even read a Christmas card."

He couldn't think of anything to say to that.

"See? You do think I'm stupid."

He sighed and sat down next to her. "Why can't you read it?"

"I just can't."

"You don't understand the words?"

"They're all scrambled up."

"And what if I do this?" He covered all but the top line of writing with his hand. Adele squinted at it and shrugged. "Can you read it now?"

"It's a bit better." She was still crying. Dan put his arm around her, and she snuggled up to him.

"Talk to me," he said gently. She remained quiet, other than the occasional sob or sniff. "They're helping you at college, yeah?" he asked. She nodded. "So what's the problem?"

"I don't want to pass it on."

"What d'you mean?"

"Like with Shu being slow."

"She'll catch up."

"But what if she's like me?"

"She is like you," Dan said. "She's beautiful."

660

She poked him in the chest. "You know what I mean."

"She's beautiful, and you're beautiful. So you can't read a card from your snotty bitch of a mother? So what? No great loss, is it?"

"I'm trying."

"I know you are. And I really don't think you're stupid. I've said it lots of times over the years, and I'm sorry. I didn't realise it hurt you so much."

She tried to smile.

"I love you, whatever."

"Even if I'm stupid?"

He laughed. "Even if you're only wearing one lot of false eyelashes."

"Oh, yeah." She giggled. She pulled them off and looked up at him. "We're nearly mid-cycle."

"I thought we were going to see Sally-Anne."

"I've had quite enough of mothers for one day, although if you'd rather get it on with Sally-Anne *daahling...*"

He pushed her back onto the bed and kicked off his shoes.

***

Kris rapped sharply on the door, casually examining his surroundings while he waited.

Andy opened up and stepped back in surprise. "I didn't expect to see you here."

Apart from their brief and awkward interchange at Cordelia's, they hadn't spoken since Kris had made it clear he was aware of what was going on, but the physiological effect was precisely the same now as it had been then, and Andy couldn't even hide it because he was wearing jogging pants.

Kris glanced down and smirked. "To think how long we've known each other. I'd never even considered that you might play for both teams too."

"That's because I don't."

"Oh, really? That's not how it's looking from over here." Kris made it very obvious that he was staring at Andy's bulge, slowly shifting his gaze to peer past him, inside the flat. "And there's your big red sofa. I bet there's plenty of room for two on that beast." He looked back at Andy and raised an eyebrow. "What's that? Fear? Desire? Incredible, isn't it? How little effort it would take to get you to fuck me?"

Andy swallowed and looked away. The way he was feeling, a couple of beers to get rid of his inhibitions and he'd probably consider it.

"And it scares the shit out of you," Kris said. "I can see it in your eyes." He moved closer and re-established eye contact. "But the thing is this, Andy. There's more to it than the sex. It's spending time together, talking and listening to each other, cooking, folding laundry, rubbing their back when they're throwing up, raising children, making a home, making love.

"So this?" Kris waved generally in the direction of Andy's crotch. "It doesn't mean you've switched teams, although I've always thought everyone swings both ways, but some people just happen to swing more one way than the other. Me? I'm right in the middle, and it's not as much fun as you'd think.

"We live in a society where we're expected to choose one person to be the great love of our lives, till death do us part, and how do you do that when even someone as extraordinary as Shaunna can't give you everything you need? But what we've got is by consent. I'm not cheating on her, and now she's not cheating on me, because I know. To start with, I just suspected, but she told me the truth. Did she tell you that?"

Andy tried not to sneer. Shaunna had told him everything, but he didn't want to get into a fight.

Kris paused so he could spend a moment studying the man before him. In spite of his apparent fear masquerading as machismo, Andy was a very good-looking guy, and maybe if things were different, Kris would have considered doing something about that, but this wasn't sexual attraction. It was the same biological imperative that leads one dog to mount another: dominance. That was why he was having to put on this whole terrifying act, because he couldn't physically challenge Andy. He wouldn't, even if he could; neither of them was even close to being alpha in their pack.

"Anyway," he said, "the rules still stand. No-one knows Shaunna and I are together, with the exception of you and perhaps Sean. That's how we want it to stay, because wonderful as our friends are, they're a conventional lot who will no doubt accept your affair far more readily than they'd accept the relationship that she, Ade and I have. So rut away, fine stag, but remember what I said. There's more to it than the sex, and if you ever hurt her..." He shrugged. "I'll kill you."

***

"Good afternoon." Alice beamed at Jason as she came into the control room.

Jason paused the playback on the track he was mixing. "Hi, Alice!" He was surprised to see her. He and Hadyn were finding it quite a trial to come in each day with all that had occurred here, but where they had no choice in the matter, she did.

"I've brought these for you, dear." She placed a folder on the desk next to the computer.

Jason frowned and opened it. "Neil's songs?" He withdrew the wad of A4 paper, covered in scribbled lyrics and chord symbols. "Why?"

"So you can play them, of course."

"Erm, thanks, Alice." He wasn't sure how to tell her that without melody lines, there was no way of knowing how the songs were meant to sound. She continued to watch him. He looked up, still frowning.

"What's wrong?" she asked.

"I really appreciate you giving these to me."

"But you don't know how they go?"

"Yeah."

Alice nodded and smiled. "It is as well that I do."

"You can sing?"

"Why, yes. Neil and I used to gig together all the time."

"You did?"

"Yes, dear. That's how we became lovers."

"Oh, right." He hadn't quite got used to her openness yet.

663

"I'm a little too old for all of that nonsense now, but I can still hold a tune well enough to teach it to someone else."

"Ah, yeah. There's our other problem. We don't have a vocalist."

Alice took her handkerchief from her pocket and sneezed into it. Or, rather, pretended to sneeze into it, attempting to cover her laughter.

"Alice?" Jason narrowed his eyes at her. "I might not see you in full aromatic colour, but I get the sneaky feeling you know something I don't." She removed the handkerchief to reveal her smile.

"Oh, Jason," she chuckled. "You are so like Alistair."

"Why? What did I say?"

"It's not just what you say. It's how you say it, how you look—everything about you. You are a wonderful young man."

Whilst they had been speaking, Hadyn had picked up his guitar and Neil's songs, and was now gently strumming through the chords. Alice tuned in to what he was playing.

"A little slower, Hadyn," she instructed. He nodded and pulled back the tempo. "That's perfect." She smiled, softly clicking her fingers and humming along to the chords. Hadyn took her beautiful light melody, busking around it, adding more colour and texture to the accompaniment. Jason closed his eyes and listened, letting his own mild synaesthesia take form inside his mind as Alice started to sing.

I wish I could see
How she sees her world
Is a rainbow,
A perfumed breeze,
A flower-hued meadow,
Blossoming trees—
I wish I could see
How she sees.
Her world.

664

The accompaniment continued, and Jason quietly left the room to get his acoustic bass, meeting Krissi halfway down the stairs. He stopped and stared at her.

"What are you doing here?"

"I came to see you."

"I thought you weren't talking to me."

"I thought *you* weren't talking to me."

"I said good morning, didn't I?"

"Well, yeah, but that's the first time you've spoken to me since the weekend."

"Sorry," Jason said, not at all apologetically. "I got all caught up with Alice, and Neil's post-mortem, and my dad…"

Krissi moved towards him and shaking her head. "No, Jay. I'm the one who should be apologising. You've been through a lot, and I should've been there."

"You've got a new boyfriend. I get it."

"Please tell me you're not jealous. You've spent months trying to get us together."

Jason smiled. "No. I'm not jealous, honestly. It's just everything's so different, and I need to get my head around it."

"Around me and Wotto?"

"And Alice, and Hadyn, and being held hostage." He looked away and took a few slow, deep breaths, just as Josh had shown him. He looked back again at Krissi's worried face. "I'm fine," he assured her, "but I had three fits on Sunday, and I was on my own."

"Oh, Jay. I'm sorry. I went to the beach with Kris and Casper."

"Is he OK?"

"Casper is, yeah," she answered with a half-smile. "I think my mum's got a new boyfriend too, but I don't want to talk about it… yet."

"OK." Jason knew her well enough to let it go.

"We need to make sure we look after each other."

"Yeah, we do," Jason agreed solemnly, and then flipped back to his all-new normal self. "So, Alice is here. That's her, singing."

Krissi held her breath and listened. "That's awesome. I don't know if I can do it justice."

"You?"

"What d'you mean, me?"

"You're going to come and sing? For us?"

"Yeah! I mean, if you don't want me to…"

Jason grinned. "None of that moaning indie crap, though."

"Oh, I'm so alone," Krissi sang in a droning, mocking tone. "My world is so black. My life is so depressing. I love death. I hate myself—"

"Yeah, yeah.." Jason laughed. "I'm just gonna get my bass. I'll see you up there."

"Cool." She continued up the stairs, then called back, "Jay?"

"Yeah?"

""Stop smiling so much or I'm gonna have to come up with a new name for you, *Gothboy*!"

***

Josh poured another over-generous shot of bourbon into Eleanor's glass and sat down again, puffing on his plastic cigar. It was only three in the afternoon, and they were quite drunk. He pressed 'play' on the remote control, and the soft jazz started up, the pair of them bobbing their heads in time to the lilting rhythm of the double bass. He pushed his cigar to the side of his mouth and talked over the muted trumpet.

"It had been a loorng and shtrange year at the Brown Shandishon-Morrrley Detective Agenshee." It was an appalling New York accent, but he didn't care, and neither did Eleanor. She pulled the front of her fedora down and clicked along to the music as he continued.

"They'd finally laid to resht the ghosht of their desheashed pal, Jeshica Lamberrt—"

Eleanor started laughing.

"What?" Josh said, drunkenly affronted.

"Jeshica," Eleanor giggled. "Shoundsh like she wash hawt!"

"She wash a babe, doll." Josh frowned. "Or should that be she wash a doll, babe?" He knocked back his bourbon in one go. "Sheesh," he shuddered. "Think I'll go make corrffee." He got up and staggered out of the room.

"Can you even find the on button?" Eleanor said.

Josh peered back into the room and nearly fell over. "What're are you shuggeshtin', doll?"

"Coffee machine?"

"Oh."

"What did you think I meant?"

"I dunno." Josh hiccupped. "Coffee," he said and scooted off in a zigzag fashion. A couple of attempts later, Eleanor followed him, turning up the music on her way and moving in time to it as she walked. It took her quite a while to get there.

"You know," she said, still boogie-ing around the kitchen and occasionally ricocheting off a cupboard, "I feel really sorry for Rob."

"Yes, me too. Fuck, fuck!" Josh shook his scalded hand. "Forgot the cup."

"I was thinking, maybe we should have a proper reunion next year. It'll be a brilliant way to celebrate us all turning forty."

"Erm, except…"

She tutted. "On average. It'll be a belated celebration for Andy and an early one for you."

"OK, OK! There's no need to get all pedantic about it." He paused to give her the opportunity to take issue with his remark, because it was he, not she, who was the pedantic one. She huffed, and he grinned at her. "I think it's an awesome idea," he said.

"So I can count you in?"

"Oh, no. What have I done?"

"Right, we're going to need a venue. I wonder if we'd get the same ballroom? And then invitations need to go out. I might see if Adele can get onto those. She's good at that sort of thing, and then we'd need to think about a DJ, and food, and…"

Josh picked up his half-cup of coffee—lucky really, as he couldn't keep it level—and headed back for the lounge, trailing behind Eleanor as she listed all of the components for the reunion that he had inadvertently signed up to helping her organise. He didn't mind, really. He was going to miss this; they had left it far too long, and now she was leaving, and the alcohol was making him melancholic.

"Are you listening?" she asked, breaking him out of his misery trance.

"What, sorry?"

She laughed gently and shook her head. "Nothing." She went and sat next to him, and they cuddled together, listening to the music and enjoying each other's company.

Iris returned and stood in the doorway watching them for a moment or so, before hobbling onwards to the kitchen, to make a cup of tea.

"Oh, look at that." She picked up Josh's phone. She knew her way around it by now and quickly located the messages between him and George. She typed as fast as she could and clicked 'send' just as Josh arrived at the kitchen doorway.

"What are you doing?" he asked.

"Nothin' at all, love. You left your phone. I was just goin' to bring it for you." She smiled and passed it to him. He went straight to the text messages.

I agree with Iris. I think you should be an artist. x

"Iris!"

"Sorry," she said, looking remorseful.

"I do agree with you, but he likes working at the farm."

"Aye, I suppose as long as he's happy…"

Josh shook his head and returned to Eleanor, taking his phone with him.

"She's just sent George a message from me."

"Oh, well. At least I'm not the only victim."

"Did she send one to you too?"

"No. Not one." She took out her phone and loaded up the dozen or so messages she had received, supposedly from Josh, telling her how upset he was that they weren't speaking, and asking her to reconsider her beliefs.

"I wondered why you said she was an interfering busybody."

"Hmm. Still. With a little help from Iris and Jeshica Lamberrt we got there in the end, hey?"

"We sure did." Josh picked up his plastic cigar again. Back on with the smooth jazz.

"Brown Shandishon-Morrrley Detective Agenshee were hot on the heelsh of their new nemeshish, the indoobidubble Irish…"

***

"There yer go, lovely." Sean placed the blueberry yoghurt crush on the table in front of Shaunna and gave her a big smile.

"Thanks." She poked at the fat straw sticking upright in the thick, lumpy liquid. "Why did I choose the yoghurt not-smoothie?"

"Because you like the suffering a little too much."

She stirred the blueberries into the yoghurt, watching as the purple hue filled the glass from top to bottom. "What shall we talk about now?"

"What would you like to talk about?"

"Anything." She pulled the straw from the glass and scooped some of the drink with it. He was watching her. She sighed. "So long as we're talking about something."

"OK, so. Dylan's started teething—"

"Done that one."

"Right. Erm, how about—"

"Did you know they did a post-mortem on Neil?"

"We did that too, and yes, I told you."

"Ah, yeah. So you did." She sighed again. Sean picked up his drink—apple crumble and custard hot milkshake.

"I hope that lot rot in prison, the suffering they've caused," he said.

Shaunna frowned.

"What?"

"I don't think I've ever heard you wish ill on anyone before."

"Did I say that out loud?"

She laughed. "Yeah. You did."

"See, there y'are again, making me say too much. Though, to tell you the truth, I've never come across anyone I wanted to wish ill on before. That Folden eejit was going to kill Sphinxy."

"When?"

"Back when he broke into the house."

"Oh. I thought you meant now." Shaunna drifted off again, like she had been doing ever since they arrived, and they were on their third drink, about to enter their third hour, hence they had run out of things to talk about, although normally they'd have happily sat in silence, but distraction was the order of the day.

"Busy, isn't it?" Sean commented.

Shaunna glanced around her and nodded.

He observed her a moment longer and switched his attention to the comings and goings of the young people, with their bags of cards and wrapping paper and gifts. The place was always busy, but today it was heaving, presumably because it was so close to Christmas, rather than there being anything different about a Thursday, as Monday was their usual day.

"Have you resigned yet?" Sean asked.

Shaunna shook her head. "I've given up trying. Hayley's just not having it. I spoke to her yesterday, about dropping my hours, and she said she could probably accommodate me."

"That's nice of her."

"That wasn't what I was trying to do. I hoped what she'd say is, 'Sorry, sweedie, bud I'll have to led you go.' And instead, she gives me a Christmas present."

Sean laughed. "She's a good boss."

"She is."

"You don't sound too sure."

"No, she is. She's wonderful."

"And you don't really want to leave anymore."

She shrugged.

"Have you opened it?"

"What?" She looked at him in total puzzlement.

"The present?" he prompted.

"Oh! Yeah. It's a day for two at the relaxation spa."

"That's not cheap."

"No, although she gets a hefty discount because Marvin does all of their plumbing work."

"The husband?"

"Yeah." Shaunna shuddered.

"So when are you going for that?"

"Not sure. I thought I'd see if Adele wanted to come with me."

"Great idea. The four of us went last Christmas, and it was fantastic. Well, I enjoyed it, Soph didn't. She came over all funny, which we know now, of course, was due to being a few weeks on with Dylan. They had warning signs up to say that some of the treatments weren't suitable for pregnant women, but we weren't aware she was at the time."

Shaunna sat back and folded her arms, watching the young couple at the next table along. They were sharing a banoffee Hot Choc and giggling as they took turns to feed each other the toffee gloop from the end of the straw.

"I guess I'd better wait, then," she said.

"For what?"

"To use my Christmas present from Hayley."

"That's good news."

"Is it?"

"For Adele and Dan, I mean."

"Adele's not pregnant."

"I thought you meant…"

She looked back at him and attempted a smile.

"Ah," he said. "Are you sure?"

"Yep. I've done three tests, all positive. And before you ask, I don't know." That answered most of his questions in one.

"Do you want to talk about it?"

"No."

The silence resumed. Shaunna stirred her drink. It had melted to normal consistency.

"Do you want to go somewhere else?" Sean asked.

"Yeah, I think I do. I'll just drink this first."

"You can leave it if you want."

"No. I'll drink it," she said. "After all—" She suddenly stopped talking and covered her face with her hands, shaking her head as it finally, properly dawned on her.

"Shaunna?"

She laughed ruefully. "I was going to say I need the calcium."

He didn't understand.

"That's what I said the last time."

"About?"

"Krissi." She sighed heavily. He reached across and moved her hands away from her face. She met his gaze, attempting a smile. "Amazing, isn't it? You finally think you're moving forward with your life, going in the right direction. And then you realise that all you've done is come full circle."

The story continues in…

A Midnight Clear (Novella)

It's a cold, desperate December when a young girl flees home, in search of food, shelter and the real Santa Claus. Stranded in George and Josh's hometown, she discovers that the spirit of Christmas can be found in the most unexpected of places. Includes the story of The Little Match Girl, by Hans Christian Andersen.

beatentrackpublishing.com/amidnightclear

* * * * *

Red Hot Christmas (Novella)

Shaunna has a complicated Christmas ahead of her. For more than twenty years, she and Kris were a couple. Now Kris has a new boyfriend, Ade, and Andy is love with Shaunna…she know what she wants, but it all adds up to a Christmas that might just be too hot to handle.

beatentrackpublishing.com/redhotchristmas

* * * * *

Two By Two (Season Six)

Two pregnancies, two babies, two troubled teens. Two psychologists hunting down the leader of a deadly cult. When Libby takes a stand against her abusive parents, Josh and George readily make her part of their family, but her parents may have been involved in something more sinister. Two unexpected guests seek sanctuary in Shaunna and Andy's new home, but that's not all. Someone is watching them.

beatentrackpublishing.com/twobytwo

* * * * *

Hiding Behind The Couch Website:
www.hidingbehindthecouch.com

About the Author

Debbie McGowan is an author and publisher based in a semi-rural corner of Lancashire, England. She writes character-driven, realist fiction, celebrating life, love and relationships. A working class girl, she 'ran away' to London at seventeen, was homeless, unemployed and then homeless again, interspersed with animal rights activism (all legal, honest ;)) and volunteer work as a mental health advocate. At twenty-five, she went back to college to study social science—tough with two toddlers, but they had a 'stay at home' dad, so it worked itself out. These days, the toddlers are young women (much to their chagrin), and Debbie teaches undergraduate students, writes novels and runs an independent publishing company, occasionally grabbing an hour of sleep where she can.

Social Media Links

Website: debbiemcgowan.co.uk
Newsletter Signup: eepurl.com/b8emHL
Blog: deb248211.blogspot.com
Facebook: facebook.com/DebbieMcGowanAuthor and facebook.com/beatentrackpublishing
Twitter: @writerdebmcg
YouTube: youtube.com/deb248211
Instagram: instagram/writerdebmcg
Google+: plus.google.com/+DebbieMcGowan
Tumblr: writerdebmcg.tumblr.com
LinkedIn: uk.linkedin.com/in/writerdebmcg
Goodreads: goodreads.com/DebbieMcGowan

By the Author

Checking Him Out Series
Checking Him Out (Book One)
Checking Him Out For the Holidays (Novella)
Hiding Out (Novella – Noah and Matty – HBTC Crossover)
Taking Him On (Book Two – Noah and Matty)
Checking In (Book Three)
The Making of Us (Book Four – Jesse and Leigh)

Seeds of Tyrone Series
~ co-written with Raine O'Tierney
Leaving Flowers (Book One)
Where the Grass is Greener (Book Two)
Christmas Craic and Mistletoe (Book Three)

Hiding Behind The Couch Series
The ongoing story of 'The Circle'…
Nine friends from high school;
Nine friends for life.

The Story So Far…
in chronological order:
novellas and short novels are 'stand-alone' stories, but tie in with the
series. Think Middle Earth—well, more Middle England, but with a
social conscience!

Beginnings (Novella)
Ruminations (Novel)
Class-A (Short Story)
Hiding Behind The Couch (Season One)

675

No Time Like The Present (Season Two)
The Harder They Fall (Season Three)
Crying in the Rain (Novel)
First Christmas (Novella)
In The Stars Part I: Capricorn–Gemini (Season Four)
Breaking Waves (Novella)
In The Stars Part II: Cancer–Sagittarius (Season Five)
A Midnight Clear (Novella)
Red Hot Christmas (Novella)
Two By Two (Season Six)
Hiding Out (Novella – CHO Crossover)
Breakfast at Cordelia's Aquarium (Short Story)
Chain of Secrets (Novella)
Those Jeffries Boys (Novel)
The WAG and The Scoundrel (Gray Fisher #1)
Reunions (Season Seven)
To Be Sure (Novella)
Tabula Rasa (Gray Fisher #2)
What A Scorcher! (Short Story)
Goth of Christmas Past (Novel)

Stand-Alone Stories

Champagne (LGBT Historical Novel)
'Time to Go' in Story Salon Big Book of Stories (Contemporary Short Story)
And The Walls Came Tumbling Down (Sci-fi Novel)
No Dice (Sci-fi Novel)
Double Six (Sci-fi Novel)
Sugar and Sawdust (M/M Romance Short Story)
Cherry Pop Valentine (M/M Romance Short Story)
Coming Up ~ co-written with Al Stewart (LGBT Short Story)
Of the Bauble (LGBT Fantasy Romance Novella)
So Long, Little Black Diamonds (Short (True) Story)
The Pastor's Last Drop (Historical Novel (Ongoing) – Wattpad)
When Skies Have Fallen (LGBT Historical Romance Novel)
A Snowy Ball (When Skies Have Fallen #1.5)
The Great Village Bun Fight (Contemporary Novella)

www.hidingbehindthecouch.com
www.debbiemcgowan.co.uk

Beaten Track Publishing

For more titles from Beaten Track Publishing,
please visit our website:

http://www.beatentrackpublishing.com

Thanks for reading!

www.ingramcontent.com/pod-product-compliance
Lightning Source LLC
Chambersburg PA
CBHW030535020726
47494CB00005B/1375